WORLDSTORM

Also by James Lovegrove

Novels
The Hope
Escardy Gap (co-written with Peter Crowther)
Days
The Foreigners
Untied Kingdom

Novellas
How the Other Half Lives
Gig

Short Fiction
Imagined Slights

For Children
The Web: Computopia
Wings
The House of Lazarus

WORLDSTORM

James Lovegrove

GOLLANCZ
LONDON

The right of James Lovegrove to be identified as the
author of this work has been asserted by him in accordance
with the Copyright, Designs and Patents Act 1988.

First published in Great Britain in 2004 by

Gollancz
An imprint of the Orion Publishing Group
Orion House, 5 Upper St Martin's Lane,
London WC2H 9EA

A CIP catalogue record for this book
is available from the British Library

ISBN 0 575 07387 X (cased)
ISBN 0 575 07388 8 (trade paperback)

Typeset at The Spartan Press Ltd,
Lymington, Hants

Printed in Great Britain by Clays Ltd, St Ives plc

www.orionbooks.co.uk

For
Montgomery James Stanley Henry Lovegrove
DoB: 30/6/03

OUTER CONTINENT

FARHSOON CHANNEL

DAMENTAINE

Phot ▪

VAIL

M

OTREA

IBAL

Domful ▪

The
Buried
City

New Gorundum

Oöfhaleyis

ARIC OCEAN

LI ✴ ISSUA

Upstream
Boat Chain

PENRESFORD

RIVER SERSA

Graveyard

Downstream
Boat Chain

SITE OF THE BATTLE
of PENRESFORD

AYN

Now that I'm sure beyond doubt of the imminence of my death, the time has come, Khollo, to set down an account of the path that has brought us here – to tell of the imperatives and the choices that have led us from the staid, moribund tranquillity of Stonehaven to the solemn, majestic tranquillity of this place.

For it hasn't been a straight path and, at its forks, whim and chance have played as much of a part in determining direction as the certainties of prevision. It'll be interesting to see, in recollection, how much has gone according to plan and how much not, how much we have achieved because we meant to and how much we have achieved because we *were* meant to. Even I, who am more sensitive in these matters than most, cannot always be sure that what I am doing is what I wish to do or what I know I have no alternative but to do. We are all borne along on tides, sometimes gentle, frequently rough. The most we can manage, by and large, is to hold our heads above water and stay afloat and hope we are swimming in roughly the right direction.

Are you cold, Khollo? I thought I saw you shiver.

[**I was in fact feeling a bit chilly when Elder Ayn asked this, but I assured him I was fine.**]

Spring is on its way, that much is sure. Winter receding, Air season yielding to Water season, the natural order. What is today's date?

[**'The twenty-fourth of Pondermonth,' I said.**]

Thank you. I've been having trouble keeping track. Just six days till Glimmermonth and the official start of spring. I have to say, however, that spring's arrival seems less confident up here in the mountains than it is elsewhere. Here, it doesn't burst on to the scene, sweeping aside the cold and the grey with an imperious unfurling of buds and blossom. Here, it is a tentative creature, offering us a breath of warmth one day only to renege on the offer the next. The sounds around us, though, are the give-away. You can hear it. Everywhere, a trickling. Rime melting, thawed snow dripping, streams crawling back to life.

Soon we will see shoots – tiny spires of green protruding miraculously from the white.

You, at any rate, will see shoots. I, who can count the days remaining to me on the fingers of both hands, will not. I know that one of the last sights these eyes of mine shall ever see is the view across the lake to the valley's opening on the far side and the mountain slopes beyond. I know that I shall be studying the way the snow on the lower part of the slopes interlaces with the rock and thinking how beautiful are the patterns thus created. I shall also be thinking how, with their mingling of white and black, the patterns remind me of the inscription on the rear wall of the Obsidian Hall at Stonehaven. Those words, whitely etched into a darkly gleaming surface in hand's-breadth capitals, which have provided a backdrop to meetings of the Council of Elders since the very first. The Stonehaven Constitution: 'Let it hereby be decreed that in this place shall the arts and offices of the first and foremost Inclination be pursued to the utmost degree of excellence, and furthermore that all who inhabit these premises shall solemnly and conscientiously promote the values of mind, intellect, rationality, logic, et cetera, et cetera, blah blah, jabber jabber . . .'

Sorry. Often those Council meetings were so boring and there was nothing else to look at. The Constitution has become etched in my memory as well as in that wall.

Funny that I shall be thinking of my former home – *our* former home – as my death approaches. Thinking of that bastion of self-serving elitism which, having lived there more decades than I care to remember, I was only too glad to leave. Thinking that, after all that has happened, I might like to return there one last time, even though there will be no possibility of that. I might like to look on my old apartment, my old haunts, the old and all too familiar faces of my erstwhile colleagues, once more before dying.

And then, having entertained these wistful thoughts, I shall raise my gaze, to view a rainbow in the sky. A perfect rainbow, broad, bright, its bands thick and sharply delineated, all seven colours distinct and shimmering. The kind of rainbow that only ever appears in the wake of the Worldstorm. To some, it's a consolatory offering, a gift of beauty to make up for all the terror and havoc the 'Storm has just caused. To others, it's the rapist's parting smile to his ravished victim.

Either way, a thing of loveliness. And the rainbow in the sky, flexed above the mountain peaks, will be reflected in the lake's mirror-smooth surface, in such a way that its ends and the reflection's almost meet. Twin rainbows, forming a near-seamless circle. A sight that will almost – almost – make the night of howling climatic rage that we'll have just endured seem worthwhile.

And then . . . then will come the blow from behind. The rock-hard impact that stoves in my skull and robs me of life. There will be no pain. It will happen too suddenly for that. A flash of light. An abrupt in-drawing of perceptions. That's all. Which is, in a way, comforting. What is not so comforting is that beyond the moment of my death I see only darkness. Nothing but a deep and endless darkness.

Now *I* am shivering, Khollo, and it is not the cold.

There's a lot of myth and misapprehension about prevision. Of all the classes of Air Inclination it's possibly the least well understood by the general populace. The common fallacy is that we can tell fortunes, foresee the futures of others. We can't, although there are those of us who do lay claim to just such an ability – charlatans who set up shop in some urban back street or travel from town to town, dunning gullible punters with astounding predictions which are, in fact, nothing more than intelligent deductions based on an understanding of human psychology bolstered by a foreknowledge of facts which their victims reveal about themselves later in the conversation. It's a clever ruse and takes some skill to pull off effectively. And funnily enough, the futures these fortune tellers predict are always rosy ones, which is perhaps why no one ever seems to doubt the veracity of what they're hearing. People want to believe in the prospect of a better tomorrow, especially if it's promised them by an authority figure, an Air Inclined no less.

It could be said that that's what I am promising too: a better to-morrow. And, it could also be said, with some validity. Well, what-ever. We shall see.

This, at any rate, is the reason I've brought you up here today, Khollo, at the cost of a certain amount of effort for you and a great amount of effort for me. Up here to this ridge overlooking the lake and the hunting lodge, by means of a steep and treacherous track etched into the mountainside by goats, deer and who knows what other beasts, and by men also, no doubt. So that I can explain to you, and to all those who through your auspices will read this account of mine, how prevision really works.

Now then, turn your head and look that way, to the east, across the ranks of mountains, row upon row of them reaching into the distance. They grow fainter the further away they are. Their colours dim from grey to purple to lilac to a hue so feeble it scarcely merits a name. Their outlines lose consistency in the haze, so that the most remote peaks are only just discernible. With my aged eyes, squinting, I can just about make out those furthest peaks – a blurred fringe against the sky. Perhaps there is another ridge beyond, and another beyond that, visible to your somewhat younger eyes.

3

[I don't recall that there was.]

Let us say, for argument's sake, that that is the past. That is how the majority of us, your kind excepted, remember our lives: as a succession of events growing dimmer and less clearly defined the further back in time they are, with the very earliest events entirely lost from view. Who can recall his birth, his infancy, his first faltering steps into self-awareness? Nobody. It is all mist and haze. Not even you, Khollo, despite your abilities, can delve that far back in your perfect memory.

[This is true, and in fact applies to the whole of my childhood, not just infancy. My mind retains in precise detail everything I've experienced since my Inclination became manifest at the age of thirteen, but prior to that my life is virtually a blank – a dull, empty mud-plain interspersed here and there with tiny scrubby outcrops of incident, all inconsequential, all unconnected. It's one of the sad drawbacks of being enshriner-class: I can remember every second of every minute of every day except from the period of my one true innocence. But I mustn't make this text about myself . . .]

Then let us turn and look westward. A similar view. More mountain ridges, arrayed to the horizon. That is the future. To me, it's no different from the past. It's the same but in the opposite direction. The closer a forthcoming event is, the more clearly I foresee it. I foresee the next instant as easily as I recall the instant just passed. I foresee that you will shiver again, Khollo – as you have done, obligingly, thank you – with as much certainty as *you* know that a moment ago you shivered.

So much for the immediate future. The deeper future is harder to make out. An ordinary person cannot always recall exactly what he did yesterday, or a week ago, or a month, a year, can he? And it's the same with prevision. I can't always know what's going to happen tomorrow or the day after. To keep with the mountain analogy, sometimes a particular 'peak' is obscured behind another one, or lost in mist, perhaps. But then I will get glimpses. Something in the present will trigger a fore-memory, like an echo of a future experience resounding back through time, Now being overlaid by a matching pattern of Yet-To-Be. It can be a word or phrase that provides this trigger, or a sight, an image, something quite inconsequential and unexpected. On the other hand, certain future events are just so dramatic and significant that I can't *not* see them coming, just as I can't shake off the remembrance of certain special occurrences in my past. And then there is the very deepest future, which is the hardest of all to divine. It is that furthest blurred pale ridge that's barely visible, or maybe the one beyond, unseen. The deepest future has always been as vague and opaque to me as the earliest past.

Until now, that is, when the future extends for me no further than the coming week and a half. Already the next ten days are sharply imaged; with just a few imprecisions here and there, patches of doubt amid the clarity. The culmination of it all looms horribly, casting its shadow backward. I'm glad, in a way, that it appears that I shall not know who my murderer is. I have a pretty good idea – the rock-hardness of the fatal blow would seem a distinct clue. But the murderer's identity falls into one of those patches of doubt. It could be that my future self does not want to know his killer. He has tried to blot out the foreknowledge, as one might try to blot out a bad memory.

[I wish *I* had the ability to blot out a bad memory. All memories, bad and good, are impossible for me to forget. But the bad ones, alas, are the ones I remember more vividly.]

He will sneak up behind me, my murderer, and will kill me in spite of the fact that I know he is coming. I'm as powerless to alter the outcome as I am to escape it. There may be some consolation in that, I don't yet know. Nor do I know why I will not attempt to defend myself as he attacks. At present, it's best if I try not to dwell on the matter.

Oh, Khollo, have I done the right thing? Has all of this, all I've struggled to achieve these past few months, been worthwhile? Or have I merely been a wilful, wayward, vainglorious old fool, wishing to rid the planet of its greatest scourge simply to assuage my own ego? Have I been mad? Am I mad?

[Elder Ayn paused here, his pale, teary old eyes seeming to invite a response from me, some kind of reassurance. I said, 'My job is to record and transcribe and be perfectly impartial, Elder Ayn. That's what you engaged me for. That's all I'm here for.' A cowardly answer, which I regret even now, and regretted then, as Elder Ayn nodded slowly and sorrowfully, having understood even before I opened my mouth that this evasion – hiding behind the mask of formality – was all he would get from me. Maybe I should have been honest. Maybe I should have told him I thought he might well be mad, or at best misguided. But then what difference would it have made?]

I do not know if I am mad. But then every madman believes he is sane and it's the rest of the world that is deranged. Perhaps the only true madness lies in thinking one is not mad. Perhaps we are all, each in his own way, unhinged.

The old, though, are more prone to delusion, are they not? High Serendipiter Marcan, Ewlin's predecessor – remember him from Stonehaven? No, he was before your time. He ended up a babbling nincompoop. We had to confine him to his apartment when one day he decided to drop his trousers and masturbate in front of a roomful of petitioners. After a while it became necessary to have someone stand guard over him twenty-four hours a day in case he should harm himself, and that still didn't stop him getting out of bed, going to his window and throwing himself off his balcony one night when the person watching over him had nodded off to sleep. Marcan was getting on. Sixty-seven, I think he was. A ripe old age. And I'm not much younger than that myself. I haven't yet fallen prey to public displays of self-abuse, but possibly that will come. *Would* come, were I to live beyond the next few days. I don't think it ever occurred to Marcan that he was crazy, not even as he plunged three hundred feet into the lagoon. I imagine that all the way down he fancied that everything was absolutely normal, that it was common practice for everyone to step off their balcony parapets and fall head-first and dash their brains out on the rocks in the shallows below.

Madness, too, is far more prevalent among us Air types than among any other Inclination. Or that's the popular prejudice at any rate, and it accords with the general view of us as highly-strung, introverted, aloof. Someone should set out to prove statistically whether or not it is so, whether Airies do go mad more easily or whether that particular honour should be accorded to the Fire Inclined instead. Perhaps that's a job for you, Khollo, when all this is over, if you decide not to return to Stonehaven.

Let me state for the record that it is my considered opinion that I am *not* mad, or if I am, that I have acted out of only the most benevolent kind of lunacy, the kind that desires nothing but the best for the world and the people of the world. I leave it to those who read this account, those who inhabit the future past the point at which my awareness runs out, to decide whether I have done well or otherwise. Arguably it's only posterity that can judge the mental fitness or unfitness of individuals, by gauging the worth of their lifetime deeds and the consequences of those deeds. Thus I dictate this account for posterity, in the hope that it will regard me leniently and even, if I am lucky, with approval.

Yet again you shiver, Khollo. The layers of blankets you have around you are not enough, eh? And the air up here is blade-sharp, is it not? One of the few blessings of old age is that one does not feel the cold so acutely. I don't know why that should be. Surely, as our skin gets thinner and our flesh less robust, cold winds should find it easier to penetrate to our bones. But maybe as our eyesight weakens and our hearing weakens, so do our other faculties weaken. The longer we live in the world, the more our senses become insulated from it.

Never mind. I spy smoke coming from the chimney down there. Our young friends have the kitchen fire going, and this evening we shall be dining, if I'm not mistaken, on venison stew, bulked out with some of those tasty root vegetables we unearthed the other day.

Let this monologue – somewhat lacking in coherence, I fear – serve as a preface to all that follows. It has enabled me, if nothing else, to establish the approach I shall take to this account and has got me over the hardest part of any new enterprise, namely the beginning of it. Let us mark that the 24th of Pondermonth in the year 687 C.D.S. is the day that I commenced my dictation to you, Khollo. We shall resume tomorrow and continue every morning for the next nine days, ending on the 2nd of Glimmermonth.

How long did it take us to climb up here? A couple of hours? The journey down, with gravity on our side, will be much quicker. However, watch your step on the way, Khollo. You will lose your footing on the track twice, though neither time at any risk to life and limb.

[On the way back down I concentrated as hard as I could on not stumbling. And naturally, perhaps because I was concentrating *too* hard, I did stumble. Twice.]

Are you ready? Then let us descend.

GREGORY

'What ought we to do?' said Tremond Brazier to his wife.

Marita Brazier, perched on the cushions of the window seat in their bedroom, continued to gaze down into the garden below. Her head was canted so that one temple was resting against the window's leaded lights, a posture which seemed to her husband both pensive and forlorn, and which was designed to give exactly that impression. A tiny square of lace-trimmed handkerchief pressed to her mouth was the finishing touch. Moments earlier, when Marita heard her husband's tread on the stairs, she had been at her writing desk going over the musical programme for the annual Brazier midsummer soirée. The desk lid was now closed. She might have been sitting at the window all morning.

Tremond repeated his question.

'I think you've already decided, haven't you,' Marita replied wearily. 'All you're after is my blessing, so that you won't feel so guilty.'

'That's not the case,' Tremond said. 'I want this to be something we both agree on. I mean, it would be best for Gregory, surely, to go and live among his own kind. At least for a while. Don't you think?'

'We're his own kind,' his wife pointed out. 'His family.'

'I know that.' It wasn't that Tremond had to be reminded. It was that, just then, he might have preferred not to be reminded. 'I know. I simply think . . . So that he can develop his Inclination fully. It would be best for him.'

'And for you?'

Tremond scowled, and Marita detected a faint whiff of singeing in the air. She wondered what object was going to suffer when her husband lost his temper (and he would, inevitably, lose his temper). The writing desk? Never. A piece of ebonised-wood furniture like that? He wouldn't dare. The bed? Likewise. Not with that damask counterpane and that hand-carved headboard. No, she reckoned it would be the vase of roses on the corner table next to the bed that would suffer. She had plucked the roses yesterday from the espalier at the northern end of the garden. They were a deep crimson red and delicately perfumed and the most vulnerable and least costly items in the room. Prime victims.

'For me,' Tremond said carefully, 'the main concern is Gregory's welfare.'

'But pride is a consideration too. "My son the Earther". Send him away from home and you won't have to be confronted by that fact every morning at the breakfast table. And you won't have to worry what other people think either. You won't have to feel the need to make apologies for him. Out of sight, and he's suddenly not a problem any more.'

'That's not true. None of that is true.'

'Oh yes? Then answer me this. Do you love Gregory?'

'Of course I do. What a question, Marita! I love both my boys.'

'Unconditionally?'

'Unconditionally.'

'Then it shouldn't matter what Gregory's Inclination is.'

'It doesn't matter. Not to me. Not at all.' The corners of Tremond's mouth twitched, a mannerism Marita had long ago come to recognise as a sign that he was being disingenuous – not that she needed such a tell-tale right then. 'What matters is that, around here, how is he going to learn to use his abilities? Hone them and make them the best they can be? He needs proper training. Willem's getting proper training, the best that money can buy. And I want the same for Gregory, and for that he has to be elsewhere.'

'But there are plenty of Earth Inclined around here. What about Sam? He could take Gregory under his wing.'

'Sam Gove is a thoroughly decent fellow. I couldn't ask for a better site foreman. But for starters, he's a strong, and even if he wasn't, Gregory needs to be trained by a professional, not by some well-intentioned amateur.'

'But isn't indestructible training terrifically brutal?'

'If Gregory's an indestructible, he has to be trained like one. But also, thinking about it, it might be good for him to spend some time in an Earth-majority community, getting to know them and himself. You could even look on it as a kind of cultural exchange.' This idea had only just occurred to Tremond. He pursued it eagerly. 'He'd come back with an insight into Earther ways, which could come in handy, very handy indeed, when he and Willem take over the business. I spend half my time liaising and negotiating with Earthers and I'm still not sure I understand how their minds work. Imagine Gregory being able to think as they do, converse with them on their own level.'

'How wonderful. As long as Brazier Brickfields gets something out of it . . .'

'Please don't take that tone with me, Marita.'

'What tone?'

'You know perfectly well what tone. Don't pretend that the business doesn't matter, that wealth isn't important. Look at the house you live in. Look at the furniture we have.' Tremond waved a hand jerkily around the room. 'Naturally grown wood, not the forced stuff from plant-sensitives' plantations. Look at your lifestyle. Good clothes shipped here all the way from Charne. Household servants. Your precious parties. All thanks to Brazier Brickfields.'

'As you never hesitate to remind me, Trem, whenever I'm foolish enough to suggest that there may be more to life than money.'

'I wouldn't have to remind you if you didn't seem so prone to forgetting.'

The smell of singeing was growing stronger and Marita could feel the temperature in the room rising. It was easy – sometimes too easy – to get her husband riled. His temper, even by Fire standards, was short, and over eighteen years of marriage she had perfected the art of making him lose it when she wanted. Dignity was important to him, and so once he lost his temper, and thus his dignity, any argument they were having was effectively over and she had won. On this particular occasion the argument didn't seem to be one that she *could* win. Tremond's mind was already made up and Gregory's fate was as good as sealed. She wasn't sure, moreover, that she wanted to win. Having Tremond explode with rage, though, would grant her a certain form of victory. Even as he lost face, she would save face by not being seen to submit to his will.

Such was the delicate politics of Tremond and Marita Brazier's marriage, a web of sparring and subtle sabotage which at one time they had treated as a game but over the years had allowed to become more routine than that, and more bitter.

'Honestly, Trem,' Marita said, 'why don't you just come out and admit it? You're ashamed of Gregory. He's a Soiler. A Browndirt. A Mudwallow. That just eats you up, doesn't it?'

'I don't deny that I would rather he had turned out to be an incendiary. I don't deny, also, that his Inclination was something of a shock. I mean, I know these things happen. Rarely, but they happen.'

'Yes, but *Earth*. Air would have been preferable. Even Water. But not Earth.'

'And you yourself aren't just the least bit disappointed?'

'No. No, in fact I'm rather pleased.'

'Oh really.'

'It makes Gregory unusual. Interesting.'

'Does it? Maybe it does, to you.' Tremond, perhaps unconsciously, touched a hand to his hair. He had the blazingly orange hair that was the mark of a pure Fire bloodline. Marita's own hair was auburn; it took on a coppery tint in summer but even then remained a shade short of the ideal.

'But to you,' she said, 'he's a stain on the family. You can't stand the idea that something that came from your loins could be so . . . so imperfect.'

'Don't forget, Marita' – Tremond touched his hair again, and this time the gesture could only be construed as deliberate – 'that he came from your loins as well.'

Marita smiled savagely. 'Ah yes. When we get down to it, it must be my fault. It can't possibly be yours. There must be something mongrel in *my* bloodline. *I* must have Earther ancestry somewhere back in the dim and distant past.' She snorted as if to show what she thought of that notion. In her own way Marita Brazier, née Scintiller, was no less conscious of breeding than her husband.

'Or could it be that someone else's loins were involved in Gregory's conception?' Tremond remarked, narrow-eyed.

His wife barked an incredulous laugh. 'You utter bastard. There's no limit to how low you'll stoop, is there?'

'Oh, and accusing me of not loving my son isn't stooping?'

'Not when it's so evidently true. Face it, Trem, you've never looked on Gregory the same way you look on Willem. Gregory's always been this . . . *awkwardness* to you. Not the elder son, not the first-born. This sort of excess offspring you don't really know what to do with.'

'I treat those boys equally.'

'No, you don't, you only think you do. And now that Gregory's turned out to be Earth Inclined, in a way you're almost relieved. It gives you a justification for not feeling so strongly for him. You're happy at the thought of packing him off to an Earth-majority community because then you'll be able to spend all your time with the son you really do care about.'

The singeing smell had become intense. Heat was radiating from the corner of the room where the roses were. She had been correct. Any moment now . . .

'I'm happy,' Tremond said, bending over his wife, jaw jutting, 'to do what I think is right for Gregory. Regardless,' he added, 'of the expense.'

'The expense, yes,' Marita echoed, staring up at him, defiantly calm. 'Expense is good. The more it costs, the clearer your conscience. In fact, for your sake let's hope sending Gregory away proves hideously expensive.'

'Damn it!' Tremond swung away from her, and at the same instant there was an incandescent flash and the roses burst into flame. They burned quickly, the stems bending, the petals curling in on themselves like mouths keeping mum. Within seconds the flowers were withered charcoal sketches of themselves, haloed in fire.

Having let Tremond vent some of his frustration, Marita, with an imperious frown, extinguished what he had ignited. The flames vanished as if sucked away into a vacuum. Twists of pale smoke began coiling up from the roses' blackened heads.

Husband and wife stared at the remains of the small conflagration, Marita placidly, Tremond with a tendon flexing in the corner of one cheek. Then, all at once, Tremond's shoulders slumped and his head drooped. After a minute of studying the floor tiles, finding solace in their terracotta regularity, he raised his head again and looked at his wife.

'I wish I didn't feel I have to do this,' he said.

It was, Marita knew, the closest she was going to get to an apology from him.

'I wish you didn't either,' she replied, and returned her gaze to the window and the garden.

Down in the garden, just out of sight of his parents' bedroom window, the son under discussion was throwing stones.

Gregory was throwing the stones at the Divided Tree, a yew which had suffered a lightning strike when young and, thanks to the ministrations of plant-sensitive gardeners, had continued to grow, although in two distinct directions, forming a Y-shape. He was aiming at the point where the Divided Tree's trunk forked, more exactly at the narrow split there, the edges of which, even after almost sixty years, still bore traces of charring. His hope was to lodge a stone in the split, but so far every shot had either rebounded off the tree or missed altogether and struck the buttressed, incurving flank of the thirty-foot brick wall immediately behind. Each time he finished propelling his entire supply of stones, he went and gathered them up and returned to the spot on the lawn from which he had thrown them and started throwing them again. It was a pleasingly active and repetitive pursuit and, for the most part, it kept him from dwelling on matters he would rather not dwell on.

For the most part. It was difficult, however, for Gregory to ignore the constant hum at the back of his mind, the knowledge that squatted there, unwanted and undeniable and smug. And every now and then he would pause to examine whichever of the stones he happened to be holding, and would study its rough rounded contours and perhaps brush off some of the soil that still clung to it, and would wonder if it was something more than merely the need for objects to hurl that had prompted him to root around in the flowerbeds and prise out this small chunk of rock and the others. And every now and then, when the process of retrieving the thrown stones took him close to the wall, he would find his hand reaching out to stroke the coarse surface of the brickwork, and he would feel the solidity of the wall and the coolness and dampness it exuded in this shady north-facing spot, and he would ask himself if he found these sensations comforting because they were familiar – because all his life the wall had embodied safety and security and sanctuary – or because of some other, more fundamental reason. Was this his affinity for things of Earth – stones, ground, dampness, clay – emerging? Was he responding at an instinctive level to the stirrings of his Inclination?

He thought not. Hoped not. But a person could no more deny his Inclination, once it manifested, than he could deny the colour of his eyes or the shape of his nose. You were what you were, once you knew *what* you were.

Having spent every day of his thirteen years of life, as far back as he could remember, believing and fully expecting that he was Fire Inclined, to find out that he was not after all was proving hard for Gregory to accept. He wanted it to be not true. He prayed that his newfound ability would, given time, mutate and re-form into something more appropriately Fire-like; or else that people could somehow be persuaded to give him the benefit of the doubt and consider what he could do a Fire attribute rather than an Earth one. The former scenario was, he knew, so unlikely as to be impossible, but the latter? His father was a wealthy man, an important man. If anyone could convince local opinion to shift, it was surely Tremond Brazier.

That was what Gregory was holding out for, the chance that his father would be able to arrange things so that everyone would politely make an exception for him and say, by consensus, *Yes, well, if you look at it in a certain light, Gregory's quite clearly Fire. And anyway he's a Brazier. Enough said.* His father's influence over the denizens of Stammeldon was unparalleled. Not even the mayor held such sway. A good quarter of the town's population worked directly for Brazier Brickfields and most of the rest owed their livelihoods in some way or other to the business. 'Stammeldon,' Gregory's father was fond of saying, just as *his* father had been fond of saying, and his father before him, 'isn't just built *of* brick, it's built *on* brick.' The town would not exist without Brazier Brickfields, and if the present owner of the business demanded that a certain fact was true, whether or not it was true the people of Stammeldon would agree it was, if they had any sense. That was what power was all about, wasn't it? Imposing your will over others. And Tremond Brazier was unquestionably a very powerful man around these parts.

Gregory believed his father would help him. His mother too. Both would do everything they could to smooth out this problem that had arisen, to make the unacceptable acceptable.

But a voice of doubt, part of the relentless troubled hum at the back of his mind, was suggesting that he might not be able to count on his parents to act with complete selflessness. That same voice seemed to be saying that he had let them down. Through no fault of his own, but nonetheless – he had let them down.

He had seen the look in his father's eyes when his father learned about the accident yesterday. He had seen bafflement turn to comprehension and then the wince that followed, the pain and disdain his father had tried to hide without success. Tremond Brazier had asked his wife to repeat, precisely, her account of what occurred, and as she had gone over it again, precisely, Gregory had watched his father's face set hard and had seen a forced, false smile appear and disappear and reappear several times.

On the previous day, Gregory had been with Willem in the garden. Their tutoring was done for the day, Professor Olgarne had gone home, and they had a couple of hours in which to amuse themselves before dinner time. Willem was experimenting with fire, as he often did, and Gregory was looking on, as he often did, because there was little he enjoyed more than watching his older brother practise the incendiary skills that he himself would, for certain, command one day. It was a foretaste of his own future.

At first Willem experimented with shapes. It was no longer an effort for him to conjure fire out of nothing. He could do it with just a frown (and sometimes a snap of his fingers, to show his brother how simple it was). After two years of pupillage under master trainer Sardon Drake, Willem had also become reasonably proficient at manipulating the flames he created. He could mould them into basic geometrical forms – sphere, cube, pyramid, cylinder, hourglass – which he could float back and forth through the air and make dart and dance. He was just beginning to be able to generate more complex objects and also greater quantities of fire.

Gregory had a very clear recollection of the moments leading up to the accident, and he appreciated that what had happened was largely his fault. Had he not been so thrilled at what Willem was up to, and so generally in awe of his big brother, he would not have urged him to

14

attempt larger and more intricate designs and would not have strayed closer and closer to them. Willem was not entirely free of blame, of course. He should have admitted that he was getting tired, and thus losing concentration, and he should have warned Gregory to move back. He was, though, relishing Gregory's delighted attention and was keen to keep impressing him.

And so he fashioned a cat, as Gregory requested, and then a dog, although it was a lumpy, malformed kind of dog and when Willem tried to get it to wag its tail the whole thing lost cohesion and collapsed into an elongated, fluctuating lambent mass, which he chose to claim was a representation of a giant dog turd, to Gregory's immense amusement. Next he attempted a horse, but he couldn't quite make it full-size. He lacked the strength yet to summon up that much flame, and anyway had over-exerted himself already. He settled for something that was closer in dimensions to a foal, and with an intense amount of concentration succeeded in animating its forelegs, so that it sort of seemed to be rearing up, almost prancing.

By this stage Gregory, who had had it drummed into him that he should keep his distance while Willem was practising, had sidled up to within a few feet of his brother, the better to appreciate the fiery display. Willem, although he knew he ought to call it a day, asked Gregory what he would like to see next, and Gregory decided he would like to see a snake.

A snake was made – a narrow crackling tube of fire with a tapered tail at one end and a flattened, triangular head at the other. Willem, pale from mental exertion, forged eyes and a mouth for the creature and got it to coil and wriggle in a suitably serpentine manner. He even managed to furnish it with a set of fangs and made it bare them menacingly. Gregory chortled, fear mixed in with the glee, as the snake flexed and lashed, golden and beautiful and surprisingly lifelike.

'Make it bigger,' he said, and Willem obliged. Soon the snake was as thick as a man's arm and twice as long.

Then Willem said, 'Put your hand up.'

'My hand?'

'Go on. I'll get it to pretend to bite you.'

Gregory gave him a dubious look.

'It'll be all right,' Willem said. 'Promise. I'll just get it to snap at you and you can snatch your hand away and make out as if it got you. Tell you what, if we get this right, we can do it for Mum and Dad at supper. Put on a little show for them. I'll make the snake, you can walk up to it, I'll make it seem to bite you, and you can fall down on the floor and pretend you're poisoned and die.'

That clinched it. Gregory liked the idea of acting out the role of a snakebite victim, with all the melodramatic writhing and screaming that it would entail. He thought his parents would find his and Willem's little playlet funny. Without further ado, he held out his hand.

Willem got the snake to rear back, drawing his inspiration from an image Professor Olgarne had projected into his and Gregory's minds during a natural history lesson. Along with the telepathic vision had come feelings of mesmerised panic, as if the snake were being viewed from the perspective of some little furry mammal that was its intended prey. Gregory was suffused with these feelings again as Willem's flame snake tensed itself to pounce. It occurred to him – almost a premonition of what was to come – that he should drop his hand. But he trusted his brother, and he put his faith in that trust over any misgivings he might be feeling, which were, anyway, nothing more than a memory of illusory impressions installed in his brain by an Air-Inclined private tutor.

The snake lunged forward like a partly-coiled length of rope being snapped straight, and Gregory's fingers were suddenly, oddly cold, as if he had dipped them in icy water, and then just as suddenly they were hot, very hot, and hurting, really hurting, and he pulled them back reflexively to escape the source of the pain, but the pain came with them. Part of the snake was still attached to his hand. The ends of his fingers were enveloped in flames. He was burning! He felt disbelief, and he shook his hand to put out the flames, but they were no ordinary flames, they had life, and the person who had given them life, Willem, was staring at them and at Gregory's hand, shocked, stupefied, not yet understanding what was going on, and now Gregory was screaming, not fake-screaming as he had imagined he would be just a few moments ago, truly screaming, and still he flagged his hand up and down but he could not shake off the grip of the fire, it was as if the snake's fangs were embedded in him, and he could smell himself, he could smell his own skin and flesh cooking . . .

Now, finally, Willem recovered his wits, and with a frantic, focused effort of will he snuffed out the flames that were burning Gregory. He also at the same time snuffed out the remains of the snake, which was hanging headless in the air. Everything fire-related winked out of existence, leaving just the two brothers in the garden, the one alarmed, the other howling.

Willem knew what to do. Before a young incendiary learned anything else in training, he learned about burns – treatment of, what to do in the event of. He grabbed Gregory and hustled him over to the nearest source of water, which was the ornamental pond where a school of large, mottled-orange fish spent their days placidly revolving and swirling. Kneeling on the paving at the pond's rim, he made Gregory stick his hand in the water. The fish, under the impression that it was feeding time, clustered near Gregory's fingertips and gaped and nibbled expectantly at the roof of their world.

'Listen, Gregory,' Willem said. 'Are you listening to me?'

Gregory, through the pain, nodded.

'Mum's going to kill me when she finds out about this. She's going to kill you too, but she's going to kill me more. So what we're going to have to say is that I was practising my fire, just like now, only what happened is you were somewhere else but then you saw me and you came running over and – and I didn't see you and you startled me and that's how you got burned. It was a complete accident. OK? That way we both of us get off not so badly. Because otherwise we're both deep in the smut. Do you understand that?' Willem's gaze was hard. 'Both of us.'

Gregory nodded again, but by that point he was barely listening to Willem any more. Something else was happening. Something he didn't quite understand.

There was no pain.

He looked down at his hand in the pond's murk. Was this common? When you were burned, the pain abruptly faded away?

'Look,' he said, frowning.

Willem followed Gregory's gaze but it was obvious that he could not see what his brother found so weirdly fascinating.

Gregory tugged against Willem's hand, which was still grasping his wrist to keep his fingers in the pond. Willem allowed Gregory to lift his hand out, and up it came, dripping, and the fish moved in on the spot where it had been and bit disappointedly at the foodless water.

'Look,' Gregory said again. 'My fingers.'

Willem stared at the fingers. When they had gone into the water they had been reddened and blistered, skin peeling away from them in ragged loops. This was not the case any more. The fingers were perhaps slightly pinker than they would ordinarily have been, but they were to all intents and purposes undamaged. The skin was smooth, but not even in that waxy way that results from burns. Willem could make out the whorls and fine ridges of Gregory's fingerprints.

He glanced back at the pond, as if its water or perhaps the fish were somehow responsible for the healing that had occurred. It was clear, however, that the source of the healing lay nowhere but with Gregory.

'You're a recuperator?' Willem breathed.

'No,' Gregory replied, and the whole thing seemed distant and incomprehensible at that moment, like a dream. 'No, I don't think so.

17

Recuperators can't fix themselves, can they? They have to get others to do it for them.'

'Then what are you?'

'I don't know. I think—'

It was at that point that their mother appeared. She told their father later that when she heard the screaming, she wasn't too concerned. It could simply have been horseplay. When there was no laughter immediately afterwards, however, she knew then that it was time to go outdoors and investigate. Finding her sons kneeling by the pond, both apparently unhurt, she was finally able to let out the breath which, she said, she had been holding all the way from the living room.

Gregory recalled her striding up to them and halting, hand on hips. She fixed her face into one of her stern interrogative looks and said, 'All right, what's going on?'

Both boys started talking at once.

'One of you,' said their mother.

'It's Gregory,' Willem said, pointing. 'He's manifested.'

Gregory held up his wet, intact hand, as if this in itself might account for everything.

'Did you spark a flame?' his mother asked. 'Did you singe yourself?'

Slowly, Gregory shook his head.

'What, then?'

The full, true story came out – not Willem's amended version of it, because that was no longer valid – and the first thing their mother did was tell Willem to go to his room, adding that he was in deep trouble and would be dealt with later. The next thing she did was take Gregory into town to see the family recuperator, despite Gregory's insistence that he was fine and nothing hurt. There was a queue in the waiting room at Dr Callentropp's surgery, but an injured Brazier was more important than anyone else, as the receptionist was only too aware, and in no time Gregory was supine on Dr Callentropp's leather examination couch and the doctor was wafting his hands over the singed fingers, assessing the damage. There was no damage, he pronounced, and Gregory dared to flash his mother a quick, haughty I-told-you-so look.

'But he was burned,' his mother said. 'Willem burned him. Try again.'

Dr Callentropp did her the courtesy of trying again. No heat radiated from his palms. There was nothing for him to cure.

'The affected area shows no sign of trauma, Mrs Brazier,' he said, sitting back down behind his desk. On the wall behind him, bracketing his head, were a pair of framed licence certificates stamped with the seal of his profession, a hand with wavy lines emanating from it. The certificates were starting to show their age, not unlike Dr Callentropp himself. On another wall there was a full-colour engraving of a human figure, life-size, one half with the skin peeled away to reveal the musculature, the other half flensed more deeply to expose bones and inner organs. Gregory, who had received treatment in this room for every single ache, sniffle and graze, never failed to find the picture gruesome.

'If this incident occurred, Mrs Brazier,' Dr Callentropp continued, 'and I do not for one moment question your word that it did, I can only assume Gregory somehow repaired the damaged tissue himself. Which would seem to indicate that . . .'

His voice trailed off as he realised the full implication of the sentence he had been about to finish. He steepled his long, elegant fingers and placed them against his lips, as if to prevent any further potentially tactless remarks escaping. His eyes were knowing and just that little bit alight.

'There will be no need,' Gregory's mother told Dr Callentropp huskily, 'to mention this matter to anyone else until Mr Brazier and I have had time to confer about it and decide on an appropriate course of action.'

'Discretion, madam, is a recuperator's watchword.'

'Nonetheless . . .'

Gregory watched his mother reach into her purse and hand over twice as much money as she would normally have paid for an appointment with Dr Callentropp – twenty leaves instead of the usual ten. He sensed that more was being bought than merely a professional service, and it was then that he began to glimpse the full implication of all that had taken place. Events had moved quickly and confusingly, but the shape of them was finally becoming clear, the possible consequences becoming clear too.

This understanding was further clarified at supper that evening, as Gregory's father was told the story of the accident once, then again. Willem had been allowed down from his room and was a surly presence at the dining table. Gregory was conscious of being the focus of the family's attention and yet at the same time being ignored by everyone. His parents were talking about him but not to him, and Willem was refusing even to glance in his direction. Gregory bristled with the injustice of the situation, but also could not help feeling that if his entire family had turned on him, their resentment must somehow be warranted. He thought several times about speaking up for himself. He shouldn't let them cold-shoulder him in this way. But doubt and shame kept undermining his resolve.

He was Earth Inclined. That was what it came down to. That was the fact which sat uncomfortably inside him – a knot of hard truth in his stomach – as he lay in bed that night, trying to sleep. Earth Inclined in a family that for generation after generation, as far back as it could trace its lineage, had been nothing but Fire.

It was this same unwelcome knowledge which continued to plague him today and which he was trying to dispel by hurling stones. Some mishap, some freak of chance, some impossibly anomalous twist of heredity, had taken the son of Fire purebreds and made him a Mud-wallow. He could have accepted being Water, although he wouldn't have wanted to go and live on an island or by the coast as most Wets did. He might have been pleased to be Air. It wouldn't have been so bad to be an Extraordinary, even, and have no Inclination at all. And of course another class of Fire Inclination would have been the best alternative by far. Better any of those than be a Mudwallow.

Gregory zinged yet another stone at the Divided Tree with a venge-ful flick of his arm, and finally achieved his goal. The stone embedded itself in the split, so snugly that, try though he might, he couldn't prise it out again. The game was over. He dumped the stones back into the flowerbeds. What to do now? He glanced in the direction of the house, hoping for inspiration.

It struck him then how much he loved the house. The thick, round-edged walls. The bricks – innumerable Brazier Brickfields bricks. The stout iron storm shutters which had, by some immense good fortune, never had to be closed in his lifetime. The gape of the long, narrow, deep-set windows. The forest of pale blue copper lightning rods that festooned the roof. Like the wall encircling it, the house spoke of sturdiness and imperturbability. It seemed so strong and heavy that it had all but fused itself with the plot of ground it rested on, like a limpet on a rock. Five times in its hundred-year history the Brazier family home had been put to the test by the Worldstorm, and five tunes it had emerged unscathed. There weren't many other buildings that could lay claim to such a feat. The house had more than earned its name, Tempest's Bane.

Gregory wondered if his Inclination wasn't again making itself felt here. He realised he was admiring qualities in the house that were, in the broadest sense, Earth qualities: endurance, solidity, stability. Was he doomed to see Earthiness everywhere? Was his Inclination taking over the way he looked at *everything*? He assured himself that he had always thought of the house in terms of its durability, and that in this respect he was simply following the example of his father, who never ceased to boast about Tempest Bane's record of 'Storm survival. Then again, it could be that even before his Inclination manifested, even as a small boy, he had been an Earther, with an Earther's tastes and preferences. All along, without knowing it, he had been swayed and influenced by the secret tides of his nature.

Aargh!

Gregory hated the way his thoughts kept turning around on themselves like this, like a dog obsessively trying to nip at a flea on its haunch. In a few painful moments the world had gone from straightforward to complicated, and he wished that his life could return to the way it was before. Manifestation was meant to be a happy event, marking a young person's first step towards adulthood. Following Willem's manifestation two years ago, their parents had held an open-house day. All of Stammeldon's smart set had turned out to celebrate, bearing gifts and smiles; it was the done thing.

Gregory had the feeling there would be no open-house day for *him*. He was Earth. It was *not* the done thing.

With a sigh, he set off disconsolately across the garden in search of some fresh distraction. As he rounded the corner of the house, he spotted Willem strolling up the driveway from the front gate.

At breakfast this morning Willem had been relatively civil. Gregory didn't think he quite yet knew what to make of having an Earther for a brother. Willem had, however, managed to escape any kind of serious punishment for the inadvertent scorching yesterday, their parents being so preoccupied with the matter of Gregory's Inclination that Willem's part in exposing it had slipped their minds. For this reason he was prepared, it seemed, not to hold a grudge. He had decided to treat Gregory more or less as normal. Benefit of the doubt, for the time being.

So Gregory would have been perfectly glad to see Willem now; the two of them might have found something to do together.

But Willem, unfortunately, was not alone. With him was Reehan Bringlight, and no sooner had Gregory registered this fact than he began to backtrack, hoping he could retreat round the side of the house before either of them saw him.

No such luck.

'A-ha!' said Reehan, raising a hand and pointing. 'It's the Little Bother.'

Gregory halted, knowing that to continue reversing would look rude (which wouldn't matter) and cowardly (which would). Had Reehan been told about him? Willem, surely, would not have been so indiscreet.

'How are you, Little Bother?' Reehan went on. He had this way, did Willem's best friend, of sounding like the most amiable person in the world, when in truth he was anything but. Willem thought Reehan was witty and sophisticated, their mother found him charming, even their father liked him. Of all the Braziers, only Gregory, it seemed, thought him a braying, arrogant idiot. Reehan was no older than Willem but felt he was entitled to look down on Gregory from a great height, as if his seniority to Gregory was more like ten years than two. His mother had died when he was very young, and Gregory had no idea what effect that might have had on him, but he was also an only child, and that, to Gregory's mind, explained a lot. Reehan knew the art of impressing adults and appearing grown-up to his peers but hadn't learned how to behave towards people younger than him because he had never needed to. Worse than that, he sneered at anything that resembled juvenility, perhaps because he had spent much of his life trying not to appear juvenile himself.

'I'm fine,' Gregory answered warily. Of the many things he hated about Reehan, that pseudo-affectionate nickname, 'Little Bother', was very near the top of the list. 'You?'

'Oh, I'm well. Very well. We've just been over to Memorial Plaza, you know.'

'Have you.'

'Chatting up some of the girls there. It's what a Freeday morning's for. How about you? What on earth have you been up to?'

There. Had there been a tiny, all but imperceptible emphasis on the word *earth*? Gregory darted a glance at Willem. Willem was just smiling. Gregory looked back at Reehan. Reehan's expression was sincere and inquisitive, but in his eyes – washed-out green eyes with lashes so pale they were almost invisible – was that the glint of mockery?

Gregory chose his words carefully, 'Nothing much. Just amusing myself.'

'Mucking around, like youngsters do,' Reehan said, with a sage nod.

Mucking. Again Gregory checked Willem's face, and this time he thought he detected a hardness about the smile, an uncertainty. If Willem *had* told Reehan what had happened yesterday, he doubtless would have sworn him to secrecy, just as their mother had Dr Callentropp. In which case, Reehan was treading a fine line: trying to taunt Gregory while at the same time not betray Willem's confidence. Why, Gregory wondered, could no one else see what a two-faced creep Reehan was? The Bringlights, like the Braziers, were a purebred Fire dynasty. Maybe Fire purebreds were blind to one another's faults. And maybe it took an outsider, an Earther, to see that.

'I've invited Reehan to stay for lunch,' Willem said.

'Fine by me,' Gregory replied, shrugging. It was, of course, not fine by him at all.

'Wouldn't want to impose or anything,' Reehan said, 'but I

understand you're having rock salmon. Isn't that right, Willem? And I just adore rock salmon.'

'I don't believe I said that, Reehan.'

A furtive flick of Willem's head finally confirmed what Gregory had suspected. Reehan, anyway, had overplayed his hand.

'Really?' Reehan said. He flashed a grin at Gregory. 'Apologies. My mistake. Not rock salmon.'

With anger and mortification boiling in his belly, Gregory watched his brother and his brother's friend continue up the driveway. When they had gone in through the front door, Gregory turned and stomped off to the garden's most secluded corner, a glade of rhododendron bushes whose blossoms were, at this time of year, head-heavy and wondrously scented. There, out of sight of anyone, he stretched himself out on the ground and gave in to his misery.

The ground was consolingly solid under him, and it didn't matter. It didn't matter that he relished the soil smell of it, that the touch of it was almost an embrace. It didn't matter.

Lunch turned out to be not as much of a trial as he feared, since, in the presence of the Brazier parents, Reehan was impeccably well-behaved. He complimented Mrs Brazier on her culinary skills, even though he knew (and she did not admit, preferring to enjoy the flattery) that the meal had been prepared by the family cook. He discussed the brick-making business with Mr Brazier with an earnestness and intellectuality that could not fail to win over any adult, and his efforts were rewarded with perhaps the ultimate accolade – 'Please call me Tremond' – although he stuck rigorously to 'Mr Brazier', as if incapable of considering himself on first-name terms with such a great man. Throughout the meal Willem had the air about him that he usually had when he brought Reehan home – proud to claim so mature and interesting a person as his friend. Gregory, for his part, kept his head down and ate.

Only at one point did Reehan dare to push his luck, and that was when he mentioned that Gregory, being thirteen, was surely due to manifest any day now. The family, he said, must be looking forward to when Gregory first demonstrated the ability to manipulate fire. Would he be training, like Reehan himself and Willem, with Sardon Drake?

Willem closed his eyes, perhaps wishing that he had kept his mouth shut after all. Meanwhile Gregory's mother, after the briefest of hesitations, answered with supreme smoothness that she, too, was expecting Gregory to manifest soon, and then, with equal smoothness, she tinkled the little bell on the tabletop that summoned the maid to come and clear away the dessert-course bowls. Willem reopened his eyes with relief, and gave Reehan a stare which, for all that it was reproachful, also contained admiration. Gregory realised why Willem had told Reehan about him. Because Willem could have no secrets from Reehan. He would do anything, say anything, to ingratiate himself with Reehan. He worshipped him.

At the end of lunch Tremond Brazier announced that there was some family business that needed to be attended to. Reehan took the hint. He said that he was expected back home anyway. He thanked Mrs Brazier for her hospitality, Mr Brazier for his conversation, and patted Willem on the back and said he would see him soon. As he left, he asked if he could pass on Mr and Mrs Brazier's regards to his father. He was told that of course he could.

In the drawing room, Gregory's father stood, the rest of the family sat. Tremond Brazier paced from end to end of the big bay window in the room's southern wall like an actor making use of the full width of the stage. He transferred his hands from his trouser pockets to his jacket pockets and back again. He shot his cuffs, cleared his throat a dozen times, flattened down his fiery hair, scratched his nose, twitched the corners of his mouth. Amid all these tics and mannerisms, he spoke. He spoke about Gregory, and about what was best for Gregory, and about what was best for the family. He spoke about the Braziers' position in Stammeldon society and about the need for maintaining the esteem with which the family was universally regarded. He added that no one should feel any shame over what had occurred, and said this looking first at his wife, then at Willem, then at the floor. He stressed that 'unfortunate turns of events' could happen in even the most orderly of bloodlines and mentioned the case of Hugo Fanyen-Flare, a contemporary of his, who had manifested telepathic abilities and gone to live at an Air enclave in the north of the country, where by all accounts he had been very happy. Hugo was now employed as part of the national messaging network, and making a very decent living at it too.

Tremond concluded his speech by saying that decisions had been taken and arrangements were being made. Gregory should expect that, within a week or so, he would be travelling. He had nothing to fear. He would be taken care of, well looked after. He must, however, accustom himself to the idea that he would not be seeing his family for a while. He would be going away, and when he came back, he would find that everything had been settled here. His absence would give the family time to gradually acclimatise friends and neighbours to the fact of his Inclination. Pave the way, so to speak, for his return. It wasn't, of course, that they were embarrassed by him. Oh no. Quite the opposite. Other people, though, were so reactionary, so quick to judge. Stammeldon was, was it not, a close-knit and deep-rooted community, highly conservative in its outlook. Anything that could be deemed out of the ordinary caused ructions. And one must bear in mind that the Worldstorm had not hit the area in almost seventeen years, and consequently there was a certain jitteriness in the town, a sense that another 'Storm visit must be impending, which didn't help matters. Nervous people were seldom calm and clear-headed and accepting people.

Tremond Brazier was not a superstitious man; otherwise, as he mentioned the Worldstorm, he would have circled a fist three times in the air and perhaps uttered the imprecation 'May it not destroy my works'. The 'Storm was not, though, something one brought into a conversation lightly, and he couldn't have been unaware that it lent his argument an unimpeachable moral authority. If the Worldstorm was a factor in his plan for Gregory, however minor, then his plan for Gregory was put beyond debate. Some things just had to be.

And so a week later, the following Freeday morning, there were suitcases in the hallway and Gregory found himself saying goodbye to his mother and Willem. He was numb – had been numb ever since his father made the announcement that he was to be sent away. For a while the numbness had been sheer disbelief, but now it was resignation. He still half hoped his parents were going to have a change of heart, but he accepted that there was nothing he himself might say that was going to bring that about. And he harboured the notion that he would only have to be away for a few days before they missed him so badly that he would be summoned back. That was the hope he nurtured inside him, a remote but plausible possibility, even as he let his mother kiss him on the cheek and Willem engage him in a brisk, manly handshake. Just a few days and he would be back here. Everyone would soon realise the mistake they had made.

Outside, on the driveway, the family coach was waiting, a mare standing patiently between its shafts. The horse had the initials BB shaved, with great precision, into her hindquarters. The traces and blinkers she wore carried the same initials, embossed in gold. Gregory's suitcases were already stacked on the back of the coach. Gregory and his father climbed into the cab. The coachman yanked the reins and the horse was urged into motion. Gregory turned and looked back at the front door, expecting to see his mother and Willem waving. Only Willem was there, framed by the porch, and the wave he offered was short-lived, his hand hovering briefly in the air in a gesture that spoke of haplessness and vague encouragement. Whatever his true feelings about the situation, Willem appeared to have persuaded himself that Gregory belonged elsewhere, at least for now. Despite that, Gregory believed that the pressure on their parents to think again would come most strongly, not from their own consciences, but from Willem. As soon as he realised what life was like without his little brother, Willem would campaign tirelessly for his return.

It was, mockingly, a beautiful day. Sunshine filled the garden, making every leaf and blade of grass glow, and once the coach was through the foot-thick, iron-banded front gates, the brilliance of the sky was magnified, becoming blinding. The streets of Stammeldon were thronged with people, all squinting or shading their eyes as they went about their Freeday leisure pursuits. In the grander quarter of town this meant gentle promenading, roadside meetings with friends and acquaintances, a quadrille of seeing-and-being-seen whose courtliness was enhanced by exaggerated dumbshows that drew attention to the magnificence of the weather – wiped foreheads, skyward sweeps of the arm, heartfelt fanning of faces. Nothing meant more, especially after seventeen 'Storm-free years, than a hot, cloudless, windless day. Now and then, too, there would be a flare of flame as two incendiaries met and each ignited a small fireball which then merged with the other's, a gesture of greeting and good earnest.

Here and there a police constable was on duty, watching out for any quickpockets who might be working the crowd – swift-class thieves who darted in, filched wallet or purse or other valuable personal effect, and darted away again, so nimbly fast that all the victim knew was a sensation like being buffeted by a sudden breeze. The constables, swift-class themselves, stood stock still, hands behind back. Only their heads moved, twitching this way and that, like those of eager birds, only faster, blurring from one angle to the next. Cudgels hung from their uniform belts, ready to be unclipped and used on any miscreants they apprehended.

The passing Brazier coach got its share of glances and greetings – Tremond Brazier and his younger son, off somewhere. More than a few people looked twice at the luggage piled up on the back, and Gregory wondered how many of them knew what was going on, what the luggage signified. It must be obvious. The rumours were surely all over town by now. He didn't think Dr Callentropp, or for that matter Reehan, would have kept their mouths shut. And the fact that Gregory's father didn't acknowledge anyone who waved to him and called out hello, but instead just kept staring stolidly straight ahead – surely that only confirmed the gossip. As the looks continued, Gregory began to wish he was invisible, like that rag-clad Extraordinary sitting over there against a wall with a cardboard sign in his lap, a scrawled request for spare change. Everyone was ignoring *him*. Gregory longed for that kind of anonymity.

In the lower reaches of Stammeldon, where the dwellings were more modest, hunkering close to the ground beneath rounded tortoise-back roofs, the street activity was faster-paced and more frenetic. Children ran to and fro, kicking balls or barging at one another in an impromptu game of sticks. Roving vendors hawked their wares, some with baskets of fruit yoked across their shoulders, others with vats of grain alcohol on their backs, others with sheaves of the scurrilous, satirical *Jarraine Jester* in their hands (the Common Tongue edition mainly, but with a few copies of the Fire and Earth language editions as well). The constables who patrolled this area were, unlike their counterparts in the posher part of town, indestructible-class. Quick-pockets weren't so common, here where the pickings were slim, and although crimes were being committed right underneath the constables' noses – infringements of the traditional Freeday ban on trade – they preferred to turn a blind eye. Their high-profile presence maintained a general level of order, and that was good enough.

As earlier, the Brazier coach drew attention, but the smiles and salutes that were directed at it seemed, to Gregory, not entirely respectful. They *looked* respectful but weren't. He wondered how many of the people they were passing were on the Brazier Brickfields payroll. Quite a few of them, probably. It wasn't a good idea to be seen to be ingratiating yourself with the boss.

And now the coach was negotiating its way through the commercial district, where the bright, broad market squares were empty except for birds taking baths in the dust, and where the shop-bordered streets which were packed on any other day of the week were deserted, and where the occasional passer-by looked lost and misdirected. Dr Callentropp's surgery came and went on the left-hand side, part of a cluster of buildings given over to the practice of recuperation.

A little further on there was a black-walled, windowless building known officially as the Stammeldon Sanatorium and unofficially as The Dampers. Here were held incendiaries who had lost, or never gained, control of their flame. For their own safety and the safety of others they were locked away in fireproof cells and kept under constant surveillance. Nobody ever spoke much about the Sanatorium, and whoever was sent there was forgotten about, never mentioned in polite conversation, effectively consigned to oblivion. To end up an inmate of The Dampers was a social, and an actual, death sentence.

Finally, the brickfields. Brazier Brickfields, the name emblazoned in a cast-iron arc above the main gates. The heart of Stammeldon (though not geographically, since it lay at the town's outskirts). The factory that supplied building materials to all of southern Jarraine and much of the north of the country, shipping its product to places as far away as the Forest Lakes, Darrow's Province and of course the national capital Charne. Seldom did Gregory come here without a sense of great excitement – today, of course, being one of the exceptions. Seldom did he approach the gates without feeling the importance the factory embodied, the significance it held both for his hometown and for his family. He loved to visit on a working day, when the vast clamp kilns were roaring away in their rows. He could watch happily for hours as the bricks, in their moulds, went into the kilns as dried clay ingots and came out again as proper fired building blocks. It was a process that never failed to enthral him – the making of something out of raw stuff, the transformation of the unformed into the purposeful.

But away from the kilns, he was just as happy seeing the clay being mixed with water until it was soft enough and could be extruded through a die into the moulds, and before that, beneficiation, when clay that was too hard or clumpy was broken down through grinders and screens until it was sufficiently smooth and malleable. These were the stages of brick manufacture that relied on the talents of strong-class Earthers.

Gregory's father had never discouraged him from going and watching the strongs as they toiled at the mixing vats and storage sheds, but neither had he ever actively encouraged him, and from this Gregory had got the impression that Earthers were a disagreeable necessity. His father would have done without them if he could have. To Gregory himself, they were strangely fascinating. Short, most of them. Dark-haired, most of them. Swarthy, stout, muscular, forever frowning and then, for no apparent reason, bursting into laughter. He found their voices guttural and coarse-sounding when they spoke their own language, and their accent, when they conversed in Common Tongue, so thick that the words were sometimes indecipherable. For all that, there was a quality about them that he admired, although it was hard to define. They seemed at heart trustworthy people, reliable people, in spite of his father constantly griping that they were liars and would steal the shirt off your back if you weren't careful.

The only Earther for whom Tremond Brazier would admit a liking was also the only Earther whom he (and Gregory) knew at all well, and this very same Earther was waiting in the main yard of the brickfields as the Brazier coach entered the premises.

Sam Gove was not a close social acquaintance. There was never any question of his visiting Tempest's Bane unless a business emergency required him to. All the same, Gregory was of the view that if his father could genuinely call anyone a friend, it was Sam. Often on his trips to the brickfields he saw the two of them laughing together. Sometimes they would bicker like an old married couple. Sam was the only person, other than Gregory's mother, who addressed Tremond as Trem.

Sam smiled as Gregory and his father climbed out of the coach, but it was a smile that seemed as much for other people's benefit as his own.

'Trem,' he nodded. There was a small travelling bag at his feet, a battered leather thing. 'Gregory.'

While the coachman hefted Gregory's luggage down from the coach, Sam shop-talked with his boss. A fresh order from Shelforn's of Charne had come in last thing yesterday – eighty pallets by the end of the month. Had they paid a deposit up front, Tremond wanted to know. Sam said they hadn't, and was told to tell them they damn well wouldn't get a single brick until they did. Shelforn's were forever trying to pull this sort of nonsense, and frankly Brazier Brickfields could do without their custom. The trouble they caused was seldom worth the profit. Had they, Tremond enquired, sent the order by ordinary post or via the telepath bureau? Telepath bureau, he was told. Then Sam should write up a demand for the deposit and send it to them by ordinary post. That would show Shelforn's how things stood.

And then it was time to go.

There wasn't anything like a formal handover, Gregory's father entrusting Sam with care of his son, Sam acknowledging the responsibility. Tremond simply looked at Gregory, then held out a hand to him, sidelong.

'Good luck,' he said.

Gregory had expected more, but that was it. His father strode back to the coach, and at that moment Gregory was all set to run after him, grab him by the sleeve, beg him to be allowed to stay. An ache of almost incalculable dimensions welled up inside him, filling his belly, his lungs, his heart, his throat. He would have wept, would have pleaded, would have grovelled in the dirt, would have done anything if it might have got his father to reconsider. He didn't care how much he might shame himself. All he understood was that the last member of his family was leaving him now. From here on, Sam notwithstanding, he was on his own. Utterly on his own.

The only thing that stopped him from going after his father was Sam's hand descending onto his shoulder. A warm, steadying weight, it secured him in place, while the coachman urged the mare round in a circle and steered for the gates. Gregory watched his father's profile in the cab window, his sharp nose, his peak of red hair, all the way until the coach turned into the road and rumbled out of view past the factory's perimeter wall. He strained to hear the sound of hooves and wheels until that, too, was gone. Then, there was nothing left. He had never felt so adrift, so bereft. He looked around him at the factory yard. At least that was familiar. He looked into the eyes of Sam, who, though tall for an Earther, wasn't much taller than him. At least Sam was familiar also.

'Come on, Gregory,' Sam said. 'Let's be on our way, shall we. Long journey ahead.'

Sam carted Gregory's suitcases in two shifts from the yard across to the wharf. There a barge was waiting. It was one of the fleet of long, broad-beamed, clinker-built vessels which brought in clay from the open-cast mines downstream in Penresford and Hallawye and transported finished bricks in either direction along the Seray river, to wherever they needed to go. Its hold at present empty, the barge floated high in the water, wavelets lapping its hull well below the water-stain level that marked how low it rode when fully laden. Its deck and pilot house were painted red and black, the Brazier Brickfields livery. On its prow, next to the woven-rope fenders, the characters 'BB17' were picked out in white.

As Sam heaved the luggage on deck, the barge's pilot watched from the stern, smoking a cigar and not offering to assist. Sam clambered aboard and helped Gregory up after him. The pilot took one last suck on the cigar and stubbed it out on the wooden gunwale. He exhaled a fumy breath.

'You've got the aft cabin,' he told Sam. Like most of the Water Inclined, he had trouble with the hard consonants of Common Tongue. 'Aft' became 'arf', 'cabin' became 'ca'in'. 'Lad's got the starboard cabin. That's on the right-hand side of the boat, in case you didn't know.'

Via a hatchway and a steep set of steps Gregory and Sam went below decks. Space here was limited: a communal area for eating and relaxation centred around a pot-bellied stove, and three sleeping cabins leading off to the stern and either side. There was room in each for a bunk, a closet, and not much else. Gregory tested the bedsprings, which crunched. Compared with his wide, plump bed at home, the bunk seemed emaciated. This was where he was going to sleep for the next two nights. This barge was his home for the next three days. A pair of portholes gave him a prisoner's view of the far bank of the Seray and the fields of corn, flax and linseed that lay beyond, parcelled by hedgerows, and beyond the fields, the hills where Freeday ramblers strolled the sheep-grazed slopes, distant dark dots moving among distant white dots.

He followed Sam back up onto the deck, where they found the pilot urinating over the side. He was muttering in his own language, and Gregory, who had observed this practice before but not at such close quarters, wondered if the man was talking to himself, to his penis, or perhaps to the sparkling yellow stream coming out of it.

'The spirits of his dead ancestors,' Sam whispered, intuiting Gregory's thoughts. 'He's asking them to make the journey easy and trouble-free.'

'And they can hear him?'

'Not just hear, they're replying.'

The pilot did indeed seem to be holding a conversation with somebody, even as he continued to piss copiously. Now and then he would stop talking and cant his head as if listening.

'They're in the river,' Sam added.

Gregory frowned. 'The spirits of his ancestors are in the river and he's pissing on them?'

'I know, doesn't seem very respectful, but in fact it's not quite that simple. The spirits aren't actually in the river, they're symbolically in the river. And of course all liquids are sacred to Wets, even urine.'

Gregory watched as the pilot's flow finally trickled to a halt. The man buttoned up his flies, turned round and grinned at his two passengers. 'All set,' he said. *All se'*. He went forward to cast off the mooring rope at the bow. As the barge began to swing out at a salient from the wharf, he trotted back to detach the aft mooring rope. All at once, the barge was drifting free and turning ponderously in the Seray's current. The pilot took up position in the pilot house, and a look of absorption came over him. Vertical grooves appeared in his leathery cheeks. The barge jerked, and jerked again, as he gained control of the river immediately around its hull. Its course straightened out, and slowly the span of turbid water between its port-side gunwale and the wharf widened. A distance Gregory could have leapt became unleapable. The barge eased into the middle of the river and picked up speed. Brazier Brickfields moved away, and Stammeldon moved away, drawing closer to itself, huddling, making itself small, until soon Gregory could see the entire town, every crimson-ochre rooftop and wall. His hometown, smoothly receding. He stared, thinking that he could never have imagined leaving it like this. Thinking, too, that in no time the town would be looming in front of him again, greeting his return. Then a bend in the river locked Stammeldon out of sight.

For several minutes there was no sound except the heavy burble of the barge's wake. Spaced out at intervals along one bank of the Seray there were fishermen, their faces shadowed beneath wide hat brims, statues of patience. Some of them glanced up as the barge passed; most were oblivious, their awareness extending no further than the ends of their lines.

Then there were no more fishermen. There was just Gregory, Sam, the pilot, the barge, and the broad brown sweep of the Seray, easing between its high green banks.

YASHU

It was the day of Swim-Through-The-Rock. The sun was already riding high and beaming warmth as Yashu set out from her aunt's cottage on the crag above Second-Cliff-Village. The air was tangy with breezes. The sea was a million-flecked dazzle of light.

Yashu had on her best dress, a plain cotton shift with a beading of tiny seashells around the neck and hem. She had drawn back two strands of hair from her temples and tied them behind her head. Around her neck was a cord of braided leather from which hung a frond of coral, one she had teethed on as an infant and ground to smoothness.

As she was leaving, her aunt told her she looked beautiful. 'Huaso will be a fool if he doesn't fall in love with you all over again,' Liyalu said, leaning on her walking-stick in the kitchen doorway. She braved one of those smiles of hers – weak, more a slackening of the jaw muscles than anything.

'Huaso *is* a fool,' Yashu replied. She said it kindly, and with a certain amount of self-deprecation.

Her aunt gave a wry nod. 'You will have a good day,' she said. '*Mala.*'

'*Mala,*' Yashu replied. 'And *mala* to you too,' she said to the goats in their pen, as she stepped onto the steep path that led down to the coastal track. The goats blinked dumbly back.

It was a long journey round from Second-Cliff-Village on the windward side of I*il to Half-Moon-Bay on the leeward, almost half a circuit of the entire island. It was a progress from rough to smooth, from rugged to undulating, from grassy steep-slope land that was useful for not much other than pasture to land whose soft folds and rich, giving earth fostered crop-fields and groves of orange and olive trees. Yashu followed the coastal track's ups and downs with a loping, easy stride-rhythm. The piece of coral knocked gently against her collarbone as she walked. She broke step only for the occasional protruding hiccup of rock which countless generations of passing soles had polished smooth but had not been able to erode to perfect flatness like the rest of the track. The route took her by Grey-Seal-Inlet, and Wave-Clash-Cove, and the series of five evenly graduating, freestanding pinnacles known as Fingers-Of-Oriñaho.

Just past there, she fell in step with a family who came from First-Cliff-Village, even further round the island. The eldest son was twelve years old, just the right age for his Flow to make itself known. It had not done so yet, but surely would after his Swim-Through-The-Rock. The father of the family asked Yashu if she herself was performing her Swim-Through-The-Rock today, although he undoubtedly could tell that she was at least two years too old. When she replied that she already had, he then enquired what her Flow was. An impertinence, she thought, but managed to restrain her irritation as she said she had none. The father nodded and said, 'Ah,' in a trying not-to-sound-pitying way. *So you're one of those*, his manner seemed to say. *One of the Dammed.*

Yashu politely wished the family *mala* and increased her pace. Soon she had put distance between her and them. Resentment simmered inside her. She told herself she should not let one idiot ruin the day for her. She thought of Huaso. The prospect of seeing him again steadied her.

At long last she rounded a turn and there was Town-By-The-Dunes spread out ahead, clustering along the curve of Half-Moon-Bay. She surveyed the bumpy, gorse-thatched roofs, the narrow zigzag streets, the numerous market squares where trade with coastliners and mainlanders was conducted. Quite the metropolis, home to nearly a thousand souls. Home, once, to Yashu herself, although she had no memory of living there. She had been only an infant when the Worldstorm came this way last and erased most of Town-By-The-Dunes. She, lucky, had survived the wrecking, the flattening, the destruction. Her parents had not. The town had been rebuilt, as it always was after a 'Storm. The bodies of her parents, along with nearly a hundred other people, had been consigned to the sea.

She turned her gaze to the beach of Half-Moon-Bay. Several dozen of her own-islanders were already gathered down there on the sand. Some were digging barbecue pits at the base of the dunes and priming them with driftwood and dried-bladderwrack kindling, over which they laid faggots of peat. Others were milling on the foreshore, greeting, chatting, looking to seaward, while the waves at their feet ebbed gradually out, leaving fine black skeins of seaweed behind. Out on the sun-sheened sea, dotted from here to the horizon, there were boats. Not mainland boats, because coastliners and mainlanders knew better than to travel to I*il on the day of Swim-Through-The-Rock.

Other-islander boats, a small fleet of them, converging on I*il from all parts of the Li*issua archipelago. From Uss, from Haroo, from Arashi, from Ra*ai, from Nyaim . . . From Shai. At least one of the boats would be from Shai, and aboard it, Yashu knew, would be Huaso. She pictured him, eager at the bows, hand shading eyes, watching as the three peaks of I*il slowly, oh-so-slowly grew larger, and perhaps urging the shaper-of-water who was in charge of the craft to propel it more quickly (and the shaper-of-water roundly ignoring him, because there was only so fast a boat could be driven, only so much water a person could displace at once). She grinned.

By the time she got down to the beach, a dozen of the boats had put in and a couple of dozen more were closing in on the shallows. The usual assortment of vessels had been pressed into service for the occasion: blunt-nosed fishing boats, ungainly-looking but uncapsize-able shore-crawlers, racy wave-skimmers with their daringly narrow freeboard, wallowing broad-beamed ferries, deep-hulled freighters, manta boats with their wing-like mesh-covered outriggers. As each made its final approach, the shaper-of-water at the stern made one last mental exertion and built up a large swell behind the craft which sent it surging forward to grind prow first into the sand. The shaper-of-water then slumped, exhausted from his efforts, and answered the thanks of his passengers with a bleary waft of the hand.

The first passengers to alight off any of the boats were almost invariably the children of Swim-Through-The-Rock age. Leaping onto the beach, they sprinted off without pausing, bound for the promon-tory at the eastern end of the bay. They scrambled along to the tip of it and stood there looking down at the Rock, which was separated from the promontory by a channel some thirty paces wide. The children's excited gesticulations were matched by their shouts and yelps, which echoed all the way across the bay. Yashu recalled how she herself had stood where they were standing, on her own Swim-Through-The-Rock day. She, too, had been excited. Nervous as well. And bitterly disappointed in the days after, when nothing happened, no Flow came. She had focused hard on distant objects, hoping she was a sharp-sight, like her aunt. She wasn't. She had tried staying underwater for long periods, hoping she was a breath-holder, and had almost drowned. She had sat for hours staring at a bucket of water, trying to mould and manipulate the bucket's contents with her mind. No use. Eventually, after long, frustrating weeks and countless failed experiments, she had had to accept the unwelcome truth. She was what mainlanders called an Extraordinary. She was without-Flow. Dammed.

'Hallo-o-o! Yashu! Hallo-o-o!'

A boat was hurtling through the waves toward landfall. A boat from

Shai. Yashu saw the clan colours of Shai painted along its gunwales – red, grey, blue, in curlicued, interleaving stripes. At the bow, just as she had pictured him, Huaso. Waving at her like a madman. Both arms flapping.

She raised a hand to wave back, and then tried to shout out a warning. The boat was going too fast. Huaso wasn't braced for the—

Too late. The boat's keel sliced into the beach, bringing the craft to an abrupt stop. Huaso went flying off forwards and fetched up with a thud in a gangly heap on the sand.

He leapt to his feet immediately. 'I'm all right!' he announced, checking his limbs and brushing himself down. 'I'm fine!' And when it was clear that he *was* fine, everyone who had witnessed the incident started laughing. The laughter erupted with such suddenness and loudness that it was obvious that people had been having a hard time keeping it in and were relieved to be able to let it out. Yashu herself could not help but contribute to it. Even Huaso chuckled, but then he was used to embarrassing himself in public, and indeed did it so often that it might be considered a habit.

'Shaihuaso,' Yashu said, coming forwards to him.

'I*ilyashu,' Huaso replied, and bowed with as much dignity as someone with his hair half covered in sand could muster.

'No serious injury?'

Huaso grinned gamely. 'Even if there was, it would mean nothing now that I am with you again.'

Before Yashu could deliver a suitably complimentary reply, she was forestalled by a high-pitched yell from the Shai boat: 'Yashu! Yashu!'

It was Zeelu, Huaso's younger sister. She vaulted off the boat, landing as gracefully as Huaso had done ungracefully. Her and Huaso's parents, Imersho and Pharralu, were waiting behind her in the queue to disembark.

'Yashu!' Zeelu came running up the sand. 'Did you see my brother just then? Ha ha! What a clumsy-bum he is! I'm doing Swim-Through-The-Rock today, did you know that? But I already have my Flow. A fish-in-the-air. Everyone agrees that's what I'm going to be. I can already float a little bit. Do you want me to show you? I can show you if you like. Look!'

The words came out in such a breathless tumble that even had Yashu for some reason not wanted a demonstration of Zeelu's Flow, she would have been hard pressed to say so. The next thing she knew, she was watching Zeelu raise herself onto tiptoes. Then, with lip-chewing concentration, Zeelu lifted one foot to horizontal, following it with the other, so that both soles were clear of the ground. She hovered unsteadily in this position for several heartbeats before her focus went and gravity reclaimed her.

'See? *Mamu* says there's no reason I shouldn't be able to make other things fly too. I'm going to be a great fish-in-the-air!'

Pharralu, joining them, admonished her daughter with a stern look. 'Zeelu, perhaps you shouldn't be showing off in front of Yashu. What did we say?'

Zeelu's cheeks flushed a faint pink. 'Oh yes. Sorry, Yashu.'

'Not to worry,' Yashu told her. 'I don't mind.'

'I*ilyashu,' said Huaso's father, with a nod of his head.

Yashu offered him a low, grave bow. 'Shaiimersho. I*il is honoured by your presence. Yours too, Shaipharralu.' Another low bow. 'It's very good to see you both.'

'The feeling is mutual,' said Pharralu, but it wasn't and both she and Yashu knew it. Pharralu was never anything less than polite to Yashu, but her politeness was false. You could hear it in her voice, like the chiming of a cracked bell. It was obvious to anyone. She didn't think much of Yashu, and Yashu knew why. Since Yashu was without-Flow, and Huaso was also without-Flow, it seemed acceptable that the two of them should get together. It seemed, in a sense, unavoidable, since their kind were not exactly spoiled for choice when it came to finding a mate. If, however, they were actually to marry, there was little chance of them having with-Flow children. On the other hand, if Huaso were able to find and marry a with-Flow girl – and likewise Yashu a with-Flow boy – then the odds on the issue of either union being with-Flow were that much greater. Pharralu, therefore, was torn between the wish for Huaso's happiness and her instinct for the greater good of Li*issua as a whole.

Imersho, too, felt that schism, but his loyalty was first and foremost to his son. There was only ever friendliness in his eyes and his voice when he spoke to Yashu. He would not mind having her as his daughter-in-law.

'*Mamu! Papo!*' Zeelu was hopping from foot to foot impatiently. 'I want to go up and have a look at the Rock now. Can I?'

Pharralu said, 'Let's all go up and look at the Rock.' It wasn't clear whether the *all* was meant to include Yashu or not. Pharralu injected a great deal of ambiguity into the word.

'I'd prefer to stay here,' Huaso said.

'Are you sure?'

'I've seen it already, *mamu*,' Huaso said simply, 'and it's not as if it holds any marvellous memories for me.'

His family headed off in the direction of the eastern promontory, with Zeelu skipping in front of her parents, begging them to walk a little faster.

'Look at her,' There was brotherly pride in Huaso's eyes, but an admixture of sorrow too. 'She couldn't be more thrilled.'

'And why shouldn't she be?' Yashu said. 'It's a big day for her.'

Huaso shrugged, nodded. 'Still . . . What it must be, to know your Flow is coming through already.'

'You mustn't envy her. It's *mala* for you just to be happy for her.'

'Oh, I am, I am. All the same . . .' He looked gloomy, like a child half his age, perhaps ready to shed tears.

'Come on, enough of that.' Yashu nudged him on the arm. 'Are you hungry? After your journey, I bet you are. And if I'm not mistaken, they've just started to cook some grilled-eel-on-stick.'

They ate their grilled-eel-on-stick sitting side by side at the top of Tallest-Dune, amid a thicket of hissing marram grass. At their feet, the beach got busier as more other-islander boats pulled in and more own-islanders traipsed down from the coastal track. The sun was launching itself ever higher. The tide crept towards its lowest ebb. Yashu and Huaso talked about what they'd been up to since they last met, which was four spring-tides ago, on Arashi, at the celebration of Anointing-New-Boats. Huaso complained about school and particularly about having to learn Common Tongue, which he was bad at and couldn't see the point of mastering since he never expected to have to use it, because he was going to be a fisherman and therefore would not have to trade with mainlanders to make a living, only with islanders and coastliners. Yashu wanted to know what he would do if some main-lander came up to him at market and wanted to buy some of his fish, and he said, 'I'd tell him this,' and made an obscene gesture peculiar to the people of Li*issua but at the same time universally intelligible, and they both giggled. Yashu then told him about her aunt, about how Liyalu's illness was continuing to creep through her body, slow and painful, and from day to day there never seemed much change in her but if you looked back not very far and remembered how she had been then and compared it to how she was now, if you considered for example that she once hardly ever used her walking-stick to get around and now depended on it almost all the time, then the deteri-oration was all too apparent. It was a grim, greedy disease Liyalu had. It seemed to eat her from within, gnawing away at her vitality. She was only forty but sometimes, particularly at the end of the day, she looked twice that. And there was no remedy for it, no cure for her condition, nothing anyone on Li*issua or on the mainland could do for her. She was just going to get worse and worse, her faculties failing, her strength trickling away, until finally, far sooner than was fair, she lost her hold on life and her spirit entered the Great-Ocean-Beyond. Yashu said all this matter-of-factly, without rancour, but around the edges of her voice there was brittleness, for she was talking about the woman who had without query or complaint taken her sister's daughter into her home and given the orphaned child as good an upbringing as anyone could ever hope for – the woman who was not just her aunt but to all intents and purposes her mother. Yashu had lost two parents already, and was facing the prospect, horribly near, of losing a third.

Huaso could think of nothing to say in response, so he laid a hand gently on Yashu's leg. It was a comforting, confirming touch – *I am here*. She studied him sidelong and was glad to be reminded that he was as good-looking as she remembered. Not handsome, not by any conventional reckoning, but he had a kind mouth, a nice symmetrical nose, deep eyes. She saw a future for herself in those eyes. She saw a life beyond the time Aunt Liyalu passed on, a life on Shai, a home for the two of them, Huaso off before dawn every morning in his boat with a shaper-of-water and a boomer among the crewmembers under his command, and she at their house, busy with children, two of them, possibly three, and minding a herd of goats, just as she did now. Shaiyashu – it was a good-sounding name, and one she had several times, when alone, uttered aloud, to see how it seemed to her ears, to give it greater reality by bringing it audibly into the world.

A shout went up from the eastern promontory, announcing that the tide was almost fully out and the ceremony would begin shortly. Yashu and Huaso got to their feet and hurried along the crest of the dunes. They reached the promontory – and a good vantage point – ahead of most of the crowd. They settled down and watched as the Swim-Through-The-Rock children formed a queue on the hand-chiselled, foot-worn steps. The steps descended to the jumping-off point, a kind of narrow natural jetty which had been festooned for the occasion with banners from all twenty islands of Li*issua, the tricolours of every clan. Adult supervisors marshalled the children, in-structing them not to shove, to keep their voices down, remain calm and wait their turn. Out in the channel, breath-holders sported and cavorted like dolphins, diving, sounding, surfacing, rolling. They put on this display as much for their own enjoyment as for the entertain-ment of the people on the promontory, although all their splashing and activity did have the additional benefit of keeping away any marine predators who might happen to be patrolling near the shore-line. The Rock, dome-shaped, imperturbable, rose above the flexing whitecapped waves, whitecapped itself from all the guano that had been deposited on it over time by resting and nesting seabirds. No human had ever set foot on it since the days of Finder-Founder Oriñaho, for whom the Rock reared out of the water as his ship approached I*il, stranding the vessel on its back so that Oriñaho, and his twenty wives, had no alternative but to disembark, swim to shore and make the island their home. Back then, all those countless generations ago, after the birth of the Worldstorm, in the time of the Great-Fissuring, I*il had had no name. Nor had Li*issua. It was Oriñaho who had given the archipelago the title of Place-Of-Respite, and who had then gone about populating it, siring two sons and two daughters by each of his wives and commanding these eighty offspring to intermarry and go forth and colonise all the islands of the archipelago. Thus were the great clans created, and to this day each still held sway over the island that bore its name.

Huaso pointed out Zeelu, fifth in the queue of not wholly quietened youngsters. Yashu made the observation that she looked about half a head taller than anyone else, and Huaso said that probably had something to do with the fact that she was so full of excitement she was floating off the ground without even realising it.

Yashu directed her gaze past the children, out to the Rock again, and focused in on its base, where it shelved away into the clear blue water, losing itself in the cloudier, bluer depths. She could just make out the mouth of the tunnel which bored through one corner of the Rock, a tide-eroded passage that was about ten paces in length and a little wider in diameter than the shoulder-breadth of a pubescent child. With the tide at its lowest ebb, as now, the tunnel's entrance and exit were only just below the surface. Holding a deep breath, you could easily submerge and wriggle through. The feat itself was not difficult. What it represented, however, was immense. If someone's Flow was not already making itself known by the time that person reached Swim-Through-The-Rock age, without fail it emerged within days of the ritual being undergone. The ritual seemed to induce its arrival – except, of course, when it came to people like her and Huaso who, for no reason other than the caprice of the spirits, had no Flow and never would.

'I told Zeelu to try and take everything in,' Huaso said. 'To concentrate on what is happening around her, to be aware of it all in such a way that she will never forget it. I barely remember *my* Swim-Through-The-Rock. It's all mist in my mind. Perhaps that's just as well, I don't know. But I want her not to be as overwhelmed by the occasion as I was. She, at least, should be able to recall every moment of this day.'

'You're a very good brother,' Yashu said, linking her arm through Huaso's. 'I'm sure she'll follow your advice.'

Huaso grimaced. 'There's always a first time, I suppose.'

Then Rhinazu, headwoman of I*il, appeared on the promontory to address a short speech to the children. Her words weren't audible from where Yashu and Huaso were sitting, but if previous form was anything to go by, she was covering the usual topics of responsibility to Li*issua, respect for clan, obedience to elders, the importance of Flow and of nurturing and developing Flow. She then stressed the symbolic significance of Swim-Through-The-Rock – a journey, via the medium of water, from the state of childhood to the state of manhood or womanhood, a kind of second birth. When she was done, she gave the nod for the ritual to commence.

The first of the children leapt from the jumping-off point into the sea. Breath-holders gathered around her and swam alongside her across the channel to the Rock. The crowds cheered encouragement as the girl gulped in a breath and ducked under, minnowing down towards the tunnel entrance with a kick of her legs. When she reappeared moments later on the far side of the tunnel, bobbing to the surface, the encouragement turned to applause. The girl was escorted back to shore while the next child in line, a boy, plunged into the water.

When Zeelu's turn came, she stepped boldly off the promontory and traversed the channel in a splashy, flailing doggy-paddle. ('Not much of a swimmer, our Zeelu,' was Huaso's comment.) With two of the breath-holders on either side of her, and another two waiting by the outlet of the tunnel, she readied herself to dive. Down she went. Moments later, up she came on the other side.

Huaso went down to hug her, and came back with the front of his shirt dampened with an imprint of her wet body. If he had looked proud before, he looked infinitely more so now. Fit to burst with it.

'So anyway,' he said. 'That's that. There's about seventy more children. How long do you think it'll take for all of them to go through?'

'I don't know,' Yashu said. She saw a conspiratorial glint in Huaso's eye and felt the corners of her mouth turning up. 'A while. Why?'

'Perhaps we could . . .' He gestured hesitantly towards the beach.

'Yes, perhaps we could.'

They stole through the crowd, hand in hand, heading back to the dunes. There, they found themselves a hollow where they were well sheltered from the onshore breeze and where the hubbub from the promontory was deliciously, illicitly distant. They weren't the only ones to have had this idea. In every other dip and cleft in the dunes, or so it seemed, there was a couple of similar age to them cuddling and canoodling. Some of the couples were going further than that, locked in positions that at first glance seemed innocent but were anything but. Furtive rocking motion and the odd ungovernable moan gave away the truth. Yashu and Huaso, in their own private trysting spot, confined themselves to deep, lascivious kissing and the hot pressure of body on body, but their hands strayed all over each other and once in a while – more than once in a while where Huaso's hands were concerned – brushed as if inadvertently over a taboo area. They teased and frustrated each other in this way until the only sensible thing they could do was roll apart. Both wanted and yet were not prepared to go further. Neither of them had the necessary self-assurance yet.

Lying on their backs, Yashu's head on Huaso's chest, they watched clouds for a while, feeling their pulse rates slowing and a sense of propriety reasserting itself. The clouds were white and sharply defined except for the wind-smeared tail each dragged behind it. Huaso likened them to ships of the sky, churning up soft furrows in their wakes.

'We'll have a house of our own when you come to live with me on Shai, Yashu,' he then said. 'I've already picked out the one. It's in Purple-Cowrie-Beach-Village. No one's lived in it for ages, and I've put in an application with the headman to be allowed to take it over. It's survived two 'Storms more or less intact, and it has seven rooms. Seven! Some of them need repairing, but that's all right, I can manage that. Some of the rendering outside needs fixing too, and the roof has holes. The good thing is, it's big enough for all of us. You, me and Liyalu.'

Yashu turned her head to look up at his face. 'You wouldn't mind Aunt Liyalu living with us?'

'Of course not. Why should I? Besides, I'd never expect you to leave her on her own to come to live with me. This way, you and I could both help look after her, we get to live together – everyone happy.'

'I don't know whether Aunt Liyalu would agree to move to Shai. She might take a lot of persuading.'

'But if you start working on her, and tell her how wonderful the house is, or will be when I've finished with it, and how beautiful Purple-Cowrie-Beach-Village is, which it is, believe me, and tell her about all the new friends she'll make on Shai, I'm sure she'll come around.'

'Aunt Liyalu's not very good at making new friends.'

'Not on I*il, maybe, but on Shai it'll be a different story.'

It was all so simple to Huaso. He had decided on a plan and could not see how anything might prevent that plan from succeeding. Yashu was both charmed by and envious of his straightforwardness. It was one of his most attractive qualities, that he had a faith in the future –

in their future together – that was utterly unhindered by doubts. Perhaps it was because he hadn't lost his parents to the Worldstorm and because he didn't live with a relative who was dying. He had experienced hardships of his own, certainly. But even discovering that he was without-Flow had not crushed his innate optimism. Life still seemed basically fair to Huaso, and Yashu was drawn to that as a hermit crab is drawn to an empty shell.

Too soon they heard the sound of people traipsing back from the Rock. The ceremony was over. Reluctantly, Yashu and Huaso drew apart, got to their feet, brushed themselves off, and descended from the dunes.

On the beach, the barbecue pits were ablaze. It wasn't long before roast food was being distributed through the crowd: lobster, crab, cobs of corn, potatoes, sizzling fish steaks. There was orange juice for the children to drink and, for the grown-ups, something also made from oranges but a little more potent, *sirassi*. Yashu and Huaso lunched with Huaso's family, and the atmosphere in their little group was convivial enough. Zeelu dominated the conversation. She was of the age when the sound of her own voice was the most important thing in the world, and her relentless chirpiness kept everyone amused.

When lunch was eaten, the storytelling show began. A troupe of fish-in-the-air puppeteers who had set up a stage on the dunes began manipulating their life-size marionettes against various backdrops. From a distance they made the elegant, articulated wooden figures strut, gesticulate, bow, swoon, skip, fight, dance, pirouette, gyrate, all to match the words of I*il's narrator-in-residence, I*ilaziano, who stood atop Tallest-Dune and bellowed out his versions of old, old tales in his boomer voice, loud enough to be heard across the entire island. These were stories which had been around as long as there had been people on Li*issua, and they told of true events that were also myths, legends that were also history. Such as: Finder-Founder Oriñaho's defiance of the Worldstorm, which he managed to scare away by shouting at it louder than its own thunder (for in Oriñaho there was every Flow, including booming). Such as: the adventures of strongman Sheelo, long-ago headman of Ra*ai, who would wrestle killer whales for sport and once ate an entire netful of sprat at a single sitting and then, suffering from a terrible stomach ache, vomited up all the fish alive. Such as: the exploits of the heroine Ussyashu, Yashu's namesake, who averted conflict between the residents of Uss and Haroo by swimming back and forth across the treacherous strait between the two islands no less than a hundred times, a feat which so impressed the warring factions that they immediately set aside their differences and sued for peace.

For each story, the stringless puppets executed a mime of gestures and dance that followed the rhythm of Aziano's words and brought the narrative to life. Some of the stage scenery also moved. Here were dark grey clouds that represented the Worldstorm, shying angrily away from Oriñaho's breast-beating bellow. Here were the killer whales that Ra*aisheelo knocked flying. Here were interleaving blue-painted boards that were the seething waters of the Uss-Haroo strait, doing their best to overwhelm a figurine representing the dauntless Ussyashu. Aziano returned again and again to certain descriptive epithets he had coined in order to set his personal stamp on the stories, while the puppeteers had their creations perform certain equivalent manoeuvres of their own devising, a combination which made the show uniquely I*il and uniquely now. Other-islander puppeteer troupes used different signature movements. Future troupes all across the archipelago would devise all-new, idiosyncratic variations for themselves. In this way, the stories were kept fresh and alive and eternal.

Everyone loved the show, children and adults alike, and there was a tumultuous round of applause at the end, with hoots and whistles. As Aziano, the puppeteers *and* the marionettes took their bows, Zeelu solemnly announced that, now that she knew she was a fish-in-the-air, she planned to become a puppeteer herself when she was older. No other job would do for her. Her mind was absolutely made up.

'And you like stories about Ussyashu, don't you?' she said to Yashu.

'I do,' Yashu said, although it would have been more accurate to say that she used to. Back when she was young. Back when she believed that anything was possible. Back before she was Dammed.

'Then I'll make sure that when I'm a puppeteer we *always* put on at least one Ussyashu story,' Zeelu said. 'Just for you.'

The show marked the culmination of the day's events. I*ilrhinazu thanked people for coming and once again congratulated the Swim-Through-The-Rock children. Then a gradual exodus to the boats began. Since Shai was one of the furthest islands away, Huaso's family were among the first to leave. Down at the water's edge, Yashu said formal farewells to Imersho and Pharralu, and also to Zeelu, who was delighted to be addressed as Shaizeelu for the first time in her life. Then Yashu turned to Huaso. He looked gloomy.

'Will you be at the celebration of Cross-The-Causeway on Oöyia the month after next?' she asked.

'If there is a boat going from Shai.'

'Then I'll see you there. We'll gorge ourselves on cockles until we're so heavy that we sink into the mud up to our knees.'

This seemed to perk him up, and when he bowed to her his mouth was trying to bend into a smile. '*Mala*, I*ilyashu.'

44

'*Mala*, Shaihuaso,' she said.

As locals helped shove the Shai boat off the sand, Huaso took his place at the prow again, standing there with his arms limp by his sides, looking back at Yashu. When the boat was afloat, its shaper-of-water turned it about on a sideways welter of water and aimed for open sea. Huaso turned too, contrariwise, and kept his gaze on Yashu until each of them was too far off to distinguish the other's face. Then he waved to her, and she waved back, until the distance between them was too great for even that gesture to be visible. Finally the boat was just one of several dispersing black dots on the horizon, and I*il, from Huaso's viewpoint, just a receding, triple-peaked silhouette, dwindling into haze.

Yashu helped her own-islanders tidy up after the revelries, tossing handfuls of food detritus off the beach into the lap of the sea. Gulls swooped in to scavenge whatever floated. Whatever sank would be nibbled up by marine creatures. The sea was all-effacing, all-embracing, all-erasing.

Once the beach was clean, Yashu made her way up to the coastal track and trod back round to the island's windward side, part of a strung-out procession of people making the same journey.

Arriving home, she was greeted by the goats. The two nannies congregated at the fence and bleated to her plaintively. Both were in need of milking, their udders hanging heavy. Meanwhile the billy stared from a short way off, his slotted gaze appraising. Yashu told the nannies she would attend to them shortly, and entered the cottage by the kitchen door, calling out Aunt Liyalu's name.

Liyalu was asleep, slumped in her favourite chair in the main room, facing the windows and the view out over the rooftops of Second-Cliff-Village to the expanse of sea beyond. Her head was angled heavily against one shoulder, and Yashu thought that this was how her aunt would look if she were to have died just now. She seemed to have no support in herself, her body sunken under its own ailing weight.

Gently she awoke her. Liyalu came round slowly, her thin hands groping at the air as though sleep were a net she was having to claw her way out of. It took her several moments to focus on her niece's face.

'Is it late afternoon already?' she said.

'Afraid so.'

'Oh shit and seaweed, I've slept most of the day away.'

'It doesn't matter.'

'It does. I was hoping to get some housework done. I just sat down for a rest . . .' She tried to get out of the chair but couldn't manage it without assistance from Yashu. 'Was it a nice day?' she asked, stretching out cramped limbs

'Mostly, yes.'

'The ceremony went well?'

'Fine.'

'And Huaso was happy to see you?'

'He was.'

'That's good then.'

Yashu changed out of her best clothes into something plainer and more practical. Then it was chores: milking the goats, washing bed-linen in the tub by the stream and hanging it out to dry, and, finally, stoking up the stove and reheating last night's rabbit stew for supper. It was a warm evening, so she and Liyalu ate at the table outdoors, lit lengthways by the rays of sunset. Controlling her hands was a struggle for Liyalu, and becoming more so as time went by and her illness worsened. As much of each trembling spoonful of stew slopped back into the bowl as made it into her mouth. Yashu found it painful to watch, but had become expert at masking her pity. The last thing Liyalu needed or expected was pity.

'You said it was "mostly" a nice day,' Liyalu said. 'Something must have squirted its ink into the water. What?'

'Just Shaipharralu. She hates me, and she tries to hide it but it's plain as anything.'

'I don't know if she hates you. It's just mothers and their sons, that's all. No girl would be good enough for her Huaso.'

'But when she talks to me, it's like her voice is dripping with vinegar. You know, sweet, but more sour than sweet. Do you think she'll ever approve of me?'

'I think,' said Liyalu, 'you should clear away the dishes and fetch me my pipe and my pouch of ninespike, please.'

Yashu did as asked, and fumblingly Liyalu gathered up pinches of the dope and tamped them into the bowl of the pipe. Then, with the aid of a match and plenty of sucking, she got the dry, dark-green shreds alight and fuming. She inhaled blissfully, holding the smoke in her lungs as long as she could. Liyalu lived most of her life having to endure rough, rasping aches all over her body, like miniature saws working away deep in her muscles, sometimes in her bones. The dope helped soothe the pain.

'Better,' she said, and dragged on the pipe a few more times before offering it to Yashu. Yashu took a couple of not-as-deep puffs before passing it back. The ninespike, grown locally, was a particularly harsh strain, and she disliked the way its smoke scraped at the back of your throat. What she did like was the mild giddiness it brought.

She thought Liyalu would be carrying on the conversation about Pharralu. When that didn't happen, she attempted to revive the subject.

'Maybe if I had Flow . . .'

'Maybe,' Liyalu replied. 'Do you know what the worst thing about this illness of mine is? Not that it's slowly killing me. Who fears entering the Great-Ocean-Beyond? And not that some part of me or other is usually hurting because of it. It's that I don't have my sharp-sight any more. That was the first thing the illness took from me. Which is usually what happens, isn't it? You know something's seriously wrong with you when your Flow starts to fade. But I used to be able to see so much. I could count the petals on a daisy at a hundred paces. I could tell you the colour of a seagull's eye a mile away. I could look down there' – she pointed at Second-Cliff-Village, now blanketing itself in a haze of chimney smoke – 'and spot wasps building a nest under somebody's eaves. On a clear day I could even make out the mainland from here. At night, there were stars visible to me that weren't visible to anybody else, hundreds of them. All gone now. The world's become dull. Drab. Like I'm peering at everything through a veil. No, not a veil. Through wool. That's how bad it is. I'm glimpsing when I used to be able to look, truly look. And I miss that so much. So much it sometimes makes me want to weep.'

Her eyes glistened, and Yashu remembered how, when she was small, she used to think that her aunt's sharp-sight didn't only bring distant objects closer – that her aunt was capable of peering into her mind and uncovering her innermost thoughts. She hadn't known then that this was an ability almost all adults had when it came to children.

'I don't mean to belittle what you're going through,' Liyalu said, stroking her niece's arm. 'I'm just saying I understand. And that things could be worse. That maybe, looked at a certain way, it's better for someone not to have Flow at all than have it and then lose it.'

'I wouldn't mind even having a not-of-the-archipelago Flow. Even that would be better.'

'What, and have to be packed off to the mainland to learn how to use it properly?'

'I'd never go! I'd never leave you!'

Liyalu's gaze was sad and fond. 'You're a good girl, Yashu. Life's been pretty unkind to you, yet you've always managed to keep your chin up and take the *mala* view. I'm so proud of you for that. If it's any consolation, I'm sure there's a purpose behind everything that's happened to you. I'm sure there's a reason why you were pulled alive and unharmed from the ruins of your parents' house, and I'm sure there's a reason why your Flow is as it is. I have no idea what the reason might be, but you should trust the spirits. They don't misguide us. Sometimes their schemes might seem a little foggy, but by and large they want what's best for all of us. Do you believe that?'

'I do.'

'Then that's all that matters.' Liyalu reached for the pouch of ninespike. 'Mind you, when I get to the Great-Ocean-Beyond, I'll be having words with them. You can count on that. "Give Yashu a break," I'll tell them. And they'd bloody well better listen.'

In spite of everything Yashu laughed. One of the things she loved most about her aunt was her irreverent streak. Liyalu observed the codes and conventions of life, but not slavishly. And it was easy to imagine her, after death, doing just as she had said – causing trouble, being ornery, refusing to let her spirit surrender gracefully to the massed anonymity of the Great-Ocean-Beyond. As obstinate as a limpet while alive, she was hardly likely to be much different when dead.

The sky dusted over with dusk. The stars sprinkled out. The moon rose, hard and pure, striping its light over a tar-black sea. Liyalu finished a second pipe of ninespike, with help from Yashu, then turned in for the night, planting a soft kiss on the crown of her niece's head before hobbling indoors. Yashu remained where she was, settling back into her seat and listening to the beat of the waves against the rocks below Second-Cliff-Village. Their rhythmic throb lulled her blood.

If there was a purpose to it all, as her aunt had said, all the misfortunes, all the things gone wrong, then fine. Yashu just wished the spirits would hurry up and reveal it.

AYN

An excellent breakfast! Those two young ones work well together in the kitchen. To think how little interest they had in each other when they first met, and now look at them. All's going as it should, Khollo. All's going as it should.

Now then. Where do I start?

Perhaps with an account of my long and distinguished career at Stonehaven.

Don't pull that face, Khollo. I'm joking. Besides, it might have been a long career but was it distinguished? High Previsionary is a grand-sounding title, and I worked my way up through the hierarchy, exceptionally hard, to attain it. But still, anyone who's ever spent any time at Stonehaven knows that a previsionary ranks right at the bottom of the ladder there. Even a High Previsionary is just the lowest of the high. Not a *practical* ability, you see. Not marketable. What good is it to anyone but myself that I know my own future? The only reason, I suspect, that there are previsionaries at Stonehaven at all is because it has always been that way. It is written into the Stonehaven constitution. The place has to play host to representatives of every single class of Air Inclination. That was the principle on which it was established all those centuries ago, and it's a principle that could no more be changed than Stonehaven itself could be damaged by the Worldstorm. Stonehaven's founders created a stronghold for all Air types. They hewed a citadel out of the rock of an extinct volcano for that purpose alone. Stonehaven is a monument to inclusivity – if you forget for a moment that it isn't open to residents from any of the other three Inclinations.

It may seem that my experiences there latterly, and I include my contretemps with High Psychometrist Ærdant, have coloured my view of Stonehaven and all that it stands for. This is undoubtedly so. Nonetheless I feel obliged to state that for a long time I was glad to live there. Not just glad, grateful. It's not easy out here in the world for a previsionary. Of all Air types, we are the ones who have the hardest time fitting in with the great mass of society. For the obvious reasons. How pointless is it to have conversations when you know in advance what the other person is about to say? How boring is it, not being able ever to be surprised by anyone? How tedious is it – tedious bordering on maddening – to live surrounded by people who seem almost like puppets, their every action conforming to your expectation? Previsionaries have a reputation for being haughty, world-weary, disdainful, and if we are, it's surely down to the fact that there is nothing new to us. We have, literally, seen it all before.

Which isn't to say that things are different in that respect for a previsionary even within a place like Stonehaven. There is still the same predictability about your fellow men. What *is* different is that your fellow men are more tolerant toward you. They understand you in a way that others – not to put too fine a point on it, but the non-Air Inclined – do not. They sympathise, even empathise. They are prepared to treat any lapses in politeness and patience, of which it's possible that I may have been guilty from time to time, as just the unfortunate by-product of prevision. Their attitude is that all we Air types are prone to our faults and foibles. It is part of the way we are. It is the price we have to pay for our exalted skills.

Please note, Khollo, a certain irony in my voice. I don't believe, any more than you do, that being Air Inclined 'exalts' us above others. Although I daresay I used to. Certainly when I was a young man, freshly installed in Stonehaven, as cocky and confident as only a young man can be, I thought myself truly a cut above the rest. Why wouldn't I? Stonehaven! My parents were proud of me for having passed the interview and been selected as an Inductee. *I* was proud of me. And I knew that as long as I played my cards right, I could live my whole life there, rise up through the ranks, join the Council of Elders, be able to count on Stonehaven's wealth and protection till I died. Why wouldn't I, under those circumstances, consider myself fortunate, privileged, special? Even more so than the average Air Inclined? You, apparently, did not ever feel that way. Am I right? You were never wholly comfortable at Stonehaven, yes? Yes. And that was why, when I decided I needed an enshriner to record this enterprise of mine for posterity, I was drawn to you and asked you to accompany me on this journey. Not only did I know you wouldn't say no, but I saw in you a fellow malcontent . . .

Actually, no, edit all that bit out, Khollo. An empty digression.

[I've disobeyed the High Previsionary's request and left it in. It is, I think, revealing. About both of us.]

Let's go back to . . . what was I saying? Something about 'faults and foibles'?

[' "Their attitude is that all we Air types are prone to our faults and foibles," ' I said. ' "It is part of the way we are. It is the price we have to pay for our exalted skills." ']

Excellent. Thank you. Carry on from '. . . part of the way we are.'

Ahum. So, while I'm not exactly unambivalent in my feelings towards Stonehaven, I am aware that without it I would have had a far less easy time of things over the course of my sixty-odd years of life. Stonehaven sheltered me. It embraced me. I was, for a long time, as much a part of it as its black rock walls, its curving, burrowing corridors, its innumerable spiral staircases, the library, the lagoon. I belonged there as the Obsidian Hall belonged there, the Balcony Grange, the Circumferential Cloister, the Cells of Solitude and Contemplation. I was thoroughly, one might even say hopelessly, immersed in the politics of the place – that long drawn-out drama of back-scratching and favour-returning and shifting allegiance with which we residents liked to entertain ourselves, that game we played with frowns of delight and smiles of deadly earnest, pretending it was just for fun but knowing deep down that it was not. Stonehaven, so vast and deep and unalterable, and we gadding about inside it, we humans with our jealousies and our ambitions, our vanities and our lust for self-furtherance. Stonehaven, eternal, and we and all that we stood for, not.

Is it any wonder, thinking about it, that I eventually wound up embarking on this attempt to do something significant, something that would have a positive effect on the entire world? After all those years when my main aim was to improve my own already privileged lot, it's not surprising that in the end I should turn around and try to improve the lot of everyone else.

[And yet I can't help thinking that Elder Ayn's grand scheme, folly or not, was at least in part intended to achieve even greater renown for himself. He'd risen as high as he could within Stonehaven. His gaze turned outward, looking for similar success in the big wide world. And perhaps, resentful of the relatively low status accorded to previsionaries at Stonehaven, he felt he had something to prove as well.]

Having said I wasn't going to discuss my career at Stonehaven, I'm aware that I am doing almost precisely that. It is necessary, though, in order to set the scene for what is to come. I was High Previsionary. I was, at the age of fifty-eight, elected to that rank by the Council of Elders, superiors who became my peers. I had cultivated the right people, made the right friends. There were rivals for the post, fellow previsionaries who, like me, had crossed that sketchily defined border between Numerary and Aspirant. I saw them off. I played the game better than they did. When my predecessor High Previsionary

Eglantine died, there was no Aspirant likelier to fill her place at the Council Table than me.

But previsionaries do not contribute materially to Stonehaven's income. As I said before, we do not possess a marketable skill, something to sell to petitioners from outside. We cannot, for example, recognise a lie the moment we hear one, as a sooth-seer can. We cannot hold, say, an item of clothing or a family heirloom in our hands and tell you its full history, as a psychometrist can. We cannot find that same family heirloom for you, if lost, by concentrating for several minutes on a sketch of the layout of your home, as a diviner can. We cannot make vast mathematical calculations and assess huge amounts of statistical data, as a numerator can. We cannot send messages for you out into the telepath network and relay the replies, as any good telepath can, nor impart with our minds some piece of knowledge you might like to acquire, as a teacher can (like the old saying: 'Those who can both send and receive, do, those who can only send, teach.'). In the Air Inclined pecking order, even serendipiters are above us, and what use are *they*?

['They make for excellent librarians,' I offered.]

Yes, fair comment. It's a good talent to be able to turn up the book someone's looking for almost before they know they need to look for it. A handy little knack.

So what are previsionaries required to do at Stonehaven? How do I and others like me earn our keep there? What are we there for, other than to complete the quota of Air-Inclined classes? We run things. We oversee the domestic staff, the kitchen staff, the scullions, the underlings. We make sure the people who keep Stonehaven in order are themselves kept in order. We are also responsible for the welfare of the poor souls incarcerated in the Cells of Solitude and Contemplation. And as High Previsionary, one gets the honour of lording it over all the other previsionaries. One is in charge of the people who are in charge of the people who do all the necessary stuff, the dirty work. It's just a couple of steps up from doing the dirty work oneself.

Supposedly previsionaries are well-equipped for this kind of employment because we can anticipate problems. And that, in a certain sense, we can do, but as I pointed out to you yesterday, Khollo, being able to foresee a problem doesn't necessarily mean you can forestall it. The real reason previsionaries have drawn the short straw at Stonehaven is because they're in no position to object. Don't like it? Bugger off into the outside world then and see how you fare there. Bet you won't be half as well off as you are now.

And I swear I did not mind. I swear I was fine about it. I knew the deal from the outset, I knew what was expected of me, and I thought it fair exchange. In return, I got a life of comfort. I got the safety of Stonehaven, which the 'Storm, even in its foulest moods, has never yet put so much as a scratch in. I got the reassurance of a daily routine. That last, believe me, is important to a previsionary. It's reassuring when the days are all racked up ahead of you one after another in a row, all but identical, like the tiles in a game of elements waiting to be turned over. The future is smoothed and blurred and . . . *planed* is a good word for it. Devoid of rough edges. Easy to handle. It's good when you know that tomorrow is going to be just like yesterday. Up at first gong. Breakfast. Supervise the cleaning up after breakfast. Listen to staff grievances. Work out menus and rosters. Attend the morning Council meeting in the Obsidian Hall. Then, before lunch, just time for a swim in the lagoon, three times across and back – marvellous exercise, though damned cold even in summer. After lunch, down to the Cells of Solitude and Contemplation, to . . .

Don't do it, Khollo. Don't. Don't yawn. Hold it back. Ha ha! I knew you wouldn't be able to. Could it be that you're finding my scintillating account of a High Previsionary's average day somewhat dull? I suspect that to anyone unfamiliar with the workings of Stonehaven, this insider's glimpse might be of some considerable interest. Equally, I understand that a narrative must not ramble, at least not too much. It must be to the point. Let us say, then, to summarise, that I welcomed the pattern of things at Stonehaven. It suited me nicely, and I it. I might wish to have been able to participate in the somewhat more glamorous work done by my non-previsionary colleagues, but one must not question one's Inclination nor envy the Inclination of others. From the start I did what was expected of me, and did it for the best part of forty years with a smile, and earned my place on the Council of Elders, and was satisfied. Or so I thought.

Disenchantment. When did the disenchantment set in? Was it before or after Traven Keech arrived? I like to think that it was after, once he and I began having those conversations of ours, but I wonder whether it might not have been before – whether the rash was already there, under the skin, latent, and Traven merely scratched it and inflamed it and brought it to the surface.

Traven, as you will remember, was a previsionary too. A young man from Damentaine, land of . . . How does the joke go?

['Land of rocks like brains and brains like rocks.']

That's the one! Those strange limestone formations that stick out from the Plain of Gaventia; ribbed and grey like exposed cerebellums. Never seen them myself. Never will. One more natural marvel that I shall die without having viewed with my own eyes. I could have travelled more, Khollo. Should have. Should have seen so much more of the world. And instead I spent forty years stuck in one place, barely venturing from its doorstep.

['We've travelled a lot recently,' I said. The High Previsionary seemed in need of encouragement just then. His voice, and face, had suddenly sunk. His body had sagged in the chair. His gaze was in-turned, shadowy. 'And besides, you were just saying how the routine at Stonehaven—']

Yes, yes, I know what I was saying. An old man is allowed his pangs of regret, isn't he? Especially an old man with just a few days left to live.

[After a minute or so's silence, he recovered himself.]

Right! Traven Keech. Came from Damentaine. A previsionary. Mentally unbalanced. Son of a telepath and a levitator, can you imagine that. Air and Water. I mean, if you must marry outside your own Inclination, fine, but Air and Water is always a potentially unstable mix. Effervescent. And up there in the wilds of Damentaine – well, the people are already a bit crazy, supposedly. The Worldstorm seems to be unusually attracted to that country, of all the countries of the Inner Continent. Could be that's *why* the people are crazy. Three times the average visits, they get there. Perhaps it's those limestone rock formations. Perhaps they attract lightning, or the 'Storm just has it in for them for some reason. Doesn't like the look of them. Thinks they stick out too much and should be flattened.

Anyhow. Traven had prevision, and it damaged him. He was given training. I mean, of course. But whoever trained him had his work cut out. Some people are simply unable to control their Inclinations, isn't that so? Just as some people cannot control a lazy eye or a twitching hand or a stutter. Traven's problem, you see, wasn't that he could see future as well as past. Rather, he could see everything at once. Past, present and future were indistinguishable from one another. He could not put them in order. From the moment he manifested, he lived in a continuum of all-time-and-any-time. Every instant of his life was happening at once. To use my analogy from yesterday, where I can see mountain ranges fading in either direction, Traven's vantage point was somewhere so high up in the sky that he could see all the mountain ranges simultaneously, with equal clarity. Not surprisingly, it drove him mad. He couldn't function in normal society. He was prone to violent outbursts. He was a danger to others and to himself. Sometimes he would harm himself, simply to prove to himself that he still existed in the here and now. Cutting your arm with a knife can be a somewhat, shall we say, sharp reminder of your own flesh-and-blood reality. And sometimes he would attack people around him, for not dissimilar reasons – to prove they were really there.

His family could not cope and applied to have him handed over into the custody of Stonehaven. The application was successful. It was, in fact, the first such application that I considered and approved after donning the High Previsionary's medal of office. Traven Keech was the first person I, as part of the Council of Elders, accepted for confinement in the Cells of Solitude and Contemplation. That and the fact that he was a previsionary made me feel a greater than usual sense of responsibility towards him. I can't deny that I also felt an odd kind of fascination in regard to him. As in the old proverb: 'We are drawn to those who walk a path which we ourselves have the fortune not to walk.'

He was an exceptionally good-looking boy, Traven. A broad, soulful face. Long eyelashes like a deer's – eyelashes any woman would be proud to possess. Scrubby, curly blond hair. Bright blue eyes. It was almost a crime, having to lock him away for the rest of his life, depriving the world of the sight of so handsome a creature. But, for his own good and everyone else's, there was no alternative. When he became violent, it was truly ugly to behold. He turned into someone else, a hideous thing, and his strength, in his desperation, was immense. It could take three, four large men to restrain him. He would flail and claw and bite like a wild animal, and scream in triumph if he drew blood, for the blood meant he wasn't imagining this moment, this wasn't some intangible memory or foresight, this was happening now.

His condition was all the more tragic and pitiable because at other times he was perfectly lucid. He would have periods of equilibrium when everything fell into order and he was no longer adrift on a sea of confused chronology. Then he was the gentlest, most affectionate, most guileless person you could ever hope to meet. He would ask about himself and about where he was and why he was there. Often he would have to have the same fact explained to him several times over, as if a cog in his inner clockwork kept slipping. There was no way he could ever have led a normal life. Incarceration was the best thing for him. But I must say that on more than one occasion I longed to unlatch his door and escort him to the main gate and set him free. Give him the chance to be just like anyone else.

The Cells of Solitude and Contemplation are on the lowest level of Stonehaven and their windows face outwards, giving a view of the Heurendon Valley to the west and the Pallian Hills in all other directions. Originally, as I understand it, they *were* used as places where a person could be alone and think on things, as their name suggests. The earliest residents of Stonehaven, as you know, were a high-minded lot. They were interested in developing their inner selves, exploring themselves as people, pondering deeply on the world and human nature. They would take it in turns to spend time down in the Cells, months on end with no one's company but their own, subsisting on meagre rations. That was the way Stonehaven was arranged back then, before the Siege forced a reappraisal of attitude a couple of centuries ago. The place used to be a retreat. Trade with outsiders was very much a sideline, a means of earning enough in the way of provisions to keep going, no more than that.

But just as Stonehaven itself is nowadays an altogether more pragmatic institution, so the Cells of Solitude and Contemplation are nowadays put to a more pragmatic use. I wouldn't say a better use, simply one which dovetails with the outlook of the present, less insular regime. That the Cells are run at the residents' own expense should not necessarily be seen as a sign of selfless generosity. Acts of charity so often are undertaken to ease the giver's conscience rather than the recipient's woes. And let us not forget that to be admitted to the Cells, a person has not only to be mad but Air Inclined.

Traven's cell faced eastwards. He got to see the dawn every morning over the Pallians and, come evening, the long wavy shadow which each hill draped over its neighbour like a friendly arm. His cell was typical in that it held a pallet bed, a small table and chair, a lidded bucket for his bodily functions and a pitcher of water, replenished every morning, for his ablutions. His window was a slot as long as your arm and not much wider, with an inner shutter that could be sealed firmly with four bolts. He was allowed books to read from the Great Library and a weekly ration of paper and ink to write with.

Scene-setting, Khollo. Not everyone will know what the living conditions in the Cells are like.

This was, and is, his home for ever more. Hardly the lap of luxury, but if it is any consolation, few of those held in the Cells of Solitude and Contemplation survive to a ripe old age. One thing or another gets to them soon enough. Dementia, ennui, suicide . . . Traven may still be alive, I don't know. Part of me hopes so, and part of me wishes, for his sake, that in the months since I last saw him he has found the only escape available to him – the freedom of death. It grieves me more to think of him still languishing in that cell than it does to think of him dead.

I don't remember how we first got talking, he and I. Talking seriously, that is. To begin with, he was just another of my duties as High Previsionary, although, as I have said, I did regard him as something of a special case. My final task, every night, was to make the rounds of the Cells, looking in through the barred window of each door, making sure the inmates were content – as content as can be expected. Some nights, the madder ones would set one another off, howling and gibbering and shrieking. A great cacophony of nonsense, horrible to endure. It was always at its worst when the 'Storm was around. The raging outside would trigger a raging inside. Never mind that there was nothing to fear. The buffeting, the changes of air pressure, doors vibrating in their frames, the way the whole of Stonehaven seemed to shiver under the 'Storm's assault – that was sufficient. Then, one could barely hear oneself think for all the clamour. The entire level rang with it. The madmen would throw themselves around in their cells. Self-harm most often occurred during the days of a visit from the Worldstorm. Suicide, too. Usually achieved by banging head against wall repeatedly.

Traven was no less prone to these fits of shouting and frenzy than anyone. But on quiet nights, and when he wasn't in one of his more bewildered frames of mind, he would always have a civil 'goodnight' for me, and I soon got into the habit of pausing by his door and enquiring if he had everything he needed.

'The only thing I need is to not be here,' he would usually reply, and then laugh, and I would laugh too.

He was intelligent but not learned, not scholarly. They don't produce great intellectuals up there in Damentaine, do they? His education had been rudimentary. He knew how to read and had been taught Common Tongue, and that was about it. He had, though, I could tell, a natural curiosity, an urge to see and discover and do, now cruelly curtailed. Under other circumstances, he might have left Damentaine and explored and wandered, drinking life in. I can imagine him, an eternal migrant, journeying wherever the whim took him and inspiring happiness and admiration wherever he went.

I took it upon myself not to let his life, and his mind, entirely go to waste. So I began bringing him books. Inmates of the Cells were permitted to read books from the library on condition that they take great care with them. It was a privilege that was seldom abused.

I chose carefully – volumes I thought would interest Traven, assuage that curiosity of his, educate him. H.C. Mellit's *Elementary Natural History*, of course, the illustrated edition with those gorgeous engravings by Olvo Luddin, an artist capable of perceiving details of the smallest of things with his sharp-sight and reproducing them with unerring accuracy. The *Geography* of Torquil. Gorong Frant's study of the development of Common Tongue, *Forging a Standard*, which, although grievously verbose, offers a robust defence against the claim that we Air types foisted our language on the rest of the world – we didn't, but since the great majority of books are written in Air it seemed logical that if the world were to have a universal language, Air should be it. And also Frant's other best-known work, *A Concordance For All*, in which he analyses the development of the Common Dating System and its gradual implementation throughout the Inner Continent. Some novels, too, including Lord Strulfana's *Storming the Crater*, which, though fictionalised, is generally held to be the most accurate and impartial of all the accounts of the Siege of Stonehaven. Even some poetry, although not wanting to alarm the lad I started him off on the straightforward stuff: some Odowhar, some Stannop, Leria Bebosh's narrative epics. Verse that scans and rhymes and tells a story.

He loved it. He leapt on it and devoured it all. Reading seemed to anchor him. As he himself said, 'I know I've read it already' – meaning that every time he opened a new book, its contents were no mystery because he had a fore-memory of finishing it – 'but while I'm actually reading, that doesn't matter. It's like following a thread. Page comes after page. I'm happy to anticipate what's coming, because that's what the writer wants me to do.' I myself have always found that knowing the end of a book in advance makes reading something of a trial, although I plod on regardless, since, obviously, I wouldn't know the end in advance if I didn't. For Traven, though, reading was a way of experiencing that quality missing from his life, seriality. It demanded some effort of concentration from him. A lot of application. But I'm pleased to say he was prepared to put in the effort. He had his lapses. Weeks would go by when he couldn't straighten his thoughts out enough even to follow one word after another in a sentence. But he would always return to a book eventually, and persevere. His progress delighted me, and he was delighted by my delight.

I put more difficult books his way, and he did not let me down. He grappled with Mard Broaste's weighty *Once In Wonder* and won. He hacked through the fat of Corval's lugubrious prose to get to the meat of *Open Musings*, that seminal work of moral philosophy. He braved the stormy waters of Aden Graice's free-form stanzas and survived. I don't kid myself that I was in any way responsible for these achievements of his. They were all his own work. All I contributed was the selection of books and some encouragement. He did the rest.

Our nightly exchanges developed from simple, casual chats into full-blown, intensive debates. We would discuss what Traven was reading or had just read, or even what he was shortly to read (we were both, after all, previsionaries), and I would perhaps steer him away from a misapprehension of an author's intent and towards a more accurate interpretation of the text, or perhaps suggest a fresh way he could view the material. I knew I should not be spending more time with one inmate than with any of the others, and I had a clear inkling that I was going to get into trouble over it somewhere down the line. There was nothing I could do about it, however. Helping Traven, watching him come on in leaps and bounds, seeing the gratitude in those blue, long-lashed eyes – it was intoxicating, nothing short of addictive. It could be that I should have extended the same treatment to inhabitants of other cells, made it look as if this was an even-handed policy for all inmates. That would have been the clever tactic, the subtle tactic. But alas, where certain aspects of behaviour are concerned, I have never been a clever or subtle man.

That rough-hewn boy from Damentaine blossomed under my care, but for all the sophistication he acquired, he retained his rustic inno-cence. You can take the boy out of the country but you can't take the country out of the boy. The Wet side of his parentage, too, showed through in so many ways. Not only did he treat his daily pitcher of water with a profound reverence – he wept once when he accidentally knocked it over and spilled its contents – but he was in thrall to various mystical notions of the kind we hear from time to time from a certain young lady of our acquaintance. Myths, stories embedded into him from birth, learned at his mother's knee, taught as true. Ideas about forces at work in the world, unseen influences that drive the machinery of life, a perpetual balancing flow of give-and-take between good and bad. It was interesting because now and then he would catch himself, as if incredulous, unable to understand why he accepted such things as true. His father's Air logicality emerging there. Mostly, though, he went along with it all, unquestioningly.

And that was how, as I changed him, he changed me.

The deeper he got into books, the more Traven found to shore up his way of seeing the world. Corval's more controversial assertions in *Open Musings*, for instance, Traven was able to use to argue in favour of the Wet view of the Worldstorm. 'Corval states that the bad deeds of every man, woman and child create a kind of resonance,' he said, 'and that that resonance cannot simply disappear into nothingness. So where does it go? Maybe it's transformed into another state. Maybe it feeds the 'Storm like coal feeds a fire.'

It could be that I am giving Traven's speech a polish it lacked, but then, clearly, I am paraphrasing his words, and mine as well. I lack the enshriner's gift for the perfect recounting of dialogue.

'Corval proceeds from the assumption that all humans are intrinsic-ally flawed,' I replied. 'He looks for some kind of moral counterweight to that. He points the finger – albeit tentatively – at the 'Storm.'

'But then what about his suggestion that errors in the past may have triggered the 'Storm?' Traven said. 'He talks about an age before history, when there wasn't a 'Storm.'

'Which accords with the Water Inclined's legends, yes. But you've read Platterney. He deals with this in his preface. Where is the evidence for an age before history? There would be records of it, surely. Remnants. Relics littered all around us. Platterney spent nearly twenty years researching, searching, before he sat down to begin work on *Origins*. He found nothing anywhere, apart from oral accounts of dubious authenticity, to show that before the development of writing and paper there was any kind of civilisation at all. We were unlettered farmers and shepherds, living much as people do now on the Outer Continent, and before that we were cave-dwellers, primitive creatures with the most rudimentary of Inclinations.'

'Couldn't the 'Storm have obliterated the evidence?'

'Possibly. But you must also realise that Corval's mention of an age before the 'Storm is, I'm convinced, meant to be ironic. It's hard to tell with someone whose grammar and syntax are so convoluted, but my impression is that he wants us to think that we – somehow – created the Worldstorm. This way we should be reminded of our own wickedness every time it blights our lives.'

'Are people whose lives are never blighted by it *not* wicked?' Traven said, a sly glint in his eye.

'I'm sure I have no idea what you mean!' I exclaimed, fingering my medal of office.

Bear in mind that our conversations were carried out through bars, Traven at his desk, or perhaps on his bed, I in the corridor, standing. Direct contact between residents and Cell inmates was prohibited. Traven and I were never once in the same room together. Our relationship was conducted on one level only, verbally, with a door between us. But sometimes words are enough.

After a time, Traven's way of thinking began to affect my own. Little by little, as he advanced his opinions to me, the task of refuting them became a struggle. What I had first thought of as unworldliness I now saw as simplicity, which is not the same thing. And in that simplicity lay complexity, for Traven's reading, which should by rights have fashioned a more enlightened and rational individual, served only to entrench him further in his inherited beliefs. And I found myself tempted. Tempted to fall in line with them. He spoke beguilingly of things beyond comprehension, things that could not be tested or proved and so must be taken on trust. I was, as a good Air Inclined, a man who believed only the evidence of his own senses. Cause and effect. Water flows downhill, drawn by gravity. A tree grows upward, drawn by sunlight. When an incendiary grasps some combustible object with his mind, he can ignite it. When we die, we die – the body shuts down, consciousness vanishes, there is no more. These are all everyday truths. The world is straightforward, predictable, explicable. Those things we cannot yet explain in empirical terms, we one day will. Or so I used to think.

Whereas Traven insisted that there are layers of truth that cannot be seen, no matter how hard one tries, and that there are unseen influences upon humans that are as great as, if not greater than, the influence of the 'Storm. Gradually, and without any deliberate effort, he was overturning the certainties of a lifetime.

Understand, Khollo, that when you are as advanced in years as I am, you do begin to wonder about yourself and your life. How have you spent your time on earth? Have you made the fullest use of it? Is there anything you would have done differently, better, if you had the chance all over again? In old age you're supposed to have made sense of the world's chaotic patterns and exist in a graceful state of wisdom. For me, however, old age turned out to bring more questions than answers. Instead of finding myself at last on solid ground, I discovered that I had strayed deeper than ever into a mire.

The physical infirmities of old age play their part, too. When the eyes have weakened, when the joints burn on cold mornings, when the bladder demands to be emptied all the time yet produces no more than a trickle, when the bowels are sluggish, when doing anything, not least defecating, seems to take twice as long as it used to . . . I don't need to go on with this list. The elderly will know what I am talking about and the young are better off not knowing. But it feels, from day to day, that the body is irreversibly falling apart and ultimately there is only one conclusion to this decline. Then, you must adopt some kind of attitude towards the prospect of your extinction, whether it is cheerful acceptance or stoic resignation or no view at all, just a wilful ignoring of the whole subject.

[What I could have said is that so many people don't even reach old age. They are whisked away from life in middle age, in youth, in infancy. Perhaps the High Previsionary should simply be grateful for his longevity. That's what I could have said, but didn't.]

Traven's conviction that a person – a personality – survives death therefore had an appeal for me. Inevitably. I could never bring myself wholly to agree with the concept, nor can I still. My argument against is as basic as this: if there is a life beyond this one, how come I, as a previsionary, cannot foresee it? Even now, I know that after I am murdered there is only a blank. Traven confessed that it was the same for him, saying that though he had ranged back and forth across the length and breadth of his life, he had never ventured any further than the extremes of its span. But he added that the place where he will go when he dies, that sea of ancestors which our Yashu also speaks of, is a separate form of existence from this one. Therefore, understandably, he could have no prevision of what it will be like. When he gets there, he will start anew, somewhat as if he is being born all over again.

'Will I go to this place too?' I once asked him. 'Even if I don't believe it exists?'

'If you believe it exists,' he said, 'you will go there.'

A marvellous roundabout logic, that. Hard to argue with.

In a last-ditch attempt to bring Traven round to a more conventional viewpoint, I presented him with a copy of Of-Jagged-Isle's *Essays*. Of-Jagged-Isle, the great explainer of Wet traditions, the great apologist-turned-debunker – he, I hoped, would be able to knock some sense into Traven. But I also hoped, at the same time, that Traven would gaily and persuasively dismiss Of-Jagged-Isle, and in so doing dismiss my own last lingering doubts. The *Essays* would force one of us into a wholehearted acceptance of the other's stance. It was the artist's final brushstroke, which either perfects the painting and assures him that he is a genius or ruins it and confirms to him that he should seek another occupation. Does that work as an analogy? Keep or omit as you see fit, Khollo.

Traven, however, was neither challenged nor provoked by Of-Jagged-Isle. On the contrary, the *Essays* enthused him. He did not perceive, or else he chose to overlook, Of-Jagged-Isle's sneering tone. He thought the essay entitled 'On Flux' a resounding defence of the principle of *mala* rather than a gimlet-eyed dissection of it. He thought 'On Hidden Depths' stated the case for a life after this life better than he ever could. And from 'On the Weight of the World' he unearthed the nugget which he – and I – transformed into the golden dream that has brought us all the way there, to this mountainous spot, this hunting lodge, this time of final fruition.

A pause. Let me soothe my throat with a draught of this excellent Tanhoutish wine. Our unwitting host has assembled himself an enviable cellar. I myself am no wine connoisseur, but the palate knows what the palate knows. Ah! A deserved reward, after so much talking. I believe the vineyards of Tanhout were all but wiped out the year before last. That makes this little drop all the more cherishable. You . . . ? Oh no, of course. Not while at work. Clouds the enshrining faculties, doesn't it.

Very well. To resume.

There is a paragraph in 'On the Weight of the World', a glancing reference to the Water-Inclined myth of the Great Fissuring. That's *fiss-uring*, not *fish-ering*, although you could be forgiven for making that mistake. Wets do go on about aquatic fauna most of the time, eh? The Great Fissuring. The time, long ago, when humans were first divided into the four Inclinations. Before then, we were all alike. A

62

rare few had Inclinations, the vast majority were as stunted and useless as Extraordinaries. Hard to conceive, is it not? A world like that. What a ghastly notion. Like everyone walking around, I don't know, hamstrung or something.

['Surely hobbling around.']

Eh?

['If they're hamstrung, they'd be hobbling around, not walking around.']

Thank you, Khollo, very much. If I'd wanted a pedant as well as an enshriner, I'd have asked for one. But just think of that community of Extraordinaries we stayed with a few months back, the Trustees of the Godhead, who put us up in such lavish style.

[A touch of sarcasm there.]

Imagine a world full of *them*. Beggars belief, doesn't it?

Anyway, the Great Fissuring. Of-Jagged-Isle says something like, 'As the 'Storm first stirred in the further reaches of the earth, so the people were rent asunder . . .' Or 'torn asunder'. Look, why don't you insert the passage I'm talking about, Khollo. You'll be able to find the book easily enough.

[Not that easily, in the event. But anyway, here it is:

As the story has it, when the Worldstorm first stirred in the distant reaches of the earth, the people of the earth were torn asunder and thrown into disarray. For a time, all was panic and terror. But out of this panic and terror and division a new order coalesced, and the four Inclinations were known, and named.

Now (Of-Jagged-Isle continues) *even when it is told in a more elaborate form than I have presented it here, this story's implication is clear. Somehow, birth of Worldstorm is equated with birth of Inclination. The one engendered the other, and the two remain inextricably linked. There are those, indeed, who see in the 'Storm's meteorological attributes each Inclination represented – Water in its rain, Air in its winds, Fire in its lightning, Earth in the ground the lightning strikes. These people (I cite the name Corval as just one example) regard the 'Storm as a fusion of human categories and argue that we and it therefore must have some fundamental connection.*

It is a tenuous line of reasoning at best, and I need not waste time dismissing it here. The notion of the Great Fissuring does, however, lead one to ponder the hypothetical possibility that, if the 'Storm made us what we are, then the reverse might also be true: we made the 'Storm what it is. If so, could we therefore not unmake it somehow? Might not some appropriate human agency be able to combat and counteract the 'Storm, perhaps even erase it entirely?

Sadly, no legend I am aware of addresses this issue, and yet again we come up against one of the essential flaws of the Water-Inclined mythos. It never speculates. It seeks only to codify, not to comment upon. It continually reinforces itself by never making demands of itself. The tellers of its tales are encouraged to elaborate but not deviate, extemporise but not extrapolate. Hence unchallenged figment persists, down through the ages, as fact.

I may be biased, but in my view Of-Jagged-Isle's book is guilty of pretty much the same crime. It's hopelessly one-sided, dressing up opinion as argument, never going to the effort of questioning its own claims. What I read of it made me both amused and irritated. I got the sense of a man trying hard to deny his own background, a man who's embarrassed that he once enjoyed these stories and who's keen to prove that he isn't so gullible any more. You can see that in the way he insists on using the Common Tongue translation of his name, never the original Water language version. But then what do I know? A lot of folk, particularly from my own Inclination, hold Of-Jagged-Isle's work in very high regard.]

On that passage – undetectably shoehorned in by my able amanuensis here – Traven and I had some of our most involved and illuminating debates. Traven floated the idea that Of-Jagged-Isle's offhand comment might provide the key to eliminating the 'Storm. Something people have often wondered about, haven't they? Something they've abjectly yearned for, not least when that great tyrant of the sky is stamping around in the vicinity, hammering down here and there with its impetuous fists. What if the 'Storm were not the untameable and everlasting phenomenon we think it is? What if it wasn't just a fact of life that we all have to put up with? What if, with the right line of attack, it could be defeated?

At first I treated the whole notion with a casual disdain. All Traven was doing, I thought, was inflating a balloon for me to prick. But still he persisted and persisted. Day after day he would bring the topic up and we would argue, sometimes rebutting one another's points before we had the chance to make them, the way previsionaries do when two or more of them get into a heated exchange. Traven was adamant that Of-Jagged-Isle had unwittingly stumbled on the one strategy that might actually work against the 'Storm. At some point in prehistory, the 'Storm and a diversification of the human race had occurred simultaneously. Might then some sort of unification of the human race not have a counterbalancing effect on the 'Storm, like weights on a pair of scales, levelling out?

I asked him what form this 'unification' might take, and Traven came up with a number of possible scenarios, most of them too absurd and impracticable to be worth relating here. One involved getting representatives of every class of the Inclinations on a hilltop together and having them all exercise their skills at once, right in the midst of a 'Storm visit. He thought the result would be the instant and permanent dispersal of the 'Storm. I thought the result would be confusion, injury and possibly even death. He also suggested taking a similar cross-section of the population and getting them to commit mass suicide. If the 'Storm were witness to the whole gamut of Inclination classes perishing at a stroke, that would satisfy its hunger for death. I pointed out that the 'Storm isn't some greedy person in search of the ultimate meal. As gluttons go, it is omnivorous and insatiable.

Still, Traven would not let it lie. He insisted he was onto something, and swap my brain for a pickled walnut if I didn't think so too.

'There must be some way,' he would say. 'Wouldn't it be amazing if I could do that for the world. From here, in my cell. Free us all!'

The upshot of all this was this scheme we concocted together. This, if you will, brainchild of ours, co-conceived by us down there in the depths of Stonehaven . . .

But I'm getting tired. The business of casting one's mind back and talking takes it out of one. So I shall conclude our session today by telling briefly of my spat with High Psychometrist Ærdant, which precipitated my departure from Stonehaven.

It's fair to say that Ærdant and I had never seen eye to eye. He was a thorn in my side almost from the beginning, and I, I hope, was a thorn in his. The other residents at Stonehaven I more or less got along with. Ærdant and I, however, shared a mutual antipathy which over the years hardened into a kind of weary loathing. I don't recall any particular incident that led us to hate each other. Some people just clash, don't they? Their characters are set that way. Ærdant was inordinately ugly, too, which didn't help. A hooked nose, thin, liver-coloured lips, a way of smiling that was more sneery than cheerful. Call me superficial.

Now then, I said earlier that I knew my association with Traven would get me into trouble, and sure enough, trouble began to loom. At first it was just a few sniping remarks across the high table in the refectory, lobbed at me from Ærdant's corner. These I could laugh off.

But then there was the occasion when I was rushing along a corridor, late for some appointment, I don't remember what, and I met Ærdant coming the other way, accompanied as ever by a gaggle of junior psychometrists. Ærdant liked to foster gormless, awestruck admiration among his pupils. He loved to have them fawn over him and worship his personality. He wasn't averse – heh heh heh – to making a complete cult of himself.

As I passed him, anyway, a barbed aside came snaking after me, meant for his juniors' ears but mine also. 'There goes Elder Ayn. Hurrying off to see his special little friend in the Cells.' Words to that effect.

Where all this was leading became clearer and clearer to me. I saw myself and Ærdant shouting at each other in the Balcony Garden, in the presence of at least two dozen other residents. I saw myself accusing him of conducting a whispering campaign against me and trying to undermine my reputation, and Ærdant retorting that there was no need to undermine a reputation already sunken so low. I saw the outcome of this slanging match. The blow that sent Ærdant reeling to the grass – a straight shot to that sneering, liver-lipped mouth of his. The shock on the faces of all who witnessed it. And then the summons to the Obsidian Hall, the grave looks from the assembled Council members, the denunciation of my conduct, the demand for an apology to Ærdant and some form of overt contrition such as a month of latrine duty and perhaps the shaving off of my hair, what little remains of it. And my response: a volley of vituperation, aimed mainly at Ærdant but taking in the other Elders on the way – an outpouring of scorn and derision, echoing to the black glossy ceiling of the hall. Hypocrites! Cowards! Fools! Self-regarding imbeciles! Smug, conceited dotards! Blustering old blowhards made soft by years of luxury and pampered living! Ignoramuses who had long ago lost any sense of perspective and feeling for their fellow men! Ossified, over-intellectualising arses! Calling them every name under the sun and a few of my own invention besides. And then, as a last dramatic flourish, snatching my medal of office from around my neck and hurling it on the Council Table, and following this with a smart about-turn and a march for the exit amid resounding silence.

I welcomed it. As these events approached, I felt a delirium of anticipation. I could hardly wait. The knowledge that I would be leaving Stonehaven, to pursue a greater destiny in the world outside, filled me with a dizzying sense of relief and joy. I had not realised till then how limited my life had been, how blinkered. Soon, in weeks, then days, then hours, I would be free.

My only regret was leaving Traven behind. I had no choice in that. I needed someone to accompany me, and made the wise decision of choosing you, Khollo, but if I could have taken Traven as well, I would have. But he would have been a liability. I could not have controlled him when he lapsed into one of his fits. He would have slowed me down, perhaps put me at risk.

I did say goodbye to him. I stood outside his cell and explained to him why I was going and what I intended to do. The timing was unfortunate, and I wish there could have been another opportunity.

Traven was lost in one of his fugues, babbling snippets of dialogue snatched from all the conversations in his life. If he heard what I said, if he was even aware of me at his door – I have no idea. The most important thing was that I told him that what I did from then on, I did for him. He would remain locked up, but I was taking his idea, his dream, out into the world. A part of him would be forever free. I made that promise to him.

There, Khollo. For now, enough.

[I'm afraid I can't let this segment of the High Previsionary's account end without adding a few final comments of my own. I've begun inserting these little parenthetical observations of mine. I might as well continue.

The High Previsionary was notorious at Stonehaven for his close relationships with certain young males, both residents and members of the domestic staff. It was one of the first facts I ever learned about him. He wasn't the only one there with a roving eye, not by a long shot. Stonehaven was a hotbed for covert sexual shenanigans. It was considered one of the perks of residency. And the higher your rank, the greater the liberties you could take with your juniors and underlings. The number of pregnant kitchen girls who were sent to recuperators to be 'cured' of their condition! I could tell a story or two. There was always some kind of scandal or other bubbling under the surface there. The fact that the place was founded inside an extinct volcano seems, under the circumstances, more than apt.

But you had to be discreet, that was the unwritten rule, and Elder Ayn was not discreet. Before my time, he had been involved in a string of dalliances which had ended in tears and recrimination – very publicly. This is the reputation which High Psychometrist Ærdant mentioned, or rather lack of reputation. This was what the High Previsionary himself was referring to when he said that where certain aspects of behaviour were concerned, he had never been a clever or subtle man. He just couldn't help himself. He got too involved. He fell in love unwisely. He fell in love, full stop. Time after time he got his heart broken. Even in old age, when he should have known better, he didn't.

You might almost admire him for that.

As for the confrontation with the High Psychometrist, it so happens that I was one of the witnesses present. I was in the Balcony Garden that morning, taking the air, enjoying the birdsong and the whisper of the leaves and the feel of lawn beneath my feet. A marvellous feat of horticulture, that place. A landscaped garden perched on a rock outcrop on the volcano's inner flank, sheltered by a broad overhang. A tiny, tranquil piece of greenery for the benefit of the residents, situated deep down in the crater, beyond even the reach of the 'Storm. The trees twist elegantly, elaborately outward, reaching for light.

The quarrel was pretty much as the High Previsionary described, although I have to say that he started it. He was the instigator. He pushed and pushed verbally till High Psychometrist Ærdant retaliated. And the punch he threw was completely unprovoked. Nothing the High Psychometrist said or did appeared to warrant it. It came right out of the blue. Yet it also looked, at least to me, premeditated. Elder Ayn entered that garden not only knowing what he would end up doing but *spoiling* for it.

I mention this just in passing. Now it's time for me to put my pen down and take a break myself.]

GREGORY

11th of Drymonth 687

He was late getting up, the last down to breakfast, as usual, but in this household it didn't seemed to matter. One more for a meal, one less, what was the difference? Sometimes he wondered if even Sol and Garla Gove knew how big their family was. Ten kids? A dozen? You couldn't go into any room without it being a whirl of activity. Someone was always fighting. Someone was always huddled down, trying to ignore the chaos. At first Gregory had found it all very hard to absorb. He had yearned for solitude. He had yearned for lots of things. Now, on the rare occasions when he did find himself alone or almost alone in the house, the quiet was unsettling; he couldn't wait for everyone to get back and the chaos to resume. Chaos was the house's natural order.

One chair at the kitchen table was vacant. Gregory pounced on it, claiming it for himself before anybody else could. A moment later, a bowl of porridge clunked down in front of him. Garla scrubbed his head in passing. Her affectionate gestures were always somewhat brutal. Her own children she more or less punched to show them she loved them. Her punishments, Gregory thought, must be incredibly harsh, but in three years he hadn't yet seen her mete one out. For all the apparent anarchy, Garla Gove ran a well-disciplined home. Her children, and Gregory, knew exactly where the line was drawn. There was no question what would happen to anyone who crossed it.

The level of mealtime jabber was raucous, but Sol, at the head of the table, was an island of calm behind his *Southern Jarraine Midweek Register*. He was studying the back page of the newspaper with a frown, no doubt dismayed by the tribulations of the Gravel Crushers, Penresford's sticks team, who had yet again fared badly at the hands of their nearest neighbours and fiercest rivals the Hallawye Badgers. Sol was the older brother, by half a minute, of Sam, but they were twins in every sense. They even wore their moustaches and hair the same way. The only overt physical difference between them was the long scar on Sol's left forearm, put there by the spade of a co-worker, an accident, a moment of inattention. The local recuperator had done his best but a cut that deep could never be mended without a trace; the flesh would not anneal perfectly. Nor could the damage done to the tendons of the arm be fully rectified. The hand, Sol's non-dominant one, could hold but not grasp. Sol Gove would never again wield a spade, never work the clayface again. He picked up odd jobs here and there around town, but the money he was receiving every month from Tremond Brazier in return for Gregory's lodging and upkeep was more than welcome. The odd jobs were mainly bookkeeping and letter-writing – Sol was good with numbers, he had nice penmanship. When the telepath bureau clerk was away or indisposed, Sol stood in for him. He sometimes took minutes at meetings of the Guild of Freemen. But casual work never paid brilliantly. And with all those mouths to feed!

No sooner had Gregory finished his porridge than the bowl was whipped away and a huge mug of milky tea was plonked in front of him. Beside him, Adana Gove was tussling with her brother Dallen over possession of a slice of bread and honey which another brother, Lorn, had decided he didn't want and had offered to the first taker. Adana had claimed it, Dallen had poached it on its way over to her. Gregory cradled the mug carefully as he sipped. A stray elbow, an unexpectedly violent shove, and the tea would end up all over him. You had to eat defensively. Adana won the contest by starting to squeal, a noise so shrill and painful that Dallen had no alternative but to stuff the slice of bread into her mouth to shut her up. Sol glanced over the top of his newspaper briefly, ascertained that nobody was dead, and resumed reading.

Suddenly, without anyone having to say anything, just some herd instinct, everyone began to get ready to go to school. The house rumbled with running feet. Exercise books were thrust into satchels. Coats were grabbed. Out into the morning air, early autumn, a tinge of frost on the rooftops, windowpanes cloudy with the cold. A wave of Goves, and one Brazier, surging along the cobbled street. One redhead bobbing amid a tide of dark-hairs. An echoing jabber of voices. The date was Thirdday the 11th of Drymonth, Gregory's eleven-hundred-and-eleventh day in exile from Stammeldon, although he had long since stopped keeping count.

The trip from Stammeldon was less than a memory. It was something that had happened nearly a quarter of a lifetime ago, an event which had left a residue in Gregory's mind rather than an indelible mark. If he looked back, which he didn't often, his main recollection was of the snaky Seray unfolding new landscapes at every turn but itself never changing. In size and speed, the river was constant. There could be slopes on either side, a gorge, and then farmland or plain – the river ploughed on. Every so often, a strand of forest, sheltered in a valley or else just lucky, having escaped being flattened by wind or burned by lightning strike. Sometimes a town, a landing – jetties and pubs and hotels. At almost every one, the pilot knew somebody to wave to, a fellow riverman. He would even bring the barge in close to shore to have a chat, which he would surely not have done were this a proper commercial journey. Or maybe he would have. On this trip, certainly, the pilot was a law unto himself. He determined everything on board: when they ate, when they dawdled, when they hove to and moored and slept. He lorded it over his little domain and his two passengers. It seemed to give him special satisfaction to be in a position of power over the foreman of Brazier Brickfields and the boss's younger son.

And so gradually on along the chocolate-brown river, passing Brazier-owned barges coming the other way, most with their holds full to capacity with clay, battling their own weight and the current. More excuses for the pilot to reduce speed, pull over, exchange a few words in Water language. He was in no hurry. He didn't have a tight schedule to keep to. This, for him, was almost a pleasure cruise. When it came to other types of river traffic, however – ferries, for example, and private skiffs – he was noticeably less companionable. Perhaps a quick, polite *parp* on the barge's horn, that was all. There was a snobbery at work: trade was what the river was really for, not travel.

How Gregory had occupied himself for the three days, he couldn't really remember. A lot of sitting and staring, either from the bows or out through the portholes of his cabin. His mother had supplied him with books to read. He didn't touch them. Sam talked to him. Left him alone mostly, but now and then struck up a conversation, telling him about Penresford and describing his brother Sol's family, the nieces and nephews, all hundred and fifty of them or however many it was. He only got to visit them about once a year – he wished it was more often – and every time he went there seemed to be a new one. He could just about name them all, in order. What their ages were, he had no idea. Ven, though, the third eldest, was the same age as Gregory. They would undoubtedly get on, the two of them. They were similar in temperament, and Ven was an indestructible, like Gregory. According to the most recent letter from Sol, Ven had just begun his training. He and Gregory would therefore be in the same training group together. That was a stroke of luck, wasn't it?

Once, and once only, Sam brought up the subject of Gregory's father. He said he could understand if Gregory did not think too highly of his father right now. It wasn't a crime to resent a parent's decision. It was forgivable. What Gregory must bear in mind was that Tremond Brazier was in a difficult position. He had more to think about than simply himself and his family. His responsibilities went deeper, wider.

'Seventeen years ago,' Sam said, to illustrate his point, 'when the 'Storm last came round to Stammeldon, we got pretty badly pounded. Right under the epicentre. It went on for a week all told. The last couple of days, the rain let up but the winds were still going strong and the lightning was crackling down. We were worried about the crops burning but we reckoned they were too soggy to catch light, and anyway they were mostly ruined already. Houses, though, that was another matter. And sure enough, a couple in the centre of town got hit. Down on Tarkby Street. Brick-built, but so what? Lightning is lightning. Up they went in flames, and do you know who one of the first incendiaries on the scene was? Your dad. Could have stayed nice and cosy in Tempest's Bane, but he demanded to be informed if anything was set alight, and soon as word reached him about the fires, off he went. Battled his way against the wind and the rain, down to Tarkby, and he was fighting the blaze all night, him and a dozen other incendiaries. He led the effort, organised everyone, rallied everyone when morale started flagging. Quite a thing to do, stand in front of a raging inferno and try to control the flames *and* direct people at the same time. He was dead on his feet by the end of it. Soot covering his face, his eyebrows singed. But he was, pardon the expression, a fucking hero. No question about it. A whole chunk of the town could have gone up in smoke if it wasn't for him, I reckon.'

There was no more to the anecdote than that. Sam wandered aft, leaving Gregory to ponder on the implications of it. Gregory, actually, had heard the story before, from Willem, who had heard it from Sardon Drake. Then, it had seemed to confirm everything Gregory believed about his father. Now, it served a similar function, but in a less positive way. Of course his father had run down to help fight the fire. Of course he had made such a dramatic, public gesture. That was what his father was all about: looking good in public.

Late on the evening of the third day of the journey, in the shadows of a murky dusk, the lights and smoke of Penresford glided into view.

Penresford was a tenth of the size of Stammeldon and far more densely packed. Whereas buildings in Stammeldon hunkered low to the ground and kept their mutual distance, in Penresford they rose 'Storm-temptingly tall, three storeys, even four, but derived their strength from proximity. Wooden-walled, shingle-roofed, they hunched shoulder to shoulder, so that it was hard to tell where one ended and another began. They stared out together, a fortress of many.

The terrain around the town was a mass of squared-off gouges – open-cast clay mines, the pinkish fat of the earth exposed, with wooden scaffolding braced in the interstices. From the mines a muddy, leaden smell drifted, detectable miles away. The Earth Inclined often lived underground but around here, as Sam had explained, that wasn't possible. Clay soil didn't make for a pleasant subterranean environment. So instead of digging their homes downward, the people of Penresford had gone upward, choosing height where they would have chosen depth.

The Gove family, at full strength, had been waiting for the barge for far too long. Gregory's first glimpse of them was not a heartening one. The children were busy savaging one another and chasing to and fro along the quayside, well past the limits of their patience. They were called to order by their mother as the barge, which should have arrived mid-afternoon, approached. They lined up. Sam was right: a hundred and fifty of them at least. Well, perhaps a dozen. They yelled and waved to their uncle. As the barge pulled in, Sam instructed the four oldest to climb aboard. He told them where his and Gregory's luggage could be found. Four eager but unskilled porters went below decks and manhandled Gregory's belongings out onto dry land. When Gregory himself disembarked, Sol Gove shook his hand roughly, a strong's grip, crushing, with much held in reserve. Garla grabbed his cheek in a painful pinch. All this served to confirm what Gregory had already decided: *I will hate it here.* But 'here' was not going to be his home for long, he remained convinced of that. A week in Penresford, two at the most – he could stick it out.

Sam Gove spent that night at his brother's house, not only for sociable reasons but also, perhaps, to help ease the transition for Gregory. He slept on the kitchen floor. A bed had been made up for Gregory in a corner of the room shared by the three eldest Gove boys, Lorn, Brayt, and Ven. They quizzed him well into the night, in whispers, asking about Stammeldon and the brickfields and his father and the river journey and other things. Did Gregory play sticks? (Some people played sticks in Stammeldon, but it wasn't a Fire sport.) Had he lived through a 'Storm visit? (In Penresford they had, five years ago, and the boys had tales to tell – the shaking, the roaring, the terror.) They had a mayor in Stammeldon, didn't they? What was that like, having things run by a single person instead of, as here, by a committee, the Guild of Freemen? (It seemed to work all right, Gregory said, no one seemed to have any complaints.)

Then the trio of Goves fell asleep, almost in unison, and Gregory was left to stare up into the dark and think of home, so far away. The mattress would not let him get comfortable. The Gove boys snored and snorted and slumber-mumbled constantly and cacophonously. He did get to sleep, in the end, but not before he had worked out how he would sneak aboard a Brazier Brickfields barge going back upstream, stow away in the hold and stay hidden there till Stammeldon. With the full complement of pilots, the trip would last a third as long as the one he had just made. Passenger ferries did call in at Penresford, but they travelled in stages, didn't operate at night, took for ever. By ferry, allowing for stopovers and missed connections, the journey could last as much as five days. By Brazier barge, he could be home in twenty-four hours. So that was his contingency plan, in case the request for him to return didn't come through soon enough.

The next morning, Sam departed. It wasn't as much of a wrench as Gregory had feared, since Sol was so like Sam that he was an effective Sam substitute. Indeed, for the next couple of days Gregory kept inadvertently calling Sol Sam, which amused everyone, although Sol pretended to take offence. 'You're wrong by half a minute,' he would say gruffly. Or: 'Nope, isn't it obvious? I'm the good-looking one.'

As for getting the children's names right, it was hopeless. The younger girls, in particular, looked all alike to Gregory and, when he mistook one for another, never hid their derision, which only made matters worse. Their capacity for embarrassing him was infinite. Dark-eyed and pretty, there was a streak of deviousness in them. They seemed innocent; they were not. And the one Gove girl who was older than him, Eda, although she was considerably more mature than her sisters, found her own way of teasing him. She nicknamed him Red-top. She didn't mean it maliciously. If anything, it was inclusive, since she also had nicknames for every one of her siblings. But often the way she said it reminded Gregory of Reehan Bringlight and his 'Little Bother'. A bad association to make.

And a week passed. It was summer, so no school. There was time to acclimatise to the Gove status quo, the clamour, the lack of privacy, the perpetual jostling for attention. Not a minute went by when Gregory didn't feel a yawning ache inside. He longed to be back at Tempest's Bane, with his own room, the liberty to do as he pleased, familiarity all around him, domestic staff to pick up the clothes he left on the floor, a pantry to be raided for snacks at any time, all that. He missed the food at home. Garla Gove was an adequate but uninspired chef, and used far less spice in her recipes than he would have liked.

Nonetheless, he was able to adapt. The temporariness of the situation made it bearable. The message from his parents must have been drafted. Perhaps it was already on its way. Via the telepathic bureau, of course, for speed. *Come back, Gregory. We were wrong. Come back.*

There was time, too, to explore Penresford, which Gregory did in the company of Ven. As Sam had predicted, the two of them did get on. Ven was the quietest of the Goves, the shyest (which wasn't saying a lot, in such an un-shy family), and Gregory liked the fact that Ven thought before he spoke, didn't just blurt out the first thing that came to mind simply because everyone else was talking and he wanted to be heard as well. The other Gove boys who had manifested were strongs like their father; Eda, the only girl old enough to have manifested, was a plant-sensitive, like her mother. Ven, as an indestructible, had bucked the trend. Gregory had that in common with him as well, although Ven had at least had the decency to remain within his family Inclination.

Ven showed Gregory the covered bazaar, a warren of corridors and passageways lit by lanterns and here and there by a shaft of daylight from an aperture in the roof. It was a place to buy fruit and vegetables and coal and other necessities of life, but it was also a clearing house for all kinds of junk and second-hand goods. Round a corner you might find a stall selling clothes which even the moths had turned their noses up at, or an alcove stuffed with items of furniture which had long ago been vacated by their woodworm tenants, or a small area of floorspace enclosed on three sides by display cabinets which contained dusty old books, knickknacks and bric-a-brac. A lot of the décor and clothing at the Gove house had, it appeared, been bought from here. Gregory looked on as customers haggled with sellers at interminable length over the price of something worth next to nothing, and he quickly discerned that it was the haggling itself, and not the purchase, that was the point of the exercise. It was an argumentative way of passing the day. Ven also showed him which greengrocers could be counted on, almost without fail, for a free apple or handful of plums. The Gove family was widely liked in Penresford, and mildly pitied. A father who could no longer do proper work, with such a brood. It didn't hurt to show a Gove child a little charity.

There were further places to buy things, dotted throughout the town's mazy cobbled streets. Many of them were to be found up alleyways which Gregory was reluctant to enter. Ven swore they were safe but the darkness and enclosedness of them intimidated Gregory. They were tunnels, essentially, with houses built over the top of them, and the shops were little more than inset kiosks. Outside, a small sign and perhaps a sample of the wares on sale. Inside, enough space for the shopkeeper and one customer, maybe two, and of course the merchandise.

One of these alleyways, however, as Ven was only too pleased to reveal, had the attraction of being the town's brothel district. It was called Hamshank Lane, and the two boys spent many an interesting hour peering from a safe distance, watching as men entered the alleyway, strolled up to the unmarked doors, knocked, and were invited inside by women, all of whom were under-dressed and over-rouged. During one unusually squirm-inducing lesson with Professor Olgarne, Gregory and Willem had been enlightened as to the reproductive practices of humans. It was hard, though, to reconcile the technical instruction Gregory had received then with the behaviour he now observed: the furtive eagerness with which the men arrived, the effusive amorousness with which they were greeted, the slow, sated air with which they departed. He sensed that he had been supplied with the rules to the game but not the refinements. There was more to it. Around the framework of facts there was a whole tapestry of mystery that Professor Olgarne had not even hinted at.

The docks were another location where Gregory and Ven could happily while away the time. All through the daylight hours barges were heaped with consignments of clay blocks, which were stacked on pallets and covered with tarpaulins to keep the dampness in. It was hypnotically fascinating to watch the loading derricks swing, propelled on the ground by teams of strong-class workers bent over arm-thick wooden spokes; to watch all that applied muscle-power and hear the chants that went with it, familiar to Gregory from the brickfields. It was useful, too, in that it helped him fine-tune his contingency plan. Getting on board a barge during working hours would be difficult – someone would surely spot him. And at night, when the docks were patrolled by sharp-sight watchmen, it would be impossible. First thing in the morning, then. Be down here early, when the watchmen were yawning and the workforce was beginning to arrive. Slip through the dockyard gates when people were at their least alert. Secrete himself beneath the tarpaulin of a pallet waiting to leave. Risky, but not dangerous. Well, being hoisted in the air by a derrick would perhaps be dangerous, but not so much that it wasn't worth attempting.

A big problem, not just with the plan but generally, was that Gregory stood out like the proverbial lone tree on a plain. He couldn't go anywhere without at least one person glancing at him, glancing again. Ginger hair and pale skin were not common in Penresford, whereas in Stammeldon, throw a stone into a crowd and you were unlikely *not* to hit someone with those attributes. Nobody stared, nobody was that rude, or that bothered, but there was no real anonymity for a Flamer in a town full of Earthers. Gregory was aware of constantly being noticed. He was, like it or not, a presence.

And when word got round – who he was and why he was there – this did nothing to lessen his curiosity value. As he passed among strangers he would frequently hear his name, or his father's name, whispered, sometimes spoken quite clearly. The longer he stayed, the more incongruous he became. The closer he got to having to put his plan into effect, the less the chance that he would be able to pull it off.

Two weeks, and no word from his family.

Three weeks.

Then training commenced.

This would have happened sooner but for the fact that Master Dan Ergall had suffered a recent bereavement, the death of his elderly mother from a sudden, catastrophic seizure. Gregory had been warned that Master Ergall was not the kindest of men anyway, and his physical appearance certainly seemed to corroborate this. He was squat, burly, furry, with a nose like a large toadstool, bifurcated in the middle, and deep furrows in his face that originated from a point between his bushy eyebrows and radiated up his forehead and down his cheeks. A scowl, for him, seemed to be less an expression, more his face's natural state of being. His one great claim to fame was that, during his former career as an endurance boxer, he had gone three hundred rounds against 'Mighty' Mike Batta and won. This was the first story anyone ever told about Master Ergall and, it seemed, the only one anyone needed to tell.

In the normal course of events, then, an intimidating man. In grief, fearsome.

The training session took place in the paved courtyard at the rear of Master Ergall's house, and from the outset it was clear that Master Ergall was nursing a deep resentment at the world. It was clear, too, that he needed someone to take that anger out on, and who better than the new lad in class, the Flamer rich kid from upriver?

'Hurts, doesn't it?' said Master Ergall, as Gregory lay on the ground, clutching the side of his head. 'A lot, I'll bet. Quite a smart. Now come on, stand up.'

Gregory, grimacing, got to his feet.

Master Ergall swatted him again, in the exact same spot.

This time, Gregory did not fall. The blow wasn't any less forceful, but it had not come out of the blue like the first one. He reeled, but stood.

'Pain,' Master Ergall announced, 'is an irrelevance. If you're going to learn anything today, all of you, learn that. Pain comes, and then it goes. Like so.' He sucked in a breath – *shvoop*. 'And why is that?'

He glanced around at the other half-dozen pupils. They had attended a couple of classes already. They knew the answer.

'Because we're indestructibles.' A haphazard intoning. 'Because we cannot be hurt.'

'Precisely. Except you can, as our new friend Gregory here is all too aware, be hurt. And pain is useful. I don't intend to train awareness of pain out of you. You need to know if you've been injured. The body needs to know. What I'm going to train out of you, in addition to all the things I intend to train *into* you, is the weakness that pain brings. You'll know when something hurts, you just won't care.'

He turned to Gregory.

'Better yet? Is it starting to fade?'

Warily, Gregory nodded.

'Anyone else would be developing a nice bruise right now,' Master Ergall said. 'Probably be feeling a lump there for the next couple of days. You won't. You're lucky. You may be a pasty-faced carrot-bonce who's too tall for his own good, but you're also an indestructible. Be proud of that. And thankful.'

'Thankful?' said Gregory, and immediately regretted opening his mouth.

'Yes,' said Master Ergall, and hit him a third time.

Escape tomorrow. Gregory lay in bed, waiting for dawn. The insomniac moon glared down through the windowpanes. Brayt was wrestling with his bedclothes, progressively knotting them around himself. Resolve was an iron clamp inside Gregory. He was not going to sleep. The moment the night sky was a shade less dark, he would be up, dressed, out, gone. At Tempest's Bane there was a clock in the hall that tolled the hours, loudly. No such amenity here, but even so he reckoned he knew what the time was. Midnight now. Now one o'clock. In summer it started to get light around four. Not long to go. Stay awake. It wasn't hard to stay awake when the success of his plan hinged on it.

He woke up and it was broad daylight outside and the other beds in the room were empty and, from down in the kitchen, he could hear the unmistakable clatter and chatter of breakfast-time. He plodded blearily, irritably, downstairs. A letter was waiting on the sideboard, from his mother, just delivered. Without a word, from him or anyone, he took it back upstairs and opened it.

Dear Gregory . . .

The weather at Stammeldon continued to be fine, for which everyone was grateful. The midsummer soirée, taking place at the height of the Fire social season, had passed off without a hitch, and if the thank-you correspondence was anything to go by the guests considered it the best yet. Master Drake had written Willem a glowing progress report, saying he was one of the most able and attentive pupils it had ever been his pleasure to train. Sam had come back announcing that he thought Gregory had settled in nicely at Penresford. All was well.

Gregory re-read every sentence, looking for more, but it wasn't there. Nothing about his absence. Nothing, even implied, that said he was missed back at home. The letter was just news. Immaculately worded, ornately penned, but just news.

His ache, for the first time, began to subside. Or rather, suddenly there seemed less space for it. The place inside him where it was contained had shrunk.

Master Ergall's courtyard had bay trees in urns at each corner. It had a well at the centre, complete with pail and winding handle. It had high walls, so that only for a couple of hours a day did the sun shine fully into it. It was a nice, civilised-looking courtyard, except that it also had thick planks erected vertically in frames for pupils to punch, and a bed of sharp gravel for them to walk over barefoot, and an array of hitting implements for Master Ergall to toughen them up with. It was a place for the generating of exhaustion and numbness and scar tissue, the giving of pain till pain was no longer an enemy. First, Master Ergall's pupils learned not to cringe when something hurt. Then they learned not to flinch. Finally they learned not to notice.

Gregory came to dread each training session, not least since Master Ergall seemed to take delight in causing him mental as well as corporeal discomfort. Quite often, when inflicting blows on each pupil one after another, he would save Gregory for last, so that Gregory would have to watch the others take their licks, his own moment of suffering delayed; and when his turn finally came, Master Ergall would have kept something in reserve – far from being worn out, he would have the energy left for several particularly swingeing flicks of rod or switch, and his eyes, which were the colour of flint, would glitter with glee as he delivered them. Nor could Gregory ever do anything to Master Ergall's satisfaction. The others were praised, sometimes; Gregory, never. When he punched a plank, he wasn't doing it hard enough. When he walked across the gravel, he was accused of going too fast and made to do it again. How was he ever going to make the most of his Inclination if he insisted on behaving like such a wimp? How was he ever going to become a true indestructible if he just danced around all the time like some twinkle-toed Stammeldoner ponce?

Every morning of a training session day Gregory would suggest to

Ven that they play truant, hide somewhere till the session was over. Ven didn't enjoy the visits to Master Ergall's any more than Gregory did, but he was more phlegmatic about them. He had to go. It was costing his parents so much money – it was costing Gregory's parents the same, of course, but relatively speaking a far smaller proportion of their income. Ven's parents could barely afford the fees. Besides, all indestructibles underwent the same treatment. The first year was the worst, that was what everyone said. Get through it, and things would improve.

This argument usually won Gregory over. An even better argument, which Ven would advance whenever Gregory was more determined than usual to bunk off training, was that Master Ergall would not be best pleased with anyone who, for no good reason, failed to attend a session. Seeing how little he liked Gregory already, it seemed unwise to give him an excuse to like him even less. And, Ven added, he himself was likely to become the object of Master Ergall's ire if Gregory didn't show up, as either he would have to invent a lie to cover for Gregory's absence – and he had no desire to get found out lying to Master Ergall – or he would have to tell the truth and then he would surely catch it for not managing to persuade Gregory to come. Gregory didn't want to get him into trouble, did he?

Gregory didn't. He was unwilling, too, for pride's sake, to let Master Ergall know how much he feared him. And so, no matter that his heart was pounding fast, no matter that he felt like he was going to be sick, he always turned up at Master Ergall's house on time. He would tell himself that he was no coward. His loathing of Master Ergall made it easier to believe this was true. He began to realise, in time, that the best way, the only way he was ever going to handle training was to nurture that loathing and never give Master Ergall the satisfaction of seeing that he was upset or intimidated. Hold out his arm to have it whacked – keep his gaze steady on Master Ergall's face and never once blink. Tread that gravel over and over – show no expression other than a grim smile of concentration.

Meanwhile, further letters came from Stammeldon. The majority from his mother, a few from Willem, none from his father. All those from his mother were like the first, a straightforward rundown of the latest happenings in the town and at Tempest's Bane. Such-and-such an order had come in for the business. So-and-so had dined at the house the other evening. Willem's missives were somewhat chattier but still had a distinct whiff of formality about them, as if written at his mother's behest and not of his own accord. Reehan Bringlight featured a lot in them. Reehan nicked a bottle of wine from his father's cellar and he and Willem got horribly drunk on it (but Gregory mustn't ever blab to mum or dad). Reehan was so advanced with his training that he could encase himself in a shell of fire, although Willem wasn't far from being able to pull off the same feat himself (the greatest risk wasn't singeing yourself but, if you weren't careful, passing out from lack of air). Willem had got himself a girlfriend, Sal-Amanda Sunglow, did Gregory remember her? He had gone out with her for a few days, at any rate, until Reehan said he had spotted her canoodling with Jirry Blaise at Memorial Plaza, and that was that. Even though Sal-Amanda denied it, it was all over. Oh, and Reehan's father had announced he was running for mayor, and Reehan was convinced their own dad should put his weight behind the election campaign because that would almost certainly swing it in Reehan's father's favour, having Tremond Brazier backing him, and wouldn't it be great, his best friend's father would then be the *other* most important and influential man in Stammeldon!

Willem at least had the decency to ask how Gregory was getting on and to invite a letter of reply, and Gregory tried several times to write one, but the task of framing sentences that didn't sound caustic and bitter, not to mention finding a quiet corner of the Gove house to sit down and compose them in, proved impossible. He wanted Willem to hear the truth about his life in Penresford, but he also didn't want to direct anger against his brother which more properly should be directed against his parents. Better to stay silent, then. More dignity that way.

Less and less did his scheme for fleeing back to Stammeldon seem viable. It was always there at the back of his mind, a possibility, but as the weeks went by it became more important to Gregory that his parents should ask him to return, that they should be the ones to give in, not him. He saw himself arriving at Tempest's Bane of his own accord, tail between legs, and he saw himself brought back formally, clattering through the gates in the coach. The son they were surprised to see again? Or the son they couldn't bear to part with for long? He had no doubt which was preferable. In the meantime, he could stand it here. Training aside, it wasn't *so* bad. Sometimes, late at night, the weight of the distance between him and home seemed insupportable. He would struggle with tears. On the whole, though, he was coping. He was making the necessary accommodations. He liked the Goves. Despite the noise and rumbustiousness, the lack of creature comforts in their home, the genial bullying that was their way with one another, they had made him feel welcome. They had made space for him, where space was at a premium. They treated him as one of them, not some special case, nor just a handy source of revenue. 'Too much Earth will smother Fire,' the saying went, but the Goves seemed to disprove it.

School was difficult, to start with. Someone who was so obviously Fire-born, someone who looked so different from everyone else, was bound to draw attention, and much of it was harmless, just looks and inquisitive frowns, but some of it was attention of the malicious kind. Sniggers. Jokes about his hair, his skin, his clothes. People pretending to smell burning when he walked into the classroom. Muttering Earth-language phrases behind his back which Ven, reluctantly, would translate for him. A constant verbal scrape, scrape, scrape, which Gregory affected to ignore but which grated on his nerves. Added to that, he had to get used to being taught as part of a large group, by teachers who relied more on blackboards and books than on tele-pathy. It was hard and tiring to project mnemonics and visual illustra-tions into the minds of twenty or more pupils at once, so the teachers employed the technique sparingly. The burden of rote-learning and memorisation fell on the pupils themselves, and his years of private tuition by Professor Olgarne had left Gregory ill-equipped for this. He floundered. For a while it looked as if he might have to drop down a year, but that would have been more humiliation than he could bear. It would also, he knew, give his tormentors further ammunition to hurl at him, so he knuckled down and forced himself to develop better learning skills. It wasn't long before he was holding his own amongst his peers, academically. He was never going to be head of the class, but his test scores displayed a marked improvement and the threat of demotion receded.

Then there was sticks. Back home, Gregory had never seen the game played properly and had only ever heard it referred to disparagingly. It was, according to his mother, a mindless pastime even by Earther standards (and that was saying something). It was an exercise in sheer brutality, she said. It was crude and dangerous and lacked any ap-parent finesse.

And all this was true, but what she hadn't mentioned – and how could she have known? – was that once you got past the violence and thuggishness of it, sticks was fantastically exciting. It was also much more sophisticated than it looked.

As an indestructible, Gregory played in the forward line. He and the other forwards took their punishment from the other team's defence, made up predominantly of strongs, while their own defence tackled the opposition's forward line. Advance and retreat, with sticks clash-ing, the school playing field a rattling battle-zone, until one side or other broke through and crossed their opponents' breach boundary. However many players crossed the breach boundary before their own breach boundary was crossed, that was how many points the team scored in that attack. The teacher refereeing the match blew his whistle as soon as one team's entire forward line were over the breach boundary or else a reverse breach, as it was known, was achieved. Then both teams returned to their respective halves of the playing field and reassembled, and the match resumed.

Thus the basics of the game, but in tactical terms, as Gregory found, sticks could be as intricate and devious as elements. There were strategies, feints, false retreats, formations, counter-formations in response to changes of strategy by the opposition, a whole raft of subtleties to complement the hammering and battering and clubbing. Stick technique was important, too. A forward's stick was more a defensive than an offensive tool. You weren't allowed to hit the other team's strongs with it, but you could use it to parry their blows and trip them up. Held out horizontally in front of you, it could act as a kind of shield, especially if the entire forward line, side by side, alternated along the row with one stick at chest height and the next at stomach level, mimicking a crenellated battlement.

No question, it was a painful sport. Gregory ended up covered in bruises every time he played. He broke fingers. Once, he was knocked cold. But bruises faded almost immediately. Broken fingers took a little longer, but they mended. He suffered no permanent side-effects from a few moments of insensibility. A blow to his face loosened a molar, but the tooth was soon rock-steady again (had he not been an indestructible, the blow would no doubt have dislodged the tooth completely). Blood flowed from a split eyebrow but the wound sealed itself within seconds. And it was worth it just for the thrill, the exultation he felt, every time he broke through the other side's defence and skipped across their breach boundary. Nothing beat that sense of triumph, earned through suffering.

And autumn became winter, and winter became spring.

Gregory would never know exactly at what point he realised he was going to remain in Penresford for the duration, but perhaps the clinching moment came when he turned fourteen. He expected, reasonably enough, that his family might want him home even for just a short while, so that they could celebrate his birthday with him. All that happened, however, was that Sam turned up on the day itself, the 21st of Sprinklemonth, ostensibly on an inspection tour of the mines but also bearing with him a letter from Gregory's mother. In it, she wished her son many happy returns and enclosed a five-leaf note for him to spend on 'something nice'. Willem had added a postscript – 'Happy birthday, Little Bother!' – and Gregory was hard pressed to decide which was worse, his mother's indifferent gift or Willem's adoption of the awful Reehan-ism. Either way, the letter spoke volumes. Gregory understood, once and for all, that he had been cut loose. As far as his family were concerned, he was elsewhere and could stay there. In his absence, he had become less of a son, less of a brother. He was now just some notion of Gregory they had, and they remembered him and thought kindly of him but he wasn't real to them any more. He could be fobbed off with a fiver. He could be addressed by a nickname coined by someone else. To his father, he probably didn't exist at all.

Gregory had grown accustomed to pain. Master Ergall, antagonistic schoolfellows, sticks. He was hardening. And hardness felt good.

Summer again in Penresford. A hot, bright afternoon in Master Ergall's courtyard. Everyone sweating hard after an hour of intensive exercise: sit-ups, press-ups, pull-ups, designed to build up the body's tolerance to muscle fatigue.

Now Master Ergall raised the thick wooden rod. Gregory put his hand out. Callused hand already, even after just a year. Knobbly-knuckled. Skin worked and waxen. The badge of an indestructible, as Master Ergall called it. The thing that told people, at a glance, what you were.

Master Ergall lifted the rod and brought it whooshing down.

Gregory felt the impact, nothing more.

In Master Ergall's flinty eyes, a tiny spark ignited.

Later, after the training session was over, he drew Gregory aside.

He didn't smile. He didn't even look pleased. But, for once, he wasn't sneering. His scowl was just marginally less in evidence.

'Not bad,' he said. 'Not bad.'

The next winter. Snow thick and deep over Penresford. A group of boys, a notorious little gang from the year above Gregory's year, thought it would be funny to pelt the Flamer with snowballs as he and Ven were leaving school. These weren't fluffy snowballs either, the kind friends chucked at one another. These were hard and compacted, little short of solid ice. Gregory and Ven retaliated. Things escalated, tempers frayed, there was a fight. Gregory had never been in an actual fight before, but sticks was a good preparation for any kind of violent confrontation. He and Ven acquitted themselves well, given that they were outnumbered and their foes were bigger. They lost, but not without honour. And from then on, the boys who had attacked them treated Gregory with an odd sort of respect. He had taken a beating from them but he had stood his ground in the first place, instead of running away. By the bullies' code, that meant he was no longer worth preying upon; he merited a wary, grudging approval. At the same time, Gregory noticed people at school weren't ragging him so much. The snide comments dwindled away. Schoolfellows who might have addressed him as 'Singe-pants' or 'Match-head' or 'Ash-hole' started calling him 'Brazier' or even 'Gregory'.

Spring, and his fifteenth birthday. Courtesy of Sam, another five-leaf note from his mother for 'something nice'. Gregory visited the market and bought a haunch of beef for Mrs Gove to roast, and, as an afterthought, some hot spices for her to roast it in. The results were mixed, but at least she tried. The spices, thereafter, remained on a kitchen shelf.

'Broken glass,' said Master Ergall, showing his pupils the contents of the bucket. 'Who'd like to be first to plunge their fist in?'
His gaze roved.
'Gregory?'

He thought he had bolted the bathroom door. He was reaching the point of climax, arch-backed, open-mouthed, when Eda Gove came barging in. Which of them was more embarrassed, it was hard to say. Certainly Gregory's face went the brighter pink, but then blushes didn't show quite as conspicuously on a dark complexion like Eda's. He beseeched her with his eyes: *don't tell anyone, if possible forget you ever saw this*. Eda nodded consent. Then, with a last quick glance down towards his lap and what lay shrivelling there in his fist, she withdrew from the bathroom, closing the door.
Coincidence or not, she never referred to him as Red-top after that. Maybe it had an unfortunate extra connotation now; or maybe she felt she couldn't and shouldn't behave towards Gregory as though he were just another of her siblings, not any more.

The day Garla Gove overheard him using an Earther swear word. Mild profanity was permitted in her house but not something as extreme as *pfharg*.
She and Eda were tending to the peonies in the house's window-boxes, stroking their stems and bright red petals to encourage them to bloom even more luxuriantly. At their touch the flowers – knots of dazzling colour amid the Penresford gloom – seemed visibly to fatten and preen. They were nearing the end of their natural lifespan but Garla and Eda would coax a few extra days of beauty out of them.
Gregory and Ven were in the backyard as well, not doing much of anything, idly talking sticks. Gregory dismissed the current Hallawye Badgers defensive line-up as a load of *pfharg*, Garla overheard, and an almighty scolding ensued.
The thing was, Gregory had not even used the word consciously. It

had just slipped out. Ven confirmed that his conversation was now liberally salted with Earth-dialect expressions. Gregory had had no idea.

'It's an honour in life to be an indestructible,' said Master Ergall. It wasn't the first time he had delivered this speech. It wouldn't be the last. 'Some folk look down on us as the lowest of the low. One step up from Extraordinaries. If that. They say all we're good for is soldiering and being constables and endurance boxers, and that may be true. But the lowest of the low? That's *pfharg*. And d'you know why it's *pfharg*? Because indestructibles suffer from very few physical ailments. Because we can expect to live to a ripe old age and in good health almost all the way. Because we endure. Not a lot endures, but we do. The 'Storm . . .'

He circled his fist three times, parodying the superstitious gesture. A fist that looked like flesh-coloured granite. A fist that could crack stone. Gregory had seen it do so.

'Not even the 'Storm can harm us. It can try. It *will* try. But it'll never succeed. A mature, fully-trained indestructible laughs at the 'Storm. He stands out in the open and dares it to do its worst. While everybody else is cowering in shelters, the indestructible goes about his business as if it's nothing more than a light spring shower he's walking around in. That's why people scorn us. It's envy, pure and simple. They can't have what we've got. They hate us for that. So be proud. What do I always say? You're paladins. Paladins . . . ?'

His pupils finished off the epithet in unison: 'Of permanence.'

'Paladins of permanence,' Master Ergall said, nodding. 'Gregory? Something amusing you?'

'No, Master Ergall.'

'You find my little catchphrases funny? They're not up to your fancy Stammeldon standards?'

'No, Master Ergall.'

'No they are or no they aren't?'

'Perhaps you'd better just thump me and get it over with, Master Ergall.'

'Good lad.'

His sixteenth birthday. A ten-leaf note from his mother this time, the doubling of the sum making her seem twice as indifferent, somehow.

Out of curiosity, and contempt, Gregory decided to spend the money on a visit to one of the prostitutes in Hamshank Lane. It took him a full hour to screw up the nerve to approach a door (chosen at random) and knock. Even in the covered, empty, dim-lit alleyway he felt horribly incongruous and exposed. Every second that passed until the door opened was a second in which his mind said run. He managed to force himself to stay put.

She seemed huge and terrifying, the woman who answered his knock. She laughed at his youngness. He thought she was going to tell him to come back when he was older. Much, much older. But there was understanding in her eyes, a hard kind of compassion. And there was a trembling ten-leaf note right under her nose.

She gestured quickly, *come in*, closed the door behind him. It was cramped and dark inside. As Gregory's eyes adjusted, he saw he was in a sort of antechamber, low-ceilinged, meanly furnished. The air smelled sweetly of incense, less sweetly of sweat and something darker, something mustier. In an alcove that could be screened off with a ragged curtain, there was a bed, a mirror, a low-burnt candle, and swags of red muslin on the walls to give the illusion of luxury.

A tenner didn't buy much, apparently. In the alcove, by guttering candlelight, the prostitute undressed herself, undressed Gregory, pushed him onto the bed, caressed him briskly, stuck him inside her, rode him. It was over very quickly. She unstraddled him and per-functorily mopped his crotch and in between her legs. Gregory left Hamshank Lane very little the wiser. Was that it? A quick spurt of pleasure, not much greater than the ones he managed by himself, and then this vague sense of shame? Maybe with more money . . .

But money wasn't the answer, he knew.

'A true indestructible,' Master Ergall said, 'should not feel much of anything.'

And so through another summer that was endlessly, suspiciously warm, cloud-free days interspersed with the occasional rainstorm, a little localised precipitation, enough to wet the land, replenish the town's cisterns and wells, keep the Seray brim-full and flowing. Weather that put people on edge because it seemed too kind, too perfect, almost an invitation to the Worldstorm to come and pay a call.

But the 'Storm resisted the temptation. It was prowling the lands to the south, by all accounts, the hot countries, the tropical latitudes it loved. Reports from the telepath network had it loitering over the Kaa-rhag Desert, a good place for it to stay, an area already so desolate and blasted that even the 'Storm couldn't make much of a difference. Then it travelled west, drawn to the steppes of Lammoran, where it laid siege to Uat, the so-called Termite Mound City, pelting it with hailstone clusters as big as a man's head, drilling holes in its rounded red walls. On from there to the coast and the merchant port of Lyrrban, which was lashed by twenty-foot waves and lost half its trading fleet in a single night. Out to sea after that, the 'Storm venting its spleen on the Aric Ocean, which could bear the punishment. Travelling in an immense circle, absorbing several smaller storms as it went. Feeding on them, some said. That was how the 'Storm kept going. It was a weather predator. It ate the climatic energy of other tempests for nourishment and strength. And maybe this was true and maybe not, but the Worldstorm's sojourn in the Aric Ocean did not bode well, because it often preceded a move north. Not always. There was a chance the 'Storm might continue west, once it was done mauling the waves and engulfing lesser storms. Cross over into the Outer Continent. Hit the coral reefs and sandbars of Danisia and on into the landmass of Faleek, the Empty Quarter (not actually empty but so sparsely populated it might as well be). There were mountain ranges there that channelled it, corralled it. The 'Storm had been known to get stuck in Faleek, like a boar snagged on a thorn bush, for months on end. One could hope that was what was going to happen now. But one had to allow for the likelihood that it might not and that the 'Storm was headed for the north-western reaches of the Inner Continent.

In Penresford, as the evenings began to shorten, talk turned again and again to the 'Storm's last visit, eight years ago. That had come in the wake of a long, benign summer like the one just passing. Which didn't mean anything, of course. The 'Storm didn't follow any rules. Did as it pleased, came when it wanted to. The time before last it had arrived in spring, after a vicious winter. But the good weather, and the 'Storm being in the Aric Ocean . . .

The telepath network kept the updates coming, the 'Storm's current position relayed from bureau to bureau in the form of addenda to paid-for messages, a service the network provided at no extra cost, knowing this only served to underscore its prestige status. The bureau building in Penresford lay on the route between the Gove house and school, and when the autumn term began Gregory would see, as he passed it each morning and each afternoon, a handful of Penresfordians hanging around outside, old people mostly, waiting for the next 'Storm report, which they then disseminated around town. Making themselves useful, but also relishing the chance to seem important and to command an attentive listenership wherever they went.

Daily, the old people were looking grimmer and more agitated. The Worldstorm seemed to have made its decision. North it was. Up towards Tanhout, where the 'Storm swerved around the wine-growing regions, sparing them on a whim, just as, on a whim, it had devastated

88

them on its previous visit. Further up into Hyleta, ploughing across Lake Oreno and the Murria Valley. Now reaching Varshet and its littoral marshes. Now Warlenvish, whose rocky shoreline it traced closely, battering it like a child running a stick along a fence.

And then, on the morning of Gregory's eleven-hundred-and-eleventh day in Penresford, he and the Gove children arrived at school to find the headmaster at the main entrance, turning pupils back. It was very simple. The 'Storm was on its way towards Jarraine. School was suspended until further notice.

Hard not to want to cheer – no school! – but hard, also, not to feel the first stirrings of anxiety. Some of the younger kids from school were crying as their mothers hurried them back home. Home was the only place to go, and Gregory and the Goves made their way back there sombrely and in silence. For the rest of the day, they helped Mrs Gove clean up the cellar and stock it with provisions; they helped Sol get ready the battens that would be nailed across the windows of the house as and when necessary. Everyone did their bit, even the very smallest Goves. It was a day of urgency and industry, but the mood was kept light. Sol sang songs and cracked jokes. These were just precautionary measures, after all. The 'Storm might not come to Jarraine. It might change its mind and head off in a completely different direction. Or it might come to Jarraine but catch Penresford a glancing blow, just brush the town. And perhaps, Sol said, Gregory was their lucky charm. Bear in mind, eight years ago the 'Storm pounded Penresford and then aimed for Stammeldon, only to veer off halfway there and head out of Jarraine altogether. Maybe having a Stammeldoner in their midst would bring Penresford some of the immunity that Stammeldon had enjoyed for over two decades now.

Everyone laughed at that. Gregory laughed. But it was odd, because he was surprised to hear himself referred to as a Stammeldoner. After more than a thousand days he was – had become – a Penresfordian.

YASHU

The clouds looked like milk gone bad. A layer of off-white overcast, with denser, yellower clots purling greasily through. Ordinary weather, an ordinary storm, did not give rise to clouds like that.

That was one sure sign. Another was the hike in temperature. The air was warm – too warm for just after sunrise in early autumn – and humid as well, even indoors. The Worldstorm's sweat, as it was known. A wave of damp heat driven ahead of the 'Storm, given off by the frenzy of its exertions.

Then there was the taste in the air, a taste like no other. Reminiscent of blood and metal. Tingling on the tongue. Once experienced, that taste was never forgotten.

Ousted from sleep by pains in her hips, Liyalu took a look out of the window, inhaled deeply through her mouth, and then, as fast as legs and stick permitted, went to wake her niece.

'It's on its way. You'd better hurry.'

Yashu's clothes were lying by the bed. She had them on in a trice. She knew her duties and the order in which she must carry them out. First, she shunted all the furniture in the cottage's main room into one corner, stacking everything behind the table, which she turned on its side to form a sort of barricade.

She then rolled up the floor rug and scattered straw in its place. For the 'Storm's duration, she and Liyalu would be sharing their accommodation with some uncouth and very messy houseguests.

Next, she fetched in faggots of dried peat from the stack beside the back door. She piled them near the stove, enough to keep it burning for at least three days.

Then she went round inserting the weatherboards into their slots on the outside of the windows. She had practised this yesterday. Warped from disuse, the boards would not slide smoothly in. She had to whack them into position with a mallet, and as she did so, she cast a glance every so often at the sky, which was like no sky she had ever seen before. She would have known. Even if fishermen had not been spreading warnings from island to island, even if talk in Second-Cliff-Village had not been about little else these past few days, she would have known what such a sky portended. Oddly, she felt calm. Excited, perhaps, but not fearful, not yet. Here it was at last, something she had only ever heard about, something she had tried countless times to imagine. No need for imagining any more. Perhaps she was calm because it almost didn't seem like it was happening. Having waited so long for the Worldstorm to appear in her life (strictly speaking, *re*appear), she found it hard to believe that the wait was finally over. There was a sense of unreality about it.

With the last weatherboard in place, the cottage's eyes tight shut, Yashu went back inside. Her aunt had lit lamps in the kitchen and the main room, and the odour of burning fish oil was already pungent. 'Time to bring the livestock in,' Liyalu said. 'Can't put it off any longer.'

The goats were fractious in their pen, scrambling this way and that with anxious, nickering bleats. As Yashu opened the gate, the billy let out an angry blare and charged at her. He was feeling threatened, and the coming 'Storm was not something he could attack but an inter-loper on his territory was. Yashu braced herself and, as the billy reached her, caught him by the horns. She was used to him; he was aggressive even at the best of times. She leaned on him, bearing down with her weight and wrestling his head to the ground. He resisted, a battle of wills as much as of strength, but in the end capitulated. When Yashu allowed him up, he was docile, and she had very little difficulty steering him over to the cottage and inside. The nannies presented even less of a problem. They did not like being without the billy and all but demanded to join him indoors. For a while, the three goats circled around in the main room, getting used to this new kind of confinement. Once they had tried unsuccessfully to nibble the edges of the overturned table and the billy had crapped on the floor, they seemed to settle in.

At this time, the barking of a dog announced the arrival of a visitor: Siaalo, from the village, bearing with him a basket of provisions. Normally, Siaalo's rangy hound Black-Tail appeared well in advance of his master. He would turn up at the door, silent and keen, hoping for a scrap of food, which he invariably got, and a few moments later Siaalo himself would come puffing into view on the path. Today, Black-Tail was sticking close to Siaalo, venturing away from his master's side only to woof fretfully at nothing and then slink back.

Dog and man were welcomed into the kitchen, where Siaalo set down the basket and unloaded a small sack of oatmeal, some potatoes, a loaf of bread, a lump of salted cod.

'I didn't know how well prepared you ladies might be,' he said. He glanced around the kitchen. The peat. The plentifully stocked shelves. 'And I should have realised the answer would be very well prepared. Never mind. It can't hurt to have some spare food around. Just in case.'

'It can't,' said Liyalu. 'And we're grateful. How are things down in the village?'

'Almost everyone's behaving themselves, nice and orderly, no one going into a panic, although as you can imagine there are one or two snapping crabs. Word is, the 'Storm should pass to the east of us. It'll clip us but we won't get the worst of it.'

'Is that true?' Yashu said. She was rubbing Black-Tail's ears, and he was letting her but not relishing it as he usually would. His tail remained inert on the floor.

'Could be. The 'Storm makes up its own mind about these things.'

'How far to the east?'

Siaalo realised what she was after. 'I wouldn't worry about Shai. I don't think they'll take a great deal more abuse there than we're going to.'

He did not stay long. He had come simply to drop off the food and make sure Liyalu and Yashu were safe and secure inside the cottage and ready for the 'Storm. For such a big man Siaalo was surprisingly shy, and it was plain to anyone with eyes that he had been deeply in love with Liyalu for a long time. Even as he promised to return to check up on them after the 'Storm had passed, his voice, his gaze, his face, everything about him spoke of a profound and abiding infatuation. And had he been any less shy, he might have admitted his feelings to Liyalu long ago. And had he been any less shy, Liyalu might not have liked him as much as she did and might not have wanted him as even just a friend. And anyway, it seemed a moot point, now that she was ill and dying. But whenever Yashu looked at Siaalo, she always felt sorry for him and was always glad that she was not quite as independent and self-reliant as her aunt. Glad that she had Huaso and needed Huaso.

Then Siaalo was gone, heading back down to Second-Cliff-Village, with Black-Tail trotting at his heels. '*Mala*,' he had said. 'See you after.' And now the wind was getting up, and it was midday but as gloomy as twilight. The cloud cover had deepened in hue almost to the colour of pus, and seagulls were wheeling and crying, grey bird-shape silhouettes against the roiling yellow. Yashu stood in the kitchen doorway, watching the world darken and feeling the wind strengthen. The sound of the gusts buffeting her ears was like the growl of far-off thunder. Then the growl of far-off thunder was like the sound of the gusts buffeting her ears. On the eastern horizon, where the sky was a field of dense black, there were flickers of lightning. They snaked sideways, silver chasing silver. Shai. Shai was somewhere under all that. But Huaso wasn't stupid. He and his family would be under cover. They would be fine.

The blackness and the lightning drew closer. Yellow overhead turned to purple. The seagulls descended out of sight, flocking to their cliff-face roosts. Yashu thought that, if she had wings, she wouldn't stay put, she would fly away as fast and as far as she could. But maybe seagulls couldn't outrace the 'Storm, or maybe they were obstinate to the point of stupidity. Or maybe – this seemed likeliest – they were just too alarmed to be thinking straight.

The thunder became more crackle than growl. The lightning bursts stained her vision, lingering as jagged streaks of blue. Liyalu suggested she come inside and close the door, but Yashu wanted to wait till the last possible moment. She wanted to see all she could see.

And now raindrops – great fat warm blobs of water flung horizont-ally, splashing against the cottage wall and against Yashu's face. The air abruptly hazed. The sea's surface dulled. With an almighty hiss, the sky let loose. A deluge. Rocks went from grey to black. Grass flattened. Gorse and heather thrashed. Second-Cliff-Village vanished from view. Liyalu again suggested Yashu come inside. Insisted, in fact, and it seemed like a sensible idea this time. Yashu shot home both bolts on the door, then lowered into place the stout retaining bar that she had never before had to use. It fit snugly into its sockets. Now the 'Storm was out there. She and Liyalu were in here. Nothing to do but sit and wait.

Rain roared onto the roof thatch. Wind rumbled and bumped around the cottage. The weatherboards shuddered, the doors rattled in their frames, the stove flue hummed and sizzled. The thunder thudded ever nearer, like vast, approaching footfalls. The lamp in the kitchen began to gutter and dim, and Liyalu refilled its oil reservoir. The din outdoors made it hard to speak at anything less than a shout. The Worldstorm demanded that it, and nothing else, be heard. The rain's impact thickened, developing into a series of sporadic thumps. Hail. The thumps gathered pace until they were a continuous violent drumming, and Yashu surveyed the ceiling. There were planks, then the roof beams overlaid with thick thatch. Several lines of defence between her and the hail, but all at once they seemed inadequate. Would they cope? Would they hold out?

She stoked the stove, a useful distraction, then ate some of the bread and salted cod Siaalo had brought. Liyalu ate too, although she looked no hungrier than Yashu felt. It was just something to do.

Eventually the hail eased off, ceding back dominance to the wind and thunder. Another refilling of the lamp. Yashu went and checked on the goats in the next room. They were huddled in one corner. Their eyes flashed in the lamplight and their long drooping ears quivered.

Was it still day? Was it night? Time had been pummelled senseless. Yashu was weary but sleep seemed unlikely. Her aunt did doze off, but this was doubtless due to her illness. It took its toll. Yashu wriggled to get comfortable in her chair, closed her eyes, tried to relax and shut the 'Storm out, but the 'Storm's shocks and surges would not let her. The cottage creaked with every detonation of thunder, leapt with every wrenching thrust of wind. It was possible to imagine the entire building coming loose from the hillside, torn free of its foundations. The 'Storm seemed to be concentrating all its efforts on doing just that. No other house on I*il was suffering so much punishment, surely. The 'Storm was focused on the cottage, it had taken a special dislike to Yashu and her aunt, it was intent on weakening the cottage's hold on the island until at last the walls gave, the roof tore off, the whole place was blown clean away and its occupants with it. The 'Storm wanted Yashu. It had failed to get her on the last visit; this time it wasn't going away empty-handed.

More waiting.

Yashu drowsed. After a while, the tumult became enervating. The constant tension, fear of the cottage being torn to pieces, wore her down. When she came to, she was surprised that she had been able to drift off at all. The roar of the 'Storm was, if anything, greater and the cottage's foothold on the island seemed even more tenuous. Yet somehow sleep, or a shallow variety of sleep, had been necessary. Stiff from the hard chair, Yashu stood up and moved around, working feeling back into her limbs. She fed the stove once more; looked in on the goats again.

Something cracked and splintered, shockingly loud, in another part of the cottage – Liyalu's bedroom, Yashu reckoned. She was all set to go and investigate, but her aunt restrained her: a hand on her arm, a shake of the head that meant leave it for now.

Yet more waiting, and Yashu began to grow impatient. Irritated with the 'Storm. Enough already. It had done its thing. There was nothing left to prove. It was powerful, it did damage. Now why not leave them alone and go and wreak havoc somewhere else?

But the 'Storm lingered, gleefully pounding at the cottage, in no hurry to move on. There was another huge, splintering crack that made the whole cottage quake and groan. Liyalu reached for Yashu's hand and gripped it with greater strength than her condition normally allowed. Yashu envisaged a section of the roof gone, a corner of the house's carapace peeled back, indoors exposed to outdoors, the elements rushing in. All at once the cottage seemed an even frailer place than before. She thought of the hull of a boat, holed – the sea seizing its chance, pouring in, dragging the boat down.

And that image sparked off another image. Huaso. Huaso talking about owning his own boat. And a bad thought settled in Yashu's mind, a dreadful thought. She tried to get rid of it but couldn't. Huaso. So much loss happened to her. Everyone close to her got taken away from her. She pictured the lightning flickering over Shai. Huaso.

Several times the intensity of the wind and thunder seemed to abate, but then the assault on the cottage would resume with sudden, fresh ferocity. Recognition that the 'Storm was finally, definitely letting up came when Liyalu said, 'Listen.' It wasn't so much what she had said as the fact that she could be heard at all. The noise outside had diminished from deafening to merely raucous. It was like somebody who had shouted himself hoarse – he wanted to keep shouting but what was coming out was a hollow, wheezy version of his voice, the same effort with less result.

Soon, startlingly soon, the wind was down to a dull, desultory huff and bluster, nothing that you wouldn't get on a breezier-than-average autumn day. Yashu made to unbar the door but Liyalu advised against. In her experience, it didn't necessarily mean a 'Storm visit was over just because things appeared to have settled down. There were false lulls. Wait a while longer. Yashu waited a while longer, until, through the sound of soft gusts, she could make out seagulls distantly squealing. That surely meant the 'Storm was past. She looked to Liyalu for permission to go out. Liyalu nodded.

The sky was pallid grey, with a weak sun glimmering low in the east like a blurred pearl. Morning, then. The slope down to Second-Cliff-Village was speckled with hail, the roofs of the village whitened with it. The sea still churned, no regularity in its waves, choppy peaks spiking and collapsing at random. The air smelled raw, empty, purged. Yashu breathed it in, glad simply to be outdoors again. Then she made a circuit of the cottage, to see what the 'Storm had done. Sure enough it was the corner where Liyalu's room was situated that had suffered. A section of the thatch had been torn off and was nowhere in sight. A couple of roof beams were absent while others were broken and sticking out at skewed angles. The planks of the ceiling had caved in. Standing upslope from the cottage, Yashu looked down through a jagged hole to see a smashed bed, broken ornaments, strewn clothing. She went back indoors to report, and Liyalu was sanguine. 'It can all be repaired or replaced. We're alive and unhurt, that's what matters.'

The goats, too, were alive and unhurt, and Yashu would have let them out but there was no pen for them to return to. The fence was now just so much tinder and flinders, and their little goat-shed was smithereens. Liyalu suggested Yashu get hold of some lengths of rope, noose the goats and tether them to a gorse bush till the fence could be rebuilt. Yashu agreed, but said that, with Liyalu's blessing, there was something else she must do too.

'Oh?'

'I need to go to Shai.'

'Shai?'

Yashu couldn't put it into words. It wasn't a foreboding, exactly. She just had to go. Go and see for herself. She had to know.

'But who'll take you?' Liyalu said. 'Nobody's going to want to venture out to sea just yet, not till everything calms down completely.'

'Somebody will.'

'Yashu . . .'

Yashu fetched her mohair overcoat and stuffed the pockets with food and a small bottle of *sirassi* which she thought she might be able to use as a bribe or a fee. Then she faced her aunt across the kitchen.

'You'll manage all right without me, won't you? For a day or two?'

'I imagine so. Siaalo will be up shortly, I expect. He can sort things out here. Deal with the goats and all that. The roof.' Liyalu forced a bleak smile. 'Go on then. Be back. I love you.'

'I love you too.'

'*Mala* '

'Let's hope so.'

Yashu took the shorter, sheerer route to Town-By-The-Dunes, over rather than round, ascending I*il's steep windward flank, bent forward, toes digging into the rain-sodden turf, till she gained the summit. She paused there briefly, overlooking a panorama of almost the entire leeward side of the island, its inlets and rocky ridges gleaming, weirdly pristine in the Worldstorm's wake. Then she began the descent. She passed the warren where she usually snared rabbits, and several dozen of its inhabitants were out and nibbling the wet grass, wary of her but too dull-witted or too hungry to be truly fearful. She passed one of the streams that supplied Town-By-The-Dunes with fresh water, and it was leaping along its downhill course, brimming with 'Storm-brought bounty. She passed bedraggled fields and sorry-looking orchards whose owners, not much less bedraggled and sorry-looking themselves, were assessing the 'Storm's ravages and starting to mend what could be mended.

Town-By-The-Dunes had lost a few roofs but, to Yashu's eyes at least, seemed reasonably unscathed. Last time (she had been told) a huge wave had come in off the sea, swept over the dunes and flooded the town, pulling down whole houses as it surged along the streets. Of those who died then, as many were drowned as were killed by collapsing buildings. This time around, the 'Storm had shown the town greater mercy, or perhaps greater indifference.

Down in Half-Moon-Bay, boat owners were checking on the state of their vessels, while numerous beachcombers were harvesting the detritus that lay strewn across the sand. Driftwood aplenty, and pebbles, useful for building work as aggregate, but there were also fish of all shapes and sizes, up to and including some of the biggest cod Yashu had ever seen, sucked up from the deeps and dumped ashore to lie there looking glum and stunned. Seals too, slumped on the sand, and albatrosses and terns, damp explosions of beak and leg and feather. An indiscriminate cull of marine life that was there to be taken advantage of, the 'Storm offering some small recompense for its many unkindnesses. *Mala* in action.

The boats were anchored in the shelter of the western promontory, at the opposite end of the bay from the Rock, and most of them appeared to have ridden out the 'Storm more or less intact. Yashu could see a couple of them listing, a couple lolling lower in the water than the rest. Some dents had occurred where gunwale had crashed against gunwale. Sprung deck planks jutted up at shallow angles. There were cracks in the boats' tough varnish. But these were sturdy craft, built with artful simplicity. Timber was a scarce commodity on Li*issua, so the archipelago's shipwrights made sure they used it plainly and used it well.

Yashu scrambled along the promontory until she was within hailing distance of the boats. 'Is anyone going to Shai?' The various boat owners glanced across at one another, then back at her. There were shrugs and head-shakes.

'What's it worth to you?' one of them asked.

'I need to go there.'

'Yes, but what's it worth?'

'It's a long way,' said another of the boat owners. 'Rough seas.'

He was tall, rangy, broad-shouldered, bearded, with the kind of sun-parched, wind-worn features that put him anywhere between thirty years old and fifty. How Huaso might look after years of seagoing, Yashu thought, and then told herself not to think that way. Not to think about the future until she was once again sure there was a future.

'I'm from Shai myself,' the man said, indicating the clan colours that adorned his boat, a shore-crawler. 'Got stuck here. Couldn't make it back before the 'Storm hit. You too?'

'No, I have . . . a friend there,' Yashu said. 'I need to see how he is.'

'That's it?'

'A good friend.'

'I see. Tell me, do you get seasick easily?'

'No.'

The man pondered a moment. 'All right then. I was going to leave it till tomorrow, but . . . Some company on the trip. Help pass the time.'

Not long after, Yashu was on board and the man, Theliñaho, was weighing anchor and nursing the shore-crawler out of the bay.

Theliñaho had said he wanted company but there wasn't much opportunity for talk once they were out on the open sea. He had to devote all of his attention to holding a steady course through the toss and tumble of the waves, while Yashu had to concentrate on keeping her balance and fending off queasiness. She hadn't lied. She didn't get seasick easily. Few islanders did. But this was no ordinary sea. It was violent and contrary and rhythmless. The agitation of the 'Storm still churned within it. Now the boat pitched, now it yawed, now it pitched and yawed at once. Waves came at it from all directions. Water so tormented was difficult to shape, and Theliñaho's weathered face was a mask of effort. Clenched teeth gleamed yellowly through his beard.

Yashu kept her gaze fixed on the horizon. Soon Ra*ai loomed up on the starboard side, with its landmark Cloud-Catch-Peak, and after Ra*ai came Oöyia. She recalled how, at Swim-Through-The-Rock, she and Huaso had agreed to meet on Oöyia for Cross-The-Causeway, which was due to take place next month. Oöyia was really two islands, one large, one small, linked by an umbilicus of mudflat which the sea exposed twice a day and which yielded, it was said, the best cockles in all of Li*issua. A grand celebration was held every autumn to commemorate this fact. It was at one such celebration, almost exactly five years ago, that Yashu and Huaso had first met.

She watched Oöyia pass by between the leaping waves, and her nausea seemed, at that point, as much a thing of soul as of body.

Then a long stretch of empty horizon, a break in the Li*issua chain. It was well past noon before the next island came in sight – Tleyis, the smallest and least populous of the twenty, home to less than a hundred inhabitants and butt of countless jokes about siblings married to siblings and unnatural relationships with livestock. Tleyis meant journey's end was near. Mallaim appeared next, and Shai not long after. Broad and rounded, Shai boasted the loveliest beaches in all the archipelago and large, precious forests nestled in the clefts of its hills. Theliñaho brought the prow round and summoned up everything he had for the final push home.

It was clear from the moment they arrived that Shai had been far worse hit than I*il. The beach at which they made landfall was littered with the wreckage of boats. Some lay cracked in two like eggshells, others were spread out over the sand, dismantled into their component timbers, a cross-brace here, an outrigger there, as if the 'Storm had casually plucked them apart and left them like that for someone else to reassemble. The owners of these shattered hulks were walking around them, scratching their heads as if wondering how to do exactly that. When Theliñaho turned up in his seaworthy vessel, envying and resentful glances were shot his way. In his exhaustion, he barely noticed.

Yashu disembarked and tendered Theliñaho formal thanks, along with the bottle of *sirassi*, which he accepted. He enquired where her friend lived and she said, 'Valley-Heart'. With a roughly northward gesture, a weary lofting of the hand, he said, 'That way.' She thanked him again, and began walking.

Her route to Valley-Heart entailed two minor detours, one around a rockslide and one around a stand of trees, several of whose number now lay prostrate across the path. When she reached the town she chose to feel a faint stab of hope because Valley-Heart, judging by its outskirts, did not seem to be in too bad shape. Roofs were gone and one house she passed appeared to have been eviscerated, its entire contents scooped neatly out, but Town-By-The-Dunes had not looked much worse, she thought. Islanders were out in the street, sweeping up, taking down their window shutters, tidying debris into heaps, neatening. They looked dazed, like people waking from a bad dream, but their actions were reassuringly methodical. Here they were, fixing things. This was what you were supposed to do.

It was a different story at the centre of town. There, buildings had not simply been uncapped or gutted, they had been crushed. Distraught householders stood staring at the flattened remnants of their homes, their faces grim and covered with dust. People held on to one another. There was a sense of communal disbelief, to which children alone seemed immune. To the adults, the ruins represented security gone, years of memories lost, possessions irreplaceably destroyed. To the children, they were there to explore and scamper over; they were playgrounds for games of Octopus and Only-Fish-In-The-Sea.

Then singing. Yashu heard the drift of massed voices, coming from the direction of Valley-Heart's main square. She recognised the melody, and as she picked her way along the rubbled streets she tried not to sing along:

Diving deep down
Darkness and slow forgetfulness
In the rinsing of the tides

Submitting themselves to unity
In the Great-Ocean-Beyond

A couple of hundred people were gathered in the main square. They lined the square's perimeter, moving their bodies in a gentle, grieving sway as they sang. Some of them were smiling, or doing their best to smile, even as the tears flowed. You ought to feel glad, had to, on behalf of the dead. The Great-Ocean-Beyond was a better place than this; the life of a spirit was a better life. That was what the song was all about.

The dead lay in the middle of the square, arranged in rows. At a glance, Yashu counted approximately forty of them. They were supine, some with their eyes closed, others gazing emptily, amazedly at the sky. All were uncovered except for a few who had had blankets drawn over them. Some of these must have been injured too horribly to look at, but the majority were small bodies – pitiably small.

Salt waters always kept warm
By our happy sorrow

Yashu steeled herself and moved forward through the singers until she had an unimpeded view of the dead. She looked from upturned face to upturned face. She scanned their lifeless features, searching, not wanting to find . . .

No Huaso. No one she recognized.

She turned to a woman next to her, who was singing in reedy, husky tones, hands clenched at her breast. She attracted the woman's attention with a polite gesture and, addressing her as 'respected Shai-islander', enquired if she knew Imersho of Valley-Heart, husband of Pharralu, father of Huaso and Zeelu. The woman responded with a slow nod.

'Where might I find him? Is he at home? Only, I'm not sure of the way to his house. I've only visited here once before.'

'Imersho left this morning for Purple-Cowrie-Beach-Village, with his family.'

'His family? All of them?'

'I don't know. I heard only that he had gone.'

The sun was warm as Yashu made her way to Purple-Cowrie-Beach-Village. The world seemed to be settling down at last. Under any other circumstances, it would have been a pleasant afternoon. She ate some of her provisions as she walked, to keep her strength up. An unfounded, defiant optimism braced her. 'With his family.' Imersho had gone to Purple-Cowrie-Beach-Village to see how Huaso's house there had fared. The whole family had gone. All four of them.

Cresting the brow of a hill, Yashu found she had reached the edge of Shai. To her right, a wide, straight beach squared the island off as surely as if it had been trimmed with ruler and blade. The woman in Valley-Heart had given careful directions, and the beach matched her description of Purple-Cowrie-Beach. Yashu looked for the village. Toward the beach's further end there was boat wreckage, and just inland from that what looked like a freshly ploughed field, but nothing she could see resembled human habitation. Reasoning that she had taken a wrong turn somewhere, she set off along the beach. There were people by the mangled boats. One of them would be able to put her on the right track.

As she got closer, she heard singing again. This was odd because you did not mourn a lost boat and commend it to the next life. Her pace quickened. Then she realised that the figures on the beach weren't looking at the boats. They were facing inland. And the boat wreckage was not, in fact, boat wreckage at all.

Then her name was called out, shrilly, and she saw Zeelu running towards her along the sand. Zeelu trying to smile, trying so hard to be brave, but her eyes were swollen and reddened, her cheeks were wet, she stumbled as she ran, and when she reached Yashu she threw herself into Yashu's arms and began sobbing against her chest.

'He went to look at the house,' Zeelu gasped out, between the sobs. 'Make sure it would be all right. He thought he could be there and back in time. Before the 'Storm . . . Before the 'Storm hit. Oh Yashu! He didn't come back. We waited for so long, and the 'Storm was so loud, and he never came back!'

AYN

Now then, where were we?

['You finished the session yesterday with the words "A part of him would be forever free. I made that promise to him." ']

Thank you. How did that seem yesterday? Did it make sense?

['My honest opinion? It seemed fine. A little disjointed, maybe . . .']

Disjointed?

['You didn't explain exactly why you left Stonehaven, what you were setting out to do.']

Everyone will know, Khollo! I left it unsaid because there's no point telling your audience something that will be quite obvious to them. They'll be living in a world that I will have changed beyond measure. They'll be reading this account fully aware of what I did. I wouldn't want to insult their intelligence.

['It just struck me as a minor flaw, Elder Ayn. Something you might want to think about amending.']

Bugger amending. Let it stand as it is. Call it, I don't know, sustaining of narrative tension, or whatever. And Khollo? How long have we known each other? Isn't it time you started calling me something other than Elder Ayn? We're not at Stonehaven any more. No need for the obsequies here.

['What should I call you?']

Annonax will do. Nax if you want to be really informal.

[I stuck with 'Elder Ayn', sometimes using the honorific 'High Previsionary'. For some reason I couldn't – still can't – think of him as the sort of person I'd know by his forename. That isn't to say I didn't like him, just that I felt it better to treat him with respect. Respect put us on different levels, kept a layer between us.]

So anyway, to resume. Oh, but a quick drink first. I'm not making the same mistake this time. Keep the whistle whetted as I go. Ah, Tanhout, Tanhout!

'I made that promise to him.' Hmmm. Very well.

Prior to leaving Stonehaven, I had made provision. Prevision equals provision, sometimes. First and foremost, I took it upon myself to engage the services of an excellent young enshriner who, as I have already said, did not strike me as happy with his lot at Stonehaven. Khollo Sharellam, bright, handsome. The son of lawyers. Hailing from the arid and drowsy uplands of Durat. His journey to Stonehaven sponsored by that country's monarch, King Xhan, after his parents were tragically taken from him. A good-natured, earnest young Inductee who, barely two years into his residency, was finding himself already thoroughly disillusioned with the pettiness and self-regard of the Stonehaven regime. A fair description?

[I nodded. Disillusioned? Yes. But dismayed might be closer to it. I had been brought up believing Stonehaven to be the acme of sophistication and . . . civilisedness, if there is such a word. Stonehaven was the place that all the Air Inclined should aspire to go to. The place where certain values and ideals of living were preserved against the ravages of the Worldstorm and the idiocy of lesser men. Intellect, embodied by the residents themselves. Knowledge and history, embodied by the library. Service to others, embodied by the petitioners and the inmates of the Cells of Solitude and Contemplation. Whatever ruin the 'Storm brought, and whatever crimes and injustices people inflicted on one another, there would always be Stonehaven. It was a repository for all that was best about the human race. Except that it turned out, when I got there, to be not like my image of it at all. It turned out to be home to just as much greed and corruption and callowness and shallowness as you'd find anywhere else. I was young. I'd expected too much. But still, I didn't make any secret of the fact that I felt bitterly let down.]

You, like me, were looking for an excuse to leave, something that would push you into taking that drastic step. I found it in Traven and my punch-up with Ærdant. You found it in me. I barely had to ask. I said I was in need of an enshriner to travel with me on a journey of great significance and record an account of my deeds. You volunteered without hesitation.

[I recall it slightly differently. Elder Ayn approached me twice before I committed to accompanying him, and he told me next to nothing about why he was travelling or where to. All he revealed was that we'd be going in search of two people and his prevision would guide us to them. It says something, though, that I agreed to go along with him anyway, despite knowing nothing more about the purpose of our journey than that. I debated whether I should go, but in my heart of hearts I knew that I did not belong at Stonehaven and never would. I applied to the Council for a temporary leave of absence and was granted it. They were very understanding. I did not tell them I was travelling with Elder Ayn, only that I needed some time away to think about life and my future. That way I was able to pretend to others, and to myself, that I'd be coming back.]

The other provision I had made took the form of several small items which I went to the trouble of appropriating from the library, the Obsidian Hall and elsewhere, and squirreled away in my apartment till they were needed. Ornaments, a beautifully bound book or two, some pieces of silverware, trinkets donated by petitioners – the sort of stuff that littered the place profligately. Not much, and nothing more than I felt was my due. I didn't regard it as stealing so much as recompensing myself for the time I would now not be spending at Stonehaven. Besides, the absence of these objects, a fraction of Stonehaven's great wealth, would not be noticed. And I needed to fund our travels somehow, for I knew that we would not necessarily be able to rely on the kindness of strangers once we were out in the big wide world. Thus a bag heavy with valuables on my back as we left. Thus departure by night, with no one to see us off but a rather somnolent gatekeeper who could barely contain his yawns as he wheeled the gate – Stonehaven's sole exit and entrance – shut behind us.

Down we went through the petitioners' camp. I say camp but it's effectively a little town, isn't it? Tents pitched everywhere, cooking-fires, horses nodding at their tethers, a few people sleeping out under the stars, but it's organised, with streets, latrine areas, and a handful of permanent structures amid the temporary – restaurants and hotels run by entrepreneurial types who pay a tithe to the Council in return for the privilege of dipping their ladles into the Stonehaven revenue stream. The camp sprawls in a kind of delta, fanning out from the volcano's base, spreading down into the Heurendon Valley. Silently we trekked through it, through the torch-lit dark, and I must confess to feeling awe at being out in the open. The sky seemed huge and black. There was more air than my lungs could take in. Of course I had ventured out from Stonehaven several times in the past, but only for a brief change of scene, never straying far. For those with their eyes on the top prize, it didn't do to leave the place for long. The ground one had gained over several years could be lost in as many days. Rivals would take advantage of one's absence.

This venturing out, besides, was different. It was for ever. Bridges well and truly burnt I was now a part of the outside world again, never to return to Stonehaven's shelter. I was going from a small, self-contained place to a place that was infinitely vast. There seemed too much of the world – too many roads I could take, too many options. I don't mind admitting I was intimidated. Not a moment went by on that first day, or for several days after, when I wasn't conscious of the immensity and the irrevocability of what I had done to myself, and didn't wish there was some way of undoing it. The further we went from Stonehaven, the more I found myself missing the security of a rock ceiling overhead and rock walls around me, not to mention the orderliness and routine I was used to. They talk of prisoners becoming institutionalised, don't they, unable to cope with the outside world after a long spell behind bars. When there aren't jailers to tèll them what to do and when to do it, when there suddenly isn't an imposed structure to their lives any more – they're overwhelmed, they go to pieces. I think I was a little like that in those first few days. I floundered. We journeyed westward, which was the way I knew we would have to go, we followed the petitioners' trail, but I'm afraid that, beyond pointing us in the right direction, I wasn't much practical help to begin with. I pretty much left it to you, Khollo, to find us places to stay for the night and to set the goal for each daily leg of the journey. I hope I was fully appreciative of your efforts, although I fear I was not.

[To be honest, he was as grumpy and inarticulate as a toddler, or a teenager.]

Now, the date of this exclaustration of ours was, for the record, the 28th of Sunmonth, 686.

['The thirtieth.']

Was it really? I must say I thought it was the 28th, but then you would remember better than I. I definitely recall that it took us three days to put the Pallian Hills out of sight, by which I mean three days before Stonehaven's black cone was no longer visible on the horizon. So that would put us just into Drymonth before there was no longer a looming reminder behind us of where we had been and what we had abandoned. We travelled on foot mostly, with the occasional stretch by stagecoach if we were feeling tired or the weather was inclement. On foot was preferable. I've never developed much of a taste for being jounced and bounced for hours on end on an inadequately-padded seat, bumping knees with strangers. Also, walking did not deplete our budget, and I knew we needed to conserve our financial resources for later.

In the stagecoaches and at the various hostelries we stopped at along the way, we met hopeful petitioners who were making the journey to Stonehaven and satisfied petitioners who were coming back. To avoid awkward questions we pretended to be petitioners ourselves, in the latter category. We were dressed appropriately, in simple travelling gear – such as these tweed trousers of mine, which aren't looking anywhere near as pristine now as when we set out. I remember, one evening, singing Stonehaven's praises to a bunch of mining prospectors from Aoterio, and the praise-singing may only have been partly tongue-in-cheek. I was still in a state of confusion. I loathed Stone-haven, but it was my home. Another evening, when I fear I was a little worse for wear for drink, I told a constable from Kraton – or was it Hyleta? – not to bother with the diviners at Stonehaven. They were all incompetent, I said, and High Diviner Ærdant was the worst and most incompetent of the lot. The constable was taking a knife, a murder weapon, to have its history read for evidence in a trial. I think, hope, he was wise enough to ignore my advice.

Then there was the time . . . this smooth-flowing enough for you, Khollo? Not too *disjointed*? Very well. There was the time, we had been on the read just over a week, and we were staying at an inn in some forsaken little hole of a town near the border between Pallia and Varshet.

['Folsa's Clearing.']

There you go. That's the one. Inn is a generous description for that particular establishment. Pub with a few lice-infested rooms-to-let above its ostlery might be more accurate.

[It wasn't quite that bad. Though to someone who had spent the past forty years cosseted in Stonehaven, perhaps it was.]

We had left the petitioners' trail by that stage, so the quality of accommodation had become, shall we say, variable. The main route to Stonehaven is a well-trodden path and the hoteliers along the way may charge the earth but at least in return they provide a decent minimum standard of bed and board. Elsewhere, it's a matter of pot luck, and in Folsa's Clearing the best that was on offer wasn't up to much. The locals were not of the friendliest, either. But in fact, when all's said and done, I blame you for what happened there, Khollo. If you'd chosen another town as our destination that day . . .

[Elder Ayn's smile. Never long-lived and never complete. His upper lip always stayed fixed. His lower lip did all the work, exposing a few of his lower teeth, which were small and thin, like grains of rice. The smile of a man who was never comfortable smiling.]

So there we were, downstairs in the pub part of the inn, eating our supper, some miserable chunks of a lamb that deserved better than to end its days boiled to the texture of putty in a broth flavoured with its own giblets and a couple of carrots. We were footsore after a day's walking, and grumpy, some of us, at the prospect of the sleepless night we were about to spend on a paper-thin mattress hopping with fleas and lice and who knows what other vermin, with the reek of horse manure wafting up from below. And there, at a nearby table, were four locals engaged in a game of elements. Farmhands they were, or artisans of some sort. Strong-class Earther, at any rate. Awash with the tasteless greyish beer they drink around those parts. Rowdy and playing extremely badly, it appeared. I foresaw myself winning money off them, and sensed the consequences of this would be undesirable . . . but anything for a little light relief in that arse-end of a place.

One of the four passed out halfway through a round, and I was up on my feet immediately and putting myself forward as his replacement. The three remaining players spotted me for an Airy straight off and asked me which class I was. They might have been drunk but they weren't entirely dumb. I said, 'What class do you think I am?' and their reply was, 'Well, as long as you're not a diviner or a telepath.' I assured them I was neither, and that was that. No sooner had I sat down than they were suggesting we play for money. Clearly I came across as someone with a bit of cash to spare and likely to be easily parted from it.

So the tiles were shuffled and lined up, face-down. I was informed I would be playing Water first off, as that was the quadrant our comatose friend had just been playing. I didn't have a problem with that. The stakes were a quarter-leaf per point. I didn't have a problem with that either. I lost the first round gracefully, knowing I wouldn't get anything like the sort of tile combination necessary to win. The second round I also lost, but deliberately. Losing made me the three men's new best friend. All at once they were grinning at me and patting me on the shoulder and asking if I'd care to up the stakes to a half-leaf per point. Of course I agreed, saying perhaps it would give me a chance to claw back some of my deficit.

After that, everything fell my way. In fact, even without knowing in advance which tiles I was going to get and where my opponents would place theirs, I would probably have beaten them. I kept turning up the most fortuitous combinations. It really was one the luckiest nights at elements I've had. When it was my turn to be Fire quadrant, for instance, I had both the Take tile and a straight run from Fire Two to Seven. Someone else put down Air One, I Took it, and that was the round sewn up. Even when I was Water, and we all know how much of a disadvantage that is, I had a Turn tile every time, and I wasn't slow in using it to punish anyone who put down the other Turn tile. On most games I would dominate at least two corners, and more often than not three. I might add that this was the oldest, most well-fingered set of tiles I had ever played with. The brown of the Earth tiles was so faded and the white of the Air tiles so grubby, it was often hard to tell one from the other. Likewise the red of the Fire tiles had paled down until it was a very similar orangey hue to that of the Water tiles, whose original bright yellow was but a tarnished memory. There was, moreover, a complicated pattern of cracks and grooves on the back of each that made them almost as distinguishable from one another upside down as right side up. Halfway through our game I had a fore-flash of someone telling me my opponents were using their familiarity with the backs of the tiles to cheat. It made no difference. Round after round, I emerged the victor. I was cheating better than them, and beating them hollow.

Needless to say, by evening's end I was not the three men's friend any more. There were sullen looks, some grumbled threats, but the landlord intervened before things turned ugly. The trio tottered off home, carrying the fourth man with them, now recovered from his lapse into insensibility. I went to bed for a restless night. Next morning, there was a constable waiting downstairs and you and I were off to jail, Khollo.

Accommodation-wise, jail wasn't a great step down. Arguably, our cells were cleaner and better appointed than our rooms at the inn had been. Certainly the rat who paid me a visit via the sanitation hole in the floor was a sleek and well-kempt ambassador for his species. It helped, I suppose, that I knew we would not have to endure internment for long. I saw us being released the following day. I only regret, Khollo, that I didn't have an opportunity when we were arrested to share that information with you.

[It seems to me that there were plenty of opportunities. Elder Ayn chose not to take one, that's all. It wasn't the last time I would be the victim of that mischievous streak of his.]

The charge was misrepresentation of Inclination. I had lied to the elements players, and my young travelling companion was an accessory because he must have known I was lying. I argued that I had not lied. The men had asked me if I belonged to two specific classes of Air Inclination, I had said I did not, and there had been no further comment on the matter. The arresting constable was one of those stolid, imperturbable indestructibles, so well suited to the job. Indestructibles aren't as fleet of foot or of mind as their swift-class colleagues, but at the same time they're less prone to rash decisions and jumping to conclusions. His massive, waxy-skinned fists looked like they brooked no nonsense but at the same time were only ever used as a last resort. He heard me out, then admitted that the three who had brought the charge against us were notorious for hustling out-of-towners. The one who had passed out had only feigned passing out, and the constable confirmed that the men could read the backs of the tiles as surely as if they were face up. He was pleased that, for once, someone had outplayed them and taken *their* money. He had had to arrest us, for form's sake, but he was going to convince the men to drop the charge and not to be such sore losers. The following morning, you and I, Khollo, were released. And that was our stay in Folsa's

Clearing. As we left the town, I remember feeling not only glad to see the back of it but, for the first time since we had set out from Stonehaven, confident. Winning at elements had restored my sense of certainty and banished my fears of being unable to cope in the outside world. That may seem incredible, such a result from just a game, but nonetheless it's true. Games give one the illusion of control. Relying on one's wits, one masters the vagaries of chance. The random becomes manipulable. That is a game's power, a game's allure. While playing, one feels that one has taken fate by the horns and tamed it – especially if one is winning. And that night, at the elements table, I had seen that things *could* go according to plan. *I could* win.

[Here, Elder Ayn replenished his wineglass.]

And so on into Varshet, and what a grim country that is! Lowland, bare, featureless, the kind of place you would expect the 'Storm to slide right over. Nothing there to snag it or waylay it. And the inhabitants a dour lot, with faces so pinched and tight any attempt to smile would probably split them in two. A people whose idea of flamboyance is wearing an item of clothing that's a slightly lighter shade of grey than normal. A people whose habitual greeting to one another is 'So I see we're still alive today' and whose definition of a friend is somebody who doesn't drop by too often and never speaks much or stays long or asks for anything. I mean, I hate to perpetuate stereotypes, but we didn't meet a single Varshetian who didn't live up to the national reputation. My theory is they live under too much sky. It's oppressive, to have all that sky overhead and so little land to offset it. They don't have horizons, just emptiness, and they retreat into themselves to escape it.

And of course where were we when the Worldstorm came up on us? Where did we have to spend two days and two nights in shelter, cooped up with some of the dullest human beings imaginable? Varshet! Because the 'Storm doesn't slide over anywhere, does it? Not at all.

We had almost reached the coast by then, and in Varshet that means the landscape is either marshland or reclaimed marshland. Either swamp and muddy estuary, or farms, villages and small towns nestled behind dykes, with a network of drainage channels running between. And it was at one of those villages, whose name is . . . Don't tell me. I want to try and get this one without your help. Tay . . . Tay-something. Tayus? Is that it? Oh, go on then.

['Tayorus.']

Ach! Nearly had it. Whatever would I do without you, Khollo? This account would be riddled with holes if you weren't on hand to plug them. Tayorus. We had stopped for lunch there when we learned that the 'Storm was headed that way. Some local chap, looking almost happy at the grimness of his news, informed us it was due to hit in about a day's time. He said the shelters in Tayorus were among the safest in all of Varshet and, for a small consideration, he was sure he could secure us a place in one of them. Result: two whole days and two whole nights stuck underground in a bunker like one of the Earthers' burial mounds. The reek of damp earth in our nostrils and, soon added to that, the reek of our fellow shelterers, roughly twenty of them in all. The booming of the 'Storm above, and every so often a sift of soil falling onto our heads and shoulders, loosened by the vibration of a thunderclap. Only one candle to see by at any time, and dry food which had been stored in the shelter so long that it tasted of earth and was probably mouldy, though there wasn't quite sufficient light to inspect it by and ascertain. A communal bucket to shit and piss in. Am I managing to convey how bad it was? And the tedium, too. Not a decent conversationalist to be found, present company excepted. In fact, our hosts seemed to frown on conversation. Whenever I tried to start one, people would glare at me as if I had just broken wind. We had to sit there in silence and endure, that was how it was supposed to be. D'you know, in a way it *was* like being buried – although I'm sure one would have more fun in a tomb.

[A pause, Elder Ayn reaching for the wine bottle again, his expression complicated. I imagine thoughts of burial had sent his mind along a certain morbid path he didn't want it to go down. Several glugs of wine hauled him back from the diversion and onto the track of his narrative again.]

I should add that, accustomed as I was to Stonehaven, that shelter in Tayorus didn't seem anything like as safe as advertised. Having had solid rock as my shield almost my entire life, mere earth braced with timber struts failed to instil me with a similar sense of impregnability. I looked ahead and saw us emerging safe and sound after the 'Storm had passed, but there were moments, especially at the height of the 'Storm's assault, when even the reliability of my own fore-memory seemed in doubt. As if the 'Storm cancels out all other factors. As if, in the face of its power, we can be sure of nothing.

I believe it was then, during that 'Storm visit, that I filled you in on true purpose of our journey. It seemed sensible, while you were in effect a captive audience. It seemed fair, too, since we weren't so far from Stonehaven that you couldn't easily return there if you wanted to. We were both more comfortable with each other by that point. The time was right for me to make a clean breast of things. I whispered my plan in your ear and left you to mull on it. The fact that you're here now would suggest you discerned some small grain of merit in it.

[Or that I lacked the imagination to think of anything else to do but remain with Elder Ayn. My first doubts about his sanity started stirring then, naturally, but for all that, I didn't yet think him mad. He had piqued my curiosity. His idea – I hate to say this, but it intrigued me. If nothing else I thought I would like to see how far he got with it.]

At last the Worldstorm's grotesque clashing and crashing died away. Our hosts insisted we stay put for a while longer, to be sure that the 'Storm was really past, and so we spent several further interminable hours in that foetid, gloomy burrow before – hurrah – permission was granted for the door to be unbolted.

The sweet air of liberty! Moist and brackish air, to be sure, but breeze-freshened and plentiful too, a treat for traumatised nose and stifled lungs. I could have breathed it in for ever, so delicious was it.

The 'Storm had dumped the equivalent of several million barrels of rain on Varshet, a country that was damp enough to start with, and now everything was thoroughly sodden. The locals encourage moss to grow on their roofs, to absorb moisture and stop it leaking through, but there had been more rain than even this preventative measure could cope with. Homes were wet inside as well as out. And the ground was positively saturated, the streets were quagmires, and the townsfolk put out planks to walk on but the planks soon sank into the mud and were of next to no use. Every field in the vicinity was one big puddle. It was lucky the farmers had gathered in the harvest just a few days earlier, otherwise the crops would have been ruined. The drainage channels between the fields were full to the brim and fast-flowing. The paths that ran alongside the channels and the footbridges that traversed them were mostly submerged. Normally Varshet was more land than water, just. Now the ratio had been reversed.

It seemed as if travel was going to be impossible, at least until things dried out a bit, and I remember you expressing concern to this effect, Khollo. I was glad to be able to reassure you that we would be on our way again soon. To be honest, I would have said that regardless of whether it was truth or not, so intolerable was the thought of spending even another hour in Tayorus. But in the event, I knew a solution to our predicament was at hand.

The Varshetians themselves need to be able to get about in all conditions. We had not been out of the shelter long before we saw our first sludgeskiff. An envoy from a neighbouring town arrived on one, to inform the inhabitants of Tayorus that the 'Storm had breached a dyke at the other town and the place was now flooded. Volunteers fetched out their own sludgeskiffs and set off with emergency supplies of food, blankets and tarpaulins, as well as with tools to help shore up the damaged dyke. They embarked on this errand of mercy with grumbles and little grace, as though it were an immense imposition on them to go to the aid of their fellow men; but give them their due, they went.

The sludgeskiff – delightful name – is basically a platform on runners, a cross between boat and sledge, and is uniquely Varshetian in that no other country I can think of would have need of such a thing and, moreover, no other country would come up with a mode of transport that requires the efforts of Earthers and Wets working in co-operation (these being the two Inclinations that dominate in Varshet). A team of strongs punt the skiff along with poles while a shaper-of-water concentrates on keeping the mud ahead as soft and unresisting as possible, easing the skiff's passage. We watched a quartet of the sludgeskiffs depart, and ungainly though they looked when stationary, once they got up speed they glided like swans, albeit much faster, throwing up fans of mud behind.

And there, I saw, was our ticket out of Tayorus right there. It wasn't difficult to negotiate the hire of a sludgeskiff for ourselves, along with the full complement of operators. Perhaps the good people of Tayorus wanted the pair of Airy outsiders to leave their town as much as the pair of Airy outsiders wanted to leave. At any rate, we were on our way that very afternoon, skimming across field and bog at a fair old lick. The strongs' muscular arms rose and fell in tireless unison; the shaper-of-water sat at the front, cross-legged and intent. A bracing, exhilarating ride! I would have been happy for it to have lasted twice as long. But by dusk we were at our destination, the coast and the port of Sweel. Or rather, what remained of the port of Sweel.

I'm sure readers will forgive me if this section of my narrative comes across as pure travelogue. Naturally those who live in Varshet or have journeyed through Varshet will know of that country's character and features already and find my descriptions of them redundant. For me, however, all this was new experience. The whole world, one might say, was new experience, and I was encountering things I had hitherto only encountered, if at all, in other people's travelogues. It interests me to convey my impressions of them. I can only hope it interests others, and anyone it does not is welcome to skip to the next section.

In other words, if they don't like it, bugger 'em.

Excise that last sentence, Khollo.

[A third glass of wine was filled and almost as quickly emptied. Elder Ayn's voice was taking on the aggressive precision of someone not yet drunk but rapidly getting that way.]

Sweel is a town built on stilts at the edge of an estuary, half of it over land, the rest over sea. When we arrived there, much of it was *in* the sea, the 'Storm having broken the legs, as it were, of many of the houses and left them slumped in the water, some up to their eaves. The town looked as if a giant child had come across some other giant child's building-block creation and, through sheer savage spite, fetched it a couple of good, hard kicks.

Our sludgeskiff crew dropped us off at a landing stage and left us there without ceremony or ado, speeding back to Tayorus through the gathering dark. A hotel called, if I'm not mistaken, The Leaping Whale provided us with accommodation for the night, and the proprietor, whose name does escape me, but it was one of those Wet names that require a person to hawk up several pints of phlegm in order to say it . . .

[‘Sha*so,’ I said, and Elder Ayn repeated the name several times, humorously spitting and spluttering over it.]

The sound of a wave seething on shingles, isn't that what one is supposed to mimic? Trust Wets to have a letter of the alphabet that nobody else uses. They're so *special*.

[The * consonant isn't actually that hard to master. It requires practice, that's all.]

He was a garrulous sort, anyway, this ‘Shacchsghso’ fellow, and if anyone reading this finds themselves in Sweel and looking for a bed for the night, my advice is don't try The Leaping Whale unless you want to have your ears worn to nubs by the constant gabble of the proprietor, who'll expatiate at great length on any subject you can think of and is an authority in all manner of fields, even ones he knows nothing about. No, *especially* ones he knows nothing about. From the moment we arrived to the moment we departed, I don't think he shut up once. He could spark conversations out of absolutely nothing. ‘Speaking of which . . .’ he would say, or ‘Now that you mention it . . .’, when no one had in fact been talking about anything at all. His wife, poor woman, was this most silent and suffering creature who had probably long ago trained herself to be deaf to everything he— Was that a discreet little clearing of the throat I just heard? Khollo? Yes? Am I rambling? Is that it?

[I suggested that the High Previsionary was perhaps in danger of committing the same crime he was accusing The Leaping Whale's proprietor of.]

Fair enough. Fuck you, but fair enough. If nothing else, the man did give us some insight into the attitude of the Water Inclined toward the demolition of their homes. It was something along the lines of a shrug and ‘We can build them again’. Likewise, the loss of life in Sweel. Nearly a dozen died under the 'Storm's assault. ‘Gone on’ was his sentiment, in essence. Gone to join their ancestors in the grand, after-death, all-pals-together jamboree that is the Great-Ocean-Beyond. Nothing to get upset about. Yes, it was a pity, people would be sad these other people were no longer around, but sooner or later the living and the dead would be reunited. A temporary separation, that was all.

So strange, Wet culture. So irrational.

So enviably irrational. Belief in something that cannot readily be proven comes naturally to them, whereas for the rest of us, if we can be bothered to try and believe in any such thing at all, constant effort is required, constant maintenance of that belief. Here am I, fighting to hope that I haven't spent the past few months pursuing an empty dream. Here am I, longing for assurance that, Air-Inclined though I may be, some kind of Great-Ocean-Beyond is waiting for me too after my death . . .

[The wine he swallowed now went down in deep, desperate draughts, and I couldn't help thinking, thanks to its redness, of blood. Some of it missed his mouth and trickled down his jowls. His teeth, which he bared in a heavy, hissing gasp when the glass was drained, were stained grey with it. His tongue, blue.]

Khollo, I have decided I am going for a walk. Some fresh air. We're done for the day.

['What about, maybe,' I said, 'if you described how we got hold of a boat and embarked on the crossing to Li*issua?']

Really?

['Just to round things off. End the "chapter" properly.']

Oh well. All right. Shasshh-whatever-his-name-is had a brother, Thaëho. Thaëho owned one of the few boats that had escaped being wrecked by the 'Storm. It was a fast, shallow vessel called a wave-skimmer or something like that. Thaëho agreed to take us to Li*issua in it, but couldn't do so for the next three days because they had to observe *cholisa*, which is some ritual-for-the-dead thing, leaving the bodies to lie for three days while the fluids inside harden and what-ever's going to leak out leaks out, then washing them, then dropping them into the sea. It's what Wets do, and during *cholisa* after a 'Storm visit no sea voyages are allowed, as a special mark of respect or something. And probably just as well, because one look at that choppy ocean and I knew I'd never have made the journey without heaving my guts up all the way. In three days the sea would be calm again, Thaëho said. So three days it was. I think the agreed fee for the trip was twenty leaves, which accounted for the last of my elements winnings at Folsa's Clearing. Thus, theretofore, henceforth, there-upon, on the third morning after we got to Sweel we put out to sea with Thaëho and went bounding across the ocean main towards the

Li*issuan archipelago, blah blah blah, chapter ends, more tomorrow. All right? That do?

[The High Previsionary rose to his feet and tottered out of the room. He was gone from the hunting lodge for the rest of the day, and around evening time we began to worry about his safety. We were just debating whether one of us should go out searching for him, when he returned, pale but sober. He went straight to bed, without eating, without a word to anybody.

I heard him later that night, moaning in his room. Whether this was due to the after-effects of the wine, or for another reason, I don't know.]

GREGORY

At the peak of the 'Storm visit, when it sounded like whole mountains were being moved overhead, Gregory felt a hand grope nervously for his. Candles would not stay lit, the 'Storm's thunder-shocks snuffing them every time, so it was pitch black in the Goves' cellar, and since Ven had been sitting next to him the last time he looked, Gregory naturally enough assumed the hand must belong to him. Also naturally enough, he wasn't about to hold hands with *Ven*, so he performed a polite but pointed act of extrication. Sixteen-year-old boys didn't clutch onto each other like girls, however scared they were.

But the hand crawled and found his hand again, and at the same time a head rested against his shoulder and Gregory felt the whisper of long hair on his neck – the person nuzzling him was not boy but girl. Eda. He knew it was her. None of the other Gove girls was her size. None of the others was tall enough to rest her head on his shoulder so easily.

All at once Gregory seemed to unfurl inside and he felt strong and strange, like a truer version of himself, a Gregory Brazier he had not really met before. Of all the people in the cellar, over all the members of her own family, Eda had sought out *him* to hold on to. Over even her father, she had chosen *him* to huddle with in the 'Storm-rocked dark. Gregory was honoured, excited, and, for Eda's sake, perhaps a little less frightened. The warmth of her touch tingled. They sat together for several hours, it seemed, and he didn't dare move, even when his backside began to grow numb, even when pins and needles hollowed one leg, for fear that moving might ruin the perfect shape of the contact between them, perhaps make Eda think he disliked her leaning on him, perhaps make her let go of his hand and sidle away. Her breath brushed his cheek. He conjured up an image of her face canted beside his. Were her eyes closed? Open? Was she looking at him, even though she couldn't see him? She was pretty, he had always thought that. Unlike the Fire girls he had known in Stammeldon, who were, as a rule, skinny and fraught-looking and too tall for themselves,

Eda was confident, rounded, short, always laughing. She was impolite in all the best ways. He had never before regarded her in any other way than as a kind of sister, but now . . . ? Now, remarkable though it was that there was room in his mind for thoughts of anything except the 'Storm, he found himself wondering how it might feel to kiss Eda and be kissed by her. How it might feel to be pressed together like this with her, but not clothed, and on their own, not surrounded by people. And from there his thoughts started chasing along all sorts of avenues of possibility, and his discomfort was greatly added to by an erection that threatened to tear the buttons from the front of his trousers.

Finally there was no alternative but to shift his weight slightly in order to relieve the pain in his bottom and restore the flow of blood to his leg (and also accommodate the erection better). Happily, instead of moving away, Eda pressed herself tighter against him.

From then on, as far as Gregory was concerned the 'Storm could have stayed overhead for ever.

The Worldstorm laid into Penresford with unusual vigour and vindictiveness. It deployed every weapon in its arsenal, hurling down lightning bolts, chucking down rain in rods, dropping hail and debris, sending wind gusts of roof-wrenching magnitude, felling walls, loosening slates and tiles and timbers and propelling them into the sides of houses with incisive force, making mortar crumble from brickwork with the reverberation of its thunder, prising away protective battens and broaching windows to wreak havoc indoors. It tormented the Seray until the river overflowed its banks and flooded the lower part of town. It tore into the dock area, reduced the derricks and wharves to kindling, and took out all the landing jetties but one. It scoured the face of the clay mines until not one scrap of scaffold was left standing. It vented all the fury that was its to command, as if Penresford and its inhabitants had committed some heinous crime for which only the direst of punishments was in order.

Hallawye was similarly chastised. At Penresford's downstream neighbour, a couple of moored barges were plucked clear from the river by the 'Storm and thrown headlong at the town, each demolishing several buildings. The whole of the southern region of Jarraine took a pounding, but Penresford and Hallawye suffered worst. For them, the 'Storm showed no mercy.

In the Goves' cellar, no one was prepared to believe it when the 'Storm finally passed on. The cacophony of crashing and rumbling continued to resound in the family's ears long after it had ceased above. Proof that their ordeal was over came when Garla Gove experimentally struck a match, applied it to the wick of a candle, and the candle stayed alight. Its steady glow revealed tired, wan faces; also revealed Gregory and Eda sitting side by side, stiffly, innocently apart.

Sol Gove tried the trapdoor in the ceiling, which afforded access to the kitchen. At first it would not budge, but he put his good arm to it, and Dallen assisted, and between them they managed to heave the trapdoor up and open, to a huge, protesting creak followed by a slap-bang-crash.

The house was chaos. The 'Storm had forced its way in and ransacked the place like a burglar. What had been blocking the way out of the cellar was the door to the kitchen, which had been torn half off its hinges and had lodged at an angle on top of the trapdoor. In the kitchen itself, crockery and cookware lay smashed and cracked; the stove flue had been yanked askew; the table was on its back with its legs in the air like a dead dog. In the main room, amid a litter of shattered glass and shredded curtain, the paraphernalia of daily life was strewn around – the books, the framed pictures, the few orna-ments Sol and Garla were proud to own, the children's toys, the armchairs. Upstairs, beds were overturned; mattresses were rain-sodden; chests of drawers had been shunted from their rightful posi-tions. The family wandered about, making an inventory of the damage, trying to take it all in. Everyone was in tears, or close to. Attempts to put things back in order were perfunctory, listless. No-body had the heart to make a proper start on the job of rectification and repair, not just yet. Gregory asked Ven if it had been this bad the last time, and Ven sourly shook his head. It hadn't. Nowhere near.

Outside, the vandalism was just as extensive. The paintwork on the front of the Goves' house looked as if someone had taken a mallet to it. This was true of every other house in the street. The roadway cobblestones were covered with a layer of rubble – fragments of roof shingle, shards of batten, bits of splintered tree branch whipped up from elsewhere, deposited here. The corpse of a neighbour's cat sprawled near the Goves' front door, its face an angry death-yowl. Lalla, the littlest Gove, saw it and started sobbing inconsolably, crying not just for the cat but for so much else. Other residents of the street were emerging from their homes, looking as dazed and appalled as the Goves and Gregory felt. Women came together and hugged. Men came together and made sombre assessments of how much work would need to be done to restore the street to its former state and how long it might take. The sky above was a cloudless, shameless blue. The autumn sun beamed warmly. It would, bar the obvious, have been a lovely day.

'Worried about Stammeldon?'

This from Sol, that evening, as the family ate a dinner of bread, cheese and preserves in the main room. No plates, no chairs, everyone hunkered on the floor in a circle with the food spread picnic-style in the middle. Sol had noticed Gregory looking pensive, chewing too slowly.

'Stammeldon?' said Gregory, with a blink. 'Yes. Yes. A bit.'

'Your parents' house is pretty much impregnable, no? I'm sure they're fine.'

Gregory thought of Tempest's Bane, iron shutters shut, shrugging off whatever the 'Storm threw at it, as it always had, as it always would. In truth, he hadn't given much consideration to the state of Stammeldon. What had been preoccupying him, until Sol spoke, was Eda. She was acting, now, as if nothing had happened in the cellar, as if snuggling up to him was of no consequence to her, she had felt like doing it, she had done it, that was that, over, forgotten. But that *wasn't* that, in Gregory's mind. The more he mused on it, the more he realised that the feelings that had been stirred up by the presence of Eda's body next to his were not new. They had been there a while, deep inside, secret even to himself, waiting. He recalled looks she had given him; the way her teasing had tailed off after the dreadful bathroom incident; how in recent months she seemed to find anything he said interesting and how he liked it that she found him interesting; how her attitude toward him had become increasingly respectful, on the level of equals, even though she was a year older. It hadn't struck him as significant, any of it – both of them growing up, that was all. Now it did. And just when Eda had clarified the situation for him at last, enlightening him in the cellar darkness, she had then gone and confused things once more by behaving no differently afterwards. No, that was not true. She *was* behaving differently. Since they had come out of the cellar, she had hardly said a word to him. He had tried to catch her gaze several times and she had studiously ignored him. It was so complicated, so unfathomable. Had he made a mistake? Had he assumed more than there was to assume? Did Eda think *she* had made a mistake?

Maybe Master Ergall was right in saying an indestructible should not feel much of anything. Maybe it was better not to feel, if all feeling brought was this ache of exposure, this humiliating bafflement. Gregory looked down at his hands and remembered that you had to keep them toughened if they were to retain their stone-like solidity. If you didn't regularly hit them against hard, rough surfaces, after a while they would start to repair themselves. Calluses would soften.

Scar tissue would give way to ordinary skin. They would be just hands again. It was a process of constant maintenance. 'Vigilance' was the word Master Ergall had used. And so with himself. Vigilance was necessary there, too. He had managed to develop an indifference to his family, his old family, his father, his mother, Willem, so that he no longer cared that they no longer cared about him. Eda had gone and created an abrasion at a fresh spot within him, but he could heal it, harden himself to it, if he tried. He resolved to try.

The next morning, Sol left to attend a town meeting organised by the Guild of Freemen. There, a picture was put together of the general condition of the town – a depressing picture – and opinions as to what to do next were solicited.

Meanwhile Garla put the household to work tidying up. With chiding and flattery she marshalled the children into a team, everyone with something to do, no one allowed to be idle for even a moment. Pieces of furniture that were beyond salvage had to be taken out into the street. Mattresses had to be lugged into the backyard to dry out. Empty windowpanes had to be patched over with cut-to-fit pieces of canvas. To the youngest children went the task of sorting through kitchen utensils, ornaments and personal belongings and separating them into two piles, one for things intact or slightly damaged, the other for things too damaged to be worth keeping. Gregory, with his unharmable hands, was given special responsibility for the disposal of broken glass and anything with sharp edges or nails sticking out of it. The house became a rush of activity, as if a second 'Storm had hit it, this one reversing the effects of the first. Now and then arguments broke out, little squalls of disagreement. A rag doll, which in one person's view was too sodden and battered to love any more, was, in its owner's view, on no account to be discarded. Criticism of a sibling's brush-and-dustpan technique, if not phrased considerately enough, could spark off a downing of tools and a tantrum. With so many people bustling about at speed, accidental and often bruising collisions could not be avoided. Garla kept a tight rein on it all, however. She was omnipresent. No sooner were voices raised than she appeared, dispensing slaps and sharp words to both parties and not in the least interested to know who had started it. No one had slept well this past couple of nights, bodies were tired, tempers were frayed, but that was no excuse. If you had the energy to argue, she said, you were obviously not working hard enough. And there were much more arduous jobs available. Clambering up onto the roof to check the chimney, for instance. Any takers for that? Well? She didn't think so.

Gregory was the model worker, the only one not to cause friction during the entire clean-up operation. He concentrated on doing what was asked of him, he discharged each task efficiently, and if he ever spoke, it was either to praise another person's efforts or to offer a polite 'excuse me' to someone in his way. He was at his very most formal whenever his and Eda's paths crossed. Putting on an expression of complete impassiveness, one he had seen his father use with his mother when they were at loggerheads over some matter relating to their social lives or the domestic staff, he would greet Eda with a nod and acknowledge her existence in some further small manner, a hand gesture or a blink, that made it clear that she was of no more significance to him than someone passing in the street. The first few times he thought he got a reaction, a narrowing of the eyes as though she had been pricked with something sharp, but after that she learned the game and matched his blankness with a blankness of her own. This, to Gregory, amounted to a victory. He had forced her to become guarded, self-protected, like him. They were even.

Sol came home at lunchtime, grim. At the town meeting it had been established that a good quarter of the houses in Penresford had suffered such severe damage that they would have to be pulled down and rebuilt from scratch. Worse news was that the death toll stood just shy of fifty. Some people had drowned in their cellars when the Seray burst its banks. Some had been crushed to death under collapsing buildings. A couple of old folk had expired of natural causes, their hearts giving out under the stress and strain of the 'Storm. It was, statistically, the worst 'Storm visit in living memory. The worst ever, some were claiming. Certainly the worst since a century ago, when Penresford had been all but wiped off the map. Back then, however, Penresford had been a fledgling town, a settlement at the river's edge, barely a tenth of its present size. The scale was just not comparable.

'Guess what, though,' Sol said, turning to Gregory. 'Stammeldon got off lightly. Again. At least, that's what the telepath bureau are saying. The links are disrupted but they're pretty certain the reports coming through from Stammeldon way are positive. Everyone thought it was going to do its usual left turn off into Damentaine, but for once it decided to go east instead, deeper into the Continent. So that's something, eh? Stammeldon safe.'

'What's the food situation?' Garla asked. 'How are we off for supplies?'

Sol framed his reply in such a way that it was clear to those above a certain age that, for the sake of the younger family members, what he was saying was not the unvarnished truth: 'Oh, I think we'll be fine. I mean, there are going to be a few difficulties, of course. Only to be expected in a town that relies on outside sources for most of its food. Trade along the river is likely to be in disarray for a while. There won't be many boats coming in and out, and besides, the docks are gone. But we have a stockpile of imperishables, which the Guild will be distributing as time goes by. I imagine, too, that we'll be able to beg off our neighbours.' He glanced back at Gregory. 'Such as Stammeldon. Your lot'll be generous, won't they?'

Gregory could hardly be spokesman for a place where he didn't live any more, but he assumed Stammeldon would respond with basic decency to a request for help and so answered the question with a vague nod. Sol, though he had been hoping for a more emphatic assurance, settled for what he got.

'See?' he said to his family. 'Nothing to worry about.'

A delegation from Penresford travelled upriver in the largest boat to have survived the 'Storm's depredations, a passenger ferry. It was a vessel designed for short hops, not the long haul, with open sides, hard benches and no inboard toilet facilities. The journey, therefore, was none too comfortable, and the Seray did not help, being swollen with rain run-off and turbid and obstreperous all the way. In places, the river rose into surging, mud-brown rollers which crashed over the ferry's narrow freeboard and threatened to swamp the boat. While everyone else hand-baled frantically, the two pilots fought to hold a steady course, and when they did finally nurse the ferry to a calmer stretch of water, they were so shattered from their exertions that it was necessary to moor for a while so that they could rest and recuperate. A further delay was caused by an uprooted tree which, swept along on the current, came out of nowhere to ram the ferry head on. Fortunately the tree did not breach the hull, but it made enough of a dent that the pilots were obliged to pull in for repairs, bracing the point of impact with slats from one of the benches and caulking it with a square of tarpaulin cut from the ferry's awning. Yet another entry in the catalogue of hindrances was the bridge at Lalmore, whose main span had collapsed in the 'Storm, leaving so much debris in the river as to make an attempt at navigation unadvisable. The inhabitants of Lalmore were working round the clock to clear a channel through, but their efforts were hampered by the Seray's height and torrential speed, and the delegation from Penresford had to wait two full days before they succeeded. In the end, it took over a week to reach Stammeldon, and the Penresfordians arrived there tired, dishevelled, irritable and bleary. They certainly looked the part of people in importunate need, but at the same time, having been through so much to get to Stammeldon, they were in no mood to accept anything less than an offer of absolute, unconditional help.

This, regrettably, they did not receive.

The present incumbent of the role of mayor of Stammeldon was Jarnley Bringlight, a man who, like his son Reehan, was a flatterer and a charmer and almost entirely devoid of empathy for his fellow human beings. From the lifts in his shoes that gave him an extra inch of height to the sweep of hair across his crown that hid a thinning patch, he had perfected the art of disguising faults, and the fault he had managed to disguise best of all, from almost everyone, was that nothing mattered to him except himself.

He received the Penresford delegation in his chambers at the town hall, he on one side of his desk, they on the other. He informed them he was very busy, there was much requiring his attention as he was sure they must realise, but he was nevertheless prepared to give them a few moments of his time. He listened as they made their plea, requesting food and, if possible, a quantity of timber with which to carry out basic building repairs, and when they had said their piece he smiled benignly, as if it would be his pleasure to donate all they asked for and more.

Then he said: 'I don't know if you noticed, gentlemen, but here in Stammeldon we've suffered too. The 'Storm may have only clipped us but it got us pretty badly all the same. At least half of our houses have some sort of structural damage and the river has flooded our farmland. You will understand, then, that before anything else we must put our own interests first.'

'Of course,' said the delegation's senior member, Horm Loffin, chief secretary of the Guild of Freemen. Loffin was an untypically tall but typically broad-shouldered strong, with a lugubrious face and an air of integrity about him that some might mistake for dullness. 'We wouldn't expect otherwise. I have to say that it looks as though the worst that's happened to your town is a few dislodged roof tiles, but that's a judgement based solely on what I've seen. I haven't, I admit, had a chance to view the whole of the town, and I'm sure you are better informed about these things than I am, Your Honour. I also have to say that yes, your fields are flooded, but there's stubble poking up above the surface of the water, and unless the 'Storm has taken to neatly scything crops close to the ground, I'd say your reapers had already been and done their job by the time the 'Storm came.'

'An observant man such as yourself, Mr Loffin,' Mayor Bringlight replied, 'must appreciate that Stammeldon is a much larger place than Penresford and has need of all the provisions it can muster. We have many more mouths to feed. I'm not refusing point blank to help you, simply saying that under the circumstances we may not have as much to spare as you expect. How much food do you actually require? What are we looking at here precisely?'

Loffin could sense the other members of the delegation champing and chafing behind him, wanting him to be more forceful with Mayor Bringlight. He himself would quite happily have grabbed the man by the collar and shaken him, if he had thought it would help. But it seemed best, for now, to keep the discussion on a polite footing. 'Enough to keep us going till trade traffic is normalised again and we've managed to get Penresford back on its feet.'

'And do you have any estimate as to how long that might take?'

'A month. A couple of months, perhaps.'

'A couple of months,' said the mayor. 'Which means quite a lot of food. Several barge-loads, I would say.'

'Penresford, Your Honour, as I don't need to remind you, is an important business ally for Stammeldon, I'd even go so far as to say a crucial one. Without our clay, there'd be no Brazier Brickfields. Without Brazier Brickfields, no Stammeldon.'

'Is that a hint of blackmail I hear?' Mayor Bringlight cupped a hand theatrically behind one ear. 'A veiled threat?'

'Not in the least.' Loffin was annoyed that his meaning could have been misconstrued in this way, and he wasn't sure if the misconstruing had not been deliberate. 'All I'm trying to say is that your town and ours are partners, have been for a long time, mutually dependent. Now we find ourselves in straitened circumstances and we're coming to you cap in hand, asking for a little charity, which we have been shown in the past in similar situations. We're not asking you to make great sacrifices, only to give us whatever you can spare and perhaps a bit more. For the sake of the longstanding relationship between the two towns. For the sake of fellow countrymen who are at risk of starvation if you don't help. It's really that simple. So will you give us what we want, Mayor Bringlight, or won't you?'

'I'd gladly give you what you want,' said Stammeldon's mayor, 'but the trouble is, what you want is too much. I'd need time to make a more exact calculation, but off the cuff I reckon the most we can afford to lend you would be perhaps fifty bushels of grain, a dozen barrels of apples, plus a few assorted crates of dried goods. You'll note I said "lend".'

'I noted that very clearly, mayor,' said Loffin, cold-voiced.

'These supplies could be provided to you only on a loan basis – the loan to be repaid in the form of a discount on future consignments of clay, the percentage of said discount to be worked out so as to represent a full and fair evaluation of the goods tendered, with a tiny amount of interest on top.' The mayor slapped his desk lightly, as if to emphasise the full stop at the end of the sentence.

'In other words, you won't even *give* us anything, you'll only sell it to us.'

'A rather stark way of putting it, but yes.'

'Even though people may die without this food?'

'I think you're exaggerating the situation somewhat.'

Loffin's anger could no longer be restrained. He lunged forward, thrusting himself across the desk until his and Bringlight's noses were almost touching. 'Come and see, Mayor Bringlight,' he said, the force of his breath making the other man blink. 'Come and see what the 'Storm did to our town. Travel down with me and I'll show you. Fifty people have died. More will die without your help.'

'Step back,' Bringlight said. As he spoke, a ball of bright white fire flared into existence directly above Loffin. Everyone in the room could feel its heat but none more so than Loffin, whose head was close enough to it that he could smell his own hair singe. 'Step back before I make you step back.'

Loffin stared at Bringlight, refusing to shy away from the fireball even though its heat was alarming. Bringlight returned the stare serenely, reflected flame-glow dancing in his green eyes.

'You wouldn't dare,' Loffin said. 'Your training prohibits it.'

'Does it? Not, perhaps, if I feel intimidated. If I feel my life is threatened by a strong leaning over me, a man who could kill me with a single punch.'

'I could, you know.'

'Absolutely. And in self-defence, I could turn your skull to cinders. One last time: step back.'

Slowly, reluctantly, with a sullen growl, Loffin eased away, letting go of the desk's edge. Where his fingers had been, there were two sets of deep, splintered gouges in the wood. The fireball continued to hover in the air like a miniature sun until, with a small, indifferent sniff, Bringlight dispensed with it.

'I've made you my best offer,' he said. 'It stands, in spite of this shamefully ill-considered outburst of yours. Go away and have a think about it.' He bent to examine some piece of paperwork in front of him. Glancing up a few seconds later, he feigned surprise that the Penresfordians were still in the room.

The delegation went away, but as far as they were concerned there was nothing to think about. They returned to their boat, silent with outrage. On board the ferry, a unanimous verdict was reached: better to accept nothing at all than accept a handout of meagre proportions, with strings attached.

Their homeward journey, with the Seray flowing with them rather than against them, at least had the compensation of being swift.

Not long after the Penresfordians exited his chambers, Mayor Bringlight paid a visit to Brazier Brickfields, where he found the proprietor in his office presiding over a company that had yet to resume manufacture in the wake of the 'Storm. Part of the problem was cracks in a number of the clamp kilns, although repairs were well in hand. The larger problem was the disruption to deliveries of raw material. The clay Tremond Brazier presently had in stock would account for perhaps a week's output. After that, he was stuck until barges were moving freely up and down the Seray again, and when that would be he had no idea. Compounding his frustration was the fact that orders were starting to come in from all parts of the country, as was always the case after a 'Storm visit. Jarraine needed rebuilding, it needed bricks to do it, and Tremond was unable to supply them. He feared that he was going to lose business to rivals in the northern regions, that other brickmakers such as Tarpen's in Leitzon were going to profit from a situation *he* should be profiting from, and he bemoaned his grandfather's decision to set up a factory many miles from the source of its product. He understood why his grandfather had done this. Who would not prefer to live in a green and scenic corner of the world like Stammeldon, rather than down there in grim, bare Penresford? But sometimes, as now, the disadvantages of a pleasant location outweighed the advantages, and perhaps if his grandfather had chosen more wisely, had been thinking more with head than heart . . .

Mayor Bringlight, never guilty of the error of putting heart before head, reckoned it would cheer Tremond Brazier up to hear the news that he, the mayor, had set in motion a process which would ultimately be of financial benefit to Brazier Brickfields, perhaps even offsetting any losses the company might incur in the short term. He related his meeting with the Penresford delegation and his attempt to establish a discount on the price of clay in return for aid to the town. That the Penresfordians had turned their noses up at the deal was not to be taken as a sign that they had rejected it outright. The negotiating had only just begun. They would go off, mull it over, and realise that they had nothing to lose by accepting the offer and everything to gain.

'So you see, Tremond, I've made good on my promise to repay you for supporting my election campaign,' Mayor Bringlight said. 'You invested in me, and here are the dividends.'

'The way things are in Penresford,' Tremond Brazier replied, 'they're really so bad that people came up here to plead for food?'

'Of course things aren't that bad,' the mayor scoffed. 'Don't believe it for a moment. I imagine that life is a little inconvenient there right now, but starvation? Please! No, this was nothing more than a case of Penresford leeching off Stammeldon, as always. They're the poor cousin, the weaker partner in the marriage. Without us, they'd be nothing. They wouldn't even exist. And if we help them, who's to say it won't encourage them to take further liberties in the future? What I was doing was reminding them who's boss. A salutary lesson. I'm sure that lot who were in my chambers this morning will be back in no time, contrite as can be. And you, my friend, will be the one to profit from their contrition.'

Mayor Bringlight let it be known, with a smile of some magnitude, that he felt he had done right by the owner of Stammeldon's prime economic engine and that he was pleased to have discharged, in one fell swoop, both his duty as mayor and his debt to his main electoral sponsor. He was surprised, then, when Tremond Brazier didn't acknowledge the good turn with unbridled enthusiasm but merely with a few words along the lines of 'the gesture is appreciated' followed by a less than subtle hint that he would like to be left alone. Mayor Bringlight walked away from the brickfields wondering at the man's ingratitude. It came down, he thought, to inheriting your business from your father. Tremond Brazier had had everything handed to him on a plate. He expected people to do things for him because he had been brought up in the belief that this was no more than his due. He had been gifted, from birth, with the certainty that the world revolved around him. Whereas Jarnley Bringlight had been born with no certainties other than that he came from pure Fire stock, which in itself was worth very little when his family had no wealth to back it up, only a legacy of squandered fortunes and misjudged attempts to marry into money. He had learned at an early age that nobody was going to do him any favours in life and that, if he was going to get on, it would have to be through his own efforts alone. First as the purchaser and renovator of a single dilapidated building in the lower part of town, then as landlord of nearly half a hundred properties in that area, and now as mayor of Stammeldon, he had earned himself the right to adopt the proud air of the self-made man, and that was something he would always have over the Tremond Braziers of this world. To them might go the easy upswing through life, the unthinking embrace of all that came their way, but they would never know the satisfaction of generating something out of nothing, making money where there had been no money before, getting rich and having nobody to credit for it but yourself. Tremond Brazier was basically an employee, one in a chain of custodians of his grandfather's business, his sole qualification for the job his parentage, and he would have to mess up severely to ruin a thriving concern like the brickfields. Jarnley Bringlight, on the other hand, could look at himself in the mirror and say, 'I am where I am because of how I am, not who I am. I am master of my own existence. I am a *man*.'

The mayor's route back to the town hall took him by one of his properties, a two-bedroom residence which he let to an Earther who worked at Brazier Brickfields. He saw that someone, the Earther's wife no doubt, had put up a new set of curtains in the upstairs window, in contravention of one of the small-print clauses of the tenancy agreement. As he carried on walking, Mayor Bringlight began mentally drafting the requisite notice of eviction.

For a long time after the mayor departed, Tremond Brazier brooded. He formed geometric fire shapes in the air and made them spin, mesmerising himself with spirals and contra-rotating concentric circles. The more he thought about what Bringlight had said, the faster and more violently the patterns turned, until a rogue sliver of flame peeled off from one and licked out at the picture on his desk, scorching it. The picture was a mezzotint of himself and his wife and sons, commissioned when Willem was five and Gregory two, the fruits of a five-minute sitting with an enshriner artist, who had then gone away and etched out the image indelibly installed in his memory. Tremond snapped the fire shapes out of existence and picked the picture up to check the damage. A bit of charring on one edge of the frame, that was all. No harm done to the print itself. He studied the artist's handiwork. Marita seated, Gregory on her lap, Willem standing next to them, himself behind. On each of the faces a smile – respectively: maternal, guileless, boyishly shy, formal. The enshriner, with his careful engraving and bur, had captured the likeness of a family Tremond no longer recognised. He looked at the way Marita and the boys were all contingent on him, the composition such that even though he stood at the rear, the eye was drawn through their figures to his. He was the apex of the picture, the focus. Had they ever really been this ideal polite-society family? Was the contentment they seemed to exude genuine, or just an artist's impression?

Sam Gove was somewhere on the premises. Tremond went in search of him.

'Sam?'

'This is the last one, Trem.' Sam gestured at the clamp kiln behind him. Two men on ladders were trowelling excess mortar from a section of new brickwork in the domed roof. 'Give it till tomorrow to set. In theory, we could have everything up and running again by Fifthday.'

Tremond drew Sam aside until they were out of earshot.

'Just been paid a call on by Mayor Bringlight.'

A slight curl of the lip indicated what Sam thought of *that*. In his view, his boss had sacrificed no small part of his reputation by allying himself so closely and overtly with Bringlight. Politics and business should never mix, and in any case, everyone knew that the greater power in Stammeldon resided not at the town hall but right here in the brickfields. Add to that Bringlight's unpopularity in the Earther community – the majority of his tenants were Earthers – and it was clear that Tremond had made a serious miscalculation. He had stooped when he should have stood aloof. When Bringlight embarked on his run for office, Tremond had consulted with Sam as to whether he should give Bringlight the backing he was after. Sam, as strongly as he dared, had advised against, but there had been other voices working on Tremond, more influential ones, closer to home. Namely, Willem and Bringlight's son Reehan. With those two as a counterweight, not even Sam's best arguments could have tipped the scales the other way.

'Some people from Penresford came to see him this morning,' Tremond said.

'Ah. About?'

'Reading between the lines, as one must with His Honour, I think Penresford is in poor shape.'

'That's what I've been hearing, too. The word coming out of the telepath bureau is that all of the southern region took a right royal battering. But if it was *really* bad news, I mean, you know, if someone we know down there was hurt, or worse . . .'

'. . . we'd have heard about it by now, wouldn't we?'

'My brother, or someone, would have got a message through.'

'Possibly has tried to and failed.'

'Possibly.'

'So, while I'm not assuming the very worst . . .'

Sam wasn't just Tremond's right-hand man. At times, he had an almost previsionary propensity for anticipating his boss's wishes. 'I'll go down to the bureau, post a message to Sol.'

'If you have to pay extra to get it bumped to the top of the sending schedule . . .'

'I'll just tell them who it's from. That should do the trick.'

The bureau was busy. A hassled-looking clerk at the outgoing-message counter was trying to explain to a queue of displeased customers that the service was operating at reduced capacity because two of the telepaths had collapsed from exhaustion and the remaining two were doing their best to keep up with demand but were near their limits.

They had been hard at it all week, coping with the usual post-'Storm increase in message traffic *and* having to take up the slack for several other local bureaus where telepaths had also gone down under the pressure of overwork or, in a couple of instances, had perished in the 'Storm. Therefore the clerk would appreciate it if people could just be a little patient and perhaps give some thought as to whether their messages were really, truly urgent.

Meanwhile, two clerks at the incoming-message counter, no less hassled-looking, were struggling to decipher a telepath's scrawled handwriting.

'Do you think that's "unharmed" or "maimed"?' one said.

'Not sure,' said the other. 'But if I were you, I'd go upstairs and double-check. Not the sort of thing you really want to get wrong, is it?'

Sam, though he could have invoked the name Brazier and jumped to the head of the queue, stood in line till his turn at the outgoing-message counter came.

'Priority communication to Penresford,' he said.

'They're all priority,' the clerk sighed, more interested in sharpening his pencil than looking to see who his next customer was.

'To Sol Gove, from Tremond Brazier.'

The clerk's head snapped up. 'Oh. Mr Gove. It's you. You know we're still only getting intermittent service down that way? The bureaus at Lalmore and Hyam Landing keep dropping out. If Mr Brazier wouldn't mind waiting a couple of days, we're more likely to be able to guarantee delivery then.'

'Mr Brazier won't wait,' Sam said. 'I think Mr Brazier's already waited long enough. Just take down the message.'

The clerk wetted his pencil tip and smoothed flat the top sheet of his pad of forms. 'Who was it to again?'

That evening, at Tempest's Bane, the Braziers ate supper with their more or less permanent houseguest Reehan. Willem's friend had not moved in with the Braziers, not exactly, but he spent so much time under their roof that he might as well have. He seemed at ease in their company, slotting snugly in with their way of life, but he impressed Marita Brazier by never appearing to take the hospitality for granted. He had to be invited to stay for a meal, never presumed that he was going to be, and always poured forth the appreciation and the thank-yous when he was. Now a young man, with a young man's lively eye and heedless self-assurance, he could be counted on to provoke and amuse and stimulate with his dinner-table chat. Sometimes Marita wondered if too much of Reehan was inhibiting Willem's development

– whenever Reehan was around, he did the talking and Willem took a back seat. And sometimes Marita felt guilty that Reehan spent more time at Tempest's Bane than he did at his own house, although she only had to remember that the boy didn't have a mother any more and her guilt evaporated. Amalda Bringlight had lost control of her flame when Reehan was very young and been sent to the Sanatorium, dying shortly after she arrived there. A terrible thing, to lose your mother like that. And sometimes, just sometimes, having Reehan there at her table made Marita forget that she had another son. Reehan occupied more than just a seat at table. He occupied a gap.

Throughout the meal Reehan made attempts to draw Tremond into conversation, but tonight Tremond was in a morose, uncommunicative mood. Marita watched her husband cut up his food methodically and slowly; saw the distraction in his eyes as he ate. Trouble at work, it could only be. When, during the dessert course, the doorbell chimed, Tremond rose and went to answer it instead of letting a member of staff greet and vet the visitor. She heard Sam's voice in the hallway. That seemed to confirm what she suspected.

Tremond said nothing about Sam's visit when he returned to the dining room, but later, when he and Marita were alone in the drawing room, he showed what Sam had brought him: the transcript of Sol Gove's reply to a telepath message he had sent earlier in the day.

Penresford in bad shape.
Gove family and guest(?) in good shape.
Food shortage a problem.
(unclear – image of brave face?)
Assistance desirable.

'Transmission problems,' Marita commented.

'The network's up the spout, according to Sam. Close to breaking point. The main thing is, at least we know for certain that Gregory's all right.' Tremond took a swig from the glass of whisky he was nursing. 'For now.'

'For now?'

'Read the message, Marita. "Food shortage a problem." '

'Yes, but Stammeldon will help tide them over, surely. We've done that in the past.'

'In the past we didn't have Jarnley Bringlight as mayor.'

'So?'

Tremond filled her in. Sam's next errand, after his trip to the telepath bureau, had been to locate the Penresford delegation and talk to them about Mayor Bringlight, telling them that Bringlight was not necessarily the final arbiter of town policy and that forces could be brought to bear on him which would change his mind regarding the provision of emergency supplies to Penresford (and indeed to Hallawye, where people were no doubt in similar straits). In the event, Sam discovered that the Penresfordians had already left, and it wasn't hard to imagine that they were pretty peeved at the way they had been treated.

'It doesn't take a pessimist,' Tremond said, 'to see that this isn't going to turn out well.'

'You think . . .'

'. . . an embargo on clay supplies.'

'That would seem something of an overreaction.'

'Hardly, Marita. This lot turn up at the town hall in person, after a long and difficult journey. I mean, they could have just sent a message but they didn't. They travelled here in order to demonstrate that this wasn't some casual request, they really do need that food. And what does Bringlight do? Tries to use it to leverage a price concession out of them. And the worst of it is, he did it for me. To return a favour. You know how *that's* going to look. The brickfields and the mayor, in each other's pockets.'

Marita could not avoid saying what she said next. It was almost her duty. 'Of course, if the brickfields and the mayor *weren't* in each other's pockets, then perhaps the chance would never arise for them to look as if they were.'

'Yes, yes, very clever, Marita. Except, I never contributed so much as one leaf to his campaign. Bringlight's rich enough that he didn't need me bankrolling him.'

'But what you gave him was infinitely more valuable than money, Trem. You gave him your name. You gave him the block vote of the brickfields workforce, and having you on his side swung most of the rest of the Earther community his way. They'd never have dreamed of electing him if he hadn't been able to say Tremond Brazier was vouching for him. The Earthers loathe him. He's not exactly well liked among our kind either, but then the other Fire candidate, who is he, that dreadful man . . .'

'Callum Furniss.'

'Yes. Everyone hates him more than they do Jarnley Bringlight. And the Earther candidate would have stood a good chance, with Furniss and Bringlight splitting the Fire vote between them, if you hadn't weighed in. There's no question: you won Bringlight that election.'

'He seemed a reasonable choice for mayor. Someone I could see eye-to-eye with. Better him than Furniss, you're right. And better him than an Earther. Willem thinks highly of him. I remember Willem saying it would be good to have someone in charge who was close to the family.'

'Are you sure it was Willem who said that?'

'Of course it was Willem.'

Marita pursed her lips. Far likelier it had been Reehan, or if it had been Willem it would have been Willem reiterating something Reehan had just said. That was how Willem was nowadays. He seemed to have no opinions of his own, only opinions copied from or sanctioned by Reehan.

'Anyway,' Tremond said, 'no one could have predicted Bringlight would go and do something quite as crass as this. I mean, business is business, but some things transcend business.'

Marita moved closer to her husband, near enough that she could have laid a hand on his shoulder had she wanted to. 'And you honestly believe Penresford is going to stop shipping clay to you as a result?'

'I honestly do.' Tremond swilled around the last sip of whisky in the glass, then tipped it down his throat. 'What have they got to lose? Nothing. Food's scarce. Their pride has been wounded. Bad enough that they have to come begging, worse that they then get snubbed. How can they let us know that they are pissed off with us and also that they're not to be screwed around with? Easy. Cut us off, like we cut them off. Tit for tat.'

'You can always get your clay from elsewhere.'

'No, I can't. You know that. Logistically, financially, it would be a nightmare. We'd have to try and tap into someone else's supplier, and you can bet we'd be made to pay through the nose for it. Assuming in the first place that another supplier would be willing to breach their exclusive contract with whichever brickmaker they're already dealing with. Then we'd have to find some way of getting it here, and that would mean new barges. The canals up north are too narrow for our fleet. One of the great advantages of using the Seray is that our barges can be almost twice as broad in the beam as the average barge and therefore carry twice the volume of cargo per trip. There's simply no way I can buy or even have built a whole new fleet of canal-gauge barges. Out of the question. We get our clay from Penresford and Hallawye, always have. That's how it's set up. Any other arrangement simply isn't possible.'

'But if there's an embargo . . .'

'Stammeldon will be on its knees in no time. I'd have to close down the brickfields, lay off the workforce temporarily. We'd be losing money like rain down a drain. I think even Bringlight can see what a disaster that would be.'

'Which means he'll end up giving the Penresfordians all they want.'

Tremond looked at his wife, a troubled light in his eyes. 'Let's hope so, Marita. Let's hope so. In the meantime, I've sent Sam on a mission.' He glanced at the clock on the mantelshelf above the fireplace. 'With any luck he's already on his way.'

'Where to?' Marita asked, although she had a feeling she knew.

'Penresford. To bring Gregory back.'

'Gregory?'

'As a precaution. In case things don't go well. I want him home. I want him safe and home.'

The barge sped down the Seray through the dark, with a good clear moon to see by and, in addition, a sharp-sight stationed on lookout at the bows to warn of low-lying obstacles and upcoming bends. The three pilots Sam had enlisted for the journey were all old hands and grumbled that on such a bright night a lookout was unnecessary. They knew the river so intimately, they could almost steer it blindfolded. However, the laws governing nocturnal navigation by commercial craft were strict, and so a lookout had had to be engaged.

The pilots, frankly, did not like the lookout. Something about him, they weren't sure what, rubbed them up the wrong way. Sam felt similarly but kept quiet about it. He had found him earlier that evening at the Uneven Keel, that noted haunt of rivermen. There had been few patrons at the pub at the time and Sam had not been spoiled for choice. In fact, there had been just the one sharp-sight on the premises. The man had responded eagerly to Sam's offer of work. His papers were in order. His Rivermen's Union accreditation document was valid, the statements on it all notarised by sooth-seer. He had boasted of several years' freelance lookout experience, not on the Seray but on Jarraine's other main waterway, the Varne. He had assured Sam that the beer he was drinking was the first of the day, which the publican corroborated. The first, at any rate, that the man had ordered at that particular establishment. Sam had still had his doubts – something didn't quite tally here – but time was pressing. The boss wanted him down at Penresford as soon as possible, and he could have lost hours scouring Stammeldon for another professional lookout.

So far, for all Sam's and the pilots' misgivings, the sharp-sight had proved his worth, and Sam felt able to relax on that front. What kept him up on deck for most of the night, however, and unable to rest in his cabin, was a constant tug of urgency. He had never, he thought, travelled down the Seray on a more important mission.

Sam was glad of the opportunity to go and see how his brother and family were faring in the aftermath of the 'Storm, but he was even gladder that he was bringing Gregory back to Stammeldon. Three years was a long time for a lad to be away from his rightful home. Even if Gregory wasn't coming back for good, he needed to see his parents and brother again and they needed to see him again.

On his irregular visits to Penresford over the past three years Sam had watched Gregory change and grow. He wondered if the Braziers would recognise him now. He wasn't the boy they had sent away. With his scarred hands and Earth language inflections – never mind that he had shot up in height and his voice had deepened – he had become someone else. Not the younger son of a well-to-do Fire family any more. He had become, if this wasn't too disloyal a thought, more interesting than that. More varied. A richer character. Better.

The river whisked against the barge's hull. The lookout's Water language cries echoed down the length of the boat.

The young man he brought home would, in Sam's opinion, be good for the Braziers to meet. He might teach them a thing or two about life outside their wealth-wombed world.

Two days later, the delegation to Stammeldon arrived back in Penresford and made their report to the Guild of Freemen.

There was disgust. There was uproar. The chairwoman of the Guild had to call the meeting to order several times and came close to declaring an adjournment so that tempers could settle down. She asked Chief Secretary Loffin whether he believed that Mayor Bringlight's decision had been in any way influenced by his close association with Tremond Brazier. Loffin replied that it was very difficult to draw any other inference. The chairman then opened the debate to the floor, inviting suggestions from Guild members as to an appropriate response. One after another, subscription-paying Penresfordians came forward and proposed, with a lesser or greater degree of vehemence, the same action. It was put to the vote, and carried unanimously.

Not another lump of clay was going Stammeldon's way till Mayor Bringlight recanted and sent down at least as much food as Penresford needed and possibly more.

A representative was despatched to Hallawye and secured a similar resolution from the Guild of Freemen there.

The embargo was on.

Having travelled through the night, the Brazier Brickfields barge ought to have overtaken the Penresford delegation's ferry somewhere around Lalmore the next morning. However, shortly after moonset, in the dark before dawn, there was an accident

Sam had retired to bed only an hour earlier, and was jolted out of

135

sleep and his bunk by a huge, crunching impact. Picking himself up off the cabin floor, he yanked his trousers on and, along with the two off-duty pilots, scrambled up onto the deck. There they found the on-duty pilot savagely berating the lookout, who was crouched against the prow, looking cowed. The barge itself was lodged nose-first in the riverbank, stuck fast.

It didn't take long to establish what had happened. The lookout had failed to warn of a bend, and the pilot (who evidently would *not* have been able to steer the Seray blindfolded) had failed to take evasive action in time.

Sam asked if the lookout had fallen asleep at his post, and the pilot told him no. 'I knew this one was a queer fish,' the pilot added.

'What do you mean?'

'This useless piece of pond scum' – the pilot spat in the lookout's general direction – 'isn't a sharp-sight at all, is he. He's Dammed.'

Sam's thought-processes were still fuddled from the crash. 'Dammed?'

'Without-Flow,' said one of the other pilots. 'Extraordinary.'

Sam, who had never known what it meant to be flabbergasted, felt that this must surely be it. 'But . . . he had documentation. All filled out and correct.'

'Forged, probably,' said the on-duty pilot. 'Or bought stolen.'

Angry now, Sam peered down at the sharp-sight. 'How did you think you'd be able to get away with this? Did you think you wouldn't be found out?'

The lookout shrugged. 'I got us this far, didn't I? And if the moon hadn't gone down . . .' He didn't seem upset at what he had done. If he regretted anything, it was that he had been caught out in his imposture. 'Do you know how hard it is to get any kind of work when you're an Extraordinary? To make any kind of decent money? Believe me, if you were in my shoes you'd have done the same.'

'No,' said Sam, with perfect honesty, 'believe me, I wouldn't.'

'What do you want doing with him, Sam?' asked one of the off-duty pilots.

'I've a few ideas,' said the on-duty pilot, cracking his knuckles.

'Just . . . just keep an eye on him, you two,' Sam said to the off-duty pair. 'You,' he told the on-duty pilot, who needed removing from the scene if violence was to be averted, 'grab a lantern and come down into the hold with me. Let's see what the damage is.'

The barge was taking on water. The fore section of the hold was already ankle-deep and filling fast. By the lantern light Sam and the pilot saw that a half-dozen planks had been stoved in at the stern, the Seray spurting enthusiastically through numerous gaps. Sam instructed the pilot to hold the river back outside the breach, creating a temporary seal. He then knelt to examine the planks more closely. None of them had actually snapped, although it was a near thing – a couple were flexed to the point of splitting but had still kept their integrity, just. Carefully, exerting maximum force with maximum precision, just his thumb tips against the wood, he began pressing the planks back in place. The danger was that one of them might break entirely while he did this, and then there would be a proper hole in the side of the boat. Set against that, with all the planks back where they should be the barge had a much improved chance of making it to the nearest boatyard. The risk was worth it.

Gently, Sam, he told himself.

Precision was sometimes a strong's weak point. Yet precision, in a world that was flimsy and full of breakable things, was vital.

The last plank creaked into position, its splintered fractures knitting, and Sam stepped back. It looked delicate, a provisional fix at best. Now, the test. He told the pilot to relax his control. All that came in were trickles through a few small fissures. Sam shrugged, relieved. It would do.

The pilot ran a length of rubberised canvas hosepipe up from the hold and out over the gunwales, and finessed the water out through it, returning river to river, until the hold was drained. Dawn broke. Sam kicked the barge off the bank, and the journey resumed with two of the pilots now in charge of steering and the third down below, keeping an eye on the leaks, ready to block the water out if they worsened. Sam, for his part, stood guard over the bogus sharp-sight and repeatedly had to fight the urge to plant a fist in his face.

The pace of travel was, of necessity, slow, and it wasn't until midday that the barge reached Lalmore. There it limped into dock, and there it was mended by a master boatwright, who happily accepted payment in the form of an official promissory note from Brazier Brickfields and happily charged an added premium for doing so. That evening, the barge was en route again, with a new lookout recruited at Lalmore. This one Sam personally vetted, writing words down on a piece of paper in increasingly small script and holding them up at thirty paces for the man to read. As for the Extraordinary who had caused so much trouble, he had been handed over into the custody of the Lalmore police. Misrepresentation of Inclination carried a minimum four-year sentence, and Sam was determined to see prosecution brought even if he had to pay for it himself. An uncharitable but consoling thought: the Extraordinary was going to get pretty rough treatment during his stay in the police cells, and he would have an even harder time in jail, if it came to that. Extraordinaries invariably ended up at the bottom of the prisoner pecking order, with all the additional suffering and abuse that that entailed.

As a consequence of the delay, it wasn't until after the embargo was declared at Penresford that the Brazier Brickfields barge, and Sam, finally arrived there.

Sam's first glimpse of the town was disheartening. He saw the roofs that had been peeled back as if they were cardboard box lids. He observed the gaping holes that had been windows. He noted a number of freshly dug graves in the burial ground to the west of town. Penresford put him in mind of someone roughed up by a bully: eyes blackened, hair wayward, clothing askew, bruises showing.

No less disheartening was the reception the barge got as it made for the one jetty that the 'Storm had left intact. A handful of Penresfordians were camped out on the jetty, and the sight of a boat from Brazier Brickfields had them instantly on their feet and jeering. Using Common Tongue laced with some particularly ripe Earth-language obscenities, they made it clear that the barge was not welcome and would not be permitted to moor. Its pilot should turn around and head home. Trade with Brazier Brickfields was suspended until further notice, and the pilot could take that message back to his Ash-hole of an employer with the compliments of all of Penresford.

Sam was not entirely surprised by this turn of events. He told the pilot to come to a halt and, standing at the prow of the barge so that the Penresfordians could see who he was, addressed them in Earth language. He said he understood that Penresford had cause for griev-ance with Stammeldon, legitimate cause, but he wasn't here for any other reason than to fetch Gregory Brazier. He would be stopping in the town only for as long as it took for Gregory to pack his bags and get on board. Could they see their way to allowing him to do that?

The Penresfordians muttered among themselves. In theory there wasn't a problem. It wouldn't do any harm to let Sam take the Brazier boy away. If Brazier senior wanted Brazier junior back, so be it. Their quarrel was with the father, not the son.

Dissenting voices, however, argued that an embargo was an em-bargo. The Guild had determined that no vessel from Stammeldon should be allowed a berth at Penresford. As a point of principle, the barge could not dock.

Someone went to the Guild to request a clarification of the embargo conditions which might help resolve this dilemma. For a while the barge sat stationary in the middle of the fast-flowing Seray, held in place by its bored pilot while the other two pilots and the lookout mur-mured sarcastic comments to each other about Earthers' intransigence and their inability to think in any way except collectively. In the end, word was brought back from the Guild that the barge had permission to dock for an hour and an hour only. This was a special, one-off dispensation and mooring rights would *not*, repeat *not*, be granted to any boat from Stammeldon again unless it was one carrying relief supplies.

As the barge pulled in, Sam leapt off onto the jetty and hurried to his brother's house. He greeted Sol with an embrace, Garla with a kiss, hugged several nephews and nieces, said how good it was to see them, then asked where Gregory was.

Gregory was in the backyard, keeping up with his training. He was kneeling in front of a bucket that contained what had once been windowpanes, and for the past hour he had been plunging his fists in, over and over. The glass was now so pulverised that it was little more than glinting dust.

When he heard Garla call his name from the house, he straightened up, brushed his knuckles off, mopped his forehead with his shirt, put the shirt back on and went indoors. As soon as he saw Sam, he knew what he had come for.

'Stammeldon,' Gregory said.

'Home, Gregory,' said Sam.

'Why? Because of the embargo? Because we could run out of food here?'

'Something like that.'

'Are my parents worried about me?'

'Yes. Yes, I think they are.'

Gregory mused for a moment.

'No, I'd rather stay.'

From the assembled Goves there were protests, expressions of surprise, ridicule. He *had* to go. What was he, an idiot? Stay in Penresford, when he'd be far better off back in Stammeldon? He must be crazy. Mad as a Wet in a desert!

'Gregory, I don't think you really have a choice,' Sam said.

'Sam, with all due respect, I do.'

'Listen.' Sam took him by the shoulder and drew him none too gently to one side. 'In all likelihood,' he said, in a low voice, 'things are going to work out fine. Stammeldon will help Penresford out, everyone will be friends again. But that may not happen, and if push comes to shove the situation could get . . . sticky. Do you understand me?'

'Of course I do. And it doesn't make any difference. I'd rather be here.'

'Gregory, I want you to be absolutely clear. You may not be safe here.'

'I'll be safe. What can hurt me? I'm an indestructible.'

'Even so.'

'Sam. I'm sorry you've had a wasted journey, but I'm not going with you, and that's final.'

Sam turned to his twin brother. 'Sol, please try and talk some sense into the kid.'

'You belong in Stammeldon, Gregory,' Sol said. 'You know that. We appreciate the sentiment. It's very loyal of you to want to stay . . .'

'I'm not staying because of loyalty.'

'Then why?'

Gregory looked from one Gove to the next, his gaze coming to rest on Eda for a fraction of a second longer than on any of the others. But it wasn't even her he was staying for. If anything, she would be a good reason for leaving. No, purely and simply he was thinking of his parents. He was thinking of their faces when Sam turned up back at Tempest's Bane without him. He envisioned stark incredulity, his father flying into a rage, probably burning something, while his mother clenched her hands bitterly to her chin. It amused him, and he fought to keep the amusement from showing. Send him away for three years, barely have any contact with him in all that time, and then just summon him back with a click of the fingers? And only because things had got awkward between Stammeldon and Penresford, not because they actually wanted him home. Worried about him? Worried, more like, about how it would look to the rest of Stammeldon if they left him to languish in Penresford.

'I have a family,' he said to Sol, to Sam, to Garla, to everyone. 'And it's here, not there.'

This was meant as an excuse, but as he said it Gregory realised it was the truth, and that put the final seal on his decision. Nothing Sam or anyone said thereafter made a difference. Gregory listened, but he was his hands. Reinforced. Impervious. Invincible. His hands.

Butting northward, the barge made good time. The Seray was at last beginning to subside, contracting to its rightful size. All that 'Storm excess, vomited out into the sea. The river gradually settling into being a regular river again.

Sam spent the journey veering between trepidation and admiration. He was not looking forward to facing Tremond and telling him his son had refused to come home. At the same time, Gregory's rejection of his parents' wishes was, it had to be said, courageous. Sam thought that, given longer, he might have been able to swing Gregory round, make him see sense. But perhaps not. Gregory had shown the entrenchedness, the obstinacy, of a true Earther, and an Earther, once he has dug his heels in, will not be moved.

And of course, Tremond Brazier did not take the news well at all. At first he was stunned. Then he was livid. And then, having bawled at Sam and set light to several objects around the house, with Marita cancelling the conflagrations out as fast as he could spark them, he went quiet. Sombre. Dangerously calm.

Tremond had already been informed, via the telepath bureau, about the embargo at Penresford. Now this business with Gregory . . . Well, enough was enough. A visit to Mayor Bringlight at the town hall, and the course of Stammeldon's policy vis-à-vis food aid was set. Not a scrap, not a drop, not a grain, not so much as an apple pip was to be sent Penresford's way until Penresford learned proper respect. Tremond Brazier was not to be denied and he was not to be defied. This kind of insolence had to be stamped down on. Penresford wanted a fight? Then it was damned well going to get one!

YASHU

One by one the bodies slipped into the sea. They were swaddled head to toe in white cloth, so that all were the same, anonymous in death. Weighted with rocks, they sank swiftly. Each glimmered through the spectrum of blueness, from aquamarine to cobalt, descending, darkening, gone.

The people of Shai sang them on their way. They stood aboard a flotilla of boats, many of which were perilously overcrowded. It had been hard finding enough good boats to go round, after the 'Storm. Shai's headman led the ceremony, firm-faced, strong-voiced, setting an example. One of his own brothers was among the dead. The headman, standing at the prow of the vessel from which the corpses were being offloaded, radiated vicarious joy.

Yashu watched. She sang. She held Zeelu's hand. Her eyes were dry, and proud. No one would see how her heart ached and how robbed she felt. She would be happy. Huaso had been taken from her but he was now in the warmth and womblike darkness of the Great-Ocean-Beyond, in company with all the ancestors up to and including Finder-Founder Oriñaho. Soon he would be losing all sense of himself, diluting gently to become one with the others. His opinions would become part and parcel of the spirits' opinions. His life experience, even though there was only sixteen-years'-worth, would add to the spirits' fund of understanding and help them shape the future course of the people-of-the-archipelago. A drop in the ocean, but every drop counted. She would be happy. She was determined to be, for Huaso's sake.

Back on Shai, it was harder to maintain this determination. Breaking away from Huaso's family, Yashu strode inland. She needed to be alone. She walked for several miles until, on a hilltop within sight of Purple-Cowrie-Beach, she sat down and wept. The tears were sorrow, but they were anger too. She wondered why she had bothered attending the funeral. The funeral was for every Shai-islander who had died, but it wasn't the same, it didn't have the same meaning, for those whose loved ones' bodies had not actually been found, and Huaso's body had not been found. She looked over at the remains of the Purple-Cowrie-Beach-Village – the torn-up foundations, the scattered debris that she had taken, at first sight, to be boat wreckage. It was clear what had happened. A tidal surge, driven by the 'Storm, sweeping inland. Raking the village flat. Clawing it down the beach. Reaping its inhabitants. Leaving not one of them, not a single corpse, behind.

So, no *cholisa* for Huaso. No washing of the body. No white wrappings. No songs sung. No dignified ceremonial plummet into the black below.

She tried to imagine his fear, the horror of his drowning. She hoped it had been quick. People said drowning was a good way to die. You felt calm, once your lungs were filled with water. You accepted it. You sank peacefully. How anyone could state this as fact, she had no idea. She supposed there were people who had nearly drowned but had been rescued at the last moment and resuscitated. But since they hadn't actually died, how could they know how it felt – really know?

Oh Huaso, the idiot! The brave, responsible idiot! Going to check on the house, thinking he could make it there and back in time. Pharralu said she had urged him to stay put but there had been no stopping him. No way was he prepared to let his and Yashu's house sit there unprotected. He had promised to run all the way to Purple-Cowrie-Beach-Village, put up the house's 'Storm defences as quickly as possible, and run all the way back home. Yashu was in no doubt that he had been true to that promise, at least the first two parts of it. But the 'Storm had moved in faster than expected. Huaso must have had to take refuge in the house. When the sea roared ashore, he hadn't stood a chance.

All his dreams of owning a fishing boat, gone.

His vision of their future together as husband and wife, gone.

Everything he and she had set their hearts on, gone.

Yashu felt a sudden, sharp loathing for the Worldstorm. The 'Storm seemed to have a particular hatred for her. It felt reasonable, and right, to hate it back.

When she couldn't cry any more – her eyes felt burned out, her throat choked dry – she returned to Valley-Heart and Huaso's family's house. It was time to leave, go back to I*il. She thanked Pharralu for letting her stay there. Pharralu had been treating her with something close to kindness these past three days. That note of fraudulence was gone from her voice, in its place a frail kind of compassion. 'He will remember you, I'm sure, Yashu,' she said. 'You will be his last thought lingering as the Great-Ocean-Beyond finally absorbs him. He did love you.'

'I know. I loved him too. Shaipharralu, you may not have thought very highly of me—'

Huaso's mother made a dismissive gesture. Whatever Yashu had to say, it didn't matter. Not any more.

Zeelu begged Yashu not to go, but Yashu said she had to. Her aunt. She couldn't leave Liyalu on her own any longer. Imersho told her he had made travel arrangements for her. A friend of his was willing to ferry her back to I*il any time she wanted. Imersho and Pharralu waved her off from the house, and Zeelu accompanied her to the outskirts of Valley-Heart, clutching onto her arm. 'Please come and see us again sometime. Don't forget about us,' she said.

Yashu promised that she wouldn't forget about them and she would come to visit.

'We are your family, sort of,' Zeelu said.

'Sort of,' said Yashu, with a smile.

Auzo, Imersho's friend, was a master shaper-of-water and was keen to test out the patching-up job he had done on his freighter. The sea had subsided to an even swell. The keel cleaved smoothly through. Near Tleyis, a school of spotted dolphins appeared and rode the bow wave for a while. Their backs broke the surface in turn. Dorsal fins flashed. Water rippled in gleaming rills over marbled hide. A long time ago Oriñaho saved the life of a beached dolphin, carrying it through the shallows until it was in water deep enough to swim away. The dolphin later repaid the favour by saving the life of one of Oriñaho's sons, who, swimming one day with his brothers and sisters, was dragged out to sea by an undertow and menaced by a shark. The dolphin saw off the shark and nudged the terrified boy back to land. Thereafter, Oriñaho declared that all dolphins were to be regarded as honorary humans. No human must ever harm one and, if one was in danger, every effort should be made to help it. The pact between humans and dolphins stood to this day. That was why dolphins always smiled.

And Auzo was smiling too, because to have dolphins ride your bow wave was an auspicious omen. It meant that your boat was in fine condition and your Flow as a shaper-of-water was good.

Just past Oöyia, Yashu and Auzo spied another boat, a wave-skimmer. The absence of clan colours indicated it was from the mainland, a coastliner's. As they drew closer, Yashu spied two people in the water not far from the wave-skimmer. Pearl-divers? It was possible, because pearl-divers favoured nippy craft like wave-skimmers to get about in. Great distances could be covered quickly, and it was not as if the boats had to carry a heavy haul like a net-full of fish.

However, they couldn't have been pearl-divers as there were no pearl-beds in this area. They weren't swimming like breath-holders, either. They didn't have that absolute self-assurance in the sea. In fact, as far as Yashu could tell, the two in the water were having some sort of argument with a third person still aboard the wave-skimmer. They were talking to him and he was yelling back and gesticulating like an irate starfish. Auzo agreed with her: it was a peculiar sight. He veered towards the wave-skimmer, pulling up within hailing distance.

One of the two swimmers, catching sight of the freighter, immediately struck out for it. The other, after some hesitation, followed. The one in front was an elderly man, judging by his white-haired, largely bald head. The other looked younger, with not many years on Yashu herself. The older man, for all that he was no breath-holder, seemed at home in the water, certainly more so than the younger. His strokes were strong and easy, and the younger man struggled to keep up.

'What's going on?' Auzo called out to the man still aboard the wave-skimmer.

'Search me,' he replied. He spoke with a coastliner accent, harder and harsher than islander cadences, roughened by constant rubbing-up against mainlanders and Common Tongue. 'I have no idea. Airheads!' He spat contemptuously in the direction of the swimmers. 'Anyway, they're your problem now. I'd rather have a sea urchin stuffed up my arse than deal with a pair like that again. Goodbye and good riddance. Here, you can have their luggage too.' The coastliner grabbed a couple of canvas bags and hurled them across the gap between the two boats. Then he turned his wave-skimmer about and scudded away on a surge of foam. By the time the swimmers reached Auzo's boat, the coastliner was halfway to the horizon.

Yashu bent down and helped the old man aboard and then, a short while later, his companion, who was exhausted by the swim, brief though it had been. As the younger man came up out of the water, she noted his skin, which was brown, browner than her own, the damp-sand colour of someone who hailed from the hot countries to the south. She also noted his wide, pale brown eyes, the gentle, rounded planes of his cheeks, the tapering, teardrop nose, and the woven, richly coloured waistcoat he was wearing. She had not seen many southerners, and certainly not one in such close proximity before. Were they all as fine-featured and brightly dressed? And were they all such lousy swimmers?

The southerner slumped down on the freighter's deck, panting, while the old man stood and calmly wrung out his shirt-tails and brushed the water from what was left of his hair. His shoes – a pair of good leather boots – hung around his neck, tied by their laces. This suggested to Yashu that, whatever the reason for it, his dip in the water had been premeditated. The southerner's canvas sandals, by contrast, were still on his feet. Or at least one of them was. The other was missing. She wondered if the southerner had leapt into the water to save the old man. But it didn't make sense, a weaker swimmer going to the aid of a stronger one.

'Thank you,' the old man said to Auzo in Water language, then continued in Common Tongue: 'I'm sorry but that's the only phrase I know. I'm grateful to you, anyway, for picking us up.'

'Would you like to tell us what you were doing there in the sea?' Auzo said. 'Did you and that coastliner have some sort of falling-out?'

The old man looked levelly at him, then at Yashu. Then he smiled, an incomplete smile, just his lower set of teeth showing. Narrow, spiny little teeth, like a fish's.

'The fellow refused to take us all the way to where we wanted to go,' he said. 'We were nearly there, and all of a sudden, quite out of the blue, he demanded extra payment or he wasn't going to go any further. Well, I wasn't having any of that. Nothing short of piracy. I thought I'd call his bluff, so I jumped into the sea. My friend here was of the same view and jumped in after me.'

Yashu gaped at the old man. Did he really think anybody would swallow a story like that? It was just plain ridiculous. Who in their right mind would try and haggle over the fare for a journey by leaping into the sea? The coastliner could simply have cruised off and left the two men there, a long way from the nearest land, further than even the strongest swimmer could swim. As bluff-calling went, it was crazy – nothing short of suicidal.

She was glad to see that Auzo felt the same way. He was regarding the old man with one eyebrow sceptically raised. But he seemed more amused by the lie than anything, whereas Yashu found it painful, like the screech of a badly played violin. She could not remember when she had ever heard someone utter such blatant nonsense. Even thinking about it set her teeth on edge.

'Are you all right, young lady?' the old man enquired, with a solicitous frown. 'You seem . . . discomfited.'

'Who are you?' Yashu said. The question came out more bluntly than intended. She wasn't well practised in Common Tongue and its niceties. Perhaps that didn't matter.

'Just two travellers.' The old man gestured inclusively at the southerner, who looked as if he was starting to recover his strength. 'We've come a long way and we're trying to get to I*il.' The attempt at pronouncing the island's name was appallingly hamfisted.

'It just so happens we're heading that way ourselves,' said Auzo.

Again, that incomplete smile. 'Well now, that *is* a lucky break, isn't it? I don't suppose you'd mind taking us there.'

Auzo seemed amenable to the idea.

'But perhaps,' said Yashu, who was already developing a wariness of the old man, 'you could have another go at explaining what happened. Why did you *really* jump off that boat?'

'I told you. Fellow tried to cheat us. You disbelieve me?'

'Who wouldn't?'

'Well, that's interesting. Because I swear it's the honest truth.'

No, he was still lying. 'I don't think so.'

'What a mistrustful creature you are. Look, whether or not what I'm saying is true, the fact remains that we're now passengers on this boat and you're bound for I*il. So why don't we just leave it at that. I mean, what are you going to do? Throw us back into the briny? And anyway . . .' He reached into one of the bags that the coastliner had thrown across. From it, after some rummaging, he drew out a gold bracelet. It was a beautiful thing, consisting of three different-coloured bands – plain gold, red gold, white gold – plaited around one another. Yashu, in spite of her feelings about the old man, would have loved to have such a bracelet on her wrist. She glanced at Auzo and could tell by his expression that he was as taken with it as she was, though perhaps more for its value than for its looks.

'For you, sir,' the old man said to Auzo. 'In return for passage to I*il.'

Auzo stepped forward and accepted the bracelet, and that was that. The boat was on the move again even before he got back to his piloting position at the stern.

For the rest of the journey, Yashu sat as far from the two strangers as she could and kept her gaze fixed on the horizon. On one occasion she did sneak a glance in the strangers' direction, and as she did so, the old man turned his head, as if he had known she was about to look. What she saw in his eyes was unsettling and made her break the contact straight away. He seemed to be familiar with her. That was the only way to describe it. He looked at her as if he knew her, this man she had never seen before in her life.

Soon, though not soon enough for Yashu, I*il appeared ahead. The three peaks. The Rock. And finally the welcoming arc of Half-Moon-Bay. Yashu leapt ashore the moment the freighter impaled itself in the sand. She wished Auzo *mala* and made for the coastal track without a backward glance.

It was close on evening by the time she reached her aunt's cottage. Black-Tail came bounding down the path to greet her and leapt around her delightedly all the way back up, almost bowling her over in his attempts to lick her face.

Siaalo was on the roof of the cottage, busy nailing back together the beams which had been exposed and broken by the 'Storm. He saluted her with a wave of his hammer.

'Missed you round here, Yashu.' He spoke around the nails he was holding between his lips. There was, she thought, just a hint of reproof in his voice. 'But we've managed.'

He didn't ask how things had gone on Shai. Indoors, however, Liyalu did, and enfolded Yashu in a tight hug when she was told.

'I hoped,' Liyalu said, 'when you didn't come back, that it was just because it was *cholisa* and you couldn't get a boat. I hoped. I begged the spirits. I asked them for it to be *cholisa* but not for anyone you knew. Oh Yashu, what can I say?'

'Nothing,' Yashu said. 'Just say nothing. I see Siaalo's put together a nice new pen for the goats. The nannies need milking. I'll get on with that.'

For two days, nothing was any different, except that everything was different. The routine of Yashu's life was unchanged, she went about her duties as normal, there were chores to be checked off and done. Siaalo mended the thatch on the roof and Liyalu was able to use her bedroom again, having spent the past few nights sleeping in Yashu's room. Yashu, in turn, was able to move from a makeshift bed in the main room back to her own room. The world re-righted itself, and Yashu's niche in it was where it had always been. She embraced ordinariness and order, and used them as a blanket to cover her thoughts. The grief, the anger, she let grate away deep within her but never summoned to the surface, never dwelled on. She moved through one moment to the next. She behaved exactly like herself. As though a performer, she acted Yashu. At evening's end, when the ninespike came out, she sucked in more of the soothing smoke than was her habit, and it made her night's sleep deep and dreamless, and that was good. Apart from this, to all appearances she was the same as ever. She was *pretending* to be the same as ever, but pretending so well, so perfectly, that most of the time even she wasn't aware she was doing it.

On the third day, she returned from a rabbit-hunting trip up over the summit of the island and found two visitors had arrived at the cottage while she was gone. Siaalo had escorted them up from Second-Cliff-Village. Liyalu had received them in and offered them refreshments. They were two weary mainlander travellers. They were the old man and the southerner.

Yashu had managed to bag a brace of nice, plump does. They

dangled, still warm, from the noose snares with which she had trapped them. She entered the main room to show off her catch to Liyalu, and there was Liyalu, and there Siaalo, and there the old man and the southerner. The latter two were at the table, tucking into bread, goat's cheese and *sirassi*. The southerner had draped his multicoloured waistcoat over the back of his chair but looked, of the two of them, the less at home.

Immediately she saw the mainlanders, Yashu made a sharp turn and headed for the kitchen, where she laid out the rabbits, grabbed a knife and prepared to gut and skin them.

Liyalu called from the main room, asking her to come back. It was odd to hear her aunt use Common Tongue. Politeness, of course, dictated that she should, but Yashu could not recall the last time she had heard her speak anything but their own language. With a great display of unwillingness, she did as asked.

'Yashu,' said Liyalu, puzzled. 'Guests.'

'I know,' was all Yashu said.

'These men say they know you,' said Siaalo.

'We've met.'

'How do they know you?' Liyalu asked.

'Ah, forgive me, I*illiyalu,' said the old man. 'My fault. If you hadn't laid on such a delicious luncheon, I would have had a chance to get round to explaining. My friend and I, on our way here from the mainland, had the good fortune to be rescued from a very awkward predicament by your niece and the man giving her a lift in his boat. She didn't tell you about this, then?'

'She didn't.'

Yashu shrugged. 'I didn't think it that big a thing.'

'Not to you, perhaps,' the old man said. 'But Khollo and I considered it more than an act of charity. It might be fair to say that you and that boat owner saved our lives. This is Khollo, by the way.' The old man motioned with his hand at the southerner, here there, a to-and-fro of introduction. 'Names weren't exchanged on the boat, were they? Khollo Sharellam, my travelling companion and personal enshriner.'

The southerner nodded to Yashu, his cheeks bulging with food.

'And I am Annonax Ayn. Formerly of Stonehaven, both of us, but we are now, for want of a better description, nomads. Citizens of the world. You've heard of Stonehaven, of course.'

'Yes,' Yashu said, 'even backward islander Wets like us have heard of Stonehaven.'

Her aunt shot her a frown. For all that the man was a mainlander, there was no need to be such a snapping crab.

'My niece,' Liyalu told Ayn, 'has suffered a bereavement recently. A close friend.'

'Really? My condolences, I*ilyashu,' said Ayn.

Yashu swatted the sympathy aside. 'Why are you here?'

The vertical lines that grooved Ayn's cheeks deepened as his mouth downturned. 'Perhaps we've come to express our appreciation,' he said. 'Perhaps we've walked halfway round your island to offer proper thanks to our rescuer.'

'No,' Yashu said, adamant, 'you've come for something else.'

Ayn revealed his lower teeth. 'A very perspicacious girl.' He turned to Liyalu. 'But then you know that already, I*illiyalu, don't you? How perspicacious your niece can be.'

In response, an odd thing. Briefly, ever so briefly, Liyalu winced. It was as though a gnat had zoomed at her face. A flicker of the eyelids, then she was calm again, controlled. If Yashu had not been looking directly at her at that moment, she might never have noticed.

A pang of pain? Her illness?

But it hadn't looked like that.

Whatever the wince meant, Liyalu's reply to Ayn was as measured as they come. 'Yashu is a girl wise beyond her years. She also appears to have taken a dislike to you, Mr Ayn, and knowing her as I do, I have to wonder why. I have to wonder whether you might not have given her a reason to dislike you.'

'My dear lady' – Ayn was all wounded innocence – 'can a man not deliver a simple compliment? But it is possible, I suppose, that I erred on the boat the other day. Some tricky point of Water etiquette that I stumbled over. In which case, I apologise.'

With, to Yashu, all the sincerity of a hungry sea snake.

'Though I must add,' he said, 'that it's a surprise to come across so exceptional a young lady. So *extraordinary* a one, if you know what I mean.'

'My niece is, yes, as you would say, an Extraordinary,' Liyalu replied, picking up on the word on which Ayn had placed a distinct, sly emphasis. 'We say without-Flow.'

'Yes, I've always considered "Flow" a particularly apt name for it. Superior to "Inclination", in that one's Inclination arrives when things are starting to flow from one's body that haven't flowed before. Semen, menstrual blood . . . Everyone should call it Flow, I think.'

Ingratiating worm, Yashu thought.

'But as it happens, I*illiyalu, you've misunderstood me. When I say extraordinary, I mean it in the literal sense of the word. Out of the ordinary.'

'What *is* he going on about?' said Siaalo in Water language.

Liyalu flicked a hand. 'Nothing, I'm sure.'

'Airheads,' Siaalo grumbled. He offered Yashu a sardonic shrug.

'I'm sorry,' said Ayn to Siaalo, 'I don't think I caught that. What did you say?'

'Mr Ayn,' Liyalu said, still controlled, still measured, 'it's not appropriate for an islander to refuse hospitality to a stranger calling at their house. It's our way. But it's also not appropriate for a guest to abuse the hospitality he has been offered.' She let the reproof hang in the air.

Ayn nodded slowly, chastened. Something was dawning on him – the knowledge that he had made a misstep, a serious one. 'I see. I see. Yes. How very clumsy of me. I assumed . . . Well, that's why I came round. Because I could see what she is. Like knows like, and all that. And I wondered how well she was coping with . . . her situation. Given that there aren't the facilities here that you'd find on the mainland. But I had no idea that— No, that's no excuse. I should have guessed. I should have worked it out as soon as I saw her. The way she behaved. Oblivious. And now, in my catastrophic idiocy, I've gone and said something I shouldn't have.'

He turned to Khollo, his shoulders haplessly hunched. 'Time we were off, my friend. I'm afraid our welcome has gone rather sour. My fault entirely. What a terrific dolt I am.'

Khollo set down, with regret, the thick slice of bread he had just cut himself.

Siaalo held the door open as Ayn and Khollo got up and gathered their things to leave. 'Thank you for coming, gentlemen. Do give our regards to the mainland.'

At the doorway, Ayn paused, then addressed himself to Yashu. 'It's really not my place to say this, I*ilyashu, but since I've done so much damage already, a little more can hardly make a difference. I think you and your aunt need to have a good long chat. It's out now. What's been said can't be unsaid. If it's any consolation, I'm sorry it had to happen this way, but maybe it's for the best. The truth should never remain hidden. You, of all people, will appreciate that.'

Yashu waited till the mainlanders were gone, then rounded on her aunt. 'The truth?' she demanded.

Liyalu would not meet her gaze. For a long time she stared at the handle of her walking-stick, which was hooked over the arm of her chair. Abruptly she grabbed the stick, creaked to her feet, and beckoned to Yashu. 'Let's go for a walk.'

Yashu accompanied her downhill and off along the coastal track. She felt queasy. Her footsteps were no less uncertain and trembling than her aunt's. Something had been kept from her, something important.

She could sense the contours of it, now that she knew it was there. The shape, the ungainly weight of it. And the more she thought about it, the more there seemed to be only one possible explanation. From what Ayn had said, hints he had dropped . . . *Like knows like.* Unwittingly he had revealed a secret, like the 'Storm tearing off that section of the cottage roof, opening the house up, exposing inside to outside.

But if the secret was what she thought it was, she wanted Liyalu to tell her. She wanted to hear it from her aunt, to see Liyalu's face as she confessed. To see Liyalu's shame.

They got as far as Grey-Seal-Inlet, a long hike for Liyalu, the furthest she had ever gone since her illness set in. The effort cost her. She sat down heavily on a rock at the edge of the precipice, wan and breathless. A couple of hundred yards below, on their secluded strip of shingle, the seals were softly yelping to one another. Above, the usual frenetic wail of seagulls. In between, Yashu and Liyalu, silent.

Then at last: 'Please understand, Yashu, that I was always going to tell you. At first I didn't because I wasn't sure. But then, as time went by and you kept reacting in a certain way to certain things I said, I *was* sure, but by that point it seemed too late, I'd put it off for too long and I was scared to tell you because it meant you would have to leave me and I was terrified of that. Who would live with me? Who would look after me? Me, dying, becoming more of a burden each day. Who would take me on? Siaalo, yes. But I couldn't live with Siaalo. I couldn't have him there in the house all day, hanging around me like Black-Tail hangs around him. A dog in the shape of a man. It would have become unbearable for both of us. Soon enough there'd have been harsh words and a friendship ruined for ever. So I made the decision . . . No, it wasn't as deliberate as that. I just let it become the absence of a decision. I told myself not to think about it, and let the matter slide away. I never lied to you, not as such. I simply hid what I knew from you and allowed you to come to the wrong conclusion about yourself. About what you were. Are. I hate myself for that. I will never forgive myself. It was unspeakably selfish of me. But I always vowed I would tell you one day, before I died. You believe that, don't you?'

Yashu let her face be blank. The love she felt for her aunt had never been as fierce as it was then, and she had never felt less like showing it.

'Yes,' said Liyalu, 'yes, I deserve the stony treatment. But however bad you want me to feel, it'll never be as bad as I actually do feel. To be quite honest, it appals me how easy it became for me to avoid the subject whenever it came up. I'd, I don't know, ignore any awkward comment you made, change the subject, ask you to go and do something for me – some clever tactic like that. I became horribly proficient at it over two years. The art, not of deceiving, but of not having to deceive. You understand? Because the last thing I wanted to do, let alone could do, was deceive you.'

There, yes. That was it. Confirmation.

'What am I?' Yashu said. 'If I'm not Dammed, if I'm something else – what? Say it. Just say it.'

Liyalu peered down into the cleft at their feet, the great deep gouge in the side of I*il. Finally she looked round at her niece, and her eyes were glassy with tears, and wide with frankness.

'On the mainland they'd call you' – Common Tongue – 'a sooth-seer.'

'I'm Air-Inclined.'

'Very much so.'

'How?'

'I don't know. It happens sometimes.'

'But my parents . . .'

'Both of them of-the-archipelago. Both Water-Inclined. But it happens sometimes, no one knows why. A kind of ancestral hiccup. Of-the-archipelago through and through, on your father's family's side, on my family's side, just typical islanders, and then . . . you.'

'A sooth-seer,' Yashu said. It was a strange, unreasonable comfort that the Common Tongue words were easy to pronounce, could almost have been Water-language words. 'I know a lie when I hear one.'

And yes, the cracked-bell sound of Pharralu's insincerity. The harsh, violin-screech resonance of Annonax Ayn's tall tale on the boat. And a dozen other small instances she could think of. For two years she had glimpsed but not grasped, sensed but not understood. It had been there, her Flow, crude, undeveloped, and she had had no way of realising.

'Yashu?'

But Yashu had stood and begun walking off, at a pace Liyalu hadn't a hope of matching. She marched away from her aunt, away from Grey-Seal-Inlet and the coastal track, over the raw, untenanted windward slopes of I*il – but the island seemed too small, she could never walk far enough, and so her feet soon led her round back to Liyalu, and she threw herself down beside her aunt and wept onto her lap, with rage, with relief, with regret, barely feeling the light soothing of Liyalu's hand on her hair. There was the 'Storm visit, there was Huaso, there was the half-smiling mainlander Ayn, there was two years of believing she was without-Flow, there was the knowledge that she was with-Flow after all, and there was the hollow pang of guilt, islander guilt, the guilt that came with letting down the clan, with being not-of-the-archipelago. There was, in all, the sheer cruelty of life, which sobbed out of her as the seals yelped below and the seagulls wailed above, creatures of sea and sky, water and air, creatures who had lungs but swam and who flew but fished, who straddled environments, who were two things at once and happy with that and belonged. They cried, Yashu cried, sounding similar, utterly unalike.

AYN

Before anything else, I think we need to discuss my funeral arrangements. Yes, now's the time. I want an Air burial, naturally, and I'd like you to assume responsibility for it. Fair enough, Khollo? I know it's a gruesome task but you've seen it done, you know what's involved, you're up to the job. It doesn't really require much skill, no matter what the professional funeral officiators say. They make such a big song and dance about it. You know, 'this way through the abdominal wall', 'that way down the medians of the arms', and so on. What it boils down to is simply being able to hold a knife and cut. Common sense, that's all. Follow the lines of the body. Any fool can do it. Not that for one moment I'm suggesting you're a fool.

The question is, are there enough carrion birds around here? At Stonehaven the crows and the buzzards and the vultures know. When they see people arrive at the Plateau of Bones on the lip of the crater, they come flocking from miles around. The word goes out along the avian grapevine and the body's a skeleton in no time. Same as at any of the officially designated Air burial sites. They have their regular customers, ready to drop by at a moment's notice for a free meal. Up here? In late winter? Perhaps a desperate eagle or two. But it must be done, that's the main thing. I will not be put under the ground, or burnt, or plopped into that lake. I will be laid out and carved up and be eaten and dispersed, as is proper. Even in death, dignity. That isn't too much to ask. All right, Khollo? You promise you'll do it? Good.

Now, where have we got to? We're on our way to the Li*issuan archipelago, correct? Bobbing merrily across the waves with our chum Thaëho, brother of the over-talkative hotelier Sha*so. So then what happened? Ah yes. Man overboard.

Forgive my chuckling, but your face when I pushed you in, Khollo. Priceless! I wish I could have given you some warning, but that would have tipped off our pilot as to what I was up to. The only way it would work was if it was a complete surprise for all concerned. And then your thrashing around, your gurgling, your struggles to keep your head above the surface . . . Most convincing. One would almost have thought you were genuinely in difficulties. But of course, you'd twigged to my plan and were putting on a terrific performance. The man who lost his footing on deck and tumbled into the sea and was in danger of drowning. Bravo!

[Elder Ayn was perfectly well aware that I'm not the best of swimmers. I wasn't even particularly happy being a passenger on Thaëho's boat, for that matter. It must have been obvious to him how uncomfortable I was, surrounded by all that water. For him then to come up behind me when I wasn't looking and give me a hearty shove between the shoulder-blades and send me head-first over the side . . . But I've mentioned that cruel streak of his before. And as he related the episode, I showed him what I thought about it by keeping my face sealed, not letting a chink of emotion come through. Not giving him the satisfaction.]

There was another boat on the horizon as Thaëho brought his vessel about so that we might retrieve you. That other boat, I knew, was the one we wanted to be on. Its presence wasn't simply convenient. There are no coincidences in the life of a previsionary. It was there because it was meant to be there in the pattern of my existence. That was its place. I knew it was coming, and to get aboard it I knew we had to stop where we did on the journey to I*il and we had to give the other boat's pilot a valid reason to stop also. And as we came back for you, Khollo, I removed my boots and laced them around my neck, because in a short time I, too, was going to have to enter the water. And then Thaëho drew up alongside you, and I think the last thing he expected to happen was that the man overboard would be joined by another man overboard. But over the side I went, plunging in. Shockingly cold it was, too. The waters around the islands of Li*issua, where shallow, are famously mild and warm. But not that far out to sea. Fair took one's breath away. But then I'd got used to cold water, thanks to my daily dips in Stonehaven's lagoon. Got to the stage where I didn't mind it at all. Even quite liked it. Good for the heart, the circulation, for sharpening the brain. I imagine your brain was pretty well sharpened by it, no?

[Sharpened like a dagger, keen to stab somebody.]

So there was poor old Thaëho, all at sea, as it were. At first maybe he thought I had jumped in to help you, but then, when all I did was tread water beside you, he must have been thoroughly perplexed. He urged us to come back aboard. He reached over the side and couldn't understand why I refused to take his hand and why I ordered you not to take it either. Understandably he got a bit miffed and there were heated words. He threatened to shape the water around us so that we'd be forced up out of it, popping up like corks onto his deck. I told him if he made us get back on the boat that way, we'd simply jump off again. By then, the other boat was close by. I called Thaëho a few choice names, so that he would lose any last shred of concern he had for us. Then he and the pilot of the other boat, Auzo, were exchanging comments in their own language, and from what I could tell Thaëho was washing his hands of us. The way he spat at us was a pretty clear indication of his feelings. A Wet never parts with a bodily fluid without good cause.

I was well on my way to Auzo's boat by that point, with you not far behind. Thaëho lobbed our luggage across, probably cursing us like mad, though I couldn't really hear him over my own splashes. Then a slim, wiry arm extending down to me, a small but strong hand inviting me to grasp it.

This was our Yashu. I*ilyashu. Yashu Of-Three-Peak-Island. This was the young woman we had travelled all that way to make the acquaintance of.

A good-looking creature. A certain ruggedness to her, characteristic of islanders. It can be a hard life, islander life, and its vicissitudes write themselves on the faces even of the young, in forceful eyes, in a graininess of the skin. Nevertheless, a good-looking creature. Brown hair bleached lighter by salt wind and sun, cut in a rough, chunky style, just touching the shoulders and with a sheared-straight fringe. A narrow face tapering to a firm chin, and a mouth with just a hint of a petulant curl to it. A boyish figure, small breasts, trim hips. Some men prefer their girls voluptuous, but were I of that particular bent I would go for someone like Yashu. None of that heaviness about her, that female ponderousness. Not the type to run to fat as most women do, especially once they've started having children. Not likely to turn into a doughy milk-cow. A sinewy girl, with strength in her every move-ment, but also a comfortable grace. Yashu. An unfortunate name, though, I must say. To me it sounds like a sneeze.

[Elder Ayn gave a practical illustration of what he meant, faking a loud sneeze and yelling 'Yashu!' as he did so. For the record, it wasn't the first time he had made this joke. He thought so highly of it, clearly, that he wanted it enshrined in his narrative.]

This was she, at any rate, and as I watched her haul you aboard, Khollo, I looked forward to the fun I was going to have revealing the truth about her Inclination. I foresaw myself at her aunt's house, dropping some very unsubtle hints and pretending to be mortified when her aunt made it apparent that I had said something I shouldn't have.

There was fun to be had right then, too. Almost the first words I spoke in Yashu's presence were a lie. I made up some outrageous fib about Thaëho trying to screw an extra fare out of us. Poor chap, perfectly honest, would never have dreamed of it, would he? And Yashu became terribly indignant, didn't believe a word I said, went into a sulk. Sooth-seers take it very hard when someone lies. It offends them deep down, like a personal insult. And even though Yashu did not know then that she was a sooth-seer, she reacted exactly as a sooth-seer would. I could see how much I had aggrieved her, and I hate to say it but I found it more than a little amusing.

Anyway, I purchased passage to I*il on Auzo's boat with a trinket of some sort . . .

[In fact quite a nice gold bracelet. A sort of triple thing, three different-coloured bands wrapped around one another. Definitely an overpayment for the relatively short journey we had to make, but Auzo had few qualms about accepting it.]

. . . and shortly we were making landfall at Sooshyarlis, or Half-Moon-Bay, the largest beach on I*il. Sooshyarlis. Did I pronounce that correctly?

[Unusually for Elder Ayn, he did.]

Yashu stomped off, still unhappy with me, and you and I, Khollo, crossed over the sand dunes to reach the town of . . . No, I'm not even going to attempt that one. Town-By-The-Dunes, in Common Tongue. A biggish place, and quiet that day, still subdued after the 'Storm visit, still recovering its equilibrium. We found lodging at a hotel somewhere in the centre. The only hotel in town, as it happens. The owner told us they didn't get many people staying overnight on I*il, mostly just merchants and seafarers who had been stranded by bad weather – in other words, who hadn't much choice in the matter. But it was a clean enough place, simply but amply furnished. There were sea-scene murals on the walls, reasonably well rendered, and each item of crockery in the dining room had tiny glazed shells inlaid around the rim. It could have been worse.

Our rooms overlooked what seemed to be a sleepy little plaza. Next morning, the sleepy little plaza was awake with noise – shouting, clattering, thumping. It sounded like a riot was going on out there but it proved to be a market. Dozens of stallholders setting up shop, laying out their wares. Fishermen returned from an early catch, with baskets brimful of glittering bounty. Local farmers with the fruits of the field on offer. Vintners with flagons of wine and distillers with flasks of the indigenous orange-based firewater, *sirassi* (the name means 'choppy seas' and after a few glasses you know why). Sellers of conch shells and cowries and pearls and narwhal-spike scrimshaw and other such fine items, for ladies to buy and beautify themselves and their homes with. Visitors from other islands and from the coast, offering merchandise that could not be found on I*il – timber, cloth, rugs, et cetera. A raucous hustle and bustle, a teem of life, the market like a reef with a human shoal milling around it, nibbling here and there, moving in wafts and twitches . . .

You know, this is all rather poetic, isn't it? I'm impressed with myself.

['Poetic,' I said, 'but perhaps also superfluous?']

Superfluous? Pah! Local colour, Khollo. Filling in the detail. A word portrait. Cut it if you like, but frankly this account will be the poorer without it.

Oh, and now I've gone and lost my thread. You shouldn't have interrupted me.

['I didn't.']

Well then, you shouldn't have let me interrupt myself. Honestly! What good are you to me if you can't keep me on the straight and narrow?

['But that's what I was trying to do.']

No, you weren't. You were— Never mind. Town-By-The-Dunes had a busy market place. Not just one but several of them. A dozen, or thereabouts. Lots of market places. There, if I'm not allowed to be poetic, I shall be prosaic. Painfully prosaic. And that very morning you went out and bought yourself a new pair of sandals because you'd somehow contrived to lose one of your old pair. All right? Still dull enough for you? And we stayed in Town-By-The-Dunes for several days and it wasn't unpleasant. The locals weren't friendly but they weren't unfriendly either. Reserved, I would say. In a remote community, outsiders are more alien than they might be elsewhere, in places not so isolated and insular. Especially outsiders who are differently-Inclined. And I noticed several people looking askance at you, Khollo. It was obvious that not many southerners came that way. Reserved, yes. A kind of wary barrier raised between us and them. Common Tongue used only reluctantly, as if a last resort. A few of the locals pretending they couldn't speak it at all. But no one ever less than polite to us. The proprietor of our hotel made sure there was always fresh water in the pitchers in our rooms. And there was that restaurant nearby whose owner showed us his cold store and boasted how a specialist shaper-of-water made new ice for him every morning to keep the food fresh. He was very proud of that, wasn't he, and I think he hoped to impress his Air clientele with it. And the seafood there and at other restaurants – quite superb. No complaints about the quality of dining in Town-By-The-Dunes! Although the cutlery – those whelk-shell knife blades could be rather blunt sometimes. And I recall us being entertained one evening by a very talented juggler who was a whatchemacall, a fish-in-the-air. The climax of his act had him floating three feet off the ground with at least twenty wooden balls hurtling around him, a kind of swirling blizzard of balls, a halo of balls – but I'm getting poetic again.

But perhaps the best thing of all about Town-By-The-Dunes was the simple fact that we weren't travelling any more. Our three-day stopover in Sweel wasn't much of a respite because we were merely waiting to move on, marking time, and meanwhile getting our ears bent all day long by Sha*so. And our sojourn in Tayorus – well, the 'Storm. Need I say more? At Town-By-The-Dunes we at last got the chance to be calm again. We deserved that. We deserved to be able to stop and take stock and relax, after many days on the road. And we had made first contact with Yashu, too, so in a different sense things were in motion. Rather than follow up that initial 'chance' encounter as soon as possible, it seemed prudent – as well as fore-ordained by prevision – to leave an interval before we and she met again. It wouldn't do to arouse her suspicions. It wouldn't do to give her cause to think that there was more to our first meeting than happenstance, that a plan was in any way afoot.

Three days seemed a decent length of time, and so on the third morning we set off round the island, finding our way to a place called Second-Cliff-Village. There, looking as lost and befuddled as only travellers can, we made enquiries. 'We're trying to find a young lady by the name of Yashu.' This brought us to the attention of one Siaalo, a big brawny giant of a man who wore his moustache in the style that a lot of the Li*issuans seemed to like, two long strands drooping down on either side of his chin like a fish's barbels. Siaalo informed us he was a friend of Yashu and also of her aunt, with whom Yashu lived. He had a dog who, as I recall, didn't take too kindly to you, Khollo.

[In truth, the dog growled at Elder Ayn just as much as at me. Siaalo told us not to mind – the dog simply didn't like not-of-the-archipelago people.]

Siaalo himself was marginally more amicable and said he'd show us the way to the aunt's house, on condition that he went with us. Very protective of her he was, you could tell.

So off we went. The dog, I'm happy to relate, was left behind.

The aunt, name of Liyalu, lived a short way uphill from the village in a low, one-storey dwelling which seemed to mimic the plot of land it was situated on. Its walls were as rocky as the hillside around it; its roof was thatched with the selfsame gorse that grew in ragged abundance there. Everywhere on I*il the houses were built from these materials, but in towns and villages, in numbers, houses become just houses. Whereas that solitary cottage gave the impression it had *sprouted* rather than been built. A natural outcropping that just so happened to have taken the shape of a cottage.

Liyalu was on her own. Yashu had set out at dawn to catch rabbits and had not yet returned. We were invited in and a small but wholesome meal was laid on for us. It's a tradition among the people of Li*issua that any stranger you permit across your threshold be fed the best food you have to offer. And a fine tradition I say. It also impressed me that Liyalu was prepared to invite us in on the strength of nothing more than an assertion that we had met her niece. Doubtless she would have been more cautious were the muscular Siaalo not on hand, but I admire her trustingness all the same.

She was clearly not a well woman, and that topic accounted for most of our conversation while we waited for Yashu to come home. Barely middle-aged, Liyalu was afflicted with one of those slow, terrible, terminal wasting diseases, and once I had made a tentative enquiry about it she seemed happy to talk about the symptoms and the prospect of death. I've gone on already about Wets and their beliefs – final immersion in the Great-Ocean-Beyond and all that – and I have little to add here on the subject except to say that Liyalu's composure was something to behold. Disregarding for the moment her conviction that a further life awaited her after this one's end, she was remarkably sanguine when discussing the months that lay ahead, during which her pain and debilitation would only worsen. In my time at Stonehaven I watched people succumb to all the excruciating declines the human body has to offer – cancer, stroke, creeping paralysis – but few if any of them displayed a fortitude to match Liyalu's. Most spent their final days in a paroxysm of fear and self-pity, forever needing to be reassured that they had used their time well and had lived good lives. With Liyalu as my example, you'll not see *me* indulging in that sort of weak-willed behaviour.

[!]

One other thing about her was apparent, at least to me. How can I put this delicately? Liyalu had no interest in the opposite sex. Whether she was attracted to her own sex, I don't know. I suspect so, but I suspect she was constrained from acting on her innate impulses by the desire for conformity that prevails among the people of Li*issua (and, as far as I'm aware, in all exclusively Water-Inclined communities). Responsibility to clan and to the archipelago as a whole matters above all else, and implicit in this is the requirement to procreate and continue the race. There is an intolerance toward any member of the community who, for whatever reason, fails to do his or her bit in that regard. So Liyalu, in order to avoid being ostracised, had partially ostracised herself by living apart from her fellow-islanders and, save for Yashu, alone. I don't know for sure if I'm right about her. But the evidence was strong, not least in her attitude toward Siaalo – the wide-eyed blitheness with which she ignored his blind devotion.

And then Yashu turned up, bearing proof of her prowess with bait and snare: two juicy rabbit carcasses. I'd have been surprised if she had been glad to see us. (A figure of speech, by the way. There is little that surprises a previsionary.) But in the event she performed the most spectacular flounce when she entered the cottage and found us there. Barely breaking stride, off to the kitchen she went. A breathtaking imperiousness! We might as well have been shit on her shoe sole, for all the level of respect she accorded us.

Her aunt managed to coax her back, and what followed saw the pair of them, her and Yashu, lured and noosed as surely as those two rabbits had been. I'm not bragging here. It was almost too easy. All I had to do was play the innocent – the typical unworldly Air Inclined. Liyalu did the rest. Perhaps she wanted it. Perhaps she had had a pretty good idea, when two Air types turned up at her door claiming acquaintance with her niece, what would ensue. It's possible she was tired of the dissembling, relieved to get it all out in the open at last. She had kept Yashu in the dark about her Inclination for two years, long enough for the guilt to fester until it was more than she could bear. Having someone come along to lance the emotional boil for her – perhaps, in the end, she was using me no less than I was using her. I don't know.

[For what it's worth, I'm inclined to agree with Elder Ayn. I think Liyalu sensed the game was up as soon as she opened the door to us. Looking back, I can see, or imagine I can see, glad resignation in her eyes as she ushered us into the cottage. As I replay the moment over and over in my mind's eye – there, yes, the transition from one kind of welcome to another.]

It was over rather quickly. The conversation, my contrived blunder. Not five minutes after Yashu arrived back home, you and I were taking our leave, in a suitable state of embarrassment. The hints I dropped about Yashu's Inclination could not have been less subtle. 'Like knows like,' I said. And I also made some play on the word *extraordinary*, allowing Liyalu her last opportunity to maintain, unconvincingly, the pretence that her niece was 'without-Flow'. I made out that I was curious to know how Yashu, as an Air Inclined, fared on an island where everyone else was a Wet. I stopped just short of blurting out that I knew she was a sooth-seer. That would have been a step too far. Showing all my tiles at once, so to speak. But again, a broad hint or two. After all, it was likely, once I'd recognised her as belonging to my own Inclination, that I'd also be able to intuit which class of Air Inclined she was. As the wise Corval says, 'A black cat looks at a tabby cat and can tell it is a cat but a cat of a different colour. It can also tell it is a cat that is not the same colour as a ginger cat, say, or a tortoiseshell cat.' You will of course, Khollo, check the quotation for accuracy.

I must admit to a certain pride at the way I orchestrated the whole event. I don't think I could have managed it any better. And you, my young friend, played your part admirably.

[Said with some sarcasm. I contributed nothing to the conversation. The way Elder Ayn was manipulating these people left me feeling deeply uncomfortable, and although I could, I suppose, have backed him up with a comment here and there, would it have helped? I doubt it. I didn't have his artfulness, or his shamelessness. Anything I said would have come out sounding absurd and sham and would have undermined his efforts rather than bolstered them. My best option seemed to be to keep silent. I made it easier by stuffing my mouth with food. Delicious cheese, tough salty bread, washed down with potent *sirassi*. While Elder Ayn insulted Liyalu's hospitality with his behaviour, I wholeheartedly embraced it.]

Now then, did anything else of note happen that day?

['Perhaps you could mention our journey back to Town-By-The-Dunes.']

Why? What about it? It was uneventful. Other than the fact that you had to turn back after we'd been walking for about ten minutes because you'd left something behind at Liyalu's house.

['My waistcoat. I left it on my chair there.']

Yes, that's it. Careless of you. Presumably you don't want such absent-mindedness preserved for posterity?

['No.']

Well, good.

['But then when I caught up with you again on the coastal track, I asked you how was it possible that Yashu could have had no idea about her Inclination, not even an inkling.']

Ah yes. Trying to beef up your role in the narrative, are you?

['Not at all. I just thought it was something that might—']

Only teasing, only teasing. As I recall, I was able to answer you by relating part of the conversation I was to have with Yashu the next day. But shall we deal with that when we actually get to it? All things in order and order in all things. Impetuous youth.

So the next morning, Yashu came to see us. Poor child, she looked wretched. As if she hadn't slept a wink. Wrung out. But then that was only to be expected. She'd just had the rug whisked out from under her. Everything she had come to understand about her life turned out to be not as she thought it was. And she had recently experienced her first 'Storm visit too, and it had brought about the death of her boyfriend, did I mention that? I didn't? Well, I hadn't actually been told then. Liyalu spoke of a bereavement, but it wasn't until later that I found out that the person who died was the boy she was intending to marry.

['All things in order, Elder Ayn?']

That's enough cheek from you!

We were breakfasting in the hotel dining room when our hotelier informed us we had a caller. In she came, and it struck me she must have been walking since well before sunrise in order to reach us so early in the day. Poor, hollow-eyed, ashen-faced, angry creature. I'd have felt sorry for her, had I not known that her sufferings then were a necessary part of the process, that good would come of them in the long run.

That's what's meant by *mala*, isn't it? I was rather hoping I'd be able to work in a reference to *mala* during this section of the narrative, while we're still, as it were, on I*il. And now I've done so. Clever me. The central tenet of Water-Inclined life. A hope, a philosophy, an affirmation, all rolled into one. The belief that good will always come out of bad. Nothing unkind happens which won't be compensated for eventually by some related or unrelated kindness. No run of luck is so dire that it won't be redeemed, sooner or later, by a run of good fortune. A consolation to even the heaviest heart.

And they don't come much heavier-hearted than Yashu was then.

She asked for a private audience with me, and though I insisted that there was nothing she could say in front of me that she couldn't say in front of you too, she was adamant that she and I speak alone; what she had to say wasn't for an enshriner's ears. So I acceded to her request, and hence the next chunk of the narrative is drawn from my memory alone, without the benefit of Khollo Sharellam's perfect recall to affirm its accuracy or amend its inaccuracies.

To find absolute solitude, we walked down through town to Half-Moon-Bay. It was a still, windless morning, and a yellowish sea-mist hung over the island. Yashu told me the islanders call this kind of mist *usurraña* – check spelling, please – which is a word related to the word for Flow but has a negative connotation. It means, in effect, a thing which fails to move or allow movement. The islanders hate it, apparently. Few fishermen venture out in such conditions. People as a whole tend to remain indoors. The mist brings a kind of stasis, and thus upsets the natural order – the natural order, for islanders, being a state of constant flux. And I have to say there was something about the smell and the thickness and the stillness of the mist, something in the way it deadened sound and reduced one's field of vision to a radius of a few yards, that I found perturbing. It almost made one feel as if the world had come to a halt, as if anything beyond one's immediate sensory sphere had ceased to exist.

Yashu led me out onto the promontory at one end of Half-Moon-Bay, along a path and down some rough steps to a flat area. Directly in front of us across a narrow channel, hidden from view by the mist, there was a large rock protruding from the sea. I'd seen this rock several times already, but Yashu, in her halting, lisping Common Tongue, explained its importance in the lives of her people. It was where Oriñaho, the mythical founding father of Li*issua, first landed and where once a year the islanders held a ceremony, a celebration to mark the manifestation of Inclination in children of the appropriate age. They swim through a tunnel worn by the tides through the rock, just below the surface. It's a sort of 'second birth' ritual, denoting passage from one section of life to another. I knew about it already from Of-Jagged-Isle's book but I let Yashu explain it to me in her own way, with her own charming simplicity of expression. Have you noticed the way she nods sometimes when she's trying to find the right word in Common Tongue? And that little knot of concentration that forms above the bridge of her nose? But it's the dental consonants she has the greatest trouble with. Traven was the same. He'd inherited many of his speech patterns from his mother. Some say it's got to do with the actual palate-shape of the Water Inclined. It doesn't lend itself to forming hard sounds. I don't know whether that's true.

Anyway, there was Yashu outlining the nature of this ceremony to me, and accompanying her the furtive lapping of waves against the island, the general susurration of the sea, the odd lone squeal of a gull, and now and then at regular intervals this huge wailing cry coming from the northernmost tip of the island. It was, in fact, the island's name being bellowed out by a boomer, using his extraordinarily loud voice to warn ships at sea not to stray too close. 'I*illlll,' he cried, approximately once every other minute. 'I*illlll.'

But for all that, it still seemed like the two of us were alone in the world, a pocket of life surrounded by an awesome pallid blankness. And then Yashu began reminiscing about her own participation in the ceremony, a couple of years ago, and the sense of shame that set in as she waited in vain, or so she thought, for her Flow to appear. How could she not have known? How could she not have realised? With hindsight, it was obvious. There were several tiny incidents, moments when someone said something that made her feel jangled and uncomfortable. What she'd thought was that her apparent lack of Flow was making her over-sensitive. She was reading too much into other people's comments, attuned for personal slights, acutely conscious that people might be dropping snide remarks about her into the conversation, perceiving insult where there was none.

I hazarded that, also, islanders were on the whole honest types. She simply hadn't been exposed to the requisite degree of mendacity.

This, she agreed, was possible. Also, it wasn't as if she interacted with other islanders on a daily basis. Her aunt's semi-isolated lifestyle was also her own. She had stopped attending school in the village in order to help look after Liyalu. On an average day she would see Liyalu and perhaps Siaalo, but no one else. And Liyalu, she had learned yesterday in the course of a long heart-to-heart conversation, had developed quite a knack for not saying anything that might come across as a lie or even a half-truth. Liyalu, you see, had figured it out. Knowing her niece as she did, she had watched her behave uncharacteristically in response to certain verbal stimuli and had deduced what this signified. Given that Yashu was Air-Inclined, Liyalu had known what would be best for her: to be sent to the mainland to receive training in her Inclination. Against this she had set her own desires – the companionship of her niece, the need for someone to look after her in her illness. She had weighed the one against the other and come to a selfish decision. Who can blame her? Can you? What it meant, though, was that she must always be scrupulously honest with Yashu, or, failing that, steer clear of any statement that might contain a hint of falsehood. In other words, in order to preserve a huge, overarching lie, she had to tell the truth at all times. A lovely irony, no?

I could tell how bitter Yashu was about this. It showed in her every hesitation, her every struggle to articulate herself correctly, the gaps in her faltering mastery of the less-familiar language. It was there, too, in her bloodshot, sleep-deprived eyes. I was moved to pat her arm at one point. You know me, not much of a one for overt displays of affection, but there we were, two alone in the world, and she seemed in need of some sort of gesture of commiseration. And I told her how much I regretted being the cause of her grief, and she, dear girl, forgave me, saying it wasn't my fault. I couldn't have known. How could I have known? In fact, she said, I had done her a favour, helping to bring the truth to light, exposing Liyalu's deceit. Not that she was criticising her aunt for what she had done. She understood Liyalu's motives perfectly. If the roles were reversed, she might well have done the same. Nonetheless she couldn't help but feel betrayed. She didn't know who she could trust any more. She felt as if everyone, everything, was against her.

That was when I learned about the young man, the fiancé, who had been taken from her by the Worldstorm on its recent visit. Huaso, his name was, from Shai. I also learned about her parents, who had been killed by the 'Storm the previous time it came round, when she was just a baby. So cruel, for someone to be singled out in this fashion, to lose parents and then future husband to the 'Storm. So unfair.

I said I wondered if her resentment of her aunt might not, to some extent at least, be misplaced resentment of the 'Storm. She considered this and replied that the two were separate, although they did perhaps overlap. She added that 'resentment', in her aunt's case, was too strong a word and, in the 'Storm's case, too weak.

I then asked why she had come to see me, why she was unburdening herself to me like this. She said she wasn't sure. She said she didn't really know me, I was something of an untried quantity, words to that effect, but she felt she could talk about herself to me for that very reason. I was an outsider. Not-of-the-archipelago. And when I left I*il, I would take all these sorrows and grievances of hers with me.

I said I was honoured to be able to fulfil so useful a function! That almost raised a smile.

And then, after a brief, pensive silence, Yashu asked me about being Air-Inclined. About Stonehaven. About sooth-seeing.

The answers I gave her were short and straight. I said being Air-Inclined was in my opinion the greatest honour there could be. I said Stonehaven was not a place she need concern herself with. And I said, not being a sooth-seer myself, I couldn't really comment on it other than to say it was a highly valued commodity, the sort of skill which, on the mainland, conferred status and renown on anyone who exercised it proficiently.

All this she took on board. I could see, from her expression, the thought processes she was working through. I let the wheels in her brain turn, not prompting her, saying nothing.

If, she said, she was to be trained as a sooth-seer, she would have to go to the mainland, wouldn't she? She couldn't learn here.

How could she learn here? I said. Who would teach her?

Couldn't I teach her?

Of course not, I said. I had no intention of staying on I*il. I was just passing through. And besides, simply because I was Air-Inclined didn't make me an expert in all classes of Air Inclination.

She said sorry, she knew it was ridiculous, she just had to make sure.

I said I was flattered but it simply wasn't within my capabilities. I was a previsionary, you see. A whole different kettle of fish.

A previsionary, she said. I knew the future.

My future, I said. Not the future of anyone else. At least, not of anyone else who wasn't in some way involved in mine.

And now she looked at me levelly, and even if I hadn't known what was coming I'd have known what was coming. If that makes sense. Her demeanour, her stiffening resolve – you didn't need prevision to be able to tell what she was building herself up to say.

'What if,' she said, and this is verbatim. Trust me, it is. 'What if, Mr Ayn the previsionary, I come travelling with you. You and your friend. To the mainland. So that I can see the mainland. So that I can see what life might be like for me as a sooth-seer on the mainland.'

'My dear,' I replied, and this is verbatim too, 'in so far as I already know that you'll be coming with us, my answer can only be yes.'

And with that, I feel we can bring this session to a close, Khollo.

GREGORY

25th of Drymonth – 27th of Drymonth 687

The graveyard afforded a good vantage-point. There, elevated above the town, Gregory and Ven observed the activity down at the river.

Yesterday a specially drafted Emergency Decree had gone out, requisitioning boats of all types – ferries, private dinghies, Brazier Brickfields barges – for the use of the Guild of Freemen. Under the terms of the decree, pilots and private owners had to surrender the vessels without let or hindrance and sign waivers allowing the Guild to do with them as it saw fit. Naturally there were cavils about such a draconian edict, but by and large the pilots and owners were sympathetic to the Guild's cause. Almost all of the boats, moreover, were damaged. It was possible that some owners, having checked the fine print in their insurance documents, were hoping that the Guild's plan for the boats might result in their total destruction. No policy covered Act of Worldstorm. Act of Man, however . . .

The Guild had then enlisted a team of volunteer strongs to put its plan into action. It would have been quicker and simpler to solicit the services of a few shapers-of-water, the very pilots the boats had been commandeered from, but Penresford was primarily an Earther town and this was primarily an Earther fight. There was something pleasingly symbolic, too, about having all those clay-miners and dock-workers out in force on the river. The town was making its own case to itself. Through the efforts of these men Penresford was able to remind itself how proud it was of its manual labourers and how insulted it felt that such fine upstanding fellows should find themselves in such desperate straits that *this* was what they had to resort to.

Shortly after breakfast, the strongs set to work. First, a pair of them drove a stanchion into the nearside bank just upstream of the town and moored a boat to it. Then some of them swam out into the river and held the boat horizontal against the current while others got on board and hauled a second boat out alongside it. They roped this boat to the first one, and the strongs in the water held the second boat in place while a third boat was brought into play. Thus a chain of river craft was built, extending all the way across the Seray to the far bank, where the last boat in line was secured to another stanchion. Just downstream of the town, an identical chain was built. Two segmented barricades were created, and the river was effectively blocked to traffic.

It took the best part of the morning to complete the job, and from the graveyard Gregory and Ven watched from start to finish, almost awed. If proof were needed that Penresford meant business, the barricading of the river was it. There was no question now: this was a town that wasn't going to take any more nonsense from those Flamers up in Stammeldon. And the embargo did not involve just Stammeldon now. Every town along the river, anyone who used the Seray to conduct trade and needed to navigate past Penresford in either direction, was going to be affected. The barricading represented a significant raising of the stakes.

'Do you think your dad'll be pissed off they're using his barges?' Ven said, while the last boat was being manhandled into position.

'I think my dad'll be pissed off whatever,' Gregory replied.

'Perhaps it'll help, though. Perhaps it'll convince him to try and get Mayor Bringlight to change his mind. You know, his own boats.'

It gave Gregory some satisfaction to say, 'If you ask me it'll do exactly the opposite. You don't know my dad. He has a terrible temper. I remember my mum seeming to spend half her life trying to get him to calm down. Sam at work, too. He just loses it sometimes. Screams and shouts and sets fire to things. Willem and I used to have to creep around whenever we heard him start. He'd go quiet to begin with. Like a kettle before it starts to whistle. You didn't want to get in his way when he went quiet like that.'

'And the barges . . .'

Gregory shook his head. 'We'll probably be able to hear him explode from here.'

'You're not at all like him, are you?' Ven said, after a while.

'I look like him. But I'm not *like* him.' Gregory held up his hands. An unconscious gesture, but he realised it illustrated his point nicely. 'Things don't get to me the way they do to him.'

Ven nodded, and glanced around the graveyard. The newer graves were already beginning to settle in, losing their humped definition, smoothing down. Soon they would be flat and overgrown with wildflowers and scrubby grass, like all the others.

'Do you think,' he said, sobered by the sight of the dead-and-buried, 'that it's going to turn violent?' He waved in the direction of the river. 'All this?'

'I don't know.'

'Some people are saying so. Me, I hope not'

'Me either.'

'But if it does, I'm prepared to get involved. I mean, this is my town, isn't it. My home.'

'I'm prepared to get involved too.'

'Honestly?'

'Honestly,' Gregory said. 'But I doubt it'll come to that. They'll get wind of it up in Charne. The government will step in.'

'You think?'

'It's likely. Well, possible. Certainly if it looks as if there's going to be violence, they'll send a squad of constables down, or soldiers, to sort it out. They'll have to.'

Ven was consoled by that thought, and would have said so had he not been interrupted by a loud, plaintive squeak from his stomach. Both boys decided to head home for lunch. There wouldn't be much to eat. The Guild was already advising that food be rationed and was doling out supplies from its stocks parsimoniously. A small meal, however, was better than nothing.

As they left the graveyard, passing between the tall drystone pillars that marked the entrance, Gregory took a look back over his shoulder. He was used now to the strangeness of the idea of planting the dead underground instead of incinerating them. It was a bit creepy to think of bodies rotting away in the earth rather than being scattered as ashes. (Burning, surely, was a much *cleaner* fate.) But he could accept it all the same, because it was the Earther way. What he didn't like about the graveyard, and would never get used to, was the small cairn that was placed on top of each grave, with a name carved into the topmost stone. As if the human remains below still, somehow, deserved to be called something. As if those who had gone still lived. Remember the dead, yes. But give them something to remember themselves by?

This got him wondering if, with his Fire upbringing, he would ever truly, completely, comfortably be an Earther. His willingness to fight for Penresford was surely a sign of which Inclination he belonged to. But was he siding with Penresford or taking a stand against Stammel-don? The two weren't necessarily the same. Was there not an element of spitefulness in his decision to stay here? Vengefulness? And if, when all was said and done, he was just getting back at his father, didn't that make him *like* his father?

Following Ven downhill to Penresford, he resolved not to care. He was making a point, that was all. Erecting barricades of his own. The chances that they would be put to the test? Minimal, he thought.

It didn't take long for word of the Penresford blockade to reach

Stammeldon. That kind of news travelled fast on the telepath network and almost as fast along the Seray itself, pilot passing it to pilot.

The telepaths, for all that they affected an air of high-minded professional detachment, loved nothing better than a sensational turn of events, a dramatic public incident. They spread it about with the eagerness of backyard gossips, lobbing their thoughts across the empty miles between them and almost immediately getting back the psychic equivalent of 'well I never' and 'tell me more' from everyone within range. The Penresford blockade had the network quivering like a breeze-blown spider web. Soon every bureau in Jarraine knew, and then every bureau in Jarraine's contiguous neighbours, and then every bureau in the northern half of the continent. At that, the news reached its natural limits. No one further out was much concerned about a local spot of bother in Jarraine. But within the radius of those close enough for it to be of interest, the initial message and regular updates raced to and fro, and the tone in which they were communicated was something akin to glee.

As for the pilots, they never made any bones about the fact that they ran titbits of information up and down the river. In part it was the currency of the job. You needed to know if there was a sinking, say, or a landslip somewhere along the Seray's length, or a temporary dearth of dock space at a certain town, or an upping of the portage fees at one of the toll stages. These things were vital if you were to discharge your piloting duties properly. But there was no denying, too, that the pilots regarded themselves as an elite, an exclusive club, and often as not the exchange of relevant data across saloon bar tables or from boat to boat, in Water language, was a means of affirming occupational solidarity. As long as you were up to date with all that was going on along the river, you were part of the brotherhood.

In Stammeldon, reports of the blockade filtered out among each of the two dominant-Inclination populations from two separate points of origin. For the Fire Inclined, it was the telepath bureau. For the Earth Inclined, it was a ferry pilot. The typically more affluent Flamers, who formed the majority of the telepath bureau's clientele, found out what was happening almost as soon as it happened. The typically less affluent Earthers had to make do with learning about it a little later, after the ferry pilot had got off shift and hurried as fast as he could to the nearest pub.

Reaction to the news was, similarly, divided along Inclination lines. The Flamers were, almost without exception, outraged and indignant. They muttered about monstrous ingratitude and castigated a sort of behaviour which, really, if you thought about it, was little short of mutiny. The Earthers on the whole took a more lenient view. The

Penresfordians' move was a proportionate response to the provocation they had received. What other option did they have? Just roll over and take it? On one point both Flamers and Earthers were in agreement: something must be done. But here, still, the disunity persisted, because on one side it was generally felt that a large contingent of men should be sent down to break the blockade by force and on the other side it was generally felt that a small diplomatic mission should be sent down to listen to the Penresfordians, find out what they wanted in return for ending the blockade, and, if it wasn't too much, give it to them.

For Tremond Brazier and Mayor Bringlight, there was no question which course of action was preferable. In fact, as far as they were concerned there *was* no other course of action. At a meeting in Tremond's office at the brickfields, the two men found they differed in only one regard, and that was whether to inform the national authorities about what they were proposing to do before or after they set about doing it. For Mayor Bringlight, political expediency dictated that he should at the very least tell Stammeldon's parliamentary representative, Stev Wilkley, that he meant to resolve the problem by action rather than negotiation. Tremond, however, pointed out that Wilkley would be constrained to go directly to parliament and relay the mayor's stated intentions to the assembled representatives, and the consensus response would undoubtedly be to order the deployment of a peacekeeping squad to head for Penresford and intervene. Soldiers from the garrison at Fort Marenkine could reach Penresford within a day, within a few hours if cavalry were mobilised. The matter would no longer be in the mayor's hands.

'But I can't not tell Wilkley,' Bringlight said. 'The terms of office are quite strict on that. "Any extension of jurisdiction beyond the municipal limits must be authorised by—"'

'What's with you, man?' snapped Tremond. 'A sudden attack of conscience?'

'The position of mayor demands the observation of certain protocols,' Bringlight said, with great exactness, and not a little regret. 'If I'm not seen to be following the rules, I could lose my job.'

'But the crucial word there is "seen". What matters is not that you tell Wilkley, but what you tell him.'

The mayor had no difficulty grasping this concept. 'I suppose I could say something like I'm taking a "vigorous, robust approach" to the matter, and leave it at that.'

'Better yet, say you're "pursuing the most profitable and immediately effective line of attack". The truth's all there. It's just a matter of interpretation.'

'Excellent. Give me a moment to write that down.'

'The point is,' Tremond said, as Bringlight scribbled on a piece of paper, 'in Charne they'll already have heard what's going on in Penresford, but if you can convince them via Wilkley that it's under control, that you're taking command of the situation, they won't lift a finger. Use soldiers? Especially cavalry? If parliament can find any excuse not to go to that expense, it'll take it.'

Bringlight shook his head, wondering at himself. 'I don't know what got into me. I must not have my head on straight this morning. Sometimes, you know, this job, you'd think you weren't actually allowed to do *anything*. All the rules and conditions attached to it – they seem there to hinder rather than help. You'd think a mayor could do as he pleases, get whatever he wants. But oh no. Try and change something, nine times out of ten you'll find there's some obscure bylaw that says you can't. You want to improve the controls on the rights of sitting tenants, say. Lo and behold it turns out that you'd have to amend the whole town constitution, and to do that—'

'Let's just stick to the problem at hand, shall we?' Tremond said with an impatient twitch.

'Yes. Yes, of course. It's just that I envy you sometimes, Tremond. No strictures on what you can and can't achieve, are there?'

Tremond dismissed the remark, not believing for one moment that it was meant sincerely. 'Anyway,' he said, 'in this particular instance the constitution's working in your favour. The Threats to Municipal Security clause – that licenses you to take pretty much whatever action you wish against Penresford.'

'Let us thank our forebears for wording it so loosely. Your grand-father in particular.'

'Indeed,' said Tremond, neutrally. 'Now then, your next task, after you've sent a message to Wilkley, is to get some men together.'

'Obviously.'

'Mostly Fire Inclined, I'd say. Incendiaries, swifts, with a couple of recuperators in support.'

'No indestructibles? No strongs?'

'Indestructibles, yes, but as long as they're constables. They'll have to obey your orders, and anyway they'll be squarely on our side. Rule of law and all that. As for strongs . . .' He gave a shrug.

'You have dozens on your payroll.'

'So?'

'These are men who owe you their jobs. Their livelihoods. And right now they're sitting idle, and still drawing a salary, no? They'll do whatever you ask them to. If they've got any sense, that is.'

'I'm minded to think they won't,' Tremond said. 'Earther sentiment is almost entirely in favour of what Penresford's up to. Inclination loyalty could prove stronger than company loyalty.'

'And of course you don't want to risk splitting your workforce down the middle or even losing employees over this.'

'You're right, I don't. Not if I don't have to.'

'Couldn't you get your tame Browndirt – what's his name? Gove? Couldn't you get him to rouse your Earther workforce to action? Someone who speaks their language, as it were.'

'Don't call him that. I find that insulting.'

Bringlight said nothing, merely arched one sandy eyebrow.

'And the answer is no,' said Tremond. 'For one thing, Sam's not around to ask. He went upriver yesterday, to the interchange depot where we transfer bricks from river barges to canal barges. The loaders up there are grumbling about the blockade and lack of work. I sent him to pacify them. He's good at that.'

Sam need not have gone. The grumbling was nothing more than the usual gripe of strong-class workers with time on their hands, pretending they disliked idleness when in fact, as long as they were still getting paid, they liked nothing more. Tremond had sent Sam up there because he had wanted him elsewhere. Sometimes it was that easy to dispense with your conscience.

'But even if he were here, I wouldn't ask him,' Tremond continued. 'I don't think we can or should rely on any Earthers to help us, other than constables. It would be a mistake to try.'

'I have tenants who are strongs. And indestructibles. I'm sure some of them would be willing to go to Penresford, given the right, shall we say, incentive.'

'It would be a mistake,' Tremond repeated.

'Well, we'll see.'

'I mean it, Jarnley. When they get there they might refuse to take part. They might even defect to the other side. Trust me: just Fire Inclined, plus indestructible-class constables.'

The mayor was reluctant to concede the argument but, in the end, made acquiescent noises.

'It's not as if there aren't going to be strongs facing us,' he said. 'Hundreds of them, I expect. But seeing as you're so set on the idea . . .'

'Even a strong,' said Tremond, 'can be burnt. Remember your elements strategy: Fire trumps Earth almost every time.'

'Depending on numbers.'

'Even so. Now, one last thing. Am I right in thinking you're taking Reehan with you to Penresford?'

'You are.'

'Are you sure that's wise?'

'On balance, yes. Reehan's furious about all this. When I told him about that Loffin fellow threatening me in my office – he even came to inspect the finger marks in my desk, to see the evidence for himself. And he can't help telling everyone he meets about it. He's absolutely incensed by it. So, you know, for him this isn't just Penresford versus Stammeldon, it's a direct personal affront. An attack on his dad. I don't think I could stop him going if I tried, short of locking him in his bedroom, and even then I know he'd escape and find a way of getting down to Penresford on his own. So it seems a better idea just to have him with me. Keep him where I can keep an eye on him. And I can't say I'm not touched. A son getting so angry and protective on his old man's account. Means I raised him right, didn't I?'

Tremond nodded, wondering if anything was being implied by that last remark. He had been freshly re-sensitised on the subject of sons. 'I'm concerned because Willem wants to go too,' he said.

'Does he?'

'He asked me this morning, shortly after breakfast. Well, told me really. Said if people were heading down to Penresford to sort out the blockade, he wanted to be a part of it.'

'And you said?'

'I fobbed him off with something like, "No decision's been made yet". Now, I suspect your boy's probably had some influence on him here.'

'And that's a bad thing?'

'Not at all, not at all. But Willem's headstrong. He's like his mother in that respect.'

'And like his father.'

'Well, perhaps. Headstrong and obstinate. Once an idea's planted in his head, it stays planted. And while I'm not exactly against the idea of him going, I'm not exactly for it either. Things could get heated down in Penresford.'

'Pun intended?'

'Slightly intended. And I realise he's eighteen now, almost a man, but still . . .'

'But still you can't stop thinking of him as your baby boy.'

'True.'

'They're never really grown up, are they? No matter how old they get. No matter how much *they* think they're grown up.' Mayor Bringlight chuckled, a close approximation of fond paternal despair. 'But listen, Tremond, that's the thing about it. Our boys *are* adults. Old enough to vote, marry, do whatever they please. And because they're adults we have to let them be free to make their own choices.

We can't keep on coddling them. I mean, Willem's already learning his way around at the factory, right? You're grooming him for the day he takes over the business. Now, that day may be far in the future, but in the meantime you're going to have to let him make decisions. Think for himself. Make mistakes if he has to. Mistakes he can learn from. It's just the way it has to be, if he's to learn to stand on his own two feet as the proprietor of Brazier Brickfields. You have to take a step back and watch him find his own way.'

'Letting him go to Penresford is helping him find his own way?'

'I think so. Just let him have the experience.'

'Even if it could get dangerous?'

'How much money have you spent on his training?' said the mayor. 'Five years of weekly sessions with Master Drake. I know precisely how much because I've spent the same. The best incendiary trainer in southern Jarraine, and doesn't he know it, the fees he charges. But if he's taught our boys anything, he's taught them how to look after themselves. How to defend themselves, keep themselves safe.'

'It still feels . . . irresponsible somehow.'

'To let him go off and have an adventure? On the contrary. As a responsible parent, it's what you have to do.'

'An adventure? I'd hardly call it that.'

'Maybe not, but that's how *he* regards it. And try forbidding him, see how far that gets you. If I tried forbidding Reehan, I know what would happen. I'd be wasting my breath. In fact, it would only make him ten times more determined. He'd defy me almost as a matter of principle.'

Tremond looked straight into Mayor Bringlight's pale green eyes.

'You'll look after Willem? If he goes? You'll keep an eye on him as if he's your own son?'

'I will.' The mayor nodded emphatically. 'Believe me, I will. Your lad will be fine, Tremond. And he'll think more of you for treating him like an adult.' Again, that fond, despairing chuckle. 'It's one of the great ironies of fatherhood, don't you think? Past a certain age, your child thinks more of you as a father the less you act like a father.'

Tremond half smiled. Misgivings still simmered away inside him, but he knew Jarnley Bringlight was correct. If Willem's mind was made up about joining the expedition to Penresford, he should not stand in his way.

At roughly the same time, Reehan and Willem were having a conversation which was roughly the same as that their fathers were having. They were in the open-sided pavilion at the rear of Master Sardon Drake's house, waiting for Master Drake to come out and begin the class. Also present were two of Master Drake's other senior pupils, Lukas Brandering and Francis Calder, who were practising the complicated art of interweaving two sets of flame. This demanded intense mental focus – maintaining control of the fire you yourself generated without, as tended to happen, inadvertently starting to manipulate the other person's as well. The pair were grimacing so hard they looked as if they were in the grip of terrible constipation.

By contrast, Reehan lounged against one of the stone pillars that supported the pavilion's roof, a picture of indolent indifference. No practising for him. No great urge to impress their trainer when he appeared. No need. He knew, and knew Master Drake knew, how good an incendiary he was. Master Drake himself had had to admit recently that he had little left to teach Reehan, and that Reehan was as adept and as powerful a pupil as had ever come under his tutelage. To the unbiased observer it might have seemed that this confession came through gritted teeth, that Master Drake would have preferred the truth to be otherwise, but Reehan had chosen to take what he had said at face value. To him it was nothing more, or less, than confirmation of a fact. Furthermore, when Master Drake had added that Reehan might wish to consider a career as a trainer himself, he had agreed that this was a possibility – but then why piss his life away like that?

Since then, a distinct frostiness had set in between Reehan and Master Drake, and neither of them, for his own reasons, could wait for the day – soon – when Reehan officially completed the course. The student had very much outgrown the teacher.

'What it boils down to,' Reehan was saying to Willem, 'is disrespect. They're showing disrespect for the whole of Stammeldon. They're showing disrespect for anyone who uses the Seray – all those pilots who can't earn a living at present because the river's blocked. They're showing disrespect, most of all, for your dad and mine. That's what really gets to me, and that's why, no question about it, someone's got to go down there and knock heads together.'

Willem was sitting cross-legged beside Reehan and gazing at a scorch mark on the flagstones in front of him, one of many such indelible black star-like stains, evidence of the misfires and over-enthusiasm of the countless pupils who had honed their skills here over the years. Possibly the mark he was looking at was one he himself had caused, once, when younger.

'I know, I know,' he said distractedly.

'I mean, those dents in the desk. I'll take you to see them sometime. Dad hasn't had them fixed yet. The man was leaning over. You can imagine it from how the dents are. Leaning over and looking my dad right in the eye. A strong. Could have snapped your neck just by breathing on you. And there were about ten others with him in the room, and just one of Dad. Sheer intimidation, that's what it was. Sheer bullying. But Dad stood up to him, and that's what we have to do. Stand up to those Sods. We can't just let them walk all over us.'

'I agree.'

'So you'll be coming? When everybody goes down to Penresford to break the blockade? You'll come along?'

'It's not definite yet that anyone's going. My dad said nothing's been decided.'

'Oh balls! Of course it's been decided. They'll start asking for volunteers this afternoon, just you see. My dad'll take the names, your dad'll supply the transportation – it's a done deal.'

Willem nodded slowly. 'If it's happening,' he said, after a pause, 'then yeah.'

'Yeah you'll sign up?'

Again, Willem nodded.

'Good man!' Reehan snapped a fireball to life in front of Willem and moulded it into the shape of a fist giving the thumbs-up sign. 'I knew I could count on you.'

Just then, Master Drake emerged from indoors. An elegant and dandyish figure, dressed as always in the latest styles – suit, shirt, shoes, tie, all from tailors and outfitters on Charne's famously fashionable Mawsom Street – he strolled to the pavilion and greeted his senior pupils with a small bow.

'Gentlemen.'

A chorus of 'Good afternoon, sir' came in reply, loudest and most obsequiously from Reehan.

Master Drake's eyes were unreadable behind the blue-tinted lenses of his spectacles. 'Shall we commence? Nice interweaving there, Lukas, Francis. Let's try all four of you at it. See how that works.'

And so, for the next couple of hours, nothing but toil and concentration. Even Reehan, by the session's end, was drained of energy. He and Willem made their way homeward in weary silence, and at the gate of Tempest's Bane parted company with just a few words. Willem crossed the garden and entered the house. In the hallway, a carpenter was hanging a new door to the dining room. The old door lay on its side, canted against the wall, showing off the head-sized, char-fringed hole which Tremond Brazier had put in it when he had learned about the Penresford blockade. To replace a solid teak door was not cheap. Willem often wondered if his father destroyed things in order to punish himself with the cost of replacing them. But it probably wasn't that calculated. His father just lashed out in the heat of the moment. Coughed up afterwards because he had to.

Lack of self-control – his father's greatest failing. That was why he made the mistakes he made.

And rectifying one of those mistakes was the task which lay before Willem now, and he didn't relish it but he was certain that he had no choice any more but to go ahead with it.

'Mum?'

'In the drawing room, dear.'

'You got a moment?'

'Of course. But don't keep shouting like that. Come and talk like a civilised person.'

She was on the sofa. A decanter of Aoterionese brandy was on the occasional table beside her. A balloon glass was in her hand. Willem thought it was perhaps a little early in the day for drinking, but why not? He found a glass, poured himself a shot, and sat and gently warmed the liquor before knocking it back at a gulp.

His mother seemed to be on uneasy terms with herself. Ever since Gregory's refusal to come home she had been like this. Brittle. Stiff. Worried. She looked at Willem expectantly. He wondered if, maybe, she had some idea what he was about to say. If she sensed it.

'I want to go to Penresford,' he said.

'Ah,' said his mother. Just a slight backward tilting of her head, a tiny upraising of her face. Hopeful. 'To show those Earthers what's what? To support you father and the mayor in their "firm stance" on the blockade?' She was quoting her husband from dinner last night, when he had outlined to her and Willem, as though before an audience of strangers, what he considered to be the correct and justified way of handling the Penresford situation.

'No, I'm not that bothered about that. I mean, Penresford's acting abominably, but I don't feel the blame lies entirely on their side.'

'How well put. I'm not sure I disagree with you, either.'

'But . . .'

'Yes?'

Willem wavered, then forged on, knowing that in this moment he had taken an irrevocable step.

'Gregory. I'm going to fetch Gregory. Grab him by the scruff of the neck and drag him all the way back if I have to. Fair enough, he's made his choice. His little act of rebellion. Point made. But there's taking a stand and then there's just being foolish, and I think he's crossed that line. And Sam couldn't force him to come back, could he? It was a nice try but Dad was wrong to send him in the first place. It should have been one of us. Me, in fact, if not Dad himself. Just to show we meant it: *come back*. Because Gregory's not a Penresfordian, no matter what he thinks, no matter how hard he would like to believe he is. He's a Stammeldoner. A Brazier. One of us. And someone needs to go down there and remind him of that, and the someone is me. I can tell him he's behaving like an idiot, it's not the time to be getting all shirty and self-righteous, not when there's a distinct possibility that people might start fighting. And I can also . . . well, I can also apologise to him. I think he deserves that. I can say sorry, because we now know how much he resents being sent away. He's made it clear. We thought he was all right with it. Sam seemed to think he was getting on OK down there. But he's obviously deeply unhappy about the whole thing, and maybe if I just say sorry, if he hears it from me, maybe that's all it'll take to get him to change his mind. And I don't care what anyone else thinks of me for that. I don't care if it makes me seem less loyal, less of a son. Because even if it does, it makes me feel like more a brother, and that's just as good.'

He stopped there, oddly out of breath. He realised he had not paused throughout the speech. The words had tumbled out of him in a heady rush. He gasped down a few gulps of air. He looked across to his mother. Her brandy balloon was trembling. He watched her reach for the decanter, pour some of the contents out with a tiny chatter-clink of glass on glass, and drink down the helping as though it were medicine.

Then she said: 'Yes.'

He thought that was it, but there was more.

'Yes. Good boy. Brave boy. Yes, bring him home. Enough's enough. Oh, I'm so proud of you. Of *course*. Tell him sorry. He'll come then. Tell him *I'm* sorry. I'm so sorry. We thought it was right. It *was* right. But he didn't know. He must have thought we loathed him. Why didn't I see? Why didn't I realise? Go down there, Willem. Don't tell your father that's why you're going. Go down there and get him. And when your father sees him, then he'll see. He'll understand. When Gregory's back here in the house, when we're all back together again . . .'

Willem knew his mother was crying. He also knew the tears would not show. It was a trick her mother had taught her, something all women incendiaries learned: how to evaporate tears as they sprang out, before they became visible. Women incendiaries did not have to be weak. They did not have to show sorrow if they didn't want to.

Willem settled back in his chair, warm inside from the brandy and from certainty. His mother had given her blessing. Beyond doubt now, he was following the correct course of action.

Volunteers trooped in and out of the town hall all afternoon and evening. They registered their names. They signed contracts of deputisation. They were told to turn up at the Brazier Brickfields docks by no later than eight tomorrow morning. Bring few personal belongings – just a change of clothes and enough food for three days.

Surprisingly, given Tremond Brazier's sensible admonition to Mayor Bringlight, several of those who signed up were strongs, tenants of properties the mayor owned. They evinced little happiness about volunteering. They added their names to the list with a surly, grudging air. To join the expedition, however, was preferable to the alternative, which was a fifty per cent increase in their rent.

Night fell, dawn came, and on a morning that was unusually balmy for the time of year, summer in autumn, more Fire season than Earth season, nearly two hundred men and women gathered at the brickfields docks. The mood was festive, convivial, as though they were all off on some holiday jaunt, not heading south for potential conflict with fellow-countrymen. In part this was bravado, in part a genuine belief that no conflict would occur – the mere presence of so many incendiaries and swifts and indestructibles would be enough to persuade the Penresfordians to dismantle the blockade and yield to Stammeldon's will.

Three Brazier Brickfields barges were waiting. At Mayor Bringlight's command, the two hundred boarded. The mayor himself, with Reehan and Willem close beside him, took up position at the bow of the frontmost barge. He yelled to its pilot, and the boat slewed away from the dockside. The other two followed. A cheer went up from the assembled company as the barges moved downstream in convoy. On the town-side bank of the Seray, a host of Stammeldoners had turned out to witness the departure and wave the expedition on its way. Again, festive. Hats fluttering to and fro. Friends calling across the water to friends. The rightness of the expedition's purpose unquestioned. The barges came to the end of the reach, rounded the bend, vanished from view.

Tremond Brazier did not watch their departure. He was present at the mustering on the docks, but soon saw that it was Jarnley Bringlight's show, his own presence supernumerary. A quick, manful handshake with Willem was both a sealing and a parting. Tremond took himself off to his office and stayed there till the hubbub on the docks dwindled away.

What did he think about? Mostly he thought about his father, for reasons he could not quite understand. Alton Brazier: a stern and unforgiving man, who raised his only son as though cultivating a professional successor, nothing more. For Alton Brazier, the business was all. Family was an obligation, but the brickfields a compulsion. He ran it forcefully, tightly, commandingly, amplifying on what *his* father had begun, turning a going concern into a market leader. His notion of small talk with his son was to describe how he had cajoled such-and-such a building firm into placing an order twenty per cent larger than it had intended to, or to crow over the latest 'Storm visit and ask Tremond to estimate the projected damage-to-profit ratio. Friendless and proud of it, Alton Brazier lived to work. He did not care that he was not well liked by his employees or by Stammeldon in general. Nor would he have cared that the crowds who turned out in such numbers at his public cremation were not there to commemorate his passing so much as to watch the old bastard burn.

Tremond considered himself both a better boss and a better parent. He had learned from his father what to do and also what not to. He had tried his best with Willem and Gregory. Gregory, he felt, was lost to him now, but that was not his fault, it was Gregory's. Willem?

A strange ache. He thought of Willem just now on the docks, looking so tall, so resolute, so like a man. He had had no choice but to give his consent when Willem asked last night to be allowed to join the expedition. That was what good parenting was about, wasn't it? Abdicating to your children responsibility for their own lives. As Jarnley had said: *Past a certain age, your child thinks more of you as a father the less you act like a father.* When they were old enough, they had to be let free in order for you and them to remain on good terms. Tremond's father had not let him free. Even when Tremond was nominally in charge of the brickfields, his father had been there all the time, breathing over his shoulder. As a consequence, he now felt nothing but a dull contempt for the man. He couldn't bear the idea of Willem feeling the same way about him when he was gone. So this was a test, then – of the breadth of his love for Willem, of Willem's independence, and ultimately of the dissimilarity between Alton Brazier and Tremond Brazier. Marita, when learning of his decision to allow Willem to go, had congratulated him. She had told him he was very brave, he was doing a good thing. He hoped she was right.

And yet . . . misgivings. Still, the misgivings.

Tremond studied the singed family portrait on his desk. He must get a new frame for that.

And now all was quiet outside, and he was alone on the premises. He went out to the docks and stood. The three barges were long out of sight. The brickfields seemed preternaturally quiet. A breeze scuttered across the main yard, twirling dust. The Seray tapped at the dock pilings like a myriad clocks ticking. Tremond, entirely at a loss what to do with himself, just stood.

No sooner were the barges embarked on their journey than news of it flashed north, east, west and south. Those telepathic tattletales couldn't keep their mind-tongues from wagging. From receptive brain to receptive brain, the images travelled. Three boats. Two hundred Stammeldoners. Downstream. And while they worked, the telepaths stayed attuned for further developments, which came piggybacking in with regular messages. Even bureau employees who were off-duty kept their awareness heightened, tapping into the network when they should have been sleeping or resting or simply enjoying their free time. It was not strictly allowed. Listening in while you weren't a functioning part of the system contravened the telepathic code of conduct. But it was common practice when exciting events were unfolding. And who could stop you? Who, apart from other telepaths, would even know?

In Penresford, it was time to get ready. Horm Loffin took charge, marshalling the townsfolk, the civilian foot soldiers who were his to deploy and who were willing to carry out whatever was asked of them. He sent sharp-sights upriver to find high ground and act as lookouts (though Water-Inclined, they were willing to pitch in and do their bit). With them went strongs who could run back with a warning when the Stammeldoners came into view. The strongs might not be fast – they certainly weren't swifts – but they wouldn't tire, they would plod energetically and remorselessly all the way.

Loffin then ordered several dozen indestructibles to man the chains of boats. The chains weren't expected to hold if attacked. Incendiaries could easily burn through the ropes which tethered the boats together and the planks which had been lashed between them to provide access from one vessel to the next. They could, if it came to it, burn the boats themselves. But they would be reluctant to do so if they saw men and women aboard; and if for some reason such scruples did not manifest, or were overcome, better for it to be indestructibles on the vessels than members of any other Inclination class.

Along either bank of the Seray, Loffin situated groups of strongs at regular intervals. He suggested that the male ones, by far the majority, take off their shirts and go bare-chested when the Stammeldon expedition arrived. Strongs seldom needed an excuse to strip to the waist, and in this instance it seemed like a better than usual idea. Broad ribcages, brawny torsos, bunched muscles – an intimidating display of physical might.

And intimidating display was what it was all about. The Guild of

184

Freemen hoped to deter the Stammeldon blockade breakers through sheer numbers. At least six hundred townspeople were out on show, beating the Stammeldon contingent by a ratio of three to one. Such overwhelming odds would surely make the Stammeldoners think again before launching any aggressive action. At the very least it would convince whoever was their spokesman to come forward with arms aloft and sue for dialogue. That was all the Guild wanted: face-to-face negotiation, diplomacy backed up by the implicit threat of force.

For a day and a night the Penresfordians waited. Hunger grumbled among them. A few neighbouring towns, in response to requests for food, had handed over a portion of their own meagre stocks, as a gesture of solidarity, albeit a token one. Other neighbouring towns had sent nothing but regrets, accompanied more often than not by expressions of unhappiness and disapproval. It was only to be expected. The river blockade was causing disruption throughout the vicinity and making life harder for people whose lives had already been made hard by the 'Storm visit. There was also, it seemed, no great depth of sympathy for the stand Penresford was taking. In principle it was fine to lock horns with another town, especially a wealthy one like Stammeldon, if you felt the other town had mistreated you. But there was no need to take matters this far, to get so militant. The way to resolve a dispute of this nature was take it to parliament and argue it out there. Jarraine had laws and everyone was governed by them. Whatever the provocation, no one entity – no person, no town – was entitled to act outside the law, just because it felt like it.

The Guild found itself able to shrug off the criticism with little difficulty. Parliament was not the answer. Things took too long to be decided up there – the lack of food was an immediate crisis demanding an immediate solution. Also, at the last count the majority of parliamentary representatives were Fire-Inclined, and no prizes for guessing which way *they* would bend in a debate on the rights and wrongs of the issue. Rather than force Stammeldon into doing what it ought, parliament was far more likely to congratulate it on adopting a fair and pragmatic line with Penresford. And who paid the greater amount annually in taxes, Stammeldon or Penresford? Tax revenue was always a measure of a town's favour in parliament.

More than that, though, there was a sense that Penresford *must* take strong action with Stammeldon; *must* respond to Mayor Bringlight's bullying like for like. And if one of the penalties for that was hunger, then so be it. And if it made Penresford a pariah within the region, then, again, so be it. Some things were more important than personal comfort or public popularity.

The sun rose through an apricot-coloured haze the next morning, a much chillier morning than the last, now more Earth season than Fire, as it should be; and the sharp-sights who had stationed themselves on top of Tantray Mount two miles north of Penresford spied the trio of barges trailing into view at the furthest bend of the river. To the strongs who were with them on the mount, the boats were mere specks in the distance, dim through a low mist. The sharp-sights, however, could make out the Brazier Brickfields identification numbers on the barges' bows and could see that the crowds of people on board consisted predominantly of redheads. They could also see the sharp-sights who had been acting as night-time guides on the barges. They waved ironically to them, and the Stammeldon sharp-sights waved back. The strongs, meanwhile, limbered up and started to run.

By the time the strongs reached Penresford, they found that most people were awake anyway, after uneasy sleeps through a night nettled with anticipation. Learning of the Stammeldoners' approach, Horm Loffin set off along the town-side bank of the river, striding past his strong-class 'troops' there as they shook the stiffness out of their limbs and stoically exposed their pectorals to the air. Loffin was emboldened by the knowledge that, late yesterday evening, a dozen pilots had come forward and said that, rather than stay on the sidelines, they wanted to participate actively in the defence of Penresford like their sharp-sight brethren. They had stipulated what they wouldn't do. They wouldn't take lives and they wouldn't manipulate water already being manipulated by another pilot. Both ran contrary to their ethics. But allowing for that, the town now had an effective tactical retort to anything the Stammeldon incendiaries might try. Ideally you fought fire with Fire Inclined, but since there weren't any of those in Penresford, fighting fire with shapers-of-water was a good second-best.

Loffin dispensed encouraging words to the left and the right, reminding the strongs that a show of strength was what he wanted from them and a show of strength was most likely all that would be required. He said something similar to the indestructibles on the upstream boat chain, as he crossed over to rouse the strongs on the far-side bank. Meanwhile, other members of the Guild committee gathered at the northern end of what remained of Penresford's docks. The men wore their Guild pins on their jacket lapels, the women wore them at their necks like brooches. They wore, too, all of them, the unmistakable straight-backed air of officialdom. Looking at them, they could have been a welcoming party; they could, equally, have been generals surveying a likely battlefield.

The trio of barges continued their stately downriver progress, and as they neared Penresford the Stammeldoners on board watched as bare-chested strongs lined up along either bank. The strongs went in for a bit of flexing and tensing. The Stammeldoners countered with mock admiration, oohing and cooing appreciatively and aping the way the strongs rolled their heads on their necks and clamped and unclamped their fists. This riled the strongs. They called out insults, 'Ash-holes', 'Match-heads', the usual stuff, interspersed with saltier Earth-language curses. The Stammeldoners responded in kind. Fire language wasn't as rich in obscenity, and certainly the words didn't have the same self-explanatory gutturalness. But then Common Tongue itself abounded in anti-Earther invective, much of it ripely onomatopoeic.

Finally, the barges arrived at the blockade and came to a grudging halt, their prows just inches from the boat chain. A heavy silence fell. At the bows of the middle barge, Mayor Bringlight drew himself to his full height, such as it was, and scanned around with an imperious air, trying to identify where and who his opposite number was among the Penresfordian ranks. His gaze came to rest on Horm Loffin, stationed halfway along the boat chain. A nod of acknowledgement, and a crackle of remembered antagonism, passed between the two men.

'Mr Loffin,' said the mayor, 'I shall ask this only once. Withdraw these boats from the river, resume the mining and shipping of clay, let Brazier Brickfields purchase the clay from you at the reduced rate we discussed, and Penresford will get the supplies it needs.'

Loffin paused before replying, as if to indicate he was at least giving thought to the mayor's request, not simply rejecting it out of hand. 'I can't do that. We can't do that. The terms you're offering are un-acceptable.'

'You'd rather starve?'

'We'll get by. We have help from other sources.'

'That's not what I've heard,' the mayor said. 'I've heard nobody's very happy with Penresford. All the way down here, at every town and landing, we've had people shout out support and tell us we're doing the right thing. You've not exactly endeared yourselves to anyone with all this.' He swept a hand to indicate the boat chain. 'So come on, let's call it a day, eh? Admit you're being unreasonable. Back down. Give way. Pride's all very well and fine, but—'

'Pride?' Loffin took a step forward so that his shins butted up against the gunwale of the boat he was on. At the same time his voice rose a notch. He had hoped to keep this civil, but already that hope seemed a forlorn one. 'Pride, Mayor Bringlight? Is that what you think this is about? You don't think this is about Stammeldon lording it over us, by any chance? You don't think, by any chance, this is about you taking advantage when we're in difficulties? Screwing us rather than helping us in our hour of need?'

Grumbles of assent rippled both ways along the boat chain.

'I think, Mr Loffin,' said the mayor of Stammeldon, 'that Penresford is behaving like the proverbial child in a tantrum, stamping on its own foot and making itself angrier as a result.'

'Then if that's your attitude,' said the chief secretary of the Guild of Freemen, 'you clearly have no understanding of the truth of the situation and you clearly do not comprehend that we, this town, are not going to give way to you, we're not going to back down, we're not going to let you ride roughshod all over us. The blockade and the embargo will stay in place till we get some form of concession out of you, and that's that.'

The grumbles of assent, louder now, spread out along the Seray's banks. The Stammledoners on the barges, not to be outdone, set up a malcontented murmuring of their own.

'No concessions,' said Mayor Bringlight. 'Just this offer. Last chance. Dismantle the blockade or we will dismantle it for you.'

To his right, Reehan clenched a fist and said, 'You tell him. Put the fucking Mudwallow in his place.' It was a private aside, but he nonetheless said it loud enough for everyone within a ten-yard radius to hear, Loffin included.

Loffin flicked a glance in Reehan's direction, decided the lad wasn't worth a moment of his time, and returned his gaze to the mayor.

'I truly wish,' he said, 'that we can avoid a violent confrontation.'

'As do I, Mr Loffin, as do I.'

'But if it comes to that, mayor, you'll find us no mean opposition. We outnumber you heavily. We have – I'm no military planner – but I'd say we have the strategic advantage here, being as we're surrounding you and also as we're on home turf. Your wisest course would be to turn back and go home. Taking on a whole town's worth of angered Earthers? Not a sensible move, in my book.'

'I'm treating that as a direct threat, witnessed here by several hundred people.'

'Treat it how you like. I'm just telling you how it is. What you're up against.'

'Oh, do shut up, Browndirt,' said Reehan. 'You're not scaring anyone.'

Mayor Bringlight rounded on his son. 'That's enough from you,' he snapped.

'But Dad, he's—'

'I said that's enough.'

Reehan sullenly tightened his mouth.

Loffin regarded the youngster with narrowed eyes. 'Your son, mayor? Yes. The family resemblance is unmistakable. A regular chip off the old block. For his sake, then, mayor, if not for your own, I suggest you leave. I suggest you give great consideration to whether you really wish to provoke hostilities. The risk that your own son might come to harm – is it worth it?'

Mayor Bringlight bristled. 'Another threat, Mr Loffin? I really don't like the turn this has taken. Implying that you'd hurt my son . . .'

'I never said that. I said there was a risk—'

'We all heard what you said. And we all know what you meant. If that's the kind of mentality we're dealing with here, then I can see we do indeed have no choice.'

'Mayor Bringlight—'

'Mr Loffin.' Firmly. With finality. 'I hereby declare, by the authority vested in me under the clause in the Stammeldon constitution pertaining to Threats to Municipal Security, that your blockade represents a direct violation of my town's interests and that I have no alternative but to arrange for its dismantling, by force if necessary. Now, I'm going to pull back and give you ten minutes to commence that dismantling yourselves. If, by the end of ten minutes, you haven't done so, I myself will order it to be done, using the manpower and capabilities at my disposal. Do you understand?'

Horm Loffin held the mayor's gaze for several long seconds, before delivering a slow, deep nod.

'Good,' said Mayor Bringlight. 'Then what happens next is entirely up to you. A peaceful settlement, or not. It's in your hands.'

He turned and instructed the pilots to reverse. The barges glided backward in formation until, a few hundred yards upriver, the mayor gave the command to halt. He then sent one of the barges over to the town-side bank, while his and the remaining barge pulled in at the far-side bank. Penresfordian strongs immediately began to gravitate towards these two locations, with the clear intention of discouraging anyone from attempting to disembark. The mayor made a great show of ignoring them, studiously consulting his pocket watch instead. Meanwhile, his fellow-Stammeldoners growled amongst themselves, debating whether Penresford would do the smart thing or not, and stoking themselves up – in the event that the answer was 'not' – for a fight. A couple of incendiaries collaborated in writing the name of their hometown in the air in tall fiery letters, which brought a low cheer from everyone around them, until the mayor ordered them to extinguish it. Not appropriate. Not yet. The mayor then turned to the sharp-sight on his barge. He asked if there was any sign of activity down at the blockade yet. The sharp-sight peered and shook his head. Not yet. Mayor Bringlight shrugged. The ten minutes were nearly up but he decided to give the Penresfordians a little while longer. Never let it be said that he was an ungenerous man.

Down at the docks, the Guild committee huddled in discussion. The chairwoman, Peta Trench, was minded to think that perhaps they should accede to Mayor Bringlight's demands. Anything to avoid trouble. Horm Loffin, on the other hand, was in no doubt. Surrender the blockade and they surrendered everything. If they gave in now, Penresford was as good as finished. You might as well just rename the town Lower Stammeldon. It was an emotive piece of rhetoric, and not even Loffin believed it fully, but having had to deal with Mayor Bringlight twice now, he was well past being reasonable.

Time was ebbing away. The arguments ranged to and fro. Was this worth fighting over? Was it worth potentially losing lives over? Opinion among the committee was divided almost evenly between yes and no. In the end, it could only be settled by a show of hands. Those in favour of dismantling the blockade? Those against?

Faces fell. So that was their decision. Well, fine. There it was. Even if it was a decision swung by just one vote, they would have to abide by it.

Loffin headed off towards the upstream boat chain, to relay the committee's verdict to the waiting townsfolk.

On the downstream boat chain, some distance from these events, Gregory and Ven stood with the other indestructibles, all of them craning their necks and trying to make out what was going on. It was a futile exercise, but what else could they do? They had been promised they would be kept abreast of the situation constantly, but the channels of communication had broken down the moment something interesting started to happen. As attention became focused on the three Stammeldon barges and the parley between Horm Loffin and Mayor Bringlight, the downstream boat chain was forgotten and the people there were left to squint and speculate. In the end, they resorted to trying to interpret the body language of the tiny figures upstream – how they stood, their collective gesturing – in order to glean some sense of where things were headed. This being an inexact science, about as useful as trying to read the mood of ants, they were little the wiser as a result, but at least it passed the time and kept their minds occupied.

At one point Gregory was asked for his opinion on how it all might turn out, based on nothing more than the fact that he had once been a

Stammeldoner and therefore might have some insight into the inner workings of a man like Mayor Bringlight. It wasn't just to appease a partisan audience that Gregory said he believed the mayor would be acting like a complete *pfharg*-head. He only had to remember the mayor's son to know that there were moral grounds for holding such a view; and of course there were actual grounds too, in that Mayor Bringlight had not exactly *not* been acting like a complete *pfharg*-head these past few days, had he? But *pfharg*-headedness aside, Gregory had no difficulty stating a simple, self-evident truth, that the mayor was unlikely to have amassed a force of Stammeldoners and travelled all this way if there wasn't, at least at the back of his mind, the thought that some kind of clash was inevitable. Otherwise why not come with just a small retinue? Why else bring two hundred people along with him?

It occurred to Gregory that he could have been dispensing such sage comments on the upstream boat chain, right in the thick of things. He envisioned himself in the midst of the Guild committee, serving as a sort of official Stammeldon expert, there to be consulted at every turn. It was a nice, heroic reverie, which lasted until he reminded himself to be realistic – daydreaming suggested a softness that was unbecoming of an indestructible.

Besides, he knew he was lucky to be on either of the boat chains at all. It was only by begging very hard, and refusing to take no for an answer, that he and Ven had managed to wangle themselves a place on the downstream chain just an hour ago. They had known they didn't stand a chance of getting onto the upstream one. For a start, Master Ergall was there, and Master Ergall had come out very firmly against the idea of any of his current set of pupils becoming involved in the defence of Penresford. (Meeting him in the street yesterday, Gregory had ventured the possibility of himself and Ven doing just that, to which Master Ergall had replied that if he caught either of them anywhere near the river in the next couple of days, he would person-ally beat the living shit out of them.) In addition, Gregory and Ven were aware that the downstream chain was regarded as by far the safer of the two, likely to be attacked, if at all, only after the other had been attacked.

Using this argument, they had been able to persuade the indestruct-ibles on it to let them join them, agreeing to the proviso that they would scurry back onto dry land at the first sign of trouble upstream. The adult indestructibles thought it charming that the two young lads were so determined to stand up and be counted. They also thought it significant, in a symbolic sense, that one of the two young-sters was Penresford's very own adopted Stammeldoner. Several of them had made a point of going over to Gregory and scrubbing a hand through his hair, as though he were a lucky mascot, and, perhaps, as though the three barge-loads of Stammeldoners could be ruffled and thrown into disarray as easily as a head of bright orange Flamer locks.

Finally the channels of communication reopened. Word was passed down in a series of yells that the Stammeldon barges were heading back upriver. There was some confusion as to whether this represented a full-scale retreat or just a tactical withdrawal. A short while later the matter was clarified: a tactical withdrawal. The Guild now had a ten-minute deadline to choose between surrender and continued resistance. The indestructibles on the downstream chain, almost without exception, expressed a preference for the latter. They turned to one another and punched fist against fist, a reminder of how unharmable they were, how impervious to pain.

All at once Gregory couldn't stop yawning. His yawns incited yawns from Ven. They were tired; they had been late to bed and up at dawn. But Gregory remembered that he often yawned like this before a sticks match. He moved his tongue and his mouth was crackly and dry, which was also the case before a sticks match some-times.

Nerves. He was scared.

Of course he was scared. This was real. This was big and serious and potentially terrible, and it was unfolding in front of him and he was here and he was witnessing it, and it was real. He understood that up until this moment the idea of conflict between the two towns had been remote, a theoretical possibility, something he couldn't imagine and hadn't wanted to. Now it was looking likely and he still couldn't imagine it, but the ignorance was no longer a comfort, it was alarming. He was standing on the brink of a huge unknown, with a dim grasp, at best, of the rage and mayhem that lay ahead. This wasn't like the Worldstorm. He had thought that, having lived through a 'Storm visit, there wasn't anything left to fear. He was wrong. This wasn't even comparable to the Worldstorm. This was man-created, not an accepted and expected fact of life. Unfamiliar, unpredictable. Uncharted territory.

'Ven?'

'Yes?'

'You all right?'

'. . . Yeah.'

'If you want to – you know.'

'No, let's hang on a bit. Because it might not . . .'

'OK.'

And now there was hush on the boat chain, and bodies were bent forward, eyes and ears were straining.

'Gregory?' Whispered.

'Yes?'

'You know my sister?'

'. . . Which one?'

'Eda.'

'Yes.'

'Can I just ask – what's going on there?'

'What?'

'Between the two of you?'

'What do you mean?'

'Only, she's pretty pissed off with you for some reason.'

'No idea why.'

'And girls only get that pissed off with someone they, you know, *like*.'

'Why bring this up now?'

'Because it just popped into my head. And because last night Eda wanted to know, she asked me, in a pissed-off way, but still, she wanted to know if you and I were still planning to do – well, this. What we're doing. And I said yes, and she said that I should tell you, if we did do what we're doing, not to do anything stupid.'

'Not to do anything stupid.'

'That's right. And she said she didn't care if you did do anything stupid, but she didn't want you to.'

'What sort of stupid? I mean, what's she talking about?'

'*I* don't know. Something reckless, I reckon. But she was saying it and I could tell, or I thought I could tell . . . But if you say there's nothing going on there, then there's nothing going on there.'

Gregory studied his friend's face and wondered whether to confess about huddling together with Eda during the 'Storm and about her cold-shouldering him afterwards (or had *he* cold-shouldered *her*?). Ven could act as his conduit to Eda. Perhaps, through him, he could find a way into how she was thinking and feeling. Of course he didn't care about her, just as she didn't care about him. He had made that vow to himself, hadn't he – nothing would get through to him, nothing would affect him. But still, there she was. Interested enough in him to ask her brother to carry a message about—

And then, from upriver, shouting. Loud.

A roar, a summoning-up of courage and anger.

The thunder of hundreds of throats yelling at once.

It echoed down the Seray, resounding between the banks, rolling over the rippled surface, faster than the current.

On the boat chain, everyone stiffened. Every spine straightened.
'All right,' said one of the indestructibles, softly, tensely. 'All right. Here it is. This is it. Here we go.'

YASHU

Yashu sat alone on the promontory. Mr Ayn had gone. The mist and chill were getting to him, he had said. Old lungs. Old bones.

Yashu listened to the pulse of the surf, echoless in the *usurraña*, a dead sound, a faint memory of clear-skied days.

Yashu, gazing into the blind white emptiness, tried to discern ancestral voices in the sound of the water. It was said that sometimes the spirits in the Great-Ocean-Beyond were audible here, in the earthly sea, murmuring in the lap and lull of the tide. In all forms of water they were present, and when you needed to hear them, when you needed guidance, you should listen close and carefully and their voices would come to you. If ever Yashu had needed guidance, it was now. Some kind of sign, a nudge to tell her she was aiming in the right direction. *Something*.

Huaso. Perhaps if Huaso could make himself heard . . .

But the waves were just waves, the sea just sea. The harder she listened, the more like itself it sounded. No voices there, just a senseless hiss. Water against rock. Water against rock. Unceasingly.

And Mr Ayn had spoken truth. Yashu might have had no formal training as a sooth-seer, but her instinct for falsehood was there and it had not registered a hint of a lie when he had said, 'My dear, in so far as I already know that you'll be coming with us, my answer can only be yes.' Yes she would be travelling with him. Yes she would be leaving with him and his southerner companion to go to the mainland. His Flow, his prevision, foresaw it, and her Flow, her sooth-seeing, confirmed it. Thus it could only be that way. Even if she didn't want to go, she would be going.

So in that sense it was no decision at all. Trying to consult the spirits, hoping for a whisper of help, had been futile. Even if they had spoken to her, whatever they said would have made no difference. Her immediate future was a foregone conclusion.

A relief, that. It didn't make Yashu's next task any easier: telling

Liyalu she was leaving. But a relief to know that her aunt could not or would not talk her out of it.

'I*illllll,' cried the boomer, distant, forlorn.

Getting to her feet, Yashu wondered if this was how it always was for Mr Ayn. Freedom from uncertainty. No such thing as choice. His path marked out and clear, with no forks in it, never any fear of the next step. She envied him that, and, in envying him, realised she no longer disliked him.

That wasn't to say she trusted him. Not yet, at any rate. But today, just now, here on the promontory, she had seen a new side to him. He had been a good audience. He had answered questions she had about herself and her Flow. Otherwise he had just let her talk. And he had done all this with, she thought, compassion. His old half-hairless head nodding. His eyes intent on her and solemn, sympathetic. They had got off to a bad start on Auzo's boat, she and he, and she felt now that the reason for this might well have been her wariness of mainlanders, innate in any islander. She hadn't given him the benefit of the doubt. He had told a lie, of course, but that might have been not to deceive her and Auzo but in order to cover up embarrassment. The real cause of his falling-out with the coastliner boat owner might have been something even pettier than money, something he was too ashamed to admit to. He seemed like a man for whom dignity was important, and there he had been on Auzo's boat, dripping wet, hauled from the sea like human flotsam, grateful but ashamed. So he had spun a small fabrication to hide an unsavoury truth. In which case, could she hold it against him?

These thoughts preoccupied Yashu as she strode back over the promontory and descended onto the sand of Half-Moon-Bay. She set off along the beach, keeping the rustle of the surf to her left, the dunes' silence to her right. Halfway along, she was roused from the depths of rumination by another sound, not far from her, to the rear.

Faint footfalls.

She didn't turn. She didn't call out. There was every chance the person the footfalls belonged to was simply a stray walker, traversing the beach, heading somewhere through the mist just like she was. No point in advertising her presence. She didn't feel like meeting anyone just then, having to chat. She would rather be alone.

The pattern of the footfalls was hasty and uncertain. For the next hundred or so paces Yashu continued to hear them, just behind. Closer to the shoreline than to the dunes. A kind of clumsy urgency about them.

Increasingly she had the sense that this wasn't someone who just so happened to be going the same way as her. Increasingly she had the suspicion she was being followed. She looked over her shoulder. Nothing but the mist. Perhaps she was being foolish. But then it wasn't common practice to be outdoors in *usurraña*. She wondered if the person was Mr Ayn, lost. He could have become disorientated on his way back to Town-By-The-Dunes. He could have veered off in entirely the wrong direction. But he had left her some while ago. He couldn't still be wandering around, could he?

It seemed sensible to Yashu to try and find out who the person was, before she did anything else. She swerved off to the right, treading stealthily over the sand, feeling it deepen as she neared the dunes. She clambered sidelong up the slope, digging her fingers into the sand's soft sift or hauling on clumps of grass, until she had gained height. Then, turning, she braced herself and waited, with every sense alert and projecting outward like an anemone's fronds.

The footfalls approached. Her ears detected the sound of breathing, slightly effortsome. The person was now almost directly in front of her. She started downslope, knees bent to control her progress. She kept her own breathing nice and slow and easy. She would sneak in at an angle from behind, move in close enough to see who this was, and then decide whether or not to establish contact. More likely than not, it was someone she had no interest in talking to, and so, once she had satisfied her curiosity as to the person's identity, she would simply melt back into the mist and leave whoever-it-was be. If it was Mr Ayn, however, she would make herself known and offer to guide him safely back to Town-By-The-Dunes. She couldn't, in all conscience, let him flail about here all day. Who knew when the mist was going to lift? It might last till evening.

As she gained level ground, she became aware that the footfalls had halted. She halted too and swivelled her head from side to side, listening. The sound of breathing was gone, engulfed in the sough of the waves. Where? Where had the footfalls' owner got to?

She started moving again, resuming the course she was already on. She scanned intently for footprints in the sand. There ought to be a line of them, heading left to right. Human spoor. A trail to follow.

Nothing. She reached the edge of the water and looked back. Not a mark on the beach to be seen, other than her own tracks.

This was puzzling, and a little disturbing. Was the other person playing some sort of game with her? Hide-and-seek in the mist? The trouble with *usurraña* was that it could throw your perceptions off-kilter, literally cloud them. It occurred to Yashu that maybe there had been no footfalls at all. She had imagined them, confusing them with her own heartbeat, or the rhythm of the surf. Something like that. A trick of the senses.

Not a reassuring thought, that she could befuddle herself so easily and hear things that weren't there. But more reassuring than the idea of somebody dogging her, stalking her, deliberately trying to unnerve her.

'I*illllll,' cried the boomer.

Head bowed, jaw set, Yashu began walking back towards the dunes, retracing her own steps.

And came across a line of footprints.

Fresh footprints which had not been there a few moments earlier.

Intersecting with her own at right angles.

Yashu felt a prickling all over her skin. All at once she remembered – and wished she hadn't – the creature of legend, the Walking Walrus, noted for its ability to mimic a human being. You saw the Walking Walrus, if at all, from a distance, but most of the time you saw just evidence of its presence. It was known to mislead you, making you think it was an islander, even someone you knew. If you investigated, perhaps tried to give chase, it eluded you and more often than not you ended up badly – stumbling over a cliff edge, for example. Finder-Founder Oriñaho was himself led astray once by the Walrus. Spying it from afar with his sharp-sight, and believing it to be one of his sons, he pursued it. Luckily, the penalty for his attempt to catch up with the creature was nothing worse than a dunking in the sea. For days afterwards, the seals laughed at him and the seagulls shrieked derision.

Yashu was not minded to think that here, right now, she was having an encounter with a semi-mythical manlike beast. Sometimes the stories were just that, stories. Nevertheless, the footfalls, the breathing, these footprints . . . It was hard to dispel the notion that *something* untoward was happening.

Tense as a trigger fish, Yashu peered around into the mist. Her instinct was to make for the dunes and find safety in the farmland beyond. Her legs, however, refused to comply. Whatever her brain was urging, her feet seemed to have taken root in the sand.

Then, to her left, a shape in the mist. A man's figure.

He was on her in an instant. He drove himself bodily into her. Hands clawed at her shoulder.

Her response was prompt and unthinking. She dropped her head, grabbed two fistfuls of clothing, yanked her attacker sideways and swung him over her leg. Next instant, he was flat on his back on the sand, the breath driven out of him. She didn't hesitate, launching herself forwards, landing on top of him, straddling his torso. Her hand came up, knuckles bunched.

A startled but familiar face stared up at her from between her knees.

'Khollo?'

Heaving for air, Khollo nodded.

Yashu's fist unclenched, then clenched again.

'What's going on? Were you following me?'

Khollo frowned, puzzled.

She had used her own language. He hadn't understood. She switched to Common Tongue and repeated the question.

'No,' Khollo wheezed. 'Well, yes. But not . . . I didn't . . .' He still couldn't draw a decent breath. He pointed at her thighs to indicate why. Her sitting on him. The pressure on his chest. 'Look, could you . . . I can't really . . .'

She considered whether he represented a threat or not. Not, she thought.

'Very well. I'll get off. But you stay where you are. Don't try to stand up unless I say so, or I'll lay you flat again.'

Khollo nodded assent, and Yashu eased her weight back onto her haunches and rose to her feet in one fluent movement.

Khollo sucked in a welcome lungful of air. He coughed on it, but soon was breathing more or less as normal again. Yashu, standing with her feet planted either side of him, studied him. There was sand stuck to his hair, and because of this she was reminded, pitifully, of Huaso. Huaso when he had tumbled onto the beach on the day of Swim-Through-The-Rock. Not far from this spot, up in the dunes, they had lain together and nuzzled and embraced and kissed. For the last time, if only they had known.

'So,' she said, sharply. 'Out with it. Explain.'

'I *was* following you, yes,' Khollo said. 'I just wanted to have a word with you. To talk.'

'Why come after me without saying anything? Why not call out my name?'

'I wanted to talk to you alone, and I didn't know if Elder Ayn was still with you. I thought if I was careful and caught up with you, I could see if the two of you were still together or not. And if you were, I'd have backed off. But then I lost track of you, it's confusing in this mist, and then I had the feeling that you'd heard me and I didn't want to startle you or make you think I was sneaking up on you, so I decided to backtrack, leave it for another time. I was trying to avoid something like *this* happening.' He patted the ground, implying his present position on it. 'And I managed to make it happen anyway,' he added ruefully.

'But you grabbed me. Attacked me.'

'No. That wasn't it. I just sort of ran into you. I didn't see you till suddenly you were there. I'm sorry. It was a complete accident.'

Nothing he'd said so far had given Yashu the least tingle of discomfort. He was being straight with her.

'All right then,' she said. 'You want to talk to me, alone. Here we are. Off you go.'

'Can I get up?'

'Not yet.'

One corner of Khollo's mouth tweaked sideways – a cock-eyed smile. 'You have me at a distinct disadvantage.'

'That doesn't bother me,' Yashu said.

'Funnily enough, me neither.'

He was amused. What kind of man was amused at being overpowered by a girl? And so easily too. Yashu felt she must be missing something here, some peculiar fineness of mainlander thinking.

'Yesterday,' she said, remembering. 'Yesterday you came back to our house shortly after you and Mr Ayn left. Was that to talk to me too?'

'I was hoping for a quick word. But you'd gone out. Just that friend of your aunt's was there, the big fellow, Siaalo.'

'He said you'd been. You forgot your waistcoat.'

'A pretext.'

'I don't know that word.'

'A pretence. A ruse. An excuse.'

'A lie?'

'Sort of. Not really.'

'So you have something you want to say to me that you don't want Mr Ayn to know about. What?'

'Just . . .' Khollo struggled to find a way of phrasing it. 'Well, I don't want you to think Elder Ayn is a bad man, that's all.'

'Ah. That's all.'

'You might have got the impression that he's a bit of a snob, and a liar as well, and he's both those things but not really. Forty-odd years in Stonehaven – the rest of the world is a strange place to him. In a way he finds it quite hostile, and he copes with that by behaving as though he's still officially a High Previsionary, looking down on people, treating us all as inferiors. It's just the way he is, but he means well.'

'I've begun to see that.'

Khollo was surprised. 'You have?'

'That he means well. Yes. The conversation he and I had just now. A kind man, I think, when he tries to be.'

'What did you talk about?'

'Is it any of your business?'

'Probably not. I thought you might be angry with him, though, after what happened yesterday.'

'He didn't do anything wrong. He just did what he thought was best.'

'So you're not angry with him.'

'Mr Ayn and I, if we had any differences, have settled them. And he's been very helpful.'

'How?'

'He's made me see what I need to do.'

'Which is?'

'You're full of questions, Khollo. Does it worry you, me and Mr Ayn getting on? Is that the problem here? Do I make you jealous? Are you worried I'm going to come between you and your friend?'

'He's not my friend, he's my employer,' Khollo replied. 'And no, I'm not jealous, or worried. If I was, would I be here? Would I be asking you not to judge him too harshly?'

Yashu could not deny the logic in that. In fact, she had merely been teasing Khollo. She had yet to forgive him for scaring her the way he had, making her think the Walking Walrus was after her, then bumbling into her. Even if he hadn't done any of this on purpose, she fully intended to make him pay.

'Mr Ayn,' she said, adopting a haughty tone, 'informed me that with proper training I could achieve great things as a sooth-seer.'

'But not here. Not on I*il.'

'No, of course not here.'

'And so he invited you to come back to the mainland with us.'

'No.'

'You're not coming?' The question was plaintive. Khollo seemed perturbed.

'I didn't say that. What happened was, I asked him to let me come with you, and he said yes. He looked ahead and saw that was how things were supposed to turn out anyway.'

'So you'll be travelling with us.'

'It looks that way. Is that a good thing?'

'Well, yes. Yes, it is.' Khollo levered himself up onto his elbows. 'Listen, Yashu—'

'Did I say you could get up?'

Khollo looked at himself. 'I'm not up. I'm part-way up.'

'I don't believe I gave you permission.'

'Will you give me permission if I ask nicely?'

She pretended to think about it. 'Maybe.'

'Please, I*ilyashu, by your leave, may I rise from this supine posture?'

Yashu didn't recognise the last two words but the general gist of the sentence was clear, as was the expression on Khollo's face, a sort of comical begging look. She nodded and lifted her foot over, so that she was no longer astride him. Khollo sat up, and then stood and started brushing sand off himself. She watched him as he did so. He glanced at her. She dropped her gaze.

'I'd appreciate it if this meeting remained our secret,' he said, when he was all but sand-free.

'You have secrets from your employer?'

'Just the one, now.'

'Why should Mr Ayn not know we met like this?'

'It wouldn't look good. He wouldn't like knowing I'd gone behind his back and pleaded to you on his behalf. He has his pride.'

Yes, and his dignity. More than ever Yashu was coming round to the idea that she had condemned Mr Ayn too hastily during their initial encounter. It said a lot about the man, too, that Khollo was prepared to go to the trouble of defending him to her. Obviously Mr Ayn was one of those people whose true quality took time to shine through. A sea urchin, in islander parlance – prickly on the outside, soft within.

'Fair enough,' she said. 'As you wish, it'll be our secret.'

'Promise?'

'Would I lie to you?'

'Unlike you, I'd never be able to tell if you did.'

He said this with a smile, a quick flash of his teeth, brightly white against his brown skin. Yashu was tempted to smile back. She kept her face straight, however, her expression stern. She still hadn't forgiven him yet. Not quite.

They parted company on an awkward note, in a fluster of 'so then' and 'all right' and 'well anyway'. Khollo swung round, checked his footprints to make sure he was facing in the right direction for Town-By-The-Dunes, and loped off, soon vanishing. Yashu waited till she could no longer hear him, then struck out in the opposite direction.

Oddly, she felt warm in the mist. All the way home, a sense of amusement, and the memory of Khollo sprawled there on his back, so readily bested.

Liyalu was pale, and quiet, and alone.

Yashu sat down in front of her, and for a long time there was silence. A weight of things to be said, almost too heavy for language to bear.

'Outside in *usurraña*?' Liyalu said eventually.

'It had to be done.'

'Dangerous on the coastal track. One false step . . .'

'I think it's a little late to start lecturing me. I went, I'm back safe, there it is.'

Liyalu sighed – a brittle, broken sound. She looked as unwell as Yashu had ever seen her. Her skin resembled driftwood, grained, worn. Her cheeks were indrawn, as though she was gradually crumbling from within.

But pity could not deter Yashu. Her course was set. She just had to come out with the words.

'I'm going away.'

There. Done. Said.

'Away?'

'To the mainland.'

'Where on the mainland? The mainland's a big place. It's the whole world, even.'

'I don't know where. Around. About. The point is to get away. To be anywhere but here.'

Liyalu took this on board, her eyelids half closing, turtle-slow.

'I see,' she said. 'Well, I suppose I should have expected it. From the moment that man Ayn arrived . . .'

'I don't know how long I'll be gone,' Yashu said. 'A while.'

'You intend to come back.'

'I think so.'

'You're not sure? You don't have a plan?'

'The plan is to be elsewhere. To see the mainland. To learn about not-of-the-archipelago life, not-of-the-archipelago people. Because I'm not-of-the-archipelago myself.'

'Of course you're of-the-archipelago. Don't be absurd.'

'My Flow isn't.'

'That's your Flow. That's not *you*.'

'I've spent two years thinking I didn't even have Flow. I want to make up for that time somehow, and I'm not going to manage to do that on I*il.'

She bit her tongue before anything else could come out. Unkind words, accusations, recriminations. This wasn't about making her aunt feel bad. This was about the two of them parting on the best terms possible.

'You hate me,' Liyalu said.

'I don't.'

'I wouldn't blame you if you did.'

'Look at me. I don't. But I am thinking it won't hurt either of us to be apart for a bit.'

'Hurt? No, no, perhaps not. I have plenty of pains anyway.' The implication was plain: *one more won't make a difference.*

'Aunt Liyalu, I'm not doing this because I want to, I'm doing this because I have to.'

'I was being unfair. You're right, I must let you go. I've been selfish enough as it is.'

'There'll be Siaalo. He can come up here every day.'

'Lucky me.'

'Make sure you're all right and you have everything you need. He won't mind doing that.'

'What a grim thought: Siaalo every day. A kind of punishment.' Liyalu twisted her mouth in a comical grimace.

Yashu couldn't suppress a snigger.

Liyalu sniggered too.

Yashu giggled.

Liyalu giggled.

Yashu laughed.

Liyalu laughed.

Then they were roaring with laughter, helpless with it, trying to prevent it, failing, setting themselves going again each time they failed, laughing not because anything was particularly funny but because nothing was and that was the joke. At one point Yashu protested that her sides hurt and Liyalu said, 'Imagine how *mine* feel!' and this sparked off a fresh burst of hilarity. They were red-faced. They were crying. Anyone hearing them from outside the cottage would have thought they were mad. But it felt good. It felt clean. It felt *mala*.

And the memory of that laughter carried them through the next couple of days, which would otherwise have been unbearably grim. As Yashu made preparations to leave – laying out clothes, selecting belongings and requisites from around the house, filling an old seal-hide satchel of Siaalo's with these items, then unpacking them and going through them and re-packing them – she only had to think of sitting there opposite Liyalu, the pair of them collapsed in hysterics, and a smile would come to her face and the job at hand no longer seemed so arduous and unreal. On a journey round to Town-By-The-Dunes to finalise arrangements with Mr Ayn, the hoots and chortles from down in Grey-Seal-Inlet had her hooting and chortling to herself. When the morning came that she was finally due to depart, the echo of the laughter was still there, in Liyalu's embrace, in the kisses she showered on Yashu, in her arms' reluctance to let go, in the tears that polished her eyes. Siaalo was present, and assured Yashu that her aunt would be well looked after till she returned. Black-Tail, for his part, trotted after her almost as far as Wave-Clash-Cove before he finally obeyed her commands to turn back.

Mr Ayn had booked passage on a coastliner ferry, one that regularly plied between Li*issua and the mainland. It was larger than the average boat, with a high quarterdeck at the stern where not one but two pilots stood, a pair of brothers, sharing control. It hauled out of Half-Moon-Bay at noon, after the markets had ceased trading for the day. Aboard were buyers and vendors from the mainland. Some had with them the wares they had purchased, Li*issuan produce, *sirassi,* shells, sponges and so on, which they would sell on to mainlander customers. Others were empty-handed apart from the cash profit they had made peddling mainlander goods to islanders. All had in common the replete look that came after a good morning's dealing had been done.

Mr Ayn himself had a not dissimilar look about him. Every now and then Yashu caught him watching her, and when their gazes met she would offer a nod or a smile and he would reciprocate, discreetly, courteously, then glance elsewhere. Khollo appeared ill at ease, and Yashu had no doubt why – a bad swimmer, out on the open water. Instead of sitting with Mr Ayn at the prow, he loitered amidships, as far from the gunwales as possible, as though he couldn't bear to be even within spitting distance of the sea.

The ferry bounded away from I*il. Yashu glanced back a few times, but for the most part kept her face forward. Ahead was where what mattered lay. There came a moment when she looked round and I*il was no longer visible. Its three peaks had slipped below the horizon line. That, then, was when she knew she had well and truly embarked on this journey. The past was out of sight, gone beneath the boisterous leap of the waves. Time blurred. Then: the mainland.

AYN

Ah, there you are, Khollo. No. No need to apologise. You overslept. It happens. I considered coming to wake you but then I thought, No, let him have a lie-in. Only fair. It's not as if I'm actually employing you, is it? Not as if you're getting paid by the hour to listen to my ramblings. Though I expect, when it's published, there'll be a fair few copies of this account sold. You shouldn't do too badly from the royalties.

Besides, the view from here has helped pass the time nicely. I've been up and about for a while. An uncomfortable night. That venison stew we had for supper, the boy put too much spice in it – too much for this old man's digestion anyway. So I got dressed before dawn and was able to watch the sun rise. It broke free of the mountains an hour ago, and I mean broke free. Leapt into the air as though the mountains had been holding it down. Suddenly, this cold clear flood of light sweeping down across the snow, blazing over the lake, inflaming everything as it went, bringing animation. The mist that had been draped over those trees down there began to swirl and thin, as though stirred by invisible fingers. It's all but gone now, a few lingering wisps left. The lake's surface was placid, and within moments it became all ripple and dazzle. The entire scene had been tranquil. No, not tranquil. Dead. No, not even dead. Waiting. That's it. Waiting. And then, at a stroke, life and beauty. A remarkable transformation. Look at it now. You'd never realise how dreary it was before, when everything was still and there was light behind the peaks but no energy, no fire. How empty, like a stage set waiting for the actors.

Not many more sunrises left for me. I'm resolved to be up to see each and every one, to make the most of the few mornings I have remaining.

[All this Elder Ayn said with his back to me, not turning round. He was standing at one of the windows in the room where we held our dictation sessions. Hands behind back, head erect, like somebody in an art gallery confronted with a great masterpiece.

The room – why not describe it? – was a kind of turret atop the hunting lodge, built, I reckon, largely for the spectacular views you got from it. It was cylindrical, with windows at regular intervals around the wall, each five feet across and fitted with defensively thick, expensively clear panes. There were soft chairs for lounging in, arrases to mask the bare stone of the walls, a fireplace. A convivial, clubby sort of décor. You could imagine, in summer, a hunting party relaxing there after a day spent down in the forest. A coterie of wealthy incendiaries, who had travelled up into the mountains using pack mules or perhaps a train of strong-class porters to carry their belongings, and bringing along with them a couple of professional swift-class beaters, experts at rousting and driving game animals. But of course the strongs and swifts would never be permitted into this room, unless perhaps they did double duty as butlers, serving refreshments. This would be very much an enclave for the hunters only, where they could review the day's events, swigging wine and congratulating one another on a successful kill or commiserating with one another on the one that got away – the deer that bounded into someone's sightline and he failed to take aim properly, failed to boil its brains where it stood, missed his mark and had to watch it bound away again unharmed.

I can't say I've ever understood the attraction of hunting for sport. But then I'm not a Flamer with more money than I know what to do with. With money, as they say, to burn.

Anyway . . .]

Does this remind you of home, Khollo? Of Durat?

['A little,' I said.

In truth, Durat's mountains are redder and starker and, to my mind, lovelier. The Khalon range, which fringes the Levasse Plateau where I was born, is a jagged cascade of crags, each rising to a steep pinnacle where only eagles have ever set foot. The colours – I could bore on for ages about the colours. Depending on the time of year and the time of day, the Khalons can be rust, crimson, blood-black, ochre, cherry purple, even pink. Sometimes they can be every shade of red at once. As a small boy, I once said I wished I could spend my entire life studying and naming every colour the Khalons could be. My father replied that it would be a noble occupation but one, unfortunately, that wouldn't pay well, if at all. I don't remember any of this conversation myself. It's lost in that void in my life, the blankness before I manifested. I only know about it because my parents mentioned it once when I was in my teens (they did their best to keep my early childhood alive for me, even as it slipped away from me inch by inch, vanishing from memory). I can imagine saying something of the kind. I like to think I was that sort of child.

And, now I've started, I can't help thinking about Durat and the

Levasse Plateau and can't help feeling a pang of yearning. Even though it's been a decade and a half since I was there last, and even though I am more than happy where I am right now, I would like to visit my homeland again sometime. See my house. See old friends I haven't set eyes on since I left for Stonehaven, find out how they've got on with their lives. Smell the arid, peppery wind that comes in off the steppes, hooting around the Khalons' summits. See the heat mirages that erase the mountains' lower portions sometimes, making them appear to float above the world. Hear the chant sung to the king every noontime, or rather to the queen these days. The Oath of Fealty. 'I pledge to my sovereign / By the height of the sun . . .' Durat, home to one of the world's last remaining monarchies. People think it a rather quaint place because of that, behind the times, and I've heard there have been republican stirrings in various quarters of the country, threats to hold a referendum and force an abdication if the results show the bulk of public opinion is against Queen Kharona. I hope that doesn't happen, and I don't think it *will* happen. Why discard something, simply to keep pace with modern opinion? Why get rid of something that has worked for centuries? Is democratic rule any better? What I witnessed in Jarraine (not wishing to pre-empt the sequence of Elder Ayn's narrative here) did not convince me that leaders voted into power are necessarily any better at the job than those who obtain the mantle of authority through birth. You might argue that heredity at least promises some kind of track record, some kind of precedent.

Yes, Durat. One day I should take my wife and children there and show them where I came from. They would probably hate it for its dryness and barrenness, and the journey would be long and costly. A dream, then. Let me be content with where I am and who I have become. But one day, maybe . . .

I've written all this down but it doesn't belong here. My additions to Elder Ayn's narrative are almost all of them unnecessary intrusions. It feels like a betrayal of his trust, not to let his words stand as they were spoken, to comment on his narration even as he narrates it.

Well, it wouldn't be the only time I betrayed his trust. Seeking out Yashu in the *usurraña*, to give just one small example. Hoping to convince her to accompany us, not knowing she had already decided to anyway.

There were – there have been – other, more significant examples.

In time, in time. We will come to those.

'A little,' I said to Elder Ayn. 'It never gets as cold in Durat, even in the depths of winter.']

We've been colder. This is nothing. A month ago the lake was frozen over, don't forget. Frozen solid, all but. And look.

[He huffed into the air.]

Just a fortnight ago you'd have seen my breath. Not long now. Spring. Then the passes will no longer be snowed in. The way will be clear for you, all of you, to leave. And I, I shall remain behind, scattered to the winds, nothing but birdshit and bones. Part of these mountains for ever. I can think of worse places.

Still, let's get to work, shall we? Lot of metaphorical ground to cover today. More of that travelogue stuff you have so little patience with. All the way from I*il to Jarraine. To be precise, all the way from I*il to the peaceful and scenic municipality of Penresford. Famed for its *fraternity* with Stammeldon and for the *warmth* of the reception it gives to visitors. Ha ha. Oh, I can be wicked at times, can't I?

Anyway. Departure from I*il aboard a scheduled ferry to the mainland. Yashu with us, her compliance having been secured through means that were, I'm proud to say, more fair than foul. A willing travelling companion. The first portion of our task successfully achieved.

We arrived near day's end at the port of Oöfhaleyis. I love that name. 'Twin-Ports-On-Sea' in Common Tongue, but Oöfhaleyis, isn't that just so much more evocative? What might come out when one is punched in the stomach. Oöfhaleyis!

There, we spent the night in the cleanest and most comfortable lodgings we had hitherto experienced. I have no hesitation in recommending the Hotel Hermit Crab to anyone who happens to find himself in Oöfhaleyis. Spacious rooms. Good restaurant. Nice mosaic floors. A bit on the steep side, price-wise, and not in the smartest of areas but then I'm not sure whether Oöfhaleyis actually has any smart—

Come now, enough with the rolling of the eyes, Khollo.

Oöfhaleyis is situated at the mouth of the mighty Seray, straddling its estuary on both sides, a two-part city. The sea around is thick with traffic, as is the river. Boats swarm like flies. The city, both halves of it, sprawls into the hills, unruly and ill-organised, white stucco salt-worn to a dirty grey, a veritable urban stain. An unimaginably noisy place, certainly in the district where we were staying. The streets filled with bustle and shouting from dawn till the small hours. Vibrant. With much entertainment to be found there to suit the jaded and the not-so-jaded palate.

Oöfhaleyis plays host to a million people, so it's said, most of them in transit, pausing on their way from hither to thither. And ten thousand of its residents are customs inspectors, so it's said too, although this may be an exaggeration. Men and women employed to examine freight manifests and bills of lading, impose portage fees, and generally make a nuisance of themselves. A threefold bureaucratic nuisance. Everything that enters the Seray from the sea, and vice versa, must be checked by one customs inspector and then double-checked by another and then triple-checked by yet another, to ensure that nobody avoids paying import or export duty. That's Oöfhaleyis's main source of revenue, the tax it levies on goods that pass through it. The city seems to exist for no other reason, and little wonder that one of the merchants on our ferry had muttered the wish that the World-storm would one day wipe the place off the map. Flatten it, as it flattened Old Corundum, and Horlan, and Mylle. A just punishment, he seemed to think.

This time around, the 'Storm had not obliged. Oöfhaleyis had got off relatively unscathed, with just the usual complement of ripped-up roofs and caved-in walls. One of its breakwaters, the huge groynes which reached into the sea to encircle the river mouth like warding arms, had had a hole knocked through it by the pounding waves. Strongs were rebuilding it, hefting the displaced rocks back into position. I watched them at work one afternoon, getting into a sweat, bare torsos glistening in the sun. How strongs love to toil topless and how aesthetically pleasing it is for the rest of us that they do. This was shortly after I had located a pawnbroker down near the docks, an obliging man who took some trinkets off me and converted them into the local currency and did not, I think, swindle me too egregiously.

However, the talk of the town was not, as one might expect, the recent 'Storm visit. It was events to the north, in Jarraine. There were rumours of trouble brewing upriver. A dispute welling up between the towns of Penresford and Stammeldon. Penresford aggrieved that Stammeldon had refused to come to its aid after the 'Storm left it battered and short of supplies. Stammeldon underestimating the depth of Penresford's resentment. Penresford electing to cease excavation and shipment of its primary natural resource, clay, in retaliation for an attempt by Stammeldon, exclusive purchasers of that natural resource, to extort more favourable terms of trade. Stammeldon responding with angry words and warnings of dire consequences.

All very exciting, the pavements and plazas and pubs of Oöfhaleyis rife with speculation as to what might ensue. A little flare-up taking place over the border in a neighbouring nation, far enough away for everyone to feel detached and yet close enough for everyone to be fascinated. I overheard a river pilot complaining that his journey up the Seray might fall foul of the hostilities, if hostilities did break out, but he was one of the few for whom the dispute had any direct impact, and it was economic impact rather than personal. The general mood was of restrained smugness, a sort of solemnly stifled glee. Clearly it was consoling to these people that the 'Storm had left misfortune in its wake but not here, not as badly here as elsewhere, nearby.

I met another pilot, one who was taking a cargo upriver, a consignment of cotton from Ibal, bound for Charne. He was agreeable to the idea of transporting three passengers as well, once a price had been fixed. We settled on a sum that seemed substantial but, he said, only just defrayed the cost of import duty on the cotton. I didn't need Yashu there to tell me that this was a lie, but it didn't matter. Getting where I wanted us to go, Penresford, was what mattered. If the pilot, Eezhalo by name, was making a bit more out of me than he claimed, what of it?

He was a chubby, cheery, thoroughly amiable sort, this Eezhalo, and he shared his boat with a ginger cat known by the exotically sonorous and vowelsome name of Aeio. We set off four days after our arrival in Oöfhaleyis, and straight away we discovered yet another of the tricks that the city has come up with to exploit its geographical situation, its stranglehold over the Seray's throat. You can't just head off along the river or out to sea once you've coughed up all the relevant fees and duties and whatnot. Oh no. You're obliged to hire an official escort dinghy to usher your boat out in either direction, and this according to a timetable that takes no account of the turning of the tide or anything like that. You leave when you're officially booked in to leave, and if you happen to be going upriver when the tide is in ebb and the river current at its strongest, you have to pay extra, because then your escort dinghy needs a pair of strongs on board in addition to a pilot. That's what happened with us. I had our departure ticket in hand, supplied by the Air actuaries at the dock offices. Eventually a boomer announced that it was our time to depart. Our boat was lashed tightly to the escort dinghy, both vessels set out together from the docks, and then, mid-channel, the strongs picked up a couple of largish boulders which were sitting on the deck of the escort dinghy, each secured to the prow with rope, and tossed them into the water. There's an undercurrent, you see, a continuous tidal influx down near the bed of the Seray that races inland for a mile or so before petering out. The tethered boulders drop into it and are caught by it and drag both boats along regardless of the surface current's direction of flow. It's ingenious. I don't mean this effort-saving method of propulsion, although it is quite ingenious. I mean how Oöfhaleyis manages to squeeze every last drop of income it can from those who pass through. You have to admire that level of dedication to profit.

[Elder Ayn paused here, as if inviting me (and readers?) to infer something, some subtle irony. Even now I'm not sure what it was, but I think he may have been trying to point out that he was doing all that he was doing for no material gain whatsoever. His scheme to defeat the 'Storm and change the world would not bring him wealth and prosperity. The most he could hope for was posthumous glory. So he scorned Oöfhaleyis for its acquisitiveness and praised himself, by implication, for his altruism. I think that's what it must have been.]

At last we were clear of Oöfhaleyis's clutches and making good time upstream. For the early portion of the journey Yashu kept to herself, sitting apart from the rest of us and occasionally petting Aeio the cat, who was very much second-in-command on board, a strutting feline first mate. He yowled a lot, as if giving orders, and if he wanted your attention he would stride right up to you and demand it. Why am I talking about a cat? I don't know. He was a character, that's all, that bold little orange puss.

Yashu was taking it all in, I could tell. Drinking in the sights and sounds of the mainland. Oöfhaleyis she had found intimidating – the crowds, the noise, the sheer pace of things happening there. She had confided in me that she would be happy to leave, and I could see her growing more relaxed by the minute as Eezhalo put distance between us and the city. Everything caught her eye. The other boats plying the Seray. The farm labourers on the bank, clearing out drainage ditches with shovels, slooshing the drenched fields dry. A bird of prey that hovered at the river's edge, supported by the merest twitches of its wings. The estates and small towns that dotted the landscape. A mill, its wheel revolving furiously in the current. The shape of clouds. A line of far-off hills. Some cows. All new to her, all fascinating. In a way I was similar. I, too, was seeing many of these things for the first time, after forty cloistered years in Stonehaven. But Yashu's eyes and mind were fresh. I could but imagine how her pure, untrammelled young brain was wondering at it all, the impression it was making on her. Beholding a world she had only ever heard about before and perhaps never expected to see in person.

What may have helped lessen the culture shock for her was that we were on a river, and on a stretch of river, moreover, so broad that at times one could not see the far bank. I noticed that in between bouts of looking around Yashu's gaze would turn to the water, as if she found comfort there and could anchor herself by concentrating on its turbulent surface.

Oöfhaleyis fancies itself as a separate city-state, self-contained, self-sufficient, but in fact it is part of Warlenvish and not even that country's capital. It is more like a goitre that has grown out of the national neck and become large enough to rival the head in size. It lacks true autonomy. It's an unfortunate excrescence. The proper capital of Warlenvish is, of course, Rommen Cas, and we passed through that great conurbation on our second day on the river. The City of Fallen Spires. Was it Joun Relzunk, in his *Wanderings*, who called it 'one of the most haunting and affecting spectacles man has created in many centuries of architectural endeavour'? I believe it was. Another reference for you to check there, Khollo.

[No need to check. It *was* Relzunk. I read *Wanderings* when I was in my late teens. Elder Ayn quoted him absolutely accurately.]

Rommen Cas was in its day what Oöfhaleyis is now, a gateway on the lower Seray, a bottleneck through which no vessel might pass uninspected and untolled. It has ten bridges spanning the river, and all but two of them are swing bridges or drawbridges, low to the water, unnavigable unless opened. Before Oöfhaleyis's rise to prominence – we're going back some eighty or ninety years – Rommen Cas was the place where they fleeced river traffic mercilessly, refusing to allow access without the proper permits presented and the, er, the pertinent payments proffered.

[A grin of satisfaction. Elder Ayn archly amused at his adroit alliteration.]

Money was made, too, from the dominant local industries, namely agriculture and metalsmithery. In short, there were a lot of rich people in Rommen Cas. Most of them Flamers, as is usually the case. That Fire business acumen, that innate drive they have to further themselves and succeed. Incendiaries, of course, particularly. That branch of the Inclination that has fostered itself and bred within its own ranks in order to become prevalent and dominant. And what happened at Rommen Cas was that these rich people got it into their heads that they would build towers. They would mark their place on earth by raising three-storey, four-storey, five-storey towers, hoisting them up above the rooftops, high, 'Storm-tauntingly high. And rapidly it evolved into a kind of competition to see who could flaunt their wealth the most ostentatiously, and soon the towers were up to seven storeys tall, and then eight. They were sprouting everywhere across the city, needling upwards, turning Rommen Cas into a forest of man-made trees. And each one, as it was constructed, used the sturdiest of building materials. Granite, reinforced with iron beams. Timber scorched and tempered to the hardness of stone by specialist incendiaries. Glass so thick not even the strongest strong could break it. No one would actually live in these towers. They were for show only. Inside they were bare and hollow and uninhabitable. But up they went regardless, and sure enough the Worldstorm came by and blew several of them over and cracked open several others with lightning bolts, and did Rommen Cas learn? Did its wealthy citizens come to their senses and see that the towers were costing lives as well and money? Because people were under the towers that toppled, and also a number of workmen had died while building them – falling from scaffolding, accidents like that.

The answer is no. Nobody came to their senses. Nobody learned a thing. The broken towers were repaired and new towers were erected. Higher, ever higher. Vaunting. And a few years later the 'Storm came along again and it blew down and it struck with lightning, and afterwards the rich tower builders looked around them and saw that these monuments to their own vanity were constantly getting knocked down and were sucking up endless sums of money, and of course they just went and commissioned yet more towers. And a third time the 'Storm visited . . .

This has all the hallmarks of a child's bedtime fable, doesn't it? 'And the moral of the story is . . .' Except that there isn't any real moral to this story, other than Wealth Doesn't Always Mean Wisdom. That third 'Storm visit was the longest and most ferocious of the lot, and it shattered almost every one of Rommen Cas's towers, and the crashing debris took more lives than ever before, and there was a groundswell of outrage among the populace, who had had enough of these pluto-crats and their arrogance and their folly. And what happened next was not a violent civic uprising. It was nastier than that. Lawyers were hired. The courts got involved. There were suits and claims for compensation. The tower builders of Rommen Cas got their come-uppance in the form of crippling payouts to the bereaved. They were bankrupted. And Rommen Cas was itself ruined, in more ways than one. It never recovered architecturally, nor did it recover financially. Its economic importance to the region was lost. Oöfhaleyis picked up the slack and has gone from strength to strength ever since.

What remains of Rommen Cas, though, is truly extraordinary. These lofty, mutilated, jagged spires jutting up wherever one looks. Some covered in moss. Some crowned with a stork's nest. Some with just a few slender struts of wood protruding into the sky, like questing fingers. Some revealing a lacy framework of corroded iron. Some whose gaping, crumbled window apertures resemble the eyes and mouths of tragic faces. Some with trees growing tentatively from the top. Some veined all over with ivy. Some looking alarmingly precarious, teetering on fragile foundations. Some little more than a couple of buttresses supporting a couple of walls. And the citizens of Rommen Cas, according to both Joun Relzunk and Eezhalo, don't dismantle these relics and have done with them once and for all because, one, they have become an integral part of the city and are now what Rommen Cas is most famed for, and two, they serve as a salutary reminder that the 'Storm is not to be defied and tempted and challenged. Anyone who does that, no matter how rich he is, is bound to come a cropper.

That's what they think in Rommen Cas, at any rate. And I . . . Well, what do you think? Do you think I'm going to come a cropper? I mean, other than being murdered in five days' time.

[Rhetorical question. I chose to treat it as one, at any rate.]

So we wended our way under or through all ten bridges, this mad lost dream of a cityscape all around us. These days the bridge tolls are minimal. A habitual user of this waterway such as Eezhalo simply stumps up an annual subscription and displays a licence placard somewhere nice and visible on his boat. The strongs who operate the bridge mechanisms know most of the regular pilots by sight, even by name. As a rule, they keep the bridges open, closing them only if an unfamiliar or unlicensed vessel happens along or, of course, if pedestrians wish to cross from one side of the river to the other. Saves effort and energy that way. The strongs just sit with their feet up and wave most of the boats through.

Downstream of Rommen Cas the Seray had already narrowed to a width of about three hundred yards. Upstream of Rommen Cas it narrowed still further, till it was about half that distance across. Gradually, of course. One wasn't aware of it happening, but then one noticed that boats going the opposite way were much closer than they were earlier, passing broadside with just a couple of dozen feet of clear water in between. Their pilots had faces, were people rather than just far-off, unidentifiable figures. And one began to get here a sense of the Seray as it's popularly thought of, the Seray of song and poetry and history. Odowhar's 'deep brown brackish flow / Contained but not confined / Shifting ceaselessly between unshifting banks'. The Seray celebrated in the slow movement of Maestro Toose's *Four Rivers* symphony. The Seray that is the setting for most of the action of Quillint's *The Lonely Ferryman*, and the novel's central allegorical conceit as well. A river that winds through seven different countries, that's the focal point around which nine major cities have aggregated, not to mention countless towns and villages. An artery that provides employment and industry for thousands. A fluid thread connecting disparate people and places and lives through the shared use of its waters.

At night we camped out on deck, under the stars. There was a bunk room down below that slept one, and Eezhalo offered it to Yashu in a very gallant gesture but she said she preferred to be up and outdoors, with us. She said she liked to hear the sound of the water lapping as she drifted off to sleep. We ate meals on deck as well, with Aeio prowling among us, asking for and getting scraps. Ruthless in that way cats are, as soon as one person had fed him a titbit and he had gulped it down, he moved on. He batted his eyelashes till he got what he wanted, then promptly turned around and used his charms on somebody else. Brazen little flirt.

One evening Eezhalo, by way of small talk, asked about us as travellers. He knew that two of us were from Stonehaven and the third had thrown her lot in with us on I*il. We seemed, he said, an odd bunch. 'Ill-assorted,' I think he said. Why leave Stonehaven? he asked. Where were we going?

Reasonable, innocent enquiries, and I had anticipated them and knew I must be careful with my answers. There was now a sooth-seer in our midst.

I told Eezhalo that I had quit Stonehaven following an altercation with a colleague, another Elder. I had disgraced myself in the eyes of the Council and, no longer feeling welcome within Stonehaven's walls, had taken myself away to explore a world I realised I knew all too little about. Khollo had agreed to come with me to enshrine and, who knows, perhaps one day immortalise in prose my exploits. Yashu had joined us for reasons it was not my place to divulge. Only she could reveal them to Eezhalo, if she so wished. Suffice to say that she was interested in seeing the world with us and that she made for a very pleasant and attractive fellow-traveller, no?

Eezhalo, who I could tell was rather smitten with Yashu, agreed, and his curiosity was satisfied by my reply. In addition, everything I had said had the ring of veracity, which meant Yashu wasn't tipped off to any ulterior motive on my part. Having had some experience of sooth-seers, being around them for forty-odd years, I had learned that the best way to deal with them is to stick to the literal truth, keep it simple, don't elaborate, be confident of your story, believe in it, trust it. You can never deceive a sooth-seer, but even the most proficient and sensitive of them cannot distinguish a part truth from the whole truth. To put it another way: it's not what you say, it's what you leave out that counts. In my case, as long as I blamed my leaving Stonehaven on the fight with High Diviner Ærdant, I had a rock-solid cover story and Yashu would be none the wiser. The fight *was*, after all, the actual, legitimate cause of my departure. You'd almost think I planned it that way, eh?

[Elder Ayn's relish for this sort of intellectual game . . .]

We were half a day's journey south of Penresford when we heard that the situation there had taken a marked turn for the worse. The townspeople, not content with imposing an embargo on clay production, had decided to block the Seray as well, preventing movement of traffic above or below that point. We passed many a disgruntled pilot moored by the side of the river, cooling his heels. Those with perishable goods on board, supposed to go north, had turned back south with the intention of offloading their cargoes someplace downstream before rot set in. Eezhalo was under the impression that the three of us desired to travel however far he could take us. Since it seemed he couldn't go beyond Penresford now, and he had no idea how long we would have to wait before he could, he offered to drop us off at the next reasonable-sized town we came to. I asked him how close to Penresford he could get us. With a rubbing of his head he said that would probably be Hallawye, a couple of miles below. I said Hallawye would suit us fine. We could walk past Penresford and perhaps catch another ride above there. Eezhalo then said he supposed I'd be wanting a partial refund, on account of he hadn't got us to Charne. To his relief, I said it wouldn't be necessary.

The rest of the way to Hallawye, progress was slow. The Seray became crowded, choked. Boats stationary along both banks. Boats that had performed an about-turn and were heading downstream. Boats still forging upstream but forced to join a meandering procession. Everything decelerating, thickening, gumming up, the nearer we got to the Penresford blockade. News was yelled from pilot to pilot. Three barges had set out from Stammeldon, bound for Penresford. Two hundred Stammeldoners were going down to confront the blockaders. Good thing too, was the general view. Confront them, bust the blockade, restore order, get everything back on an even keel. The pilots were restive, watching their profit margin shrink with every hour they spent crawling along, or not even crawling, moored.

Finally it all clogged up and ground to a halt. We were still some distance from Hallawye but there was too much traffic and not enough Seray. Boats going one way met with boats going the other and interleaved and got stuck. Nobody could move back or forth. As we became part of this jam, Eezhalo uttered an oath in Water language which must have been a severe one, judging by the way Yashu's eyebrows lifted to her hairline. 'Well, there it is,' he said, 'Sorry. End of journey.'

While the three of us readied ourselves to disembark, he chatted with another pilot, then relayed what he had learned. Things looked very grave now at Penresford. We might be better not to continue on at all, and if we did, we should certainly give the town a wide berth. The mood up there was combative. The Stammeldoners were due to arrive early tomorrow. It seemed neither side was willing to give ground. A clash was in prospect.

Looking forward, I was able to put his mind at ease. We would be all right. There was going to be conflict but the worst of it would be over by the time we reached Penresford.

We said our farewells and stepped off Eezhalo's boat and across the decks of two other boats to get to the riverbank. Eezhalo, with Aeio draped around his shoulders like a ginger stole, waved to us, and that was the last we saw of him. We struck out northward, following the twists and turns of the river for a few miles till a small, huddled town came into view, lodged between the river and hills. Hallawye.

Southern Jarraine is not a pretty place. Whether, if it had not been hit by the 'Storm a few days earlier, it would be any lovelier, I can't say. But I doubt it. The landscape is low and mean and barren, with a darkness to it as though the sky is perpetually overcast, even when the sun is shining. The hills, such as they are, mound together like lumps of half-kneaded dough. Not much grows. If anyone could bring something fruitful out of its soil, plant-sensitives could, and since they have not managed to, one can only assume the whole region simply defies fertility.

What it does have is its clay deposits. These are southern Jarraine's blessing, its redeeming feature, the only reason I can see that anyone would choose to live there. However, their presence, or rather their exploitation, has further blighted the appearance of the place. Men have hewn away huge chunks of hillside to get at them. Naturally rounded contours have been levelled off, stepped, sheared, squared, flattened. The land has been scarred with deep furrows, flensed of its valuable flesh. And there is a reek that emanates from these wounds, a ripe dank smell, one could almost say rotten, as if ruined ground putrefies. It's the smell of the clay, of course, nothing more than that, but it hangs moistly in the air and clots the nostrils and seems the very essence of decay.

Do *not* cut a word of that, Khollo. It's good stuff.

As for Hallawye, it suits its environs. It is no less unprepossessing. It is a town much like a fort, enclosed, self-surrounding. Even as we neared it, nothing about it seemed to invite entry. It loured gloomily at us with its walls, its few outward-facing windows, its crooked humpback roofs. At its immediate outskirts we passed an area of flat ground, a pitch where they play that awful game sticks, and there were teenagers practising there, charging at one another, going at it hammer and tongs. This served only to increase one's sense of unwelcomeness – the cheery violence on display, how those youngsters traded trippings and batterings and butts and punches, all for fun, all in the name of recreation, and with such seeming *joy*, even as the bruises swelled and the blood flowed.

It was evening, the sun was sinking, and there was no point in proceeding any further that day. We were weary, myself in particular, and a few nights spent outdoors will give a man a fierce craving for a bed with a mattress, a roof over his head, shelter from the wind, shutters to blot out the moonlight. Hallawye boasted a single inn, tucked away deep in its dim, convoluted heart. The Digger's Rest. Its sign showed a picture of, believe it or not, a mole. A crudely rendered, comical-looking mole, dressed in nightshirt and nightcap, slumbering in a hammock, its spade-paws tellingly caked with dirt. How I chortled over that.

There was room at the inn, or at least there were cramped cubicles available, meagrely furnished, for us to sleep in. A tasteless supper, second in inedibility only to that lamb stew monstrosity we forced down in Folsa's Clearing, was followed by a certain amount of drinking. Buying a round endeared me to the handful of surly locals for whom the inn's bar was their habitual watering-hole, and from them I gained a further perspective on the Penresford situation. Hallawye was solidly behind the stance Penresford had taken. Both towns supplied clay to Brazier Brickfields in Stammeldon and so whatever affected the one's business dealings also affected the other's. Hallawye, too, was feeling the pinch in the wake of the 'Storm. It had been especially hard during the first week, when nothing was able to get up or down the Seray. Here, they relied on river deliveries for almost all of their food, and there was only so much you could hold in storage in case of emergency, and nothing that kept indefinitely, so there had been more than a few hungry bellies in both towns while they waited for things to return to normal. Not knowing when that might be, a delegation from Penresford had gone upriver – at some personal risk – and sought a handout from Stammeldon, which the 'Storm, in one of its typically capricious moves, had spared. No handout was forthcoming. Instead: commercial blackmail by Stammeldon's mayor, in league with the owner of Brazier Brickfields.

These men of Hallawye were, I noted, in favour of Penresford's subsequent actions but not to the extent of volunteering their services to that town to help defend it against the contingent of blockade-breakers coming down from Stammeldon. They now had food again here in Hallawye (abuse it though they might with their cuisine). They had most of the ordinary comforts of life again (I use 'comfort' in the loosest sense, since it isn't the first word that springs to mind when I think of Hallawye and its appearance and accommodation). They might not have any work at present – although I didn't hear them grumbling too hard about that – and they might be having to buy in goods on credit, but they didn't foresee either state of affairs persisting for long. They were able, then, to have the best of both worlds –

standing on principle while not suffering for it. Obviously the relationship between the two towns, Penresford and Hallawye, was not as close as it appeared. Or perhaps it was too close. Over the years their proximity and similarity to each other had developed into a kind of over-familiarity. There was rivalry there, a friction. Such was the complexity of the feelings each town had for the other that, like an old married couple, they were capable of mutual love and loathing simultaneously. Hallawye was Penresford's friend through and through but saw no problem with keeping its head down while Penresford stuck its neck out. It could admire its upstream neighbour and at the same time feel no guilt about not lifting a finger to help.

I'm running dry here. Throat getting hoarse. It takes a lot of concentration, this. My aged brain isn't the free-flowing and indefatigable organ it once was. Shall we end this session there, with us in the bar of the Digger's Rest? Me retiring to bed after a couple of pints of beer and the above conversation with the locals. You and Yashu staying up a bit longer. Yashu, as I recall, starting to teach you a few words of Water language as I left. Yes? A good place to stop?

And tomorrow we get to Penresford. And what happened there. And Gregory.

GREGORY

27th of Drymonth 687

In years to come it would be called the Battle of Penresford, and it would take its place in history alongside the Siege of Stonehaven, the West Mylle Ridgeway Riots, the Hyletan Cholera Exodus and all those other memorable instances of 'Storm-born civil strife. It would have that dubious honour of being a clash not between nations, and therefore sanctioned and glamorised as war, but between factions within a nation, driven to extreme measures by extreme pressures. It would fall broadly into the category of conflicts that had at their heart a mutual misunderstanding between Inclinations, a fundamental failure on either side to fathom the other's mindset, a tragic mismatch of philosophies. And it would bear for ever the taint peculiar to all internecine violence – the knowledge that both sets of combatants had more in common than dividing them and that, with a little more effort and empathy on everyone's part, a great deal of pain and bloodshed could have been avoided.

It began with Mayor Bringlight ordering the occupants of the barge on the town-side bank and one of the two barges on the far-side bank to disembark. This command was extended to include himself, his son and Willem, and also the sharp-sight whom he had used as his 'eyes' during the ten minutes of deliberating time he had given the Guild committee. The mayor intended the sharp-sight to fulfil a similar role on the bank, relaying information from the further reaches of the battlefield.

As the Stammeldoners piled off the barges onto dry land, the Penresfordian strongs closed in with a menacing bunching of muscles. Mayor Bringlight turned to the pilot of the barge he had just alighted from and said, 'Quick as you can, down to the blockade.' The pilot gave a grim nod, and the mayor then addressed the incendiaries still aboard: 'You all know what to do. Go in there, ignite those boats, send them to the bottom of the river.' The incendiaries were full of enthusiasm for this plan. It was rare that their kind got permission to exercise their Inclination to its fullest extent. Restraint was one of an incendiary's watchwords. The ability to burn, to raze, to incinerate! – but it must be controlled and used moderately. So when you were given official license to unleash it, then you didn't hesitate and you didn't have to be asked twice. As the barge pulled away, there were grins and cheers on board.

The first and most crucial tactical error Mayor Bringlight made that day was to have forgotten, in the heat of the moment, that on the same barge was the small group of Stammeldon strongs whom he had coerced into coming. He had kept them close to hand on the trip down. Now he carelessly let them out of his sight.

With Reehan and Willem still at his side, the mayor called out to the Penresfordian strongs, who had gathered to form a rough semicircle around each of the two groups of disembarked Stammeldoners. 'This isn't a fight you want to get into,' he said, speaking to the ones in front of him, hoping his voice also carried to the ones on the opposite bank. 'You will be hurt. You will be burned. Step aside and let us do what we have to.'

'Fuck off,' growled one of the strongs close by, and others echoed him or made comments to a similar effect.

'I have no beef with you,' the mayor continued. 'You've been badly represented by your Guild committee. In defying us they've spoken for themselves, not for the will of the people of Penresford. Is it really worth being injured or, who knows, worse, for the sake of a bunch of leaders who have no one's interests at heart but their own?'

It was hardly a statement of fact but the mayor was hoping to sow seeds of doubt among the strongs which would flourish rapidly to become weeds of discord. Though no military professional, Mayor Bringlight knew the importance of psychological warfare.

The results were disappointing, however. Another chorus of 'fuck off', liberally counterpointed with Earth-language expletives.

It was a kind of stalemate. The mayor knew that somebody, most likely him, would have to make the next move. If he could delay, though, till the boats across the river started burning, then the matter would be out of his hands. The strongs would see the fires and that would doubtless prompt them to attack. The moral high ground would be his. *They started it.*

'It really would be sensible if—'

A fireball came hurtling out of nowhere, barrelling into the midst of the assembled strongs. They scattered like bowling pins.

Which of the incendiaries present had generated the fireball, none could say. It could have been any of them. Each wondered if it had been the person next to him. Only one of them, Willem, wondered this with any degree of accuracy.

Then again, if Reehan hadn't precipitated the fighting, somebody else would have. Peace was not altogether a likely prospect at this juncture, and Reehan's pre-emptive strike against the strongs did nothing more than hasten the inevitable.

A few of the strongs were singed, a few blistered. None was seriously hurt. But the shock and provocation were enough. There was an immediate counter-attack, accompanied by a roar – shared, instinctive, an inarticulate howl of anger which raised the hackles on many a Stammeldoner neck. The strongs lumbered forwards, all fist and sinew, all bulky pectoral and taut tendon.

On the opposite bank, the same. The sound of hostilities breaking out on one side of the river triggered hostilities on the other.

Meanwhile, the Brazier Brickfields barge which the mayor had sent forth to break the blockade had achieved top speed and was homing in on the upstream boat chain, now a hundred yards from it, now fifty, now thirty. The indestructibles manning the boat chain braced them-selves. It looked as if they were going to be rammed.

Range, though, was all the incendiaries required. Twenty yards was close enough. The pilot summoned up a heavy backwash at the barge's bow, bringing the craft almost instantly to a halt. No sooner had the incendiaries recovered their balance than they brought their mental focus to bear on the vessels in front of them. They summoned up the imaginary heat inside them – the idea of burning which, when imposed on a chosen objective, became real. Some went for the ropes, some the connective planks, some the boats' very timbers. The indestructibles smelled burning, heard hemp sputter and varnish crackle. Horm Loffin had had the foresight to furnish them with buckets full of earth for just this eventuality, but there was also, they knew, a contingency plan now. As flames licked upwards from the deck planking and the ropes began to smoulder and glow, the indestructibles looked towards the town, and the quayside, and the pilots, the shapers-of-water who had pledged themselves last night to the Penresford cause.

There they stood, half a dozen of them, and sure enough, all at once the surface of the Seray to the rear of the boat chain swelled, as though the river was arching its back, rising out of itself. A large blister of water formed, and on the bank the half-dozen pilots sensed one another's control, knew the extent to which each of them was work-ing, and meshed together, fusing their abilities, feeling the shared flex of non-physical muscles, and the blister grew larger, taller, sucking up more water into itself, bulging. The barge pilot could not help but feel it too, the energies amassing within the water, the pattern-threads rushing together to create this substantial flux. He did not even attempt to weigh in and retard what the other Water Inclined on the quayside were doing. He was outnumbered. It would have been futile. All he could do was watch, as everyone watched, while the blister in the Seray became a hemisphere, a liquid dome some fifteen feet in height, opaque brown and gleaming . . . then burst.

Burst in thick, arcuate plumes which gushed over the boat chain. Exploded in jets that drenched the indestructibles and extinguished the incendiaries' conflagrations. Emptied itself as though punctured. Drained out, and the river flattened with a wallop, and the boat chain and the barge rocked, and hot wood seethed and sizzled, and scorched rope steamed.

There were moments of startlement. A brief span of time for everyone to take stock and shake the water from their hair and look around. Then Master Ergall, on the boat chain, let out a braying laugh. 'Ash-holes!' he yelled to the incendiaries. The leer of triumph on his face and the straggle of his soaked hair hardly made him any more prepossessing a man. 'Nice try, Ash-holes! Weren't expecting *that*, were you?'

Which might be true, but it didn't stop the incendiaries from trying again.

Upstream, the strongs pounded into the incendiaries. The incendiaries answered with flame, great blossoming gouts of it. The strongs reeled back, nursing various degrees of burn. The incendiaries reeled back, nursing various severities of injury.

There were indestructibles there too, on the Stammeldon side. Indestructible versus strong was a close match. A well-aimed blow from a stone-hard fist could shatter a jaw, crack a tibia, snap a rib. The least slap from strong-class fingers could do the same, but the injured indestructible could quickly recover and retaliate. It was a matter of pride to members of both these classes of Inclination that they did not wield weapons. Who needed a sticks stick, say, or a shovel, or even a knife, when hands alone were sufficiently offensive implements?

Swifts from Stammeldon played their part in the proceedings by darting among the combatants, quicker than the eye could follow, all but a blur, harrying the strongs. The swifts had no qualms about bearing arms. Most being constables, they had brought their standard-issue cudgels with them and used these to hammer heads or clout the sensitive junctions of the human body, elbow, knee, knuckle, ankle, neck, anywhere where nerves clustered and bone was close to the surface. Every now and then a strong would cry out and clutch some source of sudden surprising agony, not having seen the blow coming, the person responsible for inflicting it already a good distance away. No swift, however, could sustain peak speed for long, and after a brief volley of assaults each would withdraw from the fray and find some safe spot to rest and catch his breath. The greatest danger to any swift was overexertion. You could run yourself out. You could, if not careful, burst your heart.

The fighting ranged outward from the riverbanks and back again, two masses of mêlée expanding and contracting like lungs. For all that bones were broken and blood flowed, it was skirmishing rather than out-and-out conflict. It was ugly, it was brutal, people's dander was up, their bellowing was like that of jungle creatures, but still a sense of restraint prevailed, just. No one, in other words, was killed outright or fatally wounded. Not yet. Stammeldoners and Penresfordians alike did just enough to hold the other side at bay.

This wasn't something Mayor Bringlight had counted on but it suited his battle plan nonetheless and he had no problem with it. All he wanted was to engage the Penresfordian strongs and keep them occupied while the incendiaries on the barge did their bit. A holding operation. Once the blockade was broken, the Penresfordians would, he was certain, capitulate. The symbol of their resistance being destroyed would mean the resistance itself would collapse. Then it would all be over. And if it was all over and the injuries on either side were confined to those a recuperator could fix, so much the better.

He was aggrieved when the sharp-sight informed him that the incendiaries' initial assault on the blockade had been a failure. Shapers-of-water, working for the Penresfordians? That wasn't on. The mayor had faith, however, that the incendiaries could burn harder than the shapers-of-water could dampen.

The only other slight annoyance he had to deal with during that first phase of the confrontation was his son. Reehan was chafing beside him, eager to join in the fight. Countless times he asked permission. Countless times his father flatly refused.

'It's just not going to happen, Reehan,' Mayor Bringlight said eventually, hoping to put an end to the matter. 'So shut up.'

Willem, for his part, was concentrating less on the battle and more on the lie of the land. Specifically, the way downriver to the second line of boats, which he had got a glimpse of when Mayor Bringlight was negotiating at the first line of boats. He was looking to see how he might get there. Once there, he could use the boats to cross the Seray and enter Penresford itself.

Just a few dozen yards from where he stood, there started a broad escarpment – a section of clay mine that had been worked out long ago and was now a sheer-sided ridge furred with grass and gorse. There was no one up there. Willem didn't think he would run into any Penresfordians if he scrambled up the escarpment's flank and went along its top. All he had to do was wait, bide his time. The mayor couldn't keep an eye on him for ever. His moment would come.

Downstream, the incendiaries were concentrating hard. Steam was purling up from the decks of the boat chain. The air was thick with it. Timbers hissed and spat. The doused boats would soon be tinder dry once more, and combustible.

Unbeknownst to the incendiaries, however, the strongs aboard the barge with them had put their heads together. Behind the incendiaries' backs they had discussed events in low, urgent tones. They had expressed disapproval. They had come to a consensus. They could not condone an attack on other Earthers. They could not be a party to it nor stand idly by. There was only one course of action open to them.

The result of this conspiratorial confab was a quickly hatched plan of sabotage. While the incendiaries were engrossed in their attempt to burn the boat chain a second time, the strongs distributed themselves across the deck of the barge with as much stealth and nonchalance as their heavyset frames allowed. One of them approached the pilot and, finger to lips, advised him to keep quiet and not intervene, or else. The pilot, no fool, nodded. He saw the looks on the strongs' faces, realised what they were planning, and resigned himself to the prospect of getting wet.

On the downstream boat chain, not long after hearing the strongs' defiant shout the indestructibles saw the water blister well up and burst; the wash of its collapse reached them half a minute later. More by inference than observation they gathered that the Stammeldoners had tried to use fire to breach the blockade. They reasoned that as long as the shapers-of-water could keep sousing the decks and ropes before they caught alight, the upstream boat chain would remain intact.

Distracted by the outbreak of violence, the adult indestructibles forgot about Gregory and Ven and the condition they had set for allowing the boys onto the boat chain (only until trouble started). Gregory and Ven, for their part, had no wish to get off. They were riveted by what was going on upriver, thrilled by it. To be a part of this, to be within sight of something so alarming and at the same time so momentous – how could they leave? How could they, now that it had begun, not see how it all worked out? They would make for safety if someone remembered to tell them to. Otherwise, they were staying put. Exhilaration had its own kind of weight. Fascination fed on itself, becoming an enthralled inertia.

Horm Loffin moved to the pilots' side. They were preparing to raise a second water blister and save the boat chain again. They felt strong. They could keep this up all day.

Loffin, however, suggested they hold off for a moment. He had observed what was occurring aboard the Brazier Brickfields barge. There was a good chance a second blister would not be necessary.

Crunch!
The impact shivered the barge's timbers.
Crunch! Crack! Creak!
The barge shuddered end to end, and a section of gunwale fell away, splashing into the river.

Then there were crunches and cracks and creaks in rapid succession, as the strongs set about heaving and wrenching and yanking and stomping. The barge rocked. The barge quaked. The strongs went at it with a vengeance, furious frowns on their faces. They pried. They pummelled. They snapped. Wood broke and splintered. Piece after piece of the barge was torn free and tossed overboard. The Seray's surface quickly became littered with fragments of jetsam. By the time it dawned on the incendiaries that the boat was being scuttled under them, it was too late. One of the strongs had clambered down through an access hatch into the hold. Still on the ladder, with just a few kicks he breached the hull. The barge was doomed.

To have been betrayed like this, mutiny in their midst, sparked a deep, indignant fury within the incendiaries. Having attempted to burn the boat chain and been thwarted, and been taunted when thwarted, they were already in a state of heightened aggression. Now, on top of that, *this*. The boat chain was forgotten. Every incendiary on the barge focused his attention on the strongs.

It was the ultimate incendiary taboo. On no condition did you turn the full force of your flame on another human being. From the very first day of training this was drummed into you. The step you did not take, the line you did not cross.

On Brazier Brickfields barge number BB28, the step was taken, the line crossed. Too easily. With just the tiniest shift of moral perspective, the strongs who were dismantling the boat became not people but a collective force. A danger. A threat. Earthers, already an inferior grade of human, but further dehumanised by their duplicity. Objects. *Things.*

And, to the incendiaries, *things* were permissible targets. *Things* could be incinerated.

A strong who was busy reducing the pilot house to its component planks suddenly found himself feeling hot, deep down in the pit of his stomach, as though he had a bellyful of coals. Perhaps in some dim region of his brain he knew what was happening, but his presiding thought in the instants leading up to his death was that he must have eaten something that disagreed with him. What had he had for dinner? Just the bread, cheese and cold beef his wife had packed. He'd not even tasted the Flamers' spicy grub as a couple of the other strongs had last night, bravely, trying to foster solidarity between Inclinations, showing willing. Yet his tummy was in trouble, and felt as if it was bulging, and now it hurt, yes, badly, owww, very badly, doubled-over-clutching badly, and where was that smell coming from, that roasting-pork smell? Was it coming from him?

Then there was too much pain to think, as the strong's distended abdomen split open and flame billowed from the red-lipped fissure and also jetted from his mouth and nose, and blood and flesh sizzled, and hair shrivelled to clumps, and what had been a man became a life-size marionette that lurched and staggered and writhed horribly, billowing smoke, blackening, falling to the deck without a scream.

Almost simultaneously, a second strong was stewed where he stood. Eyeballs fried in their sockets, going white like the albumen of poached eggs. Brains bubbled in the kettle of his skull.

And a third, the blood turned to steam in his veins.

And a fourth, cauterised internally, soft made hard, meat made carbon.

And a fifth, who watched his comrades fall and couldn't understand why till he looked down at his own hands and saw the skin there rippling, crackling, peeling away, flickers of fire stabbing through, his fingers turning to brands, his tendons to kindling, and the smoke, and the charring, and he beat his hands against his sides but the flames would not go out, they just grew stronger and spread up his forearms, bringing agony with them, and he turned and stumbled to the side of the barge and dived over, but even the river, though cool, did not bring relief, for as he plunged in the strong registered the appalling fact that he was still burning, he was underwater and sinking and he was *still burning* . . .

Brazier Brickfields barge BB28 began listing to starboard. River was rushing to fill the hold. The stern portion of its deck was a mass of gouges and rents and shattered wood. At the bow end, a score of incendiaries looked on with a terrible feral light in their eyes as yet another of the strongs danced the death gavotte, twisting and turning as his body succumbed to the pressures of intense internal heat. So appalled and mesmerised were the incendiaries by what they were doing – the fact that they were doing it at all – that none noticed the river rising behind them. Not in a blister this time but a wave. A tall, and now very tall, and now towering wall of water, curved, its inner surface glinting in the low sunlight. The wave hung, a teetering topaz arch, massing to top-heaviness, and now broke, descended, crashed, like a hand clamping down, and engulfed half the barge, flipping the stern upwards, and bodies were thrown this way and that, the living and the dead, scattered into the Seray amid an explosion of white turbulence, a *whoomph* of spray which reached as far as the bank, pattering down on the people there like a shower of rain.

For Horm Loffin, it had been no decision at all. 'What about the strongs?' one of the shapers-of-water had asked, and Loffin, with despair in his voice, had replied, 'They're dead. As good as. Just do it. Sink that fucking boat. Do it now!'

'Mayor!'
The sharp-sight had to shout to be heard above the sounds of combat – the cries, the *whoomph* which accompanied every ignition of flame.
'Mayor!'
Mayor Bringlight tore his gaze away from the fracas in front of him. 'Yes?'
The sharp-sight gestured downriver toward the boat chain. Mayor Bringlight peered, but all he could see were feathers of whiteness hanging in the air, slowly dispersing. He couldn't figure it out. What was this? Smoke? Steam? And where was the barge? What had become of the barge?
Then he made out a black apex protruding from the river at the epicentre of the thinning whiteness. The rear portion of the barge sticking out at an angle, like the dorsal fin of a shark. Hull, keel, and the water around it all in a ferment, leaping and lurching like a tortured thing. And in the water floated shapes – shapes in sodden clothing, shapes of men. And as the mayor watched, more of these shapes broke the surface, some thrashing, some bobbing limply up.
'What?' he demanded of the sharp-sight. 'What happened?'
Somewhat sheepishly, the sharp-sight replied that he had missed the beginning of it. He had been looking across at the fighting on the other bank. All he had seen was the river coming down and swamping the barge.
The mayor growled, 'Never mind.' He did not need to know the

details anyway. It was obvious that the Stammeldon side had suffered a serious upset. That was enough.

It was obvious, too, that restraint was a luxury his forces could no longer afford.

'Everyone!' he yelled in Fire language. 'Everyone listen!'

But there wasn't a hope of making himself heard. The ruckus was too loud, the confusion too great. He surveyed the scene and spotted a swift nearby. The swift was squatting on his hunkers, panting hard – recovering his wind in readiness to make another sortie with his cudgel.

Mayor Bringlight hurried over and instructed the swift to carry a message round to every Stammeldon combatant. The Penresfordians had sunk the barge. Stammeldoners were dead.

The message was not any longer or more complicated than that. It had no need to be. Everyone who heard it would know the appropriate response.

The swift took off in a blur, shreds of grass flying as his heels cut up the turf.

The mayor glanced across the river and knew he could get the same message across there when the swift came back. Assuming the man could swim, he could swim only marginally less fast than he could run.

Mayor Bringlight did not have the sense, as someone else might have, that events were moving beyond his control. Far from it. He felt more important, and more potent, than ever. Being honest with himself, he had expected there to be deaths. The battle's escalation to that level had, in hindsight, been almost unavoidable, and it made things easier. In a straight, no-holds-barred fight, there was no question of the outcome. Fire, unleashed, could not fail. He regretted the loss of life – the loss that had already taken place and the further loss to come. It was grim and he wished it had not had to be that way, but the Penresfordians were to blame, clearly, and would now reap the consequences of their actions. They had played with Fire.

The mayor looked back to the spot on the bank where he had been standing moments earlier. The sharp-sight was still there, hands cupped to face, scanning in the direction of the town. And of course Reehan and Willem were still there, too.

Or nearby.

The boys had moved.

But not far, surely.

Where *were* they?

It was the opportunity Willem had been waiting for. Reehan's father went off to talk to a swift, and Willem was out of his sightline, no longer hampered by proximity to him. Reehan himself was eyeing the battle, still itching to get stuck in. Everyone was focused on something other than Willem. Willem didn't hesitate.

He knew the situation was not going to get any pleasanter now that the barge had been sunk. Something was loose, something bad was in the air. A wildness. How long the fighting was going to carry on and how much worse it would get, he had no idea, but he knew he should locate Gregory as soon as he could, while things were still relatively sane. Leave it any later, and he might not get the chance.

So the moment the mayor moved away, Willem darted off, aiming for the escarpment. Halfway up the slope, he heard Reehan shout his name. He regretted keeping his friend out of this. He would explain afterwards.

As he gained the top of the slope, he heard Reehan shout again, closer this time. He turned to look back. Reehan was in hot pursuit, scurrying up the slope on all fours.

'Hey!' Reehan yelled. 'Willem! What *is* this? You're not running away, are you?'

Willem could not have Reehan thinking he was a coward. 'I'm going to find Gregory,' he said, and made to carry on.

'Wait!'

Willem, against his own wishes, waited.

A panting Reehan reached his side. 'Gregory? Ungrateful, gone-native Gregory? Snotty, I'm-too-good-for-all-of-you-so-leave-me-alone Gregory? That little brat? You're going to find *him*?'

'I said I would. Promised my mother.'

'But . . . now?'

'Yes, now. I find him, and we keep low till this is all over, and then I take him back up to Stammeldon,'

'Is this why you agreed to come down here? All along this was what you had in mind?'

Willem nodded, and was surprised to see a look of hurt enter Reehan's eyes. It hadn't occurred to him that Reehan might think he had used him and betrayed him. He felt guilty and at the same time, in an odd harsh way, pleased. It was rare that he acted without Reehan's knowledge or consent. It was untypical of their friendship. For that not to be the case, just this once, did not necessarily seem like a bad thing.

'But why didn't you say?' Reehan asked. 'Why not tell me?'

'My brother,' Willem shrugged, 'my problem.'

'But I'm your best friend.'

And with that, five small words couched in the tones of someone deeply wronged, Reehan burst Willem's bubble of defiance. Willem no longer felt guilty *and* pleased, merely guilty. That was all it took, just a reminder that they were supposed to be equals, supposed to withhold nothing from each other. Willem all at once saw how shabby he was, how selfish to have had his own agenda when it should have been Reehan's agenda too. He ached with the shame.

'I'm sorry, Reehan, I—'

Reehan dismissed the apology, and proved himself the better man, as if it needed proving, by then saying, 'Any problem of yours, Willem, is a problem of mine. You're going after Little Bother? Excellent. Then we both are. What's the plan?'

Willem could have hugged him. 'Down there,' he said, pointing. 'That second line of boats going across at the other end of the town. You can just see it. If we can get across over those, into Penresford . . .'

'Aren't there people on it?'

'I think so.'

'Will they let us over?'

'I don't know. If I tell them who I am and explain what I'm after, probably yes.'

'And you know where Gregory is in the town?'

'The Goves'. Shouldn't be too hard to find. We'll just ask a local. Gregory'll be there.'

'All right then. Seems straightforward enough. Let's go.'

Willem started off again along the escarpment. Reehan, having paused to flick a stray lock of hair from his eyes, followed. To him, Willem's plan didn't in fact seem straightforward at all. It seemed naïve and half-baked and riddled with holes. But that was fine. That didn't matter in the least. If something went awry, Reehan would be there to put it straight. By force, if need be.

Chronic bad timing saw to it that just as Willem commenced his journey down the far-side bank, one of the indestructibles on the downstream boat chain noticed that Gregory and Ven were still there when they ought not to be there. The two boys were summarily ordered back to Penresford. Having put up a token protest and had it fall on deaf ears, they made their way across from boat to boat till they alighted on the town-side bank. Both agreed they had ridden their luck as far as they could. A little longer on the boat chain would have been nice, but it was not to be. They headed for the nearest entrance into the town, knowing that there were eyes on them and that the eyes would remain on them until they got themselves safely within the perimeter of Penresford's walls.

Once in Penresford, Gregory and Ven should perhaps have gone home and rejoined the rest of the Gove household there. Ven raised the possibility, pointing out that his mother would be worried about them. This, however, was more of a disincentive than an incentive. A worried Garla Gove was an angry Garla Gove, and returning to face her wrath was not a prospect either boy relished. Instead, they decided they would try and find another spot from which to watch the action unfold. Somewhere high up. A roof? Several of the dockside buildings had staircases at the rear, with ladders at the top giving roof access.

They set off at a run. The town was near deserted, the streets theirs. They owned Penresford already, they felt. They had mapped it together, crisscrossed it countless times, staked it out to their own satisfaction, built a mythology of boyish escapades around it. Now, however, as virtually the only people moving in it, they ruled it. Down into an alley so narrow you almost had to turn sideways to get through. Along a circuit of lanes between backyards, scaring a cat which leapt in a flurry of hisses and raised fur onto the roof of an outhouse latrine. Through the corkscrewing convolutions of the bazaar, where most of the stalls were shut up but a few diehard shopkeepers had elected to remain open for business, come what may. Out towards the dockside area. Young kings of their world.

It was still silty here, where the river had flooded in. The streets had been drained but not yet cleaned, and the Seray had left its too-high tide mark on the walls, a brown film evenly coating brickwork and woodwork, in places up to waist level. The air still smelled of water. The cobbles were slippery. Gregory and Ven slowed their pace, and now they were approaching the wharf buildings through which all trade goods in Penresford passed, in one direction or the other. Gates were closed, no business being done today. But gates could be climbed. And now the boys were ascending zigzag flights of wooden stairs up the back of premises belonging to the First Freight Handling Company of Penresford, while outside the town . . .

. . . Fire scorched Earth. Figuratively. Literally. Incendiaries were letting loose, spurred by vengeance, emptied of conscience. A few held back, preferring to continue with fireballs. Most opted for the direct approach. Strongs blazed. Strongs blackened. The ground was strewn with smoking, twisted human heaps. Grass crackled to ash. Something hysterical, something disbelieving, contorted the incendiaries' faces. They couldn't stop themselves. Wouldn't have even if they could. It was easy, startlingly easy, to burn the Penresfordians. These awkward, swarthy creatures. These ungainly Earthers whose people had just killed several of the Stammeldoners' own. These brutes who, even when cooked from the inside out, kept on coming, some of them.

Lurching forwards, hands outstretched, still trying to fight when they ought to have been falling down dead. Propelled by their massive strength. Monstrous as they burned. It was startlingly easy, and it was necessary, and it was right. The incendiaries felt their Inclination coursing through them, felt the constraints of proper behaviour to be the illusions they were. Social shackles that might as well have been made of paper, so simple was it to break them. A sense of *Why not?* A sense of *Why haven't we done this before?* Because the fire was always there. Training focused it, funnelled it, constricted its use like the pupil of an eye in bright light. But the fire was always there. The possibility of being able to kill with it was always there. And yes, to lash out with it, to release its full force when the provocation was sufficient – this was good. Horribly, undeniably good.

And down by the upstream boat chain, Horm Loffin and the other Guild committee members knew that things had gone bad. Horribly, undeniably, irredeemably bad. Even at half a mile away, it was clear their own townspeople were being slaughtered. The committee members were at a loss. Paralysed. No one had had any idea it would come to this. No one had believed it possible that this was what the embargo would lead to. Perhaps some had entertained the notion – but only as the remotest of outcomes, in the very worst of circumstances. And so rapid, too, the deterioration from talking to brawling to slaying. Civilised men, suddenly going at one another like animals. The Flamers opening up with all they had. The last resort resorted to. And the committee members were afraid. Afraid of what they had unwittingly brought about. Afraid for their town.

Master Ergall on the boat chain. His habitual scowl now twice its normal density, a clenched facial knot. 'Bastards! Fucking Flamer bastards! Do you see what they're doing up there? Do you *see*?'

The boat chain no longer needed defending. The human shield on it, that ethical bulwark against incendiary attack, was redundant. It had failed. Everything had failed.

Master Ergall took the initiative. Half of his fellow-indestructibles he told to go that way, onto the far-side bank. Half the other way, onto the town-side. Since the majority of the indestructibles with him were ones who had undergone training at his hands, they obeyed without question or quibble. Fear of Master Ergall persisted even when you weren't his pupil any more.

Besides, he was right. Off the boat chain. Up the banks to where the fighting was. Absolutely. This wasn't an industrial dispute now. More than just a point of principle was at stake. Far more.

Willem and Reehan drew abreast of the upstream boat chain just as Master Ergall began chivvying people off it. By a stroke of inordinate good fortune, the two young redheads were not spotted as they hurried by along the escarpment. Attention was on events up-river.

Willem, head down, hands knifing, ran with the rock-steady stride of a man with a mission. Reehan's willingness to come along with him seemed to confirm beyond all doubt the rightness of what he was doing. Reehan would not have supported the idea of finding Gregory if he had thought it a bad one. Reehan was a good friend, the best.

Reehan, a few paces behind Willem, surveyed the further boat chain. He counted about two dozen people on it, maybe more.

No problem.

Mayor Bringlight beheld an awful beauty. On either bank of the river, the truth of Fire. Fire laid bare. This was what it could do, oh yes. The strongs, all that muscle-power – nothing compared with the untram-melled fury of incendiary minds. He watched well-built bodies flail and char. He watched Penresfordians stagger helplessly, their bulk useless to them, the might by which they earned a wage no good to them against a force that was supple and fierce and attacked from within. Their flesh could not help them when it was their flesh itself that was being crippled by incineration. One by one, he watched them succumb to a blistering death, and heard them scream, and smelled the sweet-savoury stench of human barbecue, familiar from funeral pyres on Memorial Plaza. His eyes were wide, not so much with horror as with the desire to take it all in. Foremost in his brain, this thought: *Me. I unleashed this. Me.*

Reehan. And Willem. The sharp-sight had espied the two of them heading south along the bank. Mayor Bringlight knew he should go after them. What were they up to? How dare they run off like that!

But the mayor found it difficult to move. His own son and Tremond's – but here, in front of him, the unfurling onslaught, the supremacy of Fire displayed for all to see, a lesson in Inclination. He could not tear himself away.

There were, in all, thirty indestructibles on the downstream boat chain – only one of them a woman, indestructibility being predominantly a male class of Inclination. Three of the men were constables, among them Penresford's district superintendent, no less. As for the rest, they had jobs for which their Inclination was neither a benefit nor a prerequisite. Plumbers, shopkeepers, carpenters – ordinary people.

Several had let their hard-trained hands go soft again. All enjoyed good health. All looked young for their age. But otherwise, ordinary people.

It was the superintendent who spotted the two Flamers sprinting along the bank. With a cautious growl he alerted the others. At this end of town they didn't know yet just how serious the situation upstream had become, but they were on their mettle. Something was up. A bad smell on the breeze. An up-shift in the distant sounds of battle. Something had changed, for the worse.

The Flamers were young, and the way they were running and the fact that there were only two of them struck the superintendent as curious. Assuming authority, he clambered off the barge he was aboard, onto a ferry, and from the ferry onto another barge, so that he was right by the bank when the Flamers reached the boat chain. He drew himself to his full height. He wasn't tall but he knew from experience that holding yourself straight, keeping your chin up and your chest out, added several metaphorical inches.

'Stop right there,' he told the Flamers, in a voice well accustomed to being obeyed.

The two young redheads came to a halt. Both were breathing hard, their pale cheeks flushed.

'If you're here to cause trouble, I'd advise you to think again,' said the superintendent. In truth, something – a constable's instinct – told him trouble wasn't the reason they were here, but it didn't hurt to establish who was boss right from the start. One of the Flamers, he noted, seemed familiar. In fact, he bore a distinct resemblance to Gregory Brazier, who had been on this very boat chain not five minutes earlier. Obviously, one redhead looked pretty much like another. The hair was what you saw first, the hair grabbed your attention, and other characteristics you noticed later, if at all. But even so . . .

'My name,' said the Flamer the superintendent was looking at, 'is Willem Brazier.'

'Ah yes.' The superintendent briefly congratulated himself on his powers of observation. 'It would be.'

'And I'm not here to attack you or fight you or anything,' Willem Brazier said. 'All I want is to be allowed across. I'm looking for my brother.' He gestured at his companion. '*We're* looking for my brother. Gregory Brazier.'

'I see.' The superintendent gave a quick, rueful smile. 'Well now, you've been rather unlucky.'

'How so?'

'Believe it or not, Gregory was with us right here. We sent him back into town just a short while ago. Things looked like they were getting bad up there.'

'They are,' said the other Flamer, sounding almost happy to confirm it. 'Very bad.'

'It's got nothing to do with us,' Willem Brazier said. 'We don't care about any of that. All we care about is Gregory.'

'Sounds like lies to me,' muttered one of the indestructibles in Earth language, but the superintendent raised a finger. *Hold on. One moment.*

'I swear,' said Willem. 'Gregory. I want to take him home. We both do. That's all.'

'Yes,' said his companion, with a wide-eyed nod that hinted at some secret joke being played inside his head.

The superintendent deliberated. The noise of conflict less than a mile away, just audible, was a ghastly distraction. He tried to blank it out while he made up his mind whether or not to trust these two lads, who by rights were the enemy and, like it or not, were part of whatever was happening upstream.

But they were young, late teens, still kids really, and looked honest. One of them did, at least. There seemed no reason to disbelieve Willem's claim that he was Gregory's brother, not when he and Gregory were so similar in appearance. Nor did there seem any reason to doubt he had come in search of his brother.

'Very well,' said the superintendent. 'I'm going to let you across.'

Willem shot his companion a told-you-so look. His companion just shrugged, affecting pleasant surprise.

The superintendent made an ushering gesture, a quick flick of thick fingers. Willem stepped onto the barge, the other redhead close behind. The indestructibles let them pass along the boat chain, some stepping aside courteously, others glowering. Up, down, over the connective planks the two Flamers went, with the superintendent accompanying them in order to see them safely to the other side and also to make sure they didn't try any funny business along the way.

Reaching the town-side bank, Willem jumped down. 'Thank you,' he said to the superintendent.

'You're welcome,' said the superintendent. 'That Gregory's a good lad. Everyone knows him here. We like him. For a Flamer he's almost, well, almost as good as an Earther.'

Willem took the remark in the spirit it was intended, as a piece of light mockery.

'You know where to find him, I take it,' the superintendent said.

'The Gove house.'

'And you know where that is?'

'Not really.'

The superintendent frowned. 'Well, you can't go wandering through Penresford hoping you'll just stumble across it, can you? Perhaps I should come along with you. Actually, that probably isn't a bad idea anyway, having me as an escort. For everyone's sake.'

'Would you?' said Willem. 'That'd be—'

He was unable to say any more. The moment of fragile rapprochement was rudely interrupted by a loud 'Ahem' from the other redhead, who had just joined Willem on dry land.

'Listen up, everybody,' he said. 'Gentlemen. Lady. Willem has been terribly impolite not introducing me to you all, so you won't mind if I redress the oversight. My name is Bringlight. Reehan Bringlight. My father is Jarnley Bringlight, mayor of Stammeldon.'

Mention of Jarnley Bringlight provoked murmurs and a stiffening of spines all along the boat chain.

'Yes, the man who, just under a week ago, one of your lot tried to kill.' Reehan held out his arms like a master of ceremonies. 'Now, that wasn't a nice thing to have done. Not nice at all. And I'd like to convey a message from my father in response. Something along these lines . . .'

Willem felt it, a rush of warmth, rippling the air. The boats, all of them, from one end of the chain to the other, suddenly radiating heat. Reehan's palms were splayed. Willem saw him close his eyes for a second, then open them again. A blink to refine his concentration. The temperature in the boats was rising. Willem could sense the heat's shape, feel its gathering immensity.

At last, too late, he found his voice: 'Reehan! No!'

Reehan bared his teeth.

The roof of the First Freight Handling Company of Penresford was pyramidal and sufficiently shallow-raked that Gregory and Ven could cross it without much difficulty. Slates loosened by the 'Storm presented the only real hazard. One shot out from under Ven's foot and went skittering away, disappearing down into the gap between the building and its next-door neighbour, landing with a faint *tink* three storeys below. For several panicked seconds Ven was frozen in place with his leg jutting out to the side, his body pressed to the roof, scared to move. When he realised he was safe and wasn't going to follow the slate, he grimaced and mopped his brow, making an exaggerated show of fear in order to demonstrate that he was no longer afraid.

Reaching the dockside edge of the roof, the boys settled there carefully. Each lodged himself in a half-lying position, braced by feet and elbows.

A panoramic view. The Seray visible for over a mile in either direction.

They were just beginning to survey the scene, taking stock, when the downstream boat chain exploded into flame.

YASHU

Twin-Ports-On-Sea. Yashu had had no idea that a place, any place, could be so loud. The city roared from daybreak to dusk and on through the night. It was perpetually in motion, people flooding its streets, crowd-torrents. Their clamour, as they shouted to be heard above one another, put her in mind of the Worldstorm's thunder-rumblings. Didn't they go deaf, yelling like that all the time? Or at least make themselves too hoarse to speak?

She was scared to leave the hotel. She lamented her cowardice but there was nothing she could do about it. If she ventured out into that maze of streets, that tumult of moving bodies, she thought she might get swept away. She might become lost among the crowds, driven endlessly through the city by their momentum, circulating, unable to stop, till exhaustion or starvation overtook her. Just looking down from her hotel room window on all those people was bad enough. Dizzying. Such numbers!

For her first taste of mainland life, it was not auspicious. She had to believe that the mainland wasn't all like this.

The hotel itself, too, presented problems. There was nothing wrong with the Hotel Hermit Crab, and therein lay the difficulty. Yashu had never before slept on so soft a bed, nor seen surfaces so shiny, nor experienced such a fanatical level of cleanliness. The place was spotless throughout. Staff hovered and lurked in every corner, it seemed, waiting to mop up the least speck of dust. Frequently, when she left her room even for just a few minutes, she would come back to find someone had seized the opportunity to enter it and start tidying. She wasn't comfortable with such a level of luxury and neatness. It put her on edge, as if her presence there alone dirtied her surroundings. She knew everything about the Hotel Hermit Crab was intended to make guests feel relaxed and pampered. On her it had the opposite effect.

Then there was the restaurant, where the tables were set with a bewildering array of cutlery, at least three times as many knives and forks as a person needed, all with mother-of-pearl handles engraved with an image of the marine mollusc from which the hotel took its name. The drinking glasses, similarly engraved, were so thin and fragile-looking Yashu was wary of touching them in case they snapped in her grasp. And the food was rich and strange. Familiar ingredients such as fish and vegetables were made almost unrecognisable by the addition of sauces and herbs, and the dishes were set down by the waiting staff almost as if they were things to be looked at and admired rather than consumed. What should have been a straightforward experience, eating, became complicated and lost almost all its pleasure.

Mr Ayn went out around noon every day and stayed out for the entire afternoon and well into the night. He was getting hold of money and supplies and making travel arrangements, or so he claimed. On the rare occasions she and he bumped into each other in the hotel, Yashu could tell that he found Twin-Ports-On-Sea exciting. His eyes were agleam and he couldn't stop talking about his meetings with strangers, about all the bars that the city had to offer, the nightlife. 'Vibrant' was a word he used more than once, and when Khollo explained what it meant, Yashu could see that, yes, 'vibrant' was one way of describing the city. Not necessarily the best or only way, but one way.

With Mr Ayn busy elsewhere, Yashu and Khollo ended up spending quite a bit of time in each other's company. She was surprised to discover that Khollo found Twin-Ports-On-Sea almost as intimidating as she did. He came from a quiet country, he told her. Durat. A place of desert and mountain and small, walled townships. He had only ever lived there and at Stonehaven. All this – the city, the pace, the noise – was too much for him.

One evening, over dinner, Khollo confessed that the reason Mr Ayn was enjoying himself so much here was because Twin-Ports-On-Sea had areas that catered to a man of his tastes. What he meant by this, Yashu was not sure. She asked him to explain, and reluctantly he elaborated. There were certain bars, he said, certain streets, where sexual services were bought and sold. All big cities had them, and in this one, where thousands of visitors were constantly arriving and departing, such a trade was particularly common. There were bars, too, where you could pay to watch other people copulating. Khollo suspected that that was where Elder Ayn, as he called him, was going when he went out every evening. Mr Ayn was past the age when he could take part in such activities himself, but that didn't mean they were no longer interesting to him.

'Are you sure?' Yashu asked.

'How long have we been here? Three days. It doesn't take *that* long to book a journey and get hold of some local currency, a few maps, some blankets.'

It all seemed somewhat sordid to Yashu, and more so when Khollo mentioned that the couples Mr Ayn would be watching were men, not a woman and a man. There were types like that on Li*issua, men who preferred men, women who preferred women, but as a rule the practice was frowned on. These people didn't produce offspring and thus continue their clans. More often than not, someone who was like that would quit the archipelago to live elsewhere. What good were you if you weren't helping to advance the race in any way?

'I'm supposed to trust Mr Ayn,' she said, 'and you tell me *this*?'

Khollo replied, 'It's the truth about him. I don't think he's ashamed of it and I don't think he should be.'

'Does he like you in . . . that sort of way?'

'I don't believe so.'

'You're not handsome enough, then?'

'It's not that simple.'

'So you *do* think you're handsome enough.'

He stared at her across the table, and only after several seconds did he start to smile, showing that he had realised she was teasing. This disappointed Yashu. She had been trying to speak to him as he and Mr Ayn and presumably all Air Inclined spoke, playing that sly, deadpan game whereby you never quite meant what you said or said what you meant. She hadn't done it well enough, obviously. It must take practice.

'You know, I reckon you'd make a good sooth-seer,' he said. 'You certainly can ask questions. I can well imagine you cross-examining a defendant in court, getting to the heart of their alibi.'

'In court? The law?'

'That's where most sooth-seers are employed. Or they set up in private practice, as a consultant. Or there's Stonehaven, of course, where a sworn affidavit from a sooth-seer is worth its weight in gold. A Stonehaven sooth-seer is absolutely unimpeachable.' He explained the word before she had to ask. 'Beyond criticism. No one questions their testimony. Anywhere else sooth-seers can be bribed to lie, but if you're at Stonehaven, what need do you have of extra money? The place is so wealthy anyway.'

'Tell me about sooth-seeing. I know nothing about it.'

'Well, I don't know that much myself, only what I picked up from the sooth-seers at Stonehaven. First off, there are several different grades of sooth-seer. Some hear it when a person is lying, some see it in the person's face. Some do both.'

'I think I do both.'

'Then you'll probably be doubly good at it. There are also sooth-seers who use physical contact to establish whether a lie's being told or not. They read it through their fingers. Maybe they can detect minute amounts of sweat on the skin, I don't know. And the other thing you'll have to learn, apart from just getting proficient at your Inclination, is degrees of lie. There's something called the Salcher Mendacity Scale, which grades lies according to severity, from "white" to "out-and-out", with about twenty other levels in between. You know, "necessary", "tall story", "bluff", "withholding of crucial detail", "whopper" . . .'

' "Whopper"?'

'All right, I made that one up. I don't actually know what all the names are, but there are a lot of them and some of the distinctions are so fine you can barely fit a hair between them.'

It all sounded alarmingly complicated. Yashu tried to picture herself using her Flow professionally. The idea was both intriguing and inconceivable. Too big, too remote. There would be so much to learn before she could even consider it a possibility; so much knowledge to be gained about the world before she would feel qualified to pass judgement on things its people said.

'If you did end up working in the law,' Khollo added, 'you'd meet a lot of my kind, enshriner-class. We make great lawyers and judges, you see. We memorise every case we read in the jurisprudence books. There isn't a precedent we forget. My parents were lawyers, did I tell you that?'

'No.'

'Both of them. They worked all over Durat. They even advised King Xhan from time to time on constitutional matters.'

'They sound very important.'

'They were.'

'Oh. They're dead.'

'Yes.'

Yashu hesitated. To mainlanders, what did you say? As far as they were concerned, when they perished they perished for good. They had no equivalent of the Great-Ocean-Beyond. Their spirits did not live on. Did you sympathise? Did you pity? Did you try to offer some sort of encouragement about an afterlife? Try to impose your beliefs on theirs? It was better, she thought, simpler, just to stay silent.

'It wasn't the 'Storm, if that's what you're thinking,' Khollo said. 'No, just an accident. They were riding home from another town in a carriage. An axle broke. The carriage overturned. They were killed instantly.'

'When was this?'

'Five years ago. I was seventeen. And because of who I am, how I am, my memories only go back to the time I manifested. Before then, everything's murky. So, in effect, I knew my parents for a total of just four years.' He looked dourly down at his plate. They were both eating pan-fried baby squid, and for a few moments he studied the last one on his plate, poking it around with his fork.

'I don't remember my parents at all,' Yashu said. 'The Worldstorm killed them when I was little older than a baby.'

'I didn't know that. Well, I knew they were dead. Your aunt told us when we were at your house that day, before you came home. You're an orphan too.'

'Don't you have to be a child to be an orphan? I'm not a child.'

'I think, whatever your age, if both your parents are dead you're an orphan. You can be forty years old when they go, and still, when it happens, that's it. You're parentless.' He gave a weak smile. 'But do you feel cheated? I do. Four years, it's nothing. And you – no years at all. None that you have any memory of.'

'I feel cheated,' Yashu said, nodding. 'I also feel angry. This' – she pointed to the piece of coral hung around her neck – 'this is all I have of my parents. All that the 'Storm left. It was what I gnawed on when I was small and my teeth were coming through. My mother bought it for me. The rest, the 'Storm took away. My parents' house, every scrap of their possessions, it destroyed. This was in my hand when I was pulled from the rubble.'

Khollo gestured at his multicoloured waistcoat. 'My mother bought this for me a fortnight before she died. I'll wear it till it's worn to pieces.'

'My coral will never be worn to pieces.'

Yashu gave a sorrowful laugh, and Khollo matched it with a sorrowful smile.

The next morning, at breakfast, a bleary Mr Ayn announced that they were leaving that day. He looked tired but also sated, as if he had had enough of Twin-Ports-On-Sea and it had had enough of him. As he spoke, Yashu thought of him just a few hours ago in some dim-lit dive. She imagined it to be like one of the pubs on I*il, but smokier and dingier. She pictured him sitting there watching a man mount another man. She pictured him with his half smile in place, perhaps furtively wetting his lips with his tongue every so often. Not a pleasant image. Was Khollo lying? No, he couldn't be. Wrong, then? Mistaken? Maybe.

She gathered together her belongings and took a last look around the hotel room.

She had no regrets about going. The hotel, Twin-Ports-On-Sea, this sort of lifestyle – not for her.

She, Khollo and Mr Ayn wrestled through the crowds that afternoon, making their way down to one of the vast number of quays the city boasted. Twin-Ports-On-Sea was in fact two cities perched at either side of a river mouth. The river was called the Seray, which sounded very similar to the word in Water language for 'movement'. An apt name. From bank to bank it was a frenzy of boats, their wakes further churning waters that were already choppy thanks to the Seray's current mingling with the sea's tide. So many boats. While waiting for Mr Ayn to locate the pilot whom he was paying to take the three of them upstream, Yashu saw several near-misses occur out there on the water, collisions averted at the last instant by some nifty manoeuvring. The pilots appeared to take it in their stride, all part of the process of navigating through this chaos.

A tubby shaper-of-water, Eezhalo, was to be their ferryman. He recognised Yashu as an islander the moment she stepped aboard, hailing her familiarly in their own language. He had a cat, whom he introduced to everyone as Tomcat. Yashu asked him if he couldn't have come up with a more original name. Eezhalo, not offended, said a cat was just a cat. Why call it anything else?

Eezhalo's boat was lashed to another boat. The other boat helped guide him out into the river and then gave assistance getting him upstream, using a drag anchor consisting of two roped boulders which plumbed a counter-current. The boulders were thrown overboard by a pair of Earth-Inclined men. Yashu was fascinated by the ease with which they picked up and tossed the stones, each of which must have been the equivalent of three times their own body-weight. She was put in mind of Ra*aisheelo, of Li*issuan legend. Had Sheelo, she wondered, been Earth-Inclined? His Flow not-of-the-archipelago, like hers? The stories never specified. Sheelo was an exaggerated character in general, his appetites, his strength, his physique, everything about him larger than life. It was probably too literal to think of him as just strong-class.

These two mainland Sheelos, besides, were a sullen-looking pair, and if Ra*aisheelo was famous for anything other than his strength, it was for his sense of humour. His exploits, whether heroic or humiliating, always amused him. Every story about him ended with him clutching his enormous belly and guffawing.

And now they were upstream, Twin-Ports-On-Sea behind them, and Eezhalo had sole control of his boat, and they cruised along the still-busy river, through flat landscape, beneath a big sky. Yashu watched clouds and their shadows drift over tumbled fields and sodden meadows. The Worldstorm, like a plough, left a furrow behind it, breaking, overturning. Did it anger the earth, to be tortured like this again and again? Probably no more than it angered the earth when a real plough drove through it. The earth was passive, inert, except in some regions where, she had heard, it shook from time to time, toppling houses and killing people. A kind of upside-down 'Storm, that. Just as destructive, but at least these earthquakes where confined to certain locales. Unlike the 'Storm they didn't roam, and if you wanted to avoid them, you simply didn't live where they happened.

It seemed to her that the first major city along the Seray after Twin-Ports-On-Sea might be located in an earthquake area. Rommen Cas looked to have been shaken from the foundations up several times in its history. According to Mr Ayn, however, the reason for its ruination was the 'Storm, no more, no less. He told a story about rich families building towers – towers of arrogance which the 'Storm took great delight in felling. It was a true story, too, because the relics of the towers were in evidence across the city, some of them teeteringly tall, all of them defaced and degraded and downcast. Something terrible about them, in a way. Lost and vain.

She lost count of the bridges they went under on their way through Rommen Cas. Some of them swivelled, some swung upwards like accosting arms. Men operated them, more of those mainland Sheelos.

The boat glided on. Eezhalo propelled it with a calm, effortless air. Every so often he saluted another pilot, someone he knew. They would exchange a few words as their vessels slid past each other. The boats, Yashu decided, were like floating islands, each independent yet part of a common nation. She looked at Khollo and Mr Ayn. The two of them and her – a kind of clan? Not forgetting Eezhalo and Tomcat.

Tomcat she wouldn't have minded as clan because he was what he was, a friendly creature who made no bones about the fact that he put his own interests first and foremost. To see that, you only had to watch him when there was food around, dancing attendance on anyone he thought might spare him a titbit. Eezhalo, on the other hand, failed to endear himself to her. On the evening of their very first day on the river, he invited her to share his cabin with him that night. There was a twinkle in his eye, as though he hardly expected her answer to be yes, but if that was the case then why ask her at all? She turned the offer down as politely as she could, and when Mr Ayn wanted to know what she and Eezhalo had just been talking about, she gave him an amended version: Eezhalo had told her she could use his cabin if she wished, rather than sleep on deck. She said she preferred the idea of sleeping on deck, listening to the sound of water as she fell asleep, and that at least was true, whereas the part about Eezhalo jangled as it left her lips. But it was only a small lie, designed to preserve harmony on board the boat, and Eezhalo himself made no objection to her altering what he had said when she translated it into Common Tongue. It made him seem like a courteous gentleman instead of a lecher.

A lecher he remained, however. Throughout the journey he kept up the suggestive remarks and jokey insinuations, never missing a chance to remind Yashu that he was available and she ought to feel flattered that he was paying her so much attention. But he was what, twenty years older than her? And rotund, and very hairy. There was hair bushing out of his ears. Hair on the tops of his fingers. She could not have been less attracted to anyone. But Eezhalo couldn't see that, or refused to see that, or thought it amusing not to see that. At one point she considered telling him that she had loved, and still loved, a handsome boy called Huaso who had been full of life and ambitions and next to whom a portly, middle-aged pilot was about as appetising as a plate of week-old scallops. Again, however, in order to keep life on the boat smooth and trouble-free, she refrained. She dodged around Eezhalo's comments. She learned to ignore them – just so much fish-mouth bubble-babble.

At night, as the boat strained at its moorings, she lay out under the moon and stars, beneath a blanket. It wasn't any too warm, nor any too comfortable, but it could have been worse. Mr Ayn and Khollo snored nearby, but louder than them was the Seray slapping against the planks of the hull and slopping at its own banks. She wondered whether the spirits could be heard in river water as well as sea water, and listened, not holding out much hope. Nothing. The sound was a thin echo of home, and made I*il seem even more dim and distant than it was. Each day's journey further inland was a day added to the time it would take her to get back there. Returning home was always at the back of Yashu's mind. Not if but when. She intended to stick with Mr Ayn for as long as he let her. He wanted to see the world and so did she. But there would come a time, surely, when his path and hers must separate. She couldn't see herself remaining with him indefinitely, attached like remora to shark. At some point she would either strike out on her own or else, having had enough of travel, beg leave to go back to Li*issua.

As plans went, it wasn't much of one, and sometimes the insecurity of it was overwhelming and Yashu felt breathless and scared. At other times the insecurity was exciting and she revelled in it. The 'Storm had knocked her future off-course. Once, what lay in store for her had been settled, assured. Not any more.

The *mala* of what had happened – Huaso's death and the revelation of her Flow – was that she should seize every new opportunity that came her way. She should explore. Be curious. Treat everything as an adventure. If her lot in life was never to know certainty, then she should embrace uncertainty.

And so onward, ever onward, north through this country that was called Warlenvish and then on into a country called Jarraine. The demarcation between the two was nothing more than a pair of guard-houses positioned next to pontoons on either bank, where men in uniforms checked pilots' papers and exacted toll fees. The river continued afterwards as it had before, the landscape likewise. Here, within one landmass, countries had invisible borders. The continent was not one big island but one big archipelago whose islands happened to be all pushed together, the distinctions between them decided on by people rather than made obvious by geography. In Li*issua there was a proverb: distance makes good neighbours. Did the opposite apply here?

If the reports the pilots were passing on to one another were anything to go by, then yes, it did. Trouble was brewing upstream. Two towns – if not neighbours then close allies – had fallen out over some sort of trade matter. The exact bone of contention wasn't clear, but as a result of the two towns' squabbling, the river was blockaded ahead. Some pilots had turned back, seeking other places to sell their cargoes before they spoiled. Eezhalo, who did not have to worry about this fate befalling his load of cotton, carried on. Breezily he said he reckoned matters would be resolved by the time he got to the town which was doing the blockading, Penresford.

He was wrong. Below Penresford, his boat became embroiled in a logjam. River vessels going in both directions had congested the Seray. There was no way forward and, as more boats piled in from behind, no way back. Mr Ayn decided the journey should be continued on foot. Yashu was not upset to see the back of Eezhalo. She made a great fuss of Tomcat, then snubbed Eezhalo with a curt Common Tongue 'goodbye'.

An afternoon's walking brought her, Mr Ayn and Khollo to Halla-wye, a gloomy town in a gloomy setting. Gloomier still were Halla-wye's streets, which were most of them completely under cover or else overshadowed by the upper storeys of houses that hung so closely together they looked as if they were whispering. This, Yashu understood, was the Earth-Inclined preference. Darkness. Enclosed spaces. The only hotel in town continued the theme. Its rooms were curtained-off cubicles, and the few windows it had were tiny. The air was stale-smelling and stifling from lack of light and poor ventilation. She was glad when Mr Ayn said they would be spending just the one night there.

That evening, Mr Ayn ingratiated himself with the locals, buying a round of drinks at the hotel bar and asking questions about events up at Penresford. A tale of pride and limpet-like obstinacy emerged. The locals were not, it seemed, any too delighted at the way people in the nearby town were behaving. They made noises of support but their hearts weren't in it. Again, Yashu saw that proximity didn't necessarily mean closeness. She mentioned this to Khollo, quoting the Li*issuan proverb. He said that he thought it was a good proverb and asked her to say it in her own language so he could learn it in that. He mastered the words straight away, copying her intonation exactly. He asked her to teach him a few more phrases, and she did. She was impressed at how easily he picked them up, until she recalled that this was his Flow, this was what he did, re-membering things. Mischief then overtook her, and she informed him that the sincerest and most complimentary way of greeting someone in Water language was to say, 'You have the lips of a sea-bass and a backside as big as a whale's.' Khollo dutifully repeated the words, and she pretended he had mispronounced the last one, just so that she could hear him say the sentence through again. She thought of him addressing every Water-Inclined stranger he met in the future with a solemn 'You have the lips of a sea-bass and a backside as big as a whale's', and it was a struggle not to laugh. She went on to teach him several dozen more sayings, inserting a number of boobytraps along the way. An hour passed, and when she looked up, Mr Ayn had disappeared to bed. She herself was weary, and so they called it a night.

In the morning, it was a relief to step outside the walls of Hallawye. The sun was blossoming above the hills. The air was refreshingly sharp. Mr Ayn led the way. The goal, he said, was getting to Penres-ford, or rather getting *past* Penresford. The three of them trooped along the riverbank on a well-trodden towpath. The Seray rubbed smoothly by. It was Yashu who first saw the debris. Something large and black floating in the water, drifting towards them. It seemed to be a log but as it came closer, planed edges became apparent. Wood, still, but a piece of timber. Scorched timber.

More pieces of timber came into view, pulsed along by the current. Some were scorched, some not. Some were little larger than slivers. Some were whole planks. One which looked like a section of a tree trunk, branches and all, proved to be nothing of the sort. It rolled gently over as the river carried it, revealing an arm, a hand, a face, all charred to a bark-like texture.

There was worse to come.

AYN

It's funny. When we set out from Hallawye that morning, I knew what was coming. I knew what we were going to see. There would be horrors. And yet, for all that, I was excited. The next piece of my scheme was about to fall into place. By day's end our trio would be a quartet. And this overrode all other considerations. The nastiness of the day was just something I had to get through, like when you have a decayed tooth that's too far gone for a recuperator to rescue and you have to have it pulled. Or perhaps like giving birth. The result, be it relief from pain or the arrival of a baby, makes the suffering you have to go through to achieve it almost immaterial.

We strode upriver, following a broad, beaten towpath that was the main thoroughfare linking Hallawye and Penresford. Yashu, with her clear young islander eyes, was the first to spot the wreckage in the water – fragments of what had been boats coming towards us on the current. She, too, was the first to identify human remains amid the flotsam. Bodies, burned to blackness. Immediately she murmured a few words in her own language. Hummed them, in fact. Some kind of song. Something islanders habitually sing in the presence of the dead. Her face was hard-set. Yours as well, Khollo. It was clear that the dispute at Penresford had degenerated into violence, and you suggested, did you not, that we should turn back. You knew enough about my scheme, however, to know that turning back was out of the question. Plus, it was something one had to see. The wreckage and the bodies, what they indicated, had a dreadful fascination. I felt it. We all, I'm sure, felt it. There is an instinct in man that draws him to look on ruin and devastation. Perhaps it's to remind himself that he's still alive. Perhaps it's to remind himself *why* he's still alive.

We left the towpath, aiming for the brow of a nearby hill. We climbed the hill, and there, before us, lay Penresford.

Penresford, in appearance, was much like Hallawye. Huddled, humble, closed-in. A multitude of chimney pipes sticking up above the rooftops at all sorts of angles, like tousled hair. A plucky, stalwart little town whose people had worked the land around it hard, digging into the alluvial soil, following each clay seam wherever it led until it was exhausted, then looking for the next one. Penresford sat in the midst of a sorry, manufactured baldness. It was surrounded by scars.

At its northern end there was a line of boats strung across the Seray. This, needless to say, was the means by which Penresford's inhabitants had blocked river traffic. It had had a counterpart to the south of the town, but all that remained of that was a single barge tethered to the far bank, angled downstream and half sunk. The rest had become the debris we saw earlier. On the still extant line of boats I could see people, charging to repel other people who were attempting to gain access from the far bank. To us up on the hill, they looked like ants. I might go further and say they looked like black ants and red ants – the swarthy Earthers and the redheaded Flamers, clashing. Your sceptical expression tells me the analogy doesn't work. Why?

['From that distance I couldn't tell one kind of hair colour from another.']

And if *you* couldn't, what chance did a dull-eyed old man like me have? But the image has a neatness about it, don't you feel? Oh, very well. Antlike, though, definitely antlike, were the people who were fleeing Penresford. Did you ever bash an anthill when you were a boy, Khollo, and watch the little beggars come scurrying out?

[If I did, it was before I can remember.]

That was it there. They were coming out of Penresford's southern gates, the opposite end of town from where the fighting was, a hurried exodus of women, children and the elderly, some carrying belongings, some carrying each other. Their town was doomed. They knew it. Out they came, massing in a confused, milling throng. Who could not feel pity for these people? First the 'Storm, now this. Had I been in a position to do anything to help them, I would have. But what could I have done? What could any of us have done? My role – our role – was to remain where we were and watch. This was an event to which the three of us could only be appalled spectators.

On the string of boats, the attackers were encroaching. The defenders were burning. Incendiaries were doing that which they are forbidden ever to do: they were using their fire on people. Men went up like matches. Some dived in the river to extinguish themselves. Some did not manage to and fell to the boats' decks. The attackers, by which I mean the people of Stammeldon, advanced across the boats at a steady, remorseless pace. Resistance was valiant but futile. Every headlong rush to meet the boarders ended in a burst of flame, sometimes a tiny, just audible scream. Yashu murmur-hummed her songs for the dead but after a while she gave up and lapsed into silence. She couldn't keep up. There were too many dead.

There were also Stammeldon people coming down along the bank on the same side of the river as Penresford. In their wake lay a trail of scorch marks and cinders, smouldering. It did not do to contemplate what had been there before the ground was reduced to ash. It did not do to wonder what those charred mounds were that littered the earth, seemingly fused to it.

I have read accounts of wars and battles. Incendiaries have had a part to play in conflicts throughout the ages. They have sacked towns, thrown battle lines into disarray, and yes, of course, killed. Incendiaries were involved in the Siege of Stonehaven. It was thanks to them that the gate was breached and the aggrieved rabble got inside. Incendiaries burn. It's what they do. But they burn *people* only in extremis, when the restraints of civilisation are broken, when their own lives are at stake, when a general orders them to do so, when all else has failed.

It was hard to believe, that day, that all else had failed, but it had. The evidence was right in front of us. And a terrible sight it was, too. I hope I'm conveying it accurately, doing justice to the ghastliness of it. In many ways I wish I could forget everything I saw.

[Me too. I wrote earlier that for me the bad memories always seem more prominent than the good ones. This is a case in point. Indelibly there, whenever I choose to revisit it and sometimes when I don't choose to, is a vision of fire and slaughter, the mayhem that was the Battle of Penresford. It makes me shudder to recall it, even thirteen years on.]

Soon, on the boats, the Stammeldoners were clear across to the other side, all opposition ruthlessly having been dealt with. They convened with the other Stammeldoners who were already there. It was around then that I became aware of smoke trickling up from the south-eastern quarter of Penresford. It was a precursor of things to come. Perhaps it inspired the Stammeldoners to do what they did next.

Within minutes, other columns of smoke had started to sprout at the northern end of town. We began to see flames licking up above the roofs, embers swirling skyward. Rapidly the smoke columns merged and a dark grey pall amassed in the sky over Penresford.

Fires bloomed all over the town. The riverside docks, which I could tell had already been 'Storm-battered, erupted in flames. The wharf buildings overlooking the docks went up, too. There was an explosive roar as each fresh fire ignited, and sometimes a far-off, lusty whoop from those doing the igniting. I wondered how soon they would tire, these Flamers, how soon they would deplete their inner energies and start to flag. But it was clear that a madness was upon them, a kind of hysteria, and in such a state a person can continue to utilise his Inclination well past the normal threshold. His stamina is doubled, even trebled. It's not so with us Air types. Under duress our Inclinations are apt to give out on us. But with Earthers, Wets, most classes of Flamer, there seems to be an extra reserve they can draw on in times of crisis. H. C. Mellit discusses this in the follow-up to his *Elementary Natural History*, the less well known *The Mental/Physical Divide*, in which he . . .

Book-learning. I have plenty of it but it's no substitute for experience. Forget Mellit! Forget accounts of warfare compiled by military historians who weren't there! Forget all of it! I must simply recount what I saw.

I saw people from Stammeldon driven into a frenzy that was shocking to behold. I saw incendiaries set light to things with a glee that was palpable even from, how far away were we, a mile? I saw them exercising their ability to burn, without conscience, without compunction. I saw a savagery dredged up from the very darkest recesses of the human heart, and I remember thinking then, even through my horror, that the blame for all this lay ultimately with the Worldstorm. The 'Storm was the true cause. Sometimes it could bring out the best in us. Remember Varshet? The people on the mud skiffs going to help their neighbours? But usually, more often, it brought out the worst. And I thought that soon, thanks to me, this would no longer be the case. No more 'Storm would mean no more scenes such as these. A naïve hope perhaps, but I do believe that with the main source of the world's tribulations vanquished, mankind can look forward to a safer, more peaceful future.

The former residents of Penresford, now refugees, began moving away from the burning town, uphill, towards where we stood. A few halted close by but scarcely noticed us. They had eyes only for the conflagration that was overtaking their homes and consuming what had been their lives and livelihoods. They clung to one another and dismally stared. Noon came and went, the sun at its zenith paled by the ever-thickening pall of smoke, which was now like a man-made storm cloud. Parts of Penresford were almost gone, just gutted black skeletons of buildings, which collapsed in on themselves with a tumbling cacophony of crashes and bangs and a momentary up-rush of reinvigorated flame. In places the fires were so intense they glowed white. Sparks and embers sailed away on the breeze, descending to the west of the town in a snow of soot and ash. I watched roof shingles pop and shatter, windowpanes fall in shards, fire come billowing through the hollowed frames. It would be nice to liken the blaze to a living thing, to bestow on it a metaphorical sentience, but it was anything but sentient. It was mindless, elemental, absurd in its destructiveness. The incendiaries were barely controlling it. They simply let it loose and kept adding to it. Fire and then more fire. A whole town was gradually immolated. Buildings which builders had toiled to build. Houses where people had been born and died. Streets on which, perhaps just the day before, neighbour had bid neighbour good morning. Shops whose inventory was now just so much flame fodder. There was nothing to be said. You and Yashu and I merely looked on in silence as a community's entire history went up in smoke.

Some time later – I cannot begin to speculate how much time – the fires began to subside. Penresford had become a grey husk, with here and there a corner of a building still standing proud, here and there a ribcage of roof beams showing, here and there the outline of an alleyway marked by tumbledown runs of blackened fence. Sections continued to blaze fiercely, but for the most part what could be reduced to ash and slag had been reduced to ash and slag. The smoke columns had tapered and thinned, and the cloud they had been feeding was well on its way to the horizon, dissipating as it went. It was as though the town had exhaled itself into the air, taking on a new and impermanent form.

I became aware of the sound of weeping. The townsfolk on the hillside were finally acknowledging that Penresford was gone. It was as if up until that moment there had been the chance something of it might be salvaged, something of it might have been left sufficiently intact to serve as a rallying point, a symbol of hope of recovery. But nothing. Nothing was left. And I became aware, almost simultaneously, of cheering down at the river. Perhaps in answer to the laments of the people from Penresford, the people from Stammeldon were ostentatiously congratulating each other. There was patting of backs. Hand-slaps. Laughter with a coarse, contemptuous edge. This, surely, was the most offensive sight we witnessed that day. More so than the actual ravaging and razing of Penresford – the ravagers and razers so pleased with themselves afterwards. Cheering. Crowing over the still-smouldering corpse of the town. And, by implication, over the human corpses as well. The crumbled remnants that littered both riverbanks. The bodies in the Seray itself, of which there were a score, some bobbing slowly downstream, others caught in reeds at the river's edge. Those who had been slain for having the temerity to defend their hometown. And corpses, too, in the town itself. Who knew how many had perished as Penresford blazed?

[There were losses on the other side as well. Nearly a dozen Stammeldon attackers were killed during the conflict. But I think

Elder Ayn's bias of sympathy towards Penresford is right. Once the Stammeldon incendiaries began to use their flame, the town and its population never stood a chance. The comparative toll on lives – and property – bears this out. Past a certain point the Battle of Penresford became hopelessly one-sided, more a slaughter, in fact, than a battle.]

Happily, the celebrations were short-lived. A drumming of hoof-beats announced the arrival – the too-late arrival – of a company of cavalrymen. They came thundering into view astride roan steeds whose bits were flecked with spittle and whose flanks were ribbed with sweat-froth. The cavalrymen galloped right past us, and fine figures they were, resplendent in brass helmets and scarlet tunics and tight white breeches. On his chest each had a large fireball motif embroidered in gold thread, and the man at the vanguard, who one could only assume was their leader, sported a beard so splendiferously bushy and bright orange that it itself resembled a fireball. Uttering a load 'holla!' this well-whiskered bravo urged his men on to complete the last mile of riding between them and the ruins of Penresford.

The Flamers down at the town were so wrapped up in their jubilation they didn't even notice the cavalrymen coming until the cavalrymen were almost on top of them. It would be fair to say that the fight went out of them straight away. Whatever appetite they might have had for further conflict, they suddenly lost. Even if they had not already expended their energies on burning Penresford, they would have been no match for military incendiaries, trained to a level of Inclination proficiency far exceeding that of any ordinary civilian. Here was a foe superior to them by the same margin that they were superior to Penresford's Earthers. As the cavalrymen drew level with them, reining in, their cheers dwindled. They began to look sheepish and downcast. Abashed as schoolboys, they shuffled their feet. At a stroke, the conquerors had become the conquered.

[It's a mystery how Elder Ayn, not being a sharp-sight, could make out details like facial expressions and shuffling feet from a mile off. No, I should grant him some artistic licence here. As accounts of the Battle of Penresford go, his is, to put it mildly, partial and subjective, so what does it matter if some of it is entirely his own invention? The majority of it at least has the virtue of being first-hand reportage. The same cannot be said for most of the books on the subject that have been written since.]

The cavalrymen encircled the Stammeldon group, and for a while it was hard to be sure what was going on. Some kind of discourse, it seemed. Then, next thing we knew, an order was given and the whole lot of them, soldiers and civilians, started to move off together up-stream. The cavalrymen had the people from Stammeldon completely surrounded, but if they had them under arrest or were protecting them, it was difficult to tell.

The people on the hillside with us were in no doubt which it was. Grumbles started to emanate from all around, rising to a note of incredulous anger. The soldiers and the destroyers of Penresford had struck a deal. The cavalrymen were escorting the Stammeldon incendiaries to safety. It was an Inclination thing, Flamer siding with Flamer.

Whether this was true or not, it swiftly gained the currency of truth. A few of the Penresford inhabitants set off downhill in high dudgeon, and then there was a groundswell, an avalanche, more and more joining them, until a veritable mob was making its way towards the town, all jeers and shouting and brandished fists. They circumvented the town, moving at a fast lick, in order to intercept the cavalrymen and their charges on the other side. What happened thereafter, I can't really say. There was some kind of clash, that's for sure, with sheets of fire erupting at regular intervals. By that point, you see, we had something other to do than just watch. We had business elsewhere.

'Time we were on our way,' I said, or words to that effect, and in a little procession of three we traipsed down the hillside, passing among the few townspeople still left there – small children, mothers, the elderly and infirm, and those still too numbed to have stirred themselves to join the vengeful mob. Glazed gazes barely registered us as we went by. Stunned eyes didn't do much more than flicker as we walked in front of them.

To begin with we followed much the same route the mob had taken, towards the western edge of Penresford, but I was at pains to reassure both of you that I was planning to divert even further west, away from the continuing troubles. Yashu wanted to know why we didn't simply head back to Hallawye, but I pretended not to hear. Gone a bit deaf in my old age, you know how it is. I strode on with the air of a man who knew exactly what he was doing. Which, of course, I was. And she, poor child, had no real alternative but to tag along.

Our path led us past one of those fields in which Earthers bury their dead like dogs bury bones – though without the urge to dig them up again later. You have to admit it's an odd practice, sticking the deceased in the ground like so much compost. So unclean.

[And slicing up a body so that it can become food for carrion creatures isn't?]

From there, just as we were going by, there came a low, aching moan. Again I feigned deafness, but the moan got your attention and it certainly got Yashu's. She cast around, trying to find the spot it had originated from. Then she hissed something that sounded very much like an obscenity, and she pointed, and her finger was aimed at the centre of the burial field where, beside a mound of recently turned earth, lay a body.

The body looked for all the world as if it had just emerged from the ground. It was tattered and ragged and covered in dirt, and one might reasonably have thought that this was someone who had been prematurely interred, someone who had perhaps fallen into a death-like coma and been the victim of a dreadful misdiagnosis and awoken to find himself suffocating beneath several feet of soil and had had to claw his way up out of it. That's never a danger with Air burials, is it? That kind of mistake being made.

[There's a story, most likely apocryphal, which was told to me several times at Stonehaven, about a certain High Serendipiter long ago. He's found in his bed one morning, apparently dead, no pulse detectable. He's laid out and stripped bare, all in accordance with ceremony, and then as the funeral gets under way and the first incision is made, the body startles everyone by suddenly sitting bolt upright and yelling, 'How dare you, sir! That's my arm, that is!'

In one version of the story, a previsionary present at the funeral foresees what's going to happen and intervenes a moment too late. In another version, the person wielding the knife, who is the High Serendipiter's successor, gets such a shock that he keels over dead from a heart attack. I can't say that in any version the story rings true. It sounds more like one of those tales, and there are plenty of them, which someone Air-Inclined has dreamed up to illustrate how much better it is to be Air-Inclined. Even when you're dead.]

What we were looking at, however, wasn't some self-exhumed ex-corpse. What we were looking at was a sixteen-year-old boy, grubby, redheaded, and badly burned. He was lying prone, face pressed to the ground, fingers clenched in the mound of burial dirt, his back heaving up and down erratically. One sleeve of his shirt was missing, the exposed arm scorched and peeling-skinned. A patch of that coppery hair was gone, pale white scalp showing through. What we were looking at, evidently, was somebody who had been involved in the conflict down at the town, a participant, a victim. A Flamer, too, if the hair was anything to go by.

That, at any rate, was the conclusion Yashu drew.

'It's one of them,' she said. 'One of the ones who did all the burning.' Her tone was taut, suspended halfway between alarm and contempt, and her face seemed to indicate she didn't know whether to give in to one kind of temptation and flee or another kind of temptation and go over to the boy on the ground and start belabouring him with blows. If it had come to it, I reckon she would have opted for the latter. She has a fierce, fearless streak in her, our Yashu.

At the sound of her voice, the boy's head lifted. His face, not to put too fine a point on it, was a mess. On the left side where the hair was absent, his forehead and cheek were charred, the skin cracked like a riverbed during a drought. His eye was puffed shut. Half of his upper lip was one large blister. The right side wasn't in a much better state but this was due to its rubbed-on coating of soil. Beneath that it was undamaged.

And out of this dirtied but undamaged side an eye regarded us, wide, bloodshot and baleful. An eye that had seen even worse things than we had that day, an eye that had seen much too much. I had an inkling that I knew why that eye looked the way it did, and a quick peek into my future revealed this boy, some time ahead, confessing to a tragic error of judgement he had made here at Penresford. The compassion I was going to feel for him in the future resonated back so that I felt it also right then, or at least a presentiment of it, a fore-shadowing of compassion to come.

The lad moved his hurt mouth, trying to speak. Some words emerged but they were incomprehensible, riven with pain. Not just physical pain either, a deeper pain than that. His voice carried a note of pleading, too, all of which made it eminently logical for me to say, 'We must help him.'

Yashu remonstrated, asking why we should help anybody who had been part of *that* (meaning the havoc wrought on Penresford).

My reply was a model of reasonableness: 'He's injured. We have a duty to help him as fellow human beings. But also, if we don't, what if some of the local inhabitants find him here? You saw that mob. Do you think they'd be kind to him?'

'Then he'll get what he deserves,' Yashu said, with that little knot of resolution prominent between her brows.

I said, 'Yashu, he's your age. A mere boy. We can't just leave him.'

'We can,' Yashu said, and proved it by storming off due west at a forthright pace.

'Go with her,' I told you. 'I'll catch you up.'

On my own, I ventured into the burial field, threading between the stone-marked plots till I reached the boy.

And there I permitted myself a quick gloat. As I stood over the lad who I knew to be Gregory Brazier, I enjoyed one of those all too rare moments in a previsionary's life when one's Inclination is perfectly aligned with one's intentions. I had felt the same way upon meeting Yashu, but dripping wet on the deck of a boat I was in less of a position to make the most of it. There in that burial field – which isn't the correct name for such a place. What is the correct name, do you know?

['Graveyard.']

Indeed. Much obliged. There in that graveyard, everything came together. I was at the peak of myself. How I had got there seemed less a matter of artful contrivance and more a matter of natural patterns. Meant to be rather than made to be. I stood, and at my feet lay Gregory Brazier, the second of the two crucial components of my scheme. The world seemed to revolve around us, we atop its very axis. Through prevision I had arranged things so that I would find him there. I had known that he would be there when I needed to find him. Not only was it all panning out as I knew it would, it was all panning out as I knew it *should*. I had an exultant sense of power, as opposed to the miserable sense of powerlessness that is the previsionary's usual lot. For once I was coachman rather than passenger in my own life.

Here he was, Gregory Brazier, the son of a Fire-Inclined bloodline, who was Earth-Inclined.

And already in my company I had Yashu, the daughter of a Water-Inclined bloodline, who was Air-Inclined.

Each a mingling of two different Inclinations.

And to bring them together, to have them mate and procreate, would result in that which Traven Keech had proposed would defeat the Worldstorm. A fusion of all four Inclinations. A child who embodied Air, Water, Fire and Earth all in one. A being like no other, whose very existence would tip the scales of nature back in mankind's favour.

I all but hugged myself. Then the moment passed and practicality reasserted itself.

I extended a hand down to Gregory.

And smiled at him.

And in my softest, gentlest voice said, 'Come with me.'

GREGORY

27th of Drymonth 687

Fire coursed along the downstream boat chain in a wave, crossing from one end to the other in a matter of seconds. There was no time for anyone to dive overboard or run. Boat after boat went up, the detonations like a volley of vast drumbeats. Gregory was able to wonder, briefly, how incendiaries had got to the town-side bank (he could just make out a pair of tall redheaded figures down there, orchestrating the fire). Mostly his brain was blank, too aghast to formulate thought.

Almost as soon as the inferno reached the far-side bank, the boat chain broke up. One of its smaller links, a ferry, rolled over and swiftly sank, the Seray swallowing it in a hiss of steam. The other burning vessels detached from one another with the stateliness of dancers at the music's end, a polite, mutual disengagement, each gliding off downriver at slightly different angles. A few did not get far before the weight of water flooding into their ravaged hulls started to drag on them and they began listing and then keeled over and disappeared. The rest, still roaringly ablaze, disintegrated. Caulking melted, planks popped apart, decks yawned, until the boats were large clumps of debris spread out on the river's surface, floating together but being teased further and further apart by the current. Flames continued to sputter and spark on the bits of wreckage, like tenacious tongues that couldn't finish the conversation.

Even as the boats fell to pieces there were still indestructibles aboard them, and some of the indestructibles were still alive. Gregory could see them crawling – wretched, ragged figures, seared from head to toe. Their bodies were struggling to repair their injuries, and they remained conscious. They must be conscious because they were moving through the flames, trying to get to the side and slither overboard. They were aware of what was happening and the pain they were in was something Gregory had no desire to imagine. He could not forget how much it had hurt when Willem singed his hand with that flame snake, and that had been just the tips of his fingers. Multiply it to cover every square inch of his body and you had a level of agony against which no amount of training could inure you.

In the end the dying indestructibles stopped moving, or were dragged under as the boats beneath them sank. But the sickly feeling in Gregory's stomach remained, and wasn't eased when Ven, in a whisper, said, 'We were there. Just a moment ago. That could have been us.'

That could have been them, yes. If they hadn't been told to get off the boat chain when they had, if they had somehow managed to talk the adult indestructibles into letting them stay, that could have been them on one of those floating funeral pyres, suffering as the burned indestructibles had suffered, knowing their injuries were too severe for even them to recover from, knowing they were about to die and yet their bodies were still doing their best to keep them alive, prolonging their agony.

This wasn't exciting any more. Gregory marvelled that he could ever have thought it was. This – Stammeldoners versus Penresfordians, Flamers versus Earthers – was just vicious and senseless and mad. It should not be happening. He wished it would stop, right now. But he knew that not only was it not going to stop, it was going to get worse. It was going to carry on till everyone ended up like those indestructibles, till all of Penresford ended up like that boat chain. He glanced northward. Stammeldoners were advancing implacably along either bank. He turned to Ven.

'Home,' he said, thin-lipped. 'Let's get the family. Get them out of town.'

Ven answered with a dazed nod, and he and Gregory rose and made their way back across the warehouse roof. Neither boy could recall the ladder being so loose on its mountings when they had climbed it, nor the zigzag staircase being so shaky underfoot. The world, all of a sudden, was a much less steady place.

Finally Willem recovered the power of speech.

'Reehan! Reehan, what the fuck . . . ?'

His friend turned and looked at him blankly, blandly, as if he couldn't understand what Willem was making such a fuss about. His eyes had a dreamy fullness about them – the eyes of someone who had at last, after far too long, managed to slake a thirst. Willem could not decide which was worse: what Reehan had just done or the satisfaction he exuded at having done it.

'Reehan, they were people,' he said. 'We spoke to them. They were kind to us. They did us a favour. Trusted us. People.'

'Not any more,' Reehan replied. He sounded like he was miles away.

' "Not any more"?' Willem fought, and failed, to keep an edge of hysteria out of his voice. 'You killed them, Reehan! Don't you get it? You . . . killed . . . them!'

'So? People are killing people up there, upstream. We're all doing it. They threatened Dad,' Reehan added, as if this justified everything.

'*They* didn't.' Willem waved a hand at the fragments of the boat chain smouldering their way downriver. '*They* helped us.'

'Penresfordians.' Reehan shrugged. 'Should never have been there in the first place.'

Willem felt his fist clench, his arm draw back. He had never hit anyone before. Well, Gregory a couple of times, but only as kids, only brotherly thumps. Not like this. Not out of pure, blind fury. He wanted to drive his fist into Reehan's face. Wanted to knock that awful glutted contentment out of his eyes. The only thing that prevented him was fear. An image flashed into his mind: Reehan turning his flame on *him*, not hesitating to add one more to the tally of lives he had taken, not balking at killing his best friend. Willem understood then that Reehan was insane, and it was not so much a surprise, more a revelation of the obvious. Destroying the boat chain was not something that had come out of the blue. It was the culmination of a pattern of behaviour, an action Reehan had been building up to for days, weeks, perhaps even months. His increasing contempt for Master Drake's tuition. His insistence on joining the Penresford expedition. Quietly, secretly, Reehan had been waiting for an opportunity like this. Hoping for it. And when it came, he had seized it with glee. A chance to show exactly how little society's moral guidelines meant to him. A chance to cut loose with his flame and never mind the consequences. And his flame was so powerful. Even Master Drake had had to acknowledge that. To have so much flame inside and be forced to keep it caged all the time – it would have tested the character of a far more responsible person than Reehan Bringlight.

Willem's fingers unfurled. A coward, but a wise coward.

'Besides,' Reehan said, oblivious to his friend's brief surge of loathing, 'you could have done something if you'd wanted to. I mean diverted my flame, deflected it, something like that. If you'd really wanted to.'

There was no answer to that, at least none Willem could think of which wouldn't simply feed Reehan's mad ego. *I was too shocked. Your flame's too strong for me to affect. I couldn't believe you were going to go through with it.* All he could do was shake his head dumbly, hoping his silence spoke volumes.

'In point of fact,' Reehan went on, 'you're partly to blame. If you hadn't led us down here . . .' He blinked, his gaze regaining some of its focus. 'Well, there we are, it's done now. In the past. We still have a mission, don't we? Rescuing Little Bother. So let's get on with it.' He strode briskly off, then looked round when he realised Willem wasn't beside him. 'Come on. What are you waiting for?'

It was all Willem could do to make his feet move. He dragged himself off after Reehan with a queasy heaviness in his belly. He had to stick with Reehan. He had no choice. He couldn't let him wander on his own through Penresford, not after what had just happened here. Reehan was right. In a way, Willem was to blame. And like it or not, he was probably the only person who could stop Reehan committing another atrocity.

And like it or not, another atrocity was something Reehan seemed very likely to commit.

Once or twice in his career as an endurance boxer, Master Ergall had had to face the possibility of dying. Not least during his famous, record-breaking three-hundred-round bout against 'Mighty' Mike Batta (three hundred and seven rounds, to be exact), when, towards the end, his body was so pummelled and punished that simply to remain standing took every ounce of willpower he possessed. There had come a stage when he had felt adrift inside himself, cocooned somehow from all the pain, and he had been reconciled to the idea that Batta could and would keep pounding him till some vital organ burst irreparably. It had been a curiously tranquil moment, the pro-spect of death a release, comforting in its certainty. The life of Dan Ergall had seemed a small thing, and he knew he would not be much missed. His mother would mourn him, and his manager too, each for different reasons. Other than them, there wasn't anybody for whom his death would be a great loss. Least of all himself.

That he eventually won the fight was down to the fact that, during a let-up in the barrage of blows from Batta, he realised that his op-ponent was as near collapse as he was. Batta, like him, was dead on his feet. This had spurred him to reach deep inside and summon up the last dregs of strength he needed to finish the fight.

Now, as he and a dozen other indestructibles on the far-side bank braced themselves to confront the Stammeldon forces, Master Ergall experienced that same curious sense of tranquillity. It didn't matter. Dying didn't matter. Vaguely he thought it a pity to be throwing away the further thirty or forty years he could expect to live, but when it came to the crunch – and this was very definitely the crunch – life wasn't about surviving, it was about doing. It was about actions which counted. It was about making the most of your time before the very last bell rang, announcing the onset of endless darkness.

And if he could take down a couple of those Match-head bastards before they got to Penresford, maybe slow their advance just that little bit, it would, he felt, be fair exchange for thirty or forty unlived years.

Mayor Bringlight was in the midst of the oncoming Stammeldoners. Not exactly leading them, but encouraging them forward. Master Ergall focused on him, making him his target. No point aiming low. An old boxing maxim: *go for the head*.

Master Ergall heard himself uttering a wordless battle yell. He found himself rushing towards the enemy. He was aware of the other indestructibles coming with him. He wondered if they knew the absolute freedom from fear that he knew. For their sake he hoped so.

The Stammeldoners mounted a defence, but were a fraction late in doing so. There were so many of them, compared with the indestructibles, that perhaps each thought he didn't need to respond to the indestructibles' charge; someone else would. Master Ergall managed to get within a half-dozen yards of them before the first fireball came roaring his way. It hurtled past his thigh, and he didn't feel a thing, even though a shower-burst of sparks told him he had been hit. Momentum carried him headlong into the Stammeldon ranks. They scattered to either side, and all Master Ergall saw was Mayor Bringlight directly ahead, looking fraught, calling on his men to get them, get those bloody Mudwallows now! Master Ergall accelerated, and there was a blur of movement in his path and a crack of impact across his forehead. His skull sang. He staggered. Swift. Must have been. With a cudgel. But no, it didn't hurt. It did not hurt. Master Ergall resumed his charge, and the swift came in again, catching him this time on the shoulder. Master Ergall's arm went tinglingly numb all the way to the hand. Master Ergall ran on. Mayor Bringlight. The swift, once more. But slower now, his burst of speed nearing its end. Master Ergall had no idea how he did it but he managed to catch hold of the swift's wrist as the cudgel descended. He yanked back and downward, turning the swift's own speed against him. There was a dull, rippling snap which he felt more than heard. The swift shrieked and stumbled, crashing to the ground, broken forearm flapping like a flail.

Now fewer than ten paces separated Master Ergall from Mayor Bringlight. The mayor knew Master Ergall had singled him out. You could see it in his eyes. Then an incendiary stepped between them. Master Ergall waded at him, even as the incendiary summoned up a wall of flame as big as a bedsheet. Master Ergall lowered his head, closed his eyes and plunged straight through. No pain. Then a surge of pain across the whole of the front of him. Then no pain. None that Master Ergall would acknowledge. He snapped his eyes open. The incendiary was looking startled. He looked even more startled when a horny-hard fist swung and connected with his chin. The fist was attached to an arm that was sheathed in a shirtsleeve that was alight and left a trail of smoke through the air. *That's my arm*, Master Ergall thought, dimly and with a certain relish.

The incendiary went down like a chopped tree, and Master Ergall was face to face with Mayor Bringlight. He could feel his clothes burning on him, falling away. He could feel his skin blistering and peeling. Just superficial, he told himself. His body could handle it.

Mayor Bringlight studied him, no longer fraught, intently calm. Master Ergall raised his fists. Like a fight, this was. A boxing match. Just one more boxing match, like the many dozens he'd taken part in over the years.

'Come on then,' Master Ergall growled through singed, split lips. 'Do your worst.'

Mayor Bringlight turned his mouth up at the corners.

Raised a hand.

Then there was fire.

The whole world was fire.

There was pain so great that Master Ergall could not recognise it as pain. He was encased in it. It was inside him. It was all of him.

After that, nothing.

For a moment, just a moment, Mayor Bringlight had been worried. The indestructibles had come at them so suddenly, with such unexpected ferocity, that at first glance it had seemed this counter attack might actually have some effect.

He should have known better. Surveying the roasted human remains at his feet, he let out a shivery, relieved sigh. That was it. That was the best the Penresfordians could offer. This short, squat, ugly indestructible who had made a beeline for him – see what had become of him? Indestructible, my arse! And the other incendiaries were now making short work of the rest. A scream, followed by the distinctive sizzle-crackle of superheated flesh, announced the demise of the last of them. The counterattack had been a brave effort but doomed to failure. Once the Stammeldon forces overcame their initial shock, the Earthers had not stood a chance.

Stepping around the indestructible's body, Mayor Bringlight went to check on the welfare of the incendiary the indestructible had knocked down and the swift whose arm the indestructible had broken. The incendiary was out cold while the swift was sitting up, whey-faced, cradling the broken arm with his good one. Unfortunately the recuperators who had travelled down with the Stammeldon expedition had, all three of them, been aboard the barge that was now moored upstream on the opposite bank. The mayor promised the swift that as soon as he could get a recuperator over onto this bank, he would be the first to receive treatment.

Then the mayor turned his attention to the nearer of the two boat chains. Already some incendiaries were making for it. He summoned a swift over and ordered him to run ahead and tell the incendiaries to attack quickly and without remorse. A number of indestructibles had remained on the boat chain, there to fight a rearguard action. As a last-ditch tactic, they might try to scuttle the boats in order to prevent anyone getting across. At all costs that must not be allowed to happen.

As the swift dashed off, Mayor Bringlight craned his neck and looked further downstream. The further boat chain had erupted into flame a couple of minutes ago, and it wasn't difficult to work out who was responsible. He could see no sign of Reehan, or for that matter Willem, but they were down there somewhere. No doubt it had been Reehan's idea to abscond, rather than Willem's. No doubt, too, it had been Reehan's idea to attack the boat chain. Mayor Bringlight wasn't sure whether to admire his son's initiative or be appalled at his impetuosity. What he was sure of was that when he caught up with Reehan again, there would be an almighty reckoning. The boy might be a man now but he was still a father's son and disobedience was disobedience. Reehan was too old to beat any more, but later, when all this was over, he would be on the receiving end of the severest ear-bashing he had ever known. And there would be punishments. A few weeks without his allowance, plus being put to work on the mayor's properties, clearing gutters, unclogging drains – Reehan would soon see the error of his ways.

One good thing, at least. Reehan and Willem must surely still be on the far-side bank. They couldn't have crossed the boat chain and, now that it was gone, there was no possibility of them getting to the other side. They were, in other words, safe.

Assured of this, Mayor Bringlight was once more able to devote all his energies to the conflict. He saw that the incendiaries had reached the remaining boat chain and were, per orders, quickly and mercilessly dispensing with all resistance there. He saw that the Stammeldoners on the opposite bank had drawn almost level with those on this bank and were not far from the town. The two prongs of the assault were close to meeting up. He saw that more Penresfordians were scrambling onto the boat chain from the town-side. That was good. The more of them there were on it, the less likely they would be to scuttle it.

All in all, things were going rather well, he thought. In no time his forces would be at the gates of Penresford itself. There would be more deaths, but somehow this notion no longer disturbed him. It was a bridge he had crossed a long time back. Was this, perhaps, how a general felt as the battle unfolded and victory neared? This sense of cold purposefulness? This understanding that, for success to be achieved, compromises must be made and squeamishness set aside? Mayor Bringlight was impressed that it even mattered to him. Surely a general had no qualms about that aspect of warfare. Didn't so much as question it. Get the job done. Crush the enemy. Win. Death, and death's handmaiden, destruction, were just means to an end, and if you couldn't accept that, then you had no right getting involved in conflict in the first place.

The mayor was way past caring that the fight with Penresford had its genesis in a mere trade dispute. What was important to him now was demonstrating decisively that the standpoint he had taken was the right one, and if that meant Penresford should be wiped from the map, then so be it. As far as he was concerned, nothing less than total triumph, and total vindication, would do.

One of the pilots sidled sheepishly up to Horm Loffin. After several moments of havering he started to frame a question, but Loffin, in order to spare his blushes, halted him before he got very far.

'The answer's yes,' he said. 'You can go. All of you. This isn't your fight. You've done your part. You've helped us more than we could have expected you to. We appreciate that.'

'It's not that we're scared . . .'

'No, no, of course not.'

'We'll stay if you want us to. But we can't take lives. You know that. Our beliefs.'

'There's nothing to be ashamed of. Go.'

The pilot returned to his brethren and, with looks of furtive relief all round, the group of them retreated for the nearest entrance to the town, melting into the shadows there. Loffin was inexpressibly sad to see them gone. The Stammeldoners were closing in along both river-banks, eradicating all opposition in their path. The downstream boat chain was just a memory. The defence of the town was now a rout and continued opposition to the Stammeldoners was all but futile. But for all that, the withdrawal of the pilots seemed somehow the conclusive proof that Penresford was doomed. When even your allies were deserting you . . .

Loffin took a deep breath and turned toward the remaining boat chain. Hopping up onto the gangplank, he began walking across the boats' charred and dampened decks. Other Guild committee members quickly followed his example. They knew, as he did, that it was a matter of principle. It had always been a matter of principle.

Loffin was a clay-miner and a clay-miner's son. He had worked the hills around Penresford since the age of seventeen. Until his election to the Guild committee he had spent the best part of a quarter of a century helping keep Brazier Brickfields supplied with raw material. 'Clay in his veins', as the local adage went. He thought of himself as a simple man who didn't ask much out of life except a fair deal. For himself. For everyone. He had weathered five Worldstorm visits. He had been, he believed, throughout his years, in word and in deed, a decent person. Never had he dreamed that it would all end like this. But in a way it was apt. He was, with his last few heartbeats of life, behaving decently. He need not have got onto the boat chain. He could have made some excuse. He could, like the pilots, have abandoned the field. Decency, however, decreed that he go to confront the Stammeldoners head-on.

At the other end of the boat chain red-haired men were systematically slaying indestructibles. Loffin saw Penresfordians, people he had known all his life, collapse as though struck by a stone. Smoke billowed from their mouths as they fell.

The chief secretary of the Guild committee, with his fists clenched at his sides and his colleagues right behind him, strode gamely forward.

Retracing their steps through the covered bazaar brought Gregory and Ven to its north-west exit. The Gove house was not far, and they would have covered the distance in no time but the streets, which earlier had been empty, were now crowded. Either word had spread or some instinct had taken hold. Individually or as families, Penresfordians were on the move. They had emerged from their homes and were making for the southern and western ends of town. Many of them carried personal belongings with them, nothing too large or bulky, a few small keepsakes, a few mementoes. Just as a precaution, mind. No one really, truly believed anything dire was going to happen to Penresford. But you had to be on the safe side. In case.

When the boys finally reached home, Sol was outside, looking not a little frantic. The first word out of his mouth when he caught sight of the boys was an Earther expletive so obscene, Gregory was shocked to hear him use it. The next few words were a choleric tirade which soon subsided into an expression of relief that his second eldest son and Gregory were safe and well. 'Mind you,' Sol added, 'I can't guarantee you're going to stay safe and well once the wife gets her hands on you.'

'Is everybody here?' Ven asked, eyeing the house. 'Because I think we should be getting out of town. Other people are.'

'Everybody's already gone. I sent them off about ten minutes ago, soon as we got wind that the Stammeldoners were closing in. I stayed here to wait for you two to pitch up. I'm not even going to ask where you've been. Wherever it was, you're right bloody idiots the pair of you.'

'Sorry,' Gregory said, lamely, knowing *sorry* scarcely began to make up for what he and Ven had done. It hadn't even occurred to him, until seeing the distress on Sol's face, that anyone would be alarmed by his and Ven's absence from the house. Angry he had expected but alarmed came as a disconcerting surprise.

'Yes, well, like I said, it's not me you have to worry about,' Sol replied. 'Garla's going to be relieved and delighted when she sees you again. Then she's going to break your necks. And frankly, it'll be no more than you deserve.' A thin smile appeared and disappeared beneath his moustache. 'Anyway, you're here now. So let's go. I told the family we'd meet them outside the south entrance, by Two-Arch Gate. Failing that, somewhere up the hillside. Failing *that*, Hallawye.'

'Hallawye,' said Ven. 'Who've been so very helpful to us.'

'They'll take in refugees there, if the worst comes to the worst. I'm sure of it.'

So saying, Sol took out his house key and raised it as if to lock the front door. Then, with a shake of his head, he pocketed the key again.

'Never mind,' he said under his breath, and turned and set off down the street, with Gregory and Ven following.

'Could this *be* any more of a dump?' said Reehan, looking around him with a sour sneer. 'Imagine what it was like before the 'Storm came along. Like the old joke. The sort of place where a Worldstorm visit causes a million leaves' worth of improvement.'

Willem could not deny that Penresford was no more cheery on the inside than it was on the outside. Entering it had been like exchanging daytime for twilight. The sky was visible only in narrow, irregular slivers overhead and the day's brightness, when permitted in, failed to penetrate far. Rickety wooden building leaned against rickety wooden building as if seeking mutual solace in the gloom, and there was a rank, sewagey smell in the air which, while it grew less pungent the further he and Reehan got from the river, lingered in the nostrils and added to the general impression of miasmic murkiness.

'And Little Bother wanted to stay here,' Reehan went on. 'He chose this shit-heap over Stammeldon. Unbelievable.'

That also, Willem thought, could not be denied. It did seem unbelievable that Gregory could have chosen to remain here rather than return to bright, broad, spacious, un-malodorous Stammeldon. But then there was more to Gregory's decision than mere preference. So much more that Willem wondered if he would even recognise his brother when he saw him. At the very least he expected Gregory's hair to have turned a darker shade of red from the lack of sunlight, perhaps so much darker it was as good as black.

Of course, in order to see Gregory, Willem first had to find him. So far he and Reehan had been moving through an area of town that was exclusively given over to commerce and, at present, deserted. Obviously the Goves' house was in a residential area, and to get to it they would need to ask a local for directions. Whether any of the locals would be anything other than hostile towards a pair of Flamers remained to be seen, but Willem hoped that the same sincerity which had aided them in crossing the boat chain would continue to be effective here. It had worked once so there was no reason why it shouldn't work again. Granted, the situation was different now. Willem knew now, as he had not known earlier, that he was in the company of a madman. His best friend, a hot-blooded murderer, a pyromaniac. But he simply could not afford to think about that. He had to put it out of his mind. He had to stay focused on the goal of finding Gregory, and the only way to do that was by forcing himself to pretend that Reehan's act of slaughter had been some catastrophic mental aberration, caused by a specific provocation, a particular set of circumstances. Deep within Willem there was a scream that was building up pressure and demanding release, but he kept damping it down. Later, when all this was over, he would vent it, gladly. Until then he was taking his cue from Reehan and behaving as Reehan was behaving, as if nothing had happened. This was a kind of madness in itself, but a madness with method in it, born of necessity.

Rounding a corner, Willem emerged onto a cobbled alley, a few steps ahead of Reehan. To the right the alley dead-ended but to the left it gave onto a larger thoroughfare, and Willem saw people there, Penresfordians, trooping past the alley entrance in small, hurried groups. He turned to Reehan.

'Listen, how about this? How about I just nip up that way and grab somebody and find out what we need to know?'

'And in the meantime I do what?'

'I thought maybe stay here.'

'Why?'

Why indeed? Willem felt as though he were addressing a stranger, someone whose actions he could not predict and with whom he had to weigh carefully every word he said. A stranger who happened to look exactly like Reehan Bringlight.

'Well, because two Flamers together might be intimidating. Whereas one Flamer on his own, not so bad.'

Reehan deliberated on this and seemed to agree it made sense. 'Yes, all right. Don't be long, though. Just standing here I can feel myself picking up all kinds of nasty infections.'

Moments later, Willem was at the mouth of the alley. He hung back in the shadow of a doorway, out of sight, and watched the shuffling procession of Penresfordians pass, waiting for their numbers to thin. It would be better, for all sorts of reasons, if he accosted an individual rather than a crowd.

The Penresfordians were women and children mostly, and their faces spoke of anxiety and bewilderment. Willem saw a little girl – she couldn't have been more than five – clutching her mother's hand. With her other hand she clasped a much-loved toy mole to her chest. She was snivelling and her cheeks were streaked with tears. Her mother tugged at her to keep up and at the same time made soothing noises, but the little girl could not be consoled. Over and over, in a quavering voice, she asked her mother what was happening, where they were going, why everyone was so scared.

In his mind's eye Willem flashed back to the moment when Reehan had unleashed his flame on the boat chain. The sudden uncomprehending terror on the indestructibles' faces. The way they had become silhouettes amid the fire, black shapes of men, still moving.

The pent-up scream threatened to break out of him then, and he bit his lip, literally, to prevent it from doing so.

Why not run? Just head off along the street against the flow of Penresfordians, sprinting as fast as he could? Leave Reehan behind? Now, if ever, was the time for it.

But again that sense of responsibility asserted itself. Staying close to Reehan was as much his mission as finding Gregory. It seemed that it had become Willem's lot in life to be loyal to people who didn't deserve it.

The oncoming stream of people dwindled and for a while Willem thought there would be no more and he had missed his chance, until a pair of stragglers came into view. They were an elderly couple, he sprightlier than she but both making their way at her stiff-kneed pace, his arm around her shoulders. Willem stepped out into their path.

'Please,' he said in Earth language. 'Excuse me. Hello.'

The elderly couple reacted with consternation. The woman let out a cry while her husband raised his hands and said something Willem didn't understand, although the sense of the words was quite clear from his imploring tone.

Willem had all but exhausted his meagre supply of Earth-language phrases, which he had picked up from employees at the brickfields, principally Sam. 'I'm not going to hurt you,' he said, adopting

Common Tongue. 'I just need some help, that's all. I'm looking for the Goves. Sol Gove and his family. Can you tell me where they live?'

'Sol Gove?' said the old man warily. 'Yes, I know where the house of Sol Gove is.'

'Why are you doing this, you people?' his wife piped up, jabbing a forefinger at Willem. 'You are killing everybody, we have heard. What have we done to be killed like this?'

Willem couldn't think of a satisfactory answer to that one. 'It's not my business. I'm not involved.'

'How can you not be involved?' The old man had been made brave by his wife's boldness. 'You with your red hair, with your fire. You have come here—'

'I've come here,' Willem said, painstakingly, 'for my brother, nothing else.'

'Your brother,' said the old woman.

'Gregory Brazier.'

The elderly couple appeared stunned by this. They stiffened, their eyes went wide, and Willem was puzzled. His brother's name hadn't prompted this kind of reaction from the Earthers on the boat chain. What was . . . ?

Then he sensed the heat radiating from the couple, a miniature furnace within each of them, and the old woman gargled and her husband's eyes rolled up in their sockets, and Willem immediately reached out with his mind, grasping at the source of heat in both of them and trying to suppress it, but he couldn't control it, it resisted him, growing more intense the harder he tried to contain it, writhing like some wild animal that would not be captured. The old woman clawed at her breast as though she could somehow tear out what was hurting her. The old man sagged to his knees. The heat spread through their torsos, and Willem strove to extinguish it but its tendrils were everywhere, and the old man started jerking spastically and coughing smoke, and his wife's gargling noises were hideous, and Willem realised he could save neither one. He wasn't nearly strong enough. The heat shrugged off his efforts to master it. And now the old man slumped sideways onto the street, and his wife collapsed beside him and her arm, perhaps by chance, perhaps not, fell across his body, so that in their final few seconds of life the couple were at least touching each other, a last desperate embrace.

Willem wheeled round, and there was Reehan at the alley entrance. His grin was broad and slick and sickening to behold.

What Willem felt then was beyond the ability of words to express. It came out as the bitten-back scream, a howl of sheer disgust and horror. It roared out of him, and with it roared a bolt of flame which he did not mean to unleash but which had to be expelled, like venom, like pus, something his body needed to be rid of.

The bolt of flame shot straight at Reehan but never reached him. He deflected it, making it swerve around him to explode against a nearby wall in a spray of quick-vanishing firefly flickers.

Reehan peered at the scorch pattern left on the wall, then swivelled his gaze back to Willem.

'What did you do that for?' he said, bemused. 'You could have hit me.'

'You . . . absolute . . . mindless . . . fucker!' Willem replied, gasping in his fury. 'What's got into you, Reehan? Who the blazes *are* you? I don't know who you are. You're a lunatic. A pyromaniac!'

'A pyromaniac? Oh come on, don't be absurd, Willem. This is just . . .' Reehan glanced at the elderly couple's corpses, sprawled in their death-locked posture of love. That faraway calmness was in his voice again, and that gorged, almost intoxicated look in his eyes. 'You can't be really getting all worked up over a few Earthers, can you? You, son of one of the premier Fire bloodlines? Now *that's* madness, if you ask me. Why would you, Willem Brazier, care about a few stupid Browndirts? Oh wait. Of course. Your brother's one of them. There's the answer. I should have realised. These people are family.'

That stung. 'I don't . . . They're not . . . It's not the point, Reehan. These two – I was asking them for help and you just . . . murdered them.'

'Well, they didn't look to me like they were about to help you. They looked like they were having a go at you. They might even have been about to attack you.'

'What, two sixty-year-olds?'

'They could have been strongs. Strongs stay strong right to the end, isn't that the saying? Their Inclination doesn't fade with age.'

'But . . .'

'But what, Willem?' Reehan took a step towards him. 'What were you going to say? Were you going to call me more names, perhaps? You know, I'm seriously beginning to wonder about you. The way you ran away and left me. Remember? Back on the other side of the river? That's not the sort of thing friends do, rush off without a word, pursuing some little errand of their own. And in fact you lied to me, too, didn't you? Never told me the real reason you wanted to come down here was to fetch Gregory. I thought you shared my views on Penresford. But that was only what you wanted me to think.'

'It wasn't like that.'

'Wasn't it? Seems to me like it was. And I'm offended. I'm offended you didn't trust me with the truth. Offended you conned me into believing your motive for coming down here was the same as mine.'

'Reehan . . .'

'Yes?'

All at once Willem was profoundly weary. Resignation sank through him like a boulder into a lake. He was going to have to stop this before it went any further. More Penresfordians would die by Reehan's hand unless somebody did something. The somebody, by default, was going to have to be him.

But I'm no match for him. I don't have a hope.

It didn't matter. Reehan had become a lethal liability, impossible to reason with or restrain. Here he was, menacing even his own best friend. Was anyone safe from him? What if, assuming they found Gregory, Reehan decided Little Bother was altogether too Earther, too Penresfordian, for his liking?

'Reehan, I'm sorry.'

'Yes? Well, that's something.' Reehan squared his shoulders magnanimously. 'Apology accepted.'

'No,' said Willem, 'not about any of that. About this.'

Willem aimed another bolt of flame at Reehan, this one, unlike the previous one, a conscious action. As before, Reehan deflected it with insouciant ease, but in the split-second during which his attention was distracted, Willem lunged. When it came to flame Reehan was unquestionably the superior, but in physical terms? Willem reckoned they were more or less equal.

He hit Reehan in the midriff, driving him backward into the alley and against the door which he himself had sheltered beside a couple of minutes ago. The door gave a loud crack, and next thing Willem knew he was in an office of some kind. Desks, shelves of files and ledgers, graph charts on the wall, a map of the Seray – all this he registered in a few dazed seconds as he lay on the floor trying to figure out how he had ended up here. The door. Whatever was securing it – bolt, lock, catch – must have given way under the impact. The door had sprung inward. He and Reehan had tumbled through.

Reehan . . .

Willem looked around urgently. Reehan had fetched up against one of the desks. He was groaning, rubbing the back of his head.

Willem scrambled to his feet and lurched towards Reehan. Reehan glanced up groggily, eyes unfocused. Willem crouched, seized him by the lapels, and slammed him against the desk. He slammed him again. He tried for a third time but somehow Reehan got a knee up between them. He planted his shin against Willem's chest and shoved, and Willem went staggering backwards, crashing into a desk, half-sprawling across it.

He righted himself as quickly as possible, but in the time it took, Reehan managed to regain his feet as well.

'First of all,' Reehan said, 'ow. And second of all – Willem, am I wrong or did you just attack me?'

Willem knew he couldn't hesitate. There couldn't be any let-up. Reehan must not get an opportunity to deploy his flame.

He lunged again.

Reehan turned shoulder-on and grabbed Willem's shirt as they collided. They grappled like wrestlers, straining against each other, vying for leverage, advantage. Eventually Willem got his leg behind Reehan's and wrenched him down over it. Reehan did not relinquish his grip on Willem's shirt and so they both fell, collapsing to the floor, Willem on top.

Willem punched, his fist connecting with Reehan's cheekbone. Which hurt. Willem had had no idea that delivering a proper punch hurt. Pain jolted up from his knuckles. Gritting his teeth, he punched again. This time he caught Reehan on the nose, and blood spurted out, shockingly red against Reehan's pale skin. Willem drew his fist back.

Keep hitting. Knock him out.

But his fist stayed where it was, in mid-air. He looked down at Reehan. Reehan, blood-spattered. Reehan making a high-pitched whimpering sound, like a kitten's mew. Reehan flinching in anticipation of the next blow, while blood continued to flood from his nostrils, forming a glossy crimson delta over mouth and chin.

All at once Willem no longer saw the mad, murderous creature Reehan had become, he saw just the friend he had known for years, supine beneath him, bleeding, beaten.

His arm lowered.

'Reehan, are you all right?'

Reehan's eyes snapped open. His lips pulled back, baring pinkened teeth.

'Perfectly fine. Idiot.'

Willem heard the fireball coming rather than actually saw it. A rushing noise to one side of him. He hurled himself the other way. Fierce heat shot past his ear, and an instant later the fireball struck the far wall and something ignited with a *whoof*. Before he had time even to raise his head he sensed heat amassing close by. Reehan creating another fireball. He lashed out with one of his own, sending it in what he hoped was the right direction. Everything Master Drake had drummed into him over countless lessons, every caution, every warning –

irrelevant. If he didn't respond to Reehan's attacks in kind, didn't fight fire with fire, he was finished.

His fireball failed to find its target, but in ducking to avoid it Reehan lost concentration. His own fireball, hovering in readiness, winked out of existence.

Willem levered himself up onto all fours. Reehan's first fireball had set light to some of the files and ledgers on the shelves. They were burning merrily and the flames were crawling upward, groping, hungry for further fuel. Willem turned his head, to find Reehan hunkered just a couple of yards away. Behind him the charts on the wall were also burning, courtesy of Willem's fireball.

'It's great, isn't it?' Reehan's grin was gory and feral. 'Just to let rip. Not worry about where your flame's going, who might get hit. How did you feel when you singed Little Bother's fingers in the garden? When was it, three years ago? How cut up were you over that?'

Willem blinked, smoke starting to sting his eyes. 'Very.'

'And now you just chucked a fireball at me and you didn't care, not one bit. Isn't it liberating? Doesn't it make you feel fantastic?'

There was, Willem hated to admit, some truth in this.

'I've always envied you for that,' Reehan went on. 'The fact that you burned somebody. Up till today I never knew what it was like, though I often wondered. But then I've always envied you for everything. Your family. Your home. Your surname. Your birthright. Only, now we're equals, aren't we, you and I, Willem? We both burn people. This is something we can do together. Come on, join me. We'll go look for some other Earthers.'

'No,' said Willem. 'I don't want to join you. I don't even want to fight you.'

'Oh right. You're calling a truce, I suppose. Suddenly you've decided it's not worth attacking me, now that I'm attacking you back. Funny, that.'

'You don't really want to hurt me, otherwise you'd try and do to me what you did to those old people. And I don't really want to hurt you.'

'Is that so?' Reehan smeared his fingers across his upper lip and flicked droplets of blood onto the floor. 'And I suppose whacking me in the face was just for fun. A sign of affection maybe.'

'We need to settle this.'

'Too right.'

'But not here. Somewhere else. Some other time.' The smoke was thickening. The charts, the map of the Seray, and the baize-covered board they were pinned to, had become a single rippling sheet of fire. The flames' tongue-tips were licking at the ceiling beams and the boards of the floor above. 'Let's stop this now. Help me snuff these flames out before they get out of control.'

Reehan's reply was a simple 'No', accompanied by a theatrical flourish of the hand. The leather surface of the desk nearest him, the paperwork on it, the pen and inkwell, in-tray and out-tray, all flared up in a soaring cone of flame. 'Don't you see, Willem? How much better we incendiaries are than everyone else? It's a pleasure to burn. A privilege. A privilege we should exercise whenever we can.'

Willem thought about trying to extinguish the desk, thought better of it. 'I don't see that,' he said. 'All I see is a crazy person.'

'Again with the name-calling. I warned you about that.'

'A crazy, resentful, treacherous—'

'OK, you're getting me pretty ticked off. Maybe I didn't want to hurt you before, but I'm *this* close to changing my mind.'

'I'm going.'

'What?'

'You heard.' Shakily, Willem rose. 'I've had enough. Of you. Of all of this. I don't want anything more to do with you. See that door? I'm walking out through it and going to look for Gregory on my own. You can do what you want. Stay here and burn, for all I care.'

'Willem, this is highly disappointing.'

'Tough.'

'Don't turn you back on me. Don't you dare.'

'You know what, Reehan? I used to think you were really some-thing. I used to look up to you. Admire you. And do you know how that makes me feel now? Like a complete idiot.'

'I said don't you dare turn your back. I'm serious.'

Willem turned his back and, without looking round, said, 'Good-bye, Reehan.'

'Willem!'

The doorway beckoned. In under a dozen strides Willem would be out of the burning office. If he had a plan, it was the vague hope that walking out on Reehan like this might bring him to his senses. Self-preservation, though, was also a factor. The smoke in the room had gone from eye-watering to choking, and then there was Reehan him-self, no less of a hazard to health. Exiting the office was in every respect a wise tactic.

Each step seemed to take forever. The doorway seemed to get no nearer. The nape of Willem's neck tingled, feeling exposed and vulner-able. He veered between belief that there was no way Reehan would inflict serious injury on him and belief that there was every way.

In the event, Reehan did not try to kill him, but he did, in a fit of sheer pique, summon up another fireball and toss it. Willem was almost at the threshold when he detected the fireball sparking into life behind him, a knot of denser heat amid the general combustion.

He was ready for it. He took a deep breath and ignited flame of his own, instantly encasing himself in a protective shell of fire. He sensed the fireball hurtling at him. He took the next step forwards. He could see and hear nothing except his own flame. The world was the orange haze fluctuating before his eyes, the rippling crackle in his ears, the warmth building in this lambent womb. The fireball struck, and the impact shuddered through the protective shell. Willem staggered as though he himself had been directly hit. He felt the fireball disintegrate and fragments of it, smaller fireballs, go rolling over the shell and spill out beyond. Dimly he thought he heard someone cry out. Perhaps it was himself. He took a further step, braced for Reehan to launch a follow-up, another fireball. He was sure he must be through the doorway now, out in the alley. He was also sure that he could hear voices, close to him. He debated whether or not to dispense with the shell. If there were other people around, for their sake maybe he should. Besides, he couldn't hold his breath for much—

Gregory, Ven and Sol turned onto Porters Walk, the street where the wharf district merged with the rest of the town. Here were the offices of the various Guild agencies that oversaw the flow of goods into and out of Penresford. The street was familiar enough, but what didn't belong, an ugly addition, was a pair of bodies halfway along. They lay side by side on the cobbles, their grey heads canted together as though sharing a confidence, one arm forming a bridge of physical contact between them.

The sight of the bodies prompted an oath from Sol, and he broke into a run. He knew, even before he reached them, that he was looking at two corpses, but he squatted beside them and searched for signs of life nonetheless.

'It's Mr and Mrs Lunce,' said Ven, as he and Gregory caught up with his father.

The Lunces lived a few doors down from the Goves. Their grandson, Kig, was in the year below Gregory and Ven at school.

'What happened to them?' Gregory asked.

Sol's answer was preceded by a grim twist of the lip. 'Can't you tell? Can't you smell that smell?'

Gregory could indeed detect a faint odour which pricked a latent memory: funeral pyres on Memorial Plaza. The disturbingly sweet aroma of roasting human flesh.

Mr and Mrs Lunce's bodies were, to all appearances, intact. If not for their fixed, empty stares they could have been merely sleeping.

They had been burned from the inside. Gregory's stomach curdled at the thought.

'Incendiaries,' Sol said. 'They're in the town already.'

'They're still here,' Ven said, pointing. 'Look.'

A door in a nearby alley stood wide open, and wisps of white smoke were drifting out, snaking around jamb and lintel. Just visible within was the glow of fire.

Sol straightened up. 'Boys. Go. That way. Run. Get out of here.'

'No,' said Gregory.

Sol was stalking purposefully towards the doorway, rolling up the shirtsleeve on his good right arm with his not-so-good left hand. 'For *pfharg's* sake, it wasn't a suggestion. Run. Now!'

'You run too, Dad,' said Ven.

'I'm going to deal with them.'

'No, Dad!'

Sol half turned. 'Do as I say. Go and join the family. Don't worry about me. I'll be—'

In front of him the doorway bulged with flame, like some giant bubble of burning was trying to squeeze its way out. Sol shrank back, and as he did so the bubble quivered, spasmed, and spawned several miniature versions of itself, egg-sized fireballs which shot out from its surface. Sol was able to get a hand up in front of his face, but the fireballs sprayed him all over – torso, legs, arm. One moment he was standing there, the next he was on the ground, his clothes alight, beating at himself to put out the flames, screaming.

Gregory didn't hesitate. He knew a flame shell when he saw one. He sprang forwards, his hand balling into a fist. He gauged where the head of the incendiary within the flame shell would be. His fist – rock-hard thing – swung, and he was yelling, yelling as he sometimes did during a sticks game when his side was on an attacking play and he was likely to be hit and hurt. Yelling to stiffen his resolve against the pain to come.

And there was shock as he plunged headlong into the flame shell, a kind of dreamy disbelief.

Bilious joy as his fist struck home and something crunched beneath it.

A split second in which he believed he had somehow escaped being burned.

And then the agony.

He recoiled. His arm, his chest, the side of his face, were all as one and all elsewhere, a separate part of him, attached but immersed in a realm of pure, razoring pain. Pain that had no precedent, that was outside all experience.

His vision blurred. He could feel himself breathing in short bursts but no air seemed to be getting to his lungs. There was a wall behind him. No, it was the ground. Those were buildings up above, and a silvery-blue slice of sky. And the stench was vile. Like the smell from the Lunces' bodies only much, much stronger. That was him. His own skin and flesh and hair. The hair the worst. Acrid. Sulphurous. And there was Ven, bending over him. And Ven was speaking, Gregory could see his mouth move and was sure he could hear him, but Ven might have been using Water language for all the sense his words made. Gregory wondered when the pain would start to fade. It would surely start to fade soon because he was an indestructible and indestructibles were accustomed to pain. Were friends with pain, as Master Ergall had once said. Friends with and enemies of.

And Ven began to speak intelligibly: '—Dad's hurt, it's bad, you've got to get up, Gregory, you've got to be all right, Dad's hurt and there's another of those incendiaries in there, I heard him . . .'

And Gregory was rising above the pain, was becoming the master of the pain, his body fixing it, making it good. The burned parts of him throbbed hideously with every heartbeat but they belonged to him again, weren't some outside entity bent on taking him over and subjugating him any more. The pain was a message, gruesome but also reassuring: *there has been injury, you have been damaged, but something is being done about it*. He inhaled and at last it seemed he was drinking a draught of air rather than taking sips. Clarity buzzed through his brain.

'Ven,' he croaked. 'The incendiary.'

Ven glanced towards the doorway. 'You got him. Decked him good. His flame went out the moment you hit him. He's out for the count. But Dad . . .'

Gregory tried to roll his head but it wouldn't turn more than a few degrees before the seared portion of his neck objected, sharply. Peering from the corner of his eye he could just make out Sol's right arm. The hand was performing a strange stuttery little dance on the cobbles. A reddened weal above the wrist was well on its way to becoming a grotesquely large blister.

Movement in the doorway caught his attention. Someone was crouching there. The second incendiary Ven had mentioned. He was back-lit by the flames within, his face cast in fluttering shadow, and Gregory had only an awkward, upward view of him – but there was something about his posture, the way he held his shoulders high, something that struck a chord. Gregory puzzled at the beard he was wearing, which was a kind of goatee but a particularly dark one for a redhead. Then he realised it was no goatee and its darkness was the blackness of blood.

And then he realised that he knew this man. Hardly surprising, of course. It was someone from Stammeldon – he was more likely to recognise him than not. But he didn't just know him, he knew him well.

Didn't like him.

Reehan Bringlight.

The name came rushing in like a sluice of ice water.

Taller. Older. Leaner. Blood all over his mouth. Reehan Bringlight.

He was bending over the other incendiary, the one Gregory had hit. He was talking to him in a weird, low, plaintive tone. From time to time he shook him, and the angle Gregory was looking from made it difficult to tell whether the other incendiary was responding but he didn't appear to be, and Reehan's efforts were growing more urgent and his voice was rising.

And almost, but not quite, Gregory made a deduction. Inferred something and in the same instant forgot it, as if his mind was not prepared to take that particular possibility on board as yet. He kept watching Reehan and waiting for the other incendiary to stir. Move a hand. Let out a moan, maybe. Meanwhile Ven had crawled over to his father's side and was doing much the same as Reehan, addressing him in the hope of reply and growing more and more agitated as none came. All this was counterpointed by the grumble and growl of fire. The conflagration in the office had taken hold. The flames all spoke as one, with a strident, swelling voice. They had staked their claim, the place was theirs.

Gregory clamped his teeth together and struggled to sit up. On the second attempt he succeeded, and then had to stay in that position, the breath hissing in and out of him, till the pain ebbed from unbearable to nearly bearable. Tightened skin that was trying to knit had split. Through the tatters of his shirt he glimpsed the glisten of lymph. He knew that he would heal more quickly if he just lay still. But he couldn't just lie still.

Another bout of exquisite effort brought him to his knees, both literally and in the sense of believing that he couldn't carry on. He gulped in air raggedly and felt ready to weep. But again, the pain abated, and a part of him sent out a small offering of thanks to Master Ergall. All those training sessions, three years of weekly unpleasantness, were finally paying off. Here was a true test of his Inclination, and he was, he thought, facing up to it well.

A third and final tussle with the wrenches and wracks of his burns saw him to his feet. Giddy, he waited for his head to clear. To his left,

Ven had gone quiet. Sol lay utterly still on the ground. Gregory searched for the least rise and fall of his chest. There was none.

He turned.

In the doorway, Reehan was now cradling the head of the other incendiary. Through the swirls of smoke that billowed around the pair of them, Gregory could see tears pouring down Reehan's cheeks. He followed the course of the tears to where they landed on the other incendiary's upturned face. They fell there like rain on unseeded soil, splashing in vain.

That deduction recurred, that inference of unwelcome possibility, and this time, instead of slipping away again, stayed put. Gregory knew, as if he had known all along, the identity of the other incendiary. He recognised the face without the delay it had taken to recognise Reehan's because it was one he was expecting – and dreading – to see. And he knew, with the same sort of preordained certainty, that the person the face belonged to was dead.

No, not dead. Why mince words?

Killed.

By him.

The crunch as his blow had landed.

Bones were, under the right circumstances, so brittle. A skull, fragile as an eggshell.

For all that, Willem, as he lay in Reehan's lap, looked unhurt. His eyes were half closed, his mouth half open. He looked exactly as if he were in the throes of reverie, contemplating some far-off, mildly intriguing notion. If only he would blink as Reehan's tears tumbled onto his face, if only he would wince at the way he was being sobbed over . . .

But however much Gregory wished he would, he wasn't going to. There he was – Willem, lifeless, gone. This was a fact, immutable and irreversible. This was the new truth of Gregory's existence. His brother was never blinking, or wincing, or anything, ever again, and it was *his* fist that was the cause. One blind, enraged moment, and Willem had ceased to be. It was absurd how easily it had happened. It was appalling how absurdly it had happened.

He watched Reehan reach down with a tender hand and close Willem's eyelids. He heard Reehan say, 'It's my fault, I'm sorry, it's all my fault,' and he knew this wasn't so because the blame lay right here, with him. He wanted to tell Reehan as much, fill him in on who was really responsible, but when he tried to his throat creaked like a rusty hinge; no words came out. He saw Reehan raise his head and look around with brimming, bloodshot eyes which seemed to find nothing within their scope intelligible. He waited for them to fix and focus on him. Sure enough, they did. And when they did, they grew alert, then narrowed.

'You're one of us,' Reehan said. 'You . . . you're one of *us*.'

Still Gregory could not find his voice. *No*, he wanted to say, *I'm not. Surely you know who I am. Can't you see?* It was his half-burned face, he assumed. That and the difference three years made.

Reehan slid Willem's head off his lap, letting it loll on the doorway threshold. 'Do you realise what you've done?'

All too well, Gregory thought.

'You're dead.' Reehan rose. 'You understand? You're dead, and it's not going to be a quick death either.'

He meant it, and fleetingly Gregory felt that being dead might not be such a bad thing. Rather than go on living with the knowledge of what he had done to Willem.

Then Ven spoke. All he said was Gregory's name, in a quiet, querulous voice. Gregory seemed, to Ven, not to be aware of the danger he was in. The incendiary wasn't bluffing. He was out for vengeance. Gregory needed to snap out of this daze he had fallen into, and fast.

' "Gregory"?' Reehan echoed. He did a double take, frowning at Ven then flicking his gaze back to Gregory. He cocked his head. He squinted. Assessed. And his mouth pulled into a smirk of arid amusement.

'Yes,' he said. 'Yes, of course. Burned like that and still standing . . . How many other redheaded indestructibles are there? Little Gregory. Little Bother. Oh, this is priceless. What are the chances?' A quick glance at Willem at his feet. 'You must be feeling terrible right now. You know who this is, don't you? You do, I can tell. We came for you, Willem and me. That's why we're here. We came to find you and take you back to Stammeldon, and this is the result. Oh, what have you done, Little Bother? What *have* you done?'

'Willem,' Ven breathed. 'As in . . .'

'As in his older brother,' said Reehan, nodding, not taking his eyes off Gregory. 'As in my best friend. As in a brave and honourable man who's dead. Who's lying here dead. Who did a noble thing and ended up dead in this forsaken, reeking, Mudwallow hovel of a town—'

From within the office there came a deep and ominous *crack*, followed almost instantly by a tremendous crash. Ceiling beams had burned through, floorboards had given way, and first storey plunged into downstairs. Flames and debris exploded through the doorway. Reehan was thrown forward onto the ground. Ven cowered. And Gregory . . .

. . . ran.

It wasn't panic. It wasn't cowardice. It was simply the desire to be elsewhere, anywhere but here with the sight of Willem dead before him, anywhere that wasn't the scene of the unspeakable, unpardonable deed he had done. The sudden collapse of the office triggered some basic imperative, some instinctive flight response which roused him from his stupefaction and sent him off at top speed. Penresford blurred around him. He bored through its mazy, cavelike streets. Distant detonations of pain thumped with every footstep. An impulse, a memory that seemed so old it couldn't possibly be one of his, said *Two-Arch Gate*. But he ran without direction, thinking only of absence, and escape, and oblivion.

Mayor Bringlight stepped off the upstream boat chain and onto the town-side bank with a deeply satisfied rub of the hands. He felt hilarious, as though he had just been told the greatest joke ever. Looking around, he could see no one here at the north-east corner of Penresford but Stammeldoners. The enemy had been obliterated, and his own townspeople were cheering. They were waving their arms. They were grinning. They were slapping one another on the back. Incendiaries were jetting triumphal whooshes of flame into the air.

He drank in their joy, a heady brew. He was aware that, rather than his part in guiding the battle through to a successful conclusion, what was being celebrated was the fact that the Earthers had been beaten, with light casualties on the Stammeldon side. The only name anyone was chanting was that of their hometown and not of its mayor. Nevertheless he reckoned the victory today would, given time and mature reflection, translate into personal kudos for him. Come the next mayoral election his return to office was guaranteed. Beyond that, it wasn't inconceivable that the people of Stammeldon would one day want him to represent them at a higher level, in parliament. Jarnley Bringlight, the honourable member for Stammeldon. It had a pleasing ring.

He surveyed Penresford, shabby place but in a sense *his* town now, won through conquest. What to do with it? How should he treat his prize?

The answer presented itself in the shape of a trickle of smoke coiling up above the rooftops somewhere over toward the town's southern end. Mayor Bringlight watched the smoke rise and grow denser, braiding around itself like a vaporous plait, several close-knit strands fusing into one.

At first he had thought the smoke was emanating from a chimney, but now there was too much of it for that. It was quite clearly coming from a house fire. On the hillside to the south he could see people,

Penresfordians. While the battle was under way these non-combatants had abandoned the town, and in the flurry of departure someone must have left a frying-pan on the hob or not banked the coals of a hearth fire properly. With buildings made of wood it didn't take much for an instance of domestic carelessness to become a raging inferno . . .

A raging inferno.

Within moments the mayor had the ear of the all the incendiaries present and with a few well-chosen words he had their compliance too. 'They tried to deny us a living,' he concluded. 'Let's deny them a place to live. Let's do this properly. Let's finish the job.'

Thus exhorted, the incendiaries set to work. The next few hours were one long delirious orgy of immolation, which Mayor Bringlight was content to join in rather than orchestrate. He became part of a greater whole, one among many, subsuming himself. His flame mingled with the flame of others as fire after fire was ignited on Penresford's northern edge. The fires rapidly swelled and merged and spread. Soon fully half the town was consumed by a sweeping, roaring holocaust and the sky was black with smoke, but the incendiaries did not relent. They could have relaxed their efforts and left the blaze to run its course. Short of a sudden torrential downpour of rain nothing was going to stop it until there was no more Penresford left to burn.

Instead, they continued to foster and foment the blaze. If they spied a part of a building that for some reason refused to catch alight, they caressed the flames to flow in that direction until it did. Some of them devoted themselves to the task of extinguishing any stray embers which the breeze happened to blow their way, so that nobody involved in the conflagration suffered from its adverse effects. En masse the incendiaries generated fire and fuelled fire and handled fire and revelled in the pure, unbridled, wanton joy of fire. The inferno that overtook Penresford was a thing born of collective will and it razed and annihilated and was awesome to behold. Even those of other classes of Fire Inclination were transfixed by its rapacity and immensity. The trio of recuperators, as they ran their warming hands over various wounds and broken bones, felt a cold thrill inside – to professional healers it was perversely affirming to watch unliving things be irreparably destroyed. Swifts stood stock-still and simply stared. As for the other-Inclined members of the expedition, the indestructible constables sauntered whistling, the barge pilots spat repeatedly to ward off bad luck, while the sharp-sight averted his gaze.

Then it was afternoon and Penresford was no more. Sporadic fires still sputtered and fluttered. For the most part, what had been a town and a home to a couple of thousand was now ashes and a home to none. Exhilaration winged its way through the incendiaries and alit, too, among the rest of the Stammeldoners. There was no question that something unprecedented and momentous had been done this day. An entire town reduced to zero. Only the 'Storm itself, in its very vilest tempers, could match that achievement.

Mayor Bringlight circulated among his townspeople, meting out congratulations and handclasps wherever he went. In return he at last received some of the adulation he had been hoping for. 'Good work, Mayor Bringlight.' 'Couldn't have done it without you.' 'I have to say I had my doubts, mayor, but, well, here we are.' It was one of the high points of his life. Everything, even the Stammeldoner deaths which were the price of this glory, seemed worthwhile.

A clear, commanding voice cut through the celebration, and gradually grins shrivelled and heads turned and the hubbub faded as the Stammeldoners found themselves surrounded by soldiers on horseback. Addressing them was a sturdily built and prolifically bearded man, who repeated, for the benefit of those who hadn't heard him the first and second times around, that his name was Scaldwell, Colonel Rufus Scaldwell of the First Jarrainian Mounted Flamethrowers, and that he had been sent here with the mandate of parliament itself to put an end to, as he described it, 'all this hoo-hah'.

'You're too late!' one incendiary called out, in whom the high tide of elation hadn't yet completely ebbed.

'I'm well aware of that,' Colonel Scaldwell replied testily. 'I'm also well aware that I'm talking to a bunch of absolute raving pyromaniacs. What in the name of all that's hot and bright were you thinking? Look at this. Look around you. Do you have the faintest idea what you've done?'

Up until that moment the Stammeldoners were quite clear what they had done: they had scored a famous victory and taught a town of mutinous Earthers a lesson they would never forget. Now, to their surprise, an element of uncertainty crept in. To have an authority figure like this Colonel Scaldwell berate them, to hear the frank disgust in his voice as he called them pyromaniacs. They weren't pyromaniacs . . . were they?

'I have never,' continued the colonel, 'been as ashamed of being Fire-Inclined as I am today. More to the point, of being incendiary-class. You're a disgrace, the lot of you. An affront to everything that we hold dear – dignity, rationality, continence. What's all this been about? Trade. A commodity. Clay. All this slaughter, all this destruction, over some clay!'

And now there was disgruntlement in the Stammeldon ranks. People were exchanging glances, and avoiding glances. Some spoke in low, troubled tones about making a stand and sticking up for themselves in the face of commercial blackmail. From others there were grumbled objections to being spoken to like this by a mere soldier. One or two people even suggested that Scaldwell and his men were obviously keen to get some of the same treatment that had been dished out on the Penresfordians, although these threats were couched in the softest of whispers and would never have been carried through. The Flame-throwers were an elite force, trained to a level of proficiency in their Inclination that was far above that of even the most skilled civilian. They outclassed the Stammeldoners as surely as the Stammeldoners had outclassed the Penresfordians. To attack them would have been at best folly, at worst nothing short of suicide.

Colonel Scaldwell ran his gaze imperiously across the crowd. 'Where's your leader?' he demanded. 'Which one of you's responsible for this sorry state of affairs?'

The Stammeldoners were only too ready then to give their mayor credit for bringing them here and embroiling them in a fight. Fingers pointed. Clear space appeared around him.

'Ah yes,' said the colonel. 'I was told your name. It's Mayor . . . Lightborn, is it? Burnlight? Livebrand?'

'Bringlight,' said Mayor Bringlight. 'And Colonel Scaldwell, may I say that you cannot even begin to appreciate the complexities of this issue. It's all very well bandying accusations and insults about, but anyone with any sense will—'

'Mister Bringlight, I may not possess much sense, I may not possess any at all, but I know madness when I see it. This' – Scaldwell swept an arm at ruined Penresford – 'is madness.'

Bluster hadn't worked. The mayor tried a different tack. 'It was a necessary piece of strategy. A military man such as yourself—'

Again Scaldwell interrupted. 'Strategy! Don't you even dare use that word in my presence. My *horse* knows more about strategy than you ever will.' He patted his steed's sweat-caked neck. 'No, what you've done here, all of you, is nothing more than common thuggery. Venting your anger on people and property. You didn't do it because you had to, you did it because you could. I've seen some barbaric behaviour in my time but this . . . this is something else.'

The colonel's words were hitting home. Mayor Bringlight's little impromptu army was starting to look askance at its general, wondering why they were feeling so guilt-ridden all of a sudden, wondering if it might not somehow be his fault.

The mayor, sensing the shift in mood around him, decided that a more conciliatory approach with Scaldwell was, after all, probably the best plan.

'So what's to become of us, colonel? Are we under arrest?'

'My orders were to get here, intervene, halt any violence before it could occur. Unfortunately, fast as we rode here, those orders didn't come in time, which leaves me in something of a quandary. I have no specific powers to make arrests, but at the same time I can't simply let you all go. One of my men will have to ride to the nearest town where there's a telepath bureau and get on the network and obtain fresh instructions. While that happens, I'm moving you lot away from the town. To those boats of yours I can see up that-a-way, so it'll be easier to keep you all in one place. Needless to say, you'll come quietly. No complaints. Meek as lambs. Yes?'

The Stammeldoners nodded assent and mutely allowed themselves to be marched off along the towpath on the town-side bank, with the Flamethrowers in a neat circle around them. Mayor Bringlight strode with his head down and dark thoughts revolving inside it. Scaldwell – what right did he have to be so high-handed and judgemental? Honestly, give a man a brass helmet and that big gold sun on his chest, put a few pips on his shoulders, and he thought he was the boss of the world. And didn't Inclination solidarity count for anything? Fire should stand shoulder to shoulder with Fire. It gave the wrong signal otherwise. It was why Earthers like these ones at Penresford could become so uppity.

What the mayor didn't know was that the signal being given by the Flamethrowers' escorting the Stammeldoners upriver was exactly that. To the Penresfordians who had taken refuge on the hillside to the south of town, it appeared that the Fire-Inclined soldiers were siding with the Fire-Inclined Stammeldoners. The Flamethrowers were giving Penresford's destroyers their protection, and this was intolerable.

In no time a mob had formed and was bearing down on the group of soldiers and civilians at high speed. Stones and clods of mud were plucked from the ground and hurled, along with anti-Flamer abuse. Colonel Scaldwell ordered his men to adopt defensive measures only, refusing to risk further bloodshed if at all possible. The Flamethrowers vaporised the projectiles in mid-air, but it was hard to concentrate on that and maintain strict formation around the Stammeldoners at the same time. The colonel, accordingly, ordered the deployment of fire walls. His men obeyed, erecting twenty-foot-tall blazing barriers between them and the Penresfordians and using them to ward the mob back out of throwing range. Their horses stayed admirably placid throughout, but then they were all from a bloodstock that was renowned for its strength of nerve and had also, from foalhood, had their innate animalistic fear of fire rigorously drilled out of them.

So the Fire-Inclined convoy eventually reached the barge on the town-side bank. The other barge was brought over at Colonel Scaldwell's instigation, and the Stammeldoners were steered aboard both boats. As promised, the colonel then despatched a man to Lalmore with a warrant for priority use of the telepath network, and there followed a long, mostly well-tempered wait, during which Flamethrower patrols trotted back and forth between the barges and the town, both to keep the still-fractious Penresfordians at bay and to carry out a rough inventory of the corpses that were scattered along the bank. It wasn't until an hour had passed that Mayor Bringlight's seething resentment of Scaldwell finally simmered down and he remembered that Reehan and Willem were still at large somewhere on the far side of the Seray. He managed to convey a message to the colonel that he had something important to discuss with him, and after a certain amount of wheedling he was permitted back on-to dry land for a one-to-one audience.

'Yes?'

Scaldwell was clearly in no mood for nonsense, but at least he was on foot now and the mayor wasn't going to get a crick in the neck talking to him. No longer, so to speak, on his high horse.

Mayor Bringlight swiftly and succinctly outlined the situation. Scaldwell seemed only half interested until the name Brazier was mentioned, whereupon his eyebrows lofted to the peak of his helmet and his mouth formed a big round O of concern within his beard.

'We're talking Brazier Brickfields Brazier?'

'None other.'

'Tremond Brazier's son is roaming around somewhere here?'

'And mine.'

'Well, why didn't you say anything earlier?'

Mayor Bringlight could not pass up the opportunity to score a point and even up, just a little, the imbalance between them. 'Perhaps if you hadn't kept interrupting me, colonel . . .'

Scaldwell harrumphed. 'Perhaps if you hadn't kept saying such ridiculous things. Anyway, never mind, that's neither here nor there now. I'd best put a search party together. Where did you say the Brazier boy is?'

'And my son. I don't know exactly but on the other side. That's where they were when I last saw them. I should come with you. It's easier than you just going off with a description of what they look like.'

'I don't think two teenage Fire Inclined should be that hard to identify.'

'Nevertheless.'

Scaldwell weighed up. 'All right. As one of them's your son.' He added dryly, 'I suppose it's better that paternal instinct kicks in late than not at all.'

290

Mayor Bringlight, with a barbed retort aching to leap out, held his tongue, and five minutes later he was riding pillion behind a Flame-thrower lieutenant as part of a five-strong search party headed by Scaldwell himself. They cantered down the town-side bank with a view to dismounting at the boat chain and crossing to continue on foot. In the event, however, they didn't have to travel even as far as the boat chain. There was a yell of 'Dad!' from the direction of the river, and out from the reed-thronged shallows, up the muddy bank, came Reehan. He scrambled onto the towpath, his clothing waterlogged and mud-stained, with patches of smut all over his face, a vision of bedragglement but also of heartfelt relief. He hurried to his father, who slid off the horse to greet him and, after a brief circumspect look at the filthy state he was in, embraced him.

'Are you alone?' said Scaldwell to Reehan, casting an eye along the stretch of shallows Reehan had emerged from. 'Where's the Brazier lad?'

Reehan swallowed, composed himself, and told a pitiful tale.

Soil felt good. Soil was cool. Gregory rubbed his face in it. He heaped it over himself. It balmed his burned skin but it also embedded him, shutting out the light, cocooning. It was the earth on someone's grave, but here, nonetheless, was the place to be. Here among the inhumed dead. Here, he belonged. He dug deeper, hand-spading the soil onto his head, into his hair. Granules of it trickled down the neck of his shirt. If he kept on going, burrowed down through this tilth, sooner or later he would get down far enough to be considered buried himself. Buried meant dead and dead meant at peace. All agonies, both phys-ical and otherwise, at an end. That would be more than welcome. His body was mending, itching as it mended, but inside, in his heart, something was broken beyond repair. Its fragments were like shards of glass that spiked into him constantly. An unending, ever-shifting source of hurt. Every so often he tried to force it out of himself vocally, tried to heave it up and expel it in a moan, but the moans were just sound. Nothing else came up with them. Each filled his mouth with dirt. His nostrils were filled with dirt. There was the taste of dirt at the back of his throat. He was dirt. Earth was something noble to the Earth Inclined, earth was life and living and a final resting place, but he wasn't even Earth-Inclined any more, he was lower than that. Dirt. Let him taste it, breathe it, writhe in it. Dirt.

Footfalls resounded through the ground. He felt more than heard them. At first he didn't want to look up but then, with a tug of shame, he wanted to know who was standing over him, seeing him in his prostrate misery. He would tell whoever it was to go away, fuck off, leave him be.

The old man's face was broad and wise and kindly. Gregory, blinking soil from his eyelashes, didn't recognise him but he sensed immediately: *Air-Inclined*. The old man was gazing down with a quizzical compassion. The old man, who could have no idea who Gregory was or what he was doing there in the graveyard, looked as if he would like to help.

And when he stretched out a hand and said, 'Come with me,' Gregory hesitated. Come with him? A complete stranger? Why? And where to?

But the offer was simply and sincerely phrased, and had such implications. Come with him. Go elsewhere. Have someone else make the decisions. Surrender.

Gregory dredged his arm out of the soil and reached up, placing his hand in the old man's and, with his hand, himself.

And with the old man's assistance, he got up.

And with the old man, he went.

YASHU

They tramped west, Yashu and Khollo ahead, Mr Ayn and the Fire boy some way behind. Yashu set a fast, forthright pace which she knew Khollo was hard pressed to match, Mr Ayn and the boy even harder pressed. She didn't relent, and the gap between the two pairs of them widened. Several times Khollo suggested slowing down to allow the others to catch up. He even tried saying it in her language, and made such a seaweed tangle of it that she almost laughed. Her revenge for almost laughing was to shoot back a torrent of Water words, using enough that were familiar to Khollo for him to realise she was not paying him compliments. He went quiet after that.

If only she could have put behind her the memory of what she had witnessed at Penresford as easily as she was putting the town itself behind her. At every step Yashu was hounded by images of the fighting, the fires, the refugees' fright and fury. It was something inconceivable, something beyond comprehension. As it had unfolded, in order to keep herself from screaming she had pretended she was sitting on the beach at Half-Moon-Bay in the audience for a marionette performance. It wasn't people and a town, it was puppets and painted scenery. It was a story. None of it was really happening.

But it had been really happening and it seemed to become more grotesque and vivid, not less, with distance. And there were reminders of it all around. The setting sun, as it flared and subsided on the horizon ahead, mimicked Penresford's death throes, and after it had sunk out of sight dusk moved in, as dark and gloomy as the smoke cloud that had accumulated over the burning town. Stars glowed in the twilight like sparks. The moon, with its pitted, ash-grey face, looked as if insane incendiaries had attacked it too.

She would have walked on through the night. Unlike on I*il, small and sea-surrounded, here there was a whole country she could cross, a whole continent. She could put half a world between her and Penresford. Khollo, however, eventually found the courage to speak up again, and pointed out that it was nearly dark and they should find somewhere to shelter for the night. Food would also be good, he added, if available. They hadn't eaten since breakfast.

As luck would have it, over the brow of the next hill they came upon a derelict croft, snug in the fold of a shallow valley beside a meandering brook. Khollo signalled to the other two, far behind, that they had found possible accommodation. The glimmering pale shape that was Mr Ayn raised an arm in acknowledgement.

While Khollo waited for Mr Ayn and the boy, Yashu strode downhill. By the time the other three arrived at the croft she had already secured herself prime position in the corner furthest from the doorless entrance.

Mr Ayn was not impressed with the place, but accepted that they could go further and fare worse. 'The hotels around here,' he clucked, unrolling a blanket on the hard-packed earthen floor. 'The bathroom facilities leave a lot to be desired. I bet there isn't even a decent restaurant.'

It was a cold, difficult night. Wind hissed through the chinks in the croft's stone walls. The Fire boy moaned in his sleep, and Yashu herself was restless. She dreamed fitful dreams of burning and death. At one point she was back in the graveyard where they had found the Fire boy, only this time it was Huaso writhing injured in the soil. He reached up to her as she ran to him, but before she got there the earth engulfed him, swallowing him up like quicksand. His hand vanished into the ground the instant before she could grab it. She fell to her knees and dug, spraying soil out behind her like a bone-burying dog, but he was gone.

In the morning, she emerged from the croft to find Mr Ayn down at the brook with the Fire boy. He had removed the boy's tattered shirt and was patiently hand-ladling water over him, cleaning away the grime. She noticed that the boy's burns were nowhere near as bad as they had first appeared. The cleaner he became, in fact, the less injured he looked. There were reddish blotches on the skin of his face, chest and right arm, but none of the extensive scorching and blistering she remembered from yesterday. It occurred to her that perhaps she had mistaken dirt for damage. Belatedly, the truth dawned.

Khollo came stretching and yawning out of the croft to stand beside her.

'The boy,' she said. 'He isn't Fire.'

'Hmm?'

'Look. His hands.'

With the soil sluiced off them, it was clear now that the boy's hands were abnormally large compared with the rest of him. They were hardened, too, ridged all over with calluses.

'Ah yes,' said Khollo. 'What with the red hair, you'd have thought . . .'

'We call his type a lobster.'

'Eh?'

'You know. With the big claws. The tough shell.'

'I know what a lobster is. I just didn't see how it applied. Although I do now.' Khollo studied the boy and nodded. 'Not a bad name for it, actually.'

'In Common Tongue, I can't remember what it's called.'

'Indestructible.'

A real mouthful, that. Yashu repeated it several times till she had mastered it.

'But he must have been on the same side as the other redheads, the Flamers, the ones who did the burning,' she said. 'He wasn't from Penresford.'

'Maybe,' said Khollo.

'Mr Ayn. Does he like the boy? Is that why he rescued him? Does he want him as a lover?'

'I think saving him from harm was what Elder Ayn was most worried about.'

Yashu watched the tenderness with which Mr Ayn washed the boy down. With similar tenderness, Mr Ayn took a straight razor and shaved away the boy's remaining hair, leaving him with a bald scalp and a few small nicks that repaired themselves almost instantaneously. Throughout both washing and shaving the boy just sat there, limp, as if unaware of anything that was going on. Khollo might be right about Mr Ayn's intentions. Yashu, however, wasn't so sure herself.

They had gone to bed hungry. Now they were ravenous. With the boy dried off and dressed in one of Khollo's spare shirts, they set off once more, still heading west, following the course of the brook. Mr Ayn promised them that, according to his prevision, they would soon be eating a hearty repast. Sure enough, within a couple of miles they came to a hamlet consisting of a dozen houses, along with vegetable plots, penned sheep and pigs, and some free-roaming hens. The human inhabitants were all Earthers and, as far as Yashu could judge, all members of a single extended family. A gruff, incomprehensible challenge from the family patriarch was met with a cautious Common Tongue entreaty from Mr Ayn. The patriarch, brandishing a pitchfork, gave a hesitant, clumsy reply, not in Earth language this time, but his Common Tongue was so rough it was only marginally more intelligible. Then money appeared in Mr Ayn's hand and spoke louder and more eloquently than either of them.

Under the gazes of, it seemed, the entire family, all crammed into the kitchen of the largest of the houses, the four travellers ate. On the menu was broiled mutton, boiled potatoes, roast chicken legs, and much else besides. Once everyone had got over their wariness, the Earthers proved to be hospitable and friendly. Even so, they remained curious about their guests. The four of them, Yashu knew, presented an odd mix. An islander, a southerner, a sophisticated Air gentleman, and a pale-complexioned indestructible. The boy – or, as she preferred to think of him, the lobster – was the one who intrigued the family most. He was fully healed by now, even the reddish blotches gone. His eyes, though, still had that shocked, absent look about them, and this and the fact that he barely picked at his food aroused the family's concern.

'The lad's fine,' Mr Ayn assured them. 'Just had a bit of a nasty accident, that's all.'

He proceeded to tell a story about the lobster tripping over a rock yesterday, falling and cracking his head. The lie crackled falsely in Yashu's ears, and she could tell the patriarch was not convinced by it either. He had the good grace, though, not to quibble. He also had a sizeable sum of Mr Ayn's money in his pocket, which meant he perhaps didn't feel the urge to demand absolute honesty from his guests.

Later, as they left the hamlet, Mr Ayn explained to Yashu that he was avoiding the subject of Penresford in company if possible. As they all should, he added, at least until they were out of Jarraine. 'Not everyone's going to be as easy to hoodwink as those simple peasant folk back there. And since the lad was involved somehow in that frightful business, he's unlikely to be very popular with the locals if that gets out.'

'Who is he? What do you think he did to get burned like that?'

'He'll tell us. Trust me. I've foreseen it. When he's ready, when it's necessary, he'll tell us.'

Further walking brought them to another hamlet, and after that a village, from where a broad road led to a full-blown town, which they skirted to get to another village, where they spent the night.

For the following day, and the day after that, they trekked onward through western Jarraine, remaining on foot and at Mr Ayn's insistence sticking to lesser roads and staying only in out-of-the-way villages. Other travellers on these backwoods byways were few and far between. Occasionally an ox-drawn farm cart came plodding along, and once a much faster mail coach, but for the most part the four of them were on their own. It was not particularly interesting country and they seemed to Yashu to be travelling without aim, moving just for the sake of moving. The shadow of the events at Penresford hung over them and she had the feeling that Mr Ayn was deliberately avoiding towns in case – unlikely though it was – something similar should happen again. An irrational fear, but she understood it.

Mr Ayn kept the lobster beside him at all times, and to look at them you might have thought they were father and son. No, grandfather and grandson. Yashu still could not believe that Mr Ayn's intentions toward the boy were honourable, but something offended her even more than that. The boy had usurped her place. She was now second on Mr Ayn's list of importance, no longer as interesting to him as she had been. She shouldn't have minded, but she did. Hadn't she joined him and Khollo in order to explore with them? And at the same time learn more about her Flow? Yet Mr Ayn was barely paying any attention to her any more. All the time it was the boy. Caring for the boy. Staying close to the boy.

After three days of this she began to wonder if the time hadn't come, already, for her and Mr Ayn to have a parting of the ways. Nothing about the travelling was turning out as she had hoped. Perhaps she ought to cut her losses and turn back for I*il and Aunt Liyalu.

She resolved to stick it out a little while longer. Mr Ayn kept indicating that the boy was going to snap out of this trance eventually. Then, logically, the boy would be normal again and wouldn't need the constant devotion and supervision he was getting. Mr Ayn wouldn't be endlessly preoccupied with him and would have time again for other people.

So Yashu told herself. In the meantime she kept distance between her and the lobster. At best, he was boring. He did nothing, said nothing. He walked as if in a dream. He ate only enough for basic nourishment. At worst, though, he was downright creepy. He could be sitting there at table during a meal, right across from her, looking straight at her – and yet not seeing her. His stare was miles away, glassy, lost; and that and the way he chewed listlessly at his food was almost enough to quell her own appetite.

One mealtime, she decided to conduct an experiment. Mr Ayn had nipped out to the latrine, Khollo was looking elsewhere. With a small surreptitious finger-flick she launched some of the water from her drinking glass at the lobster's face. Her aim was good. Droplets spattered his cheek and also landed on his scalp, which was downy with new-growth hair. He didn't move. Not so much as a flicker of the eyelids. Then, placidly, he raised a hand and brushed the water away. If he was aware where the water had come from, he gave no sign.

So he was there, somewhere behind those eyes. Conscious. He wasn't trapped in there through shock as a result of getting burned. He was choosing to stay in there, like an alarmed turtle indrawn into its shell.

On the fourth day after Penresford, they were deep into western Jarraine. Hilly territory, sparsely populated. The landscape was losing what little softness it had had and becoming jagged and rugged, meanly vegetated, a skin of grass over the earth with sprigs of heather and furze protruding among outcrops of harsh dark-grey rock. Every now and then Mr Ayn would enthuse about the natural beauty of the surroundings, as if this was more than enough reason to be there. For Yashu, however, the barrenness was daunting. To some degree it reminded her of the windward side of I*il, but there wasn't the sea to offset the emptiness and there wasn't the consolation of a smoother, lusher leeward side. The landscape was this, and nothing but this, in all directions.

That night the proprietor of the inn they were staying at mentioned that a group of cavalrymen had passed through only that morning, heading north to south. They had been riding hard and had stopped only to water their horses at the village well before carrying on. Now, you didn't often see soldiers round these parts, he said, and he wondered if it had anything to do with that bad affair at Penresford just recently.

Mr Ayn, straight-faced, asked what 'bad affair' that would be. The innkeeper was surprised he hadn't heard – it was the talk of the whole country – and gave a summary of the events. He ended by saying, 'Some are calling it the Battle of Penresford, but if you ask me, Massacre would be nearer the mark. And there're already repercussions. Up at Stammeldon there's been civil unrest. Earth Inclined staging protests. Questions being asked in parliament as well. You mark my words, there's going to be some kind of comeback. Somebody's going to pay.'

The innkeeper folded his brawny strong-class arms. You didn't need to look too hard to know where his sympathies lay.

It was, however, the lobster's reaction to what the innkeeper said that intrigued Yashu. For once the boy had appeared to be paying attention to what was going on around him. Only briefly, for the duration of the innkeeper's speech, but there had been a subtle yet distinct change in him. The head, cocked slightly. The eyes, looking sidelong instead of dead ahead. He had been alert and listening. And one specific phrase had, Yashu was sure, been responsible: Brazier Brickfields. She remembered the company's name from Hallawye, when patrons at The Digger's Rest had explained the origins of the dispute at Penresford. The innkeeper had used it now in the same context, and it had got the lobster's notice.

The next morning, as they were preparing to leave the inn and Mr Ayn was busy settling the bill, Yashu sidled up to the lobster and hissed the words in his ear.

There. The tiniest of flinches.

She felt abnormally pleased with herself for the rest of the day. 'Brazier Brickfields' was evidently the key to him, the means of unlocking his trance. She had no idea how to use it but reckoned an opportunity would come.

Swirling cloud cover loured overhead all morning, like a lid on the world, so low Yashu felt she could reach up and touch it. Gradually it darkened, steeping everything in gloom. Rain threatened, and at noon the threat was finally made good. A shower became a drizzle became a downpour, vertical and unrelenting. The next village the four sodden travellers arrived at was perforce their next stop. It had an inn called The No Surprises Inn, and the name was accounted for as soon as they stepped across the threshold.

'Annonax Ayn, party of four!' said a loud, welcoming voice, and a moment later the voice's owner emerged from the doorway to a back room. She was a matronly, bustling woman who was so short she barely came up to Yashu's shoulder and whose hair was such a frizzy, shapeless mop it had clearly passed beyond the power of brush or comb to tame it (and indeed several brushes and combs could be lurking within it, lost long ago). Her clothing was similarly unkempt, her blouse sleeves rucked up around her elbows, her pinafore besmirched with cookery stains, one sock loose and drooping over her shoe.

'Madam,' said Mr Ayn, with an amused bow. 'From one previsionary to another, how nice to be expected.'

'Zelzan Haak,' said the woman.

'And your name is . . . ?' said Mr Ayn.

'I am, yes, the proprietress of the No Surprises.'

'I take it, then, that you are the owner of this establishment.'

'Never an unexpected guest, that's our motto.'

'Your policy is always to know in advance who's coming.'

'Five leaves per person per room, but for you, a group rate of fifteen all in.'

'And your room rate is . . . ?'

'Thank you.'

'Very reasonable.'

Yashu frowned. Maybe it was her Common Tongue, but the pair of them seemed to be talking at cross purposes.

Khollo leaned close and whispered, 'It's a previsionary thing – anticipating the other person's next remark. Elder Ayn is letting the lady be one step ahead of him out of courtesy. He could just as easily do the same to her, but because she's the host, we're the guests, this way round is better manners.'

The back-to-front pleasantries continued for a while, till Zelzan Haak brought them to an end with a wave of her hand. 'I've made up four rooms,' she said. 'By which I mean all of our rooms. I can show you up to them if you like, but perhaps you'd rather get dried off. My husband's just this minute stoked up the fire in the inglenook . . .'

Beside the fire in the main room she plied them with peppermint tea and then bread and cold ham. While they ate under her approving eye a man wandered in. She introduced him as her husband, Lon, and Yashu noted that he had an Earther's complexion but not an Earther's build. The Earth Inclined she had encountered up to now were all stocky and sturdy but Lon Haak was more sinew than muscle, with bony wrists and a scrawny chicken-neck. He surveyed the new arrivals, his gaze lingering briefly on each of them. Then he nodded, and silently exited.

'A man of few words,' said his wife. 'He's found, being married to a previsionary, it's often better to say nothing. That way he can preserve some level of independence and mystery, and avoid all the I-knows and the I-told-you-so's. And in case you're wondering, he's that rare thing, a male plant-sensitive. Just you wait. Tonight, at supper, you'll sample some of our home-grown vegetables, and I guarantee you'll never have tasted anything to compare. He grows a mean carrot, my Lon. And what that man can do with a marrow . . . !'

She chortled at this, and Mr Ayn joined in.

'Mrs Haak,' he said, 'you have clearly been spending far too long among Earthers.'

'Oh, tell me about it,' she replied, touching his arm. 'I've picked up their sense of humour, haven't I? But then it's not that surprising. Here I am, living in the middle of nowhere, Earth Inclined all around. I get to mix with my own Inclination . . . well, hardly ever. Someone like you, Mr Ayn, comes along once in a blue moon. I used to be such a sophisticated girl, too, and now look at me.' She chortled again, 'That's what you get when you fall in love. You have to make sacrifices, and I knew when I married Lon we'd be ending up out in the boondocks where he comes from. I'm from Charne originally, you see. That's where he and I met. He was up there working for a greengrocer, helping keep the produce fresh. It was love at first sight. But city life never agreed with him and, to be honest, never with me either. So I had no qualms about moving to somewhere where the pace is slower. It suits my temperament, and my Inclination, much better. And I decided to go into the hostelry business here because, well, it's what previsionaries are good at, isn't it, Mr Ayn?'

'Some would say,' said Mr Ayn.

'Being able to anticipate guests' needs. Catering in advance.'

'It's one use to which we can put our talents.'

'Not that we get that many guests passing through this way. It's a pretty meagre living, I have to admit. But I enjoy it.'

'Tell me, Mrs Haak . . .'

'Zelzan.'

'Zelzan. This might sound like an odd question, but are we still in Jarraine?'

'Do you not have a map?'

'I do, but it doesn't mark every single village in the region. I know the border with Otrea is somewhere close by.'

'Not three miles west.' Zelzan Haak narrowed her eyes, then nodded wisely as if she had just fathomed something. Yashu could not think what. 'It's not really a border, in the sense that there isn't a manned crossing point. There's so little traffic to and fro, they don't need one. Round here the one country just sort of blends into the other. But roughly three miles or so, that's where the official boundary line lies. And then not much further west the Vail Mountains start, and who needs border guards when you've got them? So you're headed into Otrea.'

'Not necessarily.'

'I was going to say. This isn't the route you want to take if you are. The mountains are all but uncrossable from here. You need to go quite a way north or south to find a pass. Down towards Xarrid, up almost into Damentaine. And I know it's only the start of autumn but some of the northern passes are already closing. Xarrid's the better way to go anyway. There are some fascinating places down there for the tourist. The Buried City, which I've visited. Lon has family there. How it's designed, with the long shafts that ventilate the deepest parts of it and the swivelling mirrors that get sunlight down there too – amazing. And there's the Merik Necropolis, which I haven't visited. With the mummified corpses all sitting out at café tables and propped up on street corners like they're chatting. Gives me goosebumps, the whole idea of it, but I'd like to see it all the same. And the Museum of Unharmed Objects at New Gorundum. All those things the World-storm has, against all odds, spared. A single bottle from a glassblowing factory, the only one out of thousands that didn't get smashed to smithereens. The stuffed body of a sheep that survived a lightning strike that killed every other sheep in the flock. The only book to emerge intact from the destruction of the Hyletan national library. The last of Emoll Telfret's "bad luck" statuettes – although apparently another one's turned up recently so perhaps they're not such bad luck after all. Mind you, the collector who found out he owns it is desperate to get rid of it. They seem to have a way of attracting the 'Storm, those statuettes. Oh, but look at me. I'm nattering you into submission. You're weary. I'll leave you be. I've got plenty of chores I should be getting on with. If you need anything, come and ask me for it. If you don't come and ask me for it, I won't be able to have it ready for you when you do.'

The rain continued to pelt down all afternoon, and the fireside was a snug and pleasant place to be. Yashu drowsed, awoke, drowsed, and then it was evening and Zelzan Haak laid on a meal that featured copious amounts of home-grown garden produce, all of which was, as promised, delicious. Afterwards the travellers were shown to their rooms on the first floor, and Yashu washed using the water jug and basin provided, donned her nightshirt, then lowered herself onto the bed. Having snoozed most of the day she didn't believe she could be tired, but her belly was full and the rattle of the rain was soothing, a liquid lullaby. She was soon asleep again.

Then awake.

A noise had roused her. The opening and closing of a door. The front door. The rain, she noted, had stopped. She didn't know what time it was but thought it was the early hours.

She lay in the darkness, listening.

A whispered conversation, coming from downstairs. Zelzan Haak and her husband.

She was minded to roll over and try to go back to sleep. It wasn't any of her business.

But something about the tone of the conversation snagged at her curiosity. It was urgent, hurried. Furtive, even. And Zelzan Haak's voice kept rising and her husband kept trying to shush her, and the more he shushed her the louder she got.

Yashu slid off the bed, tiptoed to her door, eased it open a crack, and leaned out.

Her room was the one nearest the top of the stairs and the voices in the hallway were funnelled straight up to her. She could now hear clearly what was being said. She realised, however, that she couldn't understand any of it. The Haaks were using Earth language.

Well, she oughtn't to be eavesdropping anyway. She made to withdraw into the room and shut the door, then froze.

Perhaps she had misheard.

No, there it came again. Quite distinctly. One familiar, recognisable word standing out from the mishmash of growly Earther syllables.

Brazier.

It was too tempting. On the one hand, she would have to expose herself as someone who listened in on other people's private conversations. But on the other hand, here was a chance to find out more about this 'Brazier' business. It was even possible that the Haaks might have some piece of information that would enable her to work out how 'Brazier' and the lobster were connected. A small amount of shame was a price well worth paying for that.

She opened the door all the way with a loud flourish. The argument in the hallway broke off mid-sentence. She crossed the landing and started down the stairs, and when she was halfway down a figure appeared at the foot of the staircase, holding an oil lamp in one hand and shielding its light with the other.

'Ah yes,' said Zelzan Haak, softly, resigned. 'I*ilyashu. You're going to ask what my husband and I were just talking about. Lon, you should have consulted me before you went haring off like that. I'd have told you it wasn't going to work.'

Her husband muttered something, sounding sour and disgruntled.

'Well, never mind your civic duty. What about our duty as hosts?' She turned back to Yashu. 'Go ahead and ask. It's the way it has to be.'

'I just want to know – you were talking, and a word came up.'

'Yes. Brazier.'

'What is it? What is Brazier?'

'I think what you should be asking is *who* is it.'

'The boy with us,' Yashu said, understanding. 'The indestructible. That's his name.'

A second figure appeared at the foot of the stairs. 'A fugitive,' said Lon Haak, spitting out the words. 'A murderer. People are looking for him. Some came here just the day before yesterday. Soldiers. They want to bring him in. He killed his own brother!'

'Killed . . .'

'Yes. The moment I saw him, I knew who he was. He matched the

303

soldiers' description exactly, apart from the short hair. He was involved in that fracas over at Penresford, and he brutally attacked and killed his older brother. There's an eyewitness who saw it all. Said the attack was entirely unprovoked. He just went in swinging and smashed his brother's head open with one of those fists of his. And he's a Brazier. Gregory Brazier. And Penresford was all his father's fault, and so if soldiers are looking to arrest him and bring him to justice, I say fine, let them, he deserves it. The whole family deserves what's happened to them.'

'You say more than that actually,' said Zelzan Haak, 'don't you, Lon? Come on, you might as well tell the whole truth. Yashu here's about to admit to us that she's a sooth-seer.'

'I *am* a sooth-seer.'

'There. Go on, Lon. No point in hiding anything. Where have you just been?'

'Out,' said her husband, like a surly child caught misbehaving.

'Out where?'

'The next village but one. There's a retired telepath there, Florian Sudrin. He carries messages from time to time. He's old and not very reliable but he can still get onto the network, with a bit of effort. I was waiting for the rain to let up, and then I went out, headed over to his house, woke him . . .'

'And notified the authorities about us,' said Mr Ayn from the top of the stairs. Yashu had not heard him approach. She wondered how long he had been standing there.

'I did as any decent-minded citizen would,' said Lon Haak.

'Don't forget to mention the reward, Lon,' said his wife.

'Five hundred leaves for information leading to Gregory Brazier's arrest. It's a tidy sum, and don't tell me, Zelzan, that we couldn't do with it.'

Zelzan Haak rolled her eyes. 'Of course we could do with it, but not like this. Not from bounty on a guest.'

'Oh, and you'd rather we harboured a fugitive, a known criminal? You'd rather we turned a blind eye to lawbreakers under our roof?'

'For one thing, he's not a known criminal. He hasn't been tried and convicted yet. And for another thing . . . Oh, why am I arguing with you? There isn't time for this. Mr Ayn, perhaps you should wake the others and leave, all of you, while you can.'

'I am already dressed,' said Mr Ayn, and Yashu saw that he was. 'This is not an entirely unexpected development.'

'No, of course it isn't,' said Zelzan Haak, nodding.

'But I will get Khollo and Gregory up. And you, Yashu, should put on your day clothes and pack up. It is, as our hostess says, time to leave.'

'You're just going to let this happen?' sputtered Lon Haak to his wife. 'You're just going to let them walk out?'

Zelzan Haak shrugged. 'Nothing I can do about it. They make their getaway. It's inevitable.'

'And I suppose the fact that he and you are both Airheads has nothing to do with it.'

'Don't you start on Inclinations, Lon. Don't you even dare.'

Lon Haak grunted a few remarks in his own language and waved his fists, but his tone was thwarted and the fist-waving impotent.

Yashu went to her room, lit a candle and began gathering her belongings together and stowing them in Siaalo's satchel. As she did so, a thought struck her. What was she up to? She didn't have to leave with the others. She hadn't done anything wrong. It was only the lobster who was wanted by the authorities. Why should she have to flee too, like someone guilty? And what if, as she now suspected, Mr Ayn had been aware all along who the lobster was? What if he had taken the boy under his wing in the knowledge that it would get all of them into trouble later? It would explain his actions since Penresford – steering clear of towns, telling lies about the lobster to strangers, journeying into ever remoter parts of Jarraine. He had done everything he reasonably could to keep the boy away from people. And he had turned her and Khollo into his unwitting accomplices. He had made fugitives of them all.

The No Surprises Inn resounded with activity. Footfalls echoing through the floorboards. The Haaks down below, still bickering. Yashu stared at the satchel, running her fingers over the wrinkles in its cured seal hide. A thing redolent of I*il. She raised it to her nose, and above the sour leathery rankness she thought she could smell salt. A tang of the sea.

She heard her name called. It was called again, and then somebody came upstairs and knocked on the door. Knocked again. Then the handle turned and Khollo poked his head into the room.

'Come on. What are you waiting for? We've got to get going.'

She shook her head. 'You do. I don't.'

He was little more than a silhouette in the doorway but she could see he was taken aback. 'What do you mean?'

'Give me a reason. Tell me why we all have to run like this.'

'Because soldiers are coming.'

'So? To do what?'

'To arrest the boy. The lobster.'

'So? They're not coming to arrest *us*, are they? Just him. For killing

305

his brother. That was nothing to do with us. We're innocent. We should just stay here and then hand him over to them when they arrive. I may not know much about law on the mainland but isn't that what you're supposed to do?'

A pause. 'Yashu, it's not quite that simple.'

'Why not?'

'Well, if nothing else, we've been keeping the boy with us these past few days. That makes us accessories to the crime.'

'Does it? Not if we didn't know he committed a crime. And I didn't till just a few minutes ago. Did you?'

'No, to be honest I didn't.'

'Did Mr Ayn?'

'I can't say.'

'Do you think he did?'

'It's possible. He may have had an inkling.'

'Then he's guilty. But not us. Not you or me. And we can tell the soldiers that.'

'They might not believe us. Soldiers aren't famous for trusting other people, especially civilians. They may just think, "Take the lot of them into custody and sort it out later." I certainly wouldn't want to be around when they get here. I wouldn't want to take that risk. I don't think you should either.'

'Has Mr Ayn previsioned anything? Does he know whether we're going to escape being arrested or not?'

'All he's said is that he sees us getting across the border into Otrea. According to him they can't follow us there. It's beyond their jurisdiction. Jarrainian soldiers entering another country's territory would create all sorts of diplomatic headaches.'

'And does "us" include me?'

'He didn't say. But look, Yashu, we can't hang about. Please just come with us. If there are things you need to talk about, we'll talk about them later, when we're in Otrea.'

'No.'

'No?'

'No. I'm not happy. I didn't bargain for any of this. I feel Mr Ayn has behaved very badly. I feel . . .' She searched for the appropriate word, wishing her command of Common Tongue was better. 'Betrayed.'

Khollo glanced over his shoulder, then stepped all the way into the room and pushed the door gently to behind him. He came over to Yashu, moving into the full range of the candle's light. In its radiance his pale brown eyes took on a golden sheen. Yashu hadn't noticed this effect before, or perhaps had noticed it but not thought anything of it. It was very striking.

'I probably shouldn't say this,' he said, low-voiced, 'but I have to agree with you. Maybe I wouldn't go as far as "betrayed", but I'm definitely . . . How can I put it? Definitely beginning to wonder about Mr Ayn. Definitely having my doubts about him.'

Yashu didn't do a very good job of masking her surprise. 'You?'

'I know, I know. His personal enshriner. His loyal sidekick. It's just that lately his judgement has begun to seem . . . flawed. This thing with the boy, of course, but also in general . . .' He frowned. 'There's a saying in Durat. "A man should know when he's hitched his wagon to the wrong horse." And I'm starting to wonder if that isn't what I've done.'

'Then unhitch your wagon from him,' Yashu urged. 'We can both do it. Together. Let him and the lobster go off on their own.'

'No, I'm not staying here. Like I said, I wouldn't want to be around when the soldiers arrive.'

'So we leave at the same time but go a different way. The opposite direction. Why not?'

'Well, yes, we could. The thing is, there's more to it. I owe Elder Ayn. Without him I might never have plucked up the nerve to leave Stonehaven. But also, professionally speaking, I have an obligation to him. I agreed to accompany him and record his travels, and even though I haven't signed a contract or anything, I can't just back out on the deal. It wouldn't be right.'

'But you just said you have doubts about him.'

'Yes, I know.'

'Surely that's a good enough reason not to carry on with him. Never mind your professional duty.'

'No, I'm afraid it's not good enough. Yashu, I think what I'm trying to get at here, what I'm working my way towards, is this. I'd like you to stick with us. Please. Not for Elder Ayn's sake, not even for your own sake. For *my* sake. So that I can have an ally in all of this. Moral support. Someone I can trust. Someone who's in sympathy with me.'

He smiled at her, briefly, warily.

Winningly.

'A lot to ask, I realise,' he added. 'A huge favour. But it would make a huge difference.'

Yashu looked at his face, his glistering eyes, his candlelight-softened features, the slight hunch of his shoulders. For some reason, at that moment he reminded her of Huaso. Not so much a physical resemblance, more in his attitude, the way he was speaking to her. And as she thought of Huaso, something in her heart – she didn't want it to – gave.

'All right,' she said. 'What if we continue with Mr Ayn for a while. Just for a while. But on condition that he doesn't get us into any more trouble. Or into worse trouble.'

Khollo seemed pleased.

'And we agree that if either of us thinks he's doing that, then it's finished. We quit. Unhitch our wagons.'

'Agreed.'

'But both of us. If I go off, you have to too.'

Khollo nodded.

'A handshake on it?'

He nodded again. She proffered her hand. Khollo reached out and gripped it. She gripped back. He gripped harder. So did she. His grip was strong but hers was stronger. It became a contest and ended with a hissed oath from Khollo. He disentangled his hand from hers and waved it in the air, blowing on it, smiling. Yashu smiled too.

Five minutes later, Zelzan Haak was bidding farewell to all four of the travellers, while her husband sulked off in some corner of the house.

'Just keep heading west,' she said. 'You'll be over the border well before dawn.'

The night sky was clear, all traces of raincloud gone, and the stars' brilliance afforded just enough light to see by. The road squelched underfoot, and the land to either side was a dark mass of dripping noises, sporadic patterings, odd sucking sounds, as ground and vegetation coped with the aftermath of the deluge. Mr Ayn took the lead, Gregory Brazier close behind him, then Khollo and Yashu. Yashu had no idea if she had made a sensible decision or not, but the pact she had forged with Khollo certainly made what she was doing easier to justify to herself. If nothing else, she had struck a blow back against Mr Ayn. His close colleague was now hers. The balance in the foursome's relationships had been evened up. Now it was two and two, not three and one.

After an hour Mr Ayn announced that they had surely crossed over onto Otrean soil but to be on the safe side they ought to press on. They pressed on, and dawn gleamed into life behind them, at first just a seeping greyness that extinguished the stars, then a blush of colour, pale blues and yellows that crept across the firmament and steadied into fuller hues. Mist began to drift up from the damp earth. A few unseen birds trilled and whooped to one another across great distances, sounding more as if they were mourning the departure of night than celebrating the onset of day. The chill in the air began to fade, although each of the travellers continued to generate a wisp of vapour with every out-breath.

The sun, when it finally rose, illuminated an empty landscape, mankind's only mark on it the road, and a faint mark at that, a groove so shallow that now and then it virtually disappeared. Ahead, Yashu saw for the first time a set of mountain peaks, far-off and white, a shark's-teeth serration running along the horizon. Zelzan Haak had mentioned these yesterday and given them a name which Yashu couldn't recall just then. They were like islands in the air, a snow-capped archipelago arising from a hilly green sea. She fixed her gaze on them and kept walking.

And kept walking. The four of them had to be well inside Otrea by now but Mr Ayn said he was reluctant to leave anything to chance. There was too, he said, a destination to be reached – a place where they could stay for a few days and rest and take stock. 'We must forge ahead,' he announced. Several times, in fact, he announced this. 'A few more miles. Just a few more. Forge ahead.'

Midmorning, and fatigue was setting in, a physical and mental undertow given additional heft by lack of a full night's sleep. The landscape did not seem to change, monotonously uneven, unevenly monotonous. Yashu knew her legs were moving, knew she was repeatedly putting one foot in front of the other, but had begun to feel as if she wasn't getting anywhere. The road unrolled, always the same. The sky, likewise, always the same. The mountains did not appear to be coming any closer. Each roadside rock outcrop they passed looked much like the one before, until Yashu was almost convinced that it *was* the one before and that Mr Ayn was leading her and Khollo and Gregory Brazier around in circles. And there was an intimidating silence. The birds who had lamented dawn had gone quiet. A breeze blew – she felt it on her face, saw grass shiver in it – but it was stealthy, noiseless. Her own footfalls and those of the others, her own breathing, Mr Ayn's occasional encouraging comments, but no sound apart from these, nothing but an immense stillness which made her feel hopelessly lonely and lost. One of four tiny people, surrounded by the sheer open vastness of the world. Treading through desolation.

And the road grew fainter still until it petered out altogether, and Yashu was beginning to think Mr Ayn had misled them, somehow his prevision had got it wrong, there was no destination around here, even the road itself had decided it had nowhere to go. Then, ahead, a crag appeared. A wall of rock rising from the empty terrain, high, dark. And the road re-emerged, as if it had remembered. It scored a line straight for a deep cleft in the crag.

And Mr Ayn said, 'There!' with an expansive sweep of his arm, indicating the cleft, as if this was something he had personally laid on, his very own creation. 'I know it doesn't look much, but believe me, in there is safety. Security. *Sanctuary*.'

AYN

I was up early again this morning, in keeping with my new regime. Bet you didn't think I would stick to it. Just some passing whim, forgotten as soon as mentioned. Eh, Khollo?

[An unfair accusation. Elder Ayn had his faults but a lack of resolve wasn't one of them. He had got us to where we were, after all. Done nearly all he had set out to do since leaving Stonehaven.]

What you must realise is that the imminence of death sharpens the will considerably. Everything has to be done that one said one was going to. Recalcitrance is not an option. So I watched the sunrise. My prepenultimate sunrise. I soaked up its beauty. Such an ordinary thing, dawn. An everyday thing, one might say. The refraction of solar rays through the atmosphere, to reduce it to its bare scientific bones. Tormented light. Yet it is beautiful nonetheless. What makes it so? What is the point of its beauty? Why do those colours – those lustrous purples and fuchsias and saffrons – fall on our eyes and bounce through our retinas to the brain and make us think, helplessly, inescapably, 'Yes, that is loveliness'? And why will that rainbow in two days' time make me think the same? 'Yes, that is loveliness.' Even though I know what the rainbow has followed and what it precedes. Even though it is just tormented light too. Why do such sights work on our hearts as well as our heads? What is the purpose behind that? Does an animal look at a sunrise or a rainbow and admire? No. So why do we, we human animals?

Those Extraordinaries we stayed with thought they had the answer.

But I'm getting ahead of myself. We need to go back, do we not, to the moment I recruited Gregory to our little band. That's where we left off yesterday.

I have to say I was on something of a high in the days immediately following. I kept Gregory close to me, tended to him, nursed him. His burns healed quickly, of course, him being an indestructible, but with that large chunk of his hair missing, singed away, he looked somewhat odd. Off-kilter. It was an aesthetic kindness that I removed the rest of his hair with my shaving razor, but this depilation had a more practical purpose, too, in that I had a strong previsionary foreboding that it would serve us well to get rid of so distinguishing a characteristic.

As we walked west, away from Penresford, I stuck to Gregory like a shepherd to his flock, barely letting him out of my sight. Without that attention from me, he would have had no impetus to move or do anything. He was like an infant, entirely reliant on adult guidance and supervision. He didn't utter so much as one syllable to me or to anyone. He had been traumatised by more than just his injuries. He remained mute and uncommunicative, a silent suffering presence by my side, yet that didn't diminish one jot my feelings of protectiveness towards him. In fact, it only made them more powerful and more rewarding. At its most banal: it's nice to be needed. And Gregory needed me. Also he represented, as I believe I may have mentioned already, the second crucial component of my scheme, the other actual parent of my brainchild. The fact that I had known I was going to find him in no way detracted from the sense of triumph and euphoria I felt at actually finding him. All in all, I was a very happy chap.

It's safe to say Yashu did not regard him in the same rosy light. Having taken an instant dislike to him, her attitude didn't soften in any way over the next few days. Several times I caught her staring daggers at him, or else she affected a lack of interest in him which was too studied and self-conscious to be convincing. I daresay she was more than a little jealous, like an older sibling feeling usurped when a new baby arrives in the family. There was, however, nothing I could do about that. She would have to, *would*, come round to him in her own time.

We went west, as I said, deeper into Jarraine, into the remoter, more sparsely populated quarter of that country. We stayed in hovels, literally on the first night, on subsequent nights figuratively. Inns that were little better than hovels. The Hotel Hermit Crab seemed a long way away then! We traipsed from village to village, homes to hicks and hillbillies, and I made out that this was what I desired to do, that the region was worthy of exploration by virtue of the rugged splendour of its landscape, which was true to an extent, true enough at least not to offend the sensitivities of any untrained sooth-seers among us. The aftermath of Penresford hung over us, we were all still reeling from it, of that there's no doubt. So perhaps that's why Yashu didn't question too closely my motives for going the way we were going. Certainly it seemed that anywhere where there was less civilisation – for we had seen what ostensibly civilised people were capable of doing to one another – was a good place to be.

In the event, while we were trying to put Penresford behind us,

Penresford was busy trying to catch up. From one landlord we got wind of the fact that soldiers were combing the area. He had no idea why. I, on the other hand, did, and was glad that according to my map we were nearing the border between Jarraine and Otrea. And then we came to the inaptly named No Surprises Inn, where there *were* surprises in store – for some of us.

A torrential rainstorm gave us no choice but to avail ourselves of that hostelry, and the lady who was its host and proprietor, Zelzan Haak, turned out to be in the same Inclination class as myself, which made for some amusing conversational gamesmanship between the two of us as we first made each other's acquaintance and then attempted to divine what role each of us would play in the other's future. I knew almost straight away that we were going to be betrayed, not by the rumpled yet redoubtable Zelzan herself, but by her husband, Lon. She knew it too and was at pains to inform us how close we were to the border and safety, less than three miles. The dynamic between her and her husband was an interesting one – she Air, he, a plant-sensitive, Earth. Two Inclinations that could not have less in common, but somehow they had made it work. It was clear, though, which of them was the dominant partner. For all her skirts and domesticity, Zelzan wore the trousers in that household. And she was embarrassed, I think, by what her husband was about to do, which was why she did all she reasonably could to help us. It was an affront to her, both as an inn proprietor and as Air Inclined, that Lon was going to leave the inn that night after the rain stopped and hurry over to a neighbouring village and get word out that the reason those soldiers were searching the area, the person they were looking for, was right there under his very own roof.

There was, you see, a bounty on Gregory's head. It was Gregory the soldiers were after. He stood accused of murder, and not just any common-or-garden murder but murder of the worst kind, fratricide. He was certainly guilty of the crime but there were extenuating, indeed exonerating circumstances. It wasn't a wilful act but rather a desperately tragic error which took place in a moment of confusion and anger during Penresford's final hours. The story leading up to that moment is long and involved. Gregory has revealed it to us in dribs and drabs. Not the most forthcoming of boys. But I've pieced it together. In a nutshell, he and two members of the family he was staying with in Penresford were attacked by incendiaries, or so Gregory thought. He, naturally, retaliated. The victim of his retaliation, hidden within a flame shell, turned out to be his own brother. An awful jigsaw of events which, had even just one piece not fallen into place with such remorseless neatness, would have had a very different and far happier outcome.

That night, then, Lon Haak sneaked out and, by means of a local retired telepath, nobly and selflessly submitted information to the Jarrainian authorities that was likely to lead to the apprehension of a fugitive from justice. I wonder if he ever actually received any money, given that his tip-off ultimately proved worthless. We shall never know. When he returned home, anyway, there was his wife waiting for him with, I imagine, a rather dusty expression on her face, arms crossed, the metaphorical rolling-pin in hand. Zelzan set up a racket loud enough to rouse the entire household. I don't doubt that this was intentional. When I emerged from my room Yashu was already up and the whole sorry saga was laid out before us – Gregory's crime and Lon's betrayal, which he regarded as an act of civic-mindedness and which probably was, although a financial reward is always an irresistible incentive to do right. We packed hurriedly and prepared to depart. There was a slight delay when Yashu appeared unwilling to leave her room. I sent you up, Khollo, to coax her out, and you were successful in that task. And the reason for her dilatory behaviour – what was it again?

['The obvious, Elder Ayn. She wasn't happy to discover we'd been travelling with a murderer. She was worried that we would all be tarred with the same brush. Guilty by association. Understandable, really.']

Yes, understandable. Still, you were able to convince her to remain with us. I knew you would, but some official recognition for your powers of silver-tongued persuasion is due, and hereby given.

While you were undertaking that vital mission, Zelzan and I had the job of convincing her husband not to wake the neighbours and get them to hold us forcibly till soldiers arrived, as he was threatening to do. This we achieved through a classic previsionary's bluff. Zelzan informed her husband that he was not going to do as he said. She stated it as fact, giving it the authority of prediction. I backed her up. With the pair of us insisting that Lon had no chance of success, Lon was persuaded that he had no chance of success. He abandoned his plan and went off to sulk in a corner.

We departed the inn and went westward once more, through dark then dawn then daylight, along a road that was a mere scratch in the earth's skin. Ever westward, with the Vail Mountains now revealed on the horizon, rising from their pine-furred foothills, beckoning. At my first sight of them I experienced a pang. How could I not? There they were – here they are – the end-stop of my life. Once entered, I would never be leaving. Oh, that's an appalling sentence construction. Participle dangling all over the place like a flaccid cock. I should change it. No, forge ahead, forge ahead. In fact, wasn't that the very phrase I kept using at the time? Forge ahead. To encourage us all to keep going, even after we'd crossed the border into Otrea. To encourage myself as much as anyone, since my feet felt draggingly heavy. The mountains – deep at heart I did not want them to come closer, not even by a single stride. I think that then, if at any time, I most wished that the trajectory of my life was not so precisely plotted out. No, rather that I was not aware of its being so. Wished for the blissful ignorance of the future which is the lot of everyone but previsionaries. Wished that the Vail Mountains were nothing other than a range of peaks still sufficiently distant that I could, if I wanted to, blot them from view by raising an arm. Just rocks and snow, and not the terminal point of all I am and have ever been.

Deep sigh there, Khollo. Transcribe it if you like. 'Hahhhhh.' Or write 'Deep sigh'. Or don't bother. Up to you.

Throughout that morning there was a sense of being pursued and yet we never saw hide nor hair of anyone behind us. We must have reached Otrea well before the soldiers even got to the No Surprises, and of course they could not legitimately follow us across the border, not without risk of precipitating a diplomatic incident. All the same, the illusion was there – cavalrymen bearing down on us at the gallop while we tromped on at a comparative snail's pace. Authority in all its brass-and-leather pomp, racing to overtake us.

And then it was noon, and then noon was past, and at last we had a glimpse of journey's end. It was a lofty, sheer-sided crag running north to south, an obstacle we would have had to make a lengthy detour to circumvent. But we weren't going to circumvent it. There was, invitingly, a cleft almost directly before us. And who in their right mind can refuse to enter an inviting cleft!

I indicated to the three of you that we would find refuge therein, and led you, like mother duck and her three straggling ducklings, up to the cleft. Had this not been where the road, such as it was, terminated, nothing about the cleft would have suggested that any kind of worthwhile destination lay within. It was just a vertical divide slightly wider than one's outstretched fingertips. Nor, inside, was it any more promising-looking. The cleft was the opening to a sheer-sided gorge, of the same width, which curved deep into the crag on a shallow downward incline. The floor of the gorge was rock, with outcrops of moss and the odd puddle of stagnant rainwater. Peering in, I must say I began to have doubts about the accuracy of my own prevision. I had to run through the fore-memory of traversing this narrow defile and emerging at the other end just to make sure I wasn't mistaken. Then in I went.

After about fifty yards I realised that only Gregory was with me.

Yashu and my faithful Khollo still loitered outside the cleft. I beckoned. 'It's perfectly safe,' I said, my voice echoing, batting from rockface to rockface. You overcame your trepidation. We all four proceeded. The sides of the gorge became taller, shutting out more and more of the sky like the jaws of a vice clamping together. The ground underfoot, meanwhile, became slipperier. Down through that deepening, darkening declivity we trod. We crossed a tiny streamlet which stemmed from a trickle on the gorge's wall and dispersed across the ground in a fanning, slimy green delta. The air got cold. Our footfalls reverberated susurrantly. You've since told me, Khollo, that you began to wonder if the gorge even had an outlet; if it wasn't simply going to keep descending for ever, or perhaps narrow until it was no longer passable. No one could argue that it certainly gave that impression.

But an outlet it had, an end. After a mile and a half, I estimate, of twists and turns, the gorge opened out onto a ravine which ran crosswise, broader but with sides no less sheer and precipitous. The pebbles of an ancient riverbed crackled as we trod over them. The ravine widened and hard earth replaced the pebbles. All around us small brown mammals scurried, nipping in and out of view – some kind of gopher or ground squirrel. We slogged on, and shortly came across evidence of human habitation. There, in that unlikely spot. First of all, a fruit and vegetable plot smack-dab in the middle of the ravine. Rows of carrots, potatoes and the like, bean plants twisting up tall cones of sticks, bushes bearing a purplish berry. A good half-acre of produce encircled by a tight-woven wicker fence to keep it from predation by vermin. Then, just past that, a washing-line strung between two poles, from which hung a range of clothing – items of both male and female wear, none of which could be described as being in the best condition and some of which were just a couple of steps above rags. And not far from the washing-line, the mouth to a large cave, situated at the apex of a shallow-shelving ramp of rocks and stones that could only have been put there by human hand. A patched, ragged flap of tarpaulin hung down, screening off half of the cave-mouth and providing protection from the rain, shade from the sun, and perhaps some semblance of cosiness. The flap flexed gently in and out, wafted by the breeze that flowed along the ravine in airy emulation of the long-gone river.

The cave was impenetrably dark from a distance. From the foot of the ramp, however, it became possible to discern movement within. Figures, rising. Picking up long-handled implements of some sort. Slowly emerging to blink at us in the daylight.

There were six of them, four men and two women, and they were shaggy-haired and scrawny and clad in the same sort of clothes as we had seen drying on the washing-line, things that had seen a great deal of wear and no less tear. So tattered and shapeless was these people's attire, and so emaciated were the people themselves, that gender differences were all but erased. Only beards definitively distinguished the men from the women. Hard living had otherwise de-sexed them all.

Inordinately large eyes stared at us from skeletal faces. Bony hands clutched battered-looking homespun hoes and adzes. The way these implements were being held brandished, they looked as if they could easily be put to an altogether less innocent purpose than tilling and weeding.

We held this pose for several moments, the two groups, us and them, sizing each other up across a ten-yard gap. I heard you making uncomfortable noises beside me, Khollo. Did you not believe me when I had told you we were going to find sanctuary in that place? Or were you in the grip of some more primal disquiet? I wouldn't be surprised if it was the latter. You must have sensed an oddness about the people from the cave. Something in us always jangles in the presence of an Extraordinary, and there we were, confronted with not one but six of them.

What is the collective noun for a group of Extraordinaries? Maybe there isn't one. A blankness of Extraordinaries? A vacuum? A dearth? I ask because in the normal run of events one seldom comes across more than one or two of these rare beasts at a time. To meet half a dozen in the same spot was more than usually disconcerting. One's instinctive unease wasn't just multiplied, it was multiplied exponentially. Or perhaps an alternative mathematical metaphor: as when the product of two negatives is a positive, so the product of several Extraordinaries together is also a kind of positive, a something arisen from an accumulation of nothings, a force of absence, an aura of massed *lack*. It's an experience which, as I am amply proving, is hard to put into words. Unsettling, though, it definitely was for all of us.

Possibly we would have stood there till sunset, facing one another wordlessly, nobody ready to make the first move, but then a seventh Extraordinary came out from the cave. This man was no taller than any of the others, no more well-fleshed, no healthier in appearance, no better dressed, but he nonetheless exuded importance, stature, charisma, all the hallmarks of leadership. Lively-eyed, with streaks of silver in the hair that flared from his temples, he strode straight past his colleagues and down the rocky ramp. As he reached us his flaky lips pulled back, revealing the too-long teeth of the malnourished. This beard-breaking grin was accompanied by an outstretched hand, proffered first to me, then to you, Yashu and Gregory, in that order.

'Marius Querennion,' the man said, for all the world as if intro-ducing himself to fellow-partygoers at some smart social function. 'Forgive the wary reception. Nothing meant by it. As a rule, not many strangers pass this way, and we're always a bit shocked when they do. Please be assured that we're a peaceable lot and mean you no harm. On the contrary. Are you hungry? We can offer you a meal. Nothing fancy but it'll fill a hole.'

Thus we ended up sitting in the cave, being plied with various foodstuffs laid out on unglazed earthenware dishes. Leaves of some dark-green salady stuff, a bean-based paste, a loaf of potato-flour flatbread, and some meat as well, stringy and bitter stuff which Querennion told us came from those mammals we had seen earlier. He, too, did not know what the creature was called, but it proliferated in the ravine and was easily trapped. 'Tame and gullible,' he said, 'and if not very tasty, then at least it adds some solidity to an otherwise vegetarian diet.'

I have to admit to feeling guilty at consuming the food of people who clearly had little of it to spare, but the meal was offered so freely and with such solicitude that it would have been churlish to refuse, if not downright impolite. I saw scant such concern among my three co-travellers, who happily stuffed their faces.

[As I remember it, Elder Ayn set the pace when it came to eating and the rest of us struggled to match him. But it doesn't matter.]

Then we were given water, and astonishingly cool and fresh and clean-tasting it was. Querennion said it came from a subterranean spring and gestured deeper into the cave.

The cave itself? The part we were in, what one might term its antechamber, was large, as spacious as any mansion vestibule and not dissimilar in size to Stonehaven's Obsidian Hall. A dozen alcoves had been hewn out from the walls, each broad and deep enough for a man to stretch out in and sleep. A smaller niche next to the cavemouth made for a makeshift cooking range, with a deep groove cut length-wise to channel the fire smoke outside. These, however, were the sole adaptations that had been made to the place. There were no other concessions to creature comfort. There was no furniture and no decoration, unless you count the tarpaulin door-hanging. No candles or lanterns. Living conditions of the plainest, most primitive type imaginable. It seemed scarcely conceivable that less than a day's walk away lay the relative sophistication of the villages of south-western Jarraine. But then for those Extraordinaries what mattered was less geographical isolation, more ideological. They lived as they did by choice rather than necessity. The why was important rather than the where.

I should perhaps explain – but then it's quite obvious, isn't it? – what they were doing there in that empty, barely habitable place. They were one of those mystical sects which Extraordinaries, and it seems only Extraordinaries, are so fond of forming and joining. One hears about such sects all the time, but equally they seem like a rumour or a bad joke, just another way of stigmatising their kind. Like the name Extraordinary itself. I mean, if that isn't irony, what is?

This lot, at any rate, dubbed themselves the Trustees of the Godhead, and they had, according to Querennion, peopled that cave since time immemorial. Over the centuries their numbers had waxed and waned, sometimes reaching as many as twenty or thirty, sometimes reduced to just one. They espoused, he said, a set of old, old beliefs which survived from one occupancy to the next by means of a scrupulously maintained oral tradition.

Querennion added that he wouldn't bore us with further detail. We were Inclined, for one thing, so he would be wasting his breath, but more to the point, the worst thing a person could do, in his opinion, was try to shove his beliefs down others' throats. What he would like to do, though, if we were agreeable, was show us the cave's heart. Whatever one's viewpoint, whatever one's Inclination or lack of it, the grotto at the cave's heart was a universally awe-inspiring sight. He had taken a liking to us, he said, which was why he was making this offer. We could always refuse, he wouldn't mind.

I couldn't see the harm in taking a look, and my fore-memory of the grotto justified this decision with a tingle of anticipation. Nods between you, me and Yashu confirmed that you would like to come too. Gregory, of course, remained eminently biddable. All I had to do was take him by the hand and he blithely tagged along.

At its further end the antechamber funnelled down to become a broad, rounded tunnel. It was a nostalgic moment for me to find myself once more in a corridor that burrowed through solid rock. Had it really been a month since I left Stonehaven? It seemed that a second lifetime had gone by, that I had done as much during the past four weeks as I had in all my four decades in Stonehaven's smug, smothering embrace.

We proceeded single file, Querennion at the head, and soon the light from the cavemouth, which glimmeringly outlined the tunnel's smooth-ribbed walls, faded and we were immersed in darkness. Querennion advised us to place our feet carefully. We could, if we wanted a little extra security, brush a hand along the wall to guide ourselves, as the blind are wont to do.

We shuffled through a cool, whispering void where the only certainties were the floor underfoot, the clammy wall beneath one's fingertips, the breaths and footfalls of one's companions fore and aft. The tunnel appeared to tend downhill but it was hard to know for sure. Then – and it seemed we had been walking for an unchartably long period of time but it may not have been more than half an hour – I began to perceive Querennion in front of me again, albeit dimly, limned by a faint greenish glow ahead. His silhouette swayed against this light source which, as it grew closer, spilled along the tunnel walls to form a brightening halo around him. It was a green as of jade, milky and serene. My hand, lit by it, floated in the air like some glaucous sea-creature. From behind me I heard a hushed Air-Inclined oath . . .

[It was an eerie sight and no mistake, that green light. I wasn't sure what to make of it. What was it? What was creating it?]

. . . and then I became aware of noise emanating from the same direction as the light, a relentless patter and spatter that echoed in such a way as to suggest vastness – a huge contained space resounding with watery activity.

This, sure enough, was the noise of the grotto. The tunnel opened out and there we were. We were in an underground chamber whose dimensions had no analogue in any man-made chamber I have seen. It reached up to a height of perhaps two dozen men standing on each other's shoulders, perhaps more. Roughly cylindrical, its circumference must have measured, what, three hundred yards?

['At least.']

Great globular stalactites hung from the ceiling and similarly globular stalagmites rose from the floor, lumpen and glistening, not unlike inner organs in appearance. These and the grotto's walls were coated in some kind of phosphorescent substance – a lichen, Querennion said, which thrived in conditions of sunless damp. The level of illumination it provided seemed considerable but then that might just have been in contrast to the darkness we had passed through to get there. I doubt one could have read by it. It was akin to moonlight, flat and somehow uncertain. Abyssal viridian moonlight.

It was cold in there. Not cold enough to make one's breath visible, but almost. And did I mention the water? I mentioned the noise, but what was causing the noise were scores of drips and dribbles of water, either falling from stalactite tip to stalagmite tip or else coming down from the roof of the grotto to splash-land on the floor in eroded depressions, some of which were frying-pan shallow, others bath deep. It was a perpetual indoor rain, and each chain of droplets, sparkling in the lichen's luminosity, resembled a quivering emerald necklace. The effect was entrancing. If one stared, one began to feel that it wasn't the water that was falling, it was oneself that was rising. And the roar . . . That multiplicity of trickles, amplified by echoes and confinement, set up a din as loud as any cataract or sea-shore breakers. And the grotto's size, literally cavernous. All of it conspired to leave one dizzied and stunned.

Awe-inspiring, Querennion had said, and awe-inspiring the grotto was. Indeed, it made a chap feel very small and insignificant. Unlike the Worldstorm, which belittles with its sheer bullying brutality, here one was humbled by majesty, by wonder, a voluntary rather than enforced surrender to the might of a natural phenomenon. I felt that I could have stood on the grotto's floor and stared up, enthralled, for ever. Equally, I felt out of place, as if I didn't belong, as if I would lose all sense of myself if I stayed in the grotto too long – almost as if the grotto itself wished me to admire it but was warning me away at the same time. Too much majesty. Too much wonder.

When eventually, by mutual consent, we trooped back along the tunnel to the outer part of the cave, everything seemed thoroughly drab and ordinary. The brownness of the cave's interior. The emptiness of the ravine. The quiet daylight. The bland blue sky. Querennion and the other Extraordinaries, as if knowing how we were feeling, left us alone for a while. We four of us sat in various places on the rock ramp outside the cavemouth and husbanded our thoughts.

Yashu was the first to speak.

'We should stay here,' she said.

And for the next week we did. I can't say why exactly – what it was that made us all agree with Yashu's suggestion. Speaking for myself, while I was none too enthused about the days of discomfort and deprivation ahead, the prospect seemed acceptable simply because the grotto was there. To be able to revisit it, or just be close to it, appealed. And as Yashu had been so compliant and undemanding up till then, I had no qualms about letting her make the running for once. It was the politic thing to do. You, Khollo?

['**You announced you would like to stay, so the choice was made for me.**']

No other reason? No? Well, fair enough. Nice and pragmatic. And as for Gregory, probably much the same. Our catatonic young friend was content to do whatever the rest of us were doing.

Querennion readily consented to our request. It was as if he expected it after showing us the grotto. He said if we didn't mind living as they, the Trustees, did . . .

And so a week of eremitic existence, or should that be subsistence? At first the want of life's basic amenities was noticeable, indeed hard felt. Not just the meagre rations, the bare unaccommodating rock of the alcoves in which we slept (or tried to), the communal outdoor latrine with its stultifying stench and permanent buzzing cloud of flies.

These were bad enough. But what one was more aware of, and what made a deeper impact, was the Extraordinaries' absence of Inclination and how it impinged on their lives. To watch them, for instance, tending their produce patch – toiling hard to keep the soil irrigated and weed-free, exhausting themselves at labours which strongs would have despatched in half the time and with minimal effort. To see them at such pains to make their fruits and vegetables grow and then at even greater pains to store properly what they harvested – no plant-sensitives on hand to propagate and preserve. To note how each of them was struggling under the burden of at least one kind of ailment, be it a cold-sore, a sprain, a strained ligament, an infected scratch, toothache, even in one case an eye beginning to cloud over with a cataract – the unavailability of a recuperator evident in a myriad ways. To observe how long it took them to light a fire by rubbing two sticks together – a box of matches would have helped, an incendiary would have helped even more.

Yet the other side of the coin was that the Extraordinaries did cope. By dint of effort and application and an unyielding tenacity they wrestled with the drawbacks of their chosen lifestyle and just about emerged victorious. Being without Inclination brought with it a host of hardships, yet they had adapted. They gritted their teeth and battled on. They even, in a perhaps perverse fashion, enjoyed it. They were proving a point. No, Extraordinariness was not the encumbrance it appeared to be. Yes, one could dwell apart from the Inclined world and survive. Just.

And of course they had their faith, too, these Trustees of the Godhead. They had their beliefs to keep them steady and bolster them in their constant round of vicissitude and travail. Something grim and solemn and fitfully cheerful lit them from within. A purpose. A shared certainty.

From time to time Querennion and I would fall to discussing the sect's creed and lifestyle. More often than not he would initiate the conversations, seeking me out when he had an idle moment and softening me up with some light chitchat before broaching weightier matters. I flatter myself that he saw in me an intellectual equal, but perhaps he also saw the very embodiment of modern empiricism. I was a challenge to his orthodoxy. A test.

The precise content of our discussions I'm afraid I can't relate, not in perfect detail, because my enshriner was not on hand for any of them. They were private, one to one. I can, however, summarise them, and shall attempt to do so concisely for fear of trying my readers' patience with arguments that have been rehearsed in many another publication by commentators far wiser and more insightful than myself.

At heart all religious sects like the Trustees of the Godhead believe the same thing. That there is a higher power above us. That the human realm is governed by a numinous supreme entity, a being who is limitlessly powerful and essentially unknowable, immortal, all-seeing, a god. And that this god guides and shapes our ends. This god takes a hand, sometimes overtly, sometimes covertly, in all that we do.

Now, some sects, although not the Trustees, identify the god as the Worldstorm itself. And a very cantankerous deity this is too, perpetually angered at the behaviour of men and inflicting suffering on us at every turn. In the eyes of the Worldstorm-god we are all wrongdoers, guilty of venality and aggression and excessive love of material possessions, and in order to placate its wrath, or try to, the sects live humble, simple lives. Some of them go so far as to scourge and scarify themselves ritually. A kind of propitiatory offering to offset a greater deficit. Trying to buy respite for the rest of us with their misery and pain. Clearly works, doesn't it.

Sects such as these Querennion frowned on. He dismissed them as fanatics and said that their deification of the 'Storm was inappropriate. In a weird masochistic way they were venerating it, and the 'Storm was not a thing to be venerated. The Trustees of the Godhead – and they weren't alone in this – took the view that the 'Storm wasn't a god itself but was the tool of a god. Yes, it was there to punish men, but not so much for what they were doing, rather for what they had done once, long ago.

And at this juncture one might object, as I did, and say that if these sects' beliefs had any credibility, surely they would tally with one another. All these people would follow identical truths, or indeed one fundamental, unvarying truth. To which Querennion gave a very frosty retort, saying that some sects were muddle-headed and others were just plain wrong. He treated the objection the same way every time I raised it, with blank-eyed, blanket condemnation. Amusing, no? How the alternative viewpoints Querennion was least prepared to countenance were those that were closest to his own. Whereas the viewpoint of someone like me, antithetical to his, he hardly had a problem with.

Anyway, according to Querennion – and the Trustees' oral tradition – once, long ago, all men were worshippers of a single god. All men, moreover, were Extraordinary, or, to use Querennion's own wry euphemism, Disinclined. They lived contentedly under their god. They comported themselves in accordance with his wishes. There existed a state of mutual trust between them and him (the god is genderless but, where the neuter pronoun would be accurate, the masculine pronoun is used, both as shorthand and to reinforce a sense of personality). The entire universe was the god's handiwork, men were part of it, they happily acknowledged this fact, and all was harmonious.

But the trust was abused. The god, having become convinced that men were reliable and capable of regulating their own destinies, elected to take a remoter role in the running of things. A lackadaisical attitude, one might think, but perhaps he was bored or planning on taking retirement. For a time, anyway, men proved his faith in them right, but gradually they began to drift. As the god's influence was felt less and less, men began to succumb to their own worst tendencies. They squabbled. They stole. They fought. They cheated. They cozened. They warred. They despoiled. They plundered. They lived for self-gratification. They eschewed the noble and embraced the ignoble. And the god – somewhat belatedly, if you ask me – spotted what was going on and was, to put it mildly, peeved.

In his indignation the first thing the god did was conjure up the Worldstorm. This 'Storm was nothing like the present 'Storm. This 'Storm was significantly worse. Ten times the size, twenty times as ferocious. For an entire century it scoured the planet from end to end, scrubbing the earth's surface clean as a scullery maid might scrub a filthy flagstone floor. When it was over and the 'Storm abated somewhat, just a few scattered, embattled pockets of humanity remained. The rest was desolation.

The god took pity on these survivors. Repentant, as we often are after we lose our temper, he decided to imbue them with gifts to make up for the havoc he had inflicted on them. These gifts were the Inclinations. However, he also decided to assign different types of Inclination to different types of people. He had perceived that men had a flaw in their makeup, an intrinsic urge to seek out division and dissent. If that was how they were, then why not simply accept it. Work with it rather than change it.

And so men became Inclined. A few, however, a precious few, the god elected to keep as they were. He intended that, in them, there would survive a memory of the world as it was before the Worldstorm. In them, too, his true essence would be preserved.

'For the god resides in all of us,' Querennion said. 'He is the tree and we are his branches. He is the sap that animates everyone.'

'What, everyone?' I said. 'Even me?'

'Even you,' said Querennion.

'In which case,' I said, 'how come I'm not aware of it?'

'Because the Inclined tend not to feel him. Inclination insulates them from him. Whereas the Disinclined feel him strongly. We're more directly connected to him. It's the great compensation for the way we are. To us, you see, Inclination is the burden, not the lack of Inclination.'

The Trustees' duty was to manage without Inclination and be exemplars of what they considered a purer, truer form of existence. What their lives lacked in comfort was made up for by a sense of profound purpose. They were, in spite of all the disadvantages they lived under, happy. Or so Querennion insisted, and as I've said, there did appear to be something about them, some sort of underlying, I don't know . . . serenity?

How Querennion had come to join the Trustees' ranks was a straightforward enough tale. The son of Air-Inclined parents, both telepaths, he had struggled throughout his teens and early twenties to come to terms with his failure to manifest, shouldering the jibes and taunts of his peers, repeatedly being cut dead in the street by erstwhile boyhood friends, watching his mother and father gradually lose their social standing and become ostracised on account of him. He could look forward to a future of nothing but more of the same. What were his career prospects? His marriage prospects? Few avenues were open to him. Eventually, close to despair, and to suicide, he had the good fortune to meet another Extraordinary, a vagrant passing through his hometown, who told him about the Trustees and the grotto of which they were custodians. This is how knowledge of the sect, and others like it, is always spread. Word of mouth. Whispers passing whenever two or more Extraordinaries are gathered together. Immediately, the young Querennion knew that with the Trustees was where he belonged. He departed for the ravine as soon as he could. That had been thirty years ago. He hadn't regretted it once.

The grotto itself, he told me, wasn't simply a natural marvel. One of the Trustees' basic doctrinal tenets was that their god could be experienced there. Their god liked to make himself known from time to time. A sweeping landscape, a gorgeous sunrise or sunset, the star-flocked night sky, the plumage of a beautiful bird – these and other sights that stirred the heart, they were him. Visual reminders of his power and presence. But in certain locales, like the grotto, he revealed his magnificence the most clearly. Had I felt it, Querennion asked. Had I discerned it in the thunder and fall of that green-lit cavern? God? I didn't say that I had. I couldn't say that I had not. I merely told him I thought the grotto impressive, and he regarded me levelly and nodded and seemed to sense I had no idea of the true answer myself.

Once, during one of our conversations, I enquired of Querennion whether his beliefs were not closely allied to those of the Water Inclined, particularly of isolated Wet communities like Li*issua. His god's bestowal of Inclination and the Wets' Great Fissuring seemed to me to be only mildly divergent accounts of the same event. Did that not invalidate his sect's assertion that Extraordinaries were special, in some sense 'chosen'?

Again, a frosty response. A nerve touched. Querennion pointed out that the Water Inclined had no god.

'Oh really?' I said. 'Yashu's people have this legendary father-figure Oriñaho. A superior being. All the Water Inclination classes rolled into one. He strikes me as being remarkably analogous to *your* superior being.'

More huffing and puffing from Querennion. He said that, with Wets, the belief system they lived by was cultural, ingrained from birth. They were steeped in it and so it wasn't a matter of choice with them, merely a matter of conformity. By contrast, with Extraordinaries it was an impulse, an urge, an instinct. It arose spontaneously and was not imposed from without. For himself, journeying to this ravine had been like answering a summons. As soon as he learned of the Trustees it was as though a bell had chimed deep in his heart. The other Trustees spoke of the same sensation, he said. Irresistible inner promptings had called them here, as hunger calls a man to seek food, and this was plainly proof that theirs was the authentic form of faith, because it was elective and inwardly inspired.

When pressed on the matter, Querennion allowed that to the casual observer certain similarities might seem to exist between the two traditions, Water-Inclined and Extraordinary, but he maintained that Wets adhered to an attenuated – I think he may have used the word 'bastardised' – version. The Trustees, through zealous conservation, had clung on to the real thing.

'What's your opinion, then,' I asked, 'of the rest of the world? Those, like me, who live in almost total ignorance of your god. Who carry on oblivious, harried from time to time by the Worldstorm, not knowing the 'Storm is a continuation of a punishment first meted out on our long-ago forefathers. What good, in fact, is a punishment if the punishees don't know they're being punished?'

The 'Storm, Querennion replied, would remain a blight on the world for as long as men insisted on behaving wickedly and selfishly and without respect for others.

That, I told him, surely meant for ever.

True, he said, but then again, people might begin to realise the error of their ways. They might begin to treat one another as equals and not be so obsessed with the differences between us.

In other words, said I, they might cease to look down their noses at Extraordinaries?

That, said Querennion with a concessionary smile, would be a step in the right direction. But more generally, men might start to listen again to the voice of god inside them. There was so much rationalism in the world, so much store put by science and commerce and Inclination, so much arrogance passing for enlightenment. The tyranny of empiricism. It was time for a little humility instead, and the willing submission to a higher power. Would that be so difficult? People, after all, spoke of providence and fate all the time. They were in thrall to superstitions, especially where the Worldstorm was concerned. They acknowledged these sorts of external forces running through their lives, even if they didn't necessarily believe in them. It wasn't such a huge step from that to acknowledging one superior force, was it? A single, overarching force that controlled and drove everything.

I suggested that if he hoped for such a result, such a thoroughgoing change in human thought, then why not advertise? Why not open up his grotto to all and sundry? Let people see there what he insisted was there, his god's glory. That would help, wouldn't it?

'Turn this place into a tourist attraction?' Querennion said, and he made a great humorous show of being aghast at the idea, possibly to hide how genuinely aghast he was. 'Never in a million years. Think how that would cheapen it.'

'Not necessarily,' I said. 'I reckon you could charge a pretty hefty entrance fee.'

He was miffed at me for a whole day after that, but forgave me in the end. I do think I may have gone a bit far, proposing, even in jest, that he prostitute his sect's most sacred place. But then if a challenge was what he looking for from me, that was what he was going to get.

And speaking of that sacred place, I revisited the grotto twice during our stay, once with Querennion, once on my own. With Querennion, the purpose of the journey was to fetch water. We carried pitchers fashioned of the same stuff as the dishes the Trustees served their food on. They made all these crockery items themselves, fashioning them out of wetted earth from the ravine floor then leaving them out in the sun to bake hard. We each took a pair of empty pitchers to the grotto and set them out to catch falling water. We carried already-filled ones back, and I can tell you, that was quite an effort. Brimming with water, those pitchers were heavy and awkward to handle. It was a long trip.

Since that visit had a practical purpose, there wasn't much opportunity to pause and sight-see. The second, solo visit I undertook at night when everyone else was fast asleep. I was having particular difficulty getting comfortable in my little alcove, so I got up and ventured off down the tunnel, feeling curiously as if I was doing something daring and illicit. No one had forbidden us to visit the grotto unescorted. All the same, an undeniable sense of trespass.

The grotto was as it was. The eternally plummeting emerald rain. The lumpen accretions of stalactite and stalagmite. The relentless deafening tumult of splash and echoed splash. I surveyed it all with a coolly rational eye. I knew that the water filtered down from above through strata of porous rock, most likely originating from a subterranean aquifer. I knew that dissolved minerals, incrementally deposited over the course of millennia, had formed the grotto's giblet-like growths. I believed that the lichen was as Querennion described it. There are tiny plant-like organisms in the ocean that glow. This was the land-based equivalent. All readily explicable.

Where, then, did the feelings come from? The awe? The intimidation? Why was there clearly some sort of *presence* in that place? As though one kept glimpsing something through a veil. Movement at the periphery of one's vision, elusive, undetectable when looked at directly. The outline of a shape too massive somehow for the five senses to fathom.

Perhaps it was just disorientation. The glow, the noise, befuddling the brain.

Perhaps.

It was on our final evening with the Trustees that Querennion and I had perhaps the most intriguing, and ultimately most profitable, of all our talks. By that stage I found I had become accustomed to the Trustees' ways and no longer felt so conscious of their Extraordinariness. It was almost as if Extraordinariness was just another Inclination, different but not disturbingly so, not any more.

Briefly, Khollo, your impressions of Querennion?

[**'I thought he was pretty decent. You have to wonder what living like that for thirty years might do to a man's mind, but . . . He seemed level-headed. His intentions good. He meant well.'**]

Ah, that lethally condemning phrase. 'He meant well.'

[**'No, honestly. It's a compliment.'**]

Did he strike you as strait-laced at all?

[**'A bit.'**]

Sober? Dependable?

[**'Yes.'**]

And he had that habit, didn't he, of underlining certain remarks with a steady, penetrating stare. Either as if to make sure he had been understood correctly or else as if scanning for mockery.

[**'You had much more contact with him than I did, Elder Ayn.'**]

You're never going to call me Annonax, are you, Khollo? I'm forever to be Elder Ayn to you. Oh well. Yes, I did have much more contact with him. And that stare, to me, was the mark of someone tightly wound inside. For all his religious conviction, for all his outward calm, Querennion remained at heart bruised and embittered, still that teenager feeling aggrieved at the bad tiles life had dealt him. Being a Trustee was a balm to his sense of injustice but sometimes even that wasn't enough.

He invited me to join him for a stroll that evening. We wandered along the ravine, while those small brown mobile snacks darted around us, gambolling near the entrances to their burrows as dusk's gloaming fired the sky. About three miles from the cave we came to a rockfall. A section of the ravine's western side had slumped away, creating a rugged, sloping apron which we scaled on all fours. At the top, we sat. We were in a horseshoe-shaped concavity some one hundred feet up with perhaps a further fifty feet of ravine wall still above us. It was like sitting in the rear seats of a theatre auditorium, the ravine itself the stage. The lowering sun shed orange rays onto the opposite wall, the (as it were) backcloth. All very secluded and scenic.

Then Querennion reached down beside him and began lifting rocks away, to reveal what appeared to be, and was, a bottle. The bottle was a quarter full of some amber liquor. He grasped it by the neck, uncorked it, took a glug, and passed it to me. A very decent spot of whisky it was, nice and ripe and malty, with a far from unpleasant afterburn.

'Sometimes,' Querennion said, accepting the bottle back off me, 'I just have to get away and be on my own. No slight on my fellow-Trustees. Good people, all of them. But a man needs his solitude from time to time. Needs to be alone with his thoughts.'

'Especially a man in charge,' I said.

'Especially a man in charge,' he confirmed. 'And sometimes,' he went on, 'I'll take myself off not just for a couple of hours like this but for a number of days. I tell the others I'm going to seek vistas and contemplation. Fast for a while in the wilderness. Sharpen my mind up, away from distractions. Listen to god's voice. And it's true, I do do that. Or at any rate, I used to.'

'Where did it come from?' I asked, indicating the whisky.

'Well, that's the question, isn't it?' said Querennion. 'But first, watch this.' And he gestured towards the 'stage'. And we watched, and as the sun sank further the light it cast on the ravine wall turned from orange to rose to blood-red, and every single crack and crevice in the wall's surface was picked out in pristine relief, and here and there flecks of mica twinkled amid the deepening shadows, and then one larger shadow, the rim of the ravine wall we had our backs to, swept up like the tide to overwhelm colour with grey. All very lovely, and the loveliness by no means lessened by our continued intake of whisky.

Then, tongue loosened by the booze, Querennion began talking. What came out of him was a mishmash of certainties and doubts, hopes and fears, delivered in the slurred tones of one who did not drink much and so did not need to drink much to get drunk. I, harder-headed, mostly listened, interjecting the occasional 'yes' and 'hmm'. The image Querennion projected of the stalwart, unswerving leader crumbled away and there, beneath, lay a man as confused and questing as any other. What it boiled down to was: on the one hand, he had a responsibility to the Trustees and to the faith that bound them all together. On the other hand, what if that faith was misplaced? What if they were victims of some grand delusion? What if the rest of the world was right and there was nothing to life apart from that which could be seen and heard and touched? No god at all, only the belief in a god?

When this disconsolate outpouring had trickled to a halt, I told Querennion that I could identify with him. I said that I didn't think there was an Inclined person alive who hadn't at one time or other pondered on the possibility of some sort of deeper meaning, some sort of structure and purpose behind the apparent randomness of life. It might be, as he had stated earlier, that Inclination insulated the majority of us from a keen appreciation of anything but the material and the mundane.

'Superior beings,' he mumbled, interrupting me. 'To someone like me, you're all superior beings. And what need do superior beings have for a greater superior being?'

It might also be, I continued, that the Worldstorm hindered us in our search for order amid the chaos. For the 'Storm *was* chaos, pure and undiluted, and from its permanence and ubiquity one could only infer that chaos was the norm. The order of things was chaos.

And then – blame the whisky – I began to tell him what I was up to with Yashu and Gregory, why I had brought them together, what I hoped to achieve. It felt good to say it aloud again. I had discussed it with you, with Traven Keech, but otherwise only with myself in the debating chamber of my brain, where nothing is ever resolved beyond doubt. It felt good to lay my scheme out before someone fresh, and moreover a disinterested party, someone who stood to gain nothing by acclaiming it and lose nothing by rubbishing it. Not only that but it felt fair. Querennion had over the past week exposed himself to my scrutiny, using me as a sounding-board for his ideals and cherished conceits. Here was I, returning the favour.

'A child to defeat the Worldstorm,' he exclaimed. 'Is it possible? How?'

I told him I didn't know. One of my theories was that the child might, by its very arrival, set up some countervailing force that negated the 'Storm, as a gust of wind snuffs a flame, although I thought this unlikely. Alternatively the child might, when it reached the appropriate age, manifest some hitherto unknown Inclination – an Inclination of staggering proportions, sufficiently powerful to meet the 'Storm on equal terms and hammer it into submission. Or else the child might simply grow up into an adult who would devise some ingenious practical method of taming the 'Storm and would mobilise men and nations into putting the method into action. All I could propound with any certainty is that, as the fusion of all four Inclinations, the child surely had a unique destiny before it.

'But the chances are it's happened before,' Querennion said. 'Male and female, each a different mix of Inclination, meeting, coupling, having a baby. I can't believe, in all the generations there have been, with all the millions of people who've walked on this earth, it hasn't happened before.'

'No doubt it has,' I said. 'But neither Gregory nor Yashu is simply a "mix" of Inclination. Each is a rarity – Earth emerging from a long and scrupulously maintained Fire lineage, Air emerging from an insular, inbred Water race. A genealogical freak. The chances of two of *those* meeting are remote, and the chances of offspring resulting, infinitesimal.'

'A world without the Worldstorm,' Querennion mused. He was liking the idea. Who wouldn't? For him, however, it had an added attraction. 'Imagine if, when the 'Storm was gone, Inclination went with it. I mean, for argument's sake this is. Assuming your crackpot scheme even works. Inclination came about as recompense for the 'Storm, so it stands to reason that with the 'Storm banished Inclination would disappear too.'

I bit my tongue. For one thing – 'crackpot'? Who was this god-believing, cave-dwelling Extraordinary to call me 'crackpot'? And for another thing – no more Inclination? Now *that* was crackpot. Why I bit my tongue, though, wasn't a sudden attack of politeness. Rather, prevision was telling me Querennion was about to say something very useful and it would be unwise to antagonise him.

'Well now, listen,' he said. 'You're planning on getting the two youngsters together, and from what I've seen they're not exactly, you know' – he interlaced the fingers of both hands – 'like that. You need time and isolation, am I right? You need to get Gregory and Yashu in a place where you can work on them undisturbed. Have them face shared hardships, maybe. Forge a bond that way. Does that sound right?'

I nodded. 'That sounds like just what I need.'

'Fine,' he said. 'Then I think I know where you can go. I ought not to be doing this, but if there's just the tiniest possibility that what you're up to might succeed . . .' He picked up the whisky bottle, now almost empty, a last rinse of liquor tinkling inside it. 'Want to know where I got this from? I'll tell you.'

And the where was here, this hunting lodge. This was Querennion's destination on those infrequent excursions he made away from the ravine. He had discovered it a decade back when wandering up the mountainside genuinely for the purpose of finding solitude and fasting. The lodge had been empty but its cellar, as we know, well stocked. Querennion had roamed its rooms, seeing soft beds, sheets, pillows, windows that sealed out draughts. Tempted, he had succumbed, and spent three days and nights wallowing in pleasures he thought he had forfeited for ever. Unbending his spine onto a plush mattress. Lowering himself into the sweet, near-forgotten embrace of alcohol. Indulging mind and body until a sense of duty reasserted itself like a dash of ice water and he went scrambling back down to the cave, wracked with guilt.

But he returned to the hunting lodge. Once or twice a year, when he needed respite, up he would go. He learned that summer and early autumn was not the time to visit. That was hunting season and the lodge's owner was likely to be in residence, with friends. But in early spring and late autumn it invariably lay unoccupied. It was Querennion's own little hidey-hole then, his secret refuge from Trusteedom. In winter, of course, the lodge was unreachable. Snows surrounded it, blocking all access. During those three to four months it was cut off, a man-made island in a frozen ocean. He didn't know if people could survive there all that time but reckoned it would be feasible. Difficult but feasible.

He debated whether to tell me actually how to get to the lodge. The occasional overnight stay by one person, the odd bottle of booze missing from the cellar, could pass undetected. But four people staying for the whole winter? When the lodge's owner, that wealthy Xarridian or Otrean or whoever he was, returned in the summer, the evidence of squatters would be hard to miss and he would surely take measures to prevent further trespass on his property, with the result that Querennion would lose his secret bolthole. Then again, perhaps it was time he gave it up anyway. He never returned from one of his brief sojourns there undogged by feelings of shame.

He gave me the necessary directions, which I repeated to my enshriner at the first opportunity so that at least one of us would not forget them. We set out for the lodge the very next morning. Yashu, interestingly, did not offer any objection. She seemed perhaps sad to be leaving the cave but content to be carrying on with our little party.

It was a hard two days' walking, uphill all the way, up out of the ravine, up through pine forests, up above the treeline, finally here. We had supplies from the Trustees to keep us going, not much but enough. We spent the night on beds of pine needles, with the constellations peeping down at us through the trees' feathery fronds. The lodge came into view on the afternoon of the second day: a long, low building with a veranda along its front and this turret room its only upper storey, rising above a shelving roof supported by projecting timbers, with a broad, squat chimney stack nearby. The lodge was perched at the lip of the lake, which reflected an inverted lodge in its mirror-sheen surface. The surrounding slopes formed a natural depression, like a bowl – no, a crucible. Yes, a crucible. A thing in which raw materials are smelted and fashioned into a pure and useful form.

From then till now, this was our abode. Home for our strange four-strong family.

And there, Khollo, an end to another day's dictation. I was going to mention something I heard this very morning, not long after dawn. A particular set of sounds that would seem to mean . . . But no. I shall leave it for now. I've already gone on at greater length than usual. If repeated tomorrow, the sounds will confirm what I suspect, and I look forward to that in the calming near-certainty that they *will* be repeated tomorrow.

GREGORY

1st of Brownmonth 687 – late Innermonth 688

A manhunt, Colonel Scaldwell kept calling it, but strictly speaking it wasn't that. Their quarry was sixteen years of age. Strictly speaking, it was a boyhunt.

And if for no other reason than that, thought Reehan, it should have been a lot easier than it was turning out to be. It should, as a matter of fact, have been over by now. How could a sixteen-year-old successfully keep eluding several detachments of Jarraine's finest soldiery? One juvenile, dozens of Flamethrowers. Cavalrymen weaving back and forth across south-western Jarraine in co-ordinated formations, regularly rendezvousing, drawing together an ever-tightening mesh. But four days on, and so far the net had failed to ensnare Gregory Brazier, Little Bother, murderer. And Reehan was becoming increasingly frustrated with the lack of progress. All he wanted was to come face to face again with Willem's killer. A few minutes in Gregory's company, that was all he asked. A few minutes to make the little Mudwallow piece of shit suffer. If that wasn't possible, a few seconds would do. A few seconds was all it would take to snuff Little Bother's light out, and Reehan would be satisfied with that. But ideally, minutes. Minutes alone with Gregory. Minutes to see just how much pain a young indestructible could endure.

Such fantasies of revenge kept Reehan warm at night, warmer than the campfire around which he and the other members of the search detail were clustered. They kept him awake, too, long after everyone else had fallen asleep, long after the exhaustion of a hard day's riding should have taken its toll on him as well. A fever of anger boiled inside him. Grief was tireless. At times he wanted to yell at the snoring bodies around him: *Get up! We can't rest! We must keep going! Ride through the night if necessary!* He placated himself by manipulating the campfire flames, caressing them into the shape of a human figure which he then made contort and writhe as though in agony. He gave it a mouth that screamed and eyes that implored for release, which, eventually, reluctantly, he granted. The disturbance in the campfire's burning troubled the slumbers of his fellow-incendiaries. Colonel Scaldwell, the three non-commissioned Flamethrowers, Reehan's father – all moaned and stirred beneath their blankets until the tormented flame-figure subsided. Reehan wondered if, in their dreams, they saw visions of the same figure; if, to them, it had proper features, and a voice.

Over the past four days, when he wasn't dwelling on the sufferings he would inflict on Little Bother, Reehan's main preoccupation had been the events at Penresford and his part in them. There was no denying that he was proud of what he had done, even if the pride was mitigated somewhat by the fact that his best friend was dead and, immediately prior to that, the two of them had had a grievous falling-out. How many lives had he taken that day? Reehan reckoned it must be at least twenty, counting the Earthers on the boat bridge and the elderly couple in the town. And the adult Earther who had been with Gregory, the strong – he could be added to the total, even though his death had been incidental rather than deliberate, the result of Reehan's petulantly-flung fireball ricocheting off Willem's flame shell. Twenty-odd scorched corpses, courtesy of Reehan Bringlight. Twenty-odd fewer Browndirts cluttering up the world. Not bad going. And it would have been more, had the burning office not collapsed in on itself when it did.

It was partly the impact, mostly shock that had caused Reehan to pitch forward to the ground, and it was sheer unmitigated bad luck that caused him to crack his forehead on the cobblestones as he landed. For a while, everything had gone foggy and dull. The cobblestones had seemed an inordinately comfortable place to lie and so he had lain there, sprawled and woozy, with the back of Willem's broken head just within his field of vision.

Poor Willem, he thought. *I'm sorry we argued, truly I am.*

At last, fitfully, clarity began to filter back. Everything became a little sharper, a little more fixed in place. Raising himself up, Reehan noticed two things: one, he had a splitting headache, and two, the Earther boy, Gregory's friend, who had been crouched next to the dead strong was now standing within arm's reach, staring down. His eyes bulged. His big, fat indestructible fists were quivering.

'My father—' the boy began, but Reehan stopped him with a gesture. Something sizzled, and the boy yelped, but the coruscating burst of heat Reehan had intended to summon up wasn't there. The boy sank to his knees, gasping, and Reehan focused and tried again. Even less heat this time, scarcely a fizzle. The pain in his head wasn't helping, and he felt a yawn of emptiness inside, like a well gone dry.

Out of flame. He had used it all up, here and earlier at the boat bridge. He looked at the Earther boy, shuddering on the ground, not mortally injured but no threat to him. In a spirit of experimentation he reached out with his mind to the flames that were churning out from the office doorway. They resisted him. They would not be bent to his will. They shrugged off his attempts to prise them away from their feast of burning.

There was a moment of panic quenched by the arrival of cold, hard common sense. The loss of his flame was only temporary. Once he was rested and recovered, it would return.

Reehan knew then that he had no course left open to him but to get out of Penresford. He would have loved to finish off the Earther boy. He would have loved even more to go after Little Bother and finish *him* off. Neither, though, was possible right now, unless of course he were prepared to resort to using his bare hands, an idea he rejected on grounds of impracticability and sheer messiness.

Before turning to leave, Reehan knelt down unsteadily beside Willem. The half-open eyes gazed into the middle distance, the mouth hung stuporously agape, and Reehan wished his and Willem's last words had not been harsh ones, wished Willem had not called him those bad (and unjust) names, wished most of all that Willem would somehow suddenly stir, blink, look up, smile, be Willem again and not this absurd Willem-like mannequin, this slack-mouthed, inert, point-less *thing*.

'He'll pay,' Reehan said softly. 'Don't you worry, Willem, Little Bother will pay.'

Then off he loped, going back the way he and Willem had come, or so he thought. He got lost. Penresford's squirmy, mephitic streets baffled him. His head throbbed. His thoughts felt smothered. A left seemed like a right, a right a left. And as he became more deeply embroiled within the town and a way out continued to fail to appear, Reehan grew aware of burning. Now near, now far-off. Not the office he and Willem had set alight during their tussle. It was too great for that. Burning on an immense scale. Burning the likes of which he had never experienced before.

Soon enough he realised it was Penresford itself that was on fire. He perceived, like a choir of distant voices, the exertions of a host of incendiaries, working conjointly on the town.

His efforts to escape Penresford assumed a greater urgency then, and after a few more blind alleys and backtracks he glimpsed full daylight at the far end of a street, and next thing he knew, he was out.

Sort of. Because he had emerged onto the riverside docks. Open to the air but still part of Penresford. Derricks loomed above him, dangling their huge, pendulous hooks. The Seray sloshed against the wharf pilings. And to the north: a section of the town tumultuously on fire. The exultant leap of flames. The massing smoke. The roar.

Reehan gazed for a long time, longer than he perhaps ought to have gazed. The inferno was just . . . beautiful. He ached with regret that he could not contribute to it in any way. To be one of the incendiaries engaged in such an enterprise! The intention was obvious: the wholesale razing of Penresford. To be a part of that! All he could console himself with was that he had done his small bit to help. The office was doubtless still ablaze. Maybe the adjoining buildings were also on fire by now. It was something. It soothed his sense of impotence.

He realised he needed to get moving again. The inferno was spreading inexorably this way. He couldn't re-enter the town to find another exit, that would be stupid. He turned south, but did not get far along the docks before he reached an obstruction – a high wooden fence separating one loading company's premises from another's. The fence was unscalable, and the option of burning a hole through it was not available to him at present. This left no alternative but the river.

Reehan slid his legs over the dockside. He eased his feet towards the water. When they were almost touching it, he let himself drop, holding his breath. He expected to plunge fully under but the river was only waist-deep here. His feet hit the bottom, jarringly. He wallowed but managed to remain upright. Then it was a question of wading slowly and laboriously out towards the middle. The riverbed mud sucked around his ankles until enough of his body was submerged that he gained buoyancy. Then he swam.

He had no idea what lay downstream, other than the wreckage of the boats he had destroyed, but upstream lay his father and the other Stammeldoners and the barges they had all come in, so upstream he went. Downstream would certainly have been easier, no current to fight, but upstream called, and with a clumsy, head-erect breaststroke Reehan splashed and spluttered in that direction, against the oncoming wavelets, against the lugging undertow. No great swimmer, he. He was just sufficiently proficient at it not to drown. Leave swimming to Wets. Few Fire Inclined loved the water. He toiled on, making headway but not fast. The current all but negated his efforts. Had he put a little less into it he would have been at a standstill. To his left, wooden Penresford was incrementally cremated. He checked the progress of the fire every so often. Now the docks were going up. Now fully three quarters of the town was alight. The flames chewed, consumed, moved on, like some rapacious termite army. Ashes floated down onto the river like black confetti. The smoke was surprisingly fragrant. Reehan thought of his father. This was his doing, had to be. His vengeance on the town that had defied him. Reehan felt a surge of admiration, of love. He then thought of Willem, the body of Willem somewhere amid that seething conflagration. A pyre for his friend. The hugest funeral pyre there had ever been. A whole town incinerated in the name of Willem Brazier. Apt, that.

The upper of the two boat chains appeared ahead, and within time came closer, then close. Reehan's strength was beginning to ebb. When he finally reached the boats he aimed for a gap between two of them, struggled through, then trod water on the other side, clinging to a hull, the force of the current helping to keep him in place like a pressing hand. There had been burning aboard these boats. He glimpsed scorched paintwork and varnish and he could sense the heat still radiating above him, like a glowing shadow. He envisioned incendiaries crossing over, dispensing with the Earther opposition along the way. It confirmed that he was right, Willem wrong. Such rank hypocrisy, to possess flame and be scared to use it on people. The incendiary's superiority to others was patently obvious and should not be denied. The Airheads might be clever and tell everybody what to think, but when it came to raw power you couldn't beat an incendiary.

Reehan would have mused further along these lines had something not nudged him in the back just then. He craned his head round, and there beside him, bobbing against the side of the boat, face down, was a corpse. Roast red scalp. Singed clothing. An outstretched hand prodding him between the shoulderblades with cooked-sausage fingers.

He was thrashing away immediately, kicking up the water, propelling himself backward with jerky, fervent sweeps of the arms. The corpse rolled gently over against the boat's hull. A ruined face surfaced. The distended hand seemed to be saluting Reehan.

Not long afterwards, he was in the Seray's shallows. The mud was thick and sticky here, the reeds maliciously entangling. Utterly worn out, it was the most Reehan could do simply to wriggle to the bank. Then he could do nothing but lie supine in the mud's slimy yet strangely comfortable embrace and stare at the sky, or rather at the gobbets of smoke that trailed across the sky, black against blue.

I have been through so much today, he thought. *I have done so much. Now, surely, I am a man.*

Later, there was silence. Then voices. Hoofbeats. Then more silence. Then voices and hoofbeats again, fewer this time, softer, slower. And one of the voices he recognised. His father's.

Reehan heaved himself flopping and slopping up the vertical slope of the bank, onto dry land.

Soldiers. The mounted type. Flamethrowers. And his father with them.

Reehan had so much to tell the old man, but having hugged him (and inadvertently smeared a lot of mud onto him), what he wanted to say most of all was that Willem was dead. Willem Brazier was dead. And once he had said that, there was nothing for it but to explain how this had come to be.

The explanation was not wholly accurate. Put it this way: had a sooth-seer been present, Reehan's account of Willem's last few moments would have prompted a raised eyebrow and a rating of 'deliberate misinformation' on the Salcher Mendacity Scale. He knew, however, almost as soon as he started speaking, that the event as it had actually happened looked like it was an accident, and this would not do. He remembered Willem's flame shell suddenly dispersing, Willem crumpling, the indestructible who had struck him falling down beside him . . . Things had occurred in exactly that sequence. There was no way the indestructible, Gregory, could have known who was inside the flame shell when he attacked. Little Bother had committed a terrible, innocent error.

Which wasn't good enough for Reehan. It portrayed Willem's killing in entirely the wrong light. Mishap? No. It had to be murder. Only cold, calculated murder would suffice. Only that would measure up to the level of loss and outrage Reehan was feeling.

So the order of events changed a little. Willem dropped his flame shell. He was standing in the office doorway. It was clear who he was. It was clear he meant nobody any harm. And out of the blue, there was Gregory. He punched Willem without hesitation, with all his might. No, wait. They may have exchanged words beforehand. Reehan wasn't entirely certain about that, it had all been a bit confusing, but he seemed to recall the two brothers briefly talking. He didn't hear what they said to each other but, yes, really, it did look quite a heated exchange. Then the blur of Gregory's fist through the air. An awful sound as it connected. Willem's head snapping to the side. Willem falling.

There were other things to be mentioned, things Reehan's father wanted to know and asked about. For instance, how Reehan and Willem had got into Penresford. Why they were there.

The how Reehan sidestepped, but the why was simple: they had been looking for Gregory. It was Willem's idea and he had gone along with it. Which made what had happened all the worse, since in hoping to find Gregory and get him to safety, Willem had found

Gregory and in return the ungrateful little wretch had hit him and killed him.

Then there was the matter of the flame shell. Why, Reehan's father enquired, had Willem felt the need for one of those?

As soon as the question was raised, Reehan regretted mentioning the flame shell at all. Willem had needed it, he said, because they had just before then stumbled across a couple of Earthers. They had been in fear of their lives. He himself had been about to take the same precautionary measure – then the murder took place and all he could think about was fleeing.

His father left it at that. No more questions. Perhaps he could have pressed Reehan on the subject of getting into Penresford, which would have led inexorably backwards to the subject of the boats downstream. Reehan was expecting him to. He didn't. What he did was turn to one of the Flamethrowers, the senior officer, a man with several gold stripes on his shoulders and an enormous, well-tended red beard, who had been listening to the foregoing conversation intently.

'Colonel Scaldwell,' Reehan's father said, 'you've heard my son. Tremond Brazier's firstborn is dead. An act of wanton murder. What are you going to do about it?'

Colonel Scaldwell replied, 'I'm not sure I understand, Mayor Bringlight. There've been countless acts of wanton murder today. I'm to get all fired up about one of them in particular?'

'The son of one of Jarraine's pre-eminent industrialists, colonel! And the culprit—'

'His other son,' said Colonel Scaldwell, as if this somehow was germane.

'The culprit,' Reehan's father continued, 'has got to be somewhere around here, close by. And I'd say apprehending him is surely not just your duty, not even your most pressing task, but in actual fact your privilege.'

'My what?'

'I can't help but think, colonel, that finding and capturing Gregory Brazier would be the sort of deed from which honourable mentions result. Honourable mentions and more. A man who took the initiative in these circumstances would undoubtedly profit by it in all sorts of ways.'

Colonel Scaldwell looked askance at Reehan's father, his eyes saying he knew what the score was here. He knew when someone was trying to bamboozle him. 'I have enough on my plate already, mayor,' he said. 'I have a town that's been burned to the ground, I have a couple of hundred Stammeldoners in my custody and a baying mob of

Penresfordians to keep apart from them, I have this whole egregious mess to tidy up and you're proposing that I expend time and man-power chasing after one lone boy?'

'A murderous criminal.'

'An *alleged* murderous criminal. We have a single eyewitness to the incident, and I'm no policeman but I think you need more to base a manhunt on than that.'

'Why would Reehan invent such a story?'

'I'm not saying he did. What I'm saying is, this should wait till I have greater resources at my disposal. Reinforcements will be coming from Marenkine sometime tonight. In the morning—'

'In the morning may be too late,' said Reehan's father.

The colonel started scratching at the brass chinstrap which secured his helmet. The scratching developed into an abstract, pensive fondling of the beard. Reehan had assessed the state of play by now and could see how things stood between these two men. Colonel Scaldwell was somehow under the impression that Reehan's father, as the Stammel-doners' leader, had perpetrated a vast misdeed here. The colonel was obviously not in possession of the full facts, but Reehan's father, instead of embarking on the hopeless task of getting a dull-witted military man to comprehend the complexities of the trade dispute and escalating antagonism which had culminated in the assault on Penres-ford and its inhabitants, had decided on a different tactic. Reehan's report of Willem's murder had provided him with a handy means of diverting attention away from perceived wrongdoings onto a single, genuine wrongdoing. Once Colonel Scaldwell clicked that he had it all back to front and that Willem's murder far outweighed all the necessary and unavoidable manslaughters that had taken place today, it would be clear what the proper thing to do was. And, as had been hinted, there was potential furtherment in it for him. In Gregory's capture lay possibly a Brigadier Scaldwell, perhaps even a Major-General Scaldwell.

Reehan had to hand it to his dad. The colonel had vanity and ambition, and his father had played on this. A masterful piece of manipulation. There was, too, the bonus that, if it succeeded, Little Bother would soon be brought in. Which suited Reehan fine. He would beg to speak to him. A private audience. He would feign compassion for the kid. Shared loss. He could already feel his flame starting to come back. If the first part of Gregory's anatomy he burned was his vocal cords, Little Bother wouldn't even be able to cry out. Then time could be taken, a whole host of slow agonies inflicted, before death arrived.

The beard-fondling slowed. Colonel Scaldwell had arrived at a decision. 'We'll scout the vicinity for him,' he said. 'Five men, no more. All I can spare.'

It was less than Reehan would have hoped for but he knew it was all he was going to get. And so the search was on, and evening came, and night fell, and no Gregory Brazier was to be found. Nobody matching the description Reehan had given could be located within the immediate area. Reehan, by this time, was back aboard the two Brazier Brickfields barges with the other Stammeldoners, as was his father. He had had some food. He had changed out of his mud-caked clothes. He felt strong and confident, and the sight of the incensed Penresfordians encamped no more than a couple of hundred yards from the riverbank filled him with nothing but weary disdain. He heard their sporadic jeers and needlings, and had no reason to be the least grateful for the scarlet cordon of Flamethrowers between them and him. Let the Mudwallows attack. If they were out for Stammeldoner blood, let them come, let them try to spill it. See how far they got

When Colonel Scaldwell conveyed the bad news about Gregory, Reehan was sanguine. It was only a matter of time. Tomorrow they'd find him. He couldn't stay hidden for long. The colonel hazarded that the boy might have perished inside the town, but Reehan was sure he had not. When he had regained his senses after banging his head, there had been no Gregory in sight. Ergo, Little Bother had fled the scene. Ergo, he was out there somewhere. He didn't say as much to Colonel Scaldwell, but what he did say was that few murderers hung around after they did the deed. Someone like Gregory would have run, run like the wind. Was probably still running now.

'I'd like to think that we *will* find him,' Colonel Scaldwell said.

Reehan could tell that the notion of catching the fugitive had bedded in nicely. 'I'd like to think so too,' he said.

Around midnight, the promised reinforcements appeared. Beyond the embering ruin of Penresford, a brighter, higher glow to the south heralded their approach. They charged into view beneath a score of large fireballs which illuminated their way through the dark. It was the remainder of the First Regiment, accompanied by several members of the Light Brigade, who were riding pillion and were the ones providing the fireballs. Colonel Scaldwell straight away commanded some of the new arrivals to relieve the troops on cordon duty. The rest camped down till daybreak.

In the morning, the colonel mustered a force of forty men and informed them they were being allocated a special task. Reehan was invited to address the soldiers and furnish them with an exact account of the heinous deed he had witnessed and a detailed physical description of the guilty party. Forty pairs of cavalryman eyes were fixed on him as he spoke, forty pairs of cavalryman ears listened attentively. Reehan relished the moment, and it struck him, as he went over his version of Willem's killing aloud for the second time, that the way he was recounting it *was* the way it had happened. The more often he said it, the truer it became.

Colonel Scaldwell divided up the forty men into a dozen search details. When he mentioned that he himself would personally lead one of the details, Reehan begged to be permitted to join it. The request was turned down twice, but on the third time of asking Reehan pointed out that unlike any of the soldiers he had the advantage of actually having seen Gregory Brazier. He knew the boy well. If, say, Gregory had taken steps to alter his appearance in some way, Reehan was confident he would be able to see through the disguise. This would definitely give Colonel Scaldwell an edge. Reehan, in short, could be a very useful asset to the colonel.

Colonel Scaldwell sighed and relented. Very well, Reehan could come along.

As soon as Reehan's father learned of this, he insisted on being allowed to join the search detail too. Colonel Scaldwell balked at first, but relented eventually, saying that if he was going in for one Bring-light he might as well go in for two. 'At least this way,' he said, 'I'll be able to keep a close eye on the pair of you. How competent are you on horseback?'

The reply, in unison, was 'Very'. Again, had there been a sooth-seer present, the veracity of the claim would have been called into doubt. In fact neither Reehan nor his father was much of a rider. Both had had lessons, the basics, but in and around Stammeldon you travelled on foot or by wagon, and to go further afield you took a stagecoach or, more customarily, some form of river transport. However, with no sooth-seer handy, the colonel was obliged to take them at their word.

Reehan knew what his own motives were for wanting to join the hunt for Gregory: the sooner Little Bother was found, the sooner he could kill him. He wasn't as clear about why his father was so keen on coming along, until he realised that the Stammeldoners were getting restive. The stocks of food they had brought with them were running low. They were disgruntled at not being allowed to return home. They didn't like the way Colonel Scaldwell and the other Flamethrowers were behaving towards them, treating them as if they were prisoners, as if somehow they had committed a crime. What crime? Acrimonious looks were started to be aimed in their mayor's direction. Uneasy rumblings abounded. Some of the people on the barges were wondering, aloud, whether the mayor had not misled them – not in the sense of lied to them but in the sense of led them badly. If they *had* committed a crime, the blame for that lay not with themselves, oh no, but with the man in charge, the man who had instigated the expedition to Penresford, the man whose orders they had, as dutiful citizens, loyally followed. If they *had* committed a crime, it was only the crime of putting trust in an elected official.

All this Reehan's father had been hearing. Remarks, ostensibly not meant for his ears, were reaching his ears. Reehan had been hearing them as well, and now, given that his father appeared eager to get away from his own townspeople, he understood the reason for it. As the two of them, Bringlight junior and senior, collected their small amounts of belongings in readiness to depart, Reehan saw thinly disguised relief on his father's face. He saw congealing resentment on the faces of the Stammeldoners. His father was wise to be getting out of there. Things could have turned ugly.

Colonel Scaldwell ceded control of the Penresford situation to his trusted subordinate, Lieutenant-Colonel Simoom. Simoom would remain in charge till yet more reinforcements arrived, as they were due to by midday, under the aegis of General Samovar, no less, all the way from Fort Beacon Hill. The colonel had organised a pair of horses for the Bringlights. Two of his men had, obediently but reluctantly, surrendered their steeds. The moment Reehan climbed into the saddle of the one assigned to him, he understood that this was no docile training pony he was on. This was a vibrant, wilful thoroughbred that he would have to master. The horse stamped and sideways-pranced under his unfamiliar weight. He struggled to recall what he had been taught all those years ago. The smells of horse musk and dubbined leather helped bring some of it back. Keep your back straight. Grip with the thighs. Maintain a tight hold on the reins at all times. What else? There must have been more. The main thing, which he knew almost instinctively, was that he had to impose his will on the beast, not let it think that it was his better. That, at least, came easily to Reehan. No fucking horse was better than him.

Off they went at a trot, the group of six, Scaldwell, two Bringlights, three Flamethrowers. They were part of a general diaspora, Flame-throwers heading off in different directions in threes and fours, with cries of 'Ho!' and 'Hah!' and 'Hurrah!' The Penresfordians, who had somehow found out what mission these men were on, booed their departure and shouted out things like 'Hope you fall off!' and 'Go blind, you bastards!' along with messages specifically about Gregory Brazier, championing him. Reehan was surprised that they were on Gregory's side and wanted him to evade capture. He realised these Earthers had taken Little Bother to their bosom. He was one of their own. Well, of course he was. Gregory might look Fire, he might have been brought up Fire, but there was Earth blood in those veins, Earth marrow in those bones. Inclination drew to Inclination. It was the way. It was the only way.

Colonel Scaldwell led his party due south, skirting the still-smouldering remnants of Penresford, over the hills, past another town, Hallawye, that was similar to pre-incineration Penresford, mean and shack-like and shambolic, and onward from there, following the course of the Seray. They accelerated to a canter, and Reehan and his father were both able to cope with that, but then the colonel proposed they gallop. Within moments of the pace being upped Reehan's father took a spill, tumbling forward down his horse's neck. He rolled over on the ground, narrowly avoided being trampled under the horse's hooves, and got to his feet straight away, demonstrably unhurt. One of the non-commissioned Flamethrowers raced off to recapture the riderless mount, which seemed to think it had done the right thing by throwing off this man who did not belong on its back. Colonel Scaldwell, meanwhile, reined his own horse in and began berating Reehan's father, saying, among other things, that the mayor obviously had a highly inflated opinion of his own horsemanship. 'I thought I might regret bringing you two along,' he added hotly, 'and I already am. The last thing I need right now is to have to play nursemaid to a couple of civilians. Buck up your ideas or else!'

'It won't happen again,' Reehan's father assured him, dusting himself down.

'It had better not. If it does, that's it. You go straight back to Penresford, both of you.'

'It won't happen again,' Reehan said, with greater vehemence than his father, making it a solemn vow. He looked sternly down at the old man, and his father looked back, at first with equal sternness, then with shame.

The horse was brought back. The ride resumed. For the rest of that day, they didn't go any faster than a canter. Colonel Scaldwell stuck close to the Bringlights, offering the occasional equestrian tip. He seemed to be expecting another fall, and when by day's end it hadn't come, he seemed unsure whether to be pleased or disappointed. Reehan, for his part, was simply glad that his father had managed to stay up. Reehan would never have forgiven the old man if he had scuppered everything by becoming unsaddled a second time.

They slept under the stars. In the morning, stiff of leg, tender of backside, Reehan remounted. Another day passed, during which the colonel decided the two civilians' riding skills had improved enough that galloping could be attempted again. No one was unhorsed this time. There was a prearranged meet-up with another of the search details at some forsaken spot by the confluence of two streams. No sign of Gregory Brazier, no word from any of the other details that he had been caught. Horses having been watered, the two groups parted company. The night was spent at a remote hill farm. Food was purchased from the surly farmer, a corner of one of his fields requisitioned as a campsite.

Another day.

Another.

Then there was that night, when Reehan, sleepless as ever, tortured a proxy Gregory in the campfire flames. He still hadn't lost heart, still was convinced the search would have a successful outcome, even though Colonel Scaldwell was making noises now about calling the whole thing off, he couldn't justify the continued deployment of troops on the manhunt much longer, he had his budget to consider, and of course when you got down to it this was really a police matter, not a military matter, it wasn't in the national defence interest that Gregory Brazier be apprehended, one teenage indestructible was hardly a threat to Jarraine, and it was perfectly possible that he wasn't even *in* Jarraine any more, by now he could be in Otrea, Xarrid, you name it, even Damentaine, and that would put him indisputably outside the colonel's sphere of responsibility, then the police would have to get involved, arranging extradition and what-have-you, and that was assuming the lad was ever seen again, he might well just disappear in one of those countries, it was possible, or even make his way across the sea into the Outer Continent and *then* what were the chances of him being heard of again? Both Reehan and his father had tried to rekindle the colonel's enthusiasm for the job, but the colonel's enthusiasm was cooling fast. On top of everything, just that afternoon he had received word that General Samovar was curious to know what was going on, where the colonel was, why forty Flamethrowers were traipsing back and forth across the country like this. Colonel Scaldwell had said he reckoned he had one more day, two at the most, before the general's professed curiosity hardened into something more like displeasure and his enquiries became an order to desist and return to barracks.

When Reehan finally settled down to try to sleep, he was beset by visions of Little Bother laughing at him. In Gregory's eyes he saw manic triumph. *I killed him*, those imagined eyes seemed to be saying, *I killed your one and only friend, I did it in order to hurt you, and now I'm going to get away with it scot-free!* Four days earlier Reehan had made a claim that he had known was part fabrication, and he had been keen to kill Gregory not least because he needed to silence a person who could give the lie to his story. Gregory's death, then, had been expedient as well as desirable. Over the four days, however, things had changed. Willem's murder had mutated in Reehan's memory, becoming not what had occurred but what he believed had occurred. Obsessive mental replaying of the event had reinforced his stated version over the actual. The copy had become the original, the original had been discarded, and now Reehan knew no other truth than the one he had invented. On that basis Gregory's death was purely and simply desirable. Expediency no longer came into it. And Reehan refused even to entertain the possibility that he might not get the opportunity to confront Little Bother again, one last time. It would happen, simple as that.

His optimism was given a boost the next day. Midmorning, at another of those prearranged rendezvous with another detail, the colonel and company learned of a breakthrough in the manhunt. Apparently, back at Penresford some sort of order had been restored. General Samovar had packed the Stammeldoners off home with a sizeable military escort accompanying them both on the barges and on the riverbank. He had then set about housing some of the homeless Penresfordians at Hallawye and establishing a refugee camp for the rest. Supply lines had been organised from both Marenkine and Beacon Hill, bringing in tents, bedding and much-needed victuals. In all, the general had done much to bring comfort and balm to the traumatised townsfolk, and now a state of brittle truce existed between Flamer and Earther, with the result that the locals were providing the general with titbits of interesting information, amongst which was the fact that a trio of strangers had been sighted near the town before and during its immolation. None of the threesome was Fire-Inclined, so their presence was in all likelihood coincidental, nothing to do with the main event. However, a couple of eyewitnesses were claiming they had later seen not a threesome but a foursome making its way west, away from Penresford. Nothing was being said with any certainty, but might this revelation perhaps be relevant to the colonel's manhunt?

'Oh, singe my shorts!' Colonal Scaldwell expostulated. 'No wonder nobody's seen a lone boy if he's not actually travelling alone. We've been haring around looking in the right bloody places for the wrong bloody thing!'

To Reehan it didn't make sense. How, why, when would Little Bother have managed to hook up with three other people? It just wasn't credible.

Or was it? It smacked of a kind of deviousness, after all. The deviousness you would expect from a callous, ruthless murderer.

And all of a sudden it seemed not just credible but plausible to Reehan that Gregory would have formed an alliance like that with three strangers. Knowing that everyone would be searching for a teenager on his own, the best way to throw his pursuers off the scent would be to merge with a group.

And later that day, in the face of a gathering rainstorm, the search detail rode into a tiny hamlet where they were told that, the day before yesterday, a quartet of travellers had wandered through without stopping. None of the hamlet's inhabitants who had seen them pass would swear to it but, yes, maybe one of the four had been a teenage boy. A redhead? Possibly. The lad they'd seen had very little hair, it was all sort of close-shaven to the scalp. Ginger, what little hair he had? Might have been. Might well have been. The eyebrows . . .

That clinched it, as far as Reehan was concerned. It was Little Bother. He'd not only fallen in with others, he had altered his appearance. Sneaky, cunning Browndirt.

The rain pelted down all that afternoon. Reehan did not even feel it even though it plastered his hair to his head and soaked his clothes through to the skin. The search detail galloped west, for that was the direction the four travellers had been going in when they left the hamlet. Reehan spurred his horse on harder than he would previously have dared. The Flamethrowers were for once keeping up with him rather than the other way around, and as for his father, he was left way behind the group, gamely doing his best but nonetheless lagging by an increasing distance. At every instance of habitation, however meagre, they halted, interrogated, got no useful response, pounded onward. Darkness fell, and the rain continued to fall too, and when Colonel Scaldwell decreed that they should find shelter for the night, Reehan rounded on him. 'No!' he yelled above the downpour. 'He's close! We carry on! We've got to carry on!'

'Carry on if you like, my lad,' the colonel snapped back, 'but in these conditions you won't get far before you fall and break your neck. I couldn't care less if you do that, but I'm not risking my men's lives.'

Reehan felt his flame uncoiling inside him, licking hungrily outwards, begging for release. Flash-fry the colonel on the spot. Why not? Him and the other Flamethrowers. Obliterate them all. Go on without them.

Sense prevailed. Burning a few Earthers was one thing, but four of the most skilled and powerful incendiaries in the land? He'd never stand a chance. They would sense the attack coming. He would be toast before he so much as raised a spark.

Something must have shown in his face, some hint of what had been going through his mind, because Colonel Scaldwell fixed him with a long, deliberate stare, then shook his head in an admonitory fashion. He didn't have to say anything. The look said it all: *Don't try it, young man. I can't believe you'd even think about trying it.*

Shortly, they found a barn and a grudgingly hospitable farmer. While the horses dried off at the rate that natural evaporation allowed, the six men sped up their own drying process by warming their clothes. Steam purled rapidly off them, and for a while, by the light of an oil-lamp, the barn was as cloudy as a sauna. When the air cleared, Reehan found Colonel Scaldwell was watching him closely, circumspectly. He was annoyed with himself. He should not have permitted the colonel that glimpse of his inner workings. It wasn't his fault; the impulse to unleash his flame again had been all but irresistible. He would have to be more careful in future. He couldn't have Colonel Scaldwell wary of him. It was the colonel who was going to give him what he wanted. It was the colonel who was going to grant him his moments alone with Little Bother.

Above the rattling tattoo of the rain on the barn roof, the three noncommissioned Flamethrowers began regaling one another with barrack reminiscences – tales of training mishaps, a martinet drill instructor (now, thankfully, retired), escapades while out on patrol. None of them had seen real combat, Jarraine not having prosecuted war against another country since 676, and that a relatively minor border skirmish with Damentaine. The colonel, though, *had* seen combat, during the very same border skirmish, as but a lowly corporal, and had done so prior to that as an even lowlier lance-corporal during the Hyletan Cholera Exodus, when Varshet had called on its neighbour to the north for assistance in tackling the problem of refugees from its neighbour from the south. Varshet, with no standing army of its own, had signed a defence treaty with Jarraine back in the late 500s, which both nations had forgotten about until, in 669, Varshet suddenly had recourse to remember it and invoke it. Reluctantly, parliament sent troops down to hold back the tide of refugees flowing in from Hyleta, and a very murky business it was too, the colonel said. The refugees were nothing more than frightened civilians trying to flee a post-'Storm cholera outbreak. Whether any of them was carrying the disease was a moot point. Varshet simply did not want them on its territory. The troops, therefore, had straightforward, unambiguous orders – no one was permitted to cross the Varshet/Hyleta border and anyone who tried was to be incinerated without hesitation or mercy.

'It was,' Colonel Scaldwell said, slowly, sombrely, 'slaughter. No other word for it. Slaughter. They came like cattle. We'd give them warnings, even though we weren't required to. Shout at them to turn back immediately or face the direst consequences. They didn't listen.

Wouldn't. They were just too terrified. They came towards us, carrying their children, their chattels, all their precious portables, and we'd . . . we did as we were told. It was worst at night. They'd try to sneak past under cover of darkness, but soon as one of them was spotted the Light Brigade would ignite flares in the sky, and then we would go to work. Candles, that was what we made of them. Bursting aflame in the dark. Some shrieked. Others went up silently, as though recognising there was no alternative and just surrendering to their fate. Better a quick death by fire than a long, slow, racking death by cholera. We were there for a month, keeping Varshet safe, till Hyleta's recuperators got on top of the disease and the numbers of infected began to go down. There are very few nights when I don't dream about those refugees. I hear them screaming, but do you know what? It's the silent ones, the ones who didn't let out a peep when they died, that get me waking up in a cold sweat.'

The other three Flamethrowers listened in appropriately hushed awe, but it was towards the Bringlights that the anecdote was principally directed. The Bringlights were the colonel's true audience, as he demonstrated by tacking a moral onto the end of the tale: 'Flame is not something that you use on others willy-nilly. I don't think I'm saying anything we don't all know already, deep down. Flame is a precious, powerful gift and if you turn it on another human being, whatever the reason, you have to live with the burden of that knowledge for the rest of your days.'

Reehan, tempted to snort derisively, put on a bland expression and nodded. *Yes, how true, you're so right, colonel.*

When the lamp was extinguished and there was just the rain-drummed dark, Reehan thought of his mother. He didn't often think of her. She was a faint memory, if that. The idea of a memory. But to be in complete darkness like this and hear water all around him put him in mind of a cell at the Stammeldon Sanatorium, and from there it wasn't a huge step to his mother, who spent the last months of her life in just such a cell. He knew enough about The Dampers to have formed a picture of the living conditions there. No window in the cell. Walls, floor and ceiling of solid stone. Door of iron, with a slot at the base for meal trays and toilet bucket to be slid back and forth. Metal bed, table and chair. And all around, running through a network of brick pipes, water. Above, below, to the sides, hidden behind the stonework – bars of water. A liquid cage, there to foil any inmate attempting to burn their way out. And you could imagine the noise the pipes must make. A constant background gush and gurgle that would surely drive the cell's occupant mad, if he or she weren't mad already.

He didn't miss his mother. You could not miss what you had barely known. He used to ask about her, but his father was always reticent on the subject and he soon gave up. What he did glean was that, when he was less than two years old, his mother had started setting light to things, triggering spontaneous little fires around the house without meaning to, a book here, a handtowel there, until it was almost a daily occurrence and for everyone's safety, not least her infant son's, she had had to be packed off to The Dampers. 'A good woman,' his father once said, in one of his more forthcoming moments, 'but there was something about her, she couldn't relax, she could never be happy, and then she just started to . . . crumble. I watched it happen and there was nothing I could do. The Sanatorium was the best place for her. The only place. Now, are you home for dinner tonight or are you going over to the Braziers' again?'

Crumble. As though some crack in her personality had yawned and her flame had come leaking through.

Reehan was glad to think that this was not a trait he had inherited. His mastery of his flame was total. And it was a strength – not a weakness, as Colonel Scaldwell seemed to be implying – that he had no qualms about using his flame on people. Perhaps that was the problem with incendiaries, perhaps that was why some of them succumbed to pyromania or, like his mother, lost control: the conflict between what they could do and what they were allowed to do broke them.

It would not break Reehan because he felt no such conflict. He had passed beyond believing that restraint mattered. He had outgrown Master Drake's timid teachings. He was Reehan Bringlight, a man unfettered and fearless and free.

After midnight, the rain relented. Come dawn, the search detail was on the road once more. Less than an hour later they encountered a solitary Flamethrower coming towards them at breakneck speed. He pulled up alongside Colonel Scaldwell, saluted, said breathlessly that he had been looking for the colonel, and panted out the news he was carrying.

Not an hour later the search detail reached a village close to the Otrean border. At least twenty Flamethrowers were there already. The place was thronged with men in scarlet uniforms, and the villagers were out in force too. Bemused to find their sleepy little settlement suddenly the focus of so much military activity, they chattered amongst themselves in Earth language and directed the occasional Common Tongue comment towards the soldiers, usually something sarcastic about a Jarrainian village being invaded by its own country's troops, although the opportunists among them were also making offers of food, lodging, stabling and so on – at a price.

Colonel Scaldwell, accompanied by Reehan and his father, entered the village's only inn and were introduced to the proprietors, a married couple by the name of Haak. You could see the tension between them straight away: the husband's arms folded, the wife's head turned away, a marked absence of eye contact. When the colonel enquired about the four travellers who had been staying here scant hours ago, Mr Haak was all grievance, Mrs Haak all disdain.

'We've been over this umpteen times already,' he said.

'This is the senior officer, Lon,' said his wife. 'You'll do as he asks.'

So out it came, delivered tiredly and tonelessly like statistics learned by rote. Yesterday noon. Four travellers. Motley lot. Two Airies, one islander, and a shaven-headed boy with the colouring of a Flamer but the fists of an indestructible. Roomed them. Fed them. But that boy – he had to be the one who was wanted for murder, the one everybody was looking for.

'So, first chance I got,' said Mr Haak, 'out I went. Had somebody I know to get on the network for me. Promised him a cut in return. Seemed only fair.'

'A cut?' said the colonel. 'A cut of what?'

'Yes, very funny. Only I'm not going to receive anything now, am I, not a leaf, on account of they got away. *Somehow.*' Mr Haak aimed a vicious glance at his wife, which she successfully ignored. 'So I might as well have not bothered. Might as well not bother doing anything.'

'It was fore-ordained,' Mrs Haak said to Colonel Scaldwell. 'Nothing either of us could do about it. The gentlemen leading the group, Mr Ayn, a very nice fellow, a previsionary like me, he knew what my husband was going to do. Therefore it had to happen the way it happened.'

'You woke them up,' said her husband accusingly. 'You needn't have.'

'I had no choice. Like I said, it was fore-ordained.'

Her husband bristled at this, and suddenly the argument they were trying not to have became the argument they were having. 'Oh, that's always your excuse! "You won't be going out drinking with your friends this evening, Lon, it's fore-ordained." "There's no point snuggling up to me tonight, Lon, I'm not going to be in the mood, it's fore-ordained."'

'You married a previsionary. You must have known what it would involve.'

'Not all of us have your powers of foresight, Zelzan.'

'What I'm talking about isn't foresight, just straightforward common sense.'

'Well, obviously I don't have any of that either. But then you wouldn't expect me to, not a clod-hopping Earther like me.'

'Lon, I've never, ever called you a clod-hopping Earther. And I don't take kindly to you calling me a bobbing-headed balloon-brain in front of these people.'

'Bobbing-headed balloon-brain!'

'Mr Haak, Mrs Haak,' said Colonel Scaldwell, patting the air soothingly. 'Let's try to keep this civil, shall we? Set our domestic disagreements aside for now. Eh?'

There was a desultory shrugging of shoulders from both husband and wife.

'So these travellers,' the colonel went on, 'they left this morning.'

'Early,' said Mrs Haak. 'The small hours.'

'And they went . . . ?'

'That way.' Mr Haak nodded in a westerly direction. 'The first of your lot made it here about three hours later. They were long gone by then. A couple of your men galloped off after, but they were back within half an hour. Couldn't find 'em, and then they realised they were coming to the border and couldn't go any further.'

'The border. Otrea.'

'Yes, Otrea.'

Colonel Scaldwell drew in a deep breath and released it in a slow, whisker-fluffing hiss. The whole of his body seemed to deflate with the exhalation, inches going from his height, pounds of military bearing being shed. 'That's that, then,' he said. 'It's over. I'm calling the manhunt off.'

'What!' exclaimed Reehan. 'But you can't. You can't do that.'

'I can and I have.' The colonel turned back to the Haaks. 'Just one thing. What you said a little earlier, Mr Haak. Something about money. Care to explain that?'

'What's to explain? You know what I'm talking about. The reward money. The bounty on the boy's head. Five thousand leaves . . .' Mr Haak's voice trailed away as he saw the look of honest bafflement on Colonel Scaldwell's face. 'You haven't heard about it, have you. You don't know about any reward. There isn't any reward, is there.'

'None that I'm aware of.'

'You're sure about that?'

'I'd need to check, but no one's mentioned any such thing to me, and you think they would have.'

There was a moment's awkward silence, and then Mrs Haak sniggered. The snigger became a laugh, the laugh a guffaw, and soon her husband had joined in and both of them were shaking, helpless with mirth.

'You saw this coming,' said Mr Haak, wiping away a tear.

'I did have an inkling. After all, it was fore-ord—'

Mr Haak pressed a finger to his wife's mouth. 'Don't. Don't say it. Not right now.'

Then there was hugging and kissing, fond marital reconciliation, and Reehan couldn't stomach any more. He stormed out of the inn, disgusted beyond disgust. His father and Colonel Scaldwell emerged not long after. While the colonel went off to talk to the assembled Flamethrowers, Reehan's father came over to where Reehan was sitting, beside the village well. He tried to strike up a conversation but got no joy. Reehan just blanked him, staring fixedly into space, jaw jutting.

The colonel finished with his men and strolled over to the Bringlights with the jaunty air of someone who had tried his hardest and so did not feel the need to make apologies for failing.

'A rumour,' he said. 'That's all this reward business was. No idea how it got started or where. None of my men heard about it directly from anyone in charge. Each was told about it by someone else who said he'd been told about it by someone who'd got it from on high. Probably it was one of the locals who sparked it all off. Heard the name Brazier, thought wealth, put two and two together and got five thousand leaves. Whisper and supposition did the rest. Still, it was effective, eventually. *Almost* effective,' he corrected himself. 'In fact, now that I think of it, it wouldn't have been a bad idea to have started such a rumour myself. Maybe then, if we'd got it going sooner, we might have had more luck. Oh well.'

'That's it, is it?' said Reehan, looking up. His voice was low and venomous. 'That's all you have to say for yourself, Colonel Scaldwell? "Oh well"? After you've managed this whole thing so cackhandedly? After you've let a murderer, a brother-killer, slip through your hands? "Oh well"?'

'Now look here, lad . . .'

'Is that what you're going to say to General Samovar when you report to him?' Reehan was rising to his feet now. ' "Oh well, general, I tried, but *you know* . . ." Is that how the Jarrainian army runs itself these days? So that next time we have a war, our troops will just kind of amble into combat then turn around and give up because it's really not worth the effort. I mean why bother trying to do a job properly when it's all right just to—'

'Reehan,' said his father, a warning.

'Dad, shut up.'

'Don't you speak to me like—'

Reehan spun round and leaned towards his father till their noses were an inch apart. He couldn't recall when exactly he had grown so much taller than the old man. Or was it that his father had got smaller?

'Shut,' he said, 'up.' Then he turned back to the colonel, whose mouth was a startled oval, as though a hole had been punched through his beard. 'Frankly, Scaldwell, it astonishes me how a gutless, gumptionless moron like you could have risen so far. Must have a licked a few arses along the way, I reckon. Bet you can still taste the shit in that face-fungus of yours.'

'You jumped-up little snotrag,' came the reply, through curled lip. 'How dare you. Why, I've half a mind to—'

'Half a mind? You should be so blessed.'

The colonel jabbed a finger at him. 'If you were one of my men, I'd have you court-martialled in an instant.'

'Well, I'm not one of your men, am I?' Reehan shot back. 'And I'm unbelievably grateful for that. Having to take orders from an incompetent like you. I'd spit in your eye as soon as say "sir".'

'Reehan,' said his father, plaintive, 'what is this? What's happened to you? Why are you behaving like this? My own son, and I don't even recognise you.'

Back to his father, who had had this coming for a while: 'Because, Dad, I'm a grown-up now, in case you hadn't noticed. I'm not Jarnley Bringlight's boy any more. And because there was one person in the world that I truly liked and respected, one person who mattered in any way to me, and he's gone now and so why should I be the same as I was?'

A calculated insult, that, and it hit the old man, as hoped, like a slap in the face.

'So call off the search,' Reehan said, facing the colonel one last time. 'Fine. You're not prepared to go into Otrea. So what? I am. And I will. So fuck you, fuck your army, fuck the whole useless snuffed-out lot of you!'

The horse. When had he got up onto the horse? Reehan didn't know. But he was riding at a stately trot, cleaving a path through the throng of Flamethrowers. Behind him there were splutters from the colonel, appalled appeals from his father, and the Flamethrowers were highly amused by the spectacle, the villagers likewise – the entertainment value of other people's conflicts – and Reehan dug his heels into the horse's flanks and rose in the saddle, and then he was out of the village, alone, cantering westward, dizzyingly alone, a manly boyhunter, resoundingly alone, with the whole world before him and a single, loathed, teenage target luring him on, somewhere out there, a mobile objective, a destination in human form, Little

Bother, and Reehan knew he would know no rest until he found him, and he rode.

Did they try to follow him? His father? Scaldwell? If they did, if they got over their shock at the way he had spoken to them, if they stirred themselves to mount up and pursue, they left it too late. He gained a good head start on them, and then, in order that they couldn't catch up and try to stop him, he abandoned the road, veering left, south, accepting the challenges of slope and stream and unsmooth terrain over the easiness of timeworn track. He zigzagged for the rest of the day, until there was no possible chance that he could be found. Up and down the hills of this liminal region, where Jarraine folded into Otrea, this zone of overlap that was really neither one country nor the other. The horse seemed to relish the adventure – being put through its paces by this rider who had earned its confidence and its submission, who had supplanted its previous rider, was its only and ever master now. The horse grinned around its bit as it tackled uneven inclines and gravelly glissades; tossed its mane as it completed each successful leap across ditch or rivulet. And Reehan grinned too, with the clenched-teeth, square-lipped satisfaction of a man who had only one course to follow, one goal to aim at, one purpose to live for, and the liberty to dedicate himself to doing nothing other.

For the next three months, nothing other was what Reehan did. He rode and rode. Down into Xarrid, across into Otrea, up into Damentaine, in a giant clockwise arc. Nights on the Xarrid coast, at the resort towns which were winding down their business as the sea worked itself to a wintry froth. Days in the Buried City, where even with the sun-reflecting mirrors noon was twilight. A short stopover in Air-dominated New Gorundum, which he found a charmless place – the grid-pattern streets, the cubic buildings, everything designed and planned within an inch of its life, and everything just as it had been before the 'Storm flattened Old Gorundum back in 645, this city having been built to replicate the destroyed one exactly, stone for stone, window for window. Over the southern foothills of the Vail Mountains, where if it wasn't raining it was snowing and if it wasn't raining or snowing it was doing something in between, sending down a seepy icy sleet that made the air almost as hard to breathe as water. A fortnight in Domfil, the Otrean capital, with its tree-lined boulevards and countless museums, an enclave of culture in an otherwise gone-to-seed nation, the jewel in a tarnished crown. North via one of the main trade highways into even more gone-to-seed Damentaine.

He had luck along the way, good and bad, more bad than good. Leads that seemed to point to Gregory invariably tied themselves in knots or frayed to non-existence. He followed each one up diligently, never letting a potential sighting go uninvestigated. For a while the Buried City proved very promising, for in its lowest, most subterranean reaches all sorts of human detritus collected. The city was like a sieve for them, thieves and fugitives and other lost souls who slipped down, down, down through its levels and silted up the areas of greatest lightlessness. There, surely, was just the place where a fleeing fratricide might hide. Reehan set about scouring the vaulted alleyways, the burrowed-out plazas, the corridor-mazes of apartments that stank of vegetable rot and things more cloacal, often having to illuminate his way through the gloom with a fist-sized fireball. No Gregory. What he did find, though, on one of these forays, was a trio of knife-wielding robbers who cornered him in a low-roofed cul-de-sac and demanded every valuable he had on him. A mixed bag, they were. One an indestructible, one a shaper-of-water, one a swift. Reehan dealt with the shaper-of-water first, deeming him the most dangerous of the three. Obviously not bound by the taboos of his Inclination, the shaper-of-water could stop the blood in your veins with just a thought. Reehan made a cinder of his heart. The swift was next. His blade was at Reehan's neck the instant the shaper-of-water rolled his eyes and collapsed. It was a lethally quick lunge, and had Reehan been a split second slower in responding, his throat would have been slit. But down the swift went, screaming, steaming. Last but not least, the indestructible, and Reehan took his time. A practice run for another indestructible, a rehearsal for the agonising end of Little Bother. The trick with the burned vocal cords worked nicely. The man's chest heaved and heaved but not a sound came out except a papery, strangulated squawk. Every time the vocal cords started to mend and the squawk showed signs of developing into a full-blown cry, Reehan simply cooked them again. After an hour or so he grew bored and would have finished the robber off had he not had a better idea. He stopped burning him and let him recover. It took a while but eventually there was the light of sense again in the man's eyes, which over the course of the torture had gone dull and distant with pain. Reehan spoke to him, telling him to nod if he understood. He warned him that he would hurt him again, keep hurting him indefinitely, unless he co-operated. He said that the man must have some loot stashed away somewhere, at his house, his den, wherever that was. He didn't have to say any more. The indestructible was nodding eagerly, compliantly, and not long after that Reehan was walking away from the indestructible's foetid little hole of an apartment with a pocketful of cash along with several small trinkets and items of jewellery – not a king's ransom by any means but a worthwhile haul nonetheless, which went to fund his further travels.

New Gorundum proved fruitful in a different way. By the time he got there Reehan had become convinced that Gregory had abandoned the group of strangers he had joined and struck out on his own. At any rate, four travellers fitting the description Lon Haak had given were nowhere to be found, and you would have thought such a distinctive lot would stick in people's memories. Besides, Reehan always got more of a response when he asked about Little Bother specifically. Where enquiries about the foursome drew blank looks, more often than not whoever Reehan was speaking to would have spotted a redheaded teen recently and would not, when pressed, wholly discount the possibility that the Flamer had had an indestructible's outsize fists.

Such was the case in New Gorundum, where several separate individuals told Reehan about an itinerant carnival which had just departed after a week-long tenure in a meadow on the city's outskirts. Among the sideshow acts had been a young endurance boxer who would take on all comers, ten rounds, with a fifty-leaf prize to anyone who could put him on the mat in the allotted time. The boxer had had a shock of bright red hair, quite striking in its way.

So it was in New Gorundum, also, that Reehan got a whiff of unhappy goings-on in Stammeldon. He passed a news-stand where the news-vendor, swift-class, was gabbling his sales patter loudly and at incomprehensible speed: 'Gunnumincer, buyer Gunnumincer, layesisshun!' On the front page of the late edition of the local paper, which was actually called the Gorundum Intelligencer, Reehan spotted a headline containing his hometown's name. He scanned the first paragraph and found his father and Willem's father both mentioned. Something about legal proceedings. He would have read more but the news-vendor, slowing down to a normal rate of speech, pointed out to him that this was a news-stand not a library, and advised him to either purchase a copy or bugger off. Reehan sized up the news-stand – all those periodicals and papers, so flammable – but thought better of the idea and strode away. Stammeldon, anyway, was a closed chapter of his life. Over and done with.

He headed out of the city in pursuit of the carnival, and overtook it somewhere in the lower Vail massif, at a small alpine town where the locals were partying hard, celebrating the last few days of relatively clement weather before the snows set in for good and they would be forced to hunker indoors till spring.

The carnival was a shabby, three-cart affair. Apart from the endurance boxer, it boasted a previsionary fortune-teller ('Reads Your Future In The Elements Tiles!'), a Water levitator who performed stunts with knives ('See The Blade Halt A Hairsbreadth From His Eyeball!'), a strong who chewed and swallowed various indigestible objects ('Crockery, Pebbles, Glass – The Mighty Masticator Makes Mincemeat Of Them All!'), and an enshriner comedian who claimed to know the punchline to every joke ever cracked ('Half A Leaf To Test Him! A Whole Leaf Back If He Fails!'). Meagre pickings. Even the signs advertising the acts seemed apologetic, too weather-worn and paint-peeled for their excitable wording to convey any true zest.

Yet the townspeople, no doubt starved for entertainment, were lapping it up. Around the boxing ring in particular the mood was raucous, fuelled by high spirits and by spirits of the distilled variety. Reehan, having tethered his horse, pushed to the front of the crowd and ignored the gusts of liquor breath all around him as he raised his gaze to view the combatants.

For a moment it seemed that his quest was over, just like that. The youth in the ring, taking a pounding from a local strong, was slender enough and pale-skinned enough to be Gregory. His face could well have been Gregory's beneath all those contusions and spatters of blood. Reehan was ready to congratulate himself on his doggedness and his powers of intuition. As soon as he had learned of the carnival and its endurance boxer he had thought, *Yes, that's just the sort of low-life job Little Bother would find*, and then he had thought, *Maybe he's trying to punish himself by getting strangers to come up and beat the stuffing out of him, maybe he hates himself that much for what he did.* And now here was confirmation that he had interpreted Gregory's mindset correctly . . .

. . . only it wasn't Gregory up there in the ring. In the break between the seventh and eighth rounds, as the two combatants retired to their respective corners, Reehan observed that the indestructible did not hold himself in the same way as Little Bother. He was both broader-shouldered and bandier-legged. And Reehan could see that his face, now that the strong's repeatedly hammering fist wasn't in the way any more, was longer and more lantern-jawed than Gregory's. And although it was always hard to gauge an indestructible's age, this one looked to be in his late twenties at least. But above all else it was the hair that was wrong. It wasn't a genuine red. No hair, even a Flamer's, naturally had that kind of magenta glint. Henna had entered into the equation at some stage.

Reehan was minded to depart right then, but he stayed for the next round and, by surreptitiously raising the boxer's core temperature, giving him a raging fever to contend with as well as an opponent, made sure he lost the fight. While the victor, fifty leaves to the good, danced around the vanquished indestructible, there were howls of delight from the crowd, and the celebrations continued long after Reehan had ridden out of town and earshot.

The long, grim haul through the southern reaches of the Vails turned up few further Gregory sightings. Reehan pushed on, deeper into Otrea, simply because he had no other direction to go in. Then another of those apparent turns of good luck led him to Domfil. The weather was bitter by this stage, not as cold and snowy in the lowlands as it had been in the mountains but harsh all the same, and the Darkmonth winds gnawed. Reehan was able to keep himself warm by heating the layer of air between his skin and his clothing, but the horse was finding the conditions hard going and there was nothing he could do about that. In Domfil, where allegedly a redheaded indestructible had been spotted, Reehan reluctantly parted company with his steed. It wasn't his to sell but he sold it anyway, to an ostler who was prepared to overlook the fact that he was buying Jarrainian Flame-thrower property – tack, blanket and all – from someone who could not less resemble a cavalryman. He was getting a fine roan mount at a knockdown price so he wasn't going to quibble over something as trivial as ownership, now was he?

Giving up the horse meant Reehan had some extra cash in his pocket and no one to worry about now other than himself. Feeling in need of a bit of pampering after weeks of on-the-road exiguity, he checked into Domfil's swankiest hotel, the Citadel Plaza Hotel, so-called because it overlooked the vast, dome-shaped refuge to which those in the city's higher tax brackets could repair when the 'Storm came. By day, he ferreted through the city for Little Bother. By night, he dined well, drank well, wallowed luxuriantly in a steaming-hot bath, and slept soundly on a duckdown mattress. In no time the horse money was gone, but Reehan did not have to vacate the hotel because he had, mostly by accident, insinuated himself into the affections of a wealthy aristocratic widow who was a permanent resident of the Presidential Suite. The glamorous dowager Lady Pamwana Lantane was smitten with this lively-eyed young incendiary, and Reehan's absence during daytime on errands the nature of which he never specified made him all the more attractive to her, spicing his physical allure with a dash of mystery. She was quite happy to settle his daily room bill just to ensure his continued presence in the hotel, and he, of course, was quite happy to have the bill settled if all that was required in return was to share her ladyship's table each evening, flatter her across the starter and main course, chuckle at her every bitchy aside, and flirt with her as if it were not altogether inconceivable that a man his age and a woman hers could somehow contract a lovers' relationship. He had to admit that she wasn't ugly. She turned herself out well. Expensive clothes and corsetry and artfully applied powder and rouge disguised much of the sag and damage of late middle age. He suspected she availed herself, too, of the services of a recuperator from time to time to rejuvenate the parts of her that needed rejuvenation. Those who could afford to, did.

Alas, Lady Lantane mistook Reehan's feigned interest for real interest, and eventually made a proposition that Reehan saw no alternative but to consent to, fearing that if he turned it down his stay at the Citadel Plaza would come to an abrupt end. He acquitted himself with, he thought, honour, and reckoned that what he lacked in finesse he more than made up for in youthful stamina. Lady Lantane, for her part, seemed keen to show him all the sexual permutations she knew – teaching a new dog old tricks, as it were – and her repertoire was as extensive as her appetite. It was only, however, as he fucked her in the backside, hearing her hiss with each thrust and occasionally let out a sob, that Reehan came anywhere close to pleasure.

Come the morning, there was only repugnance. The late-rising sun, creeping in around the curtain edges, highlighted the flabby arm, the sunken milky cleavage, the dark stretched nipple showing through the organdie nightgown, the swags of loose skin under the chin, the down of hair that coated the upper lip, the bulging shoulder mole. Reehan slipped his clothes on without waking her. He helped himself to a gold necklace and some pearl stud earrings from the dressing table without waking her. He padded out of the suite without waking her. It was time to leave Domfil anyway. The Little Bother trail had gone cold there. He exited the hotel lobby for all the world as if heading out on his usual daily errand. The first outward-bound stagecoach he came across, he purchased a seat aboard.

Some time later he was with a convoy of ox-drawn merchant wagons, plodding northward into Damentaine. Never once during his three-month search for Little Bother did Reehan give up hope, but he came closest to doing so while on the road with the merchants. The pace of progress was achingly slow. The merchants' conversation was almost entirely limited to the deals they had made or planned to make. Banter meant calling one another 'cheapskate' and 'chiseller' and 'short-changer', which seemed like insults until Reehan realised that in this company they were actually compliments. He put up with it all since travelling with the convoy was the most economical and straightforward way of getting to Damentaine – the merchants were giving him free passage on condition that he kept them warm throughout the night with a massive bonfire. So he had become nocturnal, stoking flame from dusk till dawn and sleeping in the back of one of the wagons during the daylight hours. His existence was topsy-turvy. The journey was a continuum of caravanserais, a different site every night under the same stars. After a while he began to think they were getting nowhere; the merchants just drove in a loop and halted where they had begun. It was maddening.

But finally, Damentaine. Backward, poverty-stricken Damentaine. The black sheep of the Inner Continent. The country all the others were embarrassed by. The one they made jokes about, the one that always came off worse in comparisons: 'Yes, but at least we're not in Damentaine . . .' Even the Worldstorm seemed to have it in for Damentaine, and the frequent batterings the place took not only offered a climatic endorsement of international prejudice but hampered any chance its people had of improving their lot, since no sooner had they got back on their feet after one 'Storm visit than another came along to lay them flat again. The wonder of it was not that Damentainians were so resilient, but that they bothered at all. Here, surely, was a country worth leaving. Here, if anywhere, was a place you might call uninhabitable.

Stubbornly, though, they stayed put. And Reehan reckoned for several reasons that the Damentainians' harried homeland was a likely hideout for Little Bother. Firstly, Damentaine was ninety per cent Earther, and Reehan had already noted how Gregory had found acceptance among his own Inclination. Secondly, as Colonel Scaldwell had pointed out, you could disappear in a country like this one, easily. Wide open spaces, sparse population – keep on the move and no one would know where you were. Thirdly, Damentaine was one of the points where the Inner Continent was closest to the Outer (some even said it was a part of the Outer Continent that had somehow mistakenly ended up attached to the Inner). From Damentaine's tumbling western shoreline to the east coast of Ibal was little more than forty miles. Forty miles across one of the most treacherous stretches of the Aric Ocean, admittedly. The Farhsoon Channel. Forty miles of leaping, contrary seas that had claimed more than their fair share of mariners' lives. But nevertheless, the shortest, directest route between the two land-masses. If Reehan was Little Bother and wished to escape the Inner Continent as quickly and unobtrusively as possible, Damentaine was where he would set out from.

This was what Reehan was reduced to now: guesswork. The chains of hearsay he had been following had run out. It seemed there were no more leads. No one was giving him useful reports any more, or even use*less*. He was having to hunt blind.

Just across the Damentaine border the merchant convoy reached its destination, Phot, which was the capital and called itself a city but was smaller than Stammeldon and considerably more primitive, consisting of huts and longhouses and beaten-mud streets where livestock roamed as free as if in paddock or pasture. Reehan took his leave of the merchants, who were so busy setting out their stalls and rubbing their hands with glee that they barely noticed him go. The Damentainians were not famed for their bartering skills, and the merchants were looking forward to purchasing furs and sacks of salt for a small fraction of their selling price down in Otrea, and to passing off the knick-knacks and baubles they had brought with them as items of great value.

Twenty days in Damentaine, and nothing to show for it. Nothing but hunger, grumpy Earthers, desolate landscapes, grey skies. Darkmonth turned to Innermonth. The New Year came and went. Reehan saw in 688 CDS at a village near a salt mine, a relatively prosperous spot for this country, salt being the one commodity which gave Damentaine anything that nearly resembled a national economy. 'Relatively prosperous' meant that there was food and booze to spare at the New Year festivities. The local tipple was a radish-derived liquor, lethally clear, clearly lethal. Reehan downed far too much of it and then a whole lot more, because that was what everyone else was doing and because, hardly anyone knowing Common Tongue around here, he was bored and lonely. The villagers sang songs which their leering expressions told him were bawdy in the extreme. At midnight they all cheered, embraced and cheek-kissed. Even the Fire-Inclined outsider in their midst was subjected to the odd bearhug and slobbery lip-smack. Then there was yet more drinking, and Reehan remembered nothing else until he woke up on a heap of tanned deer-hides in the sprawling clutches of one of the ugliest females he had ever clapped eyes on, a veritable hog of a woman with more bodily hair than was right and proper. Her snores drilled straight through Reehan's skull, but the agonies of hangover were as nothing compared with the thought of what he might have done – from the smell of things, *had* done – with this monstrosity.

A swift would have envied the speed with which Reehan left that village. He gave no thought to direction, only to covering distance. Time blurred. It was almost with surprise that he found himself, perhaps a week later, ascending into the foothills of the Vail Mountains again. No horse now, and he was heading west to east rather than the other way round, but still he had a sense of repetition, of reiteration, and with it came a surge of renewed optimism, as if he had slipped back to near the beginning of his hunt for Gregory, as if disappointment and failure and near-despair had not yet happened. All seemed possible once more.

Cold. Savage cold. Snowdrifts that came up to the waist. Reehan kept going, melting a path through the drifts when he needed to and feeding on any specimens of wildlife that came his way – beasts small and large which he simultaneously killed and cooked. High, then higher. The inimical peaks, towering in all their whiteness, clear-cut against the sky. Whatever shelter he could find at night, he took, waking every other hour to warm himself and banish the shivers. He was dressed now in several thicknesses of Damentainian furs – that helped. And this attire made him look like an animal, and more and more he was starting to feel like one. A creature of immediacy. A thing that moved and fed and slept, slept and fed and moved. Pure. As pure as the air up here, as pure as the blue sky up here, as pure as the white snow up here.

Days. Days. Walking. More up than down. Then more down than up. Gradually Reehan realised that he had crossed the highest part of the mountains. Broken their back, and in midwinter that was no mean feat. He was descending. And if he was anywhere near where he thought he was, he was coming down towards Jarraine. Only then did it occur to him that he had gone in a circle. A wayward, eccentric circle, to be sure, but he was definitely tending back towards the point he had set out from all those months ago. He wondered if that meant anything; if it was at all significant that the apparent randomness of the boyhunt had generated a clear pattern. The only conclusion he came to, however, was that if you were dwelling on this sort of subject, you had spent too much time on your own. He needed human company again.

He found it in an unexpected place, and arguably it was not human company so much as subhuman. Down in the lower reaches of the Vails he arrived at the edge of a precipice, a deep rift in the earth which barred his way in both directions. He followed the rift's rim till he came to a spot where he thought he could clamber down. He clambered down, taking his time, pausing at intervals to evaporate the sweat from his palms when they got too slippery. Halfway, he began to wonder if he had made a wise decision. The precipice seemed to be getting sheerer, with fewer crevices and stone knobs for him to utilise. He looked up, he looked down. The way he had come appeared no more ascendable than the remainder of the journey below him appeared descendable. Of the two options, the latter was marginally more appealing. He carried on. Toeholds became handholds, over and over, until he perceived – with a relief close to joy – that the floor of the rift was just a few yards beneath him. He leapt the remaining distance. Landed jarringly. Twisted his ankle. Shit and cold buggeration!

It wasn't a sprain but the ankle was tender and would take only a limited amount of weight. Reehan peered around, taking stock. The rift had been a river once, he reckoned. That meant if he followed it, it would have to emerge somewhere eventually – somewhere nice and flat. He limped off. It was an effort. The stones that littered the ground seemed to have been put there specifically to make life difficult for somebody with a knackered ankle.

Then he rounded a corner and came to a cave and met the Extraordinaries who lived in it.

Religious nutters, he picked up on that almost straight away. Who else would be living in a cave in a ravine? An anchorite sect with doubtless a raft of strange notions about gods and what-not. It was always Extraordinaries who fell for that sort of mystical mumbo-jumbo. They used it to fill the hole where an Inclination should be. Hadn't they heard? It was all nonsense. The Airies said so, and they were the clever ones, they would know. The Airies wrote books that were full of facts and science. They said everything could be proved by observation and experimentation and what couldn't be proved that way did not exist. But still Extraordinaries went in for faith and superstition. The Wets were almost as bad, but you couldn't blame them for that, it was just how they were. Extraordinaries, coming from the other Inclinations, had no such excuse.

Reehan would have continued on, bypassing the cave and its inhabitants, but his ankle would not let him. He elected to stay with the religious nutters for one night, two if necessary, to give the injury time to mend. The Extraordinaries had better watch out, though. They had better not try and talk him into believing their rubbish. Not if they knew what was good for them.

'You've been on a long, difficult road, my young friend,' said their leader that evening to Reehan.

Anticipating a religious hard-sell, Reehan reached inside for his flame. Ready there if he needed it. He might not kill this man but he would certainly give him a singeing he'd never forget.

'No, no,' said the man, seeing the mulish look that had come over Reehan. 'It was simply an observation. I'm not about to tell you that whatever you're looking for, the answer lies with our faith. You're evidently not in the market for that sort of thing. You just look like you've been through a lot lately, that's all.'

'Yes? Really?'

'The state of your clothes. Your shoes – how worn they are. That beard.'

Beard? Reehan patted his cheeks and chin. Quite a lush outcrop of bristles there, though not in the Colonel Scaldwell league. When had that happened?

The Extraordinary copied the gesture, patting his own straggling facial growth. 'The emblem of the wayfarer, the seeker. But it's in your eyes most of all. That's where I really see it. The look of someone who's been far away and back, searching.'

Reehan thought of telling him how near the mark he was with this observation, but then what gave an Extraordinary the right to be so insightful? Besides, as a rule you didn't talk to Extraordinaries. You walked by them. Ignored them.

'Yeah, well, I've been around a bit,' he said, and that was all.

The next morning his ankle felt better but, when tested, still didn't much want to be walked on. Tomorrow, he thought, he would be able to leave. He spent the day sitting apart from the Extraordinaries, watching them go about their routine as a zoologist might watch a colony of termites or rabbits. Their hobbled haplessness was, he found, oddly endearing. He began learning their names, although only one name, that of their leader, Marius Querennion, stuck in his brain. He tried to establish which Inclination each of them would have belonged to had they manifested. Querennion was easy. He spoke Common Tongue with the fluency and refinement of Air. The others? A mixture of Fire and Earth, although by day's end Reehan had still failed to pin Inclination-origin on two of them.

It was that evening that Reehan discovered both how near he was to the village where he had started his solo boyhunt and how agonisingly close he had come to catching up with Little Bother that very same day. Querennion happened to mention the previous Inclined visitors who had come to the cave, a group of four travellers just last Brownmonth . . .

'Four?' said Reehan, breaking in on the anecdote.

Querennion nodded, and when prompted gave a description. It was them. 'You know them?' he enquired.

'Just last Brownmonth?'

'They'd come over the border from Jarraine. They stayed a week. Friends of yours?'

'Sort of.' Reehan got the rest of the information out of Querennion, and as the full monumental irony of it hit home, he began to laugh. Three months. When, if he had only stayed on the road that first day, not headed off cross-country, he might have found them right here, sheltering in this very cave. But for a simple decision to go left to avoid possible pursuit, he might never have had to wander all that time, chase all those false trails, endure everything he had endured. He might have spared himself *so much*.

He continued to laugh, and the laughter was bitter and hollow, more a cackle than anything, and when it had finally run its course he found that Querennion and the others were eyeing him strangely, as if he were mad. Oh well. Since when did he care what a bunch of Extraordinaries thought of him?

'So where did they go?' he asked.

'They . . . departed,' Querennion said warily.

'Yes, but where to? Which way did they go? Did they say?'

'No.'

'Liar.'

'Honestly. I have no idea.'

'Liar,' Reehan repeated. 'You do know.'

'That way,' said one of the other Extraordinaries, pointing to the mouth of the cave and then rightward. There was an eagerness-to-please about the action, an exaggerated helpfulness, and suddenly Reehan knew these people were scared of him.

That made him very happy.

To Querennion he said, 'This is quite simple. I will ask you one more time, and you will tell me. Where – precisely – did they go?'

Querennion's voice trembled only slightly as he said, 'For their sake I don't believe you ought to know.'

'I don't give a toss what you *believe*,' Reehan snarled. 'You can *believe* in men with wings and purple-spotted elephants for all I care. The fact is, you are clearly aware of what I am, and it isn't too big a leap of logic from there to understanding what I could do to all of you and *will* do to all of you if I don't get the information I'm after. So this is your final chance. I mean it. Have faith in me: I *will* kill you all unless you tell me.'

The Extraordinaries were in consternation, several of them urging Querennion to comply. If he did know exactly where the four travellers had gone, he should say.

Querennion's gaze remained fixed on Reehan, a war of conscience flickering in his eyes.

'You don't have to protect them,' Reehan said. 'Who are they to you? Just some Inclined people who stopped by. They probably forgot you as soon as they left you. Wherever they are now, they probably don't even remember the time they spent with you. You know how the Inclined are when it comes to Extraordinaries. Half the time you're lucky if we even notice you.'

'You argue such a convincing case,' Querennion said acidly. 'You really know how to win people round.'

'I like to think I'm terribly persuasive,' Reehan replied, with a heartless grin. 'So? Come on. Out with it. Spill the beans.'

Querennion cast a glance at his companions, and then his shoulders slumped and he sighed. 'I'm sorry,' he said.

No one seemed sure whom he was apologising to. And then Querennion sprang at Reehan, arms out, hands clawed.

It wasn't much of an assault. There wasn't a great deal of strength in Querennion's stringy muscles and undernourished bones. He hit Reehan with sufficient force to propel him back against the wall of the cave and knock the wind out of him, but Reehan was still capable of retaliating. Querennion's scream echoed sharply in the confined space.

Then there was panic. The Extraordinaries ran this way and that. Or tried to run. Reehan got three of them before they even reached the cavemouth. Another two he disposed of outside, not far from their lamentable vegetable patch. The sixth and last of them had headed inwards rather than outwards, seeking refuge in the narrow tunnel that the cave became. Reehan lit a small fireball and followed him in there, catching up with him a few hundred yards along. The man pleaded and wept, shrinking away from the fireball's crackling light. Reehan just smiled and fried his heart.

In the silence that followed the Extraordinary's death throes, Reehan became aware of a far-off whisper from the tunnel's depths. It sounded like water – an underground stream, perhaps. He was tempted to go and investigate, but there was a more urgent matter to attend to.

He returned to the main part of the cave. Querennion was not dead. Reehan had seared his internal organs, mortally wounding him, but it would take him a while yet to die. Reehan squatted down beside him and began, with artful solicitude, to coax answers from him. Querennion, in shock, rambled and babbled. Stories came out of him, snippets of things to do with his sect's faith, half-finished sentences, the occasional imprecation to his nameless god. Patiently Reehan worked on him, steering his fragmented mind again and again back to the subject of the four travellers, where they had gone, how they had got there. It took an hour but finally he thought he had all he needed. Querennion, by then, was mumbling more than speaking, incoherent more than coherent. He was sinking fast. Intermittent shudders racked him, and his eyes showed more white than iris.

Then: a last abrupt burst of lucidity. Querennion's eyes snapped open and his gaze roved, homing in on Reehan's face. His hand found somehow, and grasped, Reehan's forearm. The grip of his bony fingers was painful.

'What is your truth?' he croaked. 'Everyone has a truth deep within. What is yours?'

Reehan gave the question his full consideration. 'An end to Little Bother,' he said, 'Beyond that, who knows?'

Then Querennion was gone.

Reehan dragged all the bodies outside the cave, piled them up and cremated them. On balance, ending a half-dozen Extraordinary lives wasn't murder, it was mercy. Like putting down a lame horse or a sick dog.

The next morning, he set out, following the route he had pieced together from his interrogation of the dying Querennion. Fur-clad and forthright, Reehan Bringlight headed back up into the mountains.

YASHU

Looking around the cave at the Trustees of the Godhead, Yashu felt a profound empathy. For nearly two years she had been, or so she had thought, Dammed like them. Though no one on Li*issua had made her feel like an outcast, there had been that sense of separation between her and other islanders. Instinctively they had known she was different, and she was, just not in the way they or she had believed. These people here had experienced the same sort of rejection and, ironically, it had led them to live in a manner not unlike that of islanders. They didn't have anyone to cure them when they were unwell; they didn't have anyone to make their crops grow better. They did without the usual conveniences of mainland existence. They had made an island of their own, out here in this spot where a river once flowed copiously. An island on dry land. She recalled comparing Auzo's barge to an island too. There were islands everywhere.

With her hunger just about satisfied by the meal they had set before her, and her thirst more than quenched by the water they had offered, Yashu listened with interest as Mr Ayn talked to the Trustees' headman, Mr Querennion. Some of the conversation moved too fast for her to follow, her Common Tongue failing her on many of the longer words, but the gist was that these people had lived in the cave for a very long time, the seven of them here now being just the latest in a long line going back over the centuries. They travelled here, often from far away, and eked out a precarious existence, surviving if perhaps not thriving. They found solidarity, being among others of their kind. Solidarity and more.

But, she wondered, why here precisely? This cave? Surely there were more fertile and forgiving places to have settled in.

She soon had the answer to the puzzle. Mr Querennion extended an invitation to Mr Ayn and his three travelling companions to come with him and view something called a 'grotto'. This entailed a journey into the far reaches of the cave along a narrow, winding tunnel. For the most part they walked in utter darkness, and Yashu found herself wishing for sharp-sight like Liyalu's. Then there wouldn't have been the sense that at any moment she could stumble on the uneven floor or else crack her head against some low-hanging projection.

The tunnel went on and on, and just when she thought it was never going to have an end, a twinkle of light appeared ahead.

Yashu knew, the instant she stepped into the grotto, that this was a special place. She knew, without knowing how she knew, that there was something more here than simply that which the eye could see. She surveyed the grotto's strange, misshapen rocks; the luminous green substance that coated them; the insistent and somehow measured plummet of water from the ceiling far above, a continuous hard rain that pattered and rattled everywhere, some of it ending up in the large earthenware pitchers that the Trustees had placed at various strategic points around the grotto floor. She stared as if, by staring hard enough, she might somehow force the grotto to reveal what it was hiding. As if she could literally sooth-see the truth out of it.

Mr Querennion began talking to Mr Ayn about the luminous stuff. A kind of lichen, he said. His voice got on Yashu's nerves. She edged away until she could no longer hear him. He was about ten paces from her but his words were drowned out by the falling water.

She reached a hand into one of the chains of plunging droplets. The water pounded into her cupped palm, soon filling it and spilling over. Stingingly cold. She tipped the water out and shook her hand dry. Her palm drummed, as though the droplets were still hitting it. Someone called her name and she glanced round at Mr Ayn and the others. None of them was looking in her direction. She stared quizzically and waited for whichever of them had addressed her to do so again. It crossed her mind that it might have been the lobster. He was the closest to her. Perhaps he thought it amusing to call her name and then pretend he hadn't, just as she had thought it amusing to flick water at him the other day. She dismissed the idea. The lobster was staring dully at nothing, the way he always did, sunk deep in his own mind. He didn't have the mental wherewithal to play tricks on her. Did he?

Her name, again. And she was almost certain this time that it hadn't been any of the others who had said it. She had been looking at them. Nobody's lips had moved except Mr Querennion's, and he was talking directly to Mr Ayn.

None of them could have said it, no. But Yashu, with a tingle in her belly, began to suspect who might have.

She listened intently to the rush and roar of water. It resounded in her ears like crashing waves. Wind-whipped surf. An ocean of sound.

She strained to hear patterns in its sibilance – the shape of her name, I*ilyashu, so sibilant itself, standing proud. She thought . . . It seemed . . .

Then somebody was tapping her on the arm. Khollo. He gestured towards the tunnel. He said something she didn't make out but his meaning was clear. They were leaving, going back. She wanted to remain but could see no choice other than to go with them.

All the way through the tunnel she wondered if she had been mistaken. She wondered if she really had heard someone calling her name. She wondered if she was simply homesick – missing I*il so much that she was imagining that she could hear voices in water. Imagining that here, in this none-more-landlocked spot, she was able to hear the spirits of the Great-Ocean-Beyond.

By the time they reached the entrance part of the cave, she had persuaded herself, almost, that her ears had deceived her.

Almost.

But if there was a chance it had not been her imagination, she really had heard the spirits . . .

'We should stay here,' she said to Mr Ayn as the four of them sat outside the cave afterward, on a slope of rocks like a small pebble beach.

She was certain he would refuse the request, and was ready for that. Mr Ayn didn't seem interested in doing anything that wasn't convenient or useful for Mr Ayn. Well, he could refuse and it wouldn't make a jot of difference. She would stay here regardless. She had to revisit that grotto. She had to ascertain whether the spirits were truly there or not.

'Yes, let's,' said Mr Ayn. 'Why not?'

Yashu had a long rant prepared. She was going to complain that it would be nice for once if she was allowed to do something she wanted, rather than just going along with everybody else. Mr Ayn's response caught her by surprise. 'You mean you'd like to stay too?'

'If our hosts are agreeable,' said Mr Ayn. 'Khollo? Do you mind the idea of a brief respite from our peregrinations?'

Khollo shrugged. 'Fine by me.'

'And I think we can take Gregory's assent as read,' said Mr Ayn, with a glance at the lobster. 'Well, that's settled then. I shall have a word with Querennion. I have a feeling he won't object.'

Mr Querennion didn't object, and for a time Yashu felt a tremendous sense of achievement at having got her way. This deflated a little when she realised that Mr Ayn must have known in advance what she was going to ask and known, too, that they were predestined to stay at the cave, which would have made his agreeing to the idea a foregone conclusion. Then again, if he hadn't agreed to it, they wouldn't have been predestined to stay, in which case . . .

Oh, this previsionary stuff was complicated. You could flap around like a mackerel in a net trying to make sense of it all. Yashu decided just to be glad that things had worked out in her favour. Yes, there lay the *mala* of the situation.

Her next problem was actually getting back to the grotto. At first glance it seemed straightforward – simply stroll down the tunnel – but the more she considered it, the more complicated it became. To the Trustees of the Godhead the grotto was a hallowed place, much as the Rock was to the people of Li*issua, and she didn't think they would take too kindly to outsiders traipsing around it unsupervised. Yet she needed to go there unsupervised in order that she could spend time there alone, without being hurried or waited for by someone else. It was a tricky dilemma, and it plagued her that night as she lay in one of the cave's alcoves – purpose-designed bed areas carved out from the walls, each large enough to sleep one and not constricting as long as you didn't try to stretch out your arms sideways or upwards. Couldn't she just sneak to the grotto when the others' backs were turned? She could, but the tunnel was long and if, when returning, she happened to bump into a Trustee coming the other way, she would have no good excuse for her presence there. It would be obvious where she had just been. Asking permission to go to the grotto on her own might be the solution, but if permission wasn't granted then she would have given away her intentions and the Trustees would be on the lookout for her. They might even post a guard at the tunnel entrance.

She came to the conclusion that dead of night, when everyone was fast asleep, was the only time she might dare attempt to reach the grotto. The risk of getting caught was lessened then. If she was careful enough, stealthy enough . . .

It wasn't until two nights later that she was finally ready to implement her plan. She had established by then that the others in the cave were all sound sleepers and several of them were also profound snorers whose nasal rumblings would cover up any noise she might make as she left her alcove and headed into the tunnel. The only person there who wasn't such a sound sleeper – and she knew this already from their time on Auzo's barge – was Mr Ayn. He got up at regular intervals during the night to go and pee. Old men and their weak bladders. On Li*issue the condition was jokingly referred to as Slow-Flow, but the jest was one that had accumulated, pearl-like, around a sand grain of truth. As age reduced the speed and increased the frequency with which old men had to urinate, so too did their Flow decline in potency. Life was water, that was what it came down to.

373

Life was liquidity and movement and flux, and to be static and *usurraña* was not to live.

Once he came back from relieving himself, Mr Ayn usually took no more than a couple of minutes to drop off again. Then – and this also Yashu already knew from previous experience, unfortunately – he was one of the loudest snorers around. Here in the cave, amplified in his alcove, he made more noise than the rest put together. She had heard quieter boomers. Still, it only helped her cause. Amid this great, resonating cacophony of slumber thunder, no one could be disturbed by her sliding out from her alcove . . .

. . . tiptoeing toward the tunnel . . .

. . . groping for the entrance . . .

. . . going in.

The tunnel, as Yashu advanced tentatively along it, put her in mind of Swim-Through-The-Rock. The distance was far greater, of course, and the medium was air not water, but the principle was the same: you moved through darkness, enclosed in stone, to emerge at the other end into light. The comparison, she felt, could be taken further. Swim-Through-The-Rock brought transformation. Might this 'Walk-Through-The-Rock' bring transformation too? She hoped so. At the end she might attain what had apparently been denied her the last time – a reward, a confirmation.

Spirits, she prayed, *please be there*.

The tunnel was even longer than she remembered, and there came a point when she began to fear she had somehow taken a wrong turn. What if the tunnel forked? What if she had inadvertently gone down some side-tunnel that led nowhere? She reasoned that if there was a fork, Mr Querennion would have mentioned it last time. She kept going. It was so dark in here – even darker at night than it had been during daytime. Which was absurd, but that was how it felt. She was aware that her eyes were wide open, peering hard. That struck her as absurd, too. There was nothing to see. She might as well walk with her eyes tight shut, for all the difference it would make. Her true eyes were her fingertips as they traced the contours of the tunnel's walls and her feet as she planted them carefully one in front of the other. How long? How far? She sensed the weight of rock above her and tried not to think how deep underground she was and how fragile a thing a tunnel was. It wasn't as if the air in the tunnel was holding all that rock up, wasn't that simple – and yet it was easy to think that it *was* that simple and that there was no reason why the rock overhead shouldn't come crashing down, squashing her. Funny how, with Mr Querennion confidently leading the way, such a notion had not bothered her. Now, on her own, it bothered her greatly. She should give up. Turn back. This entire undertaking was a mistake. She was probably wasting her time anyway; she would get to the grotto and there'd be no spirits there. If she turned back now, she could soon be snug in her alcove once more, none the worse for this little night-time jaunt. She could tell herself she had tried. A noble effort, and she was more or less convinced, anyway, that the spirits' voices had been all in her mind.

But as long as there remained a shadow of doubt about the matter, she could not turn back. She could not pass up the chance to know for sure. So onward. Further and further into the tunnel's unremitting dark.

And there! Was that, ahead, the faintest hint of a glow? A greenish glow?

For a while Yashu thought not. It was just those swarming patterns of colour you saw when no other form of light was getting to your eyes.

Then she thought otherwise. The outline of the tunnel was definitely becoming visible. As were her hands, looming on either side of her. And her ears were now picking up the water-rush of the grotto.

Soon she was inside that immense chamber and indulging in a moment's self-mockery. She had really made a whale out of a sprat there, hadn't she! She only had to look at the Trustees' water pitchers, overflowing with liquid bounty, to realise how foolishly she had been behaving. The Trustees thought nothing of lugging those pitchers to and from the grotto. It was an everyday occurrence for them, that trip through the tunnel. And look at her, beset by fears and uncertainties almost every step of the way.

Mala having thus been established, Yashu ventured further into the grotto. It was possible to avoid getting drenched by the chains of water droplets. They fell in certain fixed places and more often than not there was room for a person to wind herself in-between. What could not be avoided was getting hit sidelong by the splashes the droplets made as they landed, and it wasn't long before Yashu's legs were soaked from the knees down and were going numb with cold. She aimed for the centre of the grotto, and when she was there, or as near as she could judge, she halted.

And waited.

Nothing. For a long time, a small eternity, no sound but the sound of falling water. A multiplicity of trickles and spatters.

She told herself to be patient. It was hopeless, she knew. This was a forlorn quest. But still: be patient.

Then the voices came.

Shyly at first, like a long-lost friend unsure whether to renew acquaintance. Yashu heard her name, island-prefixed as before, formal. The source of the voices seemed to be both inside her and around her. The grotto's roar made her head throb. From that throb, pulsing in time, came the spirits' voices. They spoke as one and as many. Her name overlapped with her name, until her name seemed to merge with the general hissing of water and become no name at all, just a noise, a rhythm of syllables. She thought, then, that the spirits had gone silent. A quick visit, and then something in her had driven them off. Her non-Water Flow. She was not a true islander. They had made contact out of curiosity and then decided they didn't want a part of her. She was distasteful to them.

Crushed by the cruelty of this, she nearly wept. But then the spirits returned, hushing, soothing, and her self-pity dissolved. She felt filled by the spirits' compassion, brimming with it as the Trustees' pitchers brimmed with water. The spirits' voices swirled around her and she could picture them in the Great-Ocean-Beyond, faceless entities racing in circles like an excited shoal of fish, the minnow-glimmer of ethereal bodies, the dart and flicker of soul lights in darkness, moving with shared purpose, forming and re-forming as they collectively brought comfort to a lonely islander girl far from home. They spoke, bubbling with what they had to say, telling her they were there for her, they had always been there for her, they had never abandoned her, they never would. They had been there on the crossing from I*il to the mainland, in the waves. There during the journey up the Seray from Oöfhaleyis, in the river ripples. There after Penresford in the brook beside the croft. There in the lulling rainfall at the No Surprises Inn. There even in that little seep of water she had stepped over in the rift on her way to the ravine where this cave was. Always there. She might not have heard them, she might not have been trying to hear them, but rest assured, they had been accompanying her all the way. Every spirit of every Li*issuan who ever lived, keeping a watch over her, making sure nothing happened to her that wasn't meant to happen. And now was the time to tell her so. Now was the time to confirm to her their constant attendance. Why now? Because she had drunk the grotto water. She had swallowed the very essence of this place, making it easier for her to hear the spirits speaking. She and her surroundings were in harmony. What flowed in the grotto flowed also in her. But there was another reason why the spirits had chosen this moment to converse with her. Because she needed to know that she was on the correct path. She had had her doubts. She had considered returning to I*il. And she would return to I*il. But not yet, not yet. There were things to be done in the meantime. There were joinings and partings. There were confluences and separations. She must submit herself to the tide of events. She could not fight it, nobody could. She must accept and be washed along by it. The spirits assured her everything would turn out for the best. *Mala* would win through. How? In what way? Ah, that was the beauty of *mala*. You never knew till you knew.

'Spirits . . . ?' Yashu said, aloud.

There was only the sound of water, falling. The spirits had withdrawn, vanishing quick-as-a-wink into the vastness of the Great-Ocean-Beyond. She fancied she heard a last few whispers, as of stragglers lagging behind the rest, but these could merely have been the echoes of her own voice. The spirits had come, said their piece, departed.

All at once she was weak-kneed and dizzy. The grotto's fluid din pounded through her head. She had to get out of there. Her legs worked sluggishly, muscles stiff with cold. It appeared she had been standing on that spot for quite some time, even though she could have sworn the spirits' message had lasted a matter of seconds. Moving like some arthritic old woman, she staggered around the stalagmites and dodged water droplets till she reached the tunnel entrance. In its lee she waited till her head was steadier, meanwhile massaging some feeling back into her lower limbs. Then she set off down the tunnel, with her shadow bouncing before her against the green-lit walls. Soon the light faded and her shadow merged into general blackness.

Blackness.

More blackness.

Then the main part of the cave. The dim shapes of sleepers in their alcoves. Yashu crept to her alcove. Joined the sleepers in sleep.

It wasn't till much later, past noon the next day, that Yashu was able to reflect on her experience in the grotto with anything like objectivity. The night's events seemed vague, almost as if she had dreamed it all. She hadn't, she knew that, but still she found it not altogether easy to believe that she had actually stood in the grotto, actually communed with the spirits. Perhaps it was her Airiness coming to the fore, but the dream explanation seemed preferable, and more plausible.

She engaged a couple of the Trustees in conversation, curious to know if they themselves had encountered anything similar in the grotto. She intercepted the pair as they returned from a water-fetching expedition. One of them was struggling under the burden of his full pitcher so she took it off him, much to his relief, and set it down. Then she enquired, ever so casually, about the water itself. It must be safe to drink, mustn't it? Even though it came from the grotto where there was all that glowing lichen. It surely wasn't tainted or contaminated in any way, was it?

'Shouldn't think so,' the Trustee replied, shaking out his aching arms. 'I mean, people have been drinking the stuff for centuries. I myself have been drinking it nearly ten years, and look at me.'

'Picture of health,' said his companion, and they both laughed. The Trustees were gaunt and scrawny and anything but pictures of health.

'No,' said the first, 'the stuff's safe, I'm quite sure. Why do you ask? You haven't had a bad turn or anything?'

Yashu shook her head. 'You know us Water Inclined. We're just interested in these things. Where the water comes from, the grotto – do you spend much time there?'

'Not if I can help it,' said the Trustee. 'It takes ages to reach and the place is pretty chilly.' He gave an illustrative shiver. 'As you probably noted when Querennion took you there.'

'Mostly we just go there for the water,' said the other. 'Or when we need a less tangible kind of refreshment. You know, to look at the place. It helps sometimes, when things are getting you down: just looking. But even then, never for long. It can be too much. Too impressive. It can make you a bit light-headed.'

'But then so can not eating enough,' countered the first. 'As you've seen, food's not exactly abundant around here. Which is good, because overeating dulls the mind. Hunger keeps us sharp and stops us being lazy. That happens to be one of our traditions here, and we'd stick to it even if it wasn't forced on us by necessity. But the downside is that you can get a bit weak if you're not careful.'

'We try to keep an eye on that. If anyone looks like they're ailing, they get given a small share of everyone else's rations till they start to perk up again.'

'But if you're already feeling weak and light-headed and you go into the grotto . . .'

'It can overwhelm.'

'I mean, if you pass out, you don't want to do it there.'

'Who wants to have to lug an unconscious body all the way back here?'

'And if you were on your own with no one to help, you might die of the cold. Seriously.'

'So we *could* spend lots of time there.'

'Would.'

'But' – a shrug – 'we don't. The fact that the grotto's there, that we know it's there . . .'

'That's enough for us.'

Which wasn't a huge amount of help to Yashu, although it did at least alert her to a potential hazard of visiting the grotto. If nothing else the two Trustees confirmed what she had suspected might be the case: the Trustees were unlikely to hear the spirits in the grotto since the spirits were not a feature of their belief system. To them, the place's power took on a different guise.

So it remained a possibility that there had been no spirits after all. She recalled the dizziness she had felt after the spirits' apparent visitation. As the two Trustees had said, lack of food brought light-headedness, and light-headedness could, she knew, make you imagine things that weren't there.

That night, she went back to the grotto.

And the spirits came again.

And the next night, and the next.

The information they had to impart remained the same, but it wasn't what they said that mattered so much as that she was hearing them at all. They were there – indisputably, unquestionably there. She could sense the swirl of them, almost feel the turbulence of their passing, a buffeting against her skin, as though she were physically in the Great-Ocean-Beyond with them. She was listening to Huaso, even if Huaso no longer knew he was Huaso. She was listening to her parents. To her grandparents and all the many other forebears she had never known. Ancestors without name, without number. At times it made her laugh. At times it made her cry. She rejoiced with tears; sobbed through smiles. Each day became a period of waiting, dead time. She caught up on sleep, helped the Trustees with their chores, existed. It was the nights she looked forward to, and sometimes she could scarcely contain her impatience. The sun went down so slowly. It seemed an age before everyone retired to their alcoves, a further age before everyone had sunk into the deepest part of sleep. *Come on, come on!* she wanted to urge them. *Some of us have places to be, you know.*

By her fourth night it became apparent that the spirits, happy though they still were to speak to her, were losing enthusiasm. They came, but their reassurances and encouragement were beginning to sound just that little bit perfunctory. The same stuff, over and over. Yashu could not listen to it often enough but she appreciated that the spirits themselves might be getting bored with the repetition. Perhaps they felt she was abusing the privilege of contact with them. Perhaps they had other, more important matters to attend to. It didn't do to be too greedy. She shouldn't hog their attention when she was not the only islander they had to look after.

As she left the grotto that time, she vowed to herself she would not go back.

She broke the vow. She couldn't help it. For the fifth night in a row, she trod along the tunnel. By now she had become familiar with the shape of it, the many twists and turns. By feel alone she could gauge precisely where she was along its serpentine length. She re-entered the grotto and took up her usual position at its heart. As ever – almost a routine now – she relaxed, became receptive, waited. As ever – though she didn't think she was taking it for granted – the spirits arrived in their school, clustering to her solicitously, and uttered their usual refrain. All was well. Trust them. The tide of events. Surrender. For the best. *Mala*. She imbibed their words, suckling on them sweetly because this, she was certain, was going to be absolutely the last time she visited the grotto. She wasn't going to bother the spirits any more after this. They had been more than generous with their time.

Then a change of tone. An eddy of disturbance. The spirits began to chatter agitatedly. Someone was coming. Someone was here.

Yashu looked toward the tunnel entrance, expecting to see one of the Trustees, perhaps Mr Querennion himself. She saw instead, to her surprise, Mr Ayn. He was hovering at the entrance as if unsure whether to go in or turn on his heel and head back the way he had come. In the green lichen light he looked almost sick with indecision.

Yashu ducked down and kept watching. He had not spotted her, otherwise he would have said something. She peeped over the top of a stalagmite, blinking as the occasional drip-splash hit her face. Mr Ayn continued to bob hesitantly at the grotto's edge, gazing wide-eyed in every direction. Several times he nearly stepped forward; didn't. He was perpetually on the brink of committing himself. Something held him back.

Him, the spirits whispered. Him.

What about him?

She must remain with him. Remain with him a little longer.

How much longer?

Long enough. She might not trust him, she might be wary of him. That was fine. But her course and his were still intertwined. The two of them weren't to come to a parting of the ways for some while yet.

The news settled on Yashu like a lead weight. Spend more time in Mr Ayn's company? Continue to be patronised by him, and when she wasn't being patronised, ignored? She felt like groaning.

Yes, him, the spirits went on. Trust us. Him.

Their voices were starting to tail away, dispersing into the Great-Ocean-Beyond's blackness and silence. The grotto's subterranean rainfall reasserted itself. Yashu, hunkered behind the stalagmite, watched Mr Ayn through a curtain of glittering droplets as he made one last attempt to stir himself to step forward. It didn't happen. His shoulders sank and he turned. The tunnel swallowed him.

She stayed put for another hour till the cold became too much to bear and her lips were trembling and her hands had the shakes. She nursed the faint hope that the spirits might return for a further word or two, but they were gone. Gone. An hour was more than enough time for Mr Ayn to get to the other end of the tunnel. She went in after him, and trod glumly along, wishing she had not decided to come tonight after all and blaming Mr Ayn personally for the spirits' unwelcome message about him.

By morning she had resigned herself to the spirits' edict. If they said she was to remain with Mr Ayn, then so be it. She resolved to be cheerful about it, but she couldn't deny that the thrill of communing with the spirits had been soured somewhat. The experience now had a bitter aftertaste.

Khollo noted her uncertain mood, asking, 'Have you had enough of being here, Yashu?'

She nodded. 'I think so. It's time to go.'

Khollo looked over to Mr Ayn, who was some way off up the ravine and deep in conversation with Mr Querennion. The two of them had become quite the debaters over the past few days. More often than not, if you saw one you would see the other. They entered into long and sometimes heated arguments that, as far as Yashu could gather, revolved around the Trustees' beliefs – Mr Querennion promoting, Mr Ayn repudiating. If she hadn't known already that Mr Querennion came from Air stock originally, it wouldn't have been hard to guess. His love of discussion and of the sound of his own voice – these were the giveaways.

'Whether Elder Ayn is ready to leave yet,' Khollo said, 'is another matter. Doesn't look like it to me, but you can never tell.'

'Can't you have a word with him?'

'Do you honestly think, Yashu, that I have any influence over him?'

She managed a chuckle. 'I suppose not. Perhaps *he* does, though.' She pointed to the lobster, who was sitting at the cavemouth, absently knocking one set of lumpy knuckles against the other. 'If we could somehow get him to talk to Mr Ayn . . .'

'I wouldn't count on it.'

She nodded, continuing to study the lobster. It was hard to think of him as a murderer. She had to remind herself of the fact almost every time she looked at him. Nobody could have appeared less like a killer than this boy, and over the past week Yashu had found herself becoming less and less wary in his presence. She still wasn't comfortable around him but his perpetual dazedness suggested he was, at least for now, harmless. She no longer felt she had to keep such a watchful eye on him. Although she wasn't completely lowering her guard.

In the event, no approach had to be made to Mr Ayn on the subject of leaving. That evening he returned from a long walk with Mr Querennion and announced that he wished to move on first thing tomorrow. He seemed to be in an unusually merry frame of mind, as did Mr Querennion. They even, she thought, looked drunk. But that was absurd. Drunk? Here? How?

The next day the foursome left the cave, Yashu with mixed feelings – relief and regret mainly, with a sprinkling of optimism. They trooped along the ravine, which deepened and broadened, its sides becoming progressively less steep until after a few miles it seemed entirely possible that you could climb your way out. This the travellers did. Yashu, by far the nimblest of them, led the way. She scurried up the slope, pathfinding. From this rock here to that section of loose shale there, she sprang and darted. The other three followed at their own speeds, Mr Ayn puffing and grunting at the rear.

Above the ravine they found themselves on a grassy plateau, cross-ing which they entered a pine forest. Sap scent and whispery coolness surrounded them as they walked upslope through the trees, shuffling through the soft ground-cover of fallen needles. Now and then Khollo and Mr Ayn would pause to confer. Yashu gathered that Mr. Queren-nion had provided them with directions to a residence of some kind high up in the mountains. She could not think what sort of a place it was or why they wished to go there, but such questions were no longer so important now that the spirits had spoken. Her way was smoothed. Wherever Mr Ayn went, she must go too.

Night in the forest, and then at daybreak more walking. According to Khollo, the correct landmarks were appearing in the correct order. A split rock. A fallen tree. A stream. A particular crooked mountain peak. And soon the forest was thinning, the pines being pared away as the air grew sharper, until the landscape became the kind that could not support much vegetation. The odd sprig of gorse protruding from a crevice. A scattering of wildflowers, each as bright as it was tiny, like a star.

Higher, and then Khollo began making noises to the effect that the residence ought to be appearing soon. Then it did. In a large natural basin: an improbable, incongruous house. Yashu had to blink two or three times to be sure it wasn't a hallucination. The house sat on the shore of an almost perfectly circular lake, and it reminded her, in its length and lowness, of her aunt's cottage, although it was far more robustly and expensively built. It had, too, a veranda running along the front of it, and an upper storey – a large-windowed extension jutting above the roof.

Who had built this place? Who owned it? Who lived there?

The answer to the last question was, apparently, nobody. Yashu could tell, as she got nearer to the house, that it was empty. Uninhabited buildings gave off an unmistakable air of desertion. The house, however, was not derelict. Several of the roof shingles were paler than the others, newer. Repairs had been made within the past year.

Mr Ayn explained that it was a hunting lodge, that its owner was not at present home nor likely to be till next spring, and that he felt it was a shame to let such a nice-looking place in such an agreeable spot go untenanted for long.

'You're saying that *we* should live here?' Yashu said, having digested his meaning.

'Why not?'

'It's someone else's house! We can't just walk in and – and – and act like it's ours.'

'Oh, I'm not proposing that. Simply suggesting we could . . . perch in it for a while.'

Yashu eyed him. 'Could? Or we're going to?'

'My dear, you really are starting to get the measure of prevision, aren't you?' Mr Ayn chuckled. 'But I remain open to alternative suggestions. I mean' – he swept a hand around – 'if you can see somewhere else hereabouts you think would suit.'

He had her there. It was late afternoon, the shadows were long, and the only shelter anywhere nearby was the hunting lodge. She was minded to think that spending the night in the open was preferable to invading someone else's property, minded to think that she ought to spend the night in the open purely on principle.

But . . .

But . . .

No, the hunting lodge was there. Madness not to use it. Just for tonight, anyway.

The floorboards of the veranda groaned underfoot. The front door creaked as it opened. Mr Ayn, first in, stepped aside and let Yashu pass in front of him. Inside, the air smelled musty, unstirred. She peered around the entrance area. In one corner a wooden staircase spiralled up to the first-storey room. Next to it there was a large trapdoor in the floor. A tapestry covered almost all of one wall, and depicted a hunting scene: stalwart red-haired men strode through woods in pursuit of deer that were either springing away in fear or collapsing with darts of flame issuing from their heads. At the far end of the entrance area, a corridor led off right and left.

At a nod from Mr Ayn, Yashu proceeded to explore. Along the right-hand, longer arm of the corridor there was a series of bedrooms, each identical except for the last which was larger and had bigger windows. This, she assumed, was the owner's. The bed in each room consisted of a mattress atop a sturdy wooden cot. She tested one and found it to be plush and comfortable. A wardrobe beside the bed was stuffed with blankets, pillows, and bits and pieces of warm over-clothing.

The other, shorter arm of the corridor led to a dining room with a large table, a kitchen, and then a set of more meanly furnished bedrooms, each with a pair of bunk beds that had no mattresses, just taut sections of canvas suspended within their frames. It took her a moment to work out who this inferior accommodation would be for. Servants, of course. The hunting lodge's owner was a rich man, and rich men employed servants. The smarter bedrooms were for the owner's friends. Other rich men, no doubt.

Returning to the entrance area, Yashu found it empty apart from Gregory-the-lobster, who was standing in front of the tapestry, per-haps admiring it but more likely just mesmerised by the woven colours. The trapdoor was open and she was about to go over and look in when Mr Ayn came trotting down the spiral staircase, pronouncing the view from the upper-storey room most impressive.

At almost the same moment Khollo's head poked up from the trapdoor hole. 'Quite a cache, Elder Ayn,' he said. 'Dry goods, all tightly wrapped. A supply of firewood. And, erm, just the odd bottle of wine and liquor.'

'A sensible fellow, whoever owns this place,' said Mr Ayn. 'Wise to lay in a store of provisions, just in case. You never know when the 'Storm, or something else, might strand you up here.'

'So we're going to eat his food as well?' Yashu said. 'Stay here without permission *and* raid his supplies?'

'If the alternative is starvation,' Mr Ayn replied blithely, 'then yes.'

'I still can't—'

'Of course,' said Mr Ayn, interrupting, 'we won't be eating *just* his food. We can fend for ourselves too.'

'How?'

'Observe.' Mr Ayn gestured through the open front door to the lake. At first Yashu could not see what he was indicating. She stepped out onto the veranda for a better look, and then it became clear.

The daylight was waning, the sun almost gone behind the nearest range of peaks. The air had taken on a smoky tinge, and the surface of the lake, having been like glass just a few minutes ago, was now broken by sets of concentric ripples. Each originated with a tiny, gulping *plop* and occasionally a glimpse of fin or tail. More sets of ripples appeared, and more, the patterns spreading, overlapping, con-flicting, and soon there wasn't an inch of the lake that was undisturbed. Yashu estimated there must be a thousand fish in there, and this was their evening feeding frenzy, when the air cooled and a host of gnats and small flies hovered in low and alighted on the water. Dinner for the fish, and the fish would be dinner for the lodge's residents. As long as there was the means to catch them.

Which there was. From the bountiful cellar Khollo brought up an armful of fishing tackle – rods, hooks, floats, lures, landing nets – which at Mr Ayn's instruction he laid out on the veranda.

'Between the lake and the cellar,' Mr Ayn proclaimed, 'we've all we need. We could stay here almost indefinitely.'

Yashu didn't know about 'indefinitely'. That seemed unlikely in all sorts of ways. Apart from anything else, the lodge's owner would return at some point, and Yashu had no desire to be around when he did.

But a few days. A short while. If they were frugal and didn't deplete the owner's stocks of supplies too severely. If they left the lodge just the way they had found it, or as close to that as possible.

She could hardly believe she was going along with Mr Ayn on this. It was disgraceful. She thought of how she would feel if for some reason she and Aunt Liyalu left the cottage for a few days and came back to discover it had been occupied in their absence. Even if the lodge's owner never noticed, it was still a bad thing to do.

Then again, what the owner didn't know wouldn't hurt him. And, like it or not, the spirits had told her that she was to remain with Mr Ayn.

That settled it. For the time being, the lodge had four uninvited inhabitants. A few days. A fortnight at most. They would leave before it got too cold in the mountains. When Yashu felt they had imposed themselves on the place long enough, she would insist to Mr Ayn that they moved on. She would enlist Khollo's aid in that. They had made their pact, and two voices would be more persuasive than one.

Mr Ayn claimed the largest bedroom for himself, perhaps predictably. For herself, Yashu chose the one farthest from his and nearest the hall. Gregory and Khollo berthed themselves in between.

And so a week passed, and then a fortnight passed, and with it Yashu's deadline for departure.

The lodge was very homely, that was one reason why she had no great urge to leave. Lived in, the lodge took on a life of its own. It seemed to thrive for having people in it, as if that was all it ever craved: to be used. It sat unoccupied for such long periods, and a building was built to be occupied, wasn't it? So it kept the four of them snug inside it at night, its floorboards and rafters settling around them with contented creaks. It laid its facilities open to them: kitchen, stove, cellar. *Here you go. Make yourselves at home.* It let them sit in the shade of its veranda when the sun was at its zenith and, though not hot, ferociously bright. It watched over them, benign, as they drew water from the lake to wash with and drink.

Then there was the routine which they swiftly settled into and which became a hard habit to break. Early each morning, Yashu and Khollo would go fishing. He had no skill whatsoever in this field and she was far from being an expert but, as an islander, she had the basic know-how. You couldn't live on Li*issua and not pick up a grounding in how to catch fish. Freshwater line-casting was not that different from seashore line-casting. The same basic principles applied. Besides, the lake, like the lodge, was more than obliging. The float barely had to hit the water before you would get a bite, especially at dawn when the fish were sleepy and not at their cleverest and the sun wasn't strong enough yet to force them to retreat to the bottom. Out they came, one after another, iridescent trout, surly salmon, writhing and flapping on the hook, to be scooped up in a landing net and transferred to a bucket. Yashu tutored Khollo in the art of laying out a line so that the float and lure came to rest with barely a splash. She showed him how to coax a hooked fish in gently and in stages so that the line didn't snap. He wasn't fighting the fish, she said, he was disrupting its swim-bladder and exhausting it. He quickly got the hang of this but liked to pretend that he hadn't, letting her take over if the fish was ornery, deferring to her whenever things got difficult. He also liked to chat with her as they sat side by side on the smooth rounded lakeshore stones and waited for a bite. He enquired about island life, the various rituals the Li*issuans observed, the stories that were such an integral part of their existence. At his urging she told him some of the stories, and he became a rapt audience, sometimes so absorbed in the tale she was spinning that he would not notice when one of the fishing lines went taut.

'You like the ones about Ussyashu,' he observed on one occasion. 'You tell those the best.'

'She was my heroine when I was little. I always hoped my life would be full of adventures, like hers. But . . .'

'But . . . reality.'

'Yes,' she said, nodding. 'Reality.'

In return, Khollo told her about Durat and about Stonehaven, how he missed the former and how disappointed he had been by the latter. He said he had begun to wonder whether he belonged anywhere. Home was Durat, but with his parents dead and very few relatives there, and after an absence of a couple of years, he didn't feel he could go back. And as for Stonehaven – well, that had never really been home, had it?

The fishing helped cement the alliance between them. Yashu became increasingly convinced that if she found herself at loggerheads with Mr Ayn, she could count on Khollo to take her side. She was never more sure of this than when Khollo, one morning, plucked a salmon from the catch bucket, gripped it by the head and manipulated its jaws so that it seemed to be speaking. At the same time, in a fair approximation of Mr Ayn's voice, he said, 'My dear girl, you simply have to accept that whatever I say goes. You can't argue with prevision, you know.' She was amused by the stunt, but not as amused as she was pleased.

Whatever they caught became breakfast, and whatever they didn't eat for breakfast could be served cold for lunch and supper. Down in the cellar there were jars containing dried tomatoes, pickled mushrooms, flour to coat the fish with for frying, and preserved fruits for afters. Yashu saw to it that they used – stole – these foodstuffs sparingly. The alcohol, she insisted they didn't touch, but Mr Ayn could not resist uncorking a bottle of wine every now and then.

As for Gregory-the-lobster, he did, as was his wont, nothing. He didn't help with the meals, he didn't help with the washing-up, he just hung around dumbly looking on. His hair was growing back and Yashu noted that he was not a bad-looking boy. His uncommunicativeness, however, made him unappealing, and after a while she was hardly aware of him any more. He was just *there*, like a pet or a piece of furniture, something around the house.

Mr Ayn continued to spend time with him. She often saw him talking to the boy. Softly. Confidingly. Sometimes Gregory would nod, as if Mr Ayn was getting through to him. Once she even thought she saw him smile.

Then it was the end of their third week at the lodge, and Yashu's conscience had begun nagging at her. Very soon, she thought, they should be leaving, and she said as much to Mr Ayn one mealtime. The lodge's owner could put in an appearance any day. And the temperature was dropping. The mornings were cooler than they had been, the air sharp in the lungs. They didn't want to get stuck up here once the snow fell. To which Mr Ayn replied that that would indeed be an inconvenient situation for them to have to deal with, and he understood her anxiety. Perhaps one or two more days?

She relented, reluctantly. One or two more days.

'You didn't ask him what he foresaw?' Khollo asked, later. 'When he foresaw us leaving?'

'His prevision . . . confuses me,' she said. 'Half the time I'm not sure if he isn't playing some sort of game. With me. With all of us. Tricking

387

us into doing what he wants, or making us think that what he wants is what's going to be.'

'How could he trick a sooth-seer?'

'An untrained sooth-seer, remember. And I think if anyone could, Mr Ayn could.'

Khollo shrugged. 'You might be right.'

'So I've come to the conclusion that if he's never going to give me a straight answer about what he foresees, then I shouldn't bother asking. It's a waste of breath. But in two days' time I plan on confronting him and giving him an ulti— I'm not sure of the word.'

'Ultimatum?'

'Yes. I'll say, "Either we all leave or I leave by myself." ' She looked Khollo straight in the eye. 'What I need to know is, will you join me?'

'In leaving?'

'In confronting him.'

Khollo was silent. He looked at her; lowered his eyes. She had her answer.

'I see.'

'It's not . . . You're putting me in a difficult situation, that's all.'

'No. Fine.'

'I can't, you understand. Just can't.'

'No, it's all right. I shouldn't have asked.'

'Yashu . . .'

She went to her room. She lay down on the bed. She sank bitterly into its comfort.

They had had a pact. They had shaken hands on it. Obviously Khollo had meant it at the time but had changed his mind since. She had put her trust in him. She felt a fool.

She packed her clothes into Siaalo's sealskin satchel. She acted that evening as if nothing was out of the ordinary. She was civil to everyone, even the lobster. She could see by Khollo's eyes that he thought she had forgiven him. No one had a clue that she would not be there in the morning.

Then, overnight, sudden and silent, the snows came.

AYN

So, our second-to-last dictation session. There's a lot of ground to cover today, the events of a whole four months, but I don't think I shall have trouble condensing it all into a single narrative section. And then tomorrow I envisage a brief meeting for the two of us, a few final words in the aftermath of tonight's 'Storm visit.

Yes, you wouldn't think the 'Storm was coming, would you? Looking out there at that clear, innocent sky. Trust me, by this afternoon the matter will be beyond question.

I like to think it knows. The 'Storm knows what I'm up to. It's on its way to try and stop me. It's frightened. It fears for its life, that's why it's coming. Well, too late, blight of mankind! Too late! Come and do your worst. I'm not scared of you.

[Elder Ayn rotated his hand three times in the air, clenched. He could have been shaking his fist at an enemy.]

But anyway. Enough of the breast-beating machismo. To work.

We settled in nicely at the hunting lodge. Really, the place seemed to have everything one could wish for and more. Its owner had kitted it out for all eventualities (although even he, I suspect, never anticipated being snowbound here for an entire winter). What the cellar couldn't provide with its stocks of drink and preserved goods, the lake could with its abundant fish population. Ah, Yashu, she developed a real penchant for fishing there, didn't she? She was always hesitant about drawing on the provisions in the cellar, but to her the lake was an endless source of free food, like the sea. It never occurred to her – and I never saw fit to enlighten her – that a lake like this would have to have been stocked by hand in order to teem so. In her islander innocence she didn't pause to wonder where all those trout and salmon and sturgeon had come from originally.

She spent most of her time out there at the lakeside during our first three weeks at the lodge, while the weather was still clement. As did you, Khollo, I recall. Rods in hand, the pair of you, catching our meals. What did you find to talk about, you and her? You have so little in common that I can't imagine conversation was easy, yet there you were, every time I saw you, chatting away. Mind you, Yashu appeared to be the one doing most of the chatting, you indulgently listening.

With me and Gregory, by contrast, it was the senior of us who did all the talking, while the junior said at first nothing and then very little. I had begun the process, which I knew would be a lengthy and painstaking one, of breaking down the barrier the boy had erected around himself. I needed to get through to the person within, and, to begin with, this meant hours of disquisition and monologue. To use a metaphor which an Earther would approve of: I was preparing hard ground, breaking up clods of mud, ploughing out stones, in order to create a field of tilth in which to plant the seeds of an idea.

What I said to him initially was a mixture of personal observation and things gleaned from literature. An education of sorts, with me fulfilling the role of a verbal rather than telepathic pedagogue. Whether Gregory took any of it in or not, I certainly enjoyed myself. I found I was putting my own private philosophy in order. I was having to think about my opinions and clarify and justify my own judgements. A useful rehearsal for these sessions we're having now.

For those three weeks I can confidently attest that we were a happy bunch, until towards the end when Yashu began champing at the bit. She was feeling guilty about using the hunting lodge without the owner's permission, and I daresay if the good weather had continued just that little bit longer she would have left us and my plans would have been in ruins.

But the good weather came to an abrupt (and, from my point of view, timely) end. We went to bed one night and awoke the next morning to find the world gone white. Snow coated the mountains, the distant forest, the lodge, everything but the lake, which remained a black circle, like a full stop on a gigantic blank page. Snow flitted soundlessly down from white clouds, as though the clouds were shedding themselves in flakes. Snow collected in drifts on the veranda and piled itself against the front door. Snow settled in crescents on the window mullions. Snow everywhere, and from the way it was falling it was clearly not going to stop falling for some time.

Yashu's chagrin and frustration were plain to see. The knot between her eyebrows became an angry clench and stayed that way for several days. She was moody and morose, a veritable delight to live with! Actually, for much of the time we scarcely saw her. She hid away in her room, emerging only at mealtimes to scowl at us across the table. This meant that our auxiliary angler, Khollo Sharellam, had to step into her shoes as principal food provider. His was the job of braving the frigid conditions each morning to haul our breakfast from the lake's black depths. I can still picture you out there, Khollo, huddled over your rod with copious layers of extra clothing on, resembling more a heap of laundry than a man. Although heaps of laundry don't shiver and stamp their feet for warmth, do they? Nonetheless, a sterling effort. We couldn't have managed without you.

[Words can hardly express how unpleasant it was to trudge down to the lake every day, wading through knee-deep snow, and then sit for anything up to two hours, freezing, till I had landed a big enough catch. I don't know why, but the fish seemed far more reluctant to bite than when Yashu was with me. Maybe the cold made them sluggish, or maybe I wasn't as good at catching them when she wasn't there to advise and help. Or maybe my teeth were chattering so loudly it scared them off! Hailing from Durat, where the winters are balmy and the summers broiling, I am not built for cold, and I don't like it at all. Still, at least now I shan't ever complain about an ordinary winter. I only have to recollect, in perfect piercing detail, how it felt to sit by that lake, my nose tip stinging, slowly losing all sensation in my extremities, to know that however bad a winter gets, it could always be worse.]

The days began to shorten. Brownmonth gave way to Darkmonth, the official shift from autumn to winter, although winter, of course, was well ensconced where we were. The snowfall continued, intermittent. Not every day but most days. Yashu at last graced us with her company full-time again. It had obviously sunk in that she was stuck with us. The snow was not going to vanish suddenly somehow, leaving her free to escape. She had come to terms with that, and for the most part she was civil towards us. Frosty, one might say, but polite.

Meanwhile I continued my work with Gregory. He became more and more responsive. He would answer when I asked him something, usually with a monosyllable but sometimes with a phrase, even a whole sentence. I was making headway. Little by little I learned about him, about his short life so far, about his parents and his original home in Stammeldon. Tempest's Bane – what a thing to call a house! Asking for trouble, to give a place that kind of name, yet it had lived up to it for over a hundred years, holding out gamely against the Worldstorm's onslaughts. Quite an advertisement for the Brazier family's brick-making business. Come to think of it, Tempest's Bane wouldn't be a bad sobriquet for me. Like an endurance boxer's ring nickname. *Annonax Ayn, the Tempest's Bane*. It even rhymes.

I learned also from Gregory of the parental decision that had led to his being banished to Penresford after he manifested. Harsh treatment for a boy at such a tender age, yet those Fire types have a ruthless streak in them, don't they? Whatever needs to be done, is done. And then bit by bit I uncovered the full, heartbreaking story of his lethal encounter with his brother at Penresford, and I knew why he had drawn into himself the way he had. The world was cruel, the world was bitter and deceitful. Gregory had found a place where it could hurt him no longer. He had made his mind as indestructible as his body by burying it deep within himself.

I told him he could not blame himself for what had happened. *Must* not. The death of his brother had been an accident, a desperate mistake. And by telling him so repeatedly, and through countless expressions of sorrow and sympathy, I began to persuade him the world was not wholly cruel after all. I became a beacon of kindness and understanding and compassion. That was how I succeeded in drawing him out of himself. I hooked him much the same way as you, Khollo, were hooking fish in the lake. Played him carefully. Teased the line. Reeled him slowly in.

All the while, the image of my own death was growing stronger and clearer in my mind, and with it the conviction that the agent of that death would be this boy. This boy with his rock-hard, fratricidal fists. This boy whom I was busy retrieving from inner exile, steadily bringing back to life. In saving him, I was condemning myself.

Winter set hard. Now we no longer had just snow to contend with but rapidly plummeting temperatures. At night I woke up sometimes to find the bedcovers crackling with ice. By day we went about swaddled in clothes and blankets, looking like strange perambulatory mushrooms. Thanks to the stove the kitchen was the warmest room in the house, so we tended to congregate there. Someone unearthed a set of elements tiles from a cupboard. You, was it? A lovely, posh set with tiles made from sandalwood, rosewood, yellow pine and ebony. At your instigation, we attempted to play a round at the kitchen table, but it was hopeless. Yashu couldn't follow the rules, and Gregory didn't seem bothered what tile he put down where. It might have helped while away the long evenings, the odd four-hand round of elements, but it was not to be.

We struggled on. When we weren't carrying out necessary duties, we were as physically inactive as possible. Conserving our energies, like animals in hibernation. Life had become very simple, pared down to the basics: food, water, warmth, shelter.

Unfortunately, some of those essentials were getting harder to come by. We used firewood parsimoniously, but nonetheless the pile in the cellar was shrinking fast. Then the lake began to ice over. At first just at the edges, and the ice was thin enough to be broken easily. Soon, however, it was not. The whole lake turned opaque like a cataracted eye. The ice formed a thick, solid crust, and I remember clearly the morning you came in to tell me, Khollo, that you hadn't been able to make a fishing hole. You had kicked at the ice and hammered at it with a length of wood, and failed to put a dent in it. 'What do we do now, Elder Ayn?' was your entreaty, and for the answer all I had to do was turn and look at Gregory.

It was then, when things were getting tough, that Gregory started to come into his own.

You, he and I went outside, and I invited Gregory to put those massive, misshapen fists of his to use on the ice. At first he didn't grasp my meaning, so I demonstrated – somewhat painfully, I might add. Understanding dawned, and he knelt down and set to. The first few thumps did nothing more than disperse loose snow from the ice, although they echoed in the stillness like the loudest of drumbeats. He persisted, and soon chips of ice were skittering in all directions. Cracks appeared. The chips became chunks. Remorselessly he continued thumping, the breath steaming from his mouth. He made a small crater in the ice, and all at once, with a huge wet splitting sound, a hole. He bashed away at the hole's edges, widening it, and he would have carried on pounding the ice, I'm sure, till he had cleared the entire lake surface, but I instructed him to desist. He had done enough, I told him. He had performed admirably.

We left you dipping your line into the ice hole, Khollo. Yashu was watching from the kitchen window as Gregory and I returned to the lodge. Undoubtedly she had seen him being so useful. I like to think that that was the moment when her coldness towards him began to thaw, though I may be wrong about that.

Gregory thereafter took it as his daily duty to precede you down to the lake each morning and free up the ice hole, which of course sealed itself over every night. He also found himself another task, that of collecting firewood. Around noon, when the day was at its least cold, he would set off for the pine forest and return a couple of hours later lugging some fallen log which you, Khollo, would then belabour with an axe you had unearthed in the cellar. In no time we would have faggots with which to feed the ever-hungry maw of the stove, and it became possible to keep the stove burning constantly, which not only made the lodge that bit warmer but conserved our limited supply of matches.

[Of my two main jobs at the lodge, fishing and wood-hewing, wood-hewing is definitely the one I preferred. Though that's not saying much. The lesser of two evils. But at least the exertion kept me warm while I was doing it.]

It wasn't long before Gregory started going out for almost the whole day. No sooner was the sun fully up and the ice hole reopened than he would depart for the forest, and we normally wouldn't see him again till late afternoon, as the sun was sinking. Invariably he would return dragging a log behind him, and the reasonable assumption was that he was having to go farther and farther afield in order to find suitable pieces of stove fuel, because of course any old freshly broken-off tree limb would not do – the wood had to be dry and sapless in order to burn well. I remember Yashu asking Gregory one afternoon if this was the case – if these expeditions of his were taking so much time because he was finding it harder to locate the right sort of wood. He shrugged and said maybe. An unremarkable verbal exchange which would have no place in this account were it not for the fact that it was, I am almost one hundred per cent certain, the first time the two of them actually spoke to each other. The first time in my presence, at least, which amounts to the same thing, since I was keeping such a hawkish eye on them.

Meanwhile, I sustained my efforts to prise Gregory out of his shell. Further out of his shell, I should say. It was trickier than before, with him being away and gone for a large part of the day, but I made a point of spending an hour with him each evening. To ensure we had some privacy I enlisted your help, Khollo. I had you distract Yashu while Gregory and I retreated to some quiet corner to talk. That set of elements tiles came in handy then, for you took it upon yourself to teach her the game.

[By that stage Yashu and I had . . . Let's say she and I weren't at our closest, for one reason or another. Elements seemed a good, neutral way of associating with her, a medium of communication that meant we didn't have to be anything but formal with each other.]

I never asked, did she get good at it?

['Very good. She said she couldn't see the point. Did someone become a better person than someone else by beating them at a round of elements? If not, why play? But once she got her teeth into it, she could be devious and ruthless.']

She started winning, then?

['Over all the rounds we played, I reckon the score came out pretty much even.']

Contract version? Or just simple duel?

['Duel.']

And her best quadrant pairing?

['Air/Water.']

Well, naturally. It would be. Especially against an Air opponent playing Fire/Earth.

['I like to think the quality of my teaching had something to do with it as well.']

I couldn't agree more.

And while you were stalwartly coaching Yashu in the art of elements, I in turn was coaching Gregory in the art of Yashu.

Subtlety was paramount. I couldn't simply point him in her direction and say, 'There you go, my lad, get stuck in.' That wouldn't work; would possibly have the opposite of the intended effect. I remember enough about being a teenager to know that teenagers have an intrinsic stubbornness. They can't be made to do anything they don't already want to, except by force, and even then there's no guarantee they'll comply. But if I could persuade Gregory to think that that girl there was a worthwhile goal, that it was desirable for him to desire her . . .

And she is pretty, there's no denying that – pretty in a rough-hewn, islander way. Tough and boyish, not every heterosexual male's feminine ideal, but with a certain sure-footed grace about her, a limpidity in those dark eyes, a forceful set to her jaw, attractive qualities all.

So I began by drawing Gregory's attention to her looks, and then hinting that I had seen her dart a glance at him, more than once, a furtive look of appraisal and approbation. He said he had seen nothing of the sort himself, but I assured him that he was unlikely to. Yashu wouldn't be so careless as to let him *know* she was interested in him. Women do not operate that way.

I alerted him, too, to the positive impression he was making on her with his ice-breaking and his firewood-gathering. We all appreciated what he was doing to make our lives that little bit more comfortable, but she, I was prepared to swear, was appreciating it the most.

Quicker than you can say 'lower end of the Salcher Mendacity Scale', Gregory was finding excuses to talk to Yashu. She wasn't exactly effusive in her response to his overtures, but neither did she snub him. There was a wary circling around each other, a cautious feint and parry. Both of them, in their ways, were on the defensive. But something, still, was starting.

Then, about a week before New Year, Gregory was off on one of his customary forays into the forest, and it got dark, and he hadn't come back, and try though she might Yashu could not hide her concern. She asked me no fewer than three times whether he was going to return safely, and each time my reply was the same: not only was he going to return safely, he would be bringing a rather special treat with him. She could tell I was being truthful and demanded to know what the treat was. But what good is it being a previsionary if one can't be mischievously enigmatic every once in a while?

She kept watch from the window and finally spied Gregory approaching across the moonlit snow. With a disappointed pout she said, 'That's no "treat". That's just another log.'

'Are you absolutely sure?' I said, and Yashu peered out again and then made an oh-yes-I-see kind of noise. Moments later Gregory entered the lodge, hauling the carcass of a deer behind him. A hind, beautiful, velvet-pelted, still elegant even in death, with no apparent mark of violence on her until one looked closely and saw a slight concavity on the left side of her skull. The sort of dent that might be left by a powerful, sidelong blow from an indestructible fist.

'There'll be more,' Gregory said, 'but this should do for now, don't you think?'

At first light the next day we set about butchering the deer. This was not a comfortable experience for me. In the first place, the manner in which the beast had been killed put me in mind of the manner in which I was to be killed. The same sort of blow struck by the very same hand. Then there was the cutting up of the carcass, a task which Yashu volunteered for and which she carried out with practised efficiency. I could barely watch as knife entered hide, bloody incision after bloody incision was made, skin was peeled back, ribs and tripes and flesh were exposed, and the hind was rendered down into just so much meat and offal. The inedible parts were set aside, the edible chopped into manageable lumps, and all I could think was how similar the process was to an Air burial, and how this – this gory shambles – was what was to become of me in just a few short weeks. With every cut Yashu made I felt as if it were my own body being cut. Every slice of meat that deer produced was like a slice of *me*.

I had, however, conquered my squeamishness come dinnertime. The smell of roasting venison brought the saliva rushing to my mouth, and I tucked into my steak with as much appetite as anyone at the table, wolfing down the rich-tasting stuff with gusto. If I had any residual feelings of empathy with that unfortunate ungulate whose body we were consuming – well, suffice to say that a bellyful of fresh red meat can allay almost every kind of pang.

We feasted handsomely all the way to New Year. The cellar doubled as a cold store, keeping the deer meat fresh, and we were scrupulous about burying the parts we couldn't eat deep in the ground so as not to attract unwelcome guests from the wild – wolves, say.

[Another warming labour for me: hacking out a pit in the frozen-hard earth with a mattock.]

New Year itself demanded to be celebrated, and a couple of bottles of Tanhoutish vineyards' finest put everyone in a cheery mood. Gregory was now making a point of consorting with Yashu whenever he could, and slight inebriation did wonders for breaking down both youngsters' inhibitions. Yet there was still a mutual resistance there, and Gregory, for all my exhortation, still could not 'crack' Yashu. However often I told him that she was a prize for the taking, and however often I insinuated that he was the prime candidate for taking that prize, he could not seem to find the right approach. I would suggest things for him to say – compliments, jests, enquiries – but phrases which tripped fluently and winningly from my lips sounded lame and stilted when I heard him repeat them to her. Something, still, was missing from him. He had yet to unbend completely. Even with a drop of wine inside him, he could not behave in a relaxed, confident manner, and I know that, for the fairer sex, confidence in a suitor is everything. The absence of it shrills like a warning bell.

I would have found Gregory's lack of progress with Yashu frustrating, had I not been getting fore-flashes of an imminent change in him.

It happened sometime in late Innermonth. It was when he disappeared for three days in a row, coming back on the third afternoon strangely serene, his eyes clearer and wiser than they had ever previously been. I still do not know what took place during those three days. I have asked and asked, but he refuses to say. Perhaps nothing happened. Perhaps he merely got lost and it took him three days to find his way back home and he was too embarrassed to admit it. Perhaps.

He returned with a magnificent dead buck in tow, that much I can say for sure, and he was utterly exhausted from hauling it. He slept for a full two days afterwards, and awoke voracious, and having consumed nearly an entire haunch of venison at one sitting he looked around at us and he was a new person. He was smiling and open and talkative and . . . *whole*, is the best way of putting it. As though the guilt that had hollowed him out had been expunged. As though he had at last found the piece – and the peace – that had been absent from him hitherto.

As I said, I don't know what brought this about, although I am reminded of Marius Querennion's claim that fasting for a few days in the wilderness would bring him clear-headedness and perspective. Maybe that was what Gregory had needed all along. In spite of my reassurances that he was not to blame for his brother's death, he had had to find that out for himself, out there in the snow and emptiness and altitude. With no one but himself for company for three days, he had been forced to look inward and had confronted his conscience and grappled with it and won. That, in my considered opinion, is the reason for the profound alteration that came over him. If it isn't too trite, I would say our resident indestructible learned to make his mind do what his body did of its own accord: heal.

From then on, he didn't require any further incentive from me to pursue Yashu. He made pursuing her his mission, and went about it without guile or artifice, without using any of the tactics I proposed, simply as a boy trying to win over a girl he liked the look of, the sort of mating dance one might see played out in any schoolyard or at any town-square shindig anywhere on the planet, the sort that has been going on between juveniles since time immemorial, clumsy and faltering and inexpert and, to the adult eye, quite beguiling. I having provided the initial impetus, Gregory now made all the running himself. I was redundant. All that was left for me was to sit back, observe, and gloat with quiet satisfaction as day by day it became clearer, both in my prevision and from the two youngsters' patterns of behaviour, what the inevitable outcome of this adolescent trysting was to be.

One or two instances. Scenes I recall.

Yashu demonstrating to Gregory how to prepare a fish for cooking. The cut along the belly. Rowelling out the guts with her thumb. Gregory attempting to copy her but making a botch of it, hampered by his big, ungainly hands. Yashu laughing at him, and Gregory, after a moment, laughing at himself.

The two of them sitting by the lake, much as you and she used to sit, Khollo, earlier. Crouched over the ice hole, foreheads close but not quite touching. Their breaths emerging in wisps as they chatted. The wisps entwining above their heads.

An evening when Yashu asked to see his hands. Gregory showing them to her. Letting her hold them, turn them over, inspect their leathery palms and the ridges of their knuckles. Brushing her fingertips over them and then over her own hand to feel the difference.

Overhearing them as they experimented with Yashu's sooth-sight. Gregory coming up with increasingly outlandish fabrications and finding it funny how they made Yashu screw up her face and Yashu finding it funny how funny *he* was finding it. 'I'm a purple grape.' 'My name is Gregory *Pfharg*.' 'The people of Li*issua walk around with their shoes on their heads and a squid in each hand.'

Listening to them compare notes on discovering that their Inclination was not their parents' Inclination. Gregory saying that he had felt, most of all, as if he had betrayed not just his mother and father but his whole lineage, every single Brazier there had ever been; he had let them all down. Yashu saying that it had been similar for her, when she had thought she was Dammed, and even worse when she had found out she was Air. 'We're both outcasts, aren't we, Gregory? We share that. We understand each other because of that.'

Ah, Khollo, sometimes it fair made me weep to watch them! For a corrupt old man like me, youth in all its purity and passion is surely the most sweetly painful of sights. It reminds one of everything one hoped to be and, alas, everything one has failed to become. I'm not saying Gregory and Yashu are innocents. Far from it. But to be young is to feel things intensely, all-encompassingly, with a heart that has not yet been jaded by experience. Every emotion is fresh and fierce, and I could see with those two that they were succumbing to some very fresh and fierce emotions indeed. After a while they became secretive, hoping not to betray to you and me what was going on between them, but that very secretiveness was the most glaring indicator of all. I would enter a room where moments earlier I had heard them talking, only to find them seated apart and studiously silent. I would catch the occasional furtive glance that passed between them, or the occasional, oh-so-accidental brush of hand against hand, and it was such an effort to pretend I had seen nothing! One morning I stepped out onto the veranda, and there they were, standing apart, their faces flushed with more than just the cold. Yes, it was beyond question. We had a pair of young lovers living with us now.

At what point they consummated their relationship, I'm not prepared to say. I wouldn't say even if I knew for sure, which I don't. They have been admirably discreet, and it's not my business to get into the sordid ins and outs of their private lives anyway. 'Sordid ins and outs'. Hah! Better scrub that. Put in 'details' instead. The details of their private lives.

That they *have* consummated their relationship, however, is obvious. And they have done so, I might add, fruitfully. You recall that yesterday I mentioned hearing certain sounds? Of course you do, silly question. This morning, as predicted, I heard them again. They came from the outhouse, which lies some twenty yards from the lodge, but I am a light sleeper and noise carries far when there is snow on the ground and nary a breath of wind.

Now, one person vomiting sounds much like any other person vomiting, you would think. But that's not so. I mean, one can tell when it's a woman vomiting rather than a man, can one not? Simply by the higher pitch of the retches.

And a woman vomiting first thing in the morning?

Two mornings in a row?

So now let me lace my fingers together across my belly thus, Khollo. Let me sit back in my chair and turn my head toward the view. Let the chilly morning glow of my last full day on earth light my face.

The 'Storm is coming. But I have already defeated it.

GREGORY

Cocooned.
Within.
Safe.
Like Tempest's Bane.
An impregnable wall around him.
Able to peer out.
See the world.
Unaffected by it.

The old man. The old man wanted to help him. Look after him.
Why not?
Someone else to make the choices. Because the choices Gregory himself made were always bad.
(Willem)
Nothing could go wrong if someone else was making the choices.

A glint of razor blade. Hanks of red hair tumbling into the waters of the brook, being whisked away.
Later, Gregory ran a hand over his shorn scalp.
Rough.
Like brick.

Walking. Stopping. Eating. Sleeping.
Places. People.
Out there.
Talk. Voices.
Out there.

The girl. An islander. Dark-eyed, like Eda Gove.
Water drops were splashed by her against his cheek.
They meant as little as a rain shower did to Tempest's Bane's roof.

*

401

The dark of night. The small hours.

The old man shook him awake. 'Time to leave.'

The night sky creaked open like the lid of a box to let out daytime. Air. Far-off mountains.

The cave.

The cave and its peculiar, skinny inhabitants.

The chamber that shone green and roared.

There were static days. Nothing to do. The old man left him alone.

He could feel his knuckles starting to soften. He had been taught to keep them tough.

(Willem)

He didn't want to keep them tough, but the training took over. He found himself knocking the backs of his hands against each other.

At first it stung. He heard Master Ergall's voice in his ear. He kept knocking his knuckles together. Soon it didn't sting any more.

Walking again. Uphill. Into the mountains.

There was a lake, and beside it a house. The house was no Tempest's Bane but it looked solid enough, sturdy enough.

They moved into the house. Lived there.

There were four of them – the old man, the old man's southerner enshriner, the girl, and Gregory – and they lived in the house, but only one of them, himself, was a human house. A house within a house. Doubly secure.

The old man insisted that Gregory should call him Annonax. Better yet, Nax.

Nax said he was Gregory's friend. He said Gregory looked like someone who needed a friend. He said Gregory looked like someone who had been through a lot . . .

(Willem)

. . . suffered a lot.

Nax liked to talk. Gregory let him. Sometimes he would pay attention, sometimes he wouldn't. Nax was *out there*, talking, and it was Gregory's decision whether he should listen.

The air got cold, colder, colder still. It thinned and sharpened like a whetted blade. The other three found some extra clothing to wear. Gregory was not that bothered by the cold but put some extra clothing on anyway, so as not to be left out. In here, in his own private Tempest's Bane, it got lonely sometimes. So he copied what the three of them *out there* had done. He felt less lonely as a result.

Nax spoke of the Worldstorm. He spoke of the mysteries that rationality could not yet account for and perhaps never would. He spoke of the Air Inclined and their obsession with thought and logic. He told Gregory that at times he longed to have been born Fire or Earth, or even Water. Then he would have been free of this 'burden of brain', as he put it.

Gregory murmured something about every Inclination having its own burdens. Even though the words were barely audible to himself, they nonetheless carried to *out there*. Nax heard. Nax smiled.

Snow had fallen and was falling and continued falling for days. It featherdowned the landscape. It snugged and softened the rocks and peaks.

The days shrank in on themselves. The nights dilated like a dark-adapted eye.

To Nax, Gregory talked about himself. It was really like talking to himself about himself. Nax remained *out there* and Gregory was able to believe, if he wanted to, that Nax was out of earshot. That made the talking easier, because he could say anything, without self-consciousness. Still, he steered clear of a certain subject . . .

(Willem)

. . . until it became impossible to avoid any longer. He spoke about life with his older brother and about how good it was, despite Reehan Bringlight. How good it was right up until the day he manifested. He spoke of saying goodbye to Willem that Freeday morning nearly four years ago, and from there he was led inescapably to the next time he and Willem met.

That day.

That moment.

Willem.

And as he confessed what he had done to his brother, Gregory expected to hear condemnation from *out there*. But all Nax said was that it had not been his fault. It had been a horrible accident. And Gregory knew this, had known this all along, but knowing it and hearing someone else say it were two very different things. Yes, an accident. It could not have been helped. He had not known it was Willem inside that flame shell.

Nax repeatedly told him. Not his fault. Not his fault.

Bit by bit, Gregory came to accept it.

Bit by bit, there ceased to be an *out there*.

They stepped out onto the frozen lake – Gregory, Nax, the southerner

Khollo. Nax said they needed the ice broken so that Khollo could have access to the fish beneath. Nax pounded the ice a couple of times. Gregory got the idea.

His first few blows were tentative. He wasn't sure if his hands were up to it. Other than knocking them together, he hadn't properly been keeping up with his training.

But his hands remembered. His hands knew what they were for.

Gregory barely thought of Willem at all as he punched through inches of ice and reached the water below.

The forest was glacially still. Gregory had never heard such silence. Every white pine frond hung motionless. Not the least breath of wind soughed. The only sound was Gregory himself, the tiny crunch of snow under his feet whenever he shifted his balance, the minuscule rasp of cloth against cloth as his arm swung just a fraction of a degree.

He had come here for firewood, and firewood he had found, but it was the awesome hush that was the real discovery. You could believe that time did not tick here, that the world did not turn here, that the forest had been and would be this way eternally.

His subsequent trips into the forest became lengthier, and fetching firewood was always a priority but the other priority was simply being in the forest. The cold could not harm him, as it might a non-indestructible. The silence did not judge him. In the forest, he was free.

Nax had begun mentioning the girl, Yashu. She was a topic he returned to again and again in his discussions with Gregory, and Gregory, who had not paid her much heed before, found himself doing so. At first it was simply out of curiosity, to see why Nax was so full of praise for her. She was, after all, just some islander girl Nax had picked up on his travels, and ordinarily Gregory would have had no interest in her because an islander girl would have had no interest in him or in anyone from the mainland. Islanders were insular in every sense. So why bother?

Nax, however, maintained that she *was* interested in him.

Was she?

Gregory found no evidence of it.

At first.

On perhaps his twentieth expedition into the forest, Gregory saw the deer. He walked into a clearing and there it was, some dozen yards away, at the clearing's other end. It had seen him first and had gone rigid, poised to leap away. Gregory halted and went rigid too. For a long time, neither moved a muscle. The deer kept its huge topaz eyes fixed on Gregory, seemingly too startled to decide whether it should flee. Then, with great cautiousness, it raised its head and sniffed the air. Its nose resembled a cube of liquorice, glossy and black. Gregory could see the nostrils pinch then widen, pinch then widen, as the deer assessed his scent. He knew the question it was asking itself: *Is this a predator?* Were he to move, it would have its answer. He remained utterly still.

Finally the deer bent one slender leg, turned, lofted its head and its tail, and trotted out of the clearing, into the trees. It did this at a pace that suggested it wasn't frightened, merely taking a sensible precaution. Gregory followed it with his gaze until – he must have blinked – it vanished. One moment he was looking at a deer amid pine trunks; the next, only pine trunks.

He stayed in the clearing till the sunlight was slanting through the trees, but the deer did not return.

The girl, Yashu, was a prize. That was Nax's word for her. A prize. Gregory couldn't quite see it for himself. All he saw was a shaggy-haired, sturdy-limbed islander. She wasn't even a true islander, he had discovered. She had sooth-sight. What did that make her? An Air islander? That was a complete contradiction in terms.

But then so was 'Earther Brazier'.

The third time he revisited the clearing, the deer was there again. On the previous two days he had spent hours waiting, with no sign of the deer. This time, sitting on a boulder as he had sat yesterday and the day before, he finally saw it. It nosed hesitantly out from the dappled shade of the pines and began foraging in the snow, nibbling at shoots of grass it uncovered with its nose. Perhaps it had been there on the two previous occasions, lurking out of sight among the trees, fearful, and had only today plucked up the courage to show itself. Every so often it looked up from its eating to stare straight at Gregory. Its eyes were beautifully long-lashed. Deep and demure. Its throat was a blaze of white.

It was there the next time, and the time after that it was not alone. With it were another two deer. They were skittish, obviously uneasy to be within such close proximity to a human, but the original deer was now comfortable with Gregory. It strayed to within a few feet of him. His static presence was now an accepted part of its world.

Sitting on the boulder for so long in the cold was painful. Cramps came and went. He could lose all sensation in his feet. But these were mere physical hurts and Gregory was a longstanding master of *them*.

He told no one about the deer. He returned to the lodge each evening with a log and stated that decent firewood was becoming harder to find, that was why his trips into the forest were taking so long now. Nax and Khollo had no reason to disbelieve him, but Yashu, he thought, was sceptical. As well she might be. He wasn't being dishonest, though. He just had a secret.

The deer was now so used to him, it felt safe nosing the ground right by his feet. He could have reached out and stroked its head. Its two companions were becoming less timid too, as if drawing heart from the other's boldness. A strange trust had developed between Gregory and these three creatures, fostered by his patience, his willingness and ability to sit for hours on end in the clearing, his powers of endurance.

Time and again he thought of the tapestry which hung in the hall of the hunting lodge. The scene it depicted.

Wait, he told himself.

One more day, he told himself.

Khollo and Yashu had taken to playing elements each evening. Khollo was coaching her in the basics of the game and, once she had grasped these, the finer points.

Gregory watched the two of them, head to head over the tiles.

He thought he could do that: teach her the game.

He thought he could do it better than Khollo.

A moment. A long, long moment.

Gregory knew he had only one shot at this. He had to be completely sure of himself.

The deer's head was inches from his shoulder. The deer was between bouts of foraging. Its eyes had taken on a faraway look, as if it had been struck by some passing fancy, some abstract thought flitting through its animal brain.

The moment continued.

Gregory knew he would have to be quick. Swift-class quick. In his imagination he made his move a dozen times. His fist lashed out, lashed out, lashed out.

His fist stayed by his side.

He must not miss. What a waste of all those days, all those hours spent sitting here, if he missed.

And there – the shadow of a memory – was the moment he had thrown himself into the flame shell, fist swinging. The delirious collision of knuckles with skull. He had had no thought then but that he must hurt the incendiary who had hurt Sol Gove.

That moment overlapped this one.

The deer turned its head and surveyed Gregory. Its eyes shone with a kind of wisdom. It knew. It understood. It accepted.

The *crack!* was huge in the forest silence.

The moment was over.

He had not realised why he must kill the deer until he got its carcass back to the lodge. He knew they needed food and he knew a change from their usual fishy diet would be more than welcome. But he had not realised truly why he wanted to bring the deer back dead till Yashu opened the front door to him.

He had done it for her.

He didn't tell her that. He wasn't sure how to. Even when he got a little tipsy on New Year's Eve, quaffing wine from the lodge's cellar, he couldn't explain to Yashu how or why it mattered that the deer had been an offering to her. Surely, if anyone, it ought to have been an offering to Nax, in return for retrieving him from the graveyard at Penresford and looking after him ever since. A thank-you for the many kindnesses Nax had shown him.

But no. Yashu. Yashu of I*il. I*ilyashu. That Air islander, who was almost the exact opposite of him, Fire-born Earther. That girl who was as unlike him as it was possible to imagine.

For her.

He didn't see the other two deer for almost a week, but they returned to the clearing eventually. The first one's death had sent them scuttling into the forest, but something lured them back. Were they too stupid to understand that death awaited them here as well? Perhaps. Or perhaps they remembered, more clearly than they remembered the other deer being killed, the trust they had placed in the human who sat on the boulder.

These two were stags, or rather young stags, bucks. Each had a nubbiny growth of antler, covered in peach-like winter fur. The first deer had been antler-less – a hind. Their mother? If so, it was her misguided example they were still following. Children, not understanding that a parent could get things fatally wrong.

He cultivated them carefully, as he had cultivated the hind. He let them draw near him of their own accord, nearer by the day, until he was assured they had lost all fear of him again. He had re-merged with the background, just part of the landscape.

He became so familiar with the bucks that he could tell one from another at a glance. The shape of their antlers. One's muzzle, slightly more pointed than the other's. The distinctive way one of them flicked its tail.

This one, the tail-flicker, was the more intrepid of the pair. It was the one which came more often within arm's reach. The other had a tendency to shy away if it felt it had inadvertently got too close to Gregory. Perhaps it was the wiser. It had the better memory.

The day came. Gregory looked forward to returning to the lodge that evening with his kill. It was gratifying, the way Yashu had carved up the last one. Unwrapped his gift to her, as it were. Her confident strokes with the knife. Her skill. She would do the same with this one, and he hoped then, finally, she might see, without having to be told, what the deer meant. What it symbolised.

As he descended into the forest, following a path he had grooved into the snow over repeated journeys, Gregory cast his mind back to Eda Gove and the way he and she had nearly but not quite meshed. What hadn't he said, what should he have said, that would have smoothed things out between them? He couldn't think, but it didn't matter now anyway, because Eda was in the past. Eda was in the Penresford section of his life, which was over. A new section had begun, and it had Yashu in it. Pleasing her was now his goal, and Eda he could consign to the drawer marked Oblivion. He didn't envy Khollo, who, as an enshriner, had no such drawer in his head. He was glad he had the option of forgetting.

He was in the clearing for no more than an hour before the bucks put in an appearance. They seemed strangely skittish this morning and took a long time to edge out of the forest shadows into the open, their heads questing this way and that. Something was worrying them, and Gregory wondered if there were predators in the area. Predators other than himself, that was. Wolves or even a bear. Did bears kill deer? Perhaps not, but they were certainly known to attack humans. Gregory peered around him in every direction. He knew the forest well by now. He thought he could read its moods, interpret its whispers. Something *was* awry. Something in the quality of the forest's hush felt odd to him. But he could not see anything out of place, and after a while the sense of oddness faded. Perhaps the bucks' skittishness had him imagining things that weren't there. It could be that their skittishness was, in fact, his fault. They were picking up signals from him. They knew, somehow, that today one or other of them was to die.

Yet ingrained habit proved stronger than fear, and shortly the bucks were roving close to him as usual, and Gregory stiffened, fist at the ready, waiting for the critical instant of opportunity when one of the bucks' heads would come within his arc of swing.

This time, he did it almost without thinking. It just happened. He was almost surprised to see the buck sprawled at his feet, its legs twitching as death convulsions ran through it. He glanced around, but the other buck was nowhere to be seen. His fist throbbed from the punch.

The buck on the ground shuddered its last and lay still. There were flecks of blood on the snow by its mouth. Gregory crouched down to stroke its neck, a gesture of consolation that was mostly for his own benefit.

Loud in the silence, a series of cracking sounds.

Gregory's head snapped up. What was that? Branches breaking?

A bear?

Urgently he scanned left, right, left, tensed, ready to run. Master Ergall would have no doubt had something to say like *An indestructible isn't scared of getting mauled by a bear*, but Gregory had no desire to put that to the test.

And then he thought, *It's winter. Shouldn't a bear be asleep in its cave?*

And then he thought, *I know that sound. It's a handclap.*

And it was – a slow, ironic handclap, emanating from somewhere just out of sight.

And Gregory called out, 'Hello? Who's there?'

And the handclap halted.

And a figure stepped out from behind a tree at the clearing's edge.

And for several seconds Gregory could not breathe.

Could not move.

Could not think.

And when he finally regained some semblance of self-control, all he could do was say a name.

Gasp it, really.

'Reehan.'

Reehan Bringlight was bearded, long-haired, swathed in furs, and much thinner than when Gregory had last seen him, but the biggest change that had come over him was in his eyes. Those eyes had seldom looked at Gregory with anything other than mockery or malice in them. Even when Reehan was pretending to be nice to him, the eyes had told a different story. But now they were hollowed, they were red-rimmed, their irises seemed an even paler green than they used to be. They were worn-out eyes, and what Gregory saw in them left him wishing for the good old contempt they used to contain. That, at least, had been a recognisable, human emotion. These eyes seemed to have passed beyond that into a state of eerie, etiolated grace. They and their owner had both ascended and descended. Reehan was part animal, part something else. What he was not any more was simply a human being.

'Well done. Most impressive.'

The voice, too, was not Reehan's voice of old. It sounded fragile and at the same time preternaturally calm.

Gregory knew then that he was shortly going to have to fight for his life.

'You let that deer get to know you. You gained its trust. How long did that take, I wonder. And then, when it least suspected, you belted the thing and stoved its head in. That's very much the way with you, isn't it, Little Bother? You have a fondness – indeed an aptitude – for stoving in the heads of innocent creatures.'

Gregory did not reply. What struck him most about Reehan's speech was not the accusation it contained. He might have expected that. It was the tone in which the words 'Little Bother' were phrased. No spite, no sneering or jeering. Gregory really *was* a little bother to Reehan now. That inconsequential. That insignificant.

Reehan strode across the clearing. Gregory felt himself tense up further. He would rather, all things considered, have been facing an angry bear.

'Do you know how long it's taken me to find you?' Reehan said. 'Well actually, that's self-evident, isn't it. So let me put it another way. Do you know how much trouble you've been to find? I've travelled all over the place. I've been everywhere. Even, for fuck's sake, Damentaine. Searching for *you*. You should feel honoured. I wouldn't go to that much effort for just anyone.'

Reehan came to a halt – wittingly or not, just too far away for Gregory to reach him with a single bound. Whereas Gregory was, of course, well within the range of Reehan's flame.

For now, Reehan seemed content to talk, but the attack was coming, Gregory knew. Would he even feel it, when the burning started inside him? Would he be able to respond in time?

'You took away a good friend, Little Bother, when you killed Willem. You deprived the world – you deprived *me* – of a genuinely good and decent person. I imagine you've thought about that a lot. I imagine you've congratulated yourself over and over on how clever you were. I know you hate me. You've always hated me. But I never realised how much till you showed me. You showed me how far you were prepared to go to prove your hatred. You were prepared to kill your own brother to prove it.'

'It wasn't like that,' Gregory said, and was ashamed by how shaky his voice sounded.

'I saw what I saw,' Reehan said. 'It took me ages to work out why someone would deliberately do such a thing, and then all at once I got it. It's obvious. You were jealous of me. I was closer to Willem than you. He loved me more than you. Especially when you turned out to have the wrong Inclination. You couldn't bear it that he was more of a brother to me than he ever would be to you, and so, first chance you got, you killed him. To teach *me* a lesson.' Reehan nodded to himself, fully satisfied with this rationale.

Gregory, on the other hand, was astonished. 'How can you say that? How can you honestly *think* that? You're insane! I didn't even know it was Willem. I would never have hurt him, never in my life.'

'Oh, please. I watched you do it. It couldn't have been more calculated.'

'And that's why you've spent three months tracking me down? Because you think I killed Willem to – to get at you?'

'No, I've spent three months tracking you down, Little Bother, simply to eliminate you. That's all. It's about justice. Balance. The world is a poorer place without Willem. It'll be a better place without you.'

Indignation, incredulity, intimidation – all vied within Gregory, but what came out on top was something he could not have expected.

Pity.

He looked up at Reehan and saw all the days this madman had spent, chasing from country to country in pursuit of him, hunting high and low and drawing himself into a tighter and tighter spiral of delusion as he went, until he had lost all sense of what really happened at Penresford and had substituted the facts of the event with his own invention. That was how he had kept himself going, by spurring himself on with this false memory, this lie. And Gregory's death was the culmination of the lie, the act that would make it finally, wholly true.

Yes, pity. That was all Gregory could feel for Reehan. The same rough pity he felt for the slain buck.

It would be a mercy to end Reehan's existence.

Gregory rose to his feet.

The abruptness of the move took Reehan aback.

Gregory lunged.

Reehan formed a fireball.

Gregory ducked under it.

Reehan let out a huff of air as Gregory's shoulder rammed him in the stomach.

Gregory and Reehan went tumbling together into the snow.

The fireball dispersed into nothingness.

Gregory reared back, feeling Reehan's fingers clawing at his chest. He needed room to swing, to hit.

Reehan's hands relaxed.

Heat.

Deep in Gregory's chest cavity, there was heat and wrongness. He felt the air in his windpipe become raw, unbreathable.

Somewhere distant, he heard a voice. It was Master Ergall's. It told him not to feel, just to hit.

He brought his head down onto Reehan's. Brow collided with brow. He sensed skin splitting, a rush of warm blood. His? Reehan's?

Then he had to roll away. His body was shaking, racked with uncontrollable spasms. The snow was moving under him. He knew, vaguely, that he was crawling. He had to get away, recover.

Blood pattered down onto the snow.

He was among the trees.

He tried to stand.

No good.

He lay face-down, and he was mending, it was getting easier to breathe, but so slowly, he was mending so slowly, and Reehan was back there in the clearing, regaining his strength, less badly injured . . .

Gregory urged himself onto all fours and then, with searing effort, onto his feet. He teetered, turned, looked back to the clearing.

Reehan was gone. Only one inert body on the ground there, the buck's.

Gregory started to run.

The trees blurred around him. His lungs, still incompletely healed, laboured. He put distance between himself and the clearing, aiming uphill. Higher ground. At every turn he expected to come face to face with Reehan. Where was he? The trouble was, he might not even see him before he attacked again. Reehan had the advantage of range, whereas Gregory needed to be within arm's reach in order to utilise his Inclination.

He came to a dense stand of pines and threw himself into it. Hidden, hunkered on all fours, he peered out. The forest was its usual, monumentally hushed self, and for a time all he could hear was his heart, pounding so loud that Reehan could surely hear it too.

Then, from far off, an enquiring cry: 'Little Bother?'

Downslope, but hard to tell where exactly.

'Little Bother?'

Drifting between the evergreens. Like a mother calling for her child.

'Little Botherrr . . . ?'

Gregory would have stayed put. He had a good hiding place, why give it up? He realised, however, that his dash through the forest had left a trail in the snow. There: a line of dredging footprints, leading right to where he was. A blind man could follow that. Moreover, he couldn't just lie still and hope Reehan didn't find him. Keeping on the move was the best policy for now.

With every ounce of stealth he possessed Gregory crept out from the stand of pines. He retraced his steps backward along the furrow he had cut in the snow, and then after fifty yards went off forwards again, but at an angle, cutting a fresh furrow. That ought to confuse Reehan if he did come across the tracks. Which way had Little Bother gone? How could he have gone in two directions at once?

Down below somewhere, Reehan continued to sing out that loathed nickname. Gregory gained the brow of the slope. Here ran a ledge, a horizontal pause between inclines. He headed along it, tracing a course parallel to the one Reehan appeared to be taking. Sometimes Reehan's voice was faint, sometimes loud and clear. Gregory scanned down through the pines, hoping for a glimpse of his enemy but getting none. The ledge ended, and he stopped and reviewed his options. Being higher up than Reehan gave him an edge, although not much of one. He was familiar with the lie of the land, however, and that was a definite advantage. All in all, his best tactic was to locate Reehan before Reehan located him. Sneak up on him if possible. He knew, to his dismay, that that was the only way he had a hope of winning: by bringing the fight to Reehan. Staying out of Reehan's way would buy him time but little else. Also, Reehan must know about the lodge. Why else would he be here if he didn't? And in that case, he must not be allowed to reach it. Yashu and Nax and Khollo. Gregory had their lives to consider as well as his own.

He took a step forward and one end of a pine branch cracked up through the snow. He levered the branch out from under his foot, brushed the snow off, and held it in both hands. Its heft and balance were very close to those of a sticks stick. He thought of Penresford and of the triumph he had felt whenever he crossed the opposition's breach boundary. Those days seemed long ago, far away. He tore extraneous twigs and fronds from the branch, stripping it bare. He practice-swung it a few times. He knew the branch would be of little practical help – Reehan could incinerate it with just a thought – but all the same having it in his hands felt good. Reassuring.

He set off downslope, slip-slithering through the snow, sometimes using the stick for support. Reehan was still calling, calling. So sure of himself, so arrogant. Afraid of nothing.

Soon Gregory arrived at a gully where, he knew from experience, the snow was deceptively deep. The gully appeared shallow and the

413

snow seemed no thicker there than anywhere else until you stepped on it. Then you plunged in up to your crotch and it was a struggle to extricate yourself.

Halfway along, a tree had fallen, forming a kind of bridge over the top of the gully. The tree's root bore was intact and still half embedded in the ground, meaning the tree was still alive and retained its full growth of foliage. The longer boughs drooped till their tips were touching the snow's surface to create a screen of dark green across the gully, like a frilly curtain.

Gregory assessed the scene, and a plan started to take shape. It wasn't, when fully formed, a great plan. It certainly wasn't foolproof. But in the absence of any other ideas, it would have to do.

Stick in hand, he moved along the rim of the gully, making for the tree.

Reehan paused and for the umpteenth time put his fingers to his forehead. They came away with fresh blood on them, to add to the blood that already coated them. The fresh blood, though, was sticky. Coagulating. A good sign.

For a while he had been stumbling around virtually blind. Every time he tried to open his eyes, more blood had poured into them. Handfuls of snow of had helped stem the flow and ease the pain, but he was no indestructible, he healed at the usual rate, and that little brat, that little Sod! Head-butting him like that. Fuck, it had hurt. Still hurt. And Reehan couldn't see himself getting to a recuperator any time soon, which meant the wound was going to leave a scar. A permanent reminder whenever he looked in a mirror.

Not happy. Reehan was very much not happy.

'Little Bother?' he crooned, and added under his breath, 'I'm going to burn your balls loose and cook them while you watch.'

He listened. He knew Gregory could hear him. Sooner or later he was going to goad a reply out of him.

'Little Bother?' he said yet again, and this time the murmured threat was, 'I'm going to make your eyeballs sizzle in their sockets.'

Still no answer, but somewhere out there in the trees Gregory was hiding, trembling, knowing death was coming for him.

'Little Bother?'

There! Was that . . . ?

Reehan waited, ears pricked.

Faintly the voice came again: 'I said I'm here. Over here, Ash-hole.'

Reehan loped off in the direction of Little Bother's voice. Idiot kid. Flamer family but Earther-level intelligence.

'Little Bother,' he called out. 'Listen, I'll make a deal with you. Just come out into the open and I'll kill you quickly and cleanly. That's the fairest I can be. Otherwise it'll take ages, I promise you. You'll have begged me a thousand times to finish you off before I do.'

The words echoed through the forest. Gregory's reply came echoing back: 'No, I'm not going to make it that easy for you.'

'Fine by me. Don't say I didn't offer.'

By now Reehan had Gregory's position worked out, and he homed in on it unerringly. Within a minute he was standing at the end of a gully. He peered down it to where it was traversed by a toppled pine. That, clearly, was where Gregory was, lying along the pine's trunk, secreted amongst the foliage. He called out, not expecting a response this time and not getting one. Little Bother was stupid but not that stupid. He proceeded into the gully, and with his first step found himself knee-deep in snow; with his second step, thigh-deep. Not a problem. He exercised his Inclination, and a stripe of the snow ahead of him went transparent and began to sink in on itself. In no time he had melted a channel down to the grass. He had a clear path all the way to the horizontal pine.

He walked along the channel, between its dripping, smooth-sided banks. The ground was soggy underfoot. His gaze remained fixed on the tree. Its branches hung heavy and still. You could have hidden a dozen Little Bothers amid all that greenery. He was minded to engulf the entire tree in flames and dislodge Gregory from his perch that way, but he didn't think it would be necessary. Little Bother would surely give his precise whereabouts away any moment now. And Reehan preferred, if possible, to save his flame for the torture to come.

And yes, there it was. Just as he reached the tree. The tiniest of movements among the branches to his left. A faint rustling.

Reehan sent a focused, white-hot fireball hurtling towards that part of the tree.

At the same instant, something broke free of the snow directly below his target. A shape whipped through the air, and light exploded across his vision and he went down, flailing, onto his back.

Gregory dropped the stick and hurled himself at the supine Reehan. The stick had served its purpose: he had prodded it up through the branches into the tree to give the impression that he was there, then had swung it at Reehan's head. For what he had to do next, his hands were the only weapon he needed.

The snow, which had been his ally, concealing him as he had lain in wait below the tree, all at once turned and became his enemy. It caught his legs and made him stumble. He used the momentum of the stumble to carry him forwards, but still his lunge didn't take him as far

415

as he wanted. He crashed through the side of the channel Reehan had made, landing face-first near Reehan's feet. He scrambled up onto his hands and knees and crawled onto Reehan, but the moment's delay cost him dearly. Reehan had recovered from the blow with the stick. His eyes, gleaming whitely amid the dried blood that covered his face, had their focus again.

Gregory leapt onto him, straddling his torso. He raised a fist. Reehan squinted, and Gregory felt it again, that same sensation as in the clearing, that heat and wrongness within. Reehan leered lopsidedly. The wrongness intensified. Gregory's vision began to swirl, and Reehan's face became a crimson blur. He knew he must bring his fist down, it was the only way he was going to survive this. But he could not seem to communicate the idea to his arm. The fist remained stubbornly braced in the air, quivering. At the back of his throat he tasted grilled meat. That was himself. That was what Reehan was doing to him. He must bring his fist down. Must punch. The wrongness was spreading through him. He must . . .

Reehan opened his mouth and laughed.

The laugh pierced deep into Gregory. It touched something at his core, something that had been lodged there since the day he threw that stone into the Divided Tree. It knocked it free, and Gregory was flooded with raw, enlivening relief.

This was what he needed to be. This was why he was the way he was.

His fist fell like a thunderclap.

There were two Gregorys. One Gregory lay on his back in the snow, in a trough created when he had clambered off Reehan's body and had tried to stand and had fallen sideways. The other Gregory was looking down from above on that sprawled Gregory, observing him dispassionately. This one could also see Reehan – a man-shaped mound of furs, with a bloody, mashed pulp where the head should be.

He felt nothing for either of them. Himself, at death's door. Reehan, over the threshold.

Nothing.

Night came and went in an eye-blink. Snow began falling, as though the stars themselves were plummeting from their constellation orbits. Day came and went like a flaring of a match. More snow fell, the flakes melting as they landed on Gregory's face but mantling the rest of him in soft whiteness. Night returned. Gregory, swaddled in snow, almost buried, stared deep into the vastness of the universe.

*

At daybreak, he tried to move. He felt whole, and hale, but when he raised a hand to examine it he saw that his fingertips had gone purplish-black. Frostbite. Over the course of the morning the colour lightened. By noon his fingers were pink again.

At length, he stirred once more. His first attempt at sitting up was effortful, infant-like, but after several goes he managed it. He brushed snow from him. Weakly, woozily, he stood.

Reehan was gone, and for a moment there was the appalling thought that he had recovered somehow, had risen up, and was lurking nearby, ready to attack again. But in fact he had not moved, he had just been covered. Snow had partially filled in the channel. A slight bulge in its smoothness indicated where his body lay.

Just to be sure, Gregory scraped some of the snow away. He exposed a small area of frozen gore, the tip of a shard of shattered bone. He nodded, satisfied. He straightened up.

To the clearing first, to retrieve the dead buck.

Then to the lodge.

YASHU

She rebuffed his advances until it became impossible to do so. Impossible not because she feared hurting his feelings but because she could no longer deny her own.

At first nothing he said to her seemed meant. It sounded as if someone else was talking, his words not his own, and so it was easy to remain indifferent to him. Gradually, though, he grew more confident. He emerged from within himself, and his voice no longer had such a cracked, brittle timbre. His attentiveness was both flattering and puzzling. From what she had gathered, he was a well-born Flamer boy. His Flow was Earth, but his family was very wealthy and his hometown (which was not Penresford, it turned out) was a sophisticated place where all types of Flow mixed and mingled and rubbed along. Whereas she – she was a Li*issuan, plain and simple. Why should he be interested in her? Was it just because she was there, the only female at the hunting lodge, and the same age as him? Was he just doing what boys do, perhaps in order to pass the time?

More and more she came to think not. And perhaps in order to pass the time herself – because she knew it would be weeks, even months, before she would be able to leave the lodge – she started to consider him. She started to ask herself if she minded him coming up to her, seeking her out, finding a quiet moment to say something to her; and she discovered, to her surprise, that she didn't. She had grown accustomed to the paleness of his skin and the garish redness of his hair, which was now grown close to the length it had been when she first set eyes on him in Penresford. That hair intrigued her and she wondered how it might feel to the touch. It looked as if it might feel warmer than her own.

Once he began making himself useful, he became even more intriguing. Hammering a hole in the lake ice, fetching firewood from down in the forest, and then the deer . . . These were things that mattered; they ensured that the four of them would survive this wintry ordeal, this frozen *usurraña*. The deer, in particular, was a feat. An incendiary

418

huntsman, if the hall tapestry was to be believed, could kill a deer from a distance with little difficulty, but Gregory had only his fists and, as he put it, 'a powerful patience'.

Her liking for him increased at the expense of her liking for Khollo. She couldn't forget how Khollo had reneged on their deal at the crucial moment. She wouldn't be trapped here now if he hadn't. She tried to find forgiveness inside her, and that was what persuaded her to accept when he offered to teach her elements. It would show him she wasn't *completely* angry with him. But then, having overcome her initial lack of interest in the game, she began to enjoy playing it and, even more, to enjoy beating him at it. How satisfying it was to lay down the Compass tile, say, and with that move block off his last remaining avenue of attack, and then see his crestfallen look as he tried to work out where he had slipped up and how the pupil could have outplayed the teacher in this way. Their nightly elements rounds became much more than just a tabletop contest. They confirmed that she was on an equal footing with Khollo and also, in respect of honour, his superior. A *mala* victory if ever there was one.

And *mala* played its part with regard to Gregory, for in him she could perceive something good coming out of this unpleasant situation. His efforts on everyone else's behalf were a great responsibility, and with that responsibility, which he shouldered manfully, he appeared to be coming to terms with what he had done at Penresford. She knew his frequent talks with Mr Ayn were helping too, and this served to raise Mr Ayn in her estimation. *Mala* all round.

After a while it was an effort to recall that he had murdered someone. Yashu found it hard to think of him in that light and was coming to feel that she had judged him too hastily and too harshly. From hints Mr Ayn was dropping, it appeared that there had been mitigating circumstances to the crime. Gregory was far from being a hard-hearted killer. In fact he was, as far as Yashu could gather, no less a victim than the brother who had died by his hand.

When Gregory disappeared for three days, she was beside herself with worry. She pictured him lost, in difficulties, all sorts of scenarios that brought back memories of the 'Storm visit and her conviction – proved right – that Huaso had not survived. She even envisaged Gregory abandoning them here at the lodge, striking out for civilisation because he, of all of them, could manage the journey. Would he desert them like that? She thought not, but the possibility lurked at the back of her mind.

She asked Mr Ayn if he was coming back, not holding out much hope of a straight answer. Mr Ayn, however, was unambiguous. Yes, he would be back.

'Where is he? What's happened?'

'That, my dear, I cannot tell you.'

She went in search of him. She didn't disbelieve Mr Ayn – he wasn't lying – but she couldn't simply sit indoors and wait. She had to do something. The second day that Gregory was absent, and the third, she wrapped herself in a quilt and ventured out. On the second day the snow was coming down in thick flurries and she didn't dare stray far from the lodge in case she got lost herself. She called out his name but the snow engulfed her voice. The third day was clear and bright but the previous day's snowfall hampered her. Again, she didn't get far.

That evening, Gregory staggered home with another deer. He gave no account of where he had been or why he had been absent for all that time. He slept heavily for two days straight, and while he did she peered round the door to his room several times, checking on him. Once, she went all the way into the room and sat with him for an hour, watching the steady rise and fall of his chest and the sleep tremors that sometimes overtook him. On a whim, she reached out and touched his hair, lightly so as not to disturb him. It was just hair. It felt no different from her own. She touched it again, and he stirred, mumbled and rolled away.

After he woke up, the days that followed unfolded in a pattern of inevitability. Yashu gave up questioning or resisting and simply went along with what was happening. Here they were, in this empty place, marooned in a sea of snow, and she had a right to do as she pleased, she had a right to feel happiness, and with Gregory she felt happiness. His three-day disappearance had proved that beyond doubt. She had been bereft without him; ecstatic to have him back. She liked to look at his face, which was now clear of all the troubledness that had clouded it. She liked the little interludes of conversation they had, when they would compare their lives and find, surprisingly, more similarities than disparities. She liked it when Gregory, by accident or not, would happen to touch her – contact with those big, functional, strangely handsome hands of his left her skin tingling for minutes afterwards. She liked to see that he liked all this too.

Mr Ayn and Khollo were aware of what was going on. How could they not be, with the four of them living cheek-by-jowl like this? They kept their distance as best they could in the confined space. They gave Yashu and Gregory privacy, turned a discreet eye, didn't say or do any of the things that might make two young people falling in love shy or self-conscious. Every now and then Yashu thought Khollo was looking askance at her but she reckoned it was because they were no longer playing elements every evening. He was feeling usurped. She could live with that. As for Mr Ayn, the occasional unguarded glance from him told her all she needed to know. He approved.

And did the spirits approve? She had to think so. They, after all, had urged her to stick with Mr Ayn, and they wouldn't have if they were unaware of all the possible outcomes of that advice. In which case, Huaso also approved. Huaso would want her to be happy, she was sure. Her every memory of him had him leaping about, eager to please her, always keen to do what was best for her, pained if he thought he had offended her in any way. He would want her to find someone else now that she could not have him.

The inevitability steepened and deepened. It was like a riptide tugging her out over a coastal shelf. The sea bed fell away beneath her. There was nothing to do but swim and keep swimming.

One night, he came to her room. She had, in fact, been expecting this to happen for several nights. She had given him no direct encouragement, but had hoped he would realise of his own accord that she would not mind if he took this step. He tapped tentatively at her door; entered stealthily.

'Yes?'

'I, erm, I was cold. It's cold in my room. Freezing. I thought . . .'

Her answer was to pull back the bedclothes, letting in a gust of chilly air, and him.

They nestled together, Gregory fitting himself against the contours of her body, chest to back. All night they lay like that, in the sublimeness of shared warmth. They remained fully clothed. Nothing sexual occurred. Nothing had to. The mountainside seemed miles away. The rest of the lodge did not exist. There was just this room, this bed, and the two of them in it, a pair of bodies fused so perfectly that Yashu could not tell what was her and what was Gregory, where she ended and he began.

Sometime in the heart of the night he told her about killing his brother, clearly assuming that she didn't already know about this. He told her it had been an accident and he had blamed himself for it when he shouldn't have. The matter, though, was settled now, he said. Everything was in balance again.

She listened and said nothing, just hugged him and hung on to him. *Of course*, she thought. *Of course it was an accident.* Instinctively she had known that all along. Gregory was no killer.

When she awoke, he was gone. He must have made a surreptitious exit before dawn, returning to his room so that the other two would not know where he had been. She felt empty, something missing. She rolled into the depression left in the mattress by his weight. She felt better.

He came back the next night, and the one after.

Inevitability.

The waft of his breath against her neck. The shifting of his hands, so that they were touching (but not quite) where she wanted them (but not quite) to touch her. The stir of his hips and thighs against hers.

Inevitability.

His lips on her shoulder. The fingers, so hard, that stroked her arm, her cheek, her leg. The urgency, the heat-rhythm she could feel starting to build. Pulsing.

Inevitability.

She turned over. Clothes were wrestled off, rustling, discarded, between frantic crushing kisses.

The moon was high and full outside. Its light, glowing on the snow, beamed through the window and bathed the bedroom in silver.

Gregory was on top. Yashu's fingernails dug into the skin of his back.

He lowered himself.

She raised herself.

A surge.

Pain, then no pain.

Inevitability.

Water.

Waves.

And all was liquid.

All was flow.

Mala.

Mala.

Mala.

AYN

Well.

What can I say.

To put it mildly – what a night.

If I hadn't known we were going to survive, I wouldn't have put money on it. Talk about the 'teeth of the 'Storm'. Really, it seemed like some gigantic creature had the lodge in its jaws and was shaking it from side to side. Looking out of these windows was like looking right down its maw. And the lightning flashes. I still have the after-images in my eyes. If I blink rapidly I can see them. Like bright blue roots penetrating soil.

Look, several of the windowpanes are cracked. That takes some doing. This is thick and costly glass, with a high lead content. Only the 'Storm could do that.

But I must ask, how were things down in the cellar? Everyone all right?

['Everyone is as well as can be expected.']

Good, good. Ah, hear that? A rumble. Much fainter than the last one. North-west of here. Damentaine's probably going to get another pasting. Poor Damentaine. Traven Keech once said— But it doesn't matter what Traven Keech once said. Enough of all that. Everything's nearly over. My time is nearly over. Soon, that rainbow will be appearing, and I shall exit the lodge to go and look at it. I can see it in my mind's eye already, and the mirror rainbow that gleams in the lake. A near-perfect circle of colour. We have come to where we began.

Why do I not simply stay put? Why do I not try and buck destiny by keeping my backside firmly in this chair and refusing to go outside?

Well, I could. I could.

But I won't. For, surely, the measure of a man isn't just how he lives but how he dies. If he steps out to face death with his head held high and his conscience clear, then he can be said to have lived well. I will not cower abjectly. I will meet my end with a confident smile.

The question I suppose I should ask is why I must be murdered at all. What have I done to upset him so? How have I offended him? I can't imagine. I'm referring to Gregory, of course. Last night we parted company on good terms. In fact, he tried to talk me out of spending the night up here, saying I should shelter down in the cellar with the rest of you. He was concerned for my welfare, anxious that I should not come to harm. I don't think it allayed his fears much when I told him that the Worldstorm would not be killing any of us.

Tell me, Khollo, do you perhaps have the solution to this riddle?

[I said I did not.] ·

Then there it is. Nothing I can do. I shall just have to accept that overnight the boy has developed a hatred of me as intense as it is inexplicable. One last mystery as I head towards the greatest mystery of all.

Besides, is there anything worthwhile that is brought into this world without sacrifice and suffering?

Now then, Khollo, as agreed you'll give me a suitable burial, yes? Yes. Good. And, no less important, you will at the first opportunity commit these words of mine to paper and then find a publisher for them. You promise that? Thank you. And you'll smooth and correct and redact as you see fit, amending all solecisms and fixing the places where I have been anything less than articulate? Good fellow. I know I can rely on you to do a proper job. I chose my enshriner well.

And Yashu. How is she this morning? Unwell?

['Yes. Tired on top of feeling nauseous.']

Good. I mean, not for her, obviously, but . . . you know what I mean. She's a strong girl. She will bring that child to term, I am sure. But still, I'd like you to keep an eye on her if you will, Khollo. Make certain she gets back to I*il safe and sound. You'll find the last of the valuables in a drawer in my room. There'll be enough to get all three of you home.

Her child. My brainchild. An idea made flesh. The end of the Worldstorm, conceived all those months ago by Traven and me at Stonehaven. Here, at last, quickening in Yashu's womb. In a few months, to make an appearance.

Boy or girl, I wonder.

I shall never know.

There is so much I shall never know.

But now, let me stand. Stiff legs. Unwilling to move.

I shall descend the spiral staircase.

I shall cross the hall.

I shall step out onto the veranda.

I shall walk to the lake.

I shall stand, and look, and wait.

So much to know. So much unknown.

I bid you farewell, Khollo my friend. Look after my body, and my reputation, and my legacy. If you don't, who will? I've entrusted you with so much.

Treat me kindly.

Treat me well.

GREGORY

Glimmermonth – Sunmonth 688

Within a fortnight of leaving the Vail Mountains, Gregory was back in Stammeldon.

His time at the hunting lodge was already starting to seem like a dream, even as he crossed the western highlands of Jarraine, heading for the lowlands. With every mile he put between him and the Vails it became easier to believe that all that had happened up there in that white and rarefied place had happened in his imagination. Had happened to someone asleep.

And that was for the best. To think of it any other way would have been too raw, too painful. A dream. And like all dreams, it had had to end. He had had to wake up to reality.

Stammeldon, four years since he had last laid eyes on it, looked much as he recalled. In the hazy light of a spring morning its red roofs glistened. The Seray, its eternal companion, was sheathed in a drifting veil of river mist. From a distance Stammeldon appeared to be the thriving provincial town it had always been, the model of a modern industrial municipality.

Once inside the town limits, however, Gregory soon saw that things had changed. It was Sixthday, and as he traced a route through the commercial district he expected to find the place abuzz with shoppers. The shops were open and shoppers were indeed out and about, but abuzz? That was hardly the description for the subdued faces he saw, the slow gait of the housewives and servants with their grocery baskets, the incurious gaze with which people eyed wares in windows. There was no enthusiasm in evidence, none of the customary Sixthday morning bustle (Freeday tomorrow, and food must be bought, and perhaps a new item of clothing, and something nice for the children).

Moving on, he found that the same mood prevailed in the lower quarter of town, and in the upper. Everybody was doing what they normally did – working, walking, meeting – but it was as if they no longer knew quite why. They were acting out of habit, going through the motions. Their expressions, he thought, were lost.

Nobody recognised him, but he wasn't surprised. He hadn't shaved in over two weeks, and he was taller and rangier than when anyone here last saw him. Those who did pay him any heed frowned. He knew how he must look, with his worn-out shoes and disintegrating clothes and the dust of the road seamed into his face. A vagabond. If he hadn't been walking with such obvious purpose, no doubt several people would have invited him to hurry on out of their town as fast as possible.

Familiar streets eventually led him to Tempest's Bane.

The house's outer wall was besmirched with painted graffiti – ugly accusations, mostly about Tremond Brazier, a few about Mayor Bringlight. These looked relatively fresh but there were indications of older graffiti too, scorch-marks on the brickwork where other such slogans had been burned away.

Gregory tried the gate, not thinking it would be unbarred, but it was. It swung ponderously inward, and he entered the garden.

The garden, thankfully, was unchanged. The layout and general tidiness were just as he remembered and just as they should be. The lawn was green and springy as sponge, the leaves on the trees seemed new-minted, the flowers gleamed with springtime brightness.

The house itself, however, was not in such good order. He noticed holes in many of the windows – perfect circles melted out of the glass and lead – and the front door was warped and blackened. The door, in fact, was so badly damaged that he was amazed it was still hanging on its hinges. But more amazing, and more puzzling, was why it and the perforated windows had not been repaired.

He nudged the door, and it budged, grudgingly. The house was quiet and gloomy inside. He waited in the hallway, expecting someone to come. A servant. One or other of his parents. Someone must have heard him enter.

No one came.

He called out, and there was no reply, and then there was. A querulous voice from upstairs. It took him a moment to recognise it as his mother's.

'Who is it?'

'Me. It's Gregory.'

He heard what he thought was a gasp, then a rustle of activity. He went to the foot of the stairs and peered up, noting that the paint on the banisters was browned and bubbled in several places. He noted, at the same time, that a faint, acrid odour permeated the whole house: the smell of burnt things.

His mother appeared at the head of the stairs, draping a silk robe over her nightgown as she came into view. Her hair was tied back but she had not made a good job of it. Several strands hung wild. Gregory saw streaks of silver amid the auburn.

She looked down at him, and her haggard eyes registered disbelief. *This isn't my son. It can't be.* Then, after further scrutiny, she saw past the beard, the extra foot of height, the breadth of the shoulders, to the little boy she remembered.

She swayed and collapsed to her knees, and if Gregory had been a split second slower off the mark when sprinting up to catch her, she might well have tumbled down the stairs.

'I'm alone,' she said. 'Have been for six weeks. They've all gone. The servants. Cook. The gardeners. Couldn't afford to keep them on, even if they had been willing to stay. It was Trem. Trem scared them away. When he started setting fire to things. To *everything*.'

Gregory had helped her back to the master bedroom. He had sat her in bed, propped up the pillows behind her, fetched her a glass of water, and tried not to be shocked by just how extensive the damage to the house was. The bedroom walls were pocked with black craters, plaster burned away to expose the brickwork beneath. The bedroom furniture, and the furniture in all the rooms he had passed through on his way to the kitchen, had been charred. Some items were worse off than others but few had escaped intact. Even the crockery and the cooking utensils in the kitchen had not been spared. He had had a hard time finding a glass that wasn't fire-cracked or partly melted.

'It began when Jarnley Bringlight returned from Penresford,' his mother continued. 'We knew already. What Jarnley had done. That awful man! How he had used everybody, manipulated everybody. How he had wiped Penresford out. The barges came back a week before he did, and everyone on them was saying that Jarnley had provoked the Penresfordians and the Penresfordians had retaliated, and then . . . But you must know this already.'

Gregory nodded. 'I was there.'

'Yes, you were. Oh, Gregory! My son. My boy.' She began to weep, and Gregory stroked her arm till the weeping subsided. 'But when Jarnley came back he – he just wouldn't accept that he had done anything wrong. There were bad scenes at the town hall. Crowds gathered outside. There were placards and protests. I'll say this, though, it wasn't just Earth Inclined complaining, it was everyone. They wanted Jarnley impeached, they wanted his resignation, and he kept putting out statements protesting his innocence. "Only doing my job", that sort of thing. That just served to antagonise everyone further, and it got worse when Stev Wilkley came down from Charne with several other parliamentary representatives with a brief from the rime Minister to get to the bottom of the affair. Furniss investigated, asked around, spoke to people. He even spoke to your father. And he announced his conclusions pretty quickly, and they were damning. They placed responsibility for the Battle of Penresford squarely on our mayor's shoulders, but some of it, unfortunately, on your father's as well. That was when that horrible graffiti started appearing on the wall outside. Every time we burned one lot off, something else would get painted on. Or even scorched on, which was worse. More of an insult, coming from our own Inclination. Your father was already in a bad way by then. Because of Willem, and you.'

'Because I'm supposed to have killed Willem?'

'We knew it was an accident. Not at first, admittedly. We didn't know anything at first except that you, Willem and Reehan Bringlight were all missing. We assumed the worst, and they were hollow, awful days. We spent them doing nothing, not moving, just waiting for news. Something, anything. We hoped. We held out hope. We kept hoping. Sam was down at the telepath bureau every day, every hour almost. And slowly news started to come in, in dribs and drabs. First that Willem was dead and Reehan was alive. Then that they were hunting for you on suspicion of having killed Willem. I didn't believe it for one minute, of course. I knew you hadn't. I knew it must be a mistake, you would never have done such a thing, not your own brother. Trem, though . . . Your father didn't know what to believe, and I could see it was tearing him apart. He kept saying it was his fault, he had done this, he had destroyed his family. I wish I could have comforted him but I couldn't find it in me because, well, he was right. It *was* his fault. What I did instead was ask Sam to go down to Penresford and find out whatever he could. Sam was already half out of his mind with worry. There was still so much confusion down there and he'd heard nothing about his brother and family and he was desperate. So off he went. And while he was gone, Jarnley Bringlight paid a visit.'

She paused, recollecting the event with a curl of her lip.

'That bastard. I could have incinerated him where he stood. Ought to have. He shambled in, and to start with he was behaving like it was just an ordinary social call, hello, how pleasant to see you, and so on, but soon he had set to work on your father. I eavesdropped outside your father's study and Jarnley was saying things like "We have to stick together in this, Tremond" and "I have a son too, you know, and I'm worried sick about him, he's somewhere out in the highlands, I've no idea where". Your father, to his credit, sent him away pretty sharpish. And as he showed him to the door, I remember Jarnley's parting words. All his pretence, all his arrogant showiness, had fallen away by then. I was there and I saw his face as he tried one last time to win your father over. He was pleading. Your father, he said, was his only potential ally in all the world. "They're closing in on me," he said. "I won't survive this. And I have no one. No one. Even my own son has turned on me. Do you know how humiliating that is? Yes, you probably do. And the whole town is baying for my blood. Yours too. Together we could get through this. Separately, we're both doomed. Tremond! Tremond! Help me!" And your father just closed the door on him, and put his back to the door, and for a long time stayed there, didn't move, stared at the floor, and then finally straightened up. I could see how tempted he had been. Maybe Jarnley was right, maybe together they could have weathered out that particular storm. But your father had decided it was not to be.

'That was the last we saw of Jarnley Bringlight. The last anyone saw. He went home and that very night . . . Well, the police report said it was spontaneous human combustion, but we all know what that's a euphemism for, don't we? Someone found him the next morning, his housekeeper I think, sprawled on his living-room carpet. Most of his torso was ashes. What it must take, to do that to yourself. What you must go through.

'Still, very hard to shed a tear for that man. It's Reehan I feel sorry for, wherever he is. Poor boy, he has no idea that his father is dead. I wonder if he's going to turn up soon. They say he was still looking for you when everyone else called off the search. He never found you, I take it.'

Gregory shook his head and said nothing. If you believed in a life after this one, then Reehan certainly knew his father was dead by now.

'Then Sam came back,' his mother resumed, 'and the news he brought was both good and bad. He looked awful. Hollow-eyed. Pale. His brother was among the dead at Penresford. The rest of his brother's family, however, were fine. And one of his nephews, I forget the boy's name, had a story to tell. About Willem, and Reehan, and you.'

'Ven?'

'Yes, that was him.'

So Ven was all right. And Eda and Garla and the rest of the Goves.

'And the story he had to tell . . . Well, I don't need to say, do I? Again, you were there. Right there. And Gregory? For what it's worth, I forgive you. No, not even that. That makes it sound like you did something wrong. How could you have known? You were innocent. You did the wrong thing but for all the right reasons. I love you. That's really all that matters, all that needs to be said. I never said it often enough but I will from now on, I promise. Every day. I love you. I love you.'

Gregory fought against it; failed. For several minutes he lay in his mother's arms, crying as he hadn't cried since he was little. His mother cried too.

Master Ergall was wrong. You should feel. You should feel *everything*.

'There isn't a lot more to tell,' his mother said eventually. 'Since I never believed you were guilty of what they said you'd done, I felt no different about anything. Whereas your father . . . He hadn't had that conviction, and he ought to have, and that – that was what finally broke him. That and the fact that Sam had gone straight back to Penresford and refused to have anything to do with him any more. And there was so much pressure on him now that Jarnley was no longer around. *Someone* had to be held accountable for Penresford, and with the main culprit out of the picture, the prime aider and abetter was pushed to the front. All at once it was Tremond Brazier everyone was after. Stev Wilkley came back here for a second visit, and this time he was apologetic but firm. There was mention of legal proceedings. Prosecution. Wilkley said that he would do everything he could to get your father off the hook but implied that the prospects weren't good. The authorities needed to be seen to be doing something. A big sacrifice was needed to appease people. And your father took this on board. He accepted it. He seemed calm. Resigned.

'And then all this began.' She indicated the cratered walls, the scorched furnishings, the holed windows. 'Your father went around systematically loosing off fireballs, burning everything he could find. Within a couple of days all the staff had fled – and who can blame them? And then . . .'

'Where is he now, Mum?' Gregory asked. 'Is he over at the brick-fields?'

'The brickfields? You should go and take a look sometime. If you think this place is bad, you should see what your father did there. The brickfields don't exist any more, not in any meaningful sense. So no, he isn't there.'

'Where, then?'

'Where do you think?'

For several days Gregory looked after his mother. There was a bit of cash in the house with which to buy food, and a bit more in the bank. His mother had some modest savings of her own which she was living off. He cooked for her and made sure she ate. She had lost weight. She had not been taking care of herself. Her only occupation – the only reason she ever got dressed – was tending the garden. She was out there almost every day, pruning, weeding, trimming, clipping, tying up. The house was beyond redemption but the garden wasn't. Maintaining order in it maintained some order in her life too.

Meanwhile, Gregory tried to arrange to see his father. He knew it was next to impossible. The committal had been carried out in strict accordance with regulations. Three witnesses, all former members of the Tempest's Bane domestic staff, had signed sworn, sooth-seen statements attesting to Tremond Brazier's pyromaniacal behaviour. A tribunal had been held prior to the committal order being given. The lawyer whose services Gregory enlisted looked over the paperwork and pronounced it watertight. There wasn't the tiniest loophole in it that might be exploited. He said, however, that Gregory could try and lodge an appeal on emotional grounds. The chances of success were infinitesimally small, but given the exceptional circumstances, the recent local turmoil, the fact that Gregory had not actually been present when his father was taken away . . . It was a statutory right that all family members who wished to be there should be there when someone was committed. Perhaps, the lawyer said, he could work that angle.

It took time, money, persistence, patience, money, several meetings with officials, and yet more money, but eventually, to the surprise of all, not least the lawyer, Gregory won his appeal. The lawyer, who came post-haste from the appeal hearing to convey the verdict, said a significant contributory factor had been the Brazier family's history within the community and the good standing in which, till lately, they had been held.

On the tenth of Sprinklemonth, an overcast, rain-flecked day, Gregory took his permit of visitation rights and set off for the Stammeldon Sanatorium.

'You will have quarter of an hour,' the chief custodian said, reeling off the regulations as he escorted Gregory along a cold, clammy corridor. 'Not one minute more. You will be left unattended to hold a conversation with the inmate. You will sit outside the cell door on the stool provided. You will have no physical or visual contact with the inmate. If you are caught initiating such contact you will be in breach of your visitation rights and subject to the severest of civil penalties. Is that understood?'

'Absolutely,' Gregory said, tight-lipped.

'These conditions are imposed on you as much for your own safety as anything,' the chief custodian added as, with a jangle of keys, he unlocked a cast-iron door and ushered Gregory into a second, colder, clammier corridor. 'In this place, safety is paramount. We're dealing with society's most dangerous human beings here. Whether they mean to be dangerous or not isn't for me to say. My job is to ensure they stay contained and segregated for the rest of their natural lives and to see to it that my staff – and the very occasional visitor – come to no harm. Now then . . .'

Another cast-iron door led to a staircase, which led in turn to a further corridor which was the coldest and clammiest yet. Doors were inset into either wall at regular intervals. Pipes snaked across the ceiling, some running in parallel, others intersecting at four-way junctions. They emitted a constant low gurgle. There were lanterns hung from sconces but only a couple were lit, so that the corridor was crepuscular and cave-like. Fleetingly Gregory remembered the Extraordinaries who lived in the ravine. An age ago. Part of the dream.

Near the end, positioned outside one of the doors, was the stool the chief custodian had mentioned. He directed Gregory to it, then with a frown sparked the nearest lantern into life. From the front pocket of his black overalls he took out a fob watch, consulted the dial, reminded Gregory that he had fifteen minutes only, and banged hard on the door with his fist.

'Tremond Brazier! Your guest is here.'

No sound came from within, although there was the odd muted mutter from some of the nearby cells and a muffled, plaintive cry from the cell next door to Gregory's father's. Gregory waited till the chief custodian had gone, then banged on the door again. His fist drew a sharper, more reverberant ring than the other man's had.

'Dad,' he said.

Still no sound. He studied the door, with its rivets, its reinforcing bands, its undeniable aura of solidity. There was a sliding hatch at floor level, double-bolted. Food went in that way, he presumed, and the empty tray back out. Once the door was closed on the inmate, only that hatch was ever opened.

'Dad?'

After all that effort, was this a wasted journey? Would his father refuse to speak to him?

'Gregory.'

The voice was dim and barely audible, as though it were coming from somewhere deep underground.

'Yes, Dad.'

'How – how did you manage this? I'm impressed.'

'It wasn't easy. I think it was sort of a last favour from the town to our family. I think we've used up whatever goodwill there was still left towards the Braziers.'

'You sound so different. Not like I remember at all. I didn't think it was you.'

'It's me.'

'I know. But when they told me yesterday you were coming, I thought it was just a joke. I thought they were playing a trick on me. But it *is* you.'

'Dad . . . You shouldn' t have done this.'

'What?'

'Pretended to be a pyromaniac. You shouldn't have done this to yourself. Or to Mum. You should have faced them.'

'Faced them? What for? They were going to tear me down. They were going to ruin me. I would never have got a fair hearing at any trial. This way . . . This way was for the best. This way I still have some dignity left. Not much, I admit, but some. But you – what have you been doing? Where have you been all these months?'

Gregory told him, keeping it as succinct as possible, aware that time was limited and precious. There were a few things he omitted. At no point, for instance, did he mention Reehan Bringlight. Why talk of death? There had been too much death, and in this place, which was kind of a living death for its inhabitants, the topic seemed more than usually inappropriate. Nor did he mention the circumstances under which he had left the hunting lodge in the Vails. How the dream had become tainted. He merely spoke of the 'Storm bringing things to an end, as the 'Storm usually did.

'You've been through the mill, haven't you?' said his father. 'And all thanks to me. I did this to you. And Willem, too. What happened with him. All my fault. Because I was weak and vain. Gregory, I can't even begin to say how sorry I am.'

'You don't have to. There's no need.'

'I don't expect you to forgive me.'

'There's nothing to forgive. It's done now.'

'Gregory . . .'

Soft sounds from the other side of the door. Throaty sounds, similar to the churning of the water through the pipes. Gregory said nothing; sat in the damp, ill-lit corridor; waited.

'Gregory? Son?'

'Yes, Dad?'

'Two things. You'll take care of your mother, won't you? I didn't – I didn't make provision for her before I left.'

'Of course I will. It's all sorted out. I know what we're going to do. No need to worry about her.'

'Good. Good lad.'

'What's the other thing?'

'I shouldn't ask this, but . . . You see the hatch. At the bottom of the door?'

'Yes.'

'Would you . . . ? No. Stupid idea. Don't do it. Not worth the risk.'

Gregory cast a quick glance either way along the corridor, then got down on his knees and slowly, carefully, eased back both bolts and slid the hatch open. A moment later, his father's hand appeared in the slot, groping outwards. Gregory reached for it.

His father's hand was soft and small and pale, his own scarred and hardened and large. His father let his hand be cradled by Gregory's. Gregory held it, supported it, returned its grip. For as long as he dared, he let their hands remain in contact, and then he disentangled them and, with the utmost reluctance, slid the hatch shut and bolted it.

In late Brightmonth, with their bags packed, Gregory and his mother waited for a hired wagon to come and take them to the Stammeldon docks. Marita Brazier took one last stroll around the garden, bidding it farewell. There was no saying when she would be back to tend it. If she did come back at all, she would return to an overgrown mess, nature run riot behind the thirty-foot wall of Tempest's Bane.

Gregory, for his part, had just one thing to do before they departed, also in the garden. He sought out the Divided Tree. There, still lodged in its fork, was the stone he had hurled at it almost exactly four years ago. The stone had been impossible to prise out then. Now, hooking his toughened index finger around it, he got it free with no effort at all.

He squatted down, dug a grave for the stone in the earth, and buried it.

Penresford was rising again. There wasn't yet a town but there was the skeleton of a town. The frames of houses were in place, an intricate three-dimensional lattice of uprights and joists whose gaps would shortly be filled in with planking and roof shingles. The timber had been bought with money paid from the Stammeldon municipal coffers. These reparations had been mandated by an act of parliament, but in truth the Stammeldoners did not need to be compelled to hand over the money. They did not begrudge one leaf of it. With it went their collective guilt.

The Penresfordians had overwintered in Hallawye, crowding into every spare corner and cranny of that town. It had been a cramped and sometimes squabblesome few months, and the warmer weather had arrived not a day too soon. Now, most of them were camped in tents on the hillside to the south. The resurrection of their town was a communal effort. Every evening they would look down with pride and hope on the new Penresford taking shape on the site of the old.

Marita Brazier did not enjoy living in a tent and made no bones about it. She complained about the lack of decent sanitation, the pain her back gave her every morning after a night on hard ground, and the impossibility of keeping clothes properly laundered under such conditions. But there was in her a fiercely pragmatic streak, a willingness to make the best she could of any situation. Keeping up appearances as a wealthy man's wife was as hard, in its way, as coping without life's luxuries. There had always been some form of sacrifice in her life.

Moreover, she was able to make herself useful, even indispensable. Her services as an incendiary were much in demand – cooking-fires and so on – and that was why the Penresfordians were able to put up with her complaining. The fact that she was Gregory's mother also helped.

She and Gregory shared a small section of the campsite with the Goves. She helped Garla mind the younger children during the day while the older children and Sam and Gregory were down at the town, doing their bit. She complained about the Gove offspring, of course. All that noise and rambunctiousness. But Gregory could tell she had grown fond of them, and some of the very smallest of them showed a marked preference for her over their mother. She wasn't, for one thing, as free with the physical admonishment.

Gregory himself had established something with Eda Gove. He didn't know yet what it was and didn't think she did either, but there was a rapport there, a kind of understanding. It wouldn't be able to amount to more, he felt, until the town was completely rebuilt. That was everyone's primary goal. Outside that, other concerns had to wait. But when there was a Penresford again, then he would pursue her. He knew what to do now. There was a faint, cherished memory of an islander girl whom he had had to abandon. There was that at the back of his mind as an example and as a caution, a reason to take things as they came, a lesson in what it meant to love and be loved.

Carpentry was good work, work to which someone with an indestructible's abilities and an indestructible's hands was well suited. Under the guidance of wiser and more skilled people than himself, Gregory learned the correct use of saw, plane and chisel and how to peg and dovetail and tongue-and-groove. His contributions to the rebuilding were welcomed and favourably remarked on. One of those overseeing his efforts said that he would make a good carpenter's apprentice. He had the patience, the diligence, a natural aptitude.

It could be a career for him, Gregory thought. Construction, the family trade, but not with bricks, with wood. Not using earth and fire but his own muscles, the sweat of his brow. A different kind of living for a Brazier but a no less honourable one.

Day by day, in the heat of the summer sun, Penresford re-grew.

YASHU

At first, she wasn't sure. Her bleeding had not come when it ought to. Counting back, her last menstruation had been more than four weeks ago, closer on five. But then, since the start of winter her cycle had become erratic. It was the snow, she thought. This extended *usurraña* she was living through. She was separated from the sea tides and all the other rhythms she was used to. And she knew, too, that if you weren't eating properly – and the four of them were eating adequately but not properly – it could throw your cycle out and even dry it up altogether, the body conserving its precious fluids.

No, she wasn't sure. Deep down, however, she was. She knew. Every instinct she had was telling her.

She decided to say nothing to Gregory until it was definite and undeniable. She had no idea how he would react and she didn't want to alarm him, especially if it came to nothing in the end, as was possible. You could be pregnant one moment, not pregnant the next. The process could start and then, for no appreciable cause, stop.

It troubled her that she felt she had to keep it a secret from him. Were he Huaso, she wouldn't have hesitated about telling him. Huaso, without question, would have been delighted. Gregory's response was less predictable. She trusted him, loved him, but there was still a level at which she was uncertain about him. The thought preyed on her that if they hadn't been stuck up here in the mountains he might never have looked twice at her. She believed it when he told her he loved her, everything he said to her rang with sincerity, and yet their present circumstances had played a major role in bringing them together and from time to time she couldn't help wondering how different things would have been if Mr Ayn hadn't entered their lives and swept them both along in his wake – if they had just met casually somewhere by accident (unlikely as that would have been). So many forces had acted on them from outside to get them to this place of isolation and keep them here. It seemed to her, in her more fanciful moments, that they were the victims of some kind of plan, almost. As though they were two elements tiles that had been laid carefully and thoughtfully into position.

And now this. If she *was* pregnant (and she was), what would they do? Would they stay together? Where would they go? Where would they live?

There were too many questions, too many unknowns. She resolved to put a brave face on it. Say nothing. Behave as normal. That was *mala*.

Around this time, Mr Ayn began holding daily meetings with Khollo in the lodge's upstairs room. Every morning they were up there for an hour, sometimes two, Mr Ayn talking, Khollo sometimes interjecting but otherwise silent. This was as much as she heard coming from the room, the sound of their voices. She wasn't terribly interested in hearing what was actually being said. The purpose of the meetings, as Mr Ayn explained, was to set down an account of his travels so far and at the same time enshrine some of his thoughts and opinions, with a view to possible publication later. 'After all,' he said, 'we're not going to be here much longer, are we now? Spring is approaching. A few more days and the way back down will be clear, I reckon. Might as well take this opportunity while I can.'

Spring was indeed approaching. The lake ice had melted, surprisingly suddenly, almost overnight. Snow still lay thick on the ground but it had a brittleness to it, a fragility, that seemed to suggest its lifespan was near an end. There was a crust on top that crumbled to the touch. Beneath, it was powdery and insubstantial.

The prospect of being able to leave was an exciting one. Yashu would have been completely happy about it but for two things: the pregnancy, of course, with all its attendant uncertainties, and also Gregory. He kept saying how much he was looking forward to getting out of here and returning, as he put it, 'to civilisation'. She wanted to know, but was afraid to ask, what he meant by 'civilisation' and whether or not it included her. She would not normally have been so reticent but there was such a lot riding on the answer, more than Gregory could know, and if he said the slightest thing wrong . . . Worse, if he out-and-out lied to her . . .

And then, just when her life didn't need to be made any harder, the dizzy spells started. This was confirmation of what she suspected (knew) but that didn't make it any more welcome. Without warning, she would feel drained, light-headed, as if she were falling down a well shaft. If there was someone else in the room, she would make an excuse and leave. She never actually collapsed in front of anybody, and each dizzy spell lasted only a few minutes, so no suspicions were aroused. Only Gregory noticed anything amiss with her, saying one day that she looked pale. Was she all right? Yashu, remembering her conversation with the two Trustees about lack of nourishment, told him she probably wasn't getting enough food. And it was true. Supplies certainly were running low. For all that they had been careful, the cellar was nearly empty of everything except wine. Gregory nodded, and the next morning went off on another of his hunting trips. He was unsuccessful, finding no deer, but she appreciated the attempt and wondered if she had been wrong in her judgement of him. Perhaps now was the time to come clean and tell him. He ought to know.

No. A few more days. Wait.

Then she woke up one morning feeling distinctly unwell. Gregory was still in the habit of leaving her room well before dawn, so she didn't have to worry about disturbing him as she scrambled out of bed. She made it to the outhouse in time, and afterwards clawed up some snow to rinse her mouth out with. As she traipsed miserably back to the lodge, she pondered the prospect of motherhood. This was it, the whole of her future committed to the raising of a child. Not to mention the birth itself. On the mainland, with recuperators on hand to help, the chances of giving birth safely and successfully were high. On Li*issua, the risks to both mother and baby were grave. Yet there was no question about it, if she was to bring this baby to term she would do so on I*il, with Liyalu by her side from beginning to end. Would Gregory want that? To go to I*il with her? I*il, surely, was not what someone like him, a mainlander through and through, would regard as 'civilisation'. Far from it.

Still gripped with indecision, she said nothing to him all day, but by evening she had resolved to tell him in bed that night. She would have, but at supper Mr Ayn happened to mention that the Worldstorm was on its way. Tomorrow it would be visiting them. Tomorrow night, he said, was going to be a very dark and stormy night indeed.

When Gregory came to her room, she didn't want to make love and she didn't want to talk. She just wanted to lie and hold him and be held.

'Don't you worry about the 'Storm,' he told her, gallantly. 'I'll look after you. I'll protect you.'

If only.

Her dreams were tormented. She was back in Liyalu's cottage, feeling the thunder trying to rip the earth open. Suddenly the cottage was whisked away, snapped clean off its foundations. She saw it whirling into the sky, and she and her aunt were left on the bare hillside, clinging on for dear life. Liyalu's grip failed her and she was gone. Only Yashu remained, with her fingers dug into the ground, the 'Storm wrenching at her, trying to pull her free. And then she was falling. Falling upwards. Soaring into the black boiling sky. Lightning shattered around her. Winds tossed her to and fro. The 'Storm was playing with her like a killer whale playing with the body of a seal pup before devouring it, flicking her to and fro, delighting in her helplessness . . .

She woke. It was late. The morning was beautifully clear. Not a hint of the tumult Mr Ayn said was coming.

But as the day wore on, the ominous signs started to appear. Yashu stood on the veranda and watched, occasionally going out into the open to get a better view, although the lake's edge was as far as she wandered, no further than that. First there was a slight darkening of the sky, as though smoke from an immense bonfire was hazing the sun. Then there was the wet, coppery smell in the air and the way the wind began to blow in stop-start eddies and swirls. The surface of the lake broke up into restless patterns – semicircles, curlicues, even the odd small spiral. More sinisterly, at times the wind dropped and the lake became absolutely still, like a sheet of onyx. Not a wavelet, not a ripple disturbed it. Water should not be so motionless.

By mid-afternoon distant grinds of thunder could be heard, echoing from the north. Gregory joined her on the veranda and cocked an ear. The thunder seemed to be coming no nearer but then all at once there would be a peal of it louder than any previous. Soon this level of volume had become the norm and then there would be a single, even louder peal. And so on. The 'Storm was prowling towards them, letting out snarls to let them know it was on its way.

'Following the line of the Vails,' Gregory said. 'I've heard it does that sometimes when it's heading south. Stalks along them like a cat on a fence. It may miss us, though. There's always Damentaine. The 'Storm loves Damentaine.'

'Mr Ayn seems to think it won't miss us.'

'I was just trying to be encouraging.'

'Well, don't bother. You didn't mean it.'

'Yashu?' He looked at her with concern. 'Are you OK? You've really not been yourself lately. Is it me? Have I done something to upset you?'

'The Worldstorm's coming and I don't want to be here and – and—' That was reason enough. She didn't have to say any more. 'Just leave me alone, please.'

Reluctantly, baffled, he did as asked.

And now the sky was sulphurous, and the clouds along the 'Storm's leading edge hove into view, their yellow tips like talons. Beneath her apprehension Yashu felt a dull loathing. Death and change, those were the two things the 'Storm always brought. This was the third time it had impinged on her life. Why her? Hadn't it done enough to her already? But of course the 'Storm didn't care about her, it hadn't singled her out for special attention. It was just the Worldstorm, the enemy of all. Anyone who believed it was their personal foe or set themselves up in opposition to it was destined to come off badly. That was the moral of a number of Li*issuan stories, including the tale of Scornful Uesho and the last ever escapade of Ra*aisheelo, who in his drunken old age, with his strength waning, challenged the 'Storm to a wrestling match. Only Finder-Founder Oriñaho had ever stood up to the 'Storm and won, but then he was the exception that proved the rule. No one else was Oriñaho. No one could be.

Now there wasn't a scrap of clear sky overhead. The rocky bowl in which the lake and lodge were situated was lidded with grey-and-yellow ferment. The wind was making the veranda shudder. The far-off pines were thrashing.

Khollo emerged from indoors. 'It's time,' he said. 'We need to get downstairs.'

In the hall, Gregory was at the foot of the spiral staircase, importuning Mr Ayn, was who halfway up.

'You can't go up there,' Gregory said. 'It's craziness. You need to be in the cellar, with us.'

'I shall be fine,' Mr Ayn replied. 'Believe me, I've foreseen it. First thing tomorrow, I step out of the lodge and there's a rainbow overhead and all is well, I'm well, not a scratch on me.'

'But why? Why go up there at all?'

'Can you imagine it? To sit and see the 'Storm all around you. To watch it in all its rage and immensity. Who'd pass up the chance of that?'

So saying, he brusquely turned and mounted the remaining stairs. As his feet disappeared from view, Khollo made for the trapdoor and hauled it open.

'Come on,' he said to Yashu and Gregory, with an ushering gesture.

With the trapdoor shut, the cellar was in perfect darkness. Yashu heard Khollo fumble with a box of matches. A paraffin lantern was lit, throwing its uneven glow outward. There were she and Gregory, seated with their backs to one wall of the cellar. There was Khollo, taking his place against the opposite wall. Around them, the dimpled bases of wine bottles in their racks flickered and twitched like a host of observing eyes.

The 'Storm got nearer. The ground trembled at its tread. The bottles shivered, tinkling. Yashu felt Gregory's hand cover hers on the floor. She looked across to see Khollo staring at them – specifically, at their joined hands. She couldn't fathom his expression.

442

The 'Storm growled. The wine racks creaked. The trapdoor rattled overhead.

The 'Storm pounced. It was as though some large mass suddenly landed outside.

For the next few hours, everything was this: the ground quaking, the groaning of timbers, the thunderclaps that tumbled over one another in rapid succession. The lantern having given out, the very darkness itself seemed to ripple, the 'Storm's vibrations visible. Now and then, a jar or bottle would be shaken from its perch and crash to the floor somewhere in the cellar.

Then came a lull, a blessed, resounding stretch of quiet, which Yashu knew better than to think meant the 'Storm visit was over, but still she hoped, she hoped . . .

'Yashu. Gregory.'

Khollo's voice. Coming from just inches away. She envisaged him crouching on all fours directly in front of her and Gregory. From his tone she pictured an earnest, urgent look on his face.

'Yes?' said Gregory.

'I can't do this any more,' Khollo said. 'I can't be a part of this any more. Not now.'

'A part of what?' Yashu asked.

'I'm amazed neither of you has twigged. Then again, why should you? Elder Ayn is a highly persuasive and plausible man. And pre-visionaries are always good at making people do what they want them to do and make them think they themselves wanted to do it. The authority that comes with knowledge of the future . . .'

'What are you talking about?' Gregory said.

'Why do you think you're here?' said Khollo. 'Why are you with him? You two specifically?'

'I chose to travel with him,' Yashu said.

'Did you? Or did he just let you think you did? And you, Gregory. He pulled you out of that graveyard and made you come with him. Why?'

'I – I wasn't thinking clearly at the time. It seemed simpler just to go along. He was nice to me.'

'But there we were at Penresford. Elder Ayn's a previsionary. He knew he was going to find you there.'

'So? He helped me. He looked after me. Isn't that reason enough?'

'You, an Earther with Fire-Inclined parents. And you, Yashu, a sooth-seer from islander stock. Has nothing about that struck you as at all suspect? That . . . symmetry?'

'It was just chance,' Yashu said. But was it? All at once, doubts were welling up inside her. Nothing Khollo was saying was false. She was beginning to glimpse the shape of something that appalled her, sickened her.

'You're saying Nax brought us together for a reason?' said Gregory. 'But why? What for? What was he hoping to achieve?'

'You could call it so many things. A thought experiment. A mind game. He was hoping—'

A crash of thunder broke overhead. In its wake another rolled in, and another. Gregory shouted to Khollo, demanding to know more, desperate for an explanation, but Khollo either couldn't hear or had no desire to answer. The 'Storm, after its lull, was back with renewed ferocity, and it stamped and stomped and pounded so hard Yashu could barely think straight. Mr Ayn. Mr Ayn had used them. Manipulated them. She could see it – see the pattern of his manipulation. With hindsight, it was obvious. How they had travelled. Where. When. Whom they had encountered along the way. But what it all came back to was the question Gregory had asked: why. There had to be a why. This wasn't something Mr Ayn had done on a whim. Had he done it as a kind of experiment, to see if he could bring two opposites together? Something he could publish a book about and impress all his Inclination with? Or was it just some obscure Air joke, some high-and-mighty intellectual jape she didn't have a hope of understanding? She struggled to make sense of it, and at the same time clung to one small scrap of truth, namely that she and Gregory were in love, no matter how it had come about, manipulated or not, she loved him, he loved her; and all the while, the 'Storm crashed and the 'Storm roared and the 'Storm heaved, beating at the lodge, thumping at the Vail Mountains . . .

. . . and then was gone. Not a lull this time. There wasn't that feeling of a breath being held, of the 'Storm taking a moment to ponder its next assault. The 'Storm had retreated. The thunder was pulsing between peaks elsewhere. The wind was down to a sinuous hiss.

Yashu groped beside her, expecting to find Gregory there.

Gregory was not there.

She got up, and all at once nausea hit her. The floor seemed to leap up at her. She was on her knees. She was being sick. Then she was lying curled against the wall, panting, the taste and stench of her vomit strong in her throat.

'Yashu?' It was Khollo.

'Where's Gregory?'

'He's not here?'

'I don't think so.'

'I'll light a lantern.'

He did, and shone it all around. There was glass debris on the cellar floor. Slicks of wine. No sign of Gregory.

'He's left.'

'Obviously,' she sneered.

'I'm going up to see how things are.'

She would have gone with him but when she tried to raise her head everything wavered and wobbled. She had no choice but to lay her head down and keep it there. Pathetic. So helpless. This was not her.

Khollo was gone for a long time. In the end, Yashu tried lifting her head again and found that she could. She felt weak but not ill any more. She thought, *If this is what pregnancy's like, you can keep it.* Groggily she got to her knees, then her feet. The ladder up to the trapdoor looked twice its usual height. She clambered up it, hooking her arms over the rungs for added security. As she reached the trapdoor opening Khollo appeared above her. His face was ashen. He extended a hand to her. She noticed it was trembling. She swatted it aside and continued up the ladder unaided, slithering out onto the hall floorboards.

'Did you find him?' she said. 'Gregory?'

Khollo shook his head.

'What? What's happened?'

'Perhaps you should come and see.'

He led her out. They crossed the veranda. They walked toward the lake. What had yesterday been a snowfield was now an expanse of bare ground ribbed with long thin hummocks of snow. These reminded Yashu of the way sea foam could collect on a beach, shaped into scalloped ridges by the action of wind and wave. Overhead, glimmering, was a rainbow. Its colours were faint and growing fainter right before her eyes, the sky behind showing through. Finder-Founder Oriñaho had ordered the Worldstorm to leave a rainbow in its wake after every visit as a way of apologising to people, but the 'Storm obviously did not take kindly to being told what to do and only obliged sometimes, as now.

Nearing the lakeshore, Khollo faltered. He nerved himself with a deep breath and carried on.

Yashu saw why he had hesitated.

The body lay face-down, its head in the lake's shallows. For one heart-stilling moment Yashu thought it was Gregory. He had gone out into the 'Storm and been struck by lightning. Could a bolt of lightning kill an indestructible? Quite probably.

But those were Mr Ayn's boots. Those were Mr Ayn's tweed trousers. That was the blanket Mr Ayn liked to drape himself in.

And as she got closer, Yashu saw that no lightning bolt was

445

responsible for this death. There was a cavity in the side of Mr Ayn's head, a deep dent with a crimson crescent at one end where the skin was broken. Blood streaked one side of his face. His eye, the one she could see, was open underwater. Its white gleamed dully.

She didn't have to ask who had killed him, or why. She scanned around, hoping against hope to find Gregory still here, still within view, but she knew he had gone. He couldn't stay, not after this. He was down in the forest already, striding back to his precious civilisation. There, they would accept him among them. They would never have to know what he had done up here in the mountains, this savage act of vengeance. He himself could pretend it never happened. She knew him. She knew he had done this for her and she knew, having done it, he would never be able to look her in the eye again.

'I need to bury him,' Khollo said, thinly.

He went to the lodge and returned with the largest of the carving knives from the kitchen, the same one Yashu had employed on the deer carcasses. She had thought they would be carrying Mr Ayn's body out into the lake and letting it sink there, but 'bury', of course, meant something completely different for each kind of Flow.

Khollo hauled the body fully onto dry land, turned it over and set about undressing it.

'A little help?'

Yashu, reluctantly, lent a hand, propping the body up in a sitting position so that Khollo could draw its arms out of its sleeves. The body let out a gurgle as she lowered it down. Later, when it was fully naked, it emitted a long, relaxed-sounding fart. She didn't know whether to laugh or scream.

Khollo gripped the knife, nerving himself to proceed. 'You don't have to watch,' he said.

She was already feeling unwell, and her stomach was empty. She thought she could manage. Dry-mouthed, she told Khollo to get on with it.

He held the knife tip over Mr Ayn's throat. It quivered there for several seconds, then plunged in. The next moment, Khollo was on his knees by the lake, retching.

'I don't think I can,' he said over his shoulder. The knife still stuck out from Mr Ayn's throat, an ooze of blood welling up around its blade. Khollo's cheeks were a sickly yellow. 'I have to but I don't think I can.'

Yashu studied the corpse and the knife. It wouldn't be much different from skinning and gutting the deer.

She grabbed the knife handle. Khollo told her to make four basic incisions to begin with. From throat to sternum. Inwards under the right half of the ribcage. Inwards under the left. From crotch to sternum. She complied. Now, Khollo said, she could just cut and pare as she liked. The only thing that should remain whole was the head.

Grimacing, she began to cut, and then to hew, and then to hack. The more she thought about Mr Ayn, the fiercer her actions became. The reek, the fat, the innards, the blood – this was him, all he had been, all he ever would be. Her arms were sheathed to the elbows in gore. The knife twisted against bone, shuddered through gristle. She stopped only when Khollo grasped her shoulder.

'That's enough. That'll do.'

The remains were shapeless, a thing, not a man any more. Only the head was still recognisably Mr Ayn. His eyes were fixed upwards. His mouth was open in that unconvinced smile of his.

Yashu went to the lake and methodically washed herself clean. Khollo joined her, dousing his face with water.

The rainbow was gone. The sky was a pure and perfect blue.

KHOLLO

I have waited thirteen years to do as I promised and make a record of Elder Ayn's words. I have lived for every day of those thirteen years with the ineradicable memory of our journey together and our time in the mountains. I have held back from writing anything down for fear it would somehow justify, even legitimise, what he did. I have also held back for fear of incriminating myself.

I've taken this step now because it will be our son's Swim-Through-The-Rock soon. He is almost thirteen, and although he hasn't yet shown signs of entering puberty, his Flow ought to be appearing any day, and that has prompted me to set things down and put things in order. I hoped, by committing everything to paper, I might somehow diminish it in my memory. By being out there, on the page, there might be less of it in here, in my mind. I don't feel that that has worked but I do have a sense of . . . conclusion I suppose is the word. If nothing else, thirteen years on I have discharged my final duty to Elder Ayn.

I have, contrary to his request, not edited or smoothed his account in any way. I have left his words unexpurgated and I have left in my own comments and my dialogue with him because this text is not for anybody else to read. When I have finished writing this very last section, I shall bind the manuscript up in a folder and find somewhere safe to tuck it away. Behind a drawer, or perhaps in that crack in the bedroom wall, shoved in so deep that no one will find it.

Of course, by doing so I am betraying Elder Ayn. But then I betrayed him constantly in a number of small ways during our time together and, at the end, in one major way. Let's face it, I was the least loyal 'loyal servant' a man could have.

I write this seated at the kitchen table in Liyalu's cottage. It's called that still, Liyalu's cottage, even though Liyalu herself was taken away to the Great-Ocean-Beyond some ten years ago, or, if you prefer, died. Currently, Yashu is out shopping with the children over in Town-By-The-Dunes. The children will be begging her for treats from the

448

market stalls, even Huaso, who pretends he's too old for that sort of thing, but he'll be pestering just as hard as his little sister Kharona. Yashu will give in to them. She'll buy them sweetmeats of some kind – orange treacle fritters, perhaps, or sugar candies from the mainland – while telling them how bad such things are for you. She's stern with the children, they fear her, but she can't deny them anything.

They'll be home soon, so I need to wrap this up quickly. I've been writing it in short stints, whenever I get a chance to be alone in the house, which isn't often. The paper was hard to come by and hideously costly, the pen and ink too, but that's life on I*il for you. Items which in Durat or Stonehaven were commonplace are luxuries here. It's not easy by any means, being an islander, but I've adjusted. I don't miss the mainland. Durat I do miss sometimes, but not much. I*il is home.

I never expected to stay when Yashu and I came back here after leaving the mountains. I felt I had ruined everything. I believed she hated me. She had every right to. I, after all, had been complicit in Elder Ayn's deception. She ought to have despised me almost as much as she ended up despising him.

On our way down from the mountains, however, I was her help, her guide, her companion. Not all women suffer from morning sickness, and not all of those who do are debilitated by it, but Yashu was. Without me, getting back to I*il would have been far harder for her than it was, though I don't doubt she would have managed it. While we travelled I was careful, too, to explain to her that, although I had been in on Elder Ayn's scheme all along, my reasons for repeatedly intervening and making sure she stayed with us were nothing to do with him. They were purely selfish. I wanted her to continue with us because I liked her. More than liked her.

I was, in truth, besotted with her. Had been from the outset.

I still am. Even now that she is my wife and the mother of my daughter, not a day goes by when I don't look at her and marvel.

She agreed to marry me.

Better yet, she forgave me.

It took time. While her and Gregory's baby grew inside her, and after he was born, all I was was a friend. A guest in the house. Someone who had come to visit and didn't leave. The islanders knew me as that mainlander up by Second-Cliff-Village. I was an outsider then, and remain one to this day. Even though I speak their language pretty much fluently now. Even though I participate in all their customs and rites, live as one of them. Even though mainlanders who come to the island regularly mistake me for a local. Still an outsider.

Liyalu, however, liked and accepted me – that counted for something – and after Huaso was born she took me aside and advised me to make Yashu my wife and raise Huaso as my own son. (Compare and contrast with the insidious matchmaking of Elder Ayn.) Encouraged, I did as she suggested. She died, I like to think, a happy woman, knowing her niece now had a family. I grieved for her. I knew her for less than three years and wish it had been longer.

Fortunately, Huaso was not born with his true father's colouring. Now *that* would have been a problem. I could never have passed off a redhead as my own offspring. But Yashu's complexion won out. Huaso is dark-haired and tans easily in the sun. He could conceivably be my son, and I love him as such, no less than I love Kharona, my own flesh and blood. I have brought him up as best I can, watched him grow straight and tall and true, been a father to him. I am as proud of him as I could be. I wish he genuinely were mine.

And sometimes, looking at him, I have to wonder if this isn't enough – this young, strong boy. If this, after all Elder Ayn's efforts and finagling, isn't the best possible result. Not a brainchild, just a child.

And sometimes I wonder, too, if Elder Ayn was mad. He just wanted to leave something behind, as we all do. He dressed it up in grandiose terms, talked of vanquishing the Worldstorm, but maybe this was no more than a pretext.

I try to think the best of Elder Ayn but often it's preferable to think the worst. It salves my guilty conscience to remember a callous, scheming man and not a sad and desperate man frightened of death and his own extinction. It makes the memory of our very last encounter that much less hard to bear.

Not our meeting in the upstairs room of the hunting lodge after the 'Storm visit was over.

The one after that.

When he left the lodge to view the rainbow.

When, ten minutes later, I stepped out after him, fully expecting to find him dead. I had primed Gregory to do the deed. Down in the cellar I had revealed enough about Elder Ayn's machinations to rouse Gregory to murderous anger. Elder Ayn had said several times that he was to die by Gregory's hand. When I walked out from the lodge towards the lake, I fully expected to find his corpse lying there, and perhaps Gregory nearby, satisfied, his fury vented.

I did not expect to find Elder Ayn still standing at the lakeshore, with his back to me, one hand raised to shade his eyes.

Nor did I expect to continue walking towards him, placing my feet as silently as I could.

Nor did I expect to find myself bending down, when I was a few yards from him, and picking up one of those smooth, disc-like stones that were arrayed around the lake's edge.

All I knew was that Gregory had failed me. He had left the lodge already, perhaps even while the 'Storm was still raging. Rather than take another life, kill someone else as he had killed his brother, he had absented himself from the scene. He had put himself out of temptation's way.

But if Gregory wasn't going to murder Elder Ayn, someone had to. Elder Ayn had foreseen it. He had foreseen, too, that he would not know the identity of his murderer. He would not see who killed him.

Stone in hand, I took the next step towards him, and the next. He would never know it was me. No one would ever know.

I raised the stone. I was within striking distance. I stifled a breath. It was as though I had no choice. That's what I like to believe, and every time I replay the moment in my memory, yes, I am convinced of it. I could not have prevented myself. Elder Ayn had prophesied his death at this precise instant, as he surveyed the rainbow. Yes, yes, it was a foregone conclusion and I was merely a part of it, the final piece of the jigsaw.

He had lied, though. In one small aspect.

He turned.

He saw my face.

He knew it would be me rather than Gregory.

Too late. I was already bringing the stone down.

He was smiling as the stone hit him. That smile of his. Bittersweet. It meant nothing and everything.

He was still smiling it, even as he fell.

And I am smiling it now, my own version of it.

And soon my family will be here. They're on the way back round the island, probably passing Grey-Seal-Inlet just about now. And I must pack away my pen and ink bottle and stow these pages in a secret place, never to be found.

Whatever happens from here on, happens. I'm waiting to find out what Flow – what Inclination – Huaso will have. Yashu is waiting, too. We've discussed it. We hope it will be Water. Failing that, Air. Failing that, nothing.

What we haven't discussed is what if it isn't any of these. What if it isn't even Fire or Earth.

What if it's something else altogether.

What if Elder Ayn was right.

Elder Ayn, in the last months of his life, was looking for certainty. He was looking for something to believe in. Something solid. A truth.

And that's what it comes down to. That's why this text must end here, on this uncertain note, before we have an answer.

Because truth is family and friends and honesty and life and love. All these things that can be ripped away from you without a moment's notice.

And I hope that there is no more to it than that.

And I fear – I fear – that there may be.

Acknowledgements

It's become customary for me to name-check friends and family at the back of the book and thank them for various things. So why let's break with tradition?

First off, three people – Eric Brown, Ariel, and Simon Spanton – cast an eye over the synopsis for *Worldstorm* and offered hugely useful and constructive criticism. Then my agent, Antony Harwood, helped keep me enthused and encouraged throughout the year-plus of writing and pulled me out of more than one authorial slough of despond. He and his accomplice, James Macdonald Lockhart, are grandmasters of the agenting art.

Several other people gave me unswerving support or simply were and remain good friends. They are, in no particular order: Alison Wray, Adam Roberts, Roger Levy, Ron Fortgang, Tim Mitchell, Sandy Auden, Pete Crowther, Anna Gibbons, Laurence Johnston, Julie Everton, John Hill.

Those nice folks at Orion/Gollancz deserve an honourable mention, namely Jo Fletcher, Ilona Jasiewicz, Sara Mulryan and the rest of the indefatigable sales team, Malcolm Edwards, the aforementioned Mr Spanton, and last but not least Nicola Sinclair, despite the fact that she likes to punch me.

And to round off the gushing love-in, Lou and Monty have helped make my life complete, my nights sleepless, and given my work even more of a purpose.

HOUSMAN
COUNTRY

Housman photographed by Henry Van der Weyde, *c.*1894